The Complete Escapades of The Scarlet Pimpernel

Volume 5

The Complete Escapades of The Scarlet Pimpernel

Volume 5

The Scarlet Pimpernel Looks at the World

The Way of the Scarlet Pimpernel

and

The League of the Scarlet Pimpernel

Baroness Orczy

LEONAUR

The Complete Escapades of The Scarlet Pimpernel
Volume 5
The Scarlet Pimpernel Looks at the World
The Way of the Scarlet Pimpernel
and
The League of the Scarlet Pimpernel
by Baroness Orczy

FIRST EDITION

First published under the titles
The Scarlet Pimpernel Looks at the World
The Way of the Scarlet Pimpernel
and
The League of the Scarlet Pimpernel

Leonaur is an imprint of Oakpast Ltd

ISBN: 978-1-78282-738-2 (hardcover)
ISBN: 978-1-78282-739-9 (softcover)

http://www.leonaur.com

Publisher's Notes

The views expressed in this book are not necessarily
those of the publisher.

Contents

The Scarlet Pimpernel Looks at the World

Contents

CHAPTER ONE

Sir Percy Blakeney Puts up His Quizzing-Glass

Odd's fish! but I am already beginning to wonder whether my visit to your modern world is going to be depressing or exhilarating. Lud love you, m'dears, think on it! To be compelled to be serious—really serious, mind you—through the whole length of a book; to say what I think of your modern culture; to make you see the romance of an era which you yourselves deem unbearably prosaic—*la!* the task would be impossible were it not for the fact that after taking a preliminary look round I have found that these modern times of yours are quite as romantic as were those in which I lived: they are just as full of adventure, of love and of laughter as when I and Sir Andrew and Lord Tony wore rapiers and ruffles, and Lady Blakeney danced the minuet and sang 'Eldorado' to the accompaniment of the spinet.

It would in very truth be an impossible task were it not for the delight in store for me of scoring off all those demmed dull Chauvelins, or Chambertins, of your twentieth century and of proving to them that with all their Committees of Pussyfoots and Boards of Public Morals they cannot manacle a certain little blind god we all wot of, nor can they destroy that lure of adventure and of danger which beckons to you modern young people with just as much insistence as it did to us.

Therefore, am I here now in your midst—an eighteenth-century dandy, seemingly out of place amid your plus-fours and swallow-tailed coats, but nevertheless prepared to prove my argument up to the hilt. It is demmed embarassing, believe me, to speak to you in the pages of a book and to remain invisible and inaudible the while, even though in the days of my friends Robespierre, Fouquier-Tinville and their like, my capacities in that direction were mightily embarrassing to them. But even after the first page or two I already have scored off your arrant pessimists: one hundred and fifty years ago the League of the Scarlet Pimpernel was made up of nineteen gallant English gentlemen, but now, by contrast, I can enrol under my banner hundreds of thousands—nay, millions—of men and women of every nation; all those, in fact, who worship beauty, who dream romantic dreams, who love every kind of adventure, so be it that adventure is spiced with danger. Every soldier of fortune—and your modern world counts these by the million—is really a member of this new League of the Scarlet Pimpernel.

You don't believe me? You smile? You scoff? You shrug your shoulders? By gad! if I do not succeed in proving my case within the space allotted to me in this book then I will take a ticket—not a return ticket, mind you—for old Charon's boat and never utter a word of complaint.

Now let me confess at once that yours is a strange world, even though it be not strange to me. I see changes—a power of changes, from our wigs and ruffles and rapiers, our coaches and gigs, our leisurely ways, our inconsequent aristocracy and, for the most part, contented, easy-going working-classes. You live in a rush in this twentieth century; grim earnestness pervades your whole existence; you make and accept great and marvellous wonders—miracles, I would call them—as a matter of course, simply because in your impatience and your restlessness you are always eager to get on—to get on, on, on, inventing and making things greater and more marvellous still.

But this is where the strangeness comes in: you—or, rather, the pessimistic Chauvelins amongst you—vow that romance is dead in this modern world; they speak regretfully of the good old days when Sir Percy and Lady Blakeney were the stars of London society, when a romantic love-affair or quixotic adventure met you at every turn. You find your century a dull one, and I marvelled at first whether I, too, would find it so, or would deem it necessary to tint my quizzing-glass with a roseate hue.

As a matter of fact, what do I find?

I find an age so racked with boredom, so surfeited with pleasure and novelty, that it cannot recognise the incomparable adventure of living in the midst of the most marvellous inventions devised by the ingenious brain of man; of living at a time when a man can speak to wife or friend across the width of the world; when he can put a girdle round the earth by flying through space or listen to voices that speak hundreds of miles away.

It was the fashion in my day to cultivate an air of boredom that one did not feel, but, bless me! your detachment and boredom today in the midst of all your modern marvels are neither a fad nor a pose. I see that they are very real indeed.

Strange, did I say? *La!* it is astounding.

I reckon to have enjoyed a pretty turn now and again in France with those demmed dirty fellows of the Committee of Public Safety. But what a record of heroic deeds *you* established in France less than a score of years ago when you transformed a matter of blood and mud and hate and horror into an epic of nobility and self-sacrifice and splendid comradeship to which mere words cannot attempt to do justice! My League and I were ready to take our lives in our hands when it came to spiriting an *aristo* from under the guillotine, but there is not a man among us who would hesitate to take off his hat in sincere respect and boundless admiration for the greater courage of that band of miners who recently, in a pit disaster in Yorkshire, went down unhesitatingly into the bowels of the earth to risk flame and poison-gas, death by explosion or drowning, in order to try and save their comrades, even though these were, perhaps, already beyond the hope of human aid.

You declare that romance today is dead? What, then, but romance is the story of the young nurse who a few weeks ago saved the life of her lover by drawing with her own breath and through her mouth the diphtheria poison from his throat when nothing but this difficult and dangerous method could save him from death? What, indeed, is the whole life of the great Italian inventor, Signor Marconi, but a living romance?

Nay, 'tis not romance you lack in this twentieth century. Had but one quarter as much of it come our way in the days when I frequented Richmond and Vauxhall, my faith! we should have been staggered by it. We had to seek Romance; for you it flaunts its magic before your eyes every day and in a hundred different ways. By gad! when the last word of this book is written and the last tale told, I shall feel happy in the thought that I had a sight of all that is roseate and silver in the midst of the drab existence you complain of.

Cupid, my friends, is not dead. He will never die while eyes are bright and cheeks as fair as I see them today. Mars is in durance vile for the moment—thank God for that!—and I hope soon to see you devoting his courage, his audacity and defiance of danger to the service of humanity instead of to its destruction. The steep slopes of Parnassus are still there for those who dare to climb; the golden apples of the Hesperides still grow in the enchanted garden for those who have the spirit to gather them

Look wide, you moderns! your feet may be plodding in clay, but your eyes can be raised to the eternal hills and let the memory of the Scarlet Pimpernel show you the way along the silvery paths of Romance which wind their way as deftly through your crowded city streets of today as ever they did when I followed them to Paris; for I can hear the clarion sound of high adventure as clearly now as when it called to me in the rattle of the tumbrils.

La! I find myself almost serious, and I see myself in this small book becoming more serious still; but at least, my friends, give me the credit of throwing off my cloak of badinage for the sole purpose of making you see the world or romance in which you live. For this I am ready for the time being to sacrifice my reputation, which I may modestly assure you is that of a lover of adventure, of joy and of laughter—the immortal spirit of the gay and gallant Scarlet Pimpernel.

Chapter Two

Romantic Britons

I have just chanced upon a story—the story of a mongrel dog— which interested me vastly. This dog was the friend of a group of soldiers in a dug-out during the late War, and on one occasion his opportune waking and growling warned his company of a heavy German attack which was pending, and which otherwise might have broken through a vital part of the British defensive lines. In return his name was inscribed on the roll of the company, and he was entitled thereafter to draw one man's rations daily.

A year later, in the heat of a furious enemy attack, this dog's master fell seriously wounded in the bottom of a trench, and a German attacking force poured along, past the place where he lay. In their haste they would certainly have trampled the man to death, but for the fact that Mike, one ear torn by a bullet, stood growling over his master's prostrate body; so threatening was his attitude that the hurrying Germans made shift to avoid him.

So the two were found an hour later when the trench was recaptured by a British unit; and it was all the ambulance men could do to persuade the dog, faint from loss of blood as he was, to relinquish his guard. For that episode Mike was awarded the privilege of marching on parade in front of the regiment, even before its officers and colour-sergeants. And I pray you, my friends, in what country save in romantic, sentimental England would that great honour be given even to the noblest of animals?

For England today, no less than in my own time or during the centuries that preceded me, is incurably romantic. The legend so rife in Europe of the stolid, immovable, unfeeling, bacon-and-eggs John Bull Englishman is false.

There is more real romance hidden beneath the formal Anglo-Saxon exterior than is possessed by the effervescent Gaul or the polished Roman. The reserve, the coolness, the marked difference between casual acquaintance and friendship, the adherence to convention, the general old-fashioned quiet which the Briton adopts, is an artificial wall which he builds around his inner self.

The careless observer, seeing this artificial wall, never imagines for one moment that there may be something undreamed-of behind it. It is only the serious psychologist who realises that right within those defences which guard the average Briton against being stared at more than he likes, he keeps his romantic ideals as carefully tended as a gardener does a rare and delicate plant. From his infancy he has been taught by parents and teachers how to build up his wall of reserve, how to fashion therein the gate of unbreakable self-control with the key so hidden that none may chance upon it.

At school—and, by my faith, I am happy to see how these magnificent public schools have spread and increased in number since my time—he is furthered impressed with the vital necessity of keeping every emotion and every ideal strictly concealed behind that artificial wall. And this attitude of mind soon becomes a cult—a kind of fetish. The average British schoolboy is taught that feeling and emotions are things to be ashamed of, so he keeps them carefully hidden away within himself. Whereupon thoughtless people jump to the conclusion that he hasn't any, and should they, perchance, find out their mistake, they talk at once and with bitterness of the 'perfidious, hypocritical islanders'.

Actually, your ordinary man in the street prefers not to talk about romance because he takes it very seriously. I am sure you have often seen, say, a Frenchman or a German fall on another's neck and kiss him in public; but this is not a sure indication that the two will be on speaking terms the next day. Indeed, they may not be friends at all, they may not even know each other: the act may be a mere spontaneous expression of joy engendered by the occasion of some patriotic demonstration or public rejoicing.

On our side of the Channel, on the other hand, a handshake and a few quiet words may be the outward manifestation of a lifelong

15

friendship, or the last farewell to a friend whom one may never hope to see again. And there is one other fact, m'dears, which I must mention here because it goes further than any other in refuting the fallacy that our tight little island is an old, unromantic Sobersides, and that is that in no other country in the world are there so many happy marriages. Now, why is that, I ask you?

It is because when so vital a matter as matrimony is at stake your average Briton brings out the key to that walled garden of his emotions, which he has guarded so jealously from prying eyes since his boyhood and throws open wide the gates of his secret soul; because, in short, he is incurably romantic, and looks upon marriage as the most romantic event of his life.

I could quote you instances of British romanticism by the yard, of heroic deeds which put to shame the legendary prowess of a Bayard. Think of that lion-hearted piper, not so long ago, whose regiment was ambushed by the enemy in the Afghan hill country. The men were surrounded by a hostile tribe, their ranks were breaking under a deadly fusillade, but the gallant piper just marched up and down between the ranks and continued to play one pibroch after another encouraging the wearied fighters with the skirl of his pipes; and when after a time he fell, shot in both legs, he dragged himself up to a sitting posture and continued to rally his comrades by playing steadily on, the pibroch which they loved.

There is an outcry among some of you these days that modern England and its people have become more severely practical since my time, more sternly materialistic, and that life has become, in consequence, dull and colourless. La, my friends, you have only to look at a pair of lovers wandering arm-in-arm along a country lane, or through the meadows at eventide, to realise that side by side with all that materialism there still remains in the heart of your people the old ideal of romantic love.

And to our more emotional neighbours I would say:

See how the romanticism of our people rises when occasion demands to a sublimity which, I venture to assert, has never been surpassed by any other nation. Think, my friends, of Greater Britain, the World Empire on which the sun never sets. Does it not in itself prove to you that a handful of romantic, close-tongued Islanders can and does accomplish deeds of which any people would be justly proud?

Think of the valour of this nation which you are wont to call unimaginative, setting up on arid, sun-baked or ice-bound shores its glorious Flag, the precursor and emblem of its equitable laws, ready to face a hundred perils, starvation, hostility, sometimes even torture and death, for the sake of adding a few square miles to its vast Empire, though the very names of these pioneers often remain unrecorded and forgotten.

That is what I would say to our neighbours, my friends—even I, your very own Scarlet Pimpernel. And it is the same today as it has been in the past: your true Anglo-Saxon has the love of romance buried deeply and firmly within his soul. What, think you, made Drake insist on finishing his game of bowls when the Armada was in sight, or caused that officer of Wellington's army to say grace after receiving the first French fire at Waterloo? What else can account for the thousand and one quixotic, selfless and splendid deeds which are accomplished by the average Briton every day all over the world—deeds that have caused the romantically-minded Continental peoples to speak of us in tones made up of admiration and awe as 'those mad Englishmen'?

Gadzooks! I have been spoken of as a romanticist myself; but, by my faith, in comparison with you moderns of today I begin to think that I was nothing but a practical, stolid, average Briton, or bacon-and-eggs John bull.

Ask my friend Chauvelin—he knows!

CHAPTER THREE

But Romance Does Not Come Unsought

Take my own case, m'dears! Do you know what used to be my greatest trouble in the past, that is, before I embarked on those adventures which you like to read about these days? I had wealth, good companions, a lovely home, the most charming woman in the world for a wife; nevertheless, I felt the lack of a certain savour, the spice of danger and of the unexpected in my life.

It was then that I made a discovery. I found that Romance does not come unsought, but like a capricious woman she begins by eluding her seekers and gives them no more than a few provocative glances in order to whet their appetite for more of her company. If, then, they turn from her with a shrug and a sigh and resume with but a faint murmur their daily round and common task, she will pass them scornfully by, perhaps never coming their way again. But if she encounters courage, eagerness, ambition, the desire to put fate to the touch and win or lose everything on the stake, then she will smile, beckon more insistently, and even whisper of rewards.

Now let me humbly admit that having made that discovery, I decided that the spice of life which I lacked might perchance be found in the misery, the squalor, the hatred and heroism of that great social upheaval we call the French Revolution. I went to seek romance for myself and found her so enchanting a mistress that I vow Lady Blakeney herself had often cause to complain of my new devotion!

Why should not you do the same? As I have already said in these pages, romance is as omnipresent today as she was in the world of my own time. But now, as then, she needs a manly wooing. Go out to seek her! Keep your soul for ever on the *qui vive* for adventure and novelty! Live like a knight of old, ever ready to rescue beauty in distress or to turn your weapons against the Giants Despair, Oppression, Discourtesy, and all the other thousand ogres that exist in the midst of your vaunted civilization.

Do not be content with the tabloid romance provided for you in your cinemas and theatres. You can make a better love story than the best the films can show you if only you wait till you meet your true mate and then woo her like a man. There is no stage adventure which can equal the thrill of a close competition either in work or in sport, or that of a bold and fearless move towards a longed-for goal.

Why, m'dears, in most things save in real life, whether in books, plays, films, or what you will, you can pretty well forecast in the beginning what the end of the story will be—that right will triumph over wrong, or else wrong over right; that vice will be punished in some form or other through the agency of virtue, or that virtue will find its reward in the sublimity of sacrifice. But in real life it is impossible to forecast events. If we knew beforehand with any certainty what the end of an adventure would be, where would be the zest of embarking on it? All of you who are the workers of the world and who desire to succeed have got to wage war against all manner of forces that are arraigned against you, and you have got to begin the fight, knowing well that in all probability it will be wrong—not right—that will triumph in the end unless you muster all your energy, your courage and your determination, to help you to win through.

You are no mere puppets of an author's imagination, fenced round against the attacks of trouble, care, sorrow, disappointment or fatigue. You've got to hold your own against dozens of such insidious en-to suffer smaller, though vastly more provoking

hero of romance has ever been called upon to

itating fads of your neighbours, family tempers,

heumatism, or tumbles off ladders.

e made of sterner stuff than are the fictitious

are invented for your entertainment. You can,

whole of your life one glorious adventure, one
ideal romance, by fighting bravely against bodily ills, by struggling
patiently against adverse fate. You, too, may become a hero of romance
more wonderful than the knights of old who slew fiery dragons and
conquered giants by the mere act of doing an unselfish action of helping some lame dog over a stile, or merely by winning the love and
faith of one who is dear to you.

To much of life's romance we deliberately shut our eyes, even
though it be spread in lavish abundance all around us. Take, for instance, the romance of your breakfast cup of coffee, or of the tea
which you sip quite indifferently in your parlour or your office. Now
I can remember the time when coffee and tea were luxuries that were
purchased with the blood of our fellow-men. I remember when coffee was cultivated by wretched convicts who had been condemned
to banishment for life, and when tea was brought over to England in
fast-sailing clippers whose captain and crew would risk their lives and
jeopardize their chances of a fortune in order to gain a few hours' time
in the terrible journeys they undertook across the ocean. And if you
care to look a little deeper than the mere surface of things you will
soon see that a thousand objects of use in everyday life have in their
production been the embodiment, the very essence of romance.

As it is with inanimate things, so it is with people. Your fellow-men,
m'dears, are prosaic or romantic, just as you choose to make them. Beneath the most arid surface gold may be hidden; round the most unpromising corner romance may lie in wait for you. But you must look
beneath that surface; you must venture fearlessly round the turn ahead.
In knightly days adventures did not come to the man who stayed at
home and mourned in solitude the demise of chivalry and the passing
of courage; but they did come to him who rode forth into the highways of life, stout of heart and ready of hand; and believe me, m'dears,
adventures today are not found either by your grumbler, or your slack-
er, by the cynic or the supine; they are found by those who have the
courage to seek for romance and to recognise it when they see it. In
this matter, as in many others, it is faith that moveth mountains, and if

you believe in romance it will surely come your way in the

CHAPTER FOUR

Let Modern Youth Have Its Head

Allow me, my dear friends, to congratulate you on your young bloods of today. Self-deprecation seems to have become an art with you, for everywhere I hear an outcry about modern youth's decadence. Yet when I look round me I perceive quite as much courage and as jealous a sense of honour beneath your young men's nonchalance now as was wont to hide itself with becoming modesty beneath the wigs and laces of my own hair-brained young acquaintances— Hastings, Ffoulkes, Tony, and the rest of that pleasant company. And your women are no different, either. They may not altogether despise the privilege of their sex to play havoc with our impressionable hearts, nevertheless, when occasion demands, they will rise today to heights of courage and of efficiency which surpass anything that I can remember, demmed ungallant though it be for me to say this!

Never before in the world's history has youth had such opportunities for self-expression and the attainment of success and happiness as are present today. And never before, certainly, has youth made so determined a claim to play its rightful part in contemporary affairs and to bring its boldness, initiative and enterprise to enliven and aid the caution and stability of age.

And looking at you young things of this twentieth century through my quizzing-glass, I make note of several things. You marry young nowadays, you take risks—as indeed you should—while you are still young enough to make a fresh start if perchance your first effort happen to end in failure. If you are lucky you win through while you are still young enough to enjoy the thrill of success, its power; its happiness and its responsibilities.

And, mind you, it is that horrible war that made you realise the importance of youth in the present-day scheme of life.

With a shock of surprise, you suddenly become aware that the essential sign of manliness was neither a beard nor a bald pate, but rather a virile idealism and a determination to go through with a job once started, and both of these might be the attributes of a child with hardly a bit of down showing on his upper-lip! That abysmal catastrophe was so much an affair into which youth stepped with a smile and a shrug, that since then you have come to believe in youth as a magic power, the existence of which you had not previously suspected.

I am all for giving youth its chance. Youth is the time when ideals are not yet dimmed by cynicism and bitterness. Youth dares to longer flights of vision than age's doubting sight can follow. Youth gaily takes risks which make crabbed age shake a warning head. And the amazing thing is that youth, in general, is right!

What is it that has made the American Nation so remarkable? Merely its childish readiness to believe in and try out new ideas—to experiment, in fact. It did not laugh at Edison's astonishing theories. It wrinkled its brows, puzzled a little, and then decided to back him up with money and influence. It believed in him, and thus it can now boast of having counted among its sons one of the greatest inventors the world has ever known. That is an example the older world to-day might do worse than follow, by ridding itself of its prejudices, its doubts and its fears, and having the courage to take every step which might lead to the development of the great forces of this world.

Yes, indeed I agree with those who so constantly assert that youth must have its chance. Life in the past might have been compared to a forest wherein tall pines reared their stately heads upwards to the light, whilst youth, like the stunted undergrowth, was stifled for want of the sunlight of chance. It was forced to spend its precious years striving to reach up to the level of its elders, and to reap the fruits of success when it was too weary to enjoy their savour.

I know that some of your modern idealists have talked of passing a law which would make retirement from business compulsory, say, at sixty years of age; they have even suggested that such compulsion should apply also to professional labours. That, of course, is carrying the argument to an absurd finish, because in a business undertaking experience is the most valuable asset, and in the artistic and professional worlds striving genius has no concern with age limit. It is true, perhaps, that in a good many instances your great new business concerns would, by this suggested law, be cleared of the incubus of aged and useless directors but in others they would lose the invaluable advice and assistance which experience alone can give.

Besides, age and experience themselves are necessary to the wise guiding of the headstrong spirit of youth. What pitfalls could be avoided, what obstacles overcome, what heartbreaks saved if only age would put its hard-gained knowledge at the disposal of the next generation! Of course, I know the demmed young hotheads do not suffer guidance gladly. They will not always listen to counsels of prudence indeed, they would be spiritless enough if they did; but there is such a thing as showing them tactfully the possibilities of trouble ahead, and helping them to develop their own experimental ideas, however crude they might seem to older and wiser heads. Youth is a force that no power on earth can drive, but which a silken thread can often lead—all the more easily when the thread is in the hands of a pretty woman.

Far too often in this cautious age of yours do I see well-meaning parents compelling a lad to take up a career which is not congenial to him, and in which therefore he will never succeed. Why not let him take his own risks and be content to guide him adroitly so that those risks be not too great? And heaves above! why should parents insist on having their say and more than their say in their children's choice of husband or wife? Even in my day we had come to realise that to cross the temper of a young lover is the surest way to drive him (or her) into the very embraces one fears.

Guide youth by all means, but do not seek to drive it. Give youth its chance, but do not stir it to revolt by holding the guiding-reins too tight. As with a mettlesome horse so it is with youth. Suggestion and love will in most cases call forth the very last effort of its strength, but the use of injudicious force will only result in a heart-breaking clash of opposing wills.

There is in your world of today a young and eager spirit of endeavour and of ambition; that spirit is a gift from the more general spread of education which you have brought about and developed since my time. It is for you to guide it, your task to stimulate it when it droops, to revive it should it show signs of decline. If you are content to do this the result will repay you a hundredfold.

And, egad! When in the course of the years that lie before you your men and women will have acquired not only the right to choose their own path in life, but also the strength to march boldly along it, to step over the rocks and thorns, to put a brave face after every stumble or fall, striving only to reach the summit of their ideal, then I say there will rise from out the ashes of the years of our failures the Phoenix of unconquered and unconquerable youth, with the torch of real progress in its hand, a torch that will lead this tough old world of ours to enduring happiness and peace.

Chapter Five

But Do Not Allow Progress to Become a Steamroller

And now, my friends, for a good old grumble. You will not, I hope, deny me the privilege, seeing that you have always considered grumbling the prerogative of your race.

I mean to have a doughty passage of arms with your giant machine Progress. It has served you well so far. Its very name is stimulating, inspiring—anything you like. But I foresee that soon, very soon, with all its high-sounding name and its inspiration, it will become unwieldy like a Titanic steamroller over which you will have lost control.

So long as your wonderful modern inventions, your machinery, your labour-saving devices are your obedient servants you will certainly enjoy a delightful and lazy existence; but as soon as these things become indispensable to you—that is, so soon as they dominate your life—they will rob you of your strength, of your manliness and your independence. Progress, the steamroller, will have become the master and you, his slave.

Let me, I pray, make my meaning clear. I have looked about me since the beginning of my visit to you and it strikes me pretty forcibly that the spirit of enterprise and initiative which used in my time to distinguish an Englishman—or a Scotsman or a Welshman for that matter—is fast disappearing. Education, you tell me, is spreading and brain power increasing. Faith, yes! that may well be. But what does it profit a man if he gain all the book-learning in the world and lose his power to put that knowledge to such practical use as will benefit his country first and the rest of the world as well? And what does a woman gain, even though she may know the insides of all the books ever printed, if she loses her zest in life, her joy in her home-surroundings, above all if she misses the greatest gift in the world—the gift of love.

Again, you will tell me that in no time since the beginning of things has there been such systematic cultivation of bodily health. Our young athletes of today, you say—both male and female—would put to shame the gladiators, wrestlers and Amazons of the past. And I am quite ready to admit that. I admit the importance of physical culture, of the camaraderie engendered by games, the better understanding between nations aroused by Olympic contests—but only as a means to an end.

Tell me now, m'dears, what in itself is the use of hard sinews, of prowess at tennis or football, if tough muscles and keen eyes are not going to benefit anyone else but just yourself? You certainly will feel very well in health, you will stretch your scarcely tired limbs out in front of the fire and think what a demmed fine fellow you are. Your friends will gather round you, chair you after your more signal triumphs, pat you on the back and write columns about you in the newspapers. But in what way has humanity, the great teeming millions of the world, benefited by your winning that bicycle race? What, for a matter of that, did your country gain by it?

Empires, my friends, are doomed to fall as soon as their people become followers and not leaders of men. Initiative and enterprise are the bulwarks of a nation. It is they that built up your Empire—an Empire on which the sun never sets. Be proud of it, for God's sake. Be proud of it! Do not allow it to rush to its fall while you stand in your thousands watching a football match or an automobile race. Watch these by all means, delight in them, get as excited over them as you like, join in where you can, train your muscles and your bones and your eyes, but with a greater object in view than momentary pleasure.

It was because of this seeking after physical pleasure that the great Roman Empire crumbled and was laid in the dust; it was because of this striving after pleasure only that Spain sank into insignificance; neither of these mighty nations was physically effete; the Roman gladiators were second to none, the Spaniards of the day were un-equalled at games with foils or ball. But life was gradually made easy and smooth for all but a very few. Initiative and enterprise were stifled in this scramble after pleasure. It was so much easier to loll about and watch a few playing or fighting than to venture forth as one's an-cestors had done over uncharted seas or unknown lands to discover new, enchanted worlds. Nature's mountain heights of success and her chasms of failure were gradually levelled to a smooth, safe, unbroken plain, and the mirage of equality spread its feeble rays around instead of the glorious torch of enterprise.

Above all, m'dears, beware of that false goddess Equality. She is so insidious; her voice is so alluring, it sounds so noble, we may even say so Christian. But beware!

There has never been, there is not, and there never can be such a thing as equality, and every attempt to establish so false an axiom is doomed to tragedy or farce. Nature herself has set her face against it: brains, talent, beauty, imagination, every gift physical and mental she has dealt with a lavish hand to some and parsimoniously to others. And therefore, the attempt to equalize these gifts by means of the steamroller of Progress can only result in levelling them down to the lowest faculties of man. A steamroller cannot build up; it can only crush.

During the late War would France have wished her Foch and her Clemenceau to be no more than the equal in talent and initiative to her Jacques Bonhomme? And in Russia shall simple peasant and saintly priest be moulded after the pattern of Stalin the murderer? Yet even Revolution, terrible and dangerous as it is, will do less permanent harm than this cushioned, soft soporific we term Progress. For did not France after her great revolution rise through blood and tears to a glorious resurrection, and who shall say that one day—soon, perhaps—Russia will not do the same, while all of you over here in this modern world of yours are letting yourselves go to sleep, lulled into false security by that insidious goddess, Equality and that other fetish, Progress.

Modern progress is fast outgrowing its strength. Equal education for a genius or a dunce, the taxation of the worker so that the idler may loaf, pleasures and entertainments in gaol so that the criminal might have equal opportunities for relaxation as the honest man, these and other factors in the so-called advance of civilization are like a two-edged sword.

Education should be the means of spurring the slow-witted and the unfit; taxes should never be a handicap great enough to impede success. Nevertheless, modern progress sets out to drive her steam-roller relentlessly over every individual effort to do a little better than one's neighbour, to achieve or, at any rate, attempt something in life different from other people. It tries to educate the most unfit soldier in life's army into considering himself equal to a Field-Marshal; it penalizes thrift to aid the improvident, helps to foster the selfish feeling that so long as I'm all right the rest of the world can go hang!

By my faith, is not our British Empire strong enough to give a lead to other nations in trying to get this steamroller of progress into control again? Yet even whilst I go wandering through my beloved country I find that the gospel of self and egoism has spread with alarming rapidity since my day. You, my friends, have taken the mirage of equality to be a real and shining light. In your twentieth century, taxes on hard work and thrift have ruthlessly increased, and many of you have resorted to juggling and guile in place of our old policy of outspoken truth. It is time that Britain took charge of her affairs, internal and external, with a stronger, a more firm hand.

In the times of your fathers and grandfathers which you are so fond of deriding, nearly all the great inventions, the great initiatives in the world had their origin in their brains. Great Britain led the way in science, in industry, in commerce, in the management of her Colonies. Today half the time when something new, something of world utility in science or in pleasure comes to light, it has its origin in America or in Germany, in Czecho-Slovakia, or Timbuctoo. Your fathers and grandfathers led the way to progress. Are you content to follow meekly in the wake of the steamroller? They worked, they slaved, they saved for the glory of their country and your future prosperity. Do you mean to tell me that you will go on sitting still, twiddling your thumbs and waiting for other nations to feed you with a silver spoon?

Wake up, John Bull! Look around you. Don't go lolling along the paths of life which the workers of the world have made smooth for you. Step out boldly as you did in the past on the rough road of high adventure and keep your steamroller of progress to its job of strengthening—not merely of smoothing—the trails which your gallant pioneers blazed for you at cost of their own ease and contentment, often at cost of their lives.

Do you recollect how the hero of a recent an-Arctic expedition, in order not to delay the advance of his comrades when sickness prevented him from keeping in step with them, fell out of line voluntarily and was left to perish alone in the ice? Faith! if you do not wake up there is danger that you will be lost in the drifts of obscurity. But to this falling out there will not be attached the glory of self-sacrifice, for your fame as one of the mightiest Empires the world has ever known will flicker out and die. But the world will roll on just the same.

Your shoulders are broad, friend John Bull, and you have your burden to bear in proportion to your strength. The last few years have seen many changes in the world, shifting of power and of responsibilities, and shirking of tasks. Because of the great traditions built up by your forebears, the world has looked to you more than once to put things right, to take a hand at the guiding helm, to direct the destinies of the world rather than stand by and see the reins taken out of your nerveless hands. Can you do it? Is the spirit of your race dead in you? I say it is *not*. Your hearts are as brave as they were in ages past, and now as then you scorn fear.

You have a responsibility towards the other weaker nations of the earth, a responsibility which tradition has placed upon you. Do not, in Heaven's name, allow that burden to slip off your shoulders. Remember, that if you do there are other nations ready to pick it up, to take your place in the new scheme of this world, your place in the sun, leaving you in the penumbra of oblivion.

Believe me, there's truth in what I say. Your fathers and grandfathers spent their brains and their lives freely for your country's sake. They were never content to see a rival nation usurp its place as the leader of progress and initiative. I'll never believe that you in your generation will let her down.

CHAPTER SIX

Where are You Corinthians Today?

Lord love me! when I think of the chances that a man has in your twentieth century, opportunities for amusement, for adventure and romance, I feel that the Raleighs, the Hudsons or the Cooks of the past have great cause to envy you.

Just look at your aeroplanes! What delightful surprises I could have devised in my time for my amiable friend Monsieur Chauvelin (or was it Chambertin?) could I but have equipped my beautiful *Day-Dream* with a pair of silver wings! And what about your radio, your express trains, your motor cars and great liners, not to mention your trusty friends, the telephone, electricity. Ye gods above, what an array!

At a casual glance it seems to me that ideas and ideals have changed, and that the vast number of people who complain that life today is dull and that it has none of the savour of romance which made it so joyous a thing in the time of rapiers and ruffles, are making it dull for themselves. Surely, if they would but look around they could find romance enough and to spare in the thousand new wonders of this busy modern world. But the demmed dull dogs, the croakers and the kill-joys are having it all their own way, it seems to me. They appear to be in the fashion, and Fashion's rule was always autocratic. Which—as things have turned out with you—is a vast pity.

Why have you no 'real slap-up Corinthians' now that progress is offering you new and exciting adventures every day? In my time most young men of fashion or spirit could show a neat hand and foot in the boxing-ring against the doughtiest opponent; they could ride anything ever foaled and drive against the Devil himself; and they were never backward, either, with a witty word or a gallant action.

Nor was this prowess confined to those whom Mammon had blessed. The 'prentice could sing a song or try a fall with anybody; the shopkeeper could tot up faults and virtues as well as ledgers; your tailor had a tongue as sharp in trenchant wit as his scissors were in cutting cloth.

And now, despite the fact that you possess all these new, romantic, exciting, delightful gifts from modern inventiveness, those of you who do not keep your nose close to the grindstone of money-grubbing adopt a silly air of *blasé* ignorance on the ground that knowledge is really a bore.

Now do not taunt me with the fact that I myself in my own time did ape the inanities and drolleries which were then the fashion, and no one ever wore a more vacant face of yawned more persistently than I did. I admit the soft impeachment, while reminding you that I only adopted my inane pose as a cloak in order to throw dust in the eyes of my friends at home and my enemies abroad. Whereas you young men of today seem to make a point of knowing very little more than you pretend, and of being bored with the little you do know.

If I were advising a young man of today on the way to make the most of his life—and, after all, it is the beauty of living that counts far more than the mere accumulation of riches—I would tell him to look wide, to be always ready and never afraid. The world is wider now than heretofore—a man can go adventuring and fortune-making across the seas. Modern business is so inter-related now among all the nations of the world that there is not a trade or profession which does not need foreign representatives.

I would tell him to learn, as far as lies in his power, to speak other languages besides his own. There is plenty of romantic thrill to be got out of a cheap trip across the Channel or the North Sea, and the thrill becomes greater still if you can understand what they say over there, catch their snatches of conversation, put in a word or two for yourself. It's no use saying: 'Oh, I'm not a linguist. I never could speak a word of French.' You never know what you can do till you try. Besides, you need not be a linguist to exchange a few words with pretty *Mamzelle* at Ostend or Boulogne, or the kind hostess who has made you comfortable in your holiday lodgings.

And don't forget that in life's adventure the man or woman who can speak a language or two besides his own is sure of good money. So, put up your fists, m'dears, not to meet a prize-fighter, but to tackle those few words of French or German which you can assimilate quite easily if you put your mind to it.

Take your chance in that as in everything else. Don't be afraid. So long as you are doing a clean, honourable, wholesome thing take your chance of success and face boldly the possibility of failure. There is a marvellous feeling of satisfaction and pride in having striven after something that is worthwhile, ever if that something is only your increased self-respect or your joy in having accomplished a task that at first seemed beyond your strength.

I would also advise your modern young man to spend a few moments every day in self-communion. Self-examination is so good for one. Let him ask himself the question: 'Am I a man? Can I, if opportunity arises, go out into the world? Am I brave enough to take risks? Is my heart stout enough not to flinch should danger of failure threaten me?'

At first probably your little self-satisfied ego will reply affirmatively and complacently to all the questions and will add with a sigh the usual rider: 'But, of course, luck never does come my way. Look at So-and-So! The luck he had. No wonder he got on.'

But, believe me, those feeble arguments will gradually give place to more searching self-examination. The queries: 'Am I a man? Am I brave and self-reliant?' will be followed by a more insistent: 'Am I?' And out of a true understanding of self, will come that very self-reliance, that grit, that pluck which is the one and only road to success, and which will as surely as you live lead you to the romantic heights of content, of joy, and above all of love. You will find that you have in your life today a hundred *per cent* more romance than ever came my way, even though your romance wears a sombre coat and wields a fountain-pen where we wore ruffles and buckled shoes, and for the most part were compelled to sit at home, for we had neither cars nor aeroplanes to take us about the world, nor means to learn all its wonders.

CHAPTER 7

Success? A Practical Talk to the Ambitious

I can't think what it is about your modern world, but something certainly makes me more serious than I should have dreamed of being in the days of long ago. Maybe it is your air of ardent business activity, your restless and faster moving civilization, or the world's spreading financial gloom. At least it is making me a demmed earnest critic, full of gravity and heavy words.

I stood a while ago at the exit of one of the great London railway stations, watching the faces of those who passed. And do you know, in the space of an hour, I saw—apart from those who were in conversation with friends—three smiling faces! All the rest, and there must have been many thousands, were either drawn or tense or worried or frowning. And oh! my friends, so many of them looked inconspicuous. Now I cannot bear a man to lack some sort of an air, some soupçon of dare-devilry, some outward manifestation of courage and success.

And this makes me ask you whether you individually are content to be one of the weak, ineffectual, inconspicuous little people who look with envy on those others at whose careless feet Fortune has thrown her manifold gifts? Are you content to be numbered among those who murmur dejectedly: 'Some people get all the luck! I've always been an unlucky sort'? Do you confine your share of success and happiness and efficiency to wondering how others achieve it, because if so it is entirely your own fault.

Get rid of that fallacy that 'luck' accounts for the victories won by the more forceful of your competitors. Do not deceive your better self with the false argument that all the chances go to other folk.

Get out in the cold, unflattering light of truth, m'dears; a failure stripped of comforting illusions may not cut a very pretty figure there. But the very act of shedding the cloak of self-deception will be the first step along the path which will lead you to the sunlit kingdom of success.

There is one essential key to success—sincerity. There are many other minor keys; for the gate which guards success from those that seek it may be compared to one of your new patent safes, the lock of which will only open with the aid of a certain combination of letters. But emphatically, without sincerity, no lasting success can be won in any walk of life.

Very little work that is worthwhile can be done with your tongue in your cheek, nor can it be done supinely or carelessly. We should not expect, say, a carpenter, an artist, or an instrument-maker to produce fine work while he was busy gossiping with a pal or gazing up at the skies. A consummate artist or craftsman must concentrate every energy on his task, or his work will not be worth looking at.

And the same with the rest of us. Those splendid fellows who constituted the League of the Scarlet Pimpernel did not, believe me, approach with a superior smile the serious tasks which I had the honour to set them, nor did they dally contemptuously with them. Faith! M. Chauvelin would assure you of that. Nor did any of us try to beat a retreat before our task was neatly rounded off. Gadzooks! our heads would have paid the penalty for our supineness, and your success will pay the score if you shirk.

Your splendid modern poet, Rudyard Kipling, said a very true thing when he wrote that 'Half a proper gardener's work is done upon his knees.' The spirit of that applies to all good work. You must get down to it, take off your coat, and not be afraid of hurting your hands. You must take a pride in what you do and put heart and soul into it.

The attainment of success is the hardest task ever known.

Keep a smiling face before the world, have a gay laugh always ready to help you over the stony paths of life, and a joke at your command wherewith to hearten those who feel that their burdens are heavier than they can bear. *La!* my friends—I fear me I'm but a poor example, yet I contrived to get through the task of living without ever pulling a long face, even though there were at times devilish unpleasant duties to perform. When I remember the number of times that those demned unpleasant fellows over in France spoiled the set of my cravat or made me exchange my ruffle for a coal-heaver's sack—why! I declare that I feel ready to send the members of my League down to the nether pits for the mere pleasure of another bout with them!

Courage is the keystone of success, m'dears, and so are persistence, an intense and unflagging capacity for work, and yet more work, the strength of mind to carry on in face of failure and defeat, the gift of learning wisdom from mistakes, and lastly the power of extracting every ounce of romance and idealism out of life. The demned fellow who said that success was one-tenth inspiration and nine-tenths perspiration was more than a wit—he was a prophet; though I am inclined to hate him for speaking such an unpalatable truth!

It is just as bad to allow reverses to discourage you as it is to allow success to go to your head. Success should never make you forget that even while you are still indulging in a transport or untimely bragging, you might find yourself dislodged from that particular rung of the ladder of fame which you happen to have attained. No game or battle is ever wrong till it has been fought for, nor is it won till the opponent is finally crushed.

This, at least, I see in your world of today; that it grants the guerdon of success only to those who by concentration, hard work and perseverance deserve to win it. And the surest way to win, m'dears, is to act up to the motto of one of your modern captains of industry:

'*Always do even the commonest thing uncommonly well.*'

CHAPTER 8

Your Lives are as Colourful Today as ever They Were

One of the most amazingly romantic things about your twentieth century is the way in which the women of today have dared to proclaim their independence. I don't say that every manifestation of it is altogether good—faith! there will always be hotheads who go too far in any new venture, so long as women are the demned delightful

31

creatures they insist on being—but I do feel that the general trend is in the right direction.

Well I remember how urgently Lady Blakeney used to plead that what a man could do a woman would dare, and how hard I found it to keep her from joining my League whether I would or no! And I shall never forget the trouble we had in spiriting the *grandes dames* out of France because their voluminous petticoats made it so hard to hide them under a cartload of potatoes. But, by my faith! those were happy days.

To be serious, though, modern dress for women is certainly more fitting to this era of feminine courage and enterprise than were the hoops and crinolines of old; and it certainly is more suitable for the female adventurers who range themselves in comradeship or competition with men. And it contrives to be amazingly pretty, too. To my old-fashioned mind perhaps a little more softness and femininity would add eighteenth-century charm to twentieth-century efficiency, but it isn't for an ardent admirer of the sex to grumble!

The curious thing to me is that it is women who chiefly complain that this new age is unromantic. Gadzooks! they should have sampled French Revolution times in England, when a woman dared hardly look at a man lest heads and tongues started wagging over her name in all the clubs of London. This age unromantic for women? When women can go out into the wide world as freely as did the members of my League in the olden days!

A couple of days ago I ventured—invisibly, of course—to take a chair in the lounge of a women's club in London, where a number of the pretty creatures sat drinking tea and gossiping. You must forgive the liberty, but 'twas mine own name on their lips that first aroused my curiosity.

'What a humdrum world it is nowadays!' pouted one of the speakers—a sleek-headed girl still in her twenties but who had already won for herself an important position in the world of business. 'There's no adventure, no colour left in this rotten civilization of ours. It's just an age of standardization; personal enterprise never has a chance. If a man so much as flicks another in the face forty policemen spring up out of the ground; if one gets a scratch, it's forty doctors; if one dares to be candid one is rushed off to the Law Courts to answer a charge of slander. All civilization is in league to rob us of our emotions.'

'Quite right, my dear!' replied her companion. 'If the Scarlet Pimpernel were alive today, poor man, he would probably be clapped into lunatic asylum. That's how it is now, if one shows a hunger for adventure or a mere *wanderlust* one is no longer hailed as a pioneer or a leader of men. No—one is just bundled off to the nearest psychoanalyst!'

How mistaken they were, those two very youthful critics! And how bitter in their complaints that the world had grown drearier since my time and that the modern man and woman aimed at nothing but the commonplace, rejoicing in the fact that millions and millions more of them were cut after the same pattern as themselves, with no greater ambition than to earn a 'lived respected, died lamented' epitaph from the other pigmies around! And, *la!* how blind must their bright eyes have been not to see that the restful, picturesque divinity we called 'Romance' yesterday is not dead but just transformed into a shingled, matter-of-fact, but rather startling young thing, whose claim to be thought prosaic and *blasé* has almost made us forget her divine unexpectedness!

Surely even the most sophisticated of all you moderns could not fail to be thrilled by Miss Amy Johnson's adventure, when that young woman calmly climbed into the cockpit of her aeroplane in England and set out, a young girl alone, in a flimsy affair of wood and metal and canvas, to fly half-round the world to Australia?

Were you blind to the tragic romance in the world such as a little while ago, when the youth of a dozen nations marched, laughing and singing, towards the inferno of the world's greatest battlefield—yea, and returned to it again when its wounds had been patched up, not quite laughing, perhaps, after having seen Hell and lived, but still with a smile and a song and an unfailing readiness to help a comrade?

No, m'dears, I am not talking nationally now; the same spirit was evident in all the belligerent countries—the spirit of eternal youth and romance facing the most terrible spectre that has ever sought to bring disillusionment and hopelessness upon earth. My League was gallant, but that immortal league of the adventurers of the war years, with its just as gallant sisterhood who carried on at home, makes our brilliance seem no more than that of a candle compared to the sun.

You may not find a Drake or a Columbus nowadays, or a Clive or a Brooke, because all the seas are charted and there are no fresh worlds to conquer. But I read lately of an unknown postman saving enough in his life-time from his weekly wage to found a leper hospital in India. Is that the task of a pigmy? And I see rusty tramp-steamers lying in a dozen ports around our coast, waiting their turn to venture out across the ocean, ready to sail from continent to continent whilst facing storms and gales which seem beyond the bounds of possibility for men to live through and conquer.

More can be done still, no doubt, to foster the spirit of chivalry and adventure, for only a day or two ago I read a published extract from the diary of the late Tsar of Russia, concerning myself, too. *La!* how famous one becomes through a slight appetite for amusement. 'I have been reading,' so ran the extract, 'an interesting new book—*The Elusive Pimpernel*,' and one became conscious of a wave of pity that there was no young gallant of today ready to attempt the rescue of that unfortunate man.

Be that as it may, I am still determined to champion the vital romance of your twentieth century. The colour of the picturesqueness are there; adventure calls insistently to you all; the trouble is that you will not open your eyes and see; you will not step aside from the straight and narrow road which you have traced for yourselves. But do not count me boastful, I pray, when I say that I could find just as much excitement, joy and zest in life in 1933 as ever I did in the days when I sat on a window-sill in Boulogne and scared my friend Chauvelin out of his wits.

CHAPTER NINE

And Romance still Pays

In my own time romance was appreciated and sought after because it was colourful, charming, and added savour to the dullness of life. Lud! we could hardly be said to have lived at all were it not for the romance with which we filled our days. One is apt to think, however, that in this more practical era it is a thing of the past, but I'll have you know it for a fact that romance is anything but dead. Indeed, it is very much alive, and for the simple reason that—to put it bluntly—there's money in it!

Is not the growth of a gigantic modern business the most romantic thing in the world? Lookers-on at the thrilling event are apt to think that it is all an affair of ledgers and accountants, and of 'two-three a yard' cheaper than the rival establishment opposite. Egad, no! it is an epic of courage, an Odyssey of endurance, an all-conquering hope brought to triumphant success.

Names that are writ large in the book of the world's great captains of industry are not those of slow, steady-going, conservative, over-careful plodders, but rather those of men who have faced obstacles,

disappointments with a stout heart, a gallant smile and
men who have known how to encourage the timorous
? despondent, and who have kept up their own spirit of
_____ation and endurance until the height of their ambition has
been attained.

And such men have found that there's money in romance, since
without it they would have been too deeply engrossed in counting
up the risks to seize opportunity when it came. Without their own
romanticism they would in their youth have been far too prosaic and
careful ever to dare to step forward without once looking back, or to
leave security and ease behind and take the big risk for the sake of the
big risk for the sake of the larger gain. They would, in fact, have kept
their mind's eye on safety first, and would never have dared to carry
on boldly and gallantly, ignoring the cautious warnings of age, in order
to gain the great victories which fate holds in store for inspired youth.

Now that type of man, m'dears, once his feet are firmly planted
on the road to success, will still retain all the romanticism which has
brought him where he is. You will see him building swimming-baths
and laying out playing fields for his workers so that they may indulge
in the romantic struggle for sports supremacy; you will see him holding out golden inducements to his employees to work hard for promotion, or to invent something that will increase the firm's prosperity;
and in your wonderful days of mechanical marvels a motorcar is as
good a prize for a winner in the race for success as were laurel wreaths
or silken banners in the olden days, besides being far more useful.

And now tell me, do you deem the combine of two great businesses into one as anything but romance? Is not each side taking a big
risk—the chance that the other concern might impair its own high
credit, or involve it in some unforeseen financial disaster? Such things
have happened. Such risks have to be run; and are not risks the very
element of romance? And so is success in partnership when it comes;
when W. S. Gilbert met A. S. Sullivan they set their brains to work
together, and the result was a series of some of the finest operas the
world has ever known.

True! but it is equally true that when Horrock's firm joined up
with Crewdson's all the bedrooms of the word gained promise of finer
sheets, and when Mr. Salmon and Mr. Gluckstein got together work
was found for thousands of men and women and cheaper tobacco
for millions. And though I hardly like to admit it, sheets and tobacco
are quite as romantic as operas—most households could do without

music, but not without beds, nor could they spare comforting, pleaant, delightful pipes, or good cigarettes which that romantic combine placed within reach of all.

I very much doubt if there is a single business man of any importance today whose career would not outshine in romance that of a good many fiction heroes. The late Sir Thomas Lipton was once an errand boy in Glasgow; Charles Levine, who recently flew the Atlantic to advertise his own aeroplanes, was selling newspapers at fifteen and was a millionaire before thirty; Mr. Woolworth and Mr. Selfridge, working along different lines, built up two of the world's biggest businesses from practically nothing; forty years ago, the Joel family were quite unknown. Between the obscure beginnings of these men and their present eminence runs in each case a story of almost incredible initiative, hair-raising adventures, and grim, dogged determination such as would win our thundering applause if Mr. Fairbanks showed it to us on the screen.

There is yet another way in which romance still pays in business. Men, women and love have not changed one atom in essentials since my day when powdered wigs and rapiers were Dame Fashion's decree or, if you like, since the days of cavemen. Today, as in that vague past so often called the Golden Age, the man works hardest who can win fond glances of gratitude for his pains—love glances from the woman who is his chosen mate. Love is and will ever be the greatest stimulant to a big output, to enterprising salesmanship, to brilliant engineering, or to the million unknown deeds of chivalry that are scattered throughout men's lives like the stars in the firmament.

The man of today cannot wield sword or lance or enter the lists in honour of his lady's eyebrow; but it is up to him to compete in life's list so that he may be able to give her pleasure with the gift of luxuries, however simple or small. Therefore, romance still pays, and will always pay while bright eyes are there to inspire courage. For courage makes for boldness and initiative, and these in their turn make for successful business.

Today a man cannot do as he did in the days of the Stone Age. His worth is no longer counted by the number of skins and tusks and scalps piled up outside the door of his beloved's cave. But the man who succeeds now has lost nothing in romantic glamour; in your days it is just as thrilling to earn money honestly as it used to be to kill reindeer and bears; and furs, after all, can be purchased, provided that the cost of them has been earned first.

Romance is still king in the world today—it is only his regal garb that is changed. Beauty and bravery, love and courage, are the mainsprings that drive great enterprises even now. So, do not, I pray you, bemoan the glories of the past when romance, like tis votaries, wore a somewhat cumbersome attire, but adjust your outlook to suit your wonderful modern world and, believe me, you will find as much that is romantic in the thudding mill or the teeming thoroughfare of today as ever strengthened the arm of the great knights of old, or inspired the Crusaders to conquer the Holy Land.

CHAPTER TEN

But You must Live Dangerously

I have just come across a vastly intriguing little statement—no less than this: that scientists who know how to estimate these things have stated that there are nearly twice as many people living in the world today as there were a hundred years ago. And that, surely, means that the chances of adventure and excitement are nearly twice what they were in my day. For every man, woman and child in the world may be the possible centre of romance for you. Each may be a good friend or a bitter enemy or may give you an opportunity for a generous action, for the saving of a life or the better shaping of a character.

And meanwhile you grumble because, in this age of mechanical supply, coloured portions of thrilling life are not served up to you with your breakfast coffee or trundled along in a little barrow and left at your back door while you are busy adjusting your tie and choosing a handkerchief to match your shirt. Can you wonder that I am filled with amazement?

For you have the right spirit in you still. Everywhere I wander I see a sneaking admiration for the villain in plays, films or books, and even for the clever scoundrels of real life. And I know the cause of this sneaking admiration. It is because the villain or the cinema vamp, unlike so many of the timid productions of modernity, has chosen to break through those bonds of convention, which most of you wear so patiently and so persistently that they have hardened into massive and unbreakable chains.

Free of these bonds, those others—whom we term villains and vamps—have jumped out of life's rut with almost ludicrous ease; they have taken their chance, they have filled their lungs with the intoxicating air of adventure and when luck turned against them they paid the penalty with a certain glamorous courage.

I don't mean by that, bless you, that it is a fine thing to be a villain or a scoundrel. Between ourselves, such rascals are usually demmed unpleasant and dirty. But what I do mean is that this twentieth century of yours sadly needs waking up from its lethargic sleep, and its people made to breathe again, to stretch and to live. Yes, live! not as puppets, but as men and women ready to grasp at the opportunities offered to them by fate—opportunities of fame, of fortune and adventure.

A legend was told me once, my friends, by a Hungarian lady whom I had the honour to escort out of France under the very long nose of my friend Chauvelin in the roistering days when he and his like were turning that beautiful country into shambles. This quaint little legend had its origin among the Hungarian gipsies, who vow that Fortune is a bald-headed old dame with but a single hair on her head. She flits to and fro, they declare, in and about the atmosphere where human beings dwell. But only once or at most twice does she pass close enough to any one person to allow him or her to grasp her by her single hair and to hold her till success is achieved.

That legend may seem somewhat unchivalrous, but there's common sense in it none the less. For the goddess Fortune, capricious like all her distracting sex, chooses to come within our reach at odd, unexpected moments, when perhaps we happen to be afraid or uncertain, or merely looking the other way. A stare, a doubt, a fumble, and the chance is gone. Others get there first, seize in turn that solitary hair and hold on till fame and fortune come to them instead of to us, and in an access of self-pity we are left to envy the more fortunate!

The only way, believe me, m'dears, to eliminate that chance—or rather loss of chance—is to live all the time dangerously and fully. You must, all of you, young and old, make up your minds to spurn the weak, shuffling, apologetic murmur of 'Safety first'. Do you think for one moment that your vast Empire could have thrown its boundaries beyond the setting sun if your pioneer ancestors had used that slogan as their watchword?

I see too much anxiety in the world of today on the part of parents to find sons nice safe places in banks and offices and drapers' shops, and daughters jobs behind counters and on office stools. There must needs be clerks and secretaries, of course, and men who say 'Modom' and girls who say nothing at all that's worth recording. But, in the name of all that you have held great and dear and noble in the past, do not try to mould all your children after that one pattern!

All over the world today fathers and mothers sit anxiously planning careers for their offspring. Maybe the youngsters want to be artists or soldiers or engineers. But, says mother or father, art is 'hardly respectable' (though it is lauded up to the skies if it achieves fame!); soldiers, they argue, have to sleep out under nasty wet canvas; and engineering is such a dirty job. So, the unhappy child, instead of turning dreams into great realities, is sent to Mr. Blobb's office stool for a life sentence.

It is really neither clever nor effective to sneer at the more dangerous walks of life. They may be risky or dirty, but hands can get dirtier and risk can be greater in many an office than in barracks or engineering shops. The safe, dull professions are overcrowded—filled to overflowing with smooth, little, purring people who are content and happy in their guarded lives. Meanwhile the world calls aloud for real men and real women who are fearless enough to leave the beaten track and to strike out on their own, even though their daring venture be made in the heart of a crowded city. It is the stout heart, m'dears, that matters, not the place where destiny has set you or the manner of task to which you have been called.

England is still the land of Drake, or Raleigh, of Nelson and a hundred other heroes and leaders of men. The spirit of progress still lives in her, the high endeavour, the love of adventure! Do not, in Heaven's name, allow these noble attributes of your glorious nation to be smothered beneath the pall of a deadening lethargy.

Chapter Eleven

Romantic Radio

Lud, 'tis marvellous! I vow I never dreamed of such an amazing thing! You may say it is all an affair of valves and grids, of coils and earths and aerials, of oscillation and interference. But to me it is no mere dull prosaic mechanical thing, but the most romantic invention in the world.

It keeps you at home? Nothing romantic in that, you say? Ah, but you are wrong! Home is the most romantic place in existence. Your cinema will show you magnificent hotels, glorious flats, garish nightclubs. Interesting, yes; but they pale to insignificance beside a cottage kitchen warmly lighted by a lamp, the snowy cloth set for tea, a baby sleeping in its cot, and a wife welcoming her man home after the day's work. And in the corner that wonderful little box which can bring the colour and brightness of the great world into this simple, remote workingman's home.

In times gone by, when there was no wireless, that same man

would probably have gone out after his meal to a sociable evening at the village inn. No harm in that, of course, since the type of Englishman of whom I speak does not drink more than is good for him; but not much fun in it for his wife and the youngsters at home, was there?

But since the advent of these romantic days of the wireless, that same man takes his glass of beer in his own arm-chair at home. He listens to beautiful music, clever drama, or even an interesting lecture. Between whiles he talks with his wife, plays with the baby or, perhaps, if he is a handy man, he will be able to explain to his son details about the set and how to get more perfect reception. Somehow a closer intimacy now exists between that man and his family than used to be the case. Probably, too, the money which formerly went on various kinds of gambling and betting will now go to the improvement of the wireless set and the beautifying of the home. The father of the family has become a home bird. Prosaic, you say? Romantic, says his wife and the happiness in her eyes shows which of you is right.

If it is like this in the country how much more romantic is it in the big towns! The city clerk cannot afford to take his young wife to expensive musical recitals, and only rarely to the theatre or opera. But he can and does afford to purchase a wireless set for her and then adds to it until it becomes a decorative and perfect mechanism by whose means she may listen, in the comfort of her own little home or flat, to Kreisler or Galli-Curci, or Chaliapin or Paderewski. These are gifts, indeed, and she knows it and loves him the more for it.

In these modern times there has been an alarming tendency towards taking meals and amusements outside the home, and it is this unfortunate custom which has largely been responsible for the great increase in divorce proceedings in recent years and given ground for the statement that the British nation is no longer comfortable, happy and home-loving as it used to be. But since the romantic advent of radio, men and women alike, the very young as well as those of mature years, have acquired a real incentive to look on their homes as the place where they can find all the amusement they require as well as that true happiness for which we all crave on this earth.

Can anyone doubt the very great romance that lies behind Senator Marconi's marvellous invention? Surely, no one who has visited one of the modern hospitals equipped with the latest receiving sets? Is there, indeed, anything more romantic than this new power of giving to the blind visions of the crowded stages of life, or artists' triumphs, or gentle pastoral scenes? What greater romance than the soothing of pain by recalling to the sufferer's mind through the dreamy notes of a favourite song happy moments of the past and hopes of a brighter future to come? What is there finer than the power to banish the weariness from a sick bed through the stirring scenes of a gripping radio drama?

Then think of a vessel in mid-ocean, battling against perdition, making a last gallant stand against the angry waves, and sending her appeal for help crackling through the storm-ridden air. Then think of her message being picked up by one ship after another, each one of which at once turns in her course and speeds like a grey wolf to the help of a wounded mate. The unfortunate sailors and passengers, slipping on sharply sloping decks, and clinging in agonizing despair to life, realise the romance of the radio, for without it the greater romance of living would for them soon come to an end.

One more instance and I have done. Have you never heard of an S.O.S. message calling, perhaps to a song who has been out of touch with home for years—calling to him to come to the bedside of a sick mother or father? And having heard such a message and hearing subsequently that the son did come home, a still loved prodigal, to make a pillow of his strong arms for his dying mother and did receive the kiss of forgiveness before Death closed those loving eyes in the last long sleep—having heard all that, I say you surely will not deny that one of the greatest romances of all times is the modern wireless.

There never was such a romantic thing as this, the one and only medium that can offer you in your own home, without any exertion on your part, and for an expense so trifling as to be negligible, the music, the arts, the knowledge of the entire civilized world, together with the voices of the greatest artists and scientists to interpret them for you. A waltz from Vienna, a song from Coven Garden, an opera from Milan, a recitation from Berlin, or a fox-trot from New York— you can have which you like for a few shillings yearly and the turning of a knob. It is more than romantic: it is the greatest of all the wonders of the world.

Chapter Twelve

Away to El Dorado

Where are your adventures today? Where are your pioneers, your explorers, your Hudsons, your Raleighs, your Cooks? Has the love of danger and the spirit of daring died away altogether in this twentieth century, like a grand old oak dies when choked by ivy, leaving only a gnarled and naked memory of its former beauty? Have the clinging tendrils of the money-hunger crushed all the dare-devil spirit from men's souls, so that now the most thrilling risk they dare to take is a mild flutter on the 3:30 winner at half-a-crown each way?

If it is not so, why is it that at this moment when the Colonies are crying out for men, and at home in England you have three million of them out of work, the driblet of emigrants to the El Dorado overseas is so shamefully meagre?

I know that, on reading this, hundreds of statisticians will frantically rush to their pens and ink with the purpose of proving me hopelessly wrong. They will bombard me with columns of figures, produce a barrage of information to the effect that the Colonies just now do now want immigrants, that they have no room for their own people, in fact, and generally demolish me with final proofs that the thing for young men and women to do who are jobless and hopeless in England is to sit down at home, draw the dole comfortably, and wait for something to turn up. Which is nonsense!

The thing these figure-wizards forget is that they are dealing with little cyphers in black on white sheets of paper. Whereas, I am arguing about men and women, flesh and blood and spirit, courage, high endeavour, fearlessness, enterprise and brawn. My emigrants—the kind the Colonies do want and make no secret of wanting—are what our vivid friends the Americans call 'go-getters'. They are prepared to meet difficulties and even hardships, they are clear-sighted visionaries with a definite goal ahead, and they intend to get to it if human muscle and sinew and human ingenuity can get them there. They are the spiritual descendants of the old pioneer who blazed the trail in the olden days across Africa, Australia and America.

Never before has the wider world offered such a variety of opportunities. Of course, it does not want wastrels, won't-works and failures—it is not just a vast office, warming up comfortable seats for the folk the Old Country has no use for. But it does want men—real men and real women—and for them it holds out the most glittering rewards in money, fame and happiness.

Moreover, jobs today are easier than they were even a few years ago. Hewing of wood and drawing of water are no longer the beginning and end of a pioneer's life. There is room for professional men in their thousands, for traders, for business men, for manufacturers, for policemen, for porters, in fact, for every possible branch of labour. But these men must be the best of their kind and, unless they are still young enough and willing to learn, they must be efficient craftsmen or practitioners before they think of going overseas.

But once out there they can go ahead and achieve all the success they can possibly wish for. At home every trade and profession is so overcrowded that only men of exceptional ability can make (say) a thousand pounds a year. But one man I read of recently went from a little west country town to Australia four years ago, at the age of eighteen, took up a small government concession of land on the usual condition that he cleared it in a specified time, cut and sold the timber from it, ploughed and sowed the fields, took in more land, began employing others, and now after these four years he has built himself a homestead and is not only very prosperous, but well on the road to becoming a rich man. But then he is a *man*—the sort of man to whom in the old days my League was always open. Despite the recent Australian financial and labour troubles, he made his way surely and steadily and gave the lie to the Dismal Jimmies who are always telling modern young people to stay at home and do nothing.

Take that other great country—Canada. Faith! there must be something very stimulating in the air of the great prairies, for I have met young men and women out there who came from the Old Country, but who had suddenly shed, as if by magic, the cloak of supineness and discontent which some of you are so fond of wrapping round you. You go over the great lakes in one of the luxurious C.P.R. boats, and I'll vow that you'll be struck at once with the smartness and the quiet, elegant manners of the young men and women who wait upon you in the dining-hall, the tea-room and your cabin.

Unless you feel exceptionally morose you will enter into conversation with that fair-haired young steward who has such shapely hands and wears such nice clean linen. And he will tell you that he is a University student at Toronto, that his father is a barrister or doctor or parson in the Old Country with not enough money to spend on University education for his sons; so, he—the eldest of the bunch—came out to Canada with a few pounds in his pocket and pays his 'Varsity fees himself with money which he earns during vacation time at any job that comes his way.'

Then when you land from the boat, as likely as not, the porter who carries your bag and to whom you give a fifty cents' tip, is the son of an archdeacon or the grandson of an Earl; and the chambermaid at your hotel will turn out to be the daughter of that Lady Alice Something or the Hon. Mrs. Something-else whom you met in London society. These young people out there do not consider for a moment that by their work they have come down in the social world. In the rarefied atmosphere of the Rockies work of any sort or kind is just the means of earning money—money that can be expended in education or amusement or lightening the burdens of the old people at home.

I have been vastly amused recently by reading in your newspapers various letters of protest on the subject of domestic servants. They themselves—some of them—call their occupation degrading, and I am sorry to see that in this ridiculous attitude they are backed by educated women who should know better. Degrading? Heavens above! no work efficiently done for wage loyally earned can possibly be degrading. Whether you wear a becoming white cap or whether you don't, you are doing the one thing that ennobles every character and heightens self-respect—work. You might as well argue that there is degradation in wearing the King's uniform.

It is the spirit that enters a man's or woman's soul out there in the great primitive countries that we who love our tight little Island would like to see at home.

Suppose I—even I, your old friend the Scarlet Pimpernel—had to carve my fortune today. Suppose I was still very young, but without the wealth which enabled me to satisfy my craving for adventure by pitting my wits against the tigers of the French Revolution, what would I do to save myself from dying of *ennui*? Would I, do you suppose, sit down and draw my dole, making no effort to gain more from life than ease and two square meals a day? Would I be content never to risk my precious self a yard away from the apron-strings of my Mother Country? Faith! I trust not.

I'll tell you where I'd be. I'd pack myself off steerage on one of those emigrant ships which I have seen gliding so smoothly down the Clyde or the Thames; I'd crave leave to join that gallant company of youth who, when chances look unpromising over here, set their faces boldly towards the East, the West, the North of the South, to go out (as bravely as ever my friends Tony and Ffoulkes went out to France with me) to meet high adventure wherever it may be found, and to carry the pioneer spirit—the old spirit of Mother England—to the most distant corners of the earth.

Your ancestors—those sturdy soldiers of fortune of past centuries—must look with pride on their children's children, I'll warrant, when an emigrant ship sets off so gaily from the quayside. Maybe she is only a rusty old tramp, but to the ghosts of the trapper and trader of old she is as gallant as the *Mayflower* or the *Revenge*. Her passengers seem to you and to me no more than raw youths and disappointed men, but the spirit of Hawkins and Grenville call a welcome to the blood-brothers of their long-dead shipmates, to those who sought with them in the days that are gone the land of El Dorado that lay beyond the uncharted seas.

And at least the emigrants are better adventurers than many of their critics, who shiver and draw closer to their fireside at home and shake doleful heads wisely over the chances and risks which those emigrants are ready to dare, but which the critics themselves are too supine and fearful to face.

CHAPTER THIRTEEN

The Romance of Patriotism

This is a critical moment, m'dears, in the history of the country we all love so well; indeed, it is a time of danger, or doubt and difficulty for all the world. And for this evil there is only one cure—a great and ennobling patriotism which will stimulate the citizens of every nation into serving their own country bravely and selflessly and will inspire every country throughout the world to encourage and to be of help to its neighbour.

Above all, it is imperative that England shall stand firm in the midst of this world of gloom and of doubt. For three hundred years and more all the nations have looked upon England as a small boy does on his big brother—sometimes with anger, sometimes with enmity, even with envy, but always with a certain sense of hero-worship. Spain straddled the world like a Colossus till the roll of Drake's drum sounded her death-knell; the shadow of Bonaparte darkened all Europe till a little one-armed sailor with a copybook maxim knocked out the keystone of the bogey-man's edifice of power; Germany's irresistible might, marshalled for the destruction of her rivals, was broken by the Old Bills of 'Frenches' contemptible little army'!

But England, m'dears, has a chink in her armour, an Achilles heel into which Fate will plant a poisoned dart one day. It is her strength as well as her weakness—the thing that beat the *Kaiser* as well as that which may presently rend the Union Jack to shreds. England's foreign friends are wont to say to her: 'You English, you must always have your grumble. In war it was your plum-and-apple jam; in peace it is your government. And now when the world is staggering, will you just go on grumbling and waiting for things to come right in the end? Because that way lies ruin for England,' they say, 'and ruin for England

45

would be a deadly blow for the rest of the world.' But remember, my friends, that there is still one thing which in this terrible and grave crisis can and will save our beloved country from utter collapse. It is the romance of patriotism. The sailor may forget the sea, the wooer may forget his love, but is there a Frenchman to this day who does not thrill at the sound of the name of Napoleon, or an American whose eyes do not flash when he listens to the 'Star-Spangled Banner'? And, believe me, that there is no Briton worthy of the name whose heart fails to beat a little faster while he hears around him, or joins in intoning, the lusty strains of 'God Save our King'!

Other nations are apt to say that there is very little real patriotism in England; that her peoples are nothing but a community of huckstering shopkeepers whose only thought is for their tills. In answer to this lying statement I would ask this question: 'Who were those who marched singing and jesting into the inferno of Flanders mud in 1914?' Were they mere money-grubbers? And was it the worship of Mammon that caused the glorious names of Ramillies or Blenheim, of Corunna, Trafalgar or Rorke's Drift and a score of others—names now almost illegible through the dust of ages—to be recorded on the tattered regimental banners which hang in St. Paul's Cathedral or at Windsor?

Abroad one often hears the remark—'*As safe as the Bank of England.*' Is not that the finest tribute that could be paid to the patriotism of our people to the trustworthiness and reliability which characterize our race? Wherever you may go you will find that English credit stands high. Even today, when England is fighting a grim battle to uphold her financial predominance in the world, her commercial good name has never once been questioned.

Facing the greatest crisis in her history—one which is in many ways more strenuous than that of 1914—Britain astounds the emotional Frenchman and the stern German by her *sang-froid*, by making light of what she calls unnecessary fuss, and by declaring that everything will come out all right in the end. That is her usual attitude. Her patriotism during this crisis takes the same form of fearlessness as it did whenever she was called to arms, of reluctance to talk heroics, of indulging neither in lamentations nor in boastful tirades, only in an occasional grumble before turning resolutely to the task of reconstruction.

So far so good. But in this world of interdependent relationships and interwoven commerce, credit, m'dears, and international trust are essential to the safety of every country. And I am afraid that your apparent indifference to the imminence of the peril, your casual grumbles and scornful pooh-poohs are shaking foreign confidence in Britain and engendering the fear that such an easy-going nation as you are will never have the energy to pull through so serious a crisis as the present one appears to be.

The time has come, my friends, for your patriotism to take on a new form: that of showing a more determined, aye, a graver face to the world, and of indicating by word as well as by action that Britain is able to stand firm and erect even in her present trouble. Paris, New York, Berlin, are all of them watching you anxiously. On their impressions of you much of Britain's immediate prosperity depends. World credit is a thing which rests entirely on that elusive factor—confidence. So now I ask you is this not the time for John Bull to take off his coat and give the whole world proof of his ability to face trouble?

It is no use just indulging in a drowsy grumble; the citizens of Pompeii doubtless grumbled when they were first warned that their city was threatened by a volcanic eruption, for excavations have proved that they were taken wholly unaware. England today is far more seriously threatened than they were. Then why should we not give to the rest of the world proof of what we know well in our heart of hearts: that our country is well able to take care of herself and ready to meet her troubles and to face hard facts? Not only is this attitude vital to our own existence, but to the safety and comfort of the whole world. For if England falls she would not go down alone but would drag half the world with her in a Titanic collapse. Never truer than today were the words of the poet:

> *Who stands if England fall?*
> *Who dies if England live?*

And yet, side by side with the sublime romance of true patriotism—and what I have said applies to other countries as well as to England—there is the danger of fanatical enthusiasm. Patriotism in its best and truest sense means putting the interests of one's country before one's own, doing one's utmost to make its name synonymous with peace, justice, courtesy and power, and upholding its dignity before all other nations. It is not, and never was, a sort of excuse for trumpet-blowing and sabre-rattling; it does not condone that awful and inexcusable thing—war. But of this more *anon*. Faith! I cannot bear even to breathe the words of *romance* and *patriotism* in connexion with that hideous blot on your civilization of today.

CHAPTER FOURTEEN

The Worst Blot on Your Civilization

Can you doubt for a moment what it is? Does not every thoughtful man and woman cry out against war, that hydra-headed monster which has dragged on its hated existence for centuries after other outrages and brutalities have been banished from the earth? War, the suicide of weak nations and the poisoner of strong ones; war the useless, costly incubus for the fattening and training of which hundreds of millions of pounds are wasted annually, while the poor and the diseased in every great city in Europe are clamouring, often unavailingly, for food or medical care!

In my day we thought war a romantic thing. Men hastened to don picturesque uniforms, to take sword and march in the wake of their country's banner. We took up arms in defence of other nations, for war to us meant a game, and a game in which there were definite rules to be observed. It was a game that had to be played fairly and, like any other game, it was usually enjoyed by the players.

The rival armies fought in the age-old method, hand to hand. The battle went to the strong, to those who could best endure the physical strain, or who possessed enough cunning to outwit the enemy. Let me recall to your mind the history of the capture of Quebec. It was not bloodshed and slaughter that won that glorious day. It was sheer recklessness and mother wit. Wolfe's men rowed with muffled oars over the wide St. Lawrence, silently they scaled the well-nigh inaccessible Heights of Abraham and, taking the French garrison wholly by surprise, they forced the citadel to surrender.

But modern warfare is a demmed unpleasant thing, my friends, and it is one of the few things in your twentieth-century civilization that I heartily dislike. Private quarrels are no longer settled by poisoned daggers or mailed fists. Why, then, do nations—presumably led by the keenest brains amongst them—rush to blows like quarrelsome navvies whenever their complacency is slightly disturbed?

Wars would cease to be if the man in the street had real control of affairs, such as democratic governments fatuously pretend that he has! Ask any man you meet whether he wants to get into uniform and go out into the muddy, bloody trenches, or patrol the seas, waiting to be blown to pieces by a mine or a torpedo! Not he! He is patriot enough to do it without a murmur when his country calls, but what he wants is peace. Ask any woman what she thinks of war: it is more manifestly cruel to women, perhaps, than it is to men. Watch her agony of mind and heart when she thinks of her husband or sons in hourly danger of death by shell-fire or poison gas, of her young children dying, perhaps, for want of food. Watch the women's agony and know then the hideous blot of your otherwise wonderful civilization.

It is all so wasteful nowadays! A great battleship is built today, champagne wets her bows, she slides down the slipway amid thunderous cheers, and the crowd who the pageant gives a sigh of appreciation at the grandeur and beauty of it all. Tomorrow, or in a couple of years, what is she? In peace an out-of-date scrap heap, superseded by vessels of newer design and carrying millions of the nation's money with her to the breaker's yard; in war a shell-torn, twisted, burning Hell, in which wounded and dying cry out in their last agony.

The guns, the tanks, the cases of rifles, the gay or sober uniforms— what happens to them? Progress, unable to sweep away war, ruthlessly casts them from her as she has cast aside the bow and the muzzleloader and the pike; and once again vast fortunes are dribbled away which might have been used for furthering the welfare of mankind.

You call your ministers by such obsolete titles as 'The Secretary of State for War', the 'Lords of the Admiralty', and so on. When will a generation arise that has the sense to elect a Government which will appoint a 'Secretary of State for Peace' and a 'Lord of the Merchant Service'?

You still speak of war as if it were a glorious thing. It is not! The men who saw their friends smashed and poisoned in Flanders mud, diseased in prison camps, and freezing in the North Sea—they saw this so-called noble thing at first hand, and somehow the death's head that it really is, was, for them, stripped of the bunting in which it wraps itself, and stood out in all its horror and bestiality. Civilization has made of the old, clean fighting between man and man a horrible struggle in which millions of men are sacrificed to the monster of mechanical death and mutilation, and that monster is the product of this otherwise wonderful age.

At all times there have been scoffers, and I make no doubt that they would say today that a world in which war would never find a place would no doubt be ideal, but that there are at least two objections to permanent compulsory peace. One is that army men who are trained to fighting would have nothing to do; and the second that peace-loving nations would have no protection against aggressive or greedy ones if their armed forces were entirely disbanded. Now I would contend that neither objection is worth a moment's consideration. Could not the same organisation now employed for the training of armies and the equipment of navies be turned to civil uses as state organisations for providing work instead of state weapons for purposes of butchery? Millions of money would thus be saved every year which are now spent on battleships, fighting equipment, and all the rest of the arms' departments which would then be no longer needed.

As for the insecurity of nations, why not further strengthen the hands and increase the power of the League of Nations so as to make it really an International clearing court for the settling of International disputes? And this could be easily done by organising an international police, or *gendarmerie*, a combined force whose duty would be the same as that of the usual police force in every country, only on a grand scale; namely, to see that the dictates of the clearing court are acted upon and, if necessary, to enforce obedience to the laws.

If this could be done peace would be assured for all time. And let it be the task of your generation to see that it comes about now that the world is so heartily sick of wars. A great statesman said recently that it is a 'far more difficult thing to make peace than to make war'! Egad! it is. But civilization *must* have peace if all your modern progress, of which you are so justly proud, is not to end in chaos. Emphatically, the greatest blot on your marvellous advancement towards perfection is that war is still possible. And yet it means blood, tears, hatred, murder, robbery, whole-sale destruction and unappeasable sorrow. . .

Chapter Fifteen

The Glamour of Old Things

Egad! you will write me down a croaker if I continue in the same strain. So, by your leave, we'll turn our backs on the horrors of war now and look once more on the beauty, the gentleness, the romance in which your twentieth century is so rich.

So, let us begin by talking about old things and old places: pictures, furniture, Queen Anne houses, Jacobean mantelpieces and Grinling-Gibbons carvings. What is there in them that lends them such glamour and a witchery more alluring than diamonds or pearls or a heavy banking account? I forget who wrote the lines:—

Laces and ivory, silks and gold,
Need not be new.

And there is healing in old trees;
Old roads a glamour hold.

but they are strikingly true. It is just this inexplicable glamour of age which turns your quiet and respectable citizen into a fierce collector of pictures, first editions, furniture, armour, and all manner of things that are of no practical use to him. You will see him in the sale-room with eyes flashing wrath when he sees some dusty treasure pass into the hands of a rival collector; and this in defiance of the commandment which enjoins him not to covet his neighbour's goods.

His eyes flash, did I say? Faith! but your fanatical collector of antiques can look as grim and as bloodthirsty as did those collectors of *aristos'* heads in the troubled Paris of my day.

What is it that gives old things a charm far beyond that of the glittering gewgaws of today? You may as well ask why the sunlight surpasses in splendour this demmed new flood-lighting of yours. Is it not a fact, m'dears, that when you stand in an ancient cathedral or look on the canvas of a long-dead master-hand you feel a thrill of wonder—almost of awe—which is absent when, for instance, you gaze on modern London or Paris, on the new luxury hotels and palaces and the new dwellings on the river where Hammersmith was lovely long ago?

There are certain qualities which undoubtedly lend enchantment to old things, be they works of art, buildings or what you will.

Firstly, there is the impression of loving care with which those ancient works of art were fashioned. The canvases, statuary or buildings which you treasure today as supreme examples of your predecessor's art are instinct with life and feeling because the artists who created them made each one of a definite and worthy part of his life's works. They were great men, those craftsmen of old, who understood that it is more blessed to give than to receive; and so they caught and imprisoned for posterity impressions of beauty, of strength and of wonder while the world about them clamoured for more material, quicker, more ephemeral things. By gad! I remember in the old days how the dandies of my time collected lovely objects. We filled our houses with beautiful things, Tudor and Jacobean silver, delicate, fragile china from Worcester or from France, and filmy lace from Mechlin. And now you collect my snuff-boxes and Tony's wine-glasses. The world has not changed over-much since then!

Partly, this longing to collect beautiful or rare old things is due to hero-worship, which causes you moderns to feel that the possession of, say, an authentic manuscript of Shakespeare or some other great writer of the past is worth striving for, even though this may mean a financial sacrifice, the expenditure of money which took years, perhaps, of patient toil to save. But deep down in the bottom of your hearts you are ready to admit that these mighty geniuses understood not only their own age, but, prophetically, mine also and yours. They penned the words, faded now, which you are willing to purchase just as we purchased them in our days—because you know that those words were written by them with an inspired pen and that they were written not only for their contemporaries but for you who are living now.

In the same way you are conscious of a desire to own the wares for which the artists and potters of their day had perhaps failed to find a market; you want to own them because their creators call to you over the gulf of centuries and do so in the immortal and universal language of art—a language which education is helping the world to understand more fully every day.

And then again, old things emphasise the value of leisure and of peace. You moderns are far too apt to glory in the fact that you can, by dint of turmoil and unease, crowd more action into one day than your fathers could into two. It is a passing phase, for you gain nothing by losing your appreciation of leisure. Old things, by their very contrast, recall you to the fact that while work may be a very good thing, the sense of peace which they bring is equally good.

Lastly, there is your appreciation of the value of detail in the great works of art of the past and the influence of minute factors. If you study a picture by Vermeer or a book by Chaucer you constantly come upon fresh evidence of the loving care with which the artist or the writer conveyed to the insensate vehicle of his thought the vivid sensitiveness of his own master-touch. You learn to appreciate the thoroughness which brought about the exquisite results.

And so, you love old things because they possess qualities which are not of your age and are therefore but rarely met with. In spite of the modern wonders of your era, in spite of the beauty of the world today, you love the old beauty still, the beauty of Shakespeare and of Keats, of Sir Peter Lely and Gainsborough. Accustomed as you may be to the varying contours and charms of the ladies of today, you still love to feast your eyes on the types of feminine beauty which Reynolds used to paint, and the vagaries of the naughty Lady Hamilton are forgotten beneath the magic of Romney's immortal brush.

You have your cinema today, which shows you on the same evening events that happened but a few hours ago and even goes so far as to reproduce the sound that accompanied them; but all the same, you are not averse to lingering over the beautiful word-pictures which Addison and Swift drew of their slow-moving contemporary life.

All things are welcome by contrast with others, and you hustling, bustling people of today enjoy the contrast afforded by ancient calm and perfect craftsmanship. And in my own time it was just the same; never did I enjoy the peace and sweetness of my Richmond gardens so keenly as I did after I had been shouting: '*À la Lanterne!*' with the worst of them, clad in a grimy coal-heaver's rags in the cobbled streets of old Paris.

And yet . . . Odds fish! 'tis a curious reflection, my friends, that we never appreciate beauty to the full until it is beyond our reach. Looking back on the England of my own times, it seems to me a dream of Paradise; and yet see how I used to skip across the Channel in search of adventure which would whet my appetite for the joys of home.

To me your modern England is every whit as beautiful as was mine in its day. But you, my faith! find it unbeautiful and dull. You prefer to sit in a Hepplewhite chair, turn your toes to an Adam mantlepiece and, forgetting all the marvels of today, peruse the record of my adventures among that howling Paris mob.

Gadzooks, my friends, what fools we mortals be!

Chapter Sixteen

A Word on the Importance of Universal Goodwill

Of course, modern war is intolerable. Had we in mine own time ever visualized such a nightmare we should have spent days and weeks in sack-cloth and ashes trying to think out a means by which it could be averted; certainly, we would never have tolerated it. That you moderns, boastful of your progress, should do so is almost unbelievable, all the more so when one remembers how interdependent you nations are in the world of today.

A century ago it mattered little to England, as far at least as comforts were concerned, whether she fought with the Frenchman or the Spaniard or the Russian. Cognac, cigars, snuff and caviar were no less plentiful because of a battle or two. Faith! we'd have thought demmed unkindly of a war that robbed us of these pleasant necessities of life. But your modern wars—gadzooks, my friends! ye tighten your belts at the very outset and by the time the armistice is sounded you're scarce more than miserable shadows of your former comely selves. Hunger,

53

privation, sickness, sorrow, starving children, your wives deprived of every comfort that makes life and them charming—all these horrors can be avoided if half the world lived in amity with the other half.

For the interdependence of the world of today has become a serious question. In my day Great Britain was, if not absolutely self-supporting, at least well able to provide for all her children at a pinch without suffering the miseries of food shortage or the intolerable discomforts of margarine and cotton stockings. But today matters are very different. When you get your cotton from America, your wood from Norway, your meat from the Argentine, your fruit and vegetables from France, your flour from Russia, your butter and eggs from Denmark, you are in a demmed awkward fix, my friends, when you are fighting. Even if your scattered Empire was able to provide you with all the food you need you would scarce be better off when half the seas are closed to your ships.

Therefore, the only wise thing to do is to be good friends with your neighbours; not only by word of mouth and in the columns of newspapers, but in reality. And to attain this happy object you must try and understand one another better. In the past mutual understanding was very difficult. There were no such things as travelling facilities. Your rich young bloods were the only ones who were able to make what was known as the Grand Tour; they would go to France, to Italy perhaps, to Spain hardly ever; but as they spoke no language but their own and travelled with a retinue of lackeys and horses and carriages so that they never were forced to look after themselves, it was but little they ever understood of the countries which they visited. As for the rest of the social world in England, the average Briton of his day, the man in the street, in fact, looked upon himself as the salt of the earth and upon all foreigners as its scum, to be despised if England was at peace with their outlandish country, or thrashed if they dared to go to war.

And, mind you, this attitude of mind in your tight little Island persisted well into the Victorian, the Edwardian, even the Georgian era. Shall I not be stating a truism when I say that but for it you would never have been dragged into that abominable war? With sound understanding of all the nations who started that abysmal quarrel you would have exerted your diplomacy and your tact to better effect and brought about reconciliation. But I must not talk to you about politics which have always been outside my province. My propaganda is only for love and peace.

Now that you have shaken off the more recent nightmare of national bankruptcy and once more feel hope for your country's future and determination to aid her where you can, do not in Heaven's name fall back into the archaic attitude of despising your neighbours. Think yourselves the salt of the earth by all means but remember that there is salt in other countries besides your own.

No nation today can exist without purchasing or borrowing something from its neighbours; be it articles of food or of commerce, or the product of the brains of its great men and great artists. In all the sciences and in all the arts you are interdependent and obviously you must be good friends with the man from whom you borrow. It has been said more than once that if a man is sick he should go to Germany to be diagnosed, to France to be operated on, to England to be nursed. For the past three years you, who possess artistic souls, have revelled in the masterpieces of Italy, of Holland and of France which have been brought over to your country at great risk and expense for your delectation. You can enjoy today the admirable photo-plays from America, from Germany and from France. The cost of travelling has been so reduced that you can cross over to Belgium or to France more easily than in my time one could go from London to Brighton.

And, above all, you have lived in comradeship through four terrible years and learned all there was to know of the courage, the endurance, the patriotism of those by whose side you fought—aye! I'll even venture to add that you have seen all there was to admire in your enemies.

Hang on to that thread of amity, m'dears! Do not allow it to snap in the turmoil of politics and the noise of agitators. Polemics, I know, assert that the virtues of courage, endurance and self-sacrifice are only kept alive by wars; that in time of prosperity and of peace there is no opportunity for the exercise of those wonderful qualities; but I say that such an argument is arrant nonsense. Need I quote instances? Captain Oates, whose deed of selfless valour, I, for one, cannot hear recounted without feeling a lump in my throat. And what about all those doctors—there are many of them—who in the pursuit of science have seen their limbs wither away in disease, and even then, have carried on until death put an end to their sublime self-sacrifice. Go to a pithead when there has been an explosion, and see the miners go down into what must be hell to try and rescue their comrades. Watch the lifeboat in a storm.

And these virtues, m'dears, these evidences of courage and self-sacrifice you will find in every nation. Men are men all the world over, and women of every country have been as heroic as the men.

Do not sneer at their faults; you have plenty of your own. Try and understand their little ways even if they seem strange to you at first. You can admire their virtues because you are generous to a fault; then hold out your hand to them in friendship: it will redound to your credit throughout the centuries that are to come if you are the first in these troublous times to cast aside pique and misunderstandings and, eschewing every quarrel, act up to the gospel of universal love.

CHAPTER SEVENTEEN

To the Ladies—God Bless 'Em!

Call me impertinent, put me down an ass for daring to broach the subject, but listen to me all the same. You see I had a French wife. I lived, as you know, for many years in France. I met people of all nations during my adventurous life and, in your ear, dear ladies, I made love to your adorable sex whenever and wherever any of you deigned to smile on me. So, I entreat you, to give me credit for knowing something of the subject about which I wish to speak.

How often have I heard English girls, Scottish girls—girls, in fact, of Great and Greater Britain—laugh, none too kindly sometimes, at the peculiarities of their foreign sisters. 'French women don't wash,' or 'German women are dowdy,' or 'Italians reek of garlic' are generalities which one hears emitted on every side, mostly, I'll admit, by those whose foreign experiences are confined to Boulogne or Ostend.

Mind you, when I am on the other side of the Channel I hear the same generalities: 'English women can't cook!' or 'They have eight-seven kinds of religion and only one kind of sauce' and 'They have no idea how to wear their clothes.'

And it is against these fatuous generalisations that I would like to enter a vigorous protest. I am at one with you, m'dears, in deeming my own countrywomen the cream of the earth, but do you know why that is? Simply because I understand them better than I do the beautiful creatures of other countries. Though I have travelled far and wide I was born and bred among my own people: from childhood I have romped and played with little British girls. I know their virtues and their foibles and love them for both—so do you.

You know, for instance, that not the finest chef abroad can cook fish, or game, or fry bacon better than, what is sarcastically termed, 'a good plain cook' over here. You walk down any part of London—whether it be Bond Street, Kensington High Street or Kilburn or Hammersmith, and you see just as many smart young girls tripping along as you do in

Paris or in Vienna. You are conscious of these things, and so when you hear of any disparaging remarks made about you by a foreigner you just shrug your pretty shoulders and say to yourself: 'How ignorant those *dagoes* are!'

Well, m'dears, that is where I come to the pith of my argument. The elaborate bathrooms which are to be found in your homes of today, the delicious baths in which you revel night and morning are, of course, delightful adjuncts to your comfort and love of luxury, and they are hygienic as well as cleanly. In provincial France or Italy such a luxury is unknown except in the homes of the wealthy. Girls like yourselves have to perform tragedies in five acts over a wash-hand basin night and morning instead of revelling in a bath perfumed with crystals. But this doesn't mean that the Victorian axiom: 'English people are clean, foreigners are dirty!' is true.

Even the poorest Italian *contadina* in her cottage has every one of her mattresses and pillows taken to pieces and recarded every year. In every village in Italy or in France you see the men outside the meanest-looking cottage doing that work. Now, the Scotch claim to be the cleanest amongst all other British-born people, but even they would be deemed very dirty by Italian, German or French housewives for omitting this elementary dictate of cleanliness.

That, m'dears, is only one instance of how the whole question of virtue or of sin is just a matter of point of view. In a theatre or a cinema, we all laugh at the antics of a man who has had too much to drink. In France or in Italy such antics would not raise a smile. They only create disgust. This was very much exemplified in our immortal Charlie's latest film *City Lights*. English people who went to see it in Paris were delighted with the scenes were Charlie has had much too much champagne; the French audience liked the sentimental part of the film but did not tolerate the rest.

It is all a question of the point of view, also of education; and if only you dear, lovely things would try to see your foreign sisters' point of view your men-folk, who all take their cue from you, would quickly follow suit. The universal goodwill which we all feel is the essence of our future prosperity, must begin with the little things of this world, with mutual understanding of one another's failings, the little idiosyncrasies which after all make up the characteristics of each individual nation, and which are therefore objects of keen interest and not of derision.

Why not acknowledge that though our race is, in our estimation, the chosen one of God, men of other nations have just the same love for their own land. To most Latins an Englishwoman's beauty is insipid. To most Englishmen an Italian or a Frenchwoman is not what he calls wholesome. Nature made us all different from one another, and there is a quaint proverb in Roumanian which says that: '*Mr. Frog thinks Mrs. Frog the most beautiful thing that God ever made.*' And that is what you want, m'dears: a better understanding of 'Mr. Frog's' point of view. You want comradeship these days, not isolation. The world has changed since my time. The most terrible cataclysm your modern world has known has taught you one thing and did it through blood and tears: it is that human nature is at bottom the same all the world over: men and women wherever they were born have the same ideals, the same appreciation of what is good, virtuous and beautiful. It is only a slight variation of temperament that divides one neighbour from another.

It is up to you to bridge that division over.

Chapter Eighteen
Is Love a Dry Business Nowadays?

Is it genuine or merely a pose, this attitude adopted by you moderns whenever the word 'love' occurs in real life or in fiction? You will have it that love, as apart from what you are pleased nowadays to call 'sex-appeal', either never existed save in the imagination of medieval romanticists, or if it ever did that it is long since dead, bereft of any savour or thrill.

Frankly, you would make me laugh, all of you young things of this amazing country, if this attitude of yours were not so demmed tragic. Do you mean to tell me, m'dears, that amongst your charming, sleek-headed, bright-eyed girls of today there are no Juliets, or Francescas or Heloïses, and that you have disarmed Don Cupid, broken his golden arrows and tied him down, like some dry-as-dust old clerk, to a desk in a City office? Faith! that would be a daring thing to do, for there is more power in the little god's arrows, even though they be broken, than in your most up-to-date, most deadly shrapnel. And, as I told you once before, he will have his revenge.

Only the other day at one of your smart cock-and-hen clubs I overheard a general discussion between a bevy of those same sleek-headed, carefully lipsticked young Dianas on the respective merits of the men who had been foolish enough to make love to them. They were appraising the methods these unfortunates had used in order to

58

pierce their armour of feminine scepticism, and one and all found these methods wanting—wanting in what? I asked myself and tried to disentangle the truth out of this medley of disappointments and discontent, which lent to those bright eyes a look of boredom—aye! and of age. Anyway, they all decided, over clouds of cigarette smoke, that 'love' as spoken of by the great writers of the past was only 'gammon'—I believe they called it 'rot'; and that the roseate thing of fiction was only a dry business after all.

And presently when these lovely young creatures had all fluttered away like so many butterflies, in order to alight on the high stools of the nearest American Bar, I fell to wondering whether there was not something of truth in what they said, and whether they themselves were not allowing something of the glamour of love to face into the smoke of their cigarettes or lie dim and savourless at the bottom of their cocktail-glasses.

Thus musing, I bethought me of the caveman. His manners were somewhat unpolished, shall we say, but nevertheless he had that certain dominating quality which the terse language of today has designated as 'It'. I am sure, though we have no records of his home life, that he knew how to make love—rather fiercely I should say—to his unsophisticated womankind.

Nor were the sybaritic or athletic Greeks and Romans backward in such words and deeds as would flutter any maiden's heart. And so, one might go on throughout the ages extolling the times of chivalry, when poets wrote sonnets to a lady's eyebrow, and gallant knights rode forth in armour to break a lance or lose their life in honour of the woman of their choice. Or I might remind you that in my day gentlemen crossed swords or fired at one another with pistols to settle some quarrel over a woman's favour. It was not an uncommon thing for a man to be shot dead by another—who had perhaps been his intimate friend—for no other reason than that Lady A or Mistress X had smiled equally on both.

Of course, you gay, shingled, pert young things smile at all that and shrug your thin shoulders. You call it 'tommy-rot', don't you? You sneer at your grandmothers and your grandfathers and ask how on the jolly old earth there could have been anything romantic in their bowings and scrapings, their slow-moving quadrilles or whirling polkas, with mamma or Aunt Priscilla sitting in the offing watchful lest her giddy young charge threw too many soft glances on her '*beau*'.

Faith! you may sneer at it, but believe me, m'dears, stolen fruit is passing sweet. There was something peculiarly delicious in those stolen moments in the conservatory when Aunt Priscilla wasn't looking, or in waylaying the postman for a letter which contained a few impassioned words, a discreet homage written in verse, probably.

And there was rapture in a kiss in those days of long ago, a thrill of which you cynical moderns know nothing. What is a kiss to you? You bestow and receive so many. Your mouth today is more accessible than was your grandmother's hand in the past. And that is why, m'dears, some of you—not by any means all—find love a dry business these days. There can be no romance in the love-making of an anaemic 'intellectual' to a boyish, freakish Amazon. I am talking of extreme cases, but unfortunately, they are on the increase year after year, while young people in order to be in fashion look on the love between man and maid through the muddy, horn-rimmed spectacles of modern cynicism. To them it does seem dull and dry, but only because they are too much engrossed by this selfish business called self-expression, to appreciate the subtle beauty of love. They are the people who call Beethoven's Ninth Symphony 'too horribly old-fashioned' and prefer Mr. Epstein's 'Genesis' to the soulful beauty of the Venus de Milo.

Nevertheless, m'dears, you can take it from me that love is no more a dry business today than it was in the past and thank Heaven, there are still a number of you in this go-ahead twentieth century who have experienced the thrill of a first kiss and not been ashamed to exchange love-tokens with the one destined to be your companion and helpmate throughout life.

Those of you who are so blessed will see their path strewn with the happy memories of those golden moments which alone make for contentment and happiness—fragrant rosemary treasured for remembrance in the pages of your book of life.

CHAPTER NINETEEN

Has Progress got Ahead of You?

Progress has slipped a cog. It has got ahead of you humans who are supposed to regulate its advance. During the Great War, when your backs were turned and you were attending for your lives to your own business, it took a demmed sharp advantage of you all, so much so that now, egad, you seem hardly to know where you are!

You seem suddenly to have awakened to find yourselves in the midst of an age which is not meant for you and is not altogether suited to your mentality.

This age is one or realism, rationalism, a cold-blooded, hard-headed, calculating age, and it has given your sentimental complacency a severe jolt.

Those of you who wish to be thought up-to-date at any cost have shortened your hair, you have readjusted your moral values so as to give your conscience more elasticity, you have thrown your religion overboard and assumed an attitude of cynicism and unbelief.

Your extremists, on the other hand—your early Victorians and 'dash-it-sir-things-weren't-like-this-when-I-was-a-boy'-kind-of men—have come to a sort of mental halt on small islands of age-old and rapidly disappearing sand and ordering the waves of progress to roll away out of their sight.

Meanwhile between these two extremes there is the rest of humanity—a crowding mass of ordinary, everyday folk, men and women who do their best to hide their romantic ideals, their feelings and emotions under a cloak of articiality, whilst waging their humble battle of life in an era which they cannot understand and in which they find neither sympathy nor comradeship.

Faith! the trouble some of you take to conceal what you think is your weakness, but which, in point of fact, is the essence of beauty in your nature, the hall-mark of a noble soul. But just now you are bewildered, you have been swept off your feet; you have lived through those four awful years when you saw every ideal, every gentle impulse, every sense of love and charity sacrificed to the needs of that terrible war. Your sense of security and of peace was suddenly seized upon by forces over which you had no control and hurled into the seething cauldron of a Titanic conflict wherein the demons of hatred, of distrust and of terror stirred their witches' brew.

You had suddenly lost your anchorage. The struggle for bare existence, for keeping some measure of sanity in the midst of so much horror, compelled you to wake from your dreams of tranquillity and to plunge into the nightmare of reality.

As a result, you have lost the years of transition. The time between 1914 and 1933, instead of gliding gently along its normal course, was one in which everything was artificially speeded up. The pace of living was increased an hundredfold.

In the ordinary course of events your children would have graduated to it just as you graduated from penny-farthing bicycles to your cars and your aeroplanes. But human beings have only a limited capacity for adapting themselves to new modes of life, and you have been asked to live through so many changes that you have become like a piece of elastic that has been overstretched. And you naturally feel puzzled and not a little uneasy. You are trying to be sympathetic and to understand things that shock or astonish you; you are, in fact, straining every nerve to appear hard-headed before the world, cold-blooded and what is known as modern. You have donned an armour of indifference and scepticism because civilization has run ahead of you, and you are afraid to show your true self to the world because it might scoff at the romantic ideals which you treasure in your heart.

Your pitiless psycho-analysts, who jeer at human virtue or weaknesses, would probably say that you had a superstition-complex, or a sex-complex, or some other mental ailment with a high-sounding name; but you, with all your old-fashioned beliefs, know well enough that the only complaints you suffer from are idealism, romance, love, or some silly prehistoric things like that, and you remark with a sigh of longing that the old dresses must have been very charming, or how thrilling it would have been to meet a highwayman.

What you really mean is that coquettish glances from under a coal-scuttle bonnet must have been very alluring, and that it must have been very thrilling to meet men who clung to the axiom that chivalry and courtesy are a necessary part of any gentleman's code of honour.

I could wish that you had the courage, my friends, to assert boldly with me that chivalry and love and laughter are still extant today; you know that they are; then why not proclaim it to the rest of this disillusioned world? You have felt their existence, have you not? Say on a warm summer's evening away from the bustle and noise of cities, with the right man or woman beside you? You have felt the thrill of romance then, I'll wager, so why not own to it? But all your life you have been taught that romanticism is a weakness of which you should be ashamed; so, lest your neighbours suspect you of it you adjourn to the nearest American Bar, swallow an unpleasant-tasting cocktail and do your best with a forced jest or cynical remark to dispel such an illusion.

And all the while in your innermost soul you know that you cannot get rid of that persistent streak of romance which may not belong to the age in which you live but is nevertheless a characteristic of your face.

Have you ever watched the faces of guests at one of your fashionable weddings? Serious men of business who have stolen an hour from the daily battle of life and fortune come to the ceremony in order to bestow a friendly smile and a wish for happiness on their friend; women with faces lined by age, to whom marriage has perhaps meant disillusionment, look almost beautiful when, with moist eyes and quivering lips, they murmur a silent blessing on the bride as she goes by and a beautiful prayer that she may find in her life the romance and the love which luckless fate had denied to them.

Or have you modern cynics ever watched a suburban gardener bending his back to the task of transforming his tiny plot of ground from what was a builder's scrap-heap into a small paradise filled with blossoms and flowering shrubs, a nesting-place for birds, an ideal spot where he can sit and smoke his pipe and contemplate the work of his hands?

Have you watched the street-hawker, whose bellowing voice has often grated on your sensitive ear, stoop with a smile to a small child who is afraid, to cross the road? Have you ever paused in your walk, in order to see him take the child gently by the arm and guide it safely through the traffic? Then have you watched his face—almost ashamed of the emotion that prompted this kind action—while the child, after the manner of young things, heedlessly runs away?

Now let me advise you to look out for these small incidents which occur every day in the crowded streets of your great cities, and I'll warrant that you will think as I do, that progress and rationalism have not yet succeeded in eradicating from the heart of your nation all traces of romance and of kindly, unselfish, foolish friendliness. You of your generation may try to deny it, but I know better. I know that in spite of your *blasé*, cynical attitude, you still treasure deep down in your hearts the true romanticism that is so essentially British—firm friendships, love that is as faithful as it is ardent, and with it all a light *bon-homie*, the laughter that will conceal a tear.

Romance may be foolish and out-of-date, but without it life would be like a rose without its fragrance, like an evening sky robbed of its stars. You who have it in your hearts be no longer ashamed of it. I don't say that you want to wear every emotion on your sleeve, but in Heaven's name do not allow modern cynicism to harden your hearts against romance, which is the very savour of existence—the one thing that makes men of you instead of unfeeling robots.

CHAPTER TWENTY

Give Your Children a Chance

In the Book of Books there is a commandment in which certain words occur with which even those of us who never open that Book these days are quite familiar, and which—did one ever reflect seriously on them—would give one furiously to think:

> *. . . and visit the sins of the fathers upon the children unto the third and*
> *fourth generation . . .*

Now, m'dears, in this case, whether you individually believe in God or not, is beside the point. Whether you look on those words as a divine commandment or as a mere aphorism is a matter of your own personal outlook. But you cannot deny their truth, and I will venture to add to them an entirely worldly axiom which is this: everything a man or woman does, everything he or she thinks or says, is moulding a character which, in its turn, will be handed down to another generation and to another yet.

Yours is an era, my friends, when the cry of 'Self first' and of 'Damn posterity! what has it done for me?' is heard on every side, chiefly, or course, from those who are adding to the load of weaknesses and of failures which the next generations will have to bear, from self-satisfied, self-deluded wastrels, who are content to go their slothful way along the line of least resistance, indulging in their little sins, scorning to exert any one of the gifts with which they happen to be endowed. 'Oh! what can a man do?' they are fond of saying. 'I am only one among millions. What can I do?' And having used this argument which they deem unanswerable they turn over and, figuratively speaking, go to sleep.

Would these selfish ne'er-do-wells not be wiser to remember the old fable of the bundle of sticks? Each stick by itself could easily be broken by a feeble hand, but it would take the strength of a Titan to break the bundle when the sticks were all tied together.

How many of you, I wonder, stop to think that every action of your life, good or bad, adds something of good or of evil to the character which you pass on to the next four or five generations? Have you ever realised that it is you, individually and collectively, who today are writing the history of the world a century hence? Great things are prophesied of the future—untold, unbelievable marvels! But you are writing their history *now*!

Far be it from me to suggest that it is in your power to affect altogether all the ensuing generations. But whether you will it or not you are bound to leave a legacy either of heavenly gifts or of hellish curses. If you allow your own true and simple character to be perverted out of all recognition by a sneering and cynical world you will pass it on in its warped and distorted state to your children, and to their children after them.

It is on you, m'dears, that the people of the future will look back one day, blessing you for their strength and their happiness, or cursing you for their misery or their disease. If you remain clean in heart and mind, strong, faithful and loyal, you will be giving them a fair start.

It is for you to see to it that what is dross in your generation be consumed in the furnace of your present life; for you to make the most of the many gifts with which your glorious nation is endowed— your strength of character, your patriotism, your loyalty, your love of home; for you to wage deathly warfare against all this modern cynicism, this contempt of everything that is beautiful in life or in art, this constant grubbing in the gutter in search of what is noisome, and this inability to see the glory that is around you. If you do all this, m'dears, you will ease the coming generations of their heaviest burdens.

Only think for a moment! I will quote you extreme cases first. Children of confirmed drunkards—what do they become? Drinkers themselves very often, slaves of drugs, wastrels or prostitutes.

Is there a doubt in your mind when you see a dirty, slatternly woman, lounging about the alleyways of a great city, as to what her parents were? Is it not obvious?

And what about the children of inveterate gamblers? From babyhood they have, perhaps, been stinted in their food, deprived of childish pleasures, in order to allow their selfish unnatural parents to indulge in their pet vice. Weak in health and physique, what chance will they have in life? With that pernicious example constantly before them how can their character develop on fine, straight, loyal lines?

Nor is it only those obvious vices that will trail after them a generation of diseased or decadent sufferers. The scum of your great cities, the thieves, the drunkards, the liars know quite well what heritage of diseases and misery they will ultimately bequeath to their children. But what of the ordinary average man in the street—the respectable but unthinking folk, the well-to-do, who conceal their petty vices even from themselves? What of the people who make no effort against adversity? What of those who groan and complain that the world has passed them by? What of those who are content to rail against 'bad luck'? It is to these, m'dears, that you must look for the drifters and the derelicts of tomorrow. It is their children, and their children's children who will swell the ranks of the useless and the futile of the future.

You cannot put a heavier handicap on the younger generation than the germ of laziness and supineness, for that germ will develop and spread until its hideous tentacles have smothered every noble virtue, every attribute of the intellect and of the heart.

Human nature being what it is, is fond of procrastination; it dislikes trouble, tries to avoid worry; the easy road is the one it prefers to take. These are not grave faults, I'll admit, and with your marvellous mechanical progress are not even dangerous. But there is tomorrow to think of! The future generation—your children to whom you are bequeathing a heritage which may cause the very downfall of their Empire and the destruction of their race.

What is the use of genius if it has not with it the virtues of energy and perseverance? Of what use would such great scientists as Newton and Faraday, or in your own time Edison and Marconi, have been to the world had they been content to dream of the great wonders of the universe and not applied their genius to elucidating its mysteries, and by dint of hard work succeeded in enriching the future generations with their great discoveries. I doubt not but that Nature still holds concealed many a great marvel in her ample bosom, and calmly waits for human hands to draw aside the curtain wherewith she veils them. There are, alas, many diseases still waiting for the brain that will find a way to conquer them. There are still new places to discover, new realms on which the adventurer can set his foot, new mines for the seeker after gold and precious stones. The universe is waiting to reveal its wonders to those of the next generation who have energy, courage and enterprise.

And it is in your hands that their future lies!

The man of genius who is incapable of developing within himself the great virtues of energy and perseverance will assuredly live and die nameless and unglorified; his genius will have been of no use to the world. You will soon see him slip down the social ladder and finally submerged in that low stratum where there is neither ambition nor hope of success, and where the joy of life is killed by discontent. He is a man to be both pitied and despised. He could have done something for humanity but was too lazy to accomplish it. He frittered away those grand gifts which Nature had bestowed upon him; handicapped by his own supineness, he did not even try to overcome it; and in the end he committed the unpardonable sin of transmitting that same handicap to his children 'unto the third and fourth generation'.

In Heaven's name, m'dears, remember that determination, ambition, refusal to admit defeat, are the weapons with which your children will in their time have to battle with life. Is it then not worthwhile to keep a bright edge on those weapons for their sakes; to keep them clean and burnished by constant use? For the sake of the love you bear them do not forget that every action in your life, however insignificant it may seem to you, may add one day to their happiness or to their sorrow; for children see more than you sometimes give them credit for; and it is what they see in you that goes to mould their character. Far be it from me to be a square-toes or a pussyfoot; in my day every gentleman knew how to empty his glass and thrilled at a good game of hazard; I know that you moderns enjoy these things just as we did in the past, but it is moderation that will carry you through and excess that will destroy you, for every excess means adding another twig to the rod of unhappiness with which one day Fate will smite your son or your daughter.

'Tis not for me to preach, I know. I was deemed lazy in my time, flippant, irresponsible. You perhaps judge me differently, and I, for one, know that noble latent virtues lie beneath your outward cloak of futility. All I plead for is for courage to allow your virtues to come to the surface so that your children may delight in them and their young characters be moulded after their patterns.

It is worth the effort because of the future. It is also worth the effort because through it 'self' becomes entirely subservient to the rest of humanity—humanity represented by the young ones that grow up around you and, unknown to themselves, cry out even from babyhood for the happiness and contentment which a life of courage and of initiative, of love of country and of home alone can give.

Do not let them cry out in vain.

CHAPTER TWENTY-ONE

The Unimportance of Wealth for its own Sake

Whenever I read in your newspapers that an engagement between young Society people has been broken off I cannot help but admire their courage. Their marriage had probably been engineered for them by their parents or their friends, their respective wealth and social connections had certainly been weighed in the balance on either side, and neither being found wanting it was decided that connubial bliss was bound to follow. But the young people knew better and stood firm against the conspiracy to build their happiness on the insecure foundation of wealth.

In the past—which you are, all of you, so fond of calling the good old days—it would have been very difficult for those young people to set their faces against the commands of their respective families. Custom dictated that parents should 'arrange' the future of their children, and as often as not the result was a demmed unhappy mess for the poor young things. How lucky youth is nowadays to be allowed to mould its life as it will, and I will readily admit that wealth—in terms of £. s. d. hardly ever enters into the ideal realms of a genuine love-match.

Unfortunately, one cannot blind oneself to the fact that the influence of money is very largely on the increase these days. Too often I notice that the share-pusher or fraudulent financier is accepted in certain strata of modern society. Croesus is toadied too because of the benefits which may accrue from his goodwill, and an ill-mannered millionaire is often made more welcome than a poor gentleman because of the tips he is able to give for a flutter on the Stock Exchange.

Far be it from me to assert that money has not its romantic side! I were a demmed ingrate if I did, for it was money that enabled me to indulge my passion for adventure, which I could not have done had I been a penniless rustic. Money does undoubtedly open for one the portals of a wide, wide world. It brings the many delightful luxuries of the earth within one's reach; it can satisfy one's wishes and fulfil one's desires. But it is not almighty, and somehow the very things that are beyond its reach are the most important of all.

I enjoyed my wealth; I liked the comfort it brought me and the luxuries. I loved my white-winged *Day-Dream*, my lace, my perfumes, my horses and my home. I still love the things that wealth can give. I love to see beautiful pearls round a beautiful woman's neck. I love to see her wear expensive furs, silks and dainty shoes, and all the rest of the fripperies that women love. But I do not believe in the influence of wealth as wealth, or in the power of pearl necklaces and fur coats. There are influences far greater than these.

To begin with—and I am deliberately treading here on delicate ground—there is religion. There is no money in the world that could purchase the conviction of a devout man or woman, no matter to what form of belief he or she may adhere. The pages of the world's history teem with the relations of terrible martyrdom, endured for its sake, in the early days of Christianity, or during the great religious persecutions of the Middle Ages. These facts are too well known to need reiteration, but they do serve to prove that not even life, much less wealth or honours, was thought too high a price to pay when religious convictions were at stake.

A famous statesman did once assert that *'every man has his price'*. Now that was a demmed foolish assertion on the part of that statesman: it goes to prove that he, for one, knew very little of men and of life or he would never have made it. Take your own case, m'dears; would you, if the reward was high enough, commit murder, betray your friend, or rob an old woman of her savings? Would a sackful of gold, or all the gold in the world, compensate you for the loss of love, honour, or self-respect? Egad! I'll not wait for an answer.

There is nothing in the world that will purchase the love of a woman if she be forced into a marriage with the veriest Croesus. Many a rich man has learnt that hard lesson to his cost. Diamonds and pearls, fur coats or your wonderful motor cars—every luxury a woman's heart can desire—will not command a single heartfelt caress or the true fervour of a loving kiss.

Money cannot purchase love, and it cannot purchase health. There is at least one millionaire in your world today who would give five-sixths of his entire fortune to any doctor who could cure him permanently of a troublesome, though not deadly, disease. A very well-known lady of Victorian times offered £100,000 to any physician who could rid her of a disfiguring mark on the face. Beauty-culture was not then the highly scientific study that it is today and the lady took the ugly mark with her to the grave.

Egad! do not these two instances dispose of the theory that wealth is an almighty power? And I could quote you innumerable others. But it is exceedingly pleasant, I'll admit—and so is health. Wealth has not the satisfying quality of faith, nor the rapture of love, and personally, I am of the opinion that great wealth is a source of more trouble than anything else on earth. The acquiring of it is a worry, the losing it a greater worry still. In that way it is like teeth—trouble when they come and a demmed trouble when they go!

The possession of money is, in fact, a perpetually unsatisfied ambition. The man who owns a bicycle longs to have a car; as soon as he can afford a car he wants a large one; having a larger one he wants a more expensive one, or a more exclusive make; having this he wants a yacht, and in the striving after these things he spends his life in a musty office with his ear glued to a telephone, whilst love, happiness, idealism and adventure pass him by.

And in the end money, that precious thing for the acquisition of which he has sacrificed his whole life toiling and slaving and striving, cheats him out and out, because it is powerless to obtain for him that which perhaps he wants more than anything else in the world.

Unfortunately, the tendency of today is to imagine that wealth must be gained at all costs, that nothing matters except money and the luxuries it can bring; that for its sake it is wise to sacrifice everything that the idealist holds most dear—love, conscience, art, even honour sometimes.

It is true that you cannot take love and honour to the money-lender or the pawnbroker as you can a string of pearls, but when you have them even a visit to the pawnbroker is robbed of some of its sting. You may have a hard struggle for life; you may even feel the pinch of poverty; you may have to deny yourself and those you care for many pleasant luxuries, but if you have a clean record and possess the love of one who is dear to you, you will own gems far more precious than the rarest pearls that ever came out of the sea. And what is more, these gems have a purchasing power which no money in the world ever had, or ever will have, for they can, in their turn, purchase love and friendship. Honour calls to honour, love to love, both will bring into your life that great, priceless, wonderful thing without which no life can be complete—true and loyal friends.

CHAPTER TWENTY-TWO

Who said that Petticoat Government no longer Exists?

A man, well-known in your world today, remarked recently that the world no longer bowed to the dictates of its womenkind. He talked of the old days—my days, if you like—when behind every throne in Europe there lurked the shadow of a beautiful woman. He recalled the times when no statesman dared lift a finger for fear of that powerful shadow unless he had first assured himself that it favoured his project; and he finished his talk by averring that nowadays petticoats and petticoat government have vanished together into the limbo of forgotten things. He was wrong! I have not been wandering about among you without discovering that the ladies—bless 'em—still rule, and are as captivating, bewitching and obstinate as they always were and, I trust, always will be. Odd's my life! it makes one's heart leap with joy even now to see their bright fearless eyes, coquettish as ever, turn a man into an abject slave, though the fan—lovely necessity to every flirtation once upon a time—has gone now, alas! the same way as hoops and flounces and the *frou-frou* of silk petticoats.

In the days when sticks and clubs were used alike for international or domestic arguments, it is extremely likely that skin-clad men believed that they ruled supreme. Probably there was a strident 'Woman's place is in the cave' slogan in existence even then. But all the same, even in those days, your smiling Stone-Age lady could twist the stalwart tribal chief round her finger as easily as she could twist her own glossy plaits of hair; and the local witch doctor or head councillor, whose lightest word rolled like thunder around the massed silent circle of men, was sent out grumbling by his wife from his desirable cavern residence to scrape the dirt off his feet with his spear.

And though all that happened a demmed long time ago something very similar goes on to this day! Many of the world's most famous men have confessed that all their lives they have been guided by their wife or their sweetheart or sometimes their mother. Many wonderful pictures, beautiful books, glorious pieces of music, are dedicated to the women who inspired them. Though there are many examples or men who, ruled by women, were led to cruel, unjust or foolish deeds, there are countless others where that rule has been everything that is wise and just.

But the vindication of petticoat government, m'dears, does not rest on historic records alone; it would have a poor chance of proving its case if it did. Luckily for the world's happiness it rests on more secure foundation. You surely must know many cases of ordinary everyday folk—friends, acquaintances, the man in the street—in whose life the magic of romance has turned life's rough stony roads into exquisite, rose-strewn highways, and transformed the cottage into a wondrous palace of love and of constant joy.

Even in your ultra-practical days when so many of you affect to despise romance, many a young lover would choose to be the slave of his adored rather than become the ruler of an Empire, and the rejected swain still finds the whole world, its triumphs and its rewards a hollow mockery when love is not. That is the way of true love, and it has not changed a tittle since my day or any other. It will brook no sharing of its sovereignty either with pride, with wisdom or ambition; it cares nothing for opinion of the world, powerful as that can sometimes be. Petticoat government is an autocratic form of rule, and there is no power on earth that can overthrow it if it is backed by love.

It would certainly seem that in your year of sense, 1933, you ought to banish this tyrannical petticoat rule—if indeed it chafes you, as you say it does—just as of late so many countries of the world have banished their monarchs and upset their government. I am happy to say that our own beloved country has been sane enough to set its face against the modern proneness of looking upon hereditary monarchy as an impediment to business, or as tending to distract the mind from its all-important aim of money-making; but in many countries, alas! monarchs are voted to be anachronisms, to be in the way of the steady development of reason. Let us depose our crowned kings, say the moderns, and by the same token let us hurl our queens of the petticoat from their throne. Let us rid ourselves, once and for all, of such false, out-of-date, medieval gods.

Thus, do you, m'dears, proclaim your independence from the housetops, and a good many of you in this post-war world have certainly rid yourselves of your ancient monarchies. But strive as you may against the autocratic rule of the petticoat, it is still with you. It is not in your power, nor, believe me, is it your wish to cast off woman's yoke once she has entwined herself around your heart, demanding to be worshipped, to be loved, and to rule. It is her province, my friends; she will never give it up, so you had better make up your minds to wear her fetters and pretend you like them.

You may try to abolish the word 'love' like Soviet Russia has tried to abolish Christianity, but even the most cynical amongst you may find one day that there is, perhaps, one footstep in the world the sound of which will cause a flutter in your heart, and that you will find happiness and the strength to carry on in the light of one woman's smile. You may deflect a river from its course, and in your twentieth century you have your wonderful inventions which enable you to talk to a man half a world away, to see through solid flesh as if it were transparent, or to erect buildings so high that the Tower of Babel would seem puny beside them. Nevertheless, it is a small white hand that will beckon you to the Heaven of contentment and of home or will point the way to the Hell of loneliness. With all your independence, your strength, your power to set up Governments and destroy them at your will, you are still under the sway of the most tyrannical autocracy the world has ever known.

This world is still Cupid's plaything and do believe me when I say that you have no wish for it to be otherwise. My faith! I cannot amate—nor can you, I'll warrant—what would happen if the merry little god gave up trying to play with us and left our hearts to get atrophied in their solitude. Life would not be worth the living now, would it, I ask you? Love rules most of you, the best of you, the strongest, manliest amongst you, and you had best admit it. It may be love of wife, of daughter or mother, but there is no man worthy of the name who does not toil and strive for a woman he loves. And, mind you, there is not a more jealous god than that little Cupid. If you fight him he will have his revenge. If you turn your back on him he will contrive to overload you with depression, discontent and monotony, and finally he will hand you over to the most cruel of all torturers—loneliness.

But if you bow to the sovereignty of Love, if you wear its golden fetters, it will crown you king of your little world. It will fill your life with gladness, spur you on to noble deeds, raise your hopes, stimulate your ambition and make you the real master of your fate.

CHAPTER TWENTY-THREE

Two Heads are better than One

'Pon my soul, my friends, I must congratulate you at least on this: that your generation has discovered and is not afraid to admit that a wife makes the truest comrade and the best guide an ambitious or a happy man can have. Indeed, it warms the heart to see such tributes paid to women as your great men have recently done.

See how many of your statesmen have said that but for the guidance of a woman's hand they would never have attained their high eminence in world affairs. Sir Austen Chamberlain, who is an aristocrat after mine own heart, has said:

> For thirty years my wife has been my inspiration. She has known every secret of my public life. She has sustained my courage, shared my hopes and sympathised with me in my anxieties.

Mr. Baldwin has on more than one occasion said much the same thing about his own life partner; Lord Reading, when he closed his great years of service in troubled India, said that more than once would discouragement have overcome him but for 'the lady who stood by me when times were difficult and anxious.'

Yet another of your famous statesman who would never have reached to fame alone is the Marquess of Aberdeen, who has served his country as Governor-General of Canada and as Viceroy of Ireland during the latter's most troublesome years. The book most appropriately entitled, *We Twa*, of which he and his wife are joint authors, proclaims in every page the vital truth of the ancient saying that, '*Whoso findeth a good wife findeth a great thing.*'

And in other realms than politics great or famous men have paid tribute to the white hands that guided their careers. John Galsworthy dedicated his *Forsyte Saga* to his wife, saying that without her encouragement, sympathy and criticism, he would never have won through to success. Even your amazing Mr. G. B. Shaw has for once been conventional enough to admit that he *might perhaps* have failed but for the help his wife had given him throughout his career.

My faith! I could go on quoting you instances by the yard of famous men who have said as much, but I find it difficult to choose among so many. Cromwell, that iron-hearted regicide, was never happy when parted from his wife; and she it was who once wrote those beautiful words to him: 'My life is but half a life in thine absence.' Lord John Lawrence, who helped to build our Empire in India, was once chaffed by his sister, who said that he could never rest for five minutes away from his wife's side. 'That was why I married her, madam,' he replied quietly.

But it is not in those great men, either past or present, or in their wonderful helpmates that I am most interested. My thoughts now, as always, fly to the man in the street, to the average British working or commercial man, to all those, in fact, who have found in marriage just the kind of companionship that they sought. Laurels of fame are perhaps not for them; they are not striving to reach the giddy heights of clangourous success, but in their struggles and their strivings they can hold on to a hand which is always ready to guide and to help. '*God must have loved the average woman: He made so many of them,*' was said by a great philanthropist who knew how to appreciate the wonderful qualities of the quiet, everyday housewife who sits at home and ministers to the creature comforts of the man she loves, and while darning his socks weaves into the criss-cross threads thoughts of how best she can serve him with encouragement and advice.

She it is who makes this modern world of yours seem less drab, for she causes it to glow with the effulgence of her unselfishness. She is for ever planning ways and means to save her man from petty worries and irritating cares; she it is who puts heart into him when discouragement overtakes him; she who comforts him when sorrow and disappointment seem more than he can bear.

Then I pray you, charge your glasses, ye men of this Great and Greater Britain, and drink a loyal toast to your adorable womankind. You know as well as I do that without your loving wife life would indeed make a poor show for you. Without the ladies—God bless 'em!— this whole round earth of ours would lose all its sweetness, and we, poor male creatures, would lose all our self-respect if we had no one to stand by us and tell us what demmed fine fellows we really were.

I hate that stupid old proverb which says that familiarity breeds contempt; but all the same, I fear me, that it causes us to take for granted, or cease to appreciate at its just value, the constant care, the kindliness, the thoughtfulness wherewith our working life is made easier for us. Think back on the days of your honeymoon, my friends, and how exquisite seemed to you the thousand and one little attentions which your young wife already bestowed on you. Every time you found your slippers put to warm by the fire you felt a thrill of manly satisfaction and of pride in the choice you had made of a life's companion. Do not lose this great hold you have on happiness by ceasing to notice those small attentions after the first few years of marital contentment.

The love that prompts all those small attentions is the same today as it was in the days of your betrothal. Do not blind yourself to it and take too much for granted. She is always ready to share your sorrow and make it thereby but half a trouble, and by the same token she will double your joy by sharing it with you.

It is the unfortunate lonely bachelor who 'has no one to still him and therefore must weep out his eyes'.

And to put the matter in a more prosy way, let me assure you that two heads are always better than one, especially if that other head matures thoughts only of you. The wagon that is drawn in double harness will roll without a jolt on life's highway.

Chapter Twenty-Four

Are Women really Selfish?

This, m'dears, is one of the questions everlastingly asked by man, and woman's answer to it is a Mona Lisa smile, which may be interpreted as acquiescence or scorn—as you please.

There have been, of course, many women well known in history who have appeared to be taking all and giving nothing in return, who never hesitated to destroy ruthlessly whatever stood in the way of their ambition, were it for place, for power or for love. In order to remove an obstacle that stood in their path women—demmed ungallant as it seems to say it—have been known to sacrifice the lives or friends or lovers, even the honour of their country, without granting so much as a kiss in return. Women have shown, in fact, that they can be more pitiless, more cruel than men, where their desires, their appetites or their ambition were concerned.

In the nature of things there must also have been millions of women, inconspicuous and unknown, who have acted at times with unbelievable selfishness. Women, perhaps, who have used all their arts of seduction to keep a lover at their side when honour and duty called to him to go; others who, in order to satisfy their own ambition, have tied husband or lover to their chariot wheel, and dragged him with them to heights of social or political attainments which were beyond his power to reach, with the result that a crash was inevitable, and the weak or foolish man was hurled down from those giddy heights and fell broken in heart and in spirit, unregretted, uncomforted by the very one who caused his downfall.

History has shown us many a Cleopatra in some such roles, and I know that every one of you in your own walk of life, has known of cases less famous but equally tragic.

Nevertheless, in fairness to the sex, let it be said that selfishness in its true sense is *not* always the motive power that drives these unhappy women on. Cleopatra was not intentionally selfish when she kept Antony by her side, whilst the cold ambitious Octavius had time to conquer worlds in his stead. Mrs. Warren Harding, in acting as the motive force which drove a simple farmer to the helm of one of the greatest powers in the modern world, has always appealed to me as being more a tragedy herself than even the tragic figure of her husband. And, plain Mrs. Smith, who turns her husband from an easy-going, sporting Briton into a white-faced business robot, is herself more often than not a stricken statue of self-denial.

Mark, I do not say that these women are right; merely that they are not, in the true meaning of the word, selfish.

When the pagans would have it that Cupid was blind I think they made a mistake. It is not the little god who is blind; he distributes his precious shafts judiciously enough as a rule; but his arrow points often seem to have been dipped in a virulent poison, which has the power of depriving of their sight those who have been pierced by them. And women suffer from these attacks of blindness far more frequently and more completely than men.

Watch the girl who fears or hopes for her lover. Is she selfish? Let Destiny ask her to give her life for his and see then! For herself she cares nothing, but for him—for him she will be ready to sacrifice not only her life, but the rest of the world in a single blazing funeral pyre if it would but profit him. Love's poisoned shaft has blinded her indeed.

She thinks for him, acts for him, schemes for him, plunges into evil or good impersonally for him. She sees a prize—he must have it; she recognises a goal—he must attain it. For love of him she dreams

dreams, and in her love-blindness she is obsessed by the dreams and forces his weak humanity to an impossible task.

But make no mistake. The dreams are all for him. She is willing to stand in the background, fall out by the way; she is ready to become a mere stepping-stone to his success. It would be the divine height of unselfishness were it not the blind height of folly.

Woman has a longer vision than man, but she lacks his logical faculty for estimating obstacles. Woman will try and keep her lover by her side, knowing that they would be happy together even though his name be disgraced, or his country in sore need of him. But man, whose creed is different from hers, puts her second in his thoughts. 'I could not love thee, dear, so much, loved I not honour more!' is his rule of life; he is selfish for his honour's sake, whilst she would sacrifice both her honour and his regard for her in order to keep him safely within the shelter of her arms.

It has been said that if we only had faith we could say to this mountain: 'Go hence!' and it would actually go. That is the creed of the woman who is in love. Her faith in her love is so great that, should she covet a throne for her lover and a mountain stood in his way she would try her best to move it. I always think that had St. Peter been a woman he would never have found himself sinking when he tried to walk so boldly upon the waves.

Sometimes the man also is of heroic mould and can follow the keenest flights of his chosen woman's vision and make them all come true. But such a man is rare; he is the real Fairy Prince for whom every woman pines. With a true woman as his guide and helpmate he can rise to heights supreme and when he has reached them you will find him listening to the plaudits of a wondering world, taking them all as his due, for the world, my friends, seldom sees or guesses that it was the woman who gave him all that he most needed—her help, her guidance, her sustaining love—so that he might attain his goal.

Is it not the charming contrariness in woman that makes her—demmed delicious, distracting creature that she is—dream so many uncomfortable dreams? Would woman not a million times rather be left alone in an Eden of her own creation, alone with the man she loved, no matter whether he were god or common clay, than be a dweller in a Paradise peopled and fashioned by the world outside?

That is the reason probably why most of them are glad when they find that their idol has feet of clay after all, and they can love him just as illogically and absolutely as their heart desires, with all his failings and his sins. It is heroic, this giving all for love, and women are so constituted that they actually like doing it; but a happy home, contentment and family life are really worth a thousand times more than dreams of ambition, so few of which are satisfying even when they are attained.

CHAPTER TWENTY-FIVE

Love is still Life's most Romantic Adventure

You may believe me or not, m'dears, but I can assure you that there was never yet a man or woman living who was not in search of love. Of course, you moderns, who are so thoroughly versed in psychoanalysis, will at once retort that you, for one—knowing yourself thoroughly—have never even thought of such an antiquated, ludicrous emotion as love. But let me tell you this: that even now in your practical world of today I see old and young, men and women, youths and maidens, rich and poor, married and single—all of you, in fact, hot in pursuit of the little pink god. Love, m'dears, is as vital to existence as is the sun to flowers, as is the pure air of heaven to your lungs, and all of you moderns, cynical and unbelieving though you may label yourselves, tend just as eagerly towards love as we did in the past; you are all striving—though you may not be aware of it—to struggle out of the gloom of the commonplace in order to reach the splendours of Love's fairyland.

The whole of your life, my friends, is incidental to this. It is for love's sake that a man will work so that he may have a home and comfort to offer to the woman of his choice. I doubt not that even the cave-man in his day sought the richest furs for his women and the warmest shelters for them against cold wintry weather.

Will you tell me why your shingled, boyish-looking emancipated city typist or tea-room waitress trips so gaily every morning to her work? Because she likes it? Gadzooks! does any healthy young girl really like work? Because it flatters her vanity to do man's work? Never! She does it because instinct tells her that in the world outside her home she will have a chance of one day finding her mate.

This mating instinct is passionately strong in every healthy human being, though most of you young moderns would deny it, and theorize at length about psychic affinities and sex-appeal. Those words, m'dears, are just twentieth century masks, fashioned to distort the oldest and most valuable heritage of the human race—the will to search for love.

Of course, you are ready to pulverise me with the argument that love does not by any means always lead to fairyland. More often than not its sequel is tragedy or else a drab mediocrity which is more unendurable than black despair. What you are pleased to call happiness only comes through the channel of love once in a thousand times. That is your argument, I know, and in a measure, you are right; but the reason for tragedy or mediocrity is because you young people of today are so apt to mistake the brass-farthing of sex attraction for the pure gold of love.

Love is so elusive that it is easily mistaken for dross. Perhaps it is because we want it so badly that we allow ourselves to be deluded by shams and mockeries. But you young post-war girls who are so ready to lure a man on to make love or propose marriage to you, take my advice and test your choice of a mate as carefully as if you were buying gold; nay! far more carefully, for if, after buying gold, you should find it to be base metal, you can always cast it aside and retrieve your loss by starting to bargain afresh; but if you have been foolish enough to mistake a momentary passion for true and lasting love, you will have ruined your life and could no more build it up again than you could a broken rainbow.

I am not talking now of girls who have been victimized by rogues, or of men whose affections have been broken on the wheel of some woman's caprice. These are but drops in the ocean of tragedies that come in the wake of unhappy love. The real tragedy, m'dears, of life's most romantic adventure is to be found among the millions of people who have been willing to take the cast-out shafts from Cupid's quiver and then discovered—too late, alas!—that those shafts, far from being true gold, were just poisoned darts that left incurable wounds in their heart.

How many of you, I wonder, will during this year utter the solemn vows which the churches demand from those who wish to start life together on the basis of mutual love and comradeship? And how many of you will presently regret those vows and regret them to the end of your days? For whatever may be said to the contrary, your modern easy divorce does not erase from the tablets of memory those happenings which the *decree nisi* is called upon to obliterate. The divorced man and the divorced woman may seem outwardly the same; they may behave in the same manner as before; they may smile as they did heretofore, but deep down in their hearts they know that the romance they dreamed of has received a wound which can never heal again.

If only instinct would teach you young people that happiness can only be attained by real love, and that charming woman needs to exercise more care in choosing a husband than she does in selecting a hat. Only that way, believe me, does your happiness lie.

There is such a thing as falling in love with love. The glamour of it dazzles; the object of one's adoration appears in the false light as a kind of god, a Titan amongst men. It is only when the eyes become accustomed to the surrounding gloom that the Titan shrivels to the size of a pigmy and the god is found to have feet of clay. But I well understand the glamour! How am I going to preach to you young people who are just on the threshold of life that the great adventure of love needs preparation and thought?

Too hasty enthusiasm has wrecked more exploring expeditions into Loveland than ever Arctic bergs wrecked the vessels of Pole-seeking mariners. There is a very wise parable which was told by Divine lips, and which has a universal meaning. It relates the adventures of ten virgins, five of whom were wise and five very foolish. They were waiting for the bridegroom, if you remember, and the wise virgins in anticipation of his coming kept their lamps trimmed and burning clear and bright. The foolish ones, on the other hand, neglected their lamps, allowed them to flicker out and to die for want of trimming and of oil, so that when the time came and the bridegroom knocked at the door there they were, all in the dark, unable to welcome him. All that is fiction, of course, but what a lot of truth there is in it.

Some of you foolish, charming young people are in far too great a hurry to light the lamp of your love, just letting it shed its feeble, uncertain rays on the first man or woman that comes along. For the time being it certainly does give you a sense of something big and eventful in your life, the illusion that you have laid the foundation of some great happiness. Those of you, on the other hand, who happen to be a little wiser, do not waste the light of your precious lamp. Its searching gleam will reveal pitfalls unseen in the dark. The semi-darkness of loneliness may make the path of life rather difficult, but you are content, nevertheless, to wander along quietly until such time as you see your way to pass through the gloom into the sunshine of real love.

Then, when you have found the one man or woman around whom your universe can safely revolve, you will realise how wise you were to travel on life's highway hopefully, if alone, and to reach your goal in full possession of your vitality and enthusiasm rather than to make a rush for the dazzle-light of passion and arrive dishevelled and blind.

You will no doubt remind me that in a former chapter I have entreated you to live dangerously, to take risks for the sake of the ends you have in view. I do so still: in all things of life, m'dears, be prepared to take risks, *but not in love*. Be very sure where you set your foot before you tread that wonderful path. Do not mistake the glamour of a momentary thrill for the true light of enduring love. Think twice before you dedicate your life to one who is not worthy of the sacrifice. Your gay bachelor and smart lavender-lady are happier far than those who wear the fetters of an unhappy marriage, and it is better never to have loved at all than to love amiss.

Love still is, and always will be, the most romantic adventure in life. Not for the world would I have a single one of you deliberately refuse to embark on it. All that the great adventure demands of you is a trimmed lamp, clear-sightedness to distinguish what is true gold, the love that makes the poor infinitely rich, and which will wipe away your tears; the companionship that will ease life's burden for you and ensure for your domestic happiness, the only bliss of Paradise that has survived the Fall, the spice of life that gives it all its flavour.

CHAPTER TWENTY-SIX

What is the Price of Love?

I suppose that more has been written on the subject of love than on any other subject under the sun. Proverbs, wise saws, verses, romances—their number is legion; the brains of poets and of wits, dry minds of cynics and philosophers have, in their turn, been exhausted in finding the true definition of that subtle, elusive thing we call 'love' and which only a lover understands.

And in writing about love all those prose writers and versifiers have invariably set themselves the task of inquiring as to what exactly is the price to be paid for that rarefied commodity, and whether the possession of it is built on a secure foundation. And so out of the cudgelling of great brains came the wise saws: '*When poverty comes in at the door Love flies out of the window*'; or '*Love makes beggars of kings*'; or again, '*The first sigh of love is the last of wisdom*'; and I could quote a hundred more, but all these quotations m'dears, smack more of wit than of truth.

Are all those cynics and philosophers—aye! and all those poets— going to assert that this ethereal, unsubstantial thing which brightens every life into which it enters and cheers every heart it touches, is yet so poor and feeble that it shrivels at the touch of poverty? That it is so akin to madness that it warps reason and weakens judgement? That it can have the effect of stealing away a man's riches or his strength or his wisdom? I think not. And do not be led into believing it, either. I give you my word that this modern world of yours is not yet void of great lovers, of men and women who know in their heart of hearts that the magic touch of true love is more precious even today than all the gold of Ophir, or the diamonds of Golconda.

But they will not proclaim their belief openly.

Now you know, my friends, that if you were really to search your hearts you would be ready enough to admit that love is still the greatest incentive that will spur a man to noble deeds and selfless actions, that, far from destroying wisdom and sound sense it is the whetstone of enterprise and judgement. You do not have to pay a price for love. Love is its own price: it drives away fear, it conquers pain, it makes poverty and disappointment endurable, it scorns the enmity of the envious and derides the scoffings of the cynic. It is you, who love and are loved, who are immeasurably rich and they—the jaundiced modern scoffers—who are beggars in this world. It is the great, the selfless loves of millions of men and women that mount like incense to Heaven, and the jeers and gibes of cynics that like evil-smelling smoke defile the purity of the atmosphere.

But, on the other hand, honour and duty do often exact a price which love must pay if it is to remain true to itself. When either of those two great forces call, love must often hide itself behind a veil of sorrow; I can assure you that many a time when I was in full possession of the joys and peace of my beautiful garden at Richmond and knew that Lady Blakeney was watching me with fear and doubt in the loveliest eyes that love of man ever filled with tears, I used to hear the low insistent sigh of suffering women and children in revolutionary Paris calling to me, and not even my loved one's tender arms nor her exquisite voice could then have kept me to her side.

And for you also, m'dears, suffering and sorrow are often the price which your love must pay should honour or duty call you. Most of you experienced the sorrow of parting, did you not, during the sad years of the war? You paid for the joys of love by many a heartache when you thought of *her* tears and the last kiss of farewell on the platform at Victoria Station.

And in the same way some of you, alas! must pay for the happiness which you enjoyed when things were bright and prosperous at home, by the misery of seeing those you care for suffer for want of the small comforts or luxuries you would give your heart's blood to provide for them. Where there is no love, m'dears, there can be no sorrow. Sorrow is the price you may have to pay for love; but is it not worth it? Would you not rather shed a bucketful of tears than miss the infinite joys that true love, reciprocated love alone, can give? Good old Dante, when he went to visit Hell to see how the shades were getting on there, would have it that over the gates of Hades there was graven the legend: '*For sorrow's crown of sorrow is remembering happier things*.' And this saying he got from an ancient philosopher who averred that 'In all adversity the most unhappy sort of misfortune is to have been happy.'

Faith! they may have been great men those two—they certainly were—but all the same I beg to differ from them. I'll pit my knowledge of the human heart against all their theories or their wisdom. There is a sweet fragrance in remembrance which no amount of sorrow can dispel; on the contrary, sorrow will etherealise all the thousand and one little events on which past happiness was built and turn them into a caress that will soothe the troubled mind and wipe away the tears.

And it is in times of stress that true love shines with a clearer and purer light. The sharpness of the trial will in itself purge it from the dross of complacence and selfishness which life, more often than not, is apt to mix it with. So, do not rail against love, m'dears, if you have to pay for it at times with anxiety and a few tears. The joys it gives you will more than compensate you for any measure of suffering.

And if in the end love does exact, as it unfortunately will, the greatest price of all the sorrow of life-long parting, do not even then rail against him. The Dark Angel does, alas! wield his awful sword sometimes to part young lovers, still in the rapture of their first kiss, or to sever the bonds that have held trusting comrades together for perhaps half a century.

Even then, m'dears, do not rail against love. 'It is better to have loved and lost than never to have loved at all,' so said our national poet, and with him I am in complete agreement. Sceptics and cynics may say what they like, but I will put down my profession of faith even here and now. And it is this: Love is such a mighty power that it can bridge over the black chasm which lies between life and death. Perfect love is perfect trust, and those of you who have known true love, just as I did, cannot possibly believe for a moment that it can end in this material world. Love is *not* material; it is ethereal and sublime, and as such must endure for ever. You cannot bury it, you cannot cremate it.

It is one of the attributes of eternity.

The greatest most selfless love that ever burned for man on this earth reached its sublimity on Calvary. There it triumphed, once and for all, over the terrors of Death. And men today—you, m'dears, I, the rest of the world—have learned through the grandeur of that sacrifice that human love is powerful enough to break the gates that part us from the loved one who has gone before, so that when our own time comes to cross the Great Divide we may hear the words: '*I love you. I am waiting for you*' come down to our ears from the realm of the stars, and our spirit grasp the spirit hand that beckons and points the way to the kingdom of undying love.

CHAPTER TWENTY-SEVEN

Perfect Lover, Perfect Husband?

If I were asked to decide whether men or women have more vivid imaginations, I vow 'twould not be so difficult a situation as that in which the unfortunate Paris found himself! To the ladies would I award the apple, without a doubt!

I suppose every woman has had, at some time or other in her early life, a mental picture of what a perfect lover should be: tall, handsome, strong, kind, just the smallest touch of mystery, the epitome of honour and yet adorably human. Upon my soul, a difficult dream for us poor men to live up to!

The girl sits dreaming, and in her happy, idle moments visualises a first meeting with this dream-god she has created. Hand in hand she wanders with him in her dream along winding, moonlit paths, waiting, thrilled and breathless for those three little words which, when spoken by him, will change this prosaic world into Fairyland.

And then one day she is acutely conscious of a small, glittering band on her third finger, and wonders how it has come to pass that the universe does not stand still in order to gaze enraptured on the new marvel, the perfect lover—her lover! As a matter of fact, the world has noticed the marvel, but to the girl's own friends and relations the man to whom she has become engaged is probably no more than barely good-looking, and it is extremely likely that he has some peculiarity or characteristic which they violently dislike.

Girl friends make mental resolutions that when they choose a man he shall be something quite different; already they compare their own dreams to this reality that seems to them so poor, and they smile with a certain complacent indulgence when they meet the shining eyes of the girl whose dream-lover walks by her side. Married friends are more encouraging unless, perchance, their own matrimonial venture has been unlucky, but usually their thoughts dwell on their own perfect lover, even though to others he seems but a whimsical warning of complete prosiness when seen in his own home, clad in unromantic dressing-gown and carpet slippers, grunting from the depths of a capacious armchair, and with, perhaps, a cold in his head or gout in his big toe. Odd's my life! what a dream man—to you!

To your thinking, in the halcyon time of your engagement, the world—your world—does not realise at once that the perfect lover of your dreams has come to life, whereas to you he has already taken on the form and shape of a hero of romance. What if he is of medium height and inclined to broadness? That only makes you realise what an odd mistake you made when you dreamt of him as one of those tall, ungainly, shapeless gawks! What if his nose be flattish and his eyes blue? Gadzooks! who would worship a hero with a bird-like beak and eyes like a savage? In your adolescent imagination you may (though you may not admit that you did!) have created a vague, godlike individual who looked like the illustration on the jacket of a sensational novel. But in the end what you have found is a perfect lover, a man whose character answers to your highest ideals of chivalry and manliness.

Is he less romantic than the gallant armoured knight of old, who rode over hill and dale in order to slay dragons, or to do battle against all those miscreants who refused to acknowledge the sovereignty of his lady's beauty? Of course, he is not! See the number of very real dragons he slays every day, when poverty and disappointment and threatening ill-health menace him. See how shrewdly and yet how fairly he wields his weapons of brain and muscle against clever, doughty or wealthy rivals; and yet, withal, see how chivalrous he is towards women and how kindly and gay he can be with little children.

He is the hero of your dreams, *madame*, the perfect lover of your imagination. How does he stand in your eyes when, at last, you have trod with him the magic way up to the altar, and heard right through the thunder of the Wedding March the *paean* of your victory in winning this *beau ideal* for yourself against all the world? Does the glamour of him wear thin against the hard, prosaic things of everyday life? If a man cannot be a hero to his lackey, can he possibly pose unruffled and unshaken on his pedestal before his wife's clear eyes?

Do not doubt it for a moment! You need no pedestal for the man you love; all you need for him, all he wants above all other things, is a place in your heart and to live in intimate and close companionship with you. If you, in your turn, have given him love for love, and if you have had the patience and the courage to wait till he, the bridegroom of your dreams, came to you, then marriage will surely be the portal to a realm of supreme and unchanging bliss. Your perfect lover will be the perfect husband, without whom as your helpmate and friend you can never know the perfection of life or the sublimity of romance.

In the course of years, when Father Time has laid a finger on the perfect lover and he finds increasing difficulty in persuading his hair to cover the bald patch on the top of his head, Love the Alchemist, having transmuted the evanescent metal of your girlish visions into the solid gold of conjugal happiness, will touch your eyes with magic so that you will only see the strong brave, kindly soul shining through his loving eyes. If rheumatism in the joints makes him a little slower in opening the door for you than he was forty years ago, Cupid will bewitch you, while you wait, with the understanding of the fine courage and increasing tenderness which has, for a lifetime, marked him for your perfect, gentle knight.

Your world today is no less full of magicians, giants, witches, gnomes and fairies than it was in the legendary time of King Arthur. Luck is a magician able to change your lives from drab to gold; care is a witch who can steal your beauty and line your face in a night; despair is a giant who can torture you and hold you in his iron grip until your perfect lover and perfect husband comes to your rescue as the sublime knight-errant; rebellious, unkind thoughts are demmed unpleasant little gnomes to tease you, and friendly, happy ones are the fairies that lighten your burden while you wander down the high road of life.

The Chief Magician of them all is love, love the ruler of men, the king of all the world, whom no amount of scoffing and of sneering has ever dethroned; love the dear tyrant of my time and yours, whose light no modernism can dim; love which has brightened the lives of millions of us and whose torch will be kept aflame for all the aeons to come. Let the world sneer and laugh, but if love gives the fortunate man of your choice the divine accolade and dubs him Sir Perfect Lover, or Sir Perfect Husband, then his companionship and comradeship will make every dark hour seem bright, every sorrow endurable, every joy doubly great, all through your life and in the great unknown that is to come.

CHAPTER TWENTY-EIGHT

Leaving You at the Altar

When first I made up my mind to come out into the golden light of your everyday life, I vow that I positively shivered at all the misery, the sorrow, the drabness of existence, which you yourselves led me to believe made up the sum total of your lives in this twentieth century. Much less did I relish the thought of compiling a whole book on what I feared would be a most depressing task. This work, I said, will fatigue me most atrociously; it will bore me most unhappily; I verily feared that my exuberant romanticism would be shipwrecked under the strain.

And now, here I am at the last chapter of this little book and it seems to me that the time which I have spent in this fascinating, marvellous new world of yours was but the space of a breath. I have only seen a few of its hundreds of astonishing facets, and, believe me, I feel that there are thousands more of which I have not even caught a glimpse. So, I'll console myself with the thought of another visit to you all at some future time.

I know you will forgive me if I make use of this final chapter for the benefit of those of you young moderns who will wake one morning soon to the sound of your own wedding-bells.

The latest fashion, it seems, is to treat marriage as nothing more or less than a business contract. Had this been any but my last chapter I would have resisted so monstrous a suggestion and written twenty more to make out a case for love. But things being as they are, let us by all means treat this marriage question as strictly business, and let me begin by asking you how you individually would approach a business proposition? I know little of such things, but I venture to presume that you would expect in a business partner an upright, honourable character, a clean bill of health and a full measure of discretion, ability, of sense, and of honour. Pessimists, when I started this book, might have confounded me with the argument that these things are not to be found in modern business men, but now that I know more about you all, and know that there are just as many sterling qualities to be found in your men of today as ever there were in the past, I can, in my turn, confound your pessimists.

You would also doubtless refuse to enter into business partnership with a person who looked upon the contract as a sort of slipknot. Odd's my life! if business was to be run in the slipshod manner in which some of you moderns deal with matrimony, the bankruptcy courts would be kept as busy as are the divorce courts, and the finances of the entire world would soon be engulfed in chaos.

You know as well as I do—better probably—that for a business to be successful it needs to be carried on by men or women who have brains, initiative, training and tact. But so, does marriage, m'dears! All the qualities which you expect to find in your successful business men you must look for in the partner who is to be life's companion, to whom you are going to entrust your happiness, your future and, what's more, the future of your children.

What chances, think you, would a business have if its principals knew nothing of its workings? Yet how many of you dear, irresponsible young things trip lightly up to the altar and embark on the serious business of matrimony, blissfully ignorant of how to cook a dinner, engage a maid, furnish a house or earn a regular income? No one would think of designing a public building without becoming first a qualified architect, and the law forbids any man to practise medicine without due qualifications, the result of years of strenuous study; yet one sees numberless men and women entering the serious state of marriage without the slightest idea of the duties and responsibilities it will presently entail. Can you wonder, then, that so many marriages end in recriminations, in heart-breakings and sorrow, and finally in the divorce court?

Is marriage a business? Well, we will not argue over the word. 'Tis you moderns who choose to call it so, and then deride it because, forsooth, in your estimation its profit-and-loss account points to bankruptcy. What you want to do, m'dears, is to look upon marriage as a business if you must, but also as a foundation—the only solid one—on which you can raise the edifice of lifelong happiness. By it alone can you obtain comradeship, sympathy and understanding, and that wonderful feeling that in the world there is one being whose interests are absolutely identical with yours.

All of you young moderns, I know, are fond of saying that by marriage you lose your freedom. So, you do. You lose the freedom of wandering uncared for on life's highway, the freedom of weeping alone and uncomforted when sorrow assails you. You lose the freedom of suffering in loneliness, and of being forced to bottle up your joy because there is no one who cares enough to share it with you. Well, m'dears, if that be freedom, give me all the fetters that love can forge: home ties, friendship, not to mention baby fingers that cling so tightly to the heart.

Have I lost something of glamour in your eyes now that I have made you think of me, not as the hero of a hundred adventures in the romantic days of revolutionary France, but as a romanticist who has learned that in all the adventures of life there is none to compare with the one we embark on when we set forth to choose our helpmate?

Once more, I pray you, charge your glasses, you lovely, sleek-headed, slim-legged Amazons, and you ambitious, enterprising Britons all! Drink to the master of you all—Love the King! He is all that matters in life, and in this great business of living he is the profit—worth all the gold of the Indies and all the laurel wreaths ever woven, on which you can count as a set-off against failure or disappointment or sorrow.

On this let me make my bow to you of this still young century, happy in the knowledge that your world of today is every whit as romantic as it was in the past. Your men are as gallant, your women as charming as ever they were. There is as much romance in your civilization, your commerce and your marvellous inventions, as there were in medieval jousts, in duelling or poesy. Let me express the earnest hope that I have convinced you of this. Rub your eyes, m'dears, and take another look at your world. Do not allow those demmed cynics and pessimists to be for ever pointing to mud-heaps and gutters, telling you that they are the realities of life; for I vow that real life is full to overflowing of fragrance and of beauty. Look about you, m'dears and see the loyalties, the friendships, the silent endurances and sacrifice that meet you at every turn. And then, I pray you, murmur to yourself: 'Well, I declare that demmed elusive Pimpernel of ours does know a thing or two!'

Gentlemen, your servant!

Ladies, as ever, your most devoted slave!

The Way of the Scarlet Pimpernel

Contents

Chapter 1

At an angle of the Rue de la Monnaie where it is intersected by the narrow Passage des Fèves there stood at this time a large three-storeyed house, which exuded an atmosphere of past luxury and grandeur. Money had obviously been lavished on its decoration: the balconies were ornamented with elaborately carved balustrades, and a number of legendary personages and pagan deities reclined in more or less graceful attitudes in the spandrels round the arches of the windows and of the monumental doorway. The house had once been the home of a rich Austrian banker who had shown the country a clean pair of heels as soon as he felt the first gust of the revolutionary storm blowing across the Rue de la Monnaie. That was early in '89.

After that the mansion stood empty for a couple of years. Then, when the housing shortage became acute in Paris, the revolutionary government took possession of the building, erected partition walls in the great reception and ballrooms, turning them into small apartments and offices which it let to poor tenants and people in a small way of business. A *concierge* was put in charge. But during those two years for some reason or other the house had fallen into premature and rabid decay. Within a very few months an air of mustiness began to hand over the once palatial residence of the rich foreign financier. When he departed, bag and baggage, taking with him his family and his servants, his pictures and his furniture, it almost seemed as if he had left behind him an eerie trail of ghosts, who took to wandering in and out of the deserted rooms and up and down the monumental staircase, scattering an odour of dry-rot and mildew in their wake. And although, after a time, the lower floors were all let as offices to business people, and several families elected to drag out their more or less miserable lives in the apartments up above, that air of emptiness and of decay never ceased to hang about the building, and its walls never lost their musty smell of damp mortar and mildew.

A certain amount of life did, of course, go on inside the house. People came and went about their usual avocations: in one compartment a child was born, a wedding feast was held in another, old women gossiped and young men courted: but they did all this in a silent a furtive manner, as if afraid of rousing dormant echoes; voices were never raised above a whisper, laughter never rang along the corridors, nor did light feet run pattering up and down the stairs.

Far be it from any searcher after truth to suggest that this atmosphere of silence and of gloom was peculiar to the house in the Rue de la Monnaie. Times were getting hard all over France—very hard for most people, and hard times whenever they occur give rise to great silences and engender the desire for solitude. In Paris all the necessities of life—soap, sugar, milk—were not only very dear but difficult to get. Luxuries of the past were unobtainable save to those who, by inflammatory speeches, had fanned the passions of the ignorant and the needy, with promises of happiness and equality for all. Three years of this social upheaval and of the rule of the proletariat had brought throughout the country more misery than happiness. True! the rich—a good many of them—had been dragged down to poverty or exile, but the poor were more needy than they had been before.

To see the king dispossessed of his throne, and the nobles and *bourgeois* either fleeing the country or brought to penury might satisfy a desire for retribution, but it did not warm the body in winter, feed the hungry or clothe the naked. The only equality that this glorious Revolution had brought about was that of wretchedness, and an ever-present dread of denunciation and of death. That is what people murmured in the privacy of their homes but did not dare to speak of openly. No one dared speak openly these days, for there was always the fear that spies might be lurking about, that accusations of treason would follow, with the inevitable consequences of summary trial and the guillotine.

And so, the women and the children suffered in silence, and the men suffered because they could do nothing to alleviate the misery of those they cared for. Some there were lucky enough to have got out of this hell upon earth, who had shaken the dust of their unfortunate country from their shoes in the early days of the Revolution, and had sought—if not happiness, at any rate peace and contentment in other lands. But there were countless others who had ties that bound them indissolubly to France—their profession, their business, or family ties—they could not go away: they were forced to remain in their native land and to watch hunger, penury and disease stalk the countryside, whilst the authors of all this misfortune lived a life of ease in the luxurious homes, sat round their well-filled tables, ate and drank their fill and spent their leisure hours in spouting of class-hatred and of their own patriotism and selflessness.

The restaurants of the Rue St. Honoré were thronged with merry-makers night after night. The members of the proletarian government sat in the most expensive seats at the *Opéra* and the *Comédie Française* and drove in their *barouches* to the Bois, while flaunting their democratic ideals by attending the sittings of the National Assembly stockingless and in ragged shirts and breeches. Danton kept open house at d'Arcy-sur-Aube: St. Just and Desmoulins wore jabots of Mechlin lace, and coats of the finest English cloth: Chabot had a sumptuous apartment in the Rue d'Anjou. They say to it, these men, that privations and anxiety did not come nigh them. Privations were for the rabble, who was used to them, and for *aristos* and *bourgeois*, who had never known the meaning of want: but for them, who had hoisted the flag of Equality and Fraternity, who had freed the people of France from the tyranny of kings and nobles, for them luxury had become a right, especially if it could be got at the expense of those who had enjoyed it in the past.

In this year 1792 Maître Bastien de Croissy rented a small set of offices in the three-storeyed house in the Rue de la Monnaie. He was at this time verging on middle age, with hair just beginning to turn grey, and still an exceptionally handsome man, despite the lines of care and anxiety round his sensitive mouth and the settled look of melancholy in his deep-set, penetrating eyes. Bastien de Croissy had been at one time one of the most successful and most respected members of the Paris bar. He had reckoned royal personages among his clients. Men and women, distinguished in art, politics or literature, had waited on him at his sumptuous office on the Quai de la Mégisserie. Rich, good-looking, well-born, the young advocate had been *fêted* and courted wherever he went: The king entrusted him with important financial transactions: the Duc d'Ayen was his most intimate friend: the Princesse de Lamballe was godmother to his boy, Charles-Léon.

His marriage to Louise de Vandeleur, the only daughter of the distinguished general, had been one of the social events of that season in Paris. He had been a great man, a favourite of fortune until the Revolution deprived him of his patrimony and of his income. The proletarian government laid ruthless hands on the former, by forcing him to farm out his lands to tenants who refused to pay him any rent. His income in a couple of years dwindled down to nothing. Most of his former clients had emigrated, all of them were now too poor to need legal or financial advice.

Maître de Croissy was forced presently to give up his magnificent house and sumptuous offices on the Quai. He installed his wife and child in a cheap apartment in the Rue Picpus and carried on what legal business came his way in a set of rooms which had once been the private apartments of the Austrian banker's valet. Thither he trudged on foot every morning, whatever the weather, and here he interviewed needy *bourgeois*, groaning under taxation, or out-at-elbows tradesmen on the verge of bankruptcy. He was no longer Maître de Croissy, only plain Citizen Croissy, thankful that men like Chabot or Bazire reposed confidence in him, or that the great Danton deigned to put some legal business in his way. Where six clerks had scarcely been sufficient to aid him in getting through the work of the day, he had only one now—the faithful Reversac—who had obstinately refused to take his *congé*, when all the others were dismissed.

"You would not throw me out into the street to starve, would you, *Maître?*" had been the young man's earnest plea.

"But you can find other work, Maurice," de Croissy had argued, not without reason, for Maurice Reversac was a fully qualified lawyer, he was young and active and of a surety he could always have made a living for himself. "And I cannot afford to pay you an adequate salary."

"Give me board and lodging, *Maître*," Reversac had entreated with obstinacy: "I want nothing else. I have a few *louis* put by: my clothes will last me three or four years, and by that time—"

"Yes! by that time—" Maître de Croissy sighed. He had been hopeful once that sanity would return presently to the people of France, that this era of chaos and cruelty, of persecution and oppression, could not possibly last. But of late he had become more and more despondent, more and more hopeless. When Frenchmen, after having deposed their anointed king, began to talk of putting him on his trial like a common criminal, it must mean that they had become possessed of the demon of insanity, a tenacious demon who would not easily be exorcised.

But Maurice Reversac got his way. He had board and lodging in the apartment of the Rue Picpus, and in the mornings, whatever the weather, he trudged over to the Rue de la Monnaie and aired, dusted and swept the dingy office of the great advocate. In the evenings the two men would almost invariably walk back together to the Rue Picpus. The cheap, exiguous apartment meant home for both of them, and in it they found what measure of happiness their own hearts helped them to attain. For Bastien de Croissy happiness meant home-life, his love for his wife and child. For Maurice Reversac it meant living under the same roof with Josette, seeing her every day, walking with her in the evenings under the chestnut trees of Cour de la Reine.

A little higher up the narrow Passage des Fèves there stood at this same time a small eating-house, frequented chiefly by the mechanics of the Government workshops close by. It bore the sign: "*Aux Trois Singes.*" Two steps down from the street level gave access to it through a narrow doorway. Food and drink were as cheap here as anywhere, and the landlord, a man named Furet, had the great merit of being rather deaf, and having an impediment in his speech. Added to this was the fact that he had never learned to read or write. These three attributes made of Furet an ideal landlord in a place where men with empty bellies and empty pockets were wont to let themselves go in the matter of grumbling at the present state of affairs, and at the de-vice "*Liberté, Fraternité, Égalité*" which by order of the revolutionary government was emblazoned outside and in every building to which the public had access.

Furet being deaf could not spy: being mute he could not denounce. Figuratively speaking men loosened their belts when they sat at one of the trestle tables inside the *Cabaret des Trois Singes*, sipped their sour wine and munched their meal of stale bread and boiled beans. They loosened their belts and talked of the slave-driving that went on in the Government workshops, the tyranny of the overseers, the ever-increasing cost of living, and the paucity of their wages, certain that Furet neither heard what they said nor would be able to repeat the little that he heard.

Inside the *cabaret* there were two tables that were considered privi-leged. They were no tables properly speaking, but just empty wine-casks, standing on end, each in a recess to right and left of the narrow doorway. A couple of three-legged stools accommodated two custom-ers and two only in each recess, and those who wished to avail them-selves of the privilege of sitting there were expected to order a bottle of Furet's best wine. This was one of those unwritten laws which no frequenter of the Three Monkeys every thought of ignoring. Furet, though an ideal landlord in so many respects, could turn nasty when he chose.

On a sultry evening in the late August of '92, two men were sit-ting in one of these privileged recesses in the *Cabaret des Trois Singes*.

They had talked earnestly for the past hour, always sinking their voices to a whisper. A bottle of Citizen Furet's best wine stood on the cask between them, but though they had been in the place for over an hour, the bottle was still more than half full. They seemed too deeply engrossed in conversation to waste time in drink.

One of the men was short and thick-set with dark hair and marked Levantine features. He spoke French fluently but with a throaty accent which betrayed his German origin. Whenever he wished to emphasise a point he struck the top of the wine-stained cask with the palm of his fleshy hand.

The other man was Bastien de Croissy. Earlier in the day he had received an anonymous message requesting a private meeting in the *Cabaret des Trois Singes*. The matter, the message averred, concerned the welfare of France and the safety of the king. Bastien was no coward, and the wording of the message was a sure passport to his confidence. He sent Maurice Reversac home early and kept the mysterious tryst.

His anonymous correspondent introduced himself as a representative of Baron de Batz, well known to Bastien as they agent of the Austrian Government and confidant of the Emperor, whose intrigues and schemes for the overthrow of the revolutionary government of France had been as daring in conception as they were futile in execution.

"But this time," the man had declared with complete self-assurance, "with your help, *cher maître*, we are bound to succeed."

And he had elaborated the plan conceived in Vienna by de Batz. A wonderful plan! Neither more nor less than bribing with Austrian gold some of the more venal members of their own party, and the restoration of the monarchy.

Bastien de Croissy was sceptical. He did not believe that any of the more influential Terrorists would risk their necks in so daring an intrigue. Other ways—surer ways—ought to be found, and found quickly for the king's life was indeed in peril: not only the king's but the queen's and the lives of all the royal family. But the Austrian agent was obstinate.

"It is from inside the National Convention that *M. le Baron* wants help. That he must have. If he has the co-operation of half a dozen members of the Executive, he can do the rest, and guarantee success."

Then, as de Croissy still appeared to hesitate, he laid his fleshy hand on the advocate's arm.

"*Voyons, cher maître*," he said, "you have the overthrow of this abominable Government just as much at heart as *M. le Baron,* and we none of us question your loyalty to the dynasty."

"It is not want of loyalty," de Croissy retorted hotly, "that makes me hesitate."

"What then?"

"Prudence! lest by a false move we aggravate the peril of our king." The other shrugged.

"Well! of course," he said, "we reckon that you, *cher maître*, know the men with whom we wish to deal."

"Yes!" Bastien admitted, "I certainly do."

"They are venal?"

"Yes!"

"Greedy?"

"Yes!"

"Ambitious?"

"For their own pockets, yes."

"Well then?"

There was a pause. A murmur of conversation was going on all round. Some of Furet's customers were munching noisily or drinking with a gurgling sound, others were knocking dominoes about. There was no fear of eavesdropping in this dark and secluded recess where two men were discussing the destinies of France. One was the emissary of a foreign power, the other an ardent royalist. Both had the same object in view: to save the king and his family from death, and to overthrow a government of assassins, who contemplated adding the crime of regicide to their many malefactions.

"*M. le Baron*," the foreign agent resumed with increased persuasiveness after a slight pause, "I need not tell you what is their provenance. Our Emperor is not going to see his sister at the mercy of a horde of assassins. *M. le Baron* is in his council: he will pay twenty thousand *louis* each to any dozen men who will lend him a hand in this affair."

"A dozen?" de Croissy exclaimed, then added with disheartened sigh: "Where to find them!"

"We are looking to you, *cher maître*."

"I have no influence. Not now."

"But you know the right men," the agent argued, and added significantly: "You have been watched, you know."

"I guessed."

"We know that you have business relations with members of the Convention who can be very useful to us."

"Which of them had you thought of?"

"Well! there is Chabot, for instance: the unfrocked friar."

"God in Heaven!" de Croissy exclaimed: "what a tool."

"The end will justify the means, my friend," the other retorted drily. Then he added: "And Chabot's brother-in-law Bazire."

"Both these men," de Croissy admitted, "would sell their souls, if they possessed one."

"Then there's Fabre d'Eglantine, Danton's friend."

"You are well informed."

"What about Danton himself?"

The Austrian leaned over the table, eager, excited, conscious that the Frenchman was wavering. Clearly de Croissy's scepticism was on the point of giving way before the other's enthusiasm and certainty of success. It was such a wonderful vista that was being unfolded before him. France free from the tyranny of agitation! the king restored to his throne! the country once more happy and prosperous under a stable government as ordained by God! So, thought de Croissy as he lent a more and more willing ear to the projects of de Batz. He himself mentioned several names of men who might prove useful in the scheme; names of men who might be willing to betray their party for Austrian gold. There were a good many of these: agitators who were corrupt and venal, who had incited the needy and the ignorant to all kinds of barbarous deeds, not from any striving after a humanitarian ideal, but for what they themselves could get out of the social upheaval and its attendant chaos.

"If I lend a hand in your scheme," de Croissy said presently with earnest emphasis, "it must be understood that their first aim is the restoration of our king to his throne."

"Of course, _cher maître_, of course," the other asserted equally forcibly. "Surely you can believe in _M. le Baron's_ disinterested motives."

"What we'll have to do," he continued eagerly, "will be to promise the men whom you will have chosen for the purpose, a certain sum of money, to be paid to them as soon as all the members of the Royal family are safely out of France. . . . we don't want one of the Royal Princesses to be detained as hostage, do we? . . . .Then we can promise them a further and larger sum to be paid when their Majesties make their state re-entry into their capital."

There was no doubt by now that Maître de Croissy's enthusiasm was fully aroused. He was one of those men for whom dynasty and the right of kings amounted to a religion. For him, all that he had suffered in the past in the way of privations and loss of wealth and prestige was as nothing compared with the horror which he felt at sight of the humiliations which miscreants had imposed upon his king. To save the king! to bring him back triumphant to the throne of his forbears, were thoughts and hopes that filled Bastien de Croissy's soul with intense excitement. It was only with half an ear that he listened to the foreign emissary's further scheme: the ultimate undoing of that herd of assassins. He did not care what happened once the great goal was attained. Let those corrupt knaves of whom the Austrian Emperor stood in need thrive and batten on their own villainy, Bastien de Croissy did not care.

"You see the idea, do you not, *cher maître?*" the emissary was saying.

"Yes! oh yes!" Bastien murmured vaguely.

"Get as much letter-writing as you can out of the black-guards. Let us have as much written proof of their venality as possible. Then if ever these jackals rear their heads again, we can proclaim their turpitude before the entire world, discredit them before their ignorant dupes, and see them suffer humiliation and die the shameful death which they had planned for their king."

The meeting between the two men lasted well into the night. In the dingy apartment of the Rue Picpus Louise de Croissy sat up, waiting anxiously for her husband. Maurice Reversac, whom she questioned repeatedly, could tell her nothing of Maître de Croissy's whereabouts, beyond the fact that he was keeping a business appointment, made by a new client who desired to remain anonymous. When Bastien finally came home, he looked tired, but singularly excited. Never since the first dark days of the Revolution three years ago had Louise seen him with such flaming eyes, or heard such cheerful, not to say optimistic words from his lips. But he said nothing to her about his interview with the agent of Baron de Batz, he only talked of the brighter outlook in the future. God, he said, would soon tire of the wickedness of men: the present terrible conditions could not possibly last. The king would soon come into his own again.

Louise was quickly infused with some of his enthusiasm, but she did not worry him with questions. Hers was one of those easy-going dispositions that are willing to accept things as they come without probing into the whys and wherefores of events. She had a profound admiration for and deep trust in her clever husband: he appeared hopeful for the future—more hopeful than he had been for a long time, and that was enough for Louise. It was only to the faithful Maurice Reversac that de Croissy spoke of his interview with the Austrian emissary, and the young man tried very hard to show some enthusiasm over the scheme, and to share his employer's optimism and hopes for the future.

Maurice Reversac, though painstaking and a very capable lawyer, was not exactly brilliant: against that his love for his employer and his employer's family was so genuine and so great that it gave him what amounted to intuition, almost a foreknowledge of any change, good or evil, that destiny had in store for them. And as he listened to Maître de Croissy's earnest talk, he felt a strange foreboding that all would not be well with this scheme: that somehow or other it would lead to disaster, and all the while that he sat at his desk that day copying the letters which the advocate had dictated to him—letters which were in the nature of tentacles, stretched out to catch a set of knaves—he felt an overwhelming temptation to throw himself at his employer's feet and beg him not to sully his hands by contact with this foreign intrigue.

But the temptation had to be resisted. Bastien de Croissy was not the type of man who could be swayed from his purpose by the vapourings of his young clerk, however devoted he might be. And so, the letters were written—half a score in all—requests by Citizen Croissy of the Paris bar for private interviews with various influential members of the Convention on matters of urgency to the State.

Chapter 2

More than a year had gone by since then, and Bastien de Croissy had seen all his fondly cherished hopes turn to despair one by one. There had been no break in the dark clouds of chaos and misery that enveloped the beautiful land of France. Indeed, they had gathered, darker and more stormy than before. And now had come what appeared to be the darkest days of all—the autumn of 1793. The king, condemned to death by a majority of 48 in an Assembly of over 700 members, had paid with his life for all the errors, the weaknesses, the misunderstandings of the past: the unfortunate queen, separated from her children and from all those she cared for, accused of the vilest crimes that distorted minds could invent, was awaiting trial and inevitable death.

The various political parties—the factions and the clubs—were vying with one another in ruthlessness and cruelty. Danton the lion and Robespierre the jackal were at one another's throats; it still meant the mere spin of a coin as to which would succeed in destroying the other. The houses of detention were filled to overflowing, while the guillotine did its grim work day by day, hour by hour, without distinction of rank or sex, or of age. The Law of the Suspect had just been passed, and it was no longer necessary for an unfortunate individual to do or say anything that the Committee of Public Safety might deem counter-revolutionary, it was sufficient to be suspected of such tendencies for denunciation to follow, then arrest and finally death with but the mockery of a trial, without pleading or defence.

And while the Terrorists were intent on destroying one another the country was threatened by foes without and within. Famine and disease stalked in the wake of persecution. The countryside was devastated, there were not enough hands left to till the ground and the cities were a prey to epidemics. On the frontier the victorious allied armies were advancing on the sacred soil of France. The English were pouring in from Belgium, the Russians came across the Rhine, the Spaniards crossed the gorges of the Pyrenees, whilst the torch of civil war was blazing anew in La Vendée.

Danton's cry: "To arms!" and "*La Patrie* is in danger!" resounded from end to end of the land. It echoed through the deserted cities and over the barren fields, while three hundred thousand "Soldiers of Liberty" marched to the frontiers, ill-clothed, ill-shod, ill-fed, to drive back the foreign invader from the gates of France. An epic, what? Worthy of a holier cause.

Those who were left behind, who were old, or weak, or indispensable, had to bear their share in the defence of *La Patrie*. France was transformed into an immense camp of fighters and workers. The women sewed shirts and knitted socks, salted meat and stitched breeches, and looked after their children and their homes as best they could. France came first, the home was a bad second.

It was then that little Charles-Léon fell ill. That was the beginning of the tragedy. He had always been delicate, which was not to be wondered at, seeing that he was born during the days immediately preceding the Revolution, at the time when the entire world, such as Louise de Croissy had known it, was crumbling to dust at her feet. She never thought he would live, the dear, puny mite, the precious son, whom she and Bastien had longed for, prayed for, by year until this awful winter when food became scarce and poor, and milk was almost unobtainable.

Kind old Doctor Larousse said it was nothing serious, but the child must have change of air. Paris was too unhealthy these days for deli-

cate children. Change of air? Heavens above! how was it to be got?
Louise questioned old Citizen Larousse:

"Can you get me a permit, doctor? We still have a small house in
the Isère district, not far from Grenoble. I could take my boy there."

"Yes. I can get you a permit for the child—at least, I think so—under the circumstances."

"And one for me?"

"Yes, one for you—to last a week."

"How do you mean to last a week?"

"Well, you can get the diligence to Grenoble. It takes a couple of
days. Then you can stay in your house, say, forty-eight hours to see the
child installed. Two days to come back by diligence—"

"But I couldn't come back."

"I'm afraid you'll have to. No one is allowed to be absent from
permanent domicile more than seven days. You know that, *citizeness*,
surely."

"But I couldn't leave Charles-Léon."

"Why not? There is not very much the matter with him. And
country air—"

Louise was losing her patience. How obtuse men are, even the best
of them!

"But there is no one over there to look after him," she argued.

"Surely a respectable woman from the village would—"

This time she felt her temper rising. "And you suppose that I
would leave this sick baby in the care of a stranger?"

"Haven't you a relation who would look after him? Mother? Sister?"

"My mother is dead. I have no sisters. Nor would I leave Charles-
Léon in anyone's care but mine."

The doctor shrugged. He was very kind, but he had seen this sort
of thing so often lately, and he was powerless to help.

"I am afraid—" he said.

"Citizen Larousse," Louise broke in firmly, "you must give me a
certificate that my child is too ill to be separated from his mother."

"Impossible, *citizeness*."

"Won't you try?"

"I have tried—for others—often, but it's no use. You know what
the decrees of the Convention are these days. . . . no one dares—"

"And I am to see my child perish for want of a scrap of paper?"

Again, the old man shrugged. He was a busy man and there were others. Presently he took his leave: there was nothing that he could do, so why should he stay? Louise hardly noticed his going. She stood there like a block of stone, a carved image of despair. The wan cheeks of the sick child seemed less bloodless than hers.

"Louise!"

Josette Gravier had been standing beside the cot all this time. Charles-Léon's tiny hand had fastened round one of her fingers and she didn't like to move, but she had lost nothing of what was going on. Her eyes, those lovely deep blue eyes of hers that seemed to shine, to emit light when she was excited, were fixed on Louise de Croissy. She had loved her and served her ever since Louise's dying mother, Madame de Vadeleur, confided the care of her baby daughter to Madame Gravier, the farmer's wife, Josette's mother, who had just lost her own new-born baby, the same age as Louise. Josette, Ma'me Gravier's first-born, was three years old at the time and, oh! how she took the little newcomer to her heart! She and Louise grew up together like sisters. They shared childish joys and tears. The old farmhouse used to ring with their laughter and the patter of their tiny feet. Papa Gravier taught them to ride and to milk the nanny-goats; they had rabbits of their own, chickens and runner-ducks.

Together they went to the Convent school of the Visitation to learn everything that was desirable for young ladies to know, sewing and embroidery, calligraphy and recitation, a smattering of history and geography, and the art of letter-writing. For there was to be no difference in the education of Louise de Vandeleur, the motherless daughter of the distinguished general, *aide-de-camp* to His Majesty, and of Josette Gravier, the farmer's daughter.

When, in the course of time, Louise married Bastien de Croissy, the eminent advocate at the Paris bar, Josette nearly broke her heart at parting from her lifelong friend.

Then came the dark days of '89. Papa Gravier was killed during the revolutionary riots in Grenoble; *maman* died of a broken heart, and Louise begged Josette to come and live with her. The farm was sold, the girl had a small competence; she went up to Paris and continued to love and serve Louise as she had done in the past. She was her comfort and her help during those first terrible days of the Revolution: she was her moral support now that the shadow of the guillotine lay menacing over the household of the once successful lawyer. *La Patrie* in danger claimed so many hours of her day; she, too, had to sew shirts and stitch breeches for the "Soldiers of Liberty," but her evenings, her nights, her early mornings were her own, and these she devoted to the service of Louise and of Charles-Léon.

She had a tiny room in the apartment of the Rue Picpus, but to her loving little heart that room was paradise, for here, when she was at home, she had Charles-Léon to play with, she had his little clothes to wash and to iron, she saw his great dark eyes, so like his mother's fixed upon her while she told him tales of romance and of chivalry. The boy was only five at this time, but he was strangely precocious where such tales were concerned, he seemed to understand and appreciate the mighty deeds of Hector and Achilles, of Bayard and Joan of Arc, the stories of the Crusades, of Godfrey de Bouillon and Richard of the Lionheart. Perhaps it was because he felt himself to be weak and puny and knew with the unexplainable instinct of childhood that he would never be big enough or strong enough to emulate those deeds of valour, that he loved to hear Josette recount them to him with a wealth of detail supplied by her romantic imagination.

But if Charles-Léon loved to hear these stories of the past, far more eagerly did he listen to those of today, and in the recounting of heroic adventures which not only had happened recently, but went on almost every day, Josette's storehouse of hair-raising narratives was well-nigh inexhaustible. Through her impassioned rhetoric he first heard of the heroic deeds of that amazing Englishman who went by the curious name of the Scarlet Pimpernel. Josette told him about a number of gallant gentlemen who had taken such compassion on the sufferings of the innocent that they devoted their lives to rescuing those who were persecuted and oppressed by the tyrannical government of the day. She told him how women and children, old or feeble men, dragged before a tribunal that knew of no issue save the sentence of death, were spirited away out of prison walls or from the very tumbrils that were taking them to the guillotine, spirited away as if by a miracle, and through the agency of this mysterious hero whose identity had always remained unknown, but whose deeds of self-sacrifice were surely writ large in the book of the Recording Angel.

And while Josette unfolded these tales of valour, and the boy listened to her awed and silent, her eyes would shine with unshed tears, and her lips quiver with enthusiasm. She had made a fetish of the Scarlet Pimpernel: had enshrined him in her heart like a demi-god, and this hero-worship grew all the more fervent within her as she found no response to her enthusiasm in the bosom of her adopted family, only in Charles-Léon. She was too gentle and timid to speak openly of this hero-worship to Maître de Croissy, and Louise, whom she adored, was wont to grow slightly sarcastic at the expense of Josette's imaginary hero. She did not believe in his existence at all and thought that all the tales of miraculous rescues set down to his agency were either mere coincidence or just the product of a romantic girl's fantasy. As for Maurice Reversac—well! little Josette thought him too dull and unimaginative to appreciate the almost legendary personality of the Scarlet Pimpernel, so, whenever a fresh tale got about the city of how a whole batch of innocent men, women and children had escaped out of France on the very eve of their arrest or condemnation to death, Josette kept the tale to herself, until she and Charles-Léon were alone in her little room, and she found response to her enthusiasm in the boy's glowing eyes and his murmur of passionate admiration.

When Charles-Léon's chronic weakness turned to actual, serious anaemia, all the joy seemed to go out of Josette's life. Real joy, that is; for she went about outwardly just as gay as before, singing, crooning to the little invalid, cheering Louise and comforting Bastien, who spoke of her now as the angel in the house. Every minute that she could spare she spent by the side of Charles-Léon's little bed, and when no one was listening she would whisper into his ear some of the old stories which he loved. Then if the ghost of a smile came round the child's pallid lips, Josette would feel almost happy, even though she felt ready to burst into tears.

And now, as soon as the old doctor had gone, Josette disengaged her hand from the sick child's grasp and put her arms around Louise's shoulders.

"We must not lose heart, Louise *chérie*," she said. "There must be a way out of this *impasse*."

"A way out?" Louise murmured. "Oh, if I only knew!"

"Sit down here, *chérie*, and let me talk to you."

There was a measure of comfort even in Josette's voice. It was low and a trifle husky; such a voice as some women have whose mission in life is to comfort and to soothe. She made Louise sit down in the big armchair; then she knelt down in front of her, her little hands clasped together and resting in Louise's lap.

"Listen, Louise *chérie*," she said with great excitement.

Louise looked down on the beautiful eager face of her friend; the soft red lips were quivering with excitement; the large luminous eyes were aglow with a strange enthusiasm. She felt puzzled, for it was not in Josette's nature to show so much emotion. She was always deemed quiet and sensible. She never spoke at random, and never made a show of her fantastic dreams.

"Well, darling?" Louise said listlessly: "I am listening. What is it?"

Josette looked up, wide-eyed and eager, straight into her friend's face.

"What we must do, *chérie*," she said with earnest emphasis, "is to get in touch with those wonderful Englishmen. You know who I mean. They have already accomplished miracles on behalf of innocent men, women and children, of people who were in a worse plight than we are now."

Louise frowned. She knew well enough what Josette meant: she had often laughed at the girl's enthusiasm over this imaginary hero, who seemed to haunt her dreams. But just now she felt that there was something flippant and unseemly in talking such fantastic rubbish: dreams seemed out of place when reality was so heart-breaking. She tried to rise to push Josette away, but the girl clung to her and would not let her go.

"I don't know what you are talking about, Josette," Louise said coldly at last. "This is not the time for jest, or for talking of things that only exist in your imagination."

Josette shook her head.

"Why do you say that, Louise *chérie?* Why should you deliber-ately close your eyes and ears to facts—hard, sober, solid facts that everybody knows, that everybody admits to be true? I should have thought," the girl went on in her earnest, persuasive way, "that with this terrible thing hanging over you—Charles-Léon getting more and more ill, till there's no hope of his recovery—"

"Josette!! Don't!" Louise cried out in an agony of reproach.

"I must," Josette insisted with quiet force: "it is my duty to make you look straight at facts as they are; and I say, that with this terrible thing hanging over us, you must cast off foolish prejudices and open your mind to what is the truth and will be your salvation."

Louise looked down at the beautiful, eager face turned up to hers. She felt all of a sudden strangely moved. Of course, Josette was talking nonsense. Dear, sensible, quiet little Josette! She was simple and not at all clever, but it was funny, to say the least of it, how persuasive she could be when she had set her mind on anything. Even over small things she would sometimes wax so eloquent that there was no resist-ing her. No! she was not clever, but she was extra-ordinarily shrewd where the welfare of those she loved was in question. And she adored Louise and worshipped Charles-Léon.

Since the doctor's visit Louise had felt herself floundering in such a torrent of grief that she was ready to clutch at any straw that would save her from despair. Josette was talking nonsense, of course. All the family were wont to chaff her over her adoration of the legendary hero, so much so, in fact, that the girl had ceased altogether to talk about him. But now her eyes were positively glowing with enthusiasm, and it seemed to Louise, as she gazed into them, that they radiated hope and trust. And Louise was so longing for a ray of hope.

"I suppose," she said with a wan smile, "that you are harping on your favourite string."

"I am," Josette admitted with fervour.

Then as Louise, still obstinate and unbelieving, gave a slight shrug and a sigh, the girl continued:

"Surely, Louise *chérie*, you have heard other people besides me—clever, distinguished, important people—talk of the Scarlet Pimpernel."

"I have," Louise admitted: "but only in a vague way."

"And what he did for the Maillys?"

"The general's widow, you mean?"

"Yes. She and her sister and the two children were simply snatched away from under the very noses of the guard who were taking them to execution."

"I did hear something about that," was Louise's dry comment; "but—"

"And of about the de Tournays?" Josette broke in eagerly.

"They are in England now. So, I heard."

"They are. And who took them there? The marquis was in hiding in the woods near his property: Mme. de Tournay and Suzanne were in terror for him and in fear for their lives. It was said openly that their arrest was imminent. And when the National Guard went to arrest them, Mm. de Tournay and Suzanne were gone, and the marquis was never found. You've said it yourself, they are in England now."

"But Josette darling," Louise argued obstinately, "there's nothing to say in all those stories that any mysterious Englishman had aught to do with the Maillys and the Tournays."

"Who then?"

"It was the intervention of God."

Josette shook her pretty head somewhat sadly.

"God does not intervene directly these days, my darling," she said; "He chooses great and good men to do His bidding."

"And I don't see," Louise concluded with some impatience, "I don't see what the Maillys or the Tournays have to do with me and Charles-Léon."

But at this Josette's angelic temper very nearly forsook her.

"Don't be obtuse, Louise," she cried hotly. "We don't want to get in touch with the Maillys or the Tournays. I never suggested anything so ridiculous. All I mean was that they and hundreds—yes, hundreds—of others owe their life to the Scarlet Pimpernel."

Tears of vexation rose from her loving heart at Louise's obduracy. She it was who tried to rise now, but this time Louise held her down: Poor Louise! She did so long to believe—really believe. Hope is such a precious thing when the heart is full to bursting of anxiety and sorrow. And she longed for hope and for faith: the same hope that made Josette's eyes sparkle and gave a ring of sanguine expectation to her voice.

"Don't run away, Josette," she pleaded. "You don't know how I envy you your hero-worship and your trust. But listen, darling: even if your Scarlet Pimpernel does exist—see, I no longer say that he does not—even if he does, he knows nothing about us. How then can he interfere?"

Josette drew a sigh of relief. For the first time since the hot argument had started she felt that she was gaining ground. Her faith was going to prevail. Louise's scepticism had changed: the look of despair had gone and there was a light in her eyes which suggested that hope had crept at last into her heart. The zealot had vanquished the obstinacy of the sceptic, and Josette having gained her point could speak more calmly now.

She shook her head and smiled.

"Don't you believe it, *chérie*," she said gently.

"Believe what?"

"That the Scarlet Pimpernel knows nothing about you. He does. I am sure he does. All you have to do is just to invoke him in your heart."

"Nonsense, Josette," Louise protested. "You are not pretending, I suppose, that this Englishman is a supernatural being?"

"I don't know about that," said the young devotee, "but I do know that he is the bravest, finest man that ever lived. And I know also that wherever there is a great misfortune or a great sorrow he appears like a young god, and at once care and anxiety disappear, and grief is turned to joy."

"I wish I could have your faith in miracles, my Josette."

"You need not call it a miracle. The good deeds of the Scarlet Pimpernel are absolutely real."

"But even so, my dear, what can we do? We don't know where to find him. And if we did, what could he do for us—for Charles-Léon?"

"He can get you a permit to go into the country with Charles-Léon, and to remain with him until he is well again."

"I don't believe that. Nothing short of a miracle can accomplish that. You heard what the doctor said."

"Well, I say that the Scarlet Pimpernel can do anything! And I mean to get in touch with him."

"You are stupid, Josette."

"And you are a woman of little faith. Why don't you read your Bible, and see what it says there about faith?"

Louise shrugged. "The Bible," she said coolly, "tells us about moving mountains by faith, but nothing about finding a needle in a haystack or a mysterious Englishman in the streets of Paris."

But Josette was now proof against her friend's sarcasm. She jumped to her feet and put her arms round Louise.

"Well!" she rejoined, "my faith is going to find him, that's all I know. I wish," she went on with a comic little inflection of her voice, "that I had not wasted this past hour in trying to put some of that faith into you. And now I know that I shall have to spend at least another hour driving it into Maurice's wooden head."

Louise smiled. "Why Maurice?" she asked.

"For the same reason," the girl replied, "that I had to wear myself out in order to break your obstinacy. It will take me some time perhaps, as you say, to find the Scarlet Pimpernel in the streets of Paris. I shall have to be out and about a great deal, and if I had said nothing to any of you, you and Maurice and even Bastien would always have been asking me questions: where I had been? why did I go out? why was I late for dinner? And Maurice would have gone about looking like a bear with a sore head, whenever I refused to go for a walk with him. So of course," Josette concluded *naïvely*, "I shall have to tell him."

Louise said nothing more after that: she sat with clasped hands and eyes fixed into vacancy, thinking, hoping, or perhaps just praying for hope.

But Josette having had her say went across the room to Charles-

Léon's little bed. She leaned over him and kissed him. He whispered her name and added feebly: "Tell me some more. . . . about the Scarlet Pimpernel. . . . when will he come. . . . to take me away. . . . to England?"

"Soon," Josette murmured in reply: "very soon. Do not doubt it, my precious. God will send him to you very soon."

Then without another word to Louise she ran quickly out of the room.

Chapter 3

Josette had picked up her cape and slung it round her shoulders; she pulled the hood over her fair curls and ran swiftly down the stairs and out into the street. Thoughts of the Scarlet Pimpernel had a way of whipping up her blood. When she spoke of him she at once wanted to be up and doing. She wanted to be up and doing something that would emulate the marvellous deeds of that mysterious hero of romance—deeds which she had heard recounted with bated breath by her fellow-workers in the government workshops where breeches were stitched and stockings knitted by the hundred for the "Soldiers of Liberty," marching against the foreign foe.

Josette on this late afternoon had to put in a couple of hours at the workshop. At six o'clock when the light gave out she would be free; and at six o'clock Maurice Reversac would of a certainty be outside the gates of the workshop waiting to escort her first for a walk along the Quai or the Cour la Reine and then home to cook the family supper.

She came out of the workshop on this late afternoon with glowing eyes and flaming cheeks, and nearly ran past Maurice without seeing him as her mind was so full of other things. She was humming a tune as she ran. Maurice was waiting for her at the gate, and he called to her. He felt very happy all of a sudden because Josette seemed so pleased to see him.

"Maurice!" she cried, "I am so glad you have come."

Maurice, being young and up to his eyes in love, did not think of asking her why she should be so glad. She was glad to see him and that was enough for any lover. He took hold of her by the elbow and led her through the narrow streets as far as the Quai and then over to Cour la Reine, where there were seats under the chestnut trees from which the big prickly burrs were falling fast, and split as they fell, revealing the lovely smooth surface of the chestnuts, in colour like Josette's hair; and as the last glimmer of daylight faded into evening the sparrows in the trees kicked up a great shindy, which was like a *paean* of joy in complete accord with Maurice's mood.

Nor did Maurice notice that Josette was absorbed; her eyes shone more brightly than usual, and her lips, which were so like ripe fruit, were slightly parted, and Maurice was just aching for a kiss.

He persuaded her to sit down: the air was so soft and balmy—lovely autumn evening with the scent of ripe fruit about; and those sparrows up in the chestnut trees did kick up such a shindy before tucking their little heads under their wings for the night. There were a few passers-by—not many—and this corner of old Paris appeared singularly peaceful, with a whole world of dreams and hope between it and the horrors of the Revolution. Yet this was the hour when the crowds that assembled daily on the Place de la Barrière du Trône to watch the guillotine at its dread work wandered, tired and silent, back to their homes, and when rattling carts bore their gruesome burdens to the public burying-place.

But what are social upheavals, revolutions or cataclysms to a lover absorbed in the contemplation of his beloved? Maurice Reversac sat beside Josette and could see her adorable profile with the small tip-tilted nose and the outline of her cheek so like a ripe peach. Josette sat silent and motionless at first, so Maurice felt emboldened to put out a timid hand and take hold of hers. She made no resistance and he thought of a surety that he would swoon with joy because she allowed that exquisite little hand to rest contented in his great rough palm. It felt just like a bird, soft and warm and fluttering, like those sparrows in up the trees.

"Josette," Maurice ventured to murmur after a little while, "you are glad to see me. . . . you said so. . . . didn't you, Josette?"

She was not looking at him, but he didn't mind that, for though the twilight was fast drawing in he could still see her adorable profile—that delicious tip-tilted nose and the lashes that curled like a fringe of gold over her eyes. The hood had fallen back from her head and the soft evening breeze stirred the tendrils of her chestnut-coloured hair.

"You are so beautiful, Josette," Maurice sighed, "and I am such a clumsy lout, but I would know how to make you happy. Happy! My God! I would make you as happy as the birds—without a care in the world. And all day you would just go about singing—singing—because you would have forgotten by then what sorrow was like."

Encouraged by her silence he ventured to draw a little nearer to her.

"I have seen," he murmured quite close to her ear, "an apartment that would be just the right setting for you, Josette darling: only three rooms and a little kitchen, but the morning sun comes pouring in through the big windows and there is a clump of chestnut trees in front in which the birds will sing in the spring from early dawn while you still lie in bed. I shall have got up by then and will be in the kitchen getting some hot milk for you; then I will bring you the warm milk, and while you drink it I shall sit and watch the sunshine play about in your hair."

Never before had Maurice plucked up sufficient courage to talk at such length, usually when Josette was beside him he was so absorbed in looking at her and longing for her that his tongue refused him service; for these were days when true lovers were timid and *la jeune fille* was an almost sacred being, whose limpid soul no profane word dared disturb, and Maurice had been brought up by an adoring mother in these rigid principles. This cruel and godless Revolution had, indeed, shattered many ideals and toughened the fibres of men's hearts and women's sensibilities, else Maurice would never have dared thus to approach the object of his dreams—her whom he hoped one day to have for wife.

Josette's silence had emboldened him, and the fact that she had allowed her hand to rest in his all this while. Now he actually dared to put out his arm and encircle her shoulders; he was, in fact, drawing her to him, feeling that he was on the point of stepping across the threshold of Paradise, when slowly she turned her face to him and looked him straight between the eyes. Her own appeared puzzled and there was a frown as of great perplexity between her brows.

"Maurice," she asked, and there was no doubt that she was both puzzled and astonished, "are you, perchance, trying to make love to me?"

Then, as he remained silent and looked, in his turn, both bewildered and hurt, she gave a light laugh, gently disengaged her hand and patted him on the cheek.

"My poor Maurice!" she said, "I wish I had listened sooner, but I was thinking of other things. . . ."

When a man had had the feeling that he has actually reached the gates of Paradise and that a kindly Saint Peter was already rattling his keys so as to let him in—when he has felt this for over half an hour and then, in a few seconds, is hurtled down into an abyss of disap-

116

pointment, his first sensation is as if he had been stunned by a terrific blow on the head, and he becomes entirely tongue-tied.

Bewildered and dumb, all Maurice could do was to stare at the adorable vision of a golden-haired girl whom he worshipped and who, with a light heart and a gay laugh, had just dealt him the most cruel blow that any man had ever been called upon to endure.

The worst of it was that this adorable golden-haired girl had apparently no notion of how cruel had been the blow, for she prattled on about the other things of which she had been thinking quite oblivious of the subject-matter of poor Maurice's impassioned pleading.

"Maurice dear," she said, "listen to me and do not talk nonsense."

Nonsense!! Ye gods!

"You have got to help me, Maurice, to find the Scarlet Pimpernel."

Her beautiful eyes, which she turned full upon him, were aglow with enthusiasm—enthusiasm for something in which he had no share. Nor did he understand what she was talking about. All he knew was that she had dismissed his pleading as nonsense, and that with a curious smile on her lips she was just turning a knife round and round in his heart.

And, oh, how that hurt!

But she also said that she wanted his help, so he tried very hard to get at her meaning, though she seemed to be prattling on rather inconsequently.

"Charles-Léon," she said, "is very ill, you know, Maurice dear—that is, not so very ill, but the doctor says he must have change of air or he will perish in a decline."

"A doctor can always get a permit for a patient *in extremis*—" Maurice put in, assuming a judicial manner.

"Don't be stupid, Maurice!" she retorted impatiently. "We all know that the doctor can get a permit for Charles-Léon, but he can't get one for Louise or for me, and where is Charles-Léon to go with neither of us to look after him?"

"Then what's to be done?"

"Try and listen more attentively, Maurice," she retorted. "You are not really listening."

"I am," he protested, "I swear I am!"

"Really—really?"

"Really, Josette—with both ears and all the intelligence I've got."

"Very well, then. You have heard of the Scarlet Pimpernel, haven't you?"

"We all have—in a way."

"What do you mean by 'in a way'?"

"Well, no one is quite sure if he really exists, and—"

"Maurice, don't, in Heaven's name, be stupid! You must have brains or Maître de Croissy could not do with you as his confidential clerk. So do use your brains, Maurice, and tell me if the Scarlet Pimpernel does not exist, then how did the Maillys get away—and the Frontenacs—and the Tournays—and—and...? Oh, Maurice, I hate your being so stupid!"

"You have only got to tell me, Josette, what you wish me to do," poor Maurice put in very humbly, "and I will do it, of course."

"I want you to help me find the Scarlet Pimpernel."

"Gladly will I help you, Josette; but won't it be like looking for a needle in a haystack?"

"Not at all," this intrepid little Joan of Arc asserted. "Listen, Maurice! In our workshop there is a girl, Agnes Minet, who was at one time in service with a Madame Carré, whose son Antoine was in hiding because he was threatened with arrest. His mother didn't dare write to him lest her letters be intercepted. Well, there was a public letter-writer who plied his trade at the corner of the Pont-Neuf— a funny old scarecrow he was—and Agnes, who cannot write, used sometimes to employ him to write to her *fiancé* who was away with the army. She says she doesn't know exactly how it all happened—she thinks the old letter-writer must have questioned her very cleverly, or else have followed her home one day—but, anyway, she caught herself telling him all about Antione Carré and took him and his mother safely out of France."

She paused a moment to draw breath, for she had spoken excitedly and all the time scarcely above a whisper, for the subject-matter was not one she would have liked some evil-wisher to hear. There were so many spies about these days eager for blood-money—the forty *sous* which could be earned for denouncing a "suspect."

Maurice, fully alive to this, made no immediate comment, but after a few seconds he suggested: "Shall we walk?" and took Josette by the elbow. It was getting dark now: the Cour la Reine was only poorly-lighted by a very few street lanterns placed at long intervals. They walked together in silence for a time, looking like young lovers intent on amorous effusions. The few passers-by, furtive and noiseless, took no notice of them.

"Antoine Carré's case is not the only one, Maurice," Josette resumed presently. "I could tell you dozens of others. The girls in the workshop talk about it all the time when the superintendent is out of the room."

Again, she paused, and then went on firmly, stressing her command: "You have got to help me, you know, Maurice."

"Of course, I will, Josette," Maurice murmured. "But how?"

"You must find the public letter-writer who used to have his pitch at the corner of the Pont-Neuf."

"There isn't one there now. I went past—"

"I know that. He has changed his pitch, that's all."

"How shall I know which is the right man? There are a number of public letter-writers in Paris."

"I shall be with you, Maurice, and I shall know, I am sure I shall know. There is something inside my heart which will make it beat faster as soon as the Scarlet Pimpernel is somewhere nigh. Besides—"

She checked herself, for involuntarily she had raised her voice, and at once Maurice tightened his hold on her arm. In the fast-gathering gloom a shuffling step had slided furtively past them. They could not clearly see the form of this passer-by, only the vague outline of a man stooping under a weight which he carried over his shoulders.

"We must be careful, Josette—" Maurice whispered softly.

"I know—I was carried away. But, Maurice, you will help me?"

"Of course," he said.

And though he did not feel very hopeful he said it fervently, for the prospect of roaming through the streets of Paris in the company of Josette in search of a person who might be mythical and who certainly would take a lot of finding, was of the rosiest. Indeed, Maurice hoped that the same mythical personage would so hide himself that it would be many days before he was ultimately found.

"And when we have found him," Josette continued glibly, once more speaking under her breath, "you shall tell him about Louise and Charles-Léon, and that Louise must have a permit to take the poor sick baby into the country and to remain with him until he is well."

"And you think—?"

"I don't think, Maurice," she said emphatically, "I know that the Scarlet Pimpernel will do the rest."

She was like a young devotee proclaiming the miracles of her patron saint. It was getting very dark now and at home Louise and Charles-Léon would be waiting for Josette, the angel in the house. Mechanically and a little sadly Maurice led the girl's footsteps in the direction of home. They spoke very little together after this: it seemed as if, having made her profession of faith, Josette took her loyal friend's co-operation for granted. She did not even now realise the cruelty of the blow which she had dealt to his fondest hopes. With the image of this heroic Scarlet Pimpernel so firmly fixed in her mind, Josette was not likely to listen to a declaration of love from a humble law-yer's clerk, who had neither deeds of valour nor a handsome presence wherewith to fascinate a young girl so romantically inclined.

Thus, they wandered homewards in silence—she indulging in her dreams, and he nursing a sorrow that he felt would be eternal. Up above in the chestnut trees the sparrows had gone to roost. Their *paean* of joy had ceased, only the many sounds of a great city not yet abed broke in silence of the night. Furtive footsteps still glided well-nigh soundlessly by; now and then there came a twitter, a fluttering of wings from above, or from far away the barking of a dog, the banging of a door, or the rattling of cart-wheels on the cobble-stones. And sometimes the even-ing breeze would give a great sigh that rose up into the evening air as if coming from hundreds of thousands of prisoners groaning under the tyranny of bloodthirsty oppressors, of a government that proclaimed Liberty and Fraternity from the steps of the guillotine.

And at home in the small apartment of the Rue Picpus, Josette and Maurice found that Louise had cried her eyes out until she had worked herself into a state of hysteria, while Maître de Croissy, silent and thoughtful, sat in dejection by the bedside of his sick child.

Chapter 4

The evening was spent—strangely enough—in silence and in gloom. Josette, who a few hours before had thought to have gained her point and to have brought both hope and faith into Louise's heart, found that her friend had fallen back into that state of dejection out of which nothing that Josette said could possibly drag her. Josette put this down to Bastien's influence. Bastien too had always been sceptical about the Scarlet Pimpernel, didn't believe in his existence at all. He somehow confused him in his mind with that Austrian agent Baron de Batz, of whom he had had such bitter experience. De Batz, too, had been full of schemes for rescuing the king, the royal family, and many a persecuted noble, threatened with death, but months had gone by and nothing had been done. The mint of Austrian money promised by him was never forthcoming. De Batz himself was never on the spot when he wanted. In vain had Bastien de Croissy toiled and striven his hardest to bring negotiations to a head between a certain few members of the revolutionary government who were ready to accept bribes, and the Austrian emissaries who professed themselves ready to pay.

Men like Chabot and Bazire, and Fabre d'Eglantine had been willing enough to negotiate, though their demands became more and more exorbitant as time went on and the king's peril more imminent: even Danton had thrown out hints that in these hard times a man must live, so why not on Austrian money, since French gold was so scarce? but somehow, when everything appeared to be ready, and greedy palms were already outstretched to receive the promised bribes, the money was never there, and de Batz, warned of his peril if he remained in France, had fled across the border.

And somehow the recollection of that intriguer was inextricably mixed up in de Croissy's mind with the legendary personality of the Scarlet Pimpernel.

"Josette is quite convinced of his existence," Louise had said to her husband that afternoon, when they stood together in sorrow and tears beside the sick-bed of Charles-Léon, "and that he can and will get me the permit to take our darling away into the country."

But Bastien shook his head, sadly and obstinately.

"Don't lure yourself with false hopes, my dear," he said. "Josette is an angel, but she is also a child. She dreams and persuades herself that her dreams are realities. I have had experience of such dreams myself."

"I know," Louise rejoined with a sigh.

Hers was one of those yielding natures, gentle and affectionate, that can be swayed one way or the other by an event, sometimes by a mere word; and yet at times she would be strangely obstinate, with the obstinacy of the very weak, or of the feather-pillow that seems to yield at the touch only to regain its own shape the next moment.

A word from Bastien and all the optimism which Josette's ardour had implanted in her heart froze again into scepticism and discouragement.

"If we cannot save Charles-Léon," she said, "I shall die."

Twenty-four hours had gone by since then, and today Bastien de Croissy sat alone in the small musty office of the Rue de la Monnaie. He had sent his clerk, Maurice Reversac, off early because he was a kindly man and had not forgotten the days of his own courtship and knew that the happiest hours of Maurice's day were those when he could meet Josette Gravier outside the gate of the Government workshop and take her out for a walk.

De Croissy had also sent Maurice away early because he wanted to be alone. A crisis had arisen in his life with which he desired to deal thoughtfully and dispassionately. His child was ill, would die, perhaps, unless he, the father, could contrive to send him out of Paris into the country under the care of his mother. The tyranny of this Government of Liberty and Fraternity had made this impossible; no man, woman or child was allowed to be absent from the permanent domicile without a special permit, which was seldom, if ever, granted; not unless some powerful leverage could be found to force those tyrants to grant the permit.

Now Bastien de Croissy was in possession of such a leverage. The question was: had the time come at last to make use of it? He now sat at his desk and a sheaf of letters were laid out before him. These letters, if rightly handled, would, he knew, put so much power into his hands that he could force some of the most influential members of the government to grant him anything he chose to ask.

"Get as much letter-writing as you can out of the black-guards," the Austrian emissary had said to him during that memorable interview in the *Cabaret des Trois Singes*, and de Croissy had acted on this advice. On one pretext or another he had succeeded in persuading at any rate three influential members of the existing Government to put their demands in writing. Bastien had naturally carefully preserved these letters. De Batz was going to use them for his own ends: as a means wherewith to discredit men who proclaimed their disinterestedness and patriotism from the housetops, and not only to discredit them, "but to make them suffer the same humiliation and the same shameful death which they had planned for their king."

These also had been the emissary's words at that fateful interview; and de Croissy had kept the letters up to now, not with a view to using them for his own benefit, or for purposes of blackmail, but with the earnest hope that one day chance would enable him to use them for the overthrow and humiliation of tyrants and regicides.

But now events had suddenly taken a sharp turn. Charles-Léon might die if he was not taken out of the fever-infested city, and Louise, very rightly, would not trust the sick child in a stranger's hands. And if Charles-Léon were to die, Louise would quickly follow the child to his grave.

Bastien de Croissy sat for hours in front of his desk with those letters spread out before him. He picked them up one by one, read and re-read them and put them down again. He rested his weary head against his hand, for thoughts weighed heavily on his mind. To a man of integrity, a high-minded gentleman as he had always been, the alternative was a horrible one. On one side there was that hideous thing, blackmail, which was abhorrent to him, and on the other the life of his wife and child. Honour and conscience ruled one way, and every fibre of his heart the other.

The flickering light of tallow candles threw grotesque shadows on the whitewashed walls and cast fantastic gleams of light on the handsome face of the great lawyer, with its massive forehead and nobly sculptured profile, on the well-shaped hands and hair prematurely grey.

The letter which he now held in his hand was signed "François Chabot," once a Capuchin friar, now a member of the National Convention and one of Danton's closest friends, whose uncompromising patriotism had been proclaimed on the housetops both by himself and his colleagues.

And this is what François Chabot had written not much more than a year ago to Maître de Croissy, advocate:

> My friend, as I told you in our last interview, I am inclined to listen favourably to the proposals of B. If he really disposes of the funds of which he boasts, tell him that I can get C. out of his present *impasse* and put him once more in possession of the seat which he values. Further, I and the others can keep him in a guarantee that nothing shall happen (say) for five years to disturb him again. But you can also tell B. that his proposals are futile. I shall want twenty thousand on the day that C. enters his house in the park, moreover, your honorarium for carrying this matter through must be paid by B. My friends and I will not incur any expense in connection with it."

Bastien de Croissy now took up his pen and a sheet of paper, and after a moment's reflection he transcribed the somewhat enigmatic letter by substituting names for initials, and intelligible words for those that appeared ununderstandable. The letter so transcribed now began thus:

> My friend, as I told you in our last interview, I am inclined to listen favourably to the proposals of de Batz. If he really disposes of the funds of which he boasts, tell him that I can get the king out of his present *impasse* and put him once more in possession of his throne. . .

The rest of the letter he transcribed in the same way: always substituting the words "the King" for "C." and "de Batz" for "B."; his house in the park Maître de Croissy transcribed as "Versailles."

The whole text would now be clear to anybody. Bastien then took up a number of other letters and transcribed these in the same way as he had done the first: then he made two separate packets of the whole correspondence; one of these contained the original letters, and these he slipped in the inside pocket of his coat, the other he tied loosely together and put it away with other papers in his desk. He then locked the desk and the strong box, turned out the lights in the office and finally went home.

His mind was definitely made up.

The same evening Bastien made a clean breast of all the circumstances to Louise. Maurice was there and Josette of course, and there was little Charles-Léon, who lay like a half-animate bird in his mother's arms.

For Maurice the story was not new. He had known of the first interview between de Croissy and the Austrian emissary, he had watched the intrigue developing step by step, through the good offices of the distinguished advocate. As a matter of fact, he had more than once acted as messenger, taking letters to and fro between the dingy offices of the Rue de la Monnaie and the sumptuous apartments of the Representatives of the People. He had spoken to Chabot, the unfrocked friar who lived in unparalleled luxury in the Rue d'Anjou, dressed in town like a Beau Brummel, but attended the sittings of the National Convention in a tattered coat and shoes down at heel, his hair unkempt, his chin unshaven, his hands unwashed, in order to flaunt what he was pleased to call his democratic ideals.

He saw Bazire, Chabot's brother-in-law, who hired a mudlark to enact the part of pretended assassin in order that he might raise the cry: "The royalists are murdering the patriots!" (As it happened, the pretended assassin did not turn up at the right moment, and Bazire had been left to wander alone up and down the dark *cul-de-sac* waiting to receive the stab that was to exalt him before the Convention as the victim of his ardent patriotism.) Maurice had interviewed Fabre d'Eglantine, Danton's most intimate friend, who was only too ready to see his palm greased with foreign gold, and even the ruthless and impeccable Danton had to Maurice's knowledge nibbled at the sweet biscuit held to his nose by the Austrian agent.

All these men Maurice Reversac had known, interviewed and despised. But he had also seen the clouds of bitterness and disappointment gather in Bastien de Croissy's face: he guessed more than he actually knew how one by one all the hopes born of that first interview in the *Cabaret des Trois Singes* had been laid to dust. The continued captivity of the royal family, the severance of the queen from her children had been the first heavy blows dealt to those fond hopes. The king's condemnation and death completely shattered them. Maurice dared not ask what the Austrian was doing, or what final preposterous demands had come from the Representatives of the People, which had caused the negotiations to be finally broken off. For months now, the history of those negotiations had almost been forgotten. As far as Maurice was concerned he had ceased to think of them, he only remembered the letters that had passed during that time, as incidents that might have had wonderful consequences, but had since sunk into the limbo of forgetfulness.

To Louise and Josette, on the other hand, the story was entirely new. Each heard it with widely divergent feelings. Obviously to Louise it meant salvation. She listened to her husband with glowing eyes, her lips were parted, her breath came and went with almost feverish rapidity, and every now and then she pressed Charles-Léon closer and closer to her breast. Never for a moment did she appear in doubt that here was complete deliverance from every trouble and every anxiety. Indeed, the only thing that seemed to trouble her was the fact that Bastien had withheld this wonderful secret from her for so long.

"We might have been free to leave this hell upon earth long before this," she exclaimed with passionate reproach when Bastien admitted that he had hesitated to use such a weapon for his own benefit.

"It looks so like blackmail," Bastien murmured feebly.

"Blackmail?" Louise retorted vehemently. "Would you call it murder if you killed a mad dog?"

Bastien gave a short, quick sigh. The letters were to have been the magic key wherewith to open the prison door for his king and queen: the mystic wand that would clear the way for them to their throne.

"Is not Charles-Léon's life more precious than any king's?" Louise protested passionately.

And soon she embarked on plans for the future. She would take the child into the country, and presently, if things didn't get any better, they would join the band loyal *émigrés* who led a precarious but peaceful existence in Belgium or England; Josette and Maurice would come with them, and together they would all wait for those better times which could not now be very long in coming.

"There is nothing," she declared emphatically, "that these men would dare refuse us. By threatening to send those letters to the *Moniteur* or any other paper we can force them to grant us permits, passports, anything we choose. Oh, Bastien!" she added impetuously, "why did you not think of all this before?"

Josette alone was silent. She alone had hardly uttered a word the whole evening. In silence she had listened to Bastien's exposition of the case, and to Maurice's comments on the situation, and she remained silent while Louise talked and reproached and planned. She only spoke when Bastien, after he had read aloud some of the more important letters, gathered them all together and tied them once more into a packet. He was about to slip them into his coat pocket when Josette spoke up.

"Don't do that, Bastien," she said impulsively, and stretched out her hand for the packet.

"Don't do what, my dear?" de Croissy asked.

"Let Louise take charge of the letters," the girl pleaded, "until those treacherous devils are ready to give you the permits and safe-conducts in exchange for them. You can show your transcriptions to them at first: but they wouldn't be above sticking a knife into you in the course of conversation and rifling your pockets if they knew you had the originals on you at the time."

Bastien couldn't help smiling at the girl's eagerness, but he put the packet of letters into her outstretched hand.

"You are right, Josette," he said: "you are always right. The angel in the house! What will you do with them?"

"Sew them into the lining of Louise's corsets," Josette replied.

And she never said another word after that.

Chapter 5

Louise de Croissy stood by the window and watched her husband's tall massive figure as he strode down the street on his way to the Rue de la Monnaie. When he had finally disappeared out of her sight Louise turned to Josette.

Unconsciously almost, and certainly against her better judgement, Josette felt a strange misgiving about this affair. She hadn't slept all night for thinking about it. And this morning when Bastien had set off so gaily and Louise seemed so full of hope she still felt oppressed and vaguely frightened. There is no doubt that intense love does at times possess psychic powers, the power usually called "second sight." Josette's love for Louise and what she called her "little family" was maternal in its intensity and she always averred that she knew beforehand whenever a great joy was to come to them and also had a premonition of any danger that threatened them.

And somehow this morning she felt unable to shake off a consciousness of impending doom. She, too, had watched at the window while Bastien de Croissy started out in the direction of the Rue de la Monnaie, there to pick up the packet of transcriptions and then to go off on his fateful errand; and when he had turned the angle of the street and she could no longer see him she felt more than ever the approach of calamity.

These were the last days of September: summer had lingered on and it had been wonderfully sunny all along. In the woods the ash, the oak and the chestnut were still heavy with leaf and thrushes and blackbirds still sang gaily their evening melodies, but today the weather had turned sultry: there were heavy clouds up above that presaged a coming storm.

"Why, what's the matter, Josette *chérie?*" Louise asked anxiously, for the girl, as she gazed out into the dull grey light, shivered as if with cold and her pretty face appeared drawn and almost haggard. "Are you disappointed that your mythical Scarlet Pimpernel will not, after all, play his heroic *rôle* on our stage?"

Louise said this with a light laugh, meaning only to chaff, but Josette winced as if she had been stung, and tears gathered in her eyes.

"Josette!" Louise exclaimed, full of contrition and of tenderness. She felt happy, light-hearted, proud too, of what Bastien could do for them all. Though the morning was grey and dismal, though there were only scanty provisions in the house—aye! even though Charles-Léon lay limp and listless in his little bed, Louise felt that on this wonderful day she could busy herself about her poor dingy home, singing to herself with joy. She, like Bastien himself, had never wished to emigrate, but at times she had yearned passionately for the fields and the woods of the Dauphiné where her husband still owned the family *château* and where there was a garden in which Charles-Léon could run about, where the air was pure and wholesome so that the colour could once more tinge the poor lamb's wan cheeks.

She could not understand why Josette was not as happy as she was herself. Perhaps she was depressed by the weather, and sure enough soon after Bastien started the first lightning-flash shot across the sky, and after a few seconds there came the distant rumble of thunder. A few heavy drops fell on the cobble-stones and then the rain came down, a veritable cataract, as if the sluices of heaven had suddenly been opened. Within a few minutes the uneven pavements ran with muddy streams and an unfortunate passer-by, caught in the shower, buttoned up their coat collars and bolted for the nearest doorway. The wind howled down the chimneys and rattled the ill-fitting window-panes. No wonder that Josette's spirits were damped by this dismal weather!

Louise drew away from the window, sighing: "Thank God, I made Bastien put on his thick old coat!" Then she sat down and called Josette to her. "You know, *chérie*," she said, and put loving arms round the girl's shoulders, "I didn't mean anything unkind about your hero: I was only chaffing. I loved your enthusiasm and your belief in miracles; but I am more prosy than you are, *chérie*, and prefer to pin my faith on the sale of compromising letters rather than on deeds of valour performed by a mythical hero."

To please Louise, Josette made a great effort to appear cheerful; indeed, she chided herself for her ridiculous feeling of depression, which had no reason for its existence and only tended to upset Louise. She pleaded a headache after a sleepless night.

"I lay awake," she said, with an effort to appear light-hearted, "thinking of the happy time we would all have over in the Dauphiné. It is so lovely there in the late autumn when the leaves turn to gold."

The rest of the morning Josette was obliged to spend in the Government workshops sewing shirts for the "Soldiers of Liberty," so presently when the storm began to subside she put on her cloak and hood, gave Charles-Léon a last kiss and hurried off to work. She had hoped to get her allotted task done by twelve o'clock, when Maurice could meet her and they could sally forth together in search of fresh air under the trees of Cour la Reine. Unfortunately, as luck would have it, she was detained in the workshop along with a number of other girls until a special consignment of shirts was ready for packing. When she was finally able to leave the shop, it was past one o'clock and Maurice was not waiting at the gate.

She hurried home for her midday meal, only to hear from Louise that Bastien and Maurice had already been and gone. They had snatched a morsel of food and hurried away again, for they had important work to do at the office. Louise was full of enthusiasm and full of hope. Bastien, she said, had seen Fabre d'Eglantine, also Chabot and Bazire, and had already entered into negotiations with them for the exchange of the compromising letters against permits for himself and his family—which would, of course, include Josette and Maurice—to take up permanent domicile on his estate in the Dauphiné. Bastien and Maurice, after they had imparted this joyful news and had their hurried meal, had gone back to the office. It seems that after the three interviews were over and Bastien was back at the Rue de la Monnaie, Françious Chabot had called on him with a ponderous document which he desired put into legal jargon that same afternoon.

"It will take them several hours to get through with the work," Louise went on to explain, "and when it is ready Maurice is to take the document to Citizen Chabot's apartment in Rue d'Anjoy; so, I don't suppose we shall see either of them before supper-time. Bastien says he was so amused when Chabot called at the office. His eyes were roaming round the room all the time. I am sure he was wondering in his mind where Bastien kept the letters, and I am so thankful, Josette darling, that we took your advice and have them here in safe-keeping. Do you know, Bastien declares that if those letters were published tomorrow Chabot and the lot of them, not even excepting the great Danton, would find themselves at the bar of the accused, and within the hour their heads would be off their shoulders? And serve them right, the murdering, hypocritical devils!"

After which she unfolded to her darling Josette her plans for leaving this hateful Paris within the next twenty-four hours. Dreams and hopes! Louise was full of them just now: strange that to Josette the whole thing was like a nightmare.

Chapter 6

In the late afternoon Josette had again to go back to the workshop to put in a couple of hours' more sewing. She left Louise in the apartment, engrossed in sorting out the necessary clothes required for the journey, and singing merrily like a bird. Bastien and Maurice were not expected home for some hours. Charles-Léon was asleep.

It was past eight o'clock and quite dark when Josette finally returned home to the Rue Picpus for the evening. Under the big *portcochère* of the apartment house she nearly fell into the arms of Maurice Reversac, who apparently was waiting for her.

"Oh, Maurice!" she cried, "how you frightened me!" And then, "What are you doing here?"

Instead of replying he took her by the wrist and drew her to the foot of the main staircase, away from the *concierge's* lodge, where in an angle of the wall they could be secure from prying ears and eyes. Here Maurice halted, but he still clung to her wrist, and leaned against the wall as if exhausted and breathless.

"Maurice, what is it?"

The staircase was in almost total darkness, only a feeble light filtrated down from an oil-lamp fixed on one of the landings above. Josette could not see her friend's face, but she felt the tremor that shook his arm and she heard the stertorous breath that struggled through his lips. The sense of doom, of some calamity that threatened them all, the nameless foreboding that had haunted her all day held her heart in an icy grip.

"Maurice!" she insisted.

At last he spoke; he murmured his employer's name.

"Maître de Croissy—"

Josette could scarcely repress a cry:

"Arrested?"

He shook his head.

"Not. . . ? Dead. . . ? When? How? What is it, Maurice? In God's name, tell me!"

"Murdered!"

"Murd—"

She clapped her hand to her mouth and dug her teeth into it to smother the scream which would have echoed up the well of the stairs. Louise's apartment was only up two flights. She would have heard.

"Tell me!" Josette gasped rather than spoke. She did not really understand. What Maurice had just said was so impossible. Inconceivable! She had expected a cataclysm. . . . Yes. All day she had felt like the dread hand of Doom hovering over them all. But not this! In Heaven's name, not this! Murdered? Bastien? Why, Maurice must be crazy! And she said it aloud, too.

"You are crazy, Maurice!"

"I thought I was just now."

"You've been dreaming," she insisted. For still she did not believe.

"Murdered, I tell you! Dead!"

"Where?"

"In the office. . . ."

"Then let us go. . . ."

She wanted to run. . . . out. . . . at once, but Maurice got hold of her and held her so that she could not go.

"Wait, Josette! Let me tell you first."

"Let me go, Maurice! I don't believe it. Let me go!"

Maurice had already pulled himself together. He had contrived to steady his voice, and now, with a perfectly firm grip, he pulled Josette's hand under his arm and led her out into the street. There would be no holding her back if she was determined to go. The rain-storm had turned to a nasty drizzle and it was very cold. The few passers-by who hurried along the narrow street had their coat collars buttoned closely round their necks. A very few lights glimmered here and there in the windows of the houses on either side. Street lamps were no longer lighted these days in the side streets for reasons of economy.

Out in the open Maurice put his arm round Josette's shoulder and instinctively she nestled against him. Almost paralysed with horror, she was shivering with cold and her teeth were chattering, but there was a feeling of comfort and of protection in Maurice's arm which seemed to steady her. Also, she wanted to hear every word that he said, and he did not dare raise his voice above a whisper. They walked as fast as the unevenness of the cobble-stones allowed, and now and then they broke into a run; and all the while, in short jerky sentences, Maurice tried to tell the girl something of what had happened.

"Maître de Croissy," he said, "had an interview with Citizen Chabot in the morning. . . . While he was there Chabot sent for Bazire. . . . and after that the three of them went together to Danton's lodgings—"

"You weren't with them?"

"No. . . . I was waiting at the office. Presently Maître de Croissy came back alone. He was full of hope. . . . the interview had gone off very well. . . . better than he expected. . . . Chabot and Bazire were obviously terrified out of their lives. . . . Maître de Croissy had left them with Danton, and come on to the office—"

"Yes! and then?"

"About half an hour later, Chabot called at the office. . . . alone. . . . he brought a document with him. . . . did *Madame* tell you?"

"Yes! yes!—"

"He stayed a little while talking. . . . talking. . . . explaining the document. . . . a very long one. . . . of which he wanted three copies made. . . . with additions. . . . and so on. . . . He wanted the papers back by evening—"

Maurice seemed to be gasping for breath. His voice was husky as if his throat were parched. It was difficult to talk coherently while threading one's way through the narrow streets, and once or twice he forced Josette to stand still for a moment or two, to rest against the wall while she listened.

"We went home to dinner after Chabot had gone—" Maurice went on presently. "I can't tell you just how I felt then. . . . a kind of foreboding you know—"

"Yes, I know," she said, "I felt it too. . . . last night—"

"Something in that devil's eyes had frightened me. . . . but you know Maître de Croissy. . . . he won't listen. . . . once he has made up his mind. . . . and he laughed at me when I ventured on a word of warning. . . . you know—"

"Oh, yes!" Josette sighed, "I know!"

"We went back to the office together after dinner. Maître de Croissy worked on the document all afternoon. It was ready just when the light gave out. He gave me the paper and told me to take it to Citizen Chabot. I went. Chabot kept me waiting, an hour or more. It was nearly eight o'clock when I got back to the office. The front door was ajar. I remember thinking this strange. I pushed open the door—"

He paused, and suddenly Josette said quite firmly:

"Don't tell me, Maurice. I can guess."

"What, Josette?'

"Those devils got you out of the way. They meant to filch the letters from Bastien. They killed him in order to get the letters."

"The two rooms," Maurice said, "looked as if they had been shattered by an earthquake."

"They broke everything so as to get the letters, and they killed him first."

They had reached the house in the Rue de la Monnaie. It looked no different than it had always done. Grim, grey, dilapidated. Inside the house there was that smell of damp and of mortar like in a vault. Apparently, no one knew anything as yet about what had occurred on the second floor where Citizen Croissy, the lawyer, had his office. No one challenged the young man and the girl as they hurried up the stairs. Josette as she ran was trembling in every limb, but she knew that the time had come for calmness and for courage, and with a mighty effort she regained control over her nerves. She was determined to be a help rather than a hindrance, even though horror had gripped her like some live and savage beast by the throat so that she scarcely could breathe and turned the dread in her heart to physical nausea.

Maurice had taken the precaution of locking the front door of the office, but he had the key in his pocket. Before inserting it in the keyhole he paused to take another look at Josette. If she had faltered the least bit in the world, if he had perceived the slightest swaying in her young firm body, he would have picked her up in his arms where she stood and carried her away—away from that awful scene behind the door.

He could not see her face, for the stairs were very dark, but through a dim and ghostly light he perceived the outline of her head and saw that she held it erect and her shoulders square. All he said was:

"Shall we go to the *commissariat* first?"

But she shook her head. He opened the door and she followed him in. The small vestibule was in darkness, but the door into the office was open, and here the light from the oil-lamp which dangled from the ceiling revealed the prone figure of Bastien de Croissy on the floor, his torn clothing and the convulsive twist of his hands. A heavy crowbar lay close beside the body, and all around there was a litter of broken furniture, wood, glass, a smashed inkstand with the ink still flowing out of it and staining the bit of faded carpet; sand and *débris* of paper and of string and the smashed drawers of the bureau. The strong-box was also on the floor with its metal door broken open and money and papers scattered around. Indeed, the whole place did look as if it had been shattered by an earthquake.

But Josette did not look at all that. All she saw was Bastien lying there, his body rigid in the last convulsive twitching of death. She prayed to God for the strength to go near him, to kneel beside him and say the prayers for the dead which the Church demanded. Maurice knelt down beside her, and they drew the dead man's hands together over his breast, and Josette took her rosary from her pocket and wound it round the hands; then she and Maurice recited the prayers for the dead: she with eyes closed lest if she continued to look she fell into a swoon. She prayed for Bastien's soul, and she also prayed for guidance as to what she ought to do now that Bastien was gone: for Louise was not strong and after this she would have no one on whom to lean, only on her, Josette.

When she and Maurice had finished their prayers, they sought among the *débris* for the two pewter candlesticks that used to stand on the bureau. Maurice found them presently; they were all twisted, but not broken, and close by there were the pieces of tallow candle that had fallen out of their sconces. He straightened them out, and with a screw of paper held to the lamp he lighted the candles and Josette placed them on the floor, one on each side of the dead man's head.

After which she tiptoed out of the room. Maurice extinguished the hanging lamp; he followed Josette out through the door and locked it behind him.

Then the two of them went silently and quickly down the stairs.

Chapter 7

Louise de Croissy lay on the narrow horse-hair sofa like a log. Since Josette had broken the terrible news to her, more than twenty-four hours ago, she had been almost like one dead: unable to speak, unable to eat or sleep. Even Charles-Léon's childish cajoleries could not rouse her from her apathy.

For twenty-four hours she had lain thus, silent and motionless, while Josette did her best to keep Charles-Léon amused and looked after his creature comforts as best she could. She adored Louise, but somehow at this crisis she could not help feeling impatient with the other woman's nervelessness and that devastating inertia.

After all, there was Charles-Léon to think of; all the more now as the head of the family had gone. Josette still had her mind set on finding the Scarlet Pimpernel, who of a truth was the only person in the world who could save Louise and Charles-Léon now. Josette had no illusions on the score of the new danger which threatened these two. Bastien had been murdered by Terrorists because he would not give up the letters that compromised them without getting a *quid pro quo*. They had killed him and ransacked his rooms. They might have ordered his arrest—it was so easy these days to get an enemy arrested—but no doubt feared that he might have a chance of speaking during his trial and revealing what he knew. Only dead men tell no tales.

But the letters had not been found, and at this hour there was a clique of desperate men who knew that their necks were in peril if those letters were ever made public. Josette had no illusions. Sooner or later, within a few hours perhaps, those men would strike at Louise. There would be a perquisition, arrest probably, and possibly another murder. She wanted Louise to destroy the letters, they had been the cause of this awful cataclysm, but at the slightest hint Louise had clutched at her bosom with both hands as if she would guard the letters with her life.

The next evening when Josette came home she found Louise already in bed; it was the first time she had moved from that narrow horse-hair sofa since the girl had broken the news to her. She had laid out her clothes on a chair, with her corsets ostentatiously spread out

134

on the top of the other things as if to invite attention. The packet of letters was no longer inside the lining. Josette noticed this at once, also that Louise was feigning sleep and was watching her through half-closed lids.

With well-assumed indifference Josette went about her business in the house, smoothed Louise's pillow, kissed her and Charles-Léon goodnight, and then got into bed. But she did not get much sleep, tired to death though she was. She foresaw the complications. Louise had some fixed idea about those letters, the result of shock no doubt, and was clinging to them with the obstinacy of the very weak. She had hidden them and meant to keep their hiding-place a secret, even from Josette. No doubt her nerves had to a certain extent given way, for in spite of her closed eyes as she lay on her bed there was that expression of cunning in her face which is peculiar to those whose minds are deranged.

Josette and Maurice had spent most of that day at the *Commissariat de Police*. It was a terrible ordeal from the first to last. The airless room that smelt of dirt and humanity, the patient crowd of weary men and women waiting their turn to pass into the presence of the *commissary*, the suspense of the present and the horror of the past nearly broke down Josette's fortitude. Nearly, but not quite; for she had Maurice with her, and it was wonderful what comfort she derived from his nearness. She had always been so self-reliant, so accustomed to watch over those she cared for, and cater for their creature comforts, that Maurice Reversac's somewhat diffident ways, his timid speech and dog-like devotion had tempered her genuine affection for him with a slight measure of contempt. She could not help but admire his loyalty to his employer and his disinterestedness and felt bound to admit that he was clever and learned in the law, else Bastien would not have placed reliance on his judgement, as he often did, but all the time she had the feeling that morally and physically he was a weakling, the ivy that clung rather than the oak that supported.

But since this awful trouble had come upon her, how different it all was. Josette felt just as self-reliant as in the past, for Louise and Charles-Léon were more dependent on her than ever before, but there was Maurice now, a different Maurice altogether, and he had become a force.

When their turn came to appear before the *commissary*, Josette, having Maurice at her side, did not feel frightened. They both gave their names and address in a clear voice, showed their papers and identity, and gave a plain and sincere account of the terrible events of the day before. Citizen Croissy, the well-known advocate, had been foully murdered in his office in the Rue de la Monnaie. It was their duty as citizens of the Republic to report this terrible fact to the *commissariat* of the section.

The *commissary* listened, raised his eyebrows, toyed with a paper-knife; his face was a mask of complete incredulity.

"Why should you talk of murder?" he asked.

Maurice mentioned the crowbar, the ransacked room, the scattered papers, the broken strong-box. It was clearly a case of murder for purposes of robbery.

"Any money missing?" the *commissary* asked.

"No!"

"*Eh bien!*" he remarked with a careless shrug. "You see?"

"The murder had a political motive, Citizen Commissary," Josette put in impulsively, "the assassins were not after money, but after certain papers—"

"Now you are talking nonsense," the *commissary* broke in curtly. "Murder? What fool do you suppose would resort to murder nowadays?" He checked himself abruptly, for he was on the point of letting his tongue run away with him. What he had very nearly said, and certainly had implied, was that no fool would take the risk and trouble of murder these days when it was so easy to rid oneself of an enemy by denouncing him as "suspect of treason" before the local Committee of Public Safety. Arrest, trial, and the guillotine would then follow as a matter of course, and one got forty *sous* to boot as a reward for denouncing a traitor. Then why trouble to murder?

No wonder the *commissary* checked himself in time before he had said all this: men in office had been degraded before now, if not worse, for daring to criticise the decrees of this paternal government.

"I'll tell you what I will do, *citizeness*," he said, speaking more particularly to Josette because her luminous blue eyes were fixed upon his, and he was a susceptible man; "I don't believe a word of your story, mind! but I will visit the scene of that supposed murder, and listen on the spot to the depositions of witnesses. Then we'll see."

"There were no witnesses to the crime, Citizen Commissary," Josette declared.

Whereupon the *commissary* swore loudly, blustered and threatened all false accusers with the utmost penalties the law could impose. Witnesses? There must be witnesses. The *concierge* of the house.... the other lodgers. . . . anyway, he would see, and if in the end it was definitely proved that this tale of assassination and political crime was nothing but a cock-and-bull story, well! let all false witnesses look to their own necks. . . . that was all.

"You will appear before me tomorrow," were the parting words with which the *commissary* dismissed Maurice and Josette from his presence.

No wonder that after that long and wearisome day, Josette should have lain awake most of the night a-thinking. It was very obvious that nothing would be done to bring the murderers of Bastien to justice. Perhaps she had been wrong after all to speak of "political motives" in connection with the crime: she had only moral proofs for her assertion, and those devils who had perpetrated the abominable deed would be all the more on the alert now, and Louise's peril would be greater even that before.

"Holy Virgin," she murmured *naïvely* in her prayers, "help me to find the Scarlet Pimpernel!"

On the following morning, Louise, though still listless and apathetic, rose and dressed herself without saying a word. Josette with an aching heart could not help noticing that her face still wore an expression of cunning and obstinacy, and that her eyes were still dry: Louise indeed had not shed a single tear since the awful truth had finally penetrated to her brain, and she had understood that Bastien had been foully murdered because of the letters.

With endearing words and infinite gentleness Josette did her best to soften the poor woman's mood. She drew her to Charles-Léon's bedside and murmured some of the *naïve* prayers which when they were children together they had learned at the Convent of the Visitation. Her own soulful blue eyes were bathed in tears.

"Don't try and make me cry, Josette," Louise said. These were the first words she had spoken for thirty-six hours, and her voice sounded rasping and harsh. "If I were to shed tears now I would go on crying and crying till my eyes could no longer see and then they would close in death."

"You must not talk of death, Louise," Josette admonished gently, "while you have Charles-Léon to think of."

"It is because I think of him," Louise retorted, "that I don't want to cry."

But of the letters not a word, though Josette, by hint and glance, asked more than one mute question.

"Bastien would rather have seen your tears, Louise," she said with a tone of sad reproach.

"Perhaps he will—from above—when I stand by his graveside. . . . but not now—not yet."

Louise, however, never did stand by her husband's graveside; that morning when Maurice and Josette went to the *commissariat* in order to obtain permission for the burial of Citizen Croissy, they were curtly informed that the burial had already taken place, and no amount of questioning, of entreaty and of petitions elected any further information, save that the body had been disposed of by order of what was vaguely designated as "the authorities"; which meant that it had probably been thrown in the *fosse* commune of the Jardin de Picpus— the old convent garden—the common grave where no cross or stone could mark the last resting-place of the once brilliant and wealthy advocate of the Paris bar. The reason, curtly given, for this summary procedure was that it was the usual one in the case of suicides.

Thus, was the foul murder of the distinguished lawyer classed as a case of suicide. It was useless to protest and to argue; only harm would come to Louise and Charles-Léon if either Maurice or Josette entered into any discussion on the subject. As soon as they opened their mouths they were roughly ordered to hold their peace. Maurice Reversac was commanded to accompany the Citizen Substitute to the office of the Rue de la Monnaie, there to complete certain formalities in connection with the goods and chattels belonging to "the suicide," and then officially to give up the keys of the apartment.

Chapter 8

Josette in her *naïve* little prayers had implored the Holy Virgin to aid her in finding the Scarlet Pimpernel. She was convinced that nothing could save Louise and Charles-Léon from Bastien's awful fate save the intervention of her mysterious hero, but the last two days had been so full of events that it had been quite impossible for her to begin her quest for the one man on whom in this dark hour she could pin her faith. Maurice, on the other hand, had promised that he would do his best, and this was all the more wonderful as he had not the same faith as Josette in the existence of the heroic Englishman.

Nevertheless, in order to please and cheer her, and in the intervals of running from pillar to post, from the Rue de la Monnaie to the *commissariat* and back again, he did seriously set to work to get on the track of the public letter-writer who was wont to ply his trade at the corner of the Pont-Neuf and who was supposed to be in touch with the Scarlet Pimpernel himself.

Maurice knew all the highways and by-ways of old Paris—the small eating-houses and estaminets where it was possible to enter into casual conversation with simple everyday folk who would suspect no harm in discreet inquiries. Thus, he came quite by chance on the track of what he thought might be a clue. There was, it seems, in a distant quarter of the city near the Batignolles, a funny old scarecrow who had set up his tent and carried on his trade of letter-writing for those who were too illiterate or too prudent to put pen to paper themselves. Not that Maurice believed for a moment that the scarecrow in question had anything to do with a band of English *aristos*, but he thought that the running him to earth, the walk across Paris, even though the weather was at its vilest, would take Josette out of herself for an hour or so, and turn her thoughts into less gloomy channels.

Josette readily agreed, and while Maurice was away on his melancholy errand in the Rue de la Monnaie, she promised that she would wait for him at the *Commissariat de Police*, and then they could sally forth together in quest of the hero of her dreams.

The waiting-room of the *commissariat* was large and square. The walls had at some remote time been white-washed; now they and the ceiling were of a dull grey colour, and all around there was a dado-line of dirt and grease made by the rubbing of innumerable shoulders against the lime. On the wooden benches ranged against the walls, patient, weary-looking women sat, some with shawls over their heads, others shivering in thin bodice and kirtle, and all hugging bundles or babies. One of them made room for Josette, who sat down beside her preparing to wait. There were a number of men, too, mostly in ragged breeches and tattered coats, who hung about in groups whispering and spitting on the floor or sitting on the table: nearly all of them were either decrepit or maimed.

A few children scrambled in the dirt, getting in everybody's way. The place was almost unendurably stuffy, with a mingled odour of boiled cabbage, wet clothes and damp mortar; only from time to time when the outside door was opened for someone to go in or out did a gust of cold air come sweeping through the room. Josette wished she had arranged to meet Maurice somewhere else; she didn't think she could wait much longer in this dank atmosphere. She felt very tired, too, and the want of air made her feel drowsy.

The sound of a familiar voice roused her from the state of semi-torpor into which she had fallen, blinking and rather dazed, she looked about her. Old Doctor Larousse had just come in. He had a bundle of papers in his hand and looked fussy and hurried.

"A dog's life!" he muttered in the face of anyone who listened to him. "All these papers to get signed and more than half an hour to wait, maybe, in this filthy hole!"

Josette at sight of him jumped up and intercepted him at the moment when two or three others tried to get a word with him. All day yesterday she had wished to get in touch with the old doctor, and again this morning, not so much because of Charles-Léon, but because she was getting seriously anxious about Louise. Citizen Larousse had been away from home for the past twenty-four hours: Josette had called at his rooms two or three times during the day, but always in vain.

Now she pulled the old man by the sleeve, forced him to listen to her.

"Citizen Doctor," she demanded, "at what hour can you come to the Rue Picpus and see Citizeness Croissy, who is seriously ill?"

Larousse shook her hand off his arm with unusual roughness: he was a kindly man, but apparently very harassed this morning.

"At what hour—at what hour?" he muttered petulantly. "Hark at your impudence, *citizeness!* At no hour, let me tell you—not today, anyhow! I am off to Passy as soon as I can get these cursed papers signed."

"Citizen Doctor, think of the widow! Her mind is nearly deranged. She wants—"

"Many of us want things these days, little *citizeness*," the old man said more gently, for Josette's deep blue eyes were fixed upon him and they were irresistible—would have been irresistible, that is, if he, Larousse, had not been quite so worried this morning. "I, for one, want to get to Passy, where my wife is ill with congestion of the lungs, and I shall not leave her bedside until she is well or—"

He shrugged his shoulders. He was a kind-hearted man really, but for two days he had been anxious about his wife. Josette Gravier was pretty, very pretty; she had large blue eyes that looked like a midnight sky in June when she was excited or eager or distressed, and there were delicate golden curls round her ears which always made old Larousse think of the days of his youth, of those summer afternoons when he was wont to wander out in the woods around Fontaine-bleau with his arm round a pretty girl's waist—just such a girl as Josette. But today?

No, he was not in a mood to think of the days of his youth, and he had no use for pretty girls with large blue reproachable eyes. He was much too worried to be cajoled.

"You will have to find another doctor, little *citizeness*," he concluded gruffly, "or else wait a day or two."

"How can I wait a day or two," she retorted, "with Citizeness Croissy nigh to losing her reason? Can't you imagine what she has gone through?"

The old man shrugged. He had seen so much misery, so much sorrow and pain, it was difficult to be compassionate to all. There had never been but One in this world who had compassion for the whole of humanity, and humanity repaid Him by nailing Him to a cross.

"We have to go through a lot these days, *citizeness*," the old man said, "and I do not think that your friend will lose her reason. One is apt to let one's anxiety magnify such danger. I'll come as soon as I can."

"How soon?"

"Three or four days—I cannot tell."

"But in the meanwhile, Citizen Doctor, what shall I do?"

"Give her a soothing draught."

"To what purpose? She is calm—too calm—"

"Find another doctor."

"How can I? It takes days to obtain a permit to change one's doctor. You know that well enough, citizen."

The girl now spoke with bitter dejection and the old man with growing impatience. He had freed himself quickly enough from the subtle spell of the girl's beauty: the weight of care and worry had again descended on him and hardened his heart. A queue had formed against the door which led to the *commissary's* private office, and the old doctor feared that he would lose his turn if he did not immediately take his place in the queue. The papers had got to be signed and he was longing to get away to Passy, where his wife lay sick with congestion. He tried to shake off Josette's grip on his arm, but she would not let go.

"Can you get me a permit," she pleaded, "to change our doctor?"

Oh, those permits—those awful, tiresome, cruel permits, without which no citizen of this free Republic could do anything save die! Permit to move, permit for bread, permit for meat or milk, permit to call in a doctor, a midwife or an undertaker! Permits, permits all the time!

The crowd in the room, indifferent at first, had begun to take notice of this pretty girl's importunate demands. They were here, all of them, in quest of some permit or other, the granting of which depended on the mood of the official who sat at his desk the other side of the door. If the official was harassed and tired he would be disobliging, refuse permit after permit: to a sick woman to see a doctor, to an anaemic child to receive more milk, to a man to take work beyond a certain distance from his home. He could be disobliging if he chose, for full powers were vested in him. Such were the ways of the glorious Republic which had for its motto: Liberty and Fraternity.

Such was the state of slavery into which the citizens of the free Republic had sunk. And as Josette insisted, still clinging to the doctor's arm, the men shrugged and some of them sneered. They knew that old Larousse could not get the permit for which she craved. It took days to obtain any kind of a permit: there were yards of red tape to measure out before anything of the sort could be obtained, even if the *commissary* was in one of his best moods. They were all of them sorry for the girl in a way, chiefly because she was so pretty, but they thought her foolish to be so insistent. The women gazed on her and would have commiserated with her, only that they had so many troubles of their own. And they were all so tired, so tired of hanging about in this stuffy room and waiting their turn in the queue. It was so hard to worry over other people's affairs when one was tired and had countless worries of one's own.

Now someone came out of the inner room and the queue moved on. Josette was suddenly separated from the doctor, who was probably thankful to be rid of her; with a deep sigh of dejection she went back to her seat on the bench. A few glances of pity were still cast on her, but presently the queue was able to move on again and she was soon forgotten. No one took any more notice of her. The men whispered among themselves, the women, fagged and silent, stood waiting for their turn to go in. Only one man seemed to take an interest in Josette: a tall ugly fellow with one leg who was leaning against the wall with his crutches beside him. He was dressed in seedy black with somewhat soiled linen at throat and wrist, and his hair, which was long and lanky, was tied back at the nape of the neck with a frayed-out back ribbon. He wore no hat; his shoes were down at heel and his stockings were in holes. By the look of him he might have been a lawyer's clerk fallen on evil days.

Josette did not at first notice him, until presently she had that peculiar feeling which comes to one at times that a pair of eyes were fixed steadily upon her. She looked up and encountered the man's glance, then she frowned and quickly turned her head away, for the seedy-looking clerk was very ugly, and she did not like the intentness with which he regarded her. Much to her annoyance, however, she presently became conscious that he had gathered up his crutches and hobbled towards her. The crowd made way for him, and a few seconds later he stood before her, leaning upon his crutches.

"Your pardon, *citizeness*," he said, and his voice was certainly more pleasing than his looks, "but I could not help hearing just now what you said to Citizen Larousse. . . . about your friend who is sick. . . . and your need of a doctor—"

He paused, and Josette looked up at him. He appeared timid and there certainly was not a suspicion of insolence in the way he addressed her, but he certainly was very ugly to look at. His face was the colour of yellow wax, and on his chin and cheeks there was a three days' growth of beard. His eyebrows were extraordinarily bushy and overshadowed his eyes, which were circled with purple as if from the effects of a blow. So much of his countenance did Josette take in at the first glance, but his voice had certainly sounded kindly, and poor little Josette was so devoured with anxiety just now that any show of kindness went straight to her heart.

"Then you must also have heard, citizen," she said, "that Doctor Larousse could do nothing for my friend."

"That is why," the man rejoined, "I ventured to address you, *citizeness*. I am not a doctor, only a humble apothecary, but I have some knowledge of medicine. Would you like me to see your friend?"

He had gradually dropped his voice until in the end he was hardly speaking above his breath. Josette felt strangely stirred. There was something in the way in which this man spoke which vaguely intrigued her and she couldn't make out why he should have spoken at all. She looked him straight in the eyes; her own were candid, puzzled, inquiring. If only he were less ugly, his skin less like parchment and his chin free from that stubby growth of a beard. . .

"I could come now," he said again. Then added with a light shrug, "I certainly could do your friend no harm just by seeing her, and I know of a cordial which works wonders on overstrung nerves."

Josette could never have told afterwards what it was that impelled her to rise then and to say:

"Very well, citizen. Since you are so kind, will you come with me and see my sick friend?"

She made her way to the door and he followed her, working his way through the crowd across the room on his crutches. It was he who, despite his infirmities, opened the door and held it for the girl to pass through. It was close on midday. It had ceased raining and the air was milder, but heavy-laden clouds still hung overhead and the ill-paved streets ran with yellow-coloured mud.

Josette thought of Maurice as she started to walk in the direction of the Rue Picpus. She walked slowly because of the maimed man who hobbled behind her on his crutches, covering the ground in her wake, however, with extraordinary sureness and speed. She thought of Maurice, wondering what he would think of this adventure of hers, and whether he would approve. She was afraid that he would not. Maurice was cautious—more cautious than she was—and that very morning he had warned her to be very circumspect in everything she said and did, for Louise's sake and Charles-Léon's.

"Those devils," he had said to her just before they left home, "are sure to have their eye on Madame de Croissy. They haven't found the letters, but they know that they exist, and will of a surety have another try at getting possession of them."

"We must try and leave *Madame* alone as seldom as possible," he had said later on. "Unless I am detained over this awful business I will spend most of my day with her while you are at the workshop."

Apparently, Maurice had been detained by the authorities, so Josette imagined, for he should have come to meet her at the *commissariat* before now, but when he got there presently and found her gone he would probably conclude that she had been tired of waiting and had already gone home—and he would surely follow.

All the while that Josette's thoughts had run on Maurice, she had heard subconsciously the *tap-tap* of the man's crutches half a dozen paces or so behind her; then her thoughts had gone a-roaming on the terrible past, the dismal present, the hopeless future. What, she thought, would become of Louise and Charles-Léon after this appalling tragedy? Maître de Croissy's property in the Dauphiné brought in nothing: it was administered by a faithful soul who had been bailiff on the estate for close on half a century, and he just contrived to collect a sufficiency of money by the sale of timber and agricultural produce to pay for necessary repairs and stop the buildings and the land from going to rack and ruin, but there was nothing left over to pay as much as the rent of the miserable apartment in the Rue Picpus, let alone clothes and food. Maître de Croissy had been able to make a paltry income by his profession; but now? What was to become of his widow and of his child?

And Josette's thoughts of the future had been so black, so dismal and so absorbing that she was very nearly knocked down by a passing cart. The curses of the driver and the shouts of the passers-by brought her back to present realities, and these included the nearness of her maimed companion. She turned to look for him, but he was nowhere to be seen. She stood by for quite a long time at the angle of the street, thinking perhaps that he had fallen behind and would presently overtake her. But she waited in vain. There was no sign of the strange creature in the seedy black with the one leg and the crutches, the ugly face and gentle voice.

Quite against her will and her better judgement Josette felt vaguely dismayed and disappointed. What could this sudden disappearance mean of a man who had certainly forced his companionship upon her? Why had he gone with her thus far and then vanished so unaccountably? Did he really intend to visit Louise, or was his interest in her only a blind so as to attach himself to Josette? But if so what could be his object? All these thoughts and conjectures were very disturbing. There was always the fear of spies and informers present in every man or woman's mind these days, and Josette remembered Maurice's warning to be very circumspect, and she wished now that she had insisted on waiting at the *commissariat* for Maurice's return before she embarked on this adventure with the mysterious stranger.

And then she suddenly remembered that just before coming up to the Pont-Neuf the maimed man had hobbled up close to her and asked:

"But whither are we going, *citizeness?*"

And that she had replied:

"To No. 43, in the Rue Picpus, Citizen. My friend has an apartment there on the second floor."

And now she wished she had not given a total stranger such explicit directions.

Chapter 9

The rest of the day dragged on in its weary monotony. Josette had spent an hour with Louise at dinner-time, when she had tried again, as she had done in the past ten days, to rouse the unfortunate woman from her apathy. She did not tell her about the seedy apothecary with the one leg, who had thrust himself into her company only to vanish as mysteriously as he had appeared. She was beginning to feel vaguely frightened about that man: his actions had been so very strange that the conviction grew upon her that he must be some sort of government spy.

Maurice Reversac also came in for a hurried meal at midday, and Josette spoke to him about the man at the *commissariat* who had insisted on coming with her to visit Louise and then disappeared as if the cobble-stones of the great city had swallowed him up. Maurice, who was always inclined to prudence, wished that Josette had not been quite so free in her talk with the stranger. He dreaded those government spies who undoubtedly would be detailed to watch the family of the murdered man; but whatever fears assailed him he kept them buried in his heart and indeed did his best to reassure Josette. But he did beg her to be more than ordinarily cautious. He stayed talking with her for a little while and then went away.

It was too late now to trudge all the way to the Batignolles in search of the public letter-writer, and Maurice, well aware of Josette's impetuosity at the bare mention of the Scarlet Pimpernel, thought it best to say nothing to her tonight on the subject. He was trying to put what order he could in the affairs of the late advocate, and to save what could possibly be saved out of the wreckage of his fortune for the benefit of the widow and the child.

"I have been promised a permit," he said, "to go down into the Dauphiné for a day or two. I can then see the bailiff and perhaps make some arrangement with him by which he can send *Madame* a small revenue from the estate every month. Then, if they let me carry on the practice—"

"Do you think they will?"

Maurice shrugged.

"One never knows. It all depends if lawyers are scarce now that they have killed so many. There is always some litigation afoot."

Finally, he added, with a great show of confidence which he was far from feeling:

"Don't lose heart, Josette *chérie*. Every moment of my life I will devote to making *Madame* and the boy comfortable because I know that is the way to make you happy."

But Josette found it difficult not to lose heart. She was convinced in her own mind that danger greater than ever now threatened Louise entirely because of her, Josette's, indiscretion, and that the maimed man of the *commissariat* whom she had so foolishly trusted was nothing but a government spy.

The truth did not dawn upon her, not until many hours later, after she had spent her afternoon as usual at the workshop and then came home in the late afternoon.

As soon as Josette entered the living-room she knew that the miracle had happened—the miracle to which she had pinned her faith, for which she had hoped and prayed and striven. She had left Louise lying like a log on the sofa, silent, dry-eyed, sullen, with Charles-Léon, quietly whimpering in his small bed. She found her a transformed being with eyes bright and colour in her cheeks. But it was not this sudden transformation of her friend, nor yet Louise's cry: "Josette *chérie!* You were right and I was wrong to doubt." It was something more subtle, more intangible, that revealed to this ardent devotee that the hero of her dreams had filled the air with the radiance of his personality, that he had brought joy where sorrow reigned, and security and happiness where unknown danger threatened. Louise had run up to Josette as soon as she heard the turn of the latch-key in the door. She was laughing and crying, and after she had embraced Josette she ran back into the living-room and picked Charles-Léon up in her arms and hugged him to her breast.

"My baby," she murmured, "my baby! He will get strong and well and we shall be delivered from this hateful country."

Then she put Charles-Léon down, threw herself on the sofa, and burying her face in her arms she burst into tears. She cried and sobbed; her shoulders quivered convulsively. Josette made no movement towards her: it was best that she should cry for a time. The reaction from a state of dull despair had evidently been terrific, and the poor woman's over-wrought nerves would be all the better for this outlet of tears. How could Josette doubt for a moment that the miracle had happened?

As soon as she was a little more calm, Louise dried her eyes, then she drew a much-creased paper from the pocket of her skirt and without a word held it out to Josette. It was a letter written in a bold clear hand and was addressed to Citizeness Croissy at No. 43, Rue Picpus, on the second floor, and this is what it said:

As soon as you receive this, believe that sincere friends are working for your safety. You must leave Paris and France immediately, not only for the boy's health's sake, but because very serious danger threatens you and him if you remain. This evening at eight o'clock take your boy in your arms and an empty market basket in your hand. Your *concierge* will probably challenge you; say that you are going to fetch your bread ration which you omitted to get this morning because of the bad weather. If the *concierge* makes a remark about your having the child with you, say that the Citizen Doctor ordered you to take him out as soon as the rain had ceased. Do not on any account hasten downstairs or through the *porte-cochère*, just walk quietly as if in truth you were going to the baker's shop. Then walk quietly along the street till you come to the district bakery.

There will probably be a queue waiting for rations at the door. Take your place in the queue and go in and get your bread. In the crowd you will see a one-legged man dressed in seedy black. When he walks out of the shop, follow him. Divest yourself of all fear. The League of the Scarlet Pimpernel will see you safely out of Paris and out of France to England or Belgium, whichever you wish. But the first condition for your safety and that of the child is implicit trust in the ability of the League to see you through, and, as a consequence of trust, implicit obedience.

The letter bore no signature, but in the corner, there was a small device, a star-shaped flower drawn in red ink. Josette murmured under her breath:

"The Scarlet Pimpernel! I knew that he would come."

Had she been alone she would have raised the paper to her lips, that blessed paper on which her hero's hand had rested. As it was she just held it tight in her hot little palm and hoped that in her excitement Louise would forget about it and leave it with her as a precious relic.

"And of course, you will come with me and Charles-Léon, Josette *chérie*."

Louise had to reiterate this more than once before the sense of it penetrated to Josette's inner consciousness. Even after the third repetition she still looked vague and ununderstanding.

"Josette *chérie*, of course you will come."

"But, Louise, no! How can I?" the girl murmured.

"How do you mean, how can you?"

Josette held up the precious letter.

"He does not speak of me in this."

"The English League probably knows nothing about you, Josette."

"But he does."

"How do you know?"

Josette evaded the direct question. She quoted the last few words of the letter:

"As a consequence of trust, implicit obedience."

"That does not mean—"

"It means," Josette broke in firmly, "that you must follow the directions given you in this letter, word for word. It is the least you can do, and you must do it for the sake of Charles-Léon. I am in no danger here, and I would not go if I were. Maurice will be here to look after me."

"You are talking nonsense, *chérie*. You know I would not go without you."

"You would sacrifice Charles-Léon for me?"

Then as Louise made no reply—how could she?—Josette continued with simple determination and unshaken firmness:

"I assure you, Louise *chérie*, that I am in no danger. Maurice cannot go away while he has Bastien's affairs to look after. He wouldn't go if he could, and it would be cowardly to leave him all alone here to look after things."

"But, Josette—"

"Don't say anything more about it, Louise. I am in no danger and I am not going. And what's more," she added softly, "I know that the Scarlet Pimpernel will look after me. Don't be afraid, he knows all about me."

And not another word would she say.

Louise, no doubt, knew her of old. Josette was one of those dear, gentle creatures whom nothing in the world could move once she was set on a definite purpose—especially if that purpose had in it the elements of self-sacrifice. The time, too, was getting on. It was already past seven o'clock. Louise busied herself with Charles-Léon, putting on him all the warm bits of garments she still possessed. Josette was equally busy warming up some milk, the little there was over the fire in the tiny kitchen.

At eight o'clock precisely Louise was ready. She prepared to gather the child in her arms. Josette had a big shawl ready to wrap round them both: she thrust the empty market basket over Louise's arm. Her heart ached at thought of this parting. God alone knew when they would meet again. But it all had to be done, it all had to be endured for the sake of Charles-Léon. Louise had declared her intention of going to England rather than to Belgium. She would meet a greater number of friends there.

"I will try and write to you, Josette *chérie*," she said. "My heart is broken at parting from you, and I shall not know a happy hour until we are together again. But you know, *ma chérie*, that Bastien was always convinced that this abominable Revolution could not last much longer; and—who knows?—Charlets-Léon and I may be back in Paris before the year is out."

She was, perhaps, too excited to feel the sorrow of parting quite as deeply as did Josette. Indeed, Louise was in a high state of exultation, crying one moment and laughing the next, and the hand with which she clung to Josette was hot and dry as if burning with fever. Just at the last she was suddenly shaken with a fit of violent trembling, her teeth chattered and she sank into a chair, for her knees were giving way under her.

"Josette!" she gasped. "You do not think, perchance—?"

"What, *chérie?*"

"That this. . . . this letter is all a hoax? And that we—Charles-Léon and I—are walking into a trap?"

But Josette, who still held the letter tightly clasped in her hand, was quite sure that it was not a hoax. She recalled the seedy apothecary at the *commissariat* and his gentle voice when he spoke to her, and there had been a moment when his steady gaze had drawn her eyes to him. She had not thought about it much at the time, but since then she had reflected and remembered the brief but very strange spell which seemed to have been cast over her at the moment. No, the letter was not a hoax. Josette would have staked her life on it that it was dictated, or perhaps even written, by the hero of her dreams.

"It is not a trap, Louise," she said firmly, "but the work of the finest man that ever lived. I am as convinced as that I am alive that the one-legged man in seedy black whom you will see in the bakery is the Scarlet Pimpernel himself."

It was Josette who lifted Charles-Léon and placed him in Louise's arms. A final kiss to them both and they were gone. Josette stood in the middle of the room, motionless, hardly breathing, for she tried to catch the last sound of Louise's footsteps going down the stairs. It was only after she had heard the opening and closing of the outside door of the house that she at last gave way to tears.

Just like this Josette had cried when Louise, after her marriage to Bastien de Croissy, left the little farm in the Dauphiné in order to take up her position as a great lady in Paris society. The wedding had taken place in the small village church, and everything had been done very quietly because General de Vandeleur, Louise's father, had only been dead a year and Louise refused to be married from the house of one of her grand relations. Papa and Maman Gravier and Josette were the three people she had cared for most in all the world until Bastien came along, and she had the sentimental feeling that she wished to walk straight out of the one house where her happy girlhood had been passed into the arms of the man to whom she had given her heart.

The wedding had been beautiful and gay, with the whole village hung about with flags and garlands of flowers; and previous to it there had been all the excitement of getting Louise's trousseau together, and of journeys up to Paris in order to try on the wedding gown. And Josette had been determined that no tears or gloomy looks from her should cast a shadow over her friend's happiness. It was when everything was over, when Louise drove away in the barouche *en route* for Paris, that Josette was suddenly overwhelmed with the sorrow which she had tried to hold in check for so long. Then as now she had thrown herself down on the sofa and cried out her eyes in self-pity for her loneliness. But what was the loneliness of that day in comparison with what it was now?

In those days Josette still had her father and mother: there were the many interests of the farm, the dogs, the cows, haymaking, harvesting. Now there was nothing but dreariness ahead. Dreariness and loneliness. No one to look after, no one to fuss over. No Charles-Léon to listen to tales of heroism and adventure. Only the Government workshop, the girls there with their idle chatter and their reiterated complaints: only the getting up in the morning, the munching of stale food, the stitching of shirts, and the going to bed at night!

Josette thought of all this later on when bedtime came along, and she knelt beside Charles-Léon's empty cot and nearly cried her eyes out. Nearly but not quite, for presently Maurice came home. And it was wonderful how his presence put a measure of comfort in Josette's heart. Somehow the moment she heard the turn of his latchkey in the door, and his footsteps across the hall, her life no longer appeared quite so empty. There was someone left in Paris after all, who would need care and attention and fussing over when he was sick; his future would have to be planned, suitable lodgings would have to be found for him, and life generally re-ordained according to the new conditions.

And first of all, there was the excitement of telling Maurice all about those new conditions.

Even before he came into the room Josette had jumped to her feet and hastily dried her eyes. But he saw in a moment that she had been crying.

"Josette!" he cried out, "what is it?"

"Take no notice, Maurice," Josette replied, still struggling with her tears, "I am not really crying. . . . it is only because I am so. . . . ever so happy!"

"Why? What has happened?"

"He came, Maurice," she said solemnly, "and they have gone."

Of course, Maurice could not make head or tail of that.

"He? They?" he murmured frowning. "Who came, and who has gone?"

She made him sit down on the ugly horse-hair sofa and she sat down beside him and told him about everything. Her dreams had turned to reality, the Scarlet Pimpernel had come to take Louise and Charles-Léon away out of all this danger and all this misery: he had come to take them away to England where Louise would be safe, and Charles-Léon would get quite well and strong.

"And left you here!" Maurice exclaimed involuntarily, when Josette paused, out of breath, after she had imparted the great and glorious news: "gone to safety and left you here to face—"

But Josette with a peremptory gesture put her small hand across his mouth.

"Wait, Maurice," she said, "let me tell you."

She drew the precious letter from under her *fichu*—Louise, fortunately, had not demanded its return—and she read its contents aloud to Maurice.

"Now you see!" she concluded triumphantly and fixed her glowing eyes on the young man.

"I only see," he retorted almost roughly, "that they had no right to leave you here. . . . all alone."

"Not alone, Maurice," she replied; "are you not here. . . . to take care of me?"

That, of course, was a heavenly moment in Maurice's life. Never had Josette—Josette who was so independent and self-reliant—spoken like this before, never had she looked quite like she did now, adorable always, but more so with that expression of dependence and appeal in her eyes. The moment was indeed so heavenly that Maurice felt unable to say anything. He was so afraid that the whole thing was not real, that he was only dreaming, and that if he spoke the present rapture would at once be dispelled. He felt alternately hot and cold, his temples throbbed. He tried to express with a glance all that went on in his heart. His silence and his looks did apparently satisfy Josette, for after a moment or two she explained to him just what her feelings were about the letter.

"The Scarlet Pimpernel demands trust and obedience, Maurice," she said with *naïve* earnestness. "Well! would that have been obedience if Louise had lugged me along with her? He doesn't mention me in the letter. If he had meant me to come, he would have said so."

With this pronouncement Maurice had perforce to be satisfied; but one thing more he wanted to know: what had become of the letters? But Josette couldn't tell him. Ever since Bastien's death, Louise had never spoken of them, or given the slightest hint of what she had done with them.

"Let's hope she has destroyed them," Maurice commented with a sigh.

The next day they spent in hunting for new lodgings for Maurice. Strange! Josette no longer felt lonely. She still grieved after Louise and Charles-Léon, but somehow life no longer seemed as dreary as she thought it would be.

Chapter 10

Louise, in very truth, was much too excited to feel the pang of parting as keenly as did Josette, and ever since Charles-Léon had fallen sick she had taken a veritable hatred to Paris and her dingy apartment in the Rue Picpus. The horror of her husband's death had increased her abhorrence of the place, and now hatred amounted to loathing.

Therefore, it was that she went downstairs with a light heart on that memorable evening of September. She had Charles-Léon in her arms and carried the empty market basket, with her ration card laid ostentatiously in it for anyone to see. The *concierge* was in the doorway of his lodge and asked her whither she was going. These were not days when one could tell a *concierge* to mind his own business, so Louise replied meekly:

"To the bakery, citizen," and she showed the man her ration card.

"Very late," the *concierge* remarked drily.

"The weather has been so bad all day—"

"Too bad even now to take the child out, I imagine."

"It has left off raining," Louise said still gently, "and the poor cabbage must have some fresh air; the Citizen Doctor insisted on that."

She felt terribly impatient at the delay but did not dare appear to be in a hurry, whilst the *concierge* seemed to derive amusement at keeping her standing beside his lodge. He knew her for an *aristo*, and many there were in these days who found pleasure in irritating or humiliating those who in the past had thought themselves their betters.

However, this ordeal, like so many others, did come to an end after a time; the *concierge* condescended to open the *porte-cochère* and Louise was able to slip out into the street. It had certainly left off raining, but it was very cold and damp underfoot. Louise trudged on as fast as she could, her thin shoes squelching through the mud. Fortunately, the bakery was not far, and soon she was able to take her place in the queue outside the shop. There was no crowd at this hour: a score of people at the most, chiefly women.

Louise's anxious glance swept quickly over them and at once her heart gave a jump, for she had caught sight of a maimed man on crutches, dressed in back as the mysterious letter had described. He was ahead of her in the queue, and she saw him quite distinctly when he entered the shop and stood for a moment under the lantern which hung above the door. But his face she could not clearly see, for he wore a black hat with a wide brim: a hat as shabby as his clothes. Presently he disappeared inside the shop, and Louise did not see him again until she herself had been to the counter and been served with her ration of bread. Then she saw him just going out of the shop and she followed as soon as she could.

There were still a good many people in the street, and just over the road there were two men of the Republican Guard on duty, set there to watch over the queue outside the licensed bakeries. Some of the people there were still waiting their turn, others were walking away, some in one direction, some in another. But there was no sign anywhere of the one-legged man. Louise stood for a moment in the ill-lighted street, perturbed and anxious, wondering in which direction she ought to go; her heart seemed to sink into her shoes, and she was desperately tired, too, from standing so long with the child in her arms. But with those men of the Republican Guard watching her she did not like to hesitate too long and, thoroughly heart-sick now and nigh unto despair, she began to fear that the letter and all her hopes were only idle dreams. Almost faint with fatigue and disappointment she had just turned her weary footsteps towards home when suddenly she heard the distant *tap-tap* of crutches on the cobble-stones.

With a deep sigh of relief Louise started at once to walk in the direction whence came the welcome sound. The tap-tap kept on slightly ahead of her, so all she had to do was to follow as closely as she could. With Charles-Léon asleep in her arms she had trudged on thus for about ten minutes, turning out of one street and into another, when suddenly the *tap-tap* ceased. The maimed man had paused beside an open street door; when Louise came up with him he signed to her to enter.

She hadn't the least idea where she was, but from the direction in which she had gone she conjectured that it was somewhere near the Temple. There were not many people about, and though on the way she had gone past more than one patrol of the National Guard, the men had taken no notice of her; she was just a poor woman with a child in her arms and a ration of bread in her basket; nor had they paid any heed to the maimed, seedy-looking individual hobbling along on crutches.

Now as Louise passed through the open door her guide whispered rapidly to her:

"Go up two flights of stairs and knock at the door on your right."

Strangely enough, Louise had no hesitation in obeying; though she had no idea where she would find herself she felt no fear. Perhaps she was too tired to feel anything but a longing for rest. She went up the two flights of stairs and knocked at the door which her guide had indicated. It was opened by a rough-looking youngish man in ragged clothes, unshaved, unkempt, who blinked his eyes as if he had just been roused out of sleep.

"Is it Madame de Croissy?" he asked, and Louise noted that he spoke French with a foreign accent; also, the word "*Madame*" was unusual these days. This, of course, reassured her. Her thoughts flew back to Josette and the girl's firm belief in the existence of the Scarlet Pimpernel.

The young man led the way through a narrow ill-lit passage to a room where Louise's aching eyes were greeted with the welcome sight of a table spread with a cloth on which were laid a knife and fork, a place and a couple of mugs. There was also a couch in a corner of the room with a pillow on it and a rug. It was rather cold and a solitary tallow candle shed a feeble, vacillating light on the bare white-washed walls and the blackened ceiling, but Louise thought little of all this; she sank down on a chair by the table, and the young man then said to her in his quaint stilted French:

"In one moment, *Madame*, I will bring you something to eat, for you must be very hungry; and we also have a little milk for the boy. I hope you won't mind waiting while I get everything ready for you."

He went out of the room before Louise had found sufficient energy to say "Thank you." She just sat there like a log, her purple-rimmed eyes staring into vacancy. Charles-Léon, who, luckily, had been asleep all this time, now woke and began to whimper. Louise hugged him to her bosom until the tousled young ruffian reappeared presently, carrying a tray on which there was a dish and a jug. Louise felt almost like swooning when a delicious smell of hot food and steaming milk tickled her nostrils. The young man had poured out a mugful of milk for Charles-Léon, and while the child drank eagerly Louise made a great effort to murmur an adequate "Thank you."

"It is not to me, *Madame*," the man retorted, "that you owe thanks. I am here under orders. You, too, I am afraid," he went on with a smile, "will have to submit to the will of my chief."

"Give me the orders, sir," Louise rejoined meekly. "I will obey them."

"The orders are that you eat some supper now and then have a good rest until I call you in the early morning. You will have to leave here a couple of hours before the dawn."

"Charles-Léon and I will be ready, sir. Anything else?"

"Only that you get a good sleep, for tomorrow will be wearisome. Goodnight, *Madame*."

Before Louise could say another word, the young man had slipped out of the room.

Charles-Léon slept peacefully all night cuddled up against his mother, but Louise lay awake for hours, thinking of her amazing adventure. She was up betimes, and soon after a distant church clock struck half-past four there was a knock at the door. Her young friend of the evening before had come to fetch her; he looked as if he had been up all night, and certainly he had not taken off his clothes. Louise picked Charles-Léon up, and with him in her arms she followed her friend down the stairs. Outside she found herself in a narrow street: it was quite dark because the street lanterns had already been extinguished and there was not yet a sign of dawn in the sky. Through the darkness Louise perceived the vague silhouette of a covered cart such as the collectors of the city's refuse used for their filthy trade. A small donkey was harnessed to the cart and it was bring driven apparently by a woman.

Neither the woman nor the young man spoke at the moment, but the latter intimated to Louise by a gesture that she must step into the cart. Only for a few seconds did she hesitate. The cart was indeed filthy and reeked of all sorts of horrible odours calculated to make any sensitive person sick. A kindly voice whispered in her ear:

"It cannot be helped, *Madame*, and you must forgive us: anyway, it is no worse than the inside of one of their prisons."

Her friend now took Charles-Léon from her and summoning all her courage she stepped into the cart. The child was then handed back to her and she gathered herself and him into a heap under the awning. She wanted to assure her friend that not only was she prepared for anything, but that her heart was full of gratitude for all that was being done for her. But before she could speak a large piece of sacking was thrown right over her, and over the sacking a pile of things the nature of which the poor woman did not venture to guess. As she settled herself down, as comfortably as she could, she came in contact with what appeared to be a number of bottles.

A minute or two later with much creaking of wheels and many a jerk the cart was set in motion. It went jogging along over the cobblestones of the streets of Paris at foot pace, while under the awning, smothered by a heap of all sorts of vegetable refuse, Louise de Croissy had sunk into a state of semi-consciousness.

Chapter 11

She was roused from her torpor by the loud cry of "*Halte!*" The cart came to a standstill and Louise, with sudden terror gripping her heart, realised that they had come to one of the gates of Paris where detachments of National Guard, officered by men eager for promotion, scrutinised every person who ventured in or out of the city.

The poor woman, crouching under a heap of odds and ends, heard the measured tramp of soldiers and a confused murmur of voices. Through a chink in the awning she could see that the grey light was breaking over this perilous crisis of her life. Presently a gruff commanding voice rose above the shrill croaky tones of a woman, whom Louise guessed to be the driver of the cart. The gruff voice when first it reached Louise's consciousness was demanding to see what there was underneath the awning. She could do nothing but hug the child closer to her breast, for she knew that within the next few seconds her life and his would tremble in the balance.

She hardly dared to breathe; her whole body was bathed in a cold sweat. Heavy footsteps, accompanied by short, shuffling ones, came round to the back of the cart, and a few seconds later the end flap of the awning was thrust aside and a wave of cold air swept around inside the cart. Some of it penetrated to poor Louise's nostrils, but she hardly dared to breathe. She knew that her fate and that of Charles-Léon would be decided within the next few minutes perhaps.

The gruff voice was evidently that of one in authority.

"Anyone in there?" it demanded, and to the unfortunate woman it seemed as if the heap of rubbish on the top of her was being prodded with the point of a bayonet.

"No one now, Citizen Officer," a woman's shrill voice responded, obviously the voice of the old hag who was driving the cart: "that's my son there, holding the donkey's head. He can't speak, you know, citizen. . . . never could since birth. . . . tongued-tied as the saying is. But a good lad. . . . can't gossip, you see. And here's his passport and mine!"

There was some rustle of papers, one or two muttered words and then the woman spoke again:

"I'm picking up my daughter and her boy at Champerret presently," she said: "their passports and permits are all in order too, but I haven't got them here."

"Where are you going then all of you?" the gruff voice asked, and there was more rustle of papers and a tramping of feet. The passports were being taken into the guard-room to be duly stamped.

"Only as far as Clichy, Citizen Officer. It says so on the permit. See here, Citizen. 'Permit for Citizeness Ruffin and her son Pierre to proceed to Clichy for purposes of business!' That's all in order is it not, Citizen Officer?"

"Yes! yes! that's all in order all right. And now let's see what you have got inside the cart."

"All in order. . . . of course it is—" the old woman went on, cackling like an old hen; "you don't catch Mère Ruffin out of order with authorities. Not her. Passports and permits, everything always in order, Citizen Officer. You ask any captain at the gates. They'll tell you. Mother Ruffin is always in order. . . . always. . . . in order—"

And all the while the old hag was shifting and pushing about the heap of rubbish that was lying on the top of the unfortunate Louise.

"It's not a pleasant business, mine, Citizen Officer," she continued with a doleful sigh; "but one must live, what? Citizen Arnould—you know him, don't you, citizen? Over at the chemical works—he buys all my stuff from me."

"Filthy rubbish, I call it," the officer retorted; "but don't go wasting my time, mother. Just shift that bit of sacking, and you can take your stuff to the devil for aught I care."

Louise, trembling with fear and horror, still half-smothered under the pile of rubbish, was on the point of losing consciousness. Fortunately, Charles-Léon was still asleep and she was able to keep her wits sufficiently about her to hold him tightly in her arms. Would the argument between the soldier and the old hag never come to an end?

"I am doing my best, Citizen Officer, but the stuff is heavy," the woman muttered; "and all my papers in order I should have thought. . . . . Mother Ruffin's papers always are in order, Citizen Officer. . . . Ask any captain of the guard. . . . he'll tell you—"

"*Nom d'un nom,*" the soldier broke in with an oath, "are you going to shift that sacking or shall I have to order the men to take you to the guard-room?"

"The guard-room? Me? Mère Ruffin, known all over the country as an honest patriot? You'd get a reprimand, Citizen Officer—that's what you would get for taking Mère Ruffin to the guard-room. *Bien! bien!* don't lose your temper, Citizen Officer. . . . no harm meant. . . Here! can't one of your men give me a hand?. . . . But. . . . I say—"

A click of glass against glass followed: Louise remembered the bottles that were piled up round her. After this ominous click there was a moment's silence. Sounds from the outside reached Louise's consciousness: men talking, the clatter of horses' hoofs, the rattle of wheels, challenge from the guard, cries of "*Halte!*" distant murmurs of people talking, moving, even laughing, whilst she, hugging Charles-Léon to her breast, marvelled at what precise moment she and her child would be discovered and dragged out of this noisome shelter to some equally noisome prison. The woman had ceased jabbering: the click of glass seemed to have paralysed her tongue; but only for a moment: a minute or so later her shrill voice could be heard again.

"You won't be hard on me will you, Citizen Officer?" she said dolefully.

"Hard?" the soldier retorted. "That'll depend on what you've got under there."

"Nothing to make a fuss over, Citizen Officer: a poor widow has got to live, and—"

There was another click of glass—several clicks, then a thud, the bottles tumbling one against the other, then the officer's harsh voice saying with a laugh:

"So! that's it! is it? *Absinthe?* What? You old reprobate! No wonder you didn't want me to look under that sacking."

"Citizen Officer, don't be hard on a poor widow—"

"Poor widow indeed? Where did you steal the stuff?"

"I didn't steal it, Citizen Officer. . . . I swear I didn't."

"How many bottles have you got there?"

"Only a dozen, Citizen—"

"Out with them."

"Citizen Officer—"

"Out with them I say—"

"Yes, citizen," the old woman said meekly with an audible snuffle.

She sprawled over the back of the cart, pushed some of the rubbish aside and Louise was conscious of the bottles being pulled out from round and under her. She heard the soldier say:

"Is that all?"

"One dozen, Citizen Sergeant. You can see for yourself."

The woman dropped down to the ground. Louise could hear her snuffling the other side of the awning. After which there came a terrible moment, almost the worst of this awful and protracted ordeal. The officer appeared to have given an order to one of the soldiers, who used the end of his bayonet for the purpose of ascertaining whether there were any more bottles under the sacking. What he did was to bang away with it on the pile of rubbish that still lay on the top of Louise; some of the bangs hit Louise on the legs: one blow fell heavily on one of her ankles.

The courage with which she endured these blows motionless and in silence was truly heroic. Her life and Charles-Léon's depended on her remaining absolutely still. And she did remain quite still, hugging the child to her breast, outwardly just another pile of rubbish on the floor of the cart. The boy was positively wonderful, he seemed to know that he must not move or utter a sound. Though he must have been terrified, he never cried, but just clung to his mother, with eyes tightly closed. Louise in fact came to bless the very noisomeness of the refuse which lay on top of her, for obviously the soldier did not like to touch it with his hands.

"I get most of my stuff from the hospitals," Louise could hear the old hag talking volubly to the officer; "you can see for yourself, citizen, it is mostly linen which has been used for bandages. . . . sore legs you know and all that. . . . Citizen Arnould over at the chemical works gives me good money for it. It seems they make paper out of the stuff. Paper out of linen I ask you. . . . brown or red paper I should say, for you should see some of it. . . . and all the fever they've got in the wards now. . . . yellow fever if not worse—"

"There! that'll do, Mother Ruffin," the officer broke in roughly: "all your talk won't help you. You've got to pay for taking the stuff though, and you know it. . . . and there'll be a fine for trying to smuggle—"

There followed a loud and long-winded protests on the part of the old hag; but apparently the officer was at the end of his tether and would listen to none of it, although he did seem to have a certain measure of tolerance for the woman's delinquency.

"You come along quietly, Mother," he said in the end, "it will save you trouble in the end."

He called to his men, and snuffling, cackling, protesting, the old woman apparently followed them quietly in the direction of the guard-room. At any rate Louise heard nothing more. For a long, long time she did not hear anything. The reaction after the terror of this past half hour was so great that she fell into a kind of torpor; the noises of the street only came to her ears through a kind of fog. The only feeling she was conscious of was that she must hold Charles-Léon closely to her breast.

How long this state of numbness lasted she did not know. She had lost count of time; and she had lost the use of her limbs. Her ankle where she had been hit with the flat of the soldier's bayonet had ached furiously at first: now she no longer felt the pain. Charles-Léon, she thought, must have gone to sleep, for she could just feel his even breathing against her breast.

Suddenly she was aroused by the sound, still distant, of the woman's shrill voice. It drew gradually nearer.

"Now then, Pierre, let's get on," the old hag was shrieking as she came along.

Pierre, whoever he was, had apparently remained at the donkey's head all this time. Louise from the first had suspected that he was none other than her friend of the tousled head; but who that awful old hag with the snuffle and the cackling voice she could not even conjecture. But she was content to leave it at that. Apparently those wonderful and heroic Englishmen employed strange tools in their work of mercy.

At the moment she felt far too tired and too numb even to marvel at the amazing way in which that old woman had hoodwinked the officer of the guard. As Louise returned to consciousness she could hear vaguely in the distance the soldiers laughing and chaffing and the woman muttering and grumbling:

"Making a poor woman pay for an honest trading. . . . a scandal I call it—"

"*Ohé, la mère!*" the soldiers shouted amidst loud laughter, "bring us some more of that *absinthe* tomorrow."

"Robbers! thieves! brigands!" the woman ejaculated shrilly, "catch me again coming this way—"

She apparently busied herself with putting the bottles—or some of them at any rate—back into the cart: after which the flap of the awning was again lowered: there was much creaking and shaking of the cart; soon it was once more set in motion; to the accompaniment of more laughter and many ribald jokes on the part of the soldiers, who stood watching the departure of the ramshackle vehicle and its scrubby driver.

Anon the creaking wheels resumed their jolting, axle-deep in mud, over the country roads riddled with ruts. But of this Louise de Croissy now knew little or nothing. She had mercifully once more ceased to think or feel.

Chapter 12

Days of strange adventures followed, adventures that never seemed real, only products of a long dream.

There was that halt on the wayside in the afternoon of the first day, with Paris a couple of leagues and more behind. The end flap of the awning was pulled aside and the horrible weight lifted from Louise's inert body. Glad of the relief and of the breath of clean air, she opened her eyes, then closed them again quickly at sight of the hideous old woman whose scarred and grimy face was grinning at her from the rear of the cart. A dream figure in very truth, or a nightmare! But was she not the angel in disguise who, by dint of a comedian's art, had hoodwinked the sergeant at the gate of Paris and passed through the jealously guarded barriers with as much ease as if her passengers in that filthy cart had been provided with the safest of passports?

Yet, strive how she might, Louise could see nothing in that ugly and ungainly figure before her that even remotely suggested a heroine or an angel. She gave up the attempt at fathoming the mystery and allowed herself and Charles-Léon to be helped out of the cart and, with a great sigh of gladness, she sank down on the mossy bank by the roadside and ate of the bread and cheese which the hag had placed beside her, together with a bottle of milk for the boy.

When she and Charles-Léon had eaten and drunk and she had taken in as much fresh country air as her lungs would hold, she looked about her, intending to thank that extraordinary old woman for her repeated kindness, but the latter was nowhere to be seen; also, the donkey was no longer harnessed to the cart. Somewhere in the near distance there was a group of derelict cottages and, chancing to look that way, Louise saw the woman walking towards it and leading the donkey by the bridle.

She never again set eyes on that old hag. Presently, however, a rough fellow, clad in a blue smock, who looked like a farm labourer, appeared upon the scene; he was leading a pony, and as soon as he caught Louise's glance he beckoned to her to get back into the cart. Mechanically she obeyed, and the man lifted Charles-Léon and placed him in his mother's arms. He harnessed the pony to the cart, and once more the tumble-down vehicle went lumbering along the muddy country lanes. Fortunately, though the sky was grey and the wind boisterous, the rain held off most of the time. For three days and nights they were on the road, sleeping when they could, eating whatever was procurable on the way.

They never once touched the cities but avoided them by circuitous ways; always a pony, or sometimes a donkey, was harnessed to the cart, but the same rough-looking farm labourer held the reins the whole time. Two or three times a day he would get down, always in the vicinity of some derelict building or other into which he would disappear, and presently he would emerge once more leading a fresh beast of burden. Once or twice he would be accompanied on those occasions by another man as rough-looking as himself, but for the most part he would attend to the pony or donkey alone.

There were some terrible moments during those days, moments when Louise felt that she must choke with terror. Her heart was in her mouth, for patrols of soldiers would come riding or marching down the road, and now and again there would be a cry of "*Halte!*" and a brief colloquy would follow between the sergeant in command and the driver of the cart. But apparently—thank God for that—the cart and its rustic driver appeared too beggarly and insignificant to arouse suspicion or to engage for long the attention of the patrols.

The worst moment of all occurred in the late afternoon of the third day. The driver had turned the cart off the main road into a narrow lane which ran along the edge of a ploughed field. It was uphill work and the pony had done three hours' work already, dragging the rickety vehicle along muddy roads. Its pace got slower and slower. The wind blew straight from the north-east, and Louise felt very sick and cold, nor could she manage to keep Charles-Léon warm: the awning flapped about in the wind and let in gusts of icy draught all round.

When presently the driver pulled up and came round to see how she fared, she ventured to ask him timidly whether it wouldn't be possible to find some sheltered spot where they could all spend the night in comparative warmth for the child. At once the man promised to do his best to find some derelict barn or cottage. He turned into a ploughed field and soon disappeared from view. Louise remained shivering in the cart with Charles-Léon hugged closely to her under her shawl. She had indeed need of all her faith in the wonderful Scarlet Pimpernel to keep her heart warm, while her body was racked with cold.

She had no notion of time, of course; and sundown meant nothing when all day the sky had been just a sheet of heavy, slate-coloured clouds. A dim grey light still hung over the dreary landscape, while slowly the horizon veiled itself in mist. The driver had been gone some time when Louise's sensitive ears caught the distant sound of horses' hoofs splashing in the mud of the road. It was a sound that always terrified her. Up to now nothing serious had happened, but it was impossible to know when some meddlesome or officious Sergeant might with questions and suspicions shatter at one fell swoop all the poor woman's hopes of ultimate safety.

The patrol—for such it certainly was—was coming at a fair speed along the main road. Perhaps, thought Louise, the soldiers would ride past the corner of the lane and either not see the cart or think it not worth investigating. Bitterly she reproached herself for her want of endurance. If she had not sent the driver off to go in search of a shelter for the night, he would have driven on at least another half kilometre and then surely the cart would not have been sighted from the road. And, what's more, she would not have been alone to face this awful contingency.

For contingency it certainly was. Anything—the very worst— might happen now, for the man was not there to answer harsh questions with gruff answers, he was not there with his ready response and his amazing knack of averting suspicions. Louise was alone and she heard the squad of soldiers turn into the lane. Her heart seemed to cease beating. A moment or two later the man in command cried "*Halte!*" and himself drew rein close to the rear of the cart.

"Anyone there?" he queried in a loud voice.

Oh! for an inspiration to know just what to say in reply!

"There's someone under there," the soldier went on peremptorily; "who is it?"

More dead than alive, Louise was unable to speak.

The sergeant then gave the order! "*Allons!* just see who is in there; and," he added facetiously, "let's hear where the driver of this elegant *barouche* has hidden himself."

There was some clatter and jingle of metal: the sound of men dismounting, the pawing and snorting of horses. Through the chinks in the awning Louise could perceive the dim light of a couple of dark lanterns like two yellow eyes staring. Then the awning in the rear of the cart was raised, the lantern lit up the interior and Louise was discovered crouching in the distant corner on a pile of sacking, hugging Charles-Léon.

"*Ohé! la petite mère!*" the sergeant called out not unkindly: "come out and lets have a look at you."

Louise crawled out of the darkness, still hugging Charles-Léon. The evening was drawing in. She wondered vaguely if anything in her appearance would betray that she was no rustic, but an unfortunate, fleeing the country. She looked wearied to death, dishevelled and grimy. The sergeant leaning down from his saddle peered into her face.

"Who is in charge of your *barouche, petite mère?*" he asked.

"My—my—husband," Louise contrived to stammer through teeth that were chattering.

"Where is he?"

"Gone to the village. . . . to see if we can get. . . . a bed. . . . for the night—"

"Hm!" said the sergeant. And after a moment or two: "Suppose you let me see your papers."

"Papers?" Louise murmured.

"Yes! Your passports, what?"

"I haven't any papers."

"How do you mean you haven't any papers?" the sergeant retorted, all the kindliness gone out of his voice.

"My husband—" Louise stammered again.

"Oh! you mean your husband has got your papers?"

Louise, no longer able to utter a sound, merely nodded.

"And he's gone to the village?"

Another nod.

"Where is the village?"

Louise shook her head.

"You mean you don't know?"

The man paused for a moment or two. Clearly there was something unusual in this helpless creature stranded in the open country with a child in her arms, and no man in sight belonging to her.

"Well!" he said after a moment or two, during which he vainly tried to peer more closely in Louise's face, "you'll come along with us now, and when your husband finds the *barouche* gone he will know where to look for you."

"You get into your carriage, *petite mère*," he added; "one of the men will drive you."

So shaken and frightened was Louise that she could not move. Her knees were giving way under her. Two men lifted her and Charles-Léon into the cart. They were neither rough nor unkind—family men perhaps with children of their own—or just machines performing their duty. Louise could only wonder what would happen next. Crouching once more in the cart, she felt it give a lurch as one man scrambled into the driver's seat. He took the reins and clicked his tongue, and the pony had just answered to a flick of the whip when from the ploughed field there came loud cries of "*Ohé!*" coming right out of the evening mist. Louise didn't know if she could feel relief or additional terror when she heard that call. It was her rustic friend coming back at full speed. He was running and came to a halt in the lane breathless and obviously exhausted.

"Sergeant," he cried, gasping for breath, "give a hand. . . . on your life give a hand. . . . a fortune, sergeant, if we get him now."

The soldier, taken aback by the sudden appearance of this madman—he thought of him as such—fell to shouting: "What's all this?" and had much ado to hold his horse, which had shied and reared at the strident noise. The other soldiers—there were only four of them—were in a like plight, and for a moment or two there was a good deal of confusion which the quickly gathering darkness helped to intensify.

"What's all this?" the sergeant queried again as soon as the confusion subsided. "Here! you!" he commanded: "are you the owner of this aristocratic vehicle!"

"I am," the man replied.

"And is that your wife and child inside?"

"They are. But in Satan's name, sergeant—"

"Never mind about Satan now. You just get into your stylish vehicle and turn your pony's head round; you are coming along with me."

"Where to?"

"To Abbeville, *parbleu*. And if your papers are not in order—"

"If you go to Abbeville, sergeant," the man declared, still panting with excitement, "you lose the chance of a lifetime. . . . there's a fortune for you and me and these honest patriots waiting for us in the middle of this ploughed field."

"The man's mad," the sergeant declared. "*Allons*, don't let's waste any more time. *En evant!*"

"But I tell you I saw him, Citizen Sergeant," the man protested.

"Saw whom? The devil?"

"Worse. The English spy."

It was the sergeant's turn to gasp and to pant.

"The English spy?" he exclaimed.

"Him they call the Scarlet Pimpernel!" the man asserted hotly.

"Where?" the sergeant cried.

And the four men echoed excitedly! "Where?"

The man pointed towards the ploughed field.

"I went to look for a shelter for the night for my wife and child. I came to a barn. I heard voices. I drew near. I peeped in. *Aristos* I tell you. A dozen of them. All talking gibberish. English, what? And drinking. Drinking. Some of them were asleep on the straw. They mean to spend the night there."

He paused, breathless, and pressed his grimy hands against his chest as if every word he uttered caused him excruciating pain. The words came from his throat in short jerky sentences. Clearly, he was on the verge of collapse. But now the sergeant and his men were as eager, as excited as he was.

"Yes! yes! go on!" they urged.

"They are there still," the man said, trying to speak clearly: "I saw them. Not ten minutes ago. I ran away, for I tell you they looked like devils. And one of them is tall. . . . tall like a giant. . . . and his eyes—"

"Never mind his eyes," the sergeant broke in gruffly: "I am after those English devils. There's a reward of ten thousand *livres* for the capture of their chief. . . . and promotion—" he added lustily.

He turned his horse round in the direction of the field and called loudly "*Allons!*"

The driver halloed after him.

"But what about me, Citizen Sergeant?"

"You can follow. In what direction did you say?"

"Straight across," the man replied. "See that light over there. . . . keep it on your right. . . . and then follow the track. . . . and there's a gap in the hedge—"

But the sergeant was no longer listening. No doubt visions of ten thousand *livres* and fortune rising to giddy heights rose up before him out of the fast-gathering gloom. He was not going to waste time. The men followed him, as eager as the jingle of their accoutrements, the creaking of damp leather, the horses snorting and pawing the wet earth. The flap of the awning had been lowered again: she couldn't see anything, but she heard the welcome sounds, and no longer felt the cold.

"My baby, my baby," she murmured, crooning to Charles-Léon, "I do believe that God is on our side."

The cart moved along. She didn't know in which direction. The pony was going at foot-pace: probably the driver was leading it, for the darkness now was intense—the welcome darkness that enveloped the wanderers as in a black shroud. At first Louise could not help thinking of that sergeant and the soldiers. What would they do when they found that they had been hoodwinked? They would scour the countryside of course to find traces of the cart. Would they succeed in the darkness of the night? She dared not let her thoughts run on farther. All she could do was to press Charles-Léon closer and closer to her heart and to murmur over and over again: "I do believe that God is on our side."

He was indeed, for the night passed by and there was no further sign of the patrol. After a time, the cart came to a standstill and the driver came round, and helped her and Charles-Léon to descend. They all sheltered in the angle of a tumble-down wall which had once been part of a cottage. The man wrapped some sacking round Louise and the child and she supposed she slept, for she remembered nothing more until the light of dawn caused her to open her eyes.

The next day they came in sight of Calais. The driver pulled up and bade Louise and the child descend. Louise knew nothing of this part of France. It appeared to her unspeakably dreary and desolate. The earth was of a drab colour, so different to the rich reddish clay of the Dauphiné, and instead of the green pastures and golden cornfields, still scrubby grass grew in irregular tufts here and there. The sky was grey and there was a blustering wind which brought with it a smell of fish and salt water. The stunted trees, with their branches all tending away from the sea, had the mournful appearance of a number of attenuated human beings who were trying to run away and were held back by their fettered feet. Calais lay far away on the right, and there was only one habitation visible in this desolate landscape. This was a forlorn and dilapidated-looking cottage on the top of the cliff to the west: its roof was all crooked on the top like a hat that has been blown aside by the wind. The driver pointed to the cottage and said to Louise:

"That is our objective now, *Madame*, but I am afraid it has to be reached on foot. Can you do it?"

This was the first time that the man spoke directly to Louise. His voice was serious and kindly, nevertheless she was suddenly conscious of a strange pang of puzzlement and doubt—almost of awe: for the man spoke in perfect French, the language of a highly educated man. Yet he had the appearance of a rough country boor: his clothes were ragged, he wore neither shirt nor stockings: of course, his unshaved cheeks and chin added to his look of scrubbiness and his face and hands were far from clean. At first, when he replaced the horrible old hag on the driver's seat of the cart, Louise had concluded that he was one of that heroic band of Englishmen who were leading her and Charles-Léon to safety, but this conclusion was soon dispelled when the man spoke to the several patrols of soldiers who met them on the way. She had heard him talk to them, and also the night before, during those terrible moments in the lane; and he had spoken in the guttural *patois* peculiar to the peasantry of Northern France.

But now, that pleasant, cultured voice, the elegant diction of a Parisian! Louise did not know what to make of it. Had she detected the slightest trace of a foreign accent she would have understood, and gone back to her first conclusion, that here was one of those heroic Englishmen of whom Josette was wont to talk so ecstatically. But a French gentleman, masquerading in country clothes, what could it mean?

The poor woman's nerves were so terribly on edge that one emotion would chase away another with unaccountable speed. For the past few hours she had felt completely reassured—almost happy—but now, just a few words uttered by this man whom she had learned to trust sent her back into a state of panic, and the vague fears which she had experienced when first she left her apartment in the Rue Picpus once more reared their ugly heads. It was stupid of course! A state bordering on madness! But Louise had not been quite normal since the tragic death of Bastien.

And suddenly she clutched at her skirt, in the inner pocket of which she had stowed the packet of letters which already had cost Bastien de Croissy his life. But the letters were no longer there. She searched and searched, but the packet had indubitably gone. Then she was seized with wild panic. Pressing the child to her bosom she turned as if to fly. Whither she knew not, but to fly before the hideous arms of those vengeful Terrorists were stretched out far enough to get hold of Charles-Léon.

But before she had advanced one step in this wild career a strange sound fell upon her ear, a sound that made her pause and look vaguely about her to find out how it was that le *bon Dieu* had sent this heaven-born protector to save her and the boy. The sound was just a pleasant mellow laugh, and then the same kindly voice of a moment ago said quietly:

"This is yours, I believe, *Madame.*"

Instinctively she turned like a frightened child, hardly daring to look. Her glance fell first on the packet of letters which she had missed and which was held out to her by a very grimy yet strangely beautiful hand: from the hand her eyes wandered upwards along the tattered sleeve and the bent shoulder to the face of the driver who had been the silent companion of her amazing three days' adventure. And out of that face a pair of lazy deep-set blue eyes regarded her with obvious amusement, whilst the aftermath of that pleasant mellow laugh still lingered round the firm lips.

With her eyes fixed upon that face, which seemed like a mask over a mystical entity, Louise took the packet of letters. Her trembling lips murmured an awed "Who are you?" whereat the strange personage replied lightly, "For the moment your servant, *Madame,* only anxious to see you safely housed in yonder cottage. Shall we proceed?"

All Louise could do was to nod and then set off as briskly as she could, so as to show this wonderful man how ready she was to follow him in all things. He had already taken the pony out of the cart and set Charles-Léon on its back. The cart he left by the roadside, and he walked beside the pony steadying Charles-Léon with his arm. Thus, the little party climbed to the top of the cliff. It was very heavy going, for the ground was soft and Louise's feet sank deeply into the sand; but she dragged herself along bravely, although she felt like a somnambulist, moving in a dream-walk to some unknown, mysterious destination, a heaven peopled by heroic old hags and rough labourers with unshaven cheeks and merry, lazy eyes. The cottage on the cliff was not so dilapidated as it had appeared in the distance. The man brought the pony to a halt and pushed open the door. Louise lifted Charles-Léon down and followed her guide into the cottage. She found herself in a room in which there was a table, two or three chairs and benches, and an iron stove in which a welcome fire was burning.

Two men were sitting by the fire and rose as Louise, half-fainting with fatigue, staggered into the room. Together they led her to an inner room where there was a couch, and on this she sank breathless and speechless. Charles-Léon was then laid beside her: the poor child looked ghastly, and Louise, with a pitiable moan, hugged him to her side. One of the men brought her food and milk, whilst the other placed a pillow to her head. Louise, though only half-conscious at this moment, felt that if only she had the strength she would have dragged herself down on her knees and kissed the hands of those rough-looking men in boundless gratitude.

She remained for some time in a state of torpor, lying on the couch holding the boy closely to her. The door between the two rooms was ajar: a welcome warmth from the iron stove penetrated to the tired woman's aching sinews. A vague murmur of voices reached her semi-consciousness. The three men whom she regarded as her saviours were talking together in whispers. They spoke in English, of which Louise understood a few sentences. Now and again that pleasant mellow laugh which she had already heard came to her ears, and somehow it produced in her a sense of comfort and of peace. One of the three men, the one with the mellow laugh, seemed to be in command of the others, for he was giving them directions of what they were to do with reference to a boat, a creek and a path down the side of a cliff, and also to a signal with which the others appeared to be familiar.

But the voices became more and more confused; the gentle murmur, the pleasant roar of the fire acted as a lullaby, and soon Louise fell into a dreamless sleep.

Chapter 13

A pleasant, cultured voice, speaking French with a marked foreign accent, roused Louise out of her sleep. She opened her eyes still feeling dazed and not realising for the moment just where she was. One of the young men whom she had vaguely perceived the night before was standing under the lintel of the door.

"I hope I haven't frightened you, *Madame*," he now said, "but we ought to be getting on the way."

It was broad daylight, with a grey sky heavy with clouds that threatened rain, and a blustering wind that moaned dismally down the chimney. From the distance came the regular booming of the breakers against the cliffs. It was a sound Louise had never heard in her life before and she could not help feeling alarmed at the prospect of going on the sea with Charles-Léon so weak and ill, even though salvation and hospitable England lay on the other side. But she had made up her mind that however cowardly she felt in her heart of hearts, she would bear herself bravely before her heroic friends. As soon as the young man had gone, she made herself and the boy ready for the journey— the Great Unknown as she called it with a shudder of apprehension.

There was some warm milk and bread for her and Charles-Léon on the table in the other room. She managed to eat and drink and then said bravely: "We are quite ready now, *Monsieur*."

The young man guided her to the front door of the house. Here she expected to see once more the strange and mysterious man who had driven her all the way from Paris in the ramshackle vehicle and who throughout four long wearisome days and nights had never seemed to tire, and never lost his ready wit and resourcefulness in face of danger from the patrols of the National Guard.

Not seeing him or the cart she turned to her new friend.

"What has happened to our elegant *barouche?*" she asked with a smile, "and the pony?"

"They wouldn't be much use down the cliff-side, *Madame*," he replied; "I hope you are not too tired to walk—"

"No, no! of course not, but—"

"And one of us will carry the boy."

"I didn't mean that," she rejoined quickly.

"What then?"

"The. . . . driver who brought us safely here. . . . he was so kind. . . . so. . . . so wonderful. . . . I would love to see him again. . . . if only to thank him—"

The young man remained silent for a minute or two, then when Louise insisted, saying: "Surely, I could speak to him before we go?" he said rather curtly, she thought: "I am afraid not, *Madame*."

She would have liked to have insisted still more urgently, thinking it strange that this young man should speak so curtly of one who deserved all the eulogy and all the recognition that anyone could give for his valour and ingenuity, but somehow, she had the feeling that for some obscure reason or other the subject of that wonderful man was distasteful to her new friend, and that she had better not inquire further about him. Anyway, she was so surrounded by mysteries that one more or less did not seem to matter.

Just then she caught sight of another man who was coming up the side of the cliff. He kept his head bent against the force of the wind, which was very boisterous and made going against it very difficult. Soon he reached the top of the cliff. He greeted Louise with a pleasant "*Bonjour, Madame,*" uttered with a marked English accent. Indeed, to Louise he looked, just like the other, a fine, upstanding young foreigner, well-groomed despite the inclemency of the weather and the primitiveness of his surroundings. The two men exchanged a few words together which Louise did not understand, after which one of them said, "*En route!*" and the other added in moderately good French, "I hope you are feeling fit and well, *Madame*; you have another tiring day before you."

Louise assured him that she was prepared for any amount of fatigue; he then took Charles-Léon in his arms; his friend took hold of Louise by the elbow, and led the way down the cliff, carefully guiding her tottering footsteps.

At the foot of the cliff the little party came to a narrow creek, and Louise perceived a boat hidden in a shallow cave in the rock. Guided by her friends Louise crept into the cave and stepped into the boat. The young men made her as comfortable as they could and gently laid Charles-Léon in her arms. Except for gentle words of encouragement to the little boy now and then, they spoke very little, and Louise, who by now was in a kind of somnambulistic state, could only nod her thanks when one or the other of them asked if she felt well, or offered her some scanty provisions for herself and Charles-Léon.

The party sat in the boat during the whole of the day, until it was quite dark. In this distance far out at sea Louise's aching eyes perceived from time to time ships riding on the waves. Charles-Léon was frightened at first, and crouched against his mother, and when the waves came tumbling against the rocks and booming loudly he hid his little head under her shawl. But after a time, the reassuring voices of the young Englishmen coupled with boyish curiosity induced him to look at the ships; he listened to childish sea-faring yarns told by one or the other of them: soon he became interested and, like his mother, felt no longer afraid.

Poor Louise, was, of course, terribly ignorant of all matters connected with the sea, as she had never been as much as near it in her life. She only knew vaguely the meaning of the word tide, and when the young men spoke of "waiting for the tide" before putting out to sea, she did not know what they meant. She fell to wondering whether they would all presently cross La Manche in the tiny rowing boat which was not much bigger than those in which she and Josette with Papa and Maman Gravier were wont in the olden days to go out for picnics on the Isère. But she asked no questions. Indeed, by now she felt that she had permanently lost the use of her tongue.

Soon the evening began to draw in. A long twilight slowly melted into the darkness of a moonless night. Looking towards the sea it seemed to Louise that she was looking straight at a heavy black curtain—like a solid mass of gloom. The wind continued unabated, and now that she could no longer see the sea, and only heard its continuous roar, Louise once more felt that hideous, cold fear grinding at her heart. Those terrifying waves seemed to come nearer and nearer to the sheltering cave, while the breakers broke on the stony beach with a sound like thunder. As was quite natural, her terror communicated itself to the child. He refused to be comforted, and though the two men did all they could to soothe him, and one of them knelt persistently beside Louise, whispering words of encouragement in the child's ear, poor little Charles-Lèon continued to shiver with terror.

Through the dismal howling of the wind and the booming of the waves no other sound penetrated to Louise's ears. After a while the young men too remained quite silent: they were evidently waiting for the signal of which they had spoken together the night before.

What that signal was Louise did not know. She certainly heard no strange sound, but the men did evidently hear something, for, suddenly and without a word, they seized their oars and pushed the boat off and out of the cave. This was perhaps on the whole the most terrifying moment in Louise's extraordinary adventure. The boat seemed to be plunging straight into a wall of darkness. It rocked incessantly, and poor Louise felt horribly sick. Presently she felt that she was being lifted to her feet and held in a pair of strong arms which carried her upwards through the darkness, whither she knew not at the time, but a little while later it occurred to her that perhaps she had died of fright, and that as of a matter of fact she had not awakened in Paradise. She was lying between snow-white, lavender-scented sheets, her aching head rested on a downy pillow, and a kindly voice was persuading her to sip some hot-spiced wine, which she did. It certainly proved to be delicious.

And there was Charles-Léon sitting opposite to her on the knee of a ruddy-faced, tow-haired sailor who was holding a mug of warm milk to the child's trembling lips. All that and more did indeed confirm Louise's first impression that this was not the cruel, hard world with which she was all too familiar, but rather an outpost of Paradise—if not the blessed heavens themselves.

The movement of the ship, alas! made Louise feel rather sick after a time, and this was an unpleasant and wholly earthly sensation which caused her to doubt her being in the company of angels. But indeed, she was so tired that soon she fell asleep, in spite of the many strange noises around and above her, the creaking of wood, the soughing of the wind and the lashing of the water against the side of the ship.

When she woke after several hours' sleep the pale rosy light of dawn came creeping in through the port-hole. It was in very truth a rosy dawn, an augury of the calm and beauty that was now in store for the long-suffering woman. She was in England at last, she and her child: together they were safe from those assassins who had done Bastien to death and would probably have torn Charles-Léon from her breast before they sent her to the guillotine.

Le Bon Dieu had indeed been on their side.

Chapter 14

And while Louise lived through the palpitating events of those fateful days Josette Gravier was quietly taking up the threads of life again. They were not snapped; they had only slipped for a few hours out of her hands, and life, of course, had to go on just the same. She would be alone after this in the apartment of the Rue Picpus: the small rooms, the tiny kitchen seemed vast now that all those whom Josette had cared for had gone. Strangely enough she was not anxious about Louise's fate; her faith was so immense, her belief in the Scarlet Pimpernel so absolute that she was able to go through the days that followed in comparative peace of mind whilst looking forward to Maurice's return.

He had obtained a permit, lasting six or seven days, to visit the de Croissy estates in the Dauphiné. The permit had been granted before Louise's departure was known to the authorities, or probably she and Charles-Léon, as sole heirs of Bastien de Croissy, would have been classed as *émigrés*: all their property would then be automatically confiscated and no one but government officials allowed to administer it. Maurice spent five days of his leave in the diligence between Paris and Grenoble, and one in consultation with the old bailiff on the Croissy estate, trying to extract from him a promise that he would send to Mademoiselle Gravier on behalf of Madame de Croissy a small sum of money every month for rent and the bare necessities of life. Maurice hoped that after Josette had paid the rent out of this money she would contrive to send the remainder over to England as soon as she knew where to find Louise.

Josette had a little money of her own which she kept in her stocking, and she also received a few *sous* daily pay for the work which she did in the government shops—stitching, knitting, doing up parcels for the "Soldiers of Liberty" who were fighting on the frontiers against the whole of Europe and keeping the great armies of Prussia and Austria at bay. If the rent of the apartment could be paid with monies sent from the Croissy estate, Josette was quite sure that she could live on her meagre stipend. Penury in the big cities, and especially in Paris, was appalling just now. Sugar and soap were unobtainable, and the scarcity of bread was becoming more and more acute.

Queues outside the bakeries began to assemble as early as four o'clock in the morning to wait for the distribution of two ounces of bread, which was all that was allowed per person per day; and the two ounces consisted for the most part of bran and water. The baker favoured Josette because of her pretty face, but she was obliged to go for her ration very early in the morning because she had to be at the workshop by eight o'clock, and if she queued up later in the day Citizen Loquin would sometimes run out of bread before all his customers were served.

When Maurice came back from Grenoble life for Josette became more cheerful. He had found a tiny room for himself under the roof of another house in the Rue Picpus and had at once fallen back into his old habit of calling for Josette in the late afternoon at the government shop when the day's work was done, and together the two of them would go arm-in-arm for a walk up the Champs Élysées or sometimes as far as the Bois. Maurice would bring what meagre provisions they could afford for their supper, and they would sit under the chestnut trees, now almost shorn of leaves and munch sour bread and dig their young teeth into an apple.

Sometimes they would stroll into the town to see the illuminations, for there were illuminations on more than one day every week. What the wretched poverty-stricken, tyrant-ridden citizens of Paris rejoiced for on those evenings heaven alone knew! Certain it is that though tallow and grease were scarce, innumerable candles and lamps were lit, time after time, on some pretext or other, such as the passing of some decree which had a momentary popularity, or the downfall of a particular member of the Convention who had—equally momentarily—become unpopular with the mob. Such occasions were marked, in addition to the brilliant lighting of the city, by a great deal of noise and cheering, as an ill-clad, ill-fed mob thronged the streets, cheering their Robespierre or their Danton, and booing all the poor wretches who had been decreed traitors to the Republic on that day, and whose trial, condemnation and death on the guillotine would—just as night inevitably follows day—follow within twenty-four hours.

Maurice and Josette, jostled by the crowd, neither booed nor cheered: they seldom knew what the rejoicings and illuminations were for, but the movement, the lights and the noise took them out of themselves and caused them to forget for an hour or two the ever-growing problem of how to go on living. Once or twice when Maurice had carried through successfully a bit of legal business, he would buy a couple of tickets for the theatre, and he and Josette would listen enthralled to the sonorous verses of Corneille or Racine as declaimed by Citizen Talma or laugh their fill over the drolleries of Mascarille or Monsieur Jourdain.

Sunday had been officially abolished by decree of the Convention in the new calendar, but Decadi came once every ten days with a half-holiday for Josette; then, if the day was fine, the two of them would hire a boat and Maurice would row up the river as far as Suresnes, and he and Josette would munch their sour bread and their apples under the trees by the towpath, and watched the boats gliding up and down the Seine and long for the freedom to drift downstream away from the noise and turmoil of the city, and away from the daily horrors of the guillotine and countless deaths of innocents which would for ever remain a stain on the fair fame of the country which they loved.

Maurice had never spoken again of love to Josette. He was not an ordinary lover, for he had intuition, and his love was entirely unselfish. So few lovers have a direct apprehension of the right moment for declaring their feelings; those that have this supreme gift will often succeed where others less sensitive will fail because they have not approached the loved one when she was in a receptive mood. Maurice knew that his hour had not yet come. Josette was still in a dream-state of adoration for a hero whom she had never seen. She was too young and too unsophisticated to analyse her own feelings; too ignorant of men and of life to take Maurice altogether seriously. As a friend or a brother, she cared for him more than she had ever cared for another living soul, not excepting Louise; she trusted him, she relied on him: had she not said on that never-to-be-forgotten occasion: "Are you not here to take care of me?"

But for the time being her thoughts were too full of that other man's image to add idealism to her affection. And so even though these autumn days were calm and sweet, though the wood-pigeons still cooed in the forests and the black-birds whistled in the chestnut trees, Maurice did not speak of love to Josette; although at times he suffered so acutely from her ingenuousness that tears would well up to his eyes and the words which he forced himself not to utter nearly choked him; yet he did not tell her how he loved her, and how he ached with the longing to take her in his arms, to bury his face in her golden curls, or press his burning lips on her sweet, soft mouth.

He was happy in this, that he was in a measure working for her; all her little pleasure, all the small delicacies which he brought her, and which she munched with the relish of a young animal, came to her through his exertions. He had automatically slipped into his late employer's practice. It did not amount to much, but he was a fully qualified advocate, and as clerk to Citizen Croissy, had become known to the latter's clients. A part of the money which he earned he put by for *Madame* because he considered that it was her due, but there was always a little over which Maurice set aside for the joy of giving Josette some small treat—tickets at the theatre, an excursion into the country, or an intimate little dinner at one of the cheap restaurants. Strange, indeed, that in the midst of the most awful social upheaval the world has ever known, life for many, like Josette Gravier and Maurice Reversac, could go on in such comparative calm.

Three weeks and more went by before Josette had any news of Louise. But one evening when she came home after her walk with Maurice she found that a letter had been thrust under the door of the apartment. It was from Louise, it said:

My Josette *chérie*
We are in England, Charles-Léon and I, and the man who has wrought this miracle is none other than the mysterious hero of

whom you have so often dreamed. I have received word that this letter will reach you. That word was signed with the device which stands for courage and self-sacrifice—a small scarlet flower, my Josette, the Scarlet Pimpernel. I am completely convinced now that I owe my salvation and that of Charles-Léon to your English hero.

Here in England no one doubts it. He is the national hero, and people speak of him with bated breath as of a godlike creature, whom only the elect have been privileged to meet in the flesh. It is generally believed that he is a high-born English gentleman who devotes his life to saving the weak and the innocent from the murderous clutches of those awful Terrorists in France. He has a band of followers, nineteen in number, who obey his commands without question, and under his leadership constantly risk their precious lives in the cause of humanity. It is difficult to understand why they do this: some call it the sublimity of self-sacrifice, others the love of sport and adventure, innate in every Englishman. But God alone can judge of motives.

My darling Josette, you will be happy to know that we are at peace and comfortable now, my poor lamb and I, though my heart is filled with sorrow at being parted from you. Daily do I pray to God that you may come to me someday soon. Remember me to Maurice. He is a brave and loyal soul. I will not tell you of the hopes which I nurse for your future and his. You will have guessed these long ago. I am afraid that he would refuse to come away from Paris just yet, but if you can, Josette, would join me here in England—and you can do that any day with the aid of the Scarlet Pimpernel—we could bide our time quietly until the awful turmoil has subsided, which, by God's will, it soon must, and then return to France, when you and Maurice could be happily united.

As to my adventures from the moment when I left our apartment with Charles-Léon in my arms until the happy hour when we landed here in England I can tell you nothing. My lips are sealed under a promise of silence, and implicit obedience to the wishes of my heroic rescuers is the only outward token of my boundless gratitude that I can offer them.

But I can tell you something of our arrival in Dover. I was still very sea-sick, but the feeling of nausea left me soon after

I had set foot on solid ground. We walked over to a delightful place, a kind of tavern it was, though not a bit like our *cafés* or restaurants. Later on, when I was rested, I made a note of the sign which was painted on a shield outside the door; it was 'The Fisherman's Rest,' and, in English, such places are called inns. I have prayed God ever since I crossed that threshold that you, my Josette *chérie* might see it one day.

Here for the first time since I left Paris I came in contact with people of my own sex. The maid who showed me to a room where I could wash and rest was a sight for sore eyes: so clean, so fresh, so happy! So different to our poor girls in France nowadays—underfed, ill-clothed, in constant terror of what the near future might bring. These little maids over here go about their work singing—singing, *chéie!* Just think of it! Of late I have never heard anyone sing except you!

We spent the best part of the day at 'The Fisherman's Rest.' In the afternoon we posted to Maidstone, where we now are the guests of some perfectly charming English people. I cannot begin to tell you, *chérie*, of the kindness and hospitality of these English families who take us in, poor *émigrés*, feed us and clothe us and look after us until such time as we can get resources of our own. I wish our good Maurice could send me a remittance from time to time, but that, I know, is impossible. But I will try to get some needlework to do; you know how efficient I was always considered, even at the convent, in sewing and embroidery. I do not wish to be a burden longer than I can help to my over-kind hosts.

How this letter will reach you I know not, but I know that it will reach you, because a day or two ago the post brought me a mysterious communication saying that any letter of mine sent to the *Bureau des Émigrés*, Fitzroy Square, London, will be delivered to any address in France. This is only one of the many wonderful happenings that have occurred since I left Paris. It seems such a long time ago now, and our little apartment in the Rue Picpus seems so far, so very far away. I have forgotten nothing. Josette *chérie*, even though my memory has been over-clouded by all the strange events which have befallen me.

So little have I forgotten that many a time and very bitterly have I reproached myself that I lent such an inattentive ear when you spoke to me about the mysterious English hero who goes by the name of the Scarlet Pimpernel, and of his no less heroic followers. Had I believed in you and them sooner, my Bastien might be beside me even now. The Scarlet Pimpernel, my Josette, is real, very real indeed. He and his nineteen lieutenants have saved the lives of hundreds of innocents: his name here is on everybody's lips, but no one knows who he is. He works in the dark, under that quaint appellation, and those of us who owe our lives to him have, so far as we know, never set eyes on him.

Well! it is a problem the solution of which I shall probably never know. All I can do is to keep sacred in my heart the memory of all that that man has done for me.

That is all, my Josette. I hope and pray to Almighty God that someday soon it may be your good fortune to come to me—to come to England under the tender care of the man whom you have almost deified. When that happy day comes you will find your Louise's arms stretched out in loving welcome.

Your devoted friend.

Louise.

P.S.—I still have the letters.

Josette could scarcely read the welcome missive to the end. Her eyes were dim with tears. She loved Louise as she had always done, and she adored Charles-Léon, and somehow this letter, coming from far-off England, quickened and accentuated the poignancy of parting: she spent many hours sitting at the table under the lamp with Louise's letter spread out before her. One sentence in it she read over and over again, for it expressed just what she herself felt in her heart for the hero of her dreams, Louise had written:

All I can do, is to keep sacred the memory of all that that man has done for me.

Chapter 15

Josette had read on so late into the night and been so excited over what she read that sleep had quite gone out of her eyes. She could not get to sleep for thinking of Louise and her adventures, of the Scarlet Pimpernel, and also of Maurice Reversac. Poor Maurice! Whatever happened he would have his burden to bear here in Paris. For the sake of the dead, and because of Louise and Charles-Léon, he must carry on his work and trust to God to see him safely through.

That day, for the first time since his return from the Dauphiné, Maurice was not at his usual place outside the gate of the workshop, waiting for Josette to come out. Josette, slightly disappointed, knew, of course, that it must be the exigencies of business that had kept him away. But when the evening hour came and again no Maurice at the gate, Josette was anxious. Before she went home she went over to Maurice's lodgings down the street to inquire from the *concierge* if, perchance, Maurice was ill. She knew that nothing but illness could possibly have kept him from his evening walk with her, or from sending her a message. But the *concierge* had seen and heard nothing of Maurice since morning when he started off as usual for the office.

Nothing would do after that but Josette must go off, then and there, to the Rue de la Monnaie. She had not been near the place since that awful day when she saw Maître de Croissy lying dead in his devastated office; and when she turned the angle of the street and saw at a hundred paces farther along the *porte-cochère* of the house where the terrible tragedy had occurred, she was suddenly overcome with an awful prescience of doom. So powerful was this sense of forewarning that she could no longer stand on her feet but was obliged to lean against the nearest wall while trying to conquer sheer physical nausea. A horrible, nameless terror assailed her: she was trembling in every limb. However, after a few moments she regained control over herself, chided herself for her weakness, and walked with comparative coolness to the *porte-cochère*, which had not yet been closed for the night.

Again, that awful feeling of giddiness and nausea. The house had always worn that dismal air of desolation and decay with a pervading odour of damp mortar and putrid vegetables. Josette knew its history: she knew that it had once been the fine abode of a rich foreign banker who had fled the country at the first outbreak of the Revolution, that it had stood empty for two or three years, then been appropriated by the State, a *concierge* put in office, and the house let out in apartments and offices. She had often been to the house and always disliked the sight of it, its air of emptiness despite the fact that most of the apartments were inhabited: the courtyard and stairs looked to her as if they were peopled by ghosts.

Josette went up to the *concierge's* lodge and asked if Citizen Reversac were still in his office. The *concierge* eyed her with a quizzical glance. He had seen the pretty girl in the company of Citizen Reversac before now. His sweetheart, no doubt—ah, well! these things were of every-day occurrence these days. Mothers lost their sons, wives their husbands: it was no good grieving over other people's troubles or commiserating over their misfortunes.

"Citizen Reversac was here this morning, little *citizeness*," the *concierge* said in response to Josette's reiterated question, "but. . . . you know—"

"What?"

"He was arrested this morning—"

"Arr—?"

"Easy, easy, little *citizeness*," the *concierge* rejoined quickly, and with outstretched hand steadied Josette, who looked as if she would measure her length outside his lodge. "These things," he added with a shrug, "happen every day. Why, my own sister less than a week ago—"

Josette did not hear what he said. He went rambling on about his sister whose only son had been arrested, and who was breaking her heart this very day because the boy had been guillotined.

"He was not a bad lad either, my nephew; and a good patriot; but there! one never knows."

"One never knows!" Josette murmured mechanically, stupidly, staring at the *concierge* with great unseeing eyes. The man felt really sorry for the girl. She was so very pretty, that mouth of hers had been fashioned for smiles, those blue eyes made only to shine with merriment, and those chestnut curls to tempt a man to sin. Ah, well, one never knows! These things happened every day!

Chapter 16

How Josette reached home that evening she never knew. She seemed to have spent hours and hours in repeating to herself: "It cannot be true!" and "It must be a mistake."

"He has done nothing!" she murmured from time to time, and then: "In a few days they will set him free again! They must! He has done nothing! Such an innocent!"

But in her heart, she knew that innocents suffered these days as often as the guilty. Only a short time ago she had been called on to fill the *rôle* comforter. She could not help thinking of Louise and of that awful tragedy which was the precursor of the present cataclysm. But now she had to face this trouble alone: there was no one in whom she could confide, no one who could give her a word of advice or comfort. And when she found herself alone at last in the apartment of the Rue Picpus, where every stick of furniture, every door and every wall reminded her of those whom she loved and proclaimed her present loneliness, she realised the immensity of that cataclysm.

She felt that with Maurice gone she had nothing more to live for. The dreariness of days without his kindly voice to cheer her, his loving arm to guide her, was inconceivable. It looked before her like a terrifying nightmare. And she pictured to herself Maurice's surprise and indignation at his arrest, his protestations of innocence, his final courage in face of the inevitable. She thought of him in one of the squalid overcrowded prisons, thinking of her, linking his hands tightly together in a proud attempt to appear unconcerned, indifferent to his fate before his fellow-prisoners.

Maurice! Josette never knew till now how she cared for him. Love?. . . . No! She did not know what love was, nor did she believe that the desperate ache which she had in her heart at thought of Maurice had anything to do with the love that poets and authors spoke about. On the contrary, she thought that what she felt for Maurice was far stronger and deeper than the thing people called "love." All she knew was that she suffered intensely at this moment, that his image haunted her in a way it had never done before.

She recalled every moment that of late she had spent with him, every trick of his voice, every expression of his face: his kind grey eyes, the gentle smile around his lips, the quaint remarks he would make at times which had often made her laugh. Above all, she was haunted at this hour with the remembrance of a mellow late summer's evening when she chaffed him because he had spoken to her of love. How sad he was that evening, whilst she never thought for a moment that he had been serious.

"Maurice! Maurice!" she cried out in her heart; "if those devils take you from me I shall never know a happy hour again."

But it was not in Josette's nature to sit down and mope. Her instinct was to be up and doing, whatever happened and however undecipherable the riddle set by Fate might be. And so, in this instance also. The arrest of Maurice was in truth the knock-down blow: at this juncture Josette could not have imagined a more overwhelming catastrophe. As she was alone in the apartment she indulged in the solace of tears. She cried and cried till her eyes were inflamed and her head ached furiously: she cried because of the intense feeling of loneliness and desolation that gave her such a violent pain in her heart which nothing but a flood of tears seemed able to still.

But having had her cry, she pulled herself together, dried her tears, bathed her face, then sat down to think or, rather, to remember. With knitted brows and concentrated force of will she tried to recall all that Bastien de Croissy had said to Louise the evening when first he spoke of the letters and she, Josette suggested stitching the packet in the lining of Louise's corsets. These letters were more precious than any jewels on earth, for they were to be the leverage wherewith to force certain influential members of the Convention to grant Louise a permit to take her child into the country, to remain with him and nurse him back to health and strength. The possession of those letters had been the cause of Bastien de Croissy's terrible death. They were seriously compromising to certain influential representatives of the people, proofs probably of some black-hearted treason to their country. The possession of them was vitally important to their writers, so important that they chose the way of murder rather than risk revelation. A man on trial, a man condemned to death might have the chance of speaking. It is only the dead who cannot speak.

So now for the knowledge of who were the writers of the letters. And Josette, her head buried in her hands, tried to recall every word which Bastien had spoken the night before his death, while she, Josette, sat under the light of the lamp, stitching the precious packet into the lining of Louise's corsets. But unfortunately, at one moment during the evening her mind, absorbed in the facts themselves, had been less retentive than usual. Certain it is that at this desperately critical moment she could not recall a single name that Bastien had mentioned, and after his death, Louise, with the obstinacy of the half-demented, had guarded the letters with a kind of fierce jealousy; she had taken them to England with her, with what object God only knew—probably none! Just obstinacy and without definite consciousness.

It was in the small hours of the morning that Josette had an inspiration. It was nothing less, and it so comforted her that she actually fell asleep, and as soon as she was washed and dressed ran out into the street. She ran all the way to the corner of the Pont des Arts, where vendors of old books and newspapers had their booths. She bought a bundle of back numbers of Le Moniteur and, hugging it under her cape, she ran back to the Rue Picpus.

The Moniteur gave the reports of the sittings of the Convention day by day, the debates, the speeches. Josette, whilst sitting by herself the night before with her mind still in a whirl with the terrible news of Maurice's arrest, had not been able to recall a single name mentioned by Bastien in connection with the letters, but with the back numbers of the Moniteur spread out before her, with the names of several members of the Convention staring at her in print, the task of reconstructing the conversation for that night became much easier. For instance, she did remember Louise exclaiming at one moment: "But he is Danton's most intimate friend!" and Bastien saying then: "All three of them are friends of Danton."

And shrewd little Josette concentrated on the *Moniteur* until she came upon the report of a debate in the Convention over a proposition put forward by Citizen Danton. Who were his friends? Who his supporters? he had a great number, for he was still at the height of his popularity: they agreed and debated and perorated, and Josette while she read, murmured their names repeatedly to herself: "Desmoulins, Desmoulins, Desmoulins—no! that wasn't it. Hérault, Hérault de Séchelles—no! Delacroix—no, again no! Chabot?. . . . Chabot—?" And slowly memory brought the name back to her mind—Chabot! That was one of the names! Chabot, Danton's friend. "Yes!" Bastien had said at one moment, "an unfrocked Capuchin friar!" and Louise had uttered an exclamation of horror.

Chabot! that certainly was one of the names. And Josette read on; taxed her memory, forced it to serve her purpose. More names which meant nothing, and then one that stood out! Fabre d'Eglantine— Danton's most intimate friend! Chabot and Fabre—two names! And then a third one—Bazire! Josette had paid no attention at the time. She had heard Bastien mention those names, but only vaguely, and her brain had only vaguely registered them; but now they came back. Memory had served her a good turn.

Fabre, Chabot, Bazire! Josette had no longer any doubt as to who the men were who had written the letters, letters that were the powerful leverage wherewith to force them to grant whatever might be asked of them: a permit for Louise, freedom for Maurice Reversac.

Josette had not been sufficiently care-free up to now to note that the weather was like, but now, with a sense almost of gladness in her heart, she threw open the window and looked up at the sky. She only had a small glimpse of it because the Rue Picpus was narrow and the houses opposite high, but she did have a glimpse of clear blue, the blue of which Paris among all the great cities of Europe can most justifiably boast, translucent and exhilarating. The air was mild. There was no trace of wintry weather, of rain or of cold. The sun was shining and she, Josette, was going to drag Maurice out of the talons of those revolutionary birds of prey.

From far away came the dismal sound of the bell of St. Germain, booming out the morning hour. Another day had broken over the unfortunate city, another day wherein men waged a war to the death one against the other, wherein they persecuted the innocent, heaped crime upon crime, injustice upon injustice, flouted religion and defied God; another day wherein ruled the devils of hate and dolour, of tribulation and of woe. But Josette did no longer think of devils or of sorrow. She was going to be the means of opening the prison gates for Maurice.

Chapter 17

Since the day when Charlotte Corday forced her way into the apartment of Citizen Marat and plunged a dagger into the heart of that demagogue, the more prominent members of the revolutionary government were wont to take special precautions to guard their valuable lives.

Thus, the conventionnel François Chabot in his magnificent apartment in the Rue d'Anjou made it a rule that every person desirous of an interview with him must be thoroughly searched for any possible concealed weapon before being admitted to his august presence. The unfrocked friar proclaimed loudly his patriotism, declared his readiness to die a martyr like Marat, but he was taking no risks. He had married a very rich and very beautiful young wife. Whilst professing in theory the most rigid *sans-culottism*, he lived in the greatest possible luxury, ate and drank only of the best, wore fine clothes, and surrounded himself with every comfort that his wife's money could buy.

Josette did indeed appear as a humble suppliant when, having mounted the carpeted stairs which led up to the first floor of that fine house in the Rue d'Anjou, she found herself face to face with a stalwart janitor at the door of François Chabot's apartment.

"Your business?" he demanded.

"To speak with Citizen Chabot," Josette replied.

"Does the citizen expect you?"

"No, but when he knows of the business which has brought me here he will not refuse to see me."

"That is as it may be, but you cannot pass this door without stating your business."

"It is private, and for Citizen Chabot's private ear alone."

The stalwart looked down on the dainty figure before him. Being a man, he looked down with considerable pleasure, for Josette in her neat kirtle and well-fitting bodice, her frilled muslin cap perched coquettishly on her chestnut curls, was exceedingly pleasant to look on. Her blue eyes did not so much as demand that her wish to speak with Citizen Chabot should not be peremptorily denied.

The janitor pulled himself up and his waistcoat down, passed his hand over his bristly cheek, hemmed and hawed and cleared his throat, then, unable apparently to resist the command of those shining eyes any longer, he said finally:

"I will see what can be done, *citizeness*."

"That is brave of you," Josette said demurely, and then added: "Where shall I wait?" which translated into ordinary language meant: "You would not surely allow me to wait outside the door where any passer-by might behave in an unseemly manner towards me?"

At any rate this was how the janitor interpreted Josette's simple query. He opened the door on the thickly carpeted, richly furnished vestibule and said: "Wait here, *citizeness*."

Josette went in. It was years since she had seen such beautiful furniture, such tall mirrors and rich gildings, years since she had trodden on such soft carpets, and these were the days when woman had to go shoeless, and children died for want of nourishment, whilst men like Chabot preached equality and fraternity, and loudly proclaimed the simplicity and abnegation of their lives. Josette's astonishment at all this luxury caused her to open wide her eyes, and when those blue eyes were opened wide, men, even the most stalwart, became like putty.

"Sit down there, *citizeness*," the magnificent janitor said, "whilst I go and inquire if the Citizen Representative will see you."

Josette sat down and waited. Two or three minutes later the janitor returned. As soon as he caught sight of Josette he shook his head, then said:

"Not unless you will state your business. And," he added, "you know the rule: no one is admitted to speak with any Representatives of the People without being previously searched."

"Give me pen and paper," Josette rejoined, "that I may state my business in writing."

When the man brought her pen and paper she wrote:

"Dead men tell no tales, but the written words endure."

She folded the paper, then demanded wax and a seal. Presumably the man couldn't read, but one never knew. A seal was safer and Chabot himself would be grateful to her for having thought of it. A few moments later she found herself in a small room, bare of furniture or carpet, into which the janitor had ushered her after he had taken her written message to the Citizen Representative. A middle-aged woman, who was probably the housekeeper, passed her rough hands all over Josette's young body, dived into her shoes, under her muslin *fichu*, and even under her cap. Satisfied that there was no second Charlotte Corday intent on assassination, she called the janitor back and handed an indignant if silent Josette back to him. The audience could now be granted with safety.

Such were the formalities attendant upon a request for an audience with one of the representatives of the people in this glorious era of Equality and Fraternity.

Chapter 18

François Chabot was at this time about forty years of age. A small, thin, nervy-looking creature with long nose, thick lips, arched eyebrows above light brown eyes, and a quantity of curly hair which swept the top of his high coat-collar at the back, covering it with grease. He was dressed in the height of fashion, with a very short waist and long tails to his coat. His neck was swathed in a high stock collar, and his somewhat receding chin rested on a voluminous jabot of muslin and lace.

Josette, who had been ushered into his presence with so much ceremony, eyed him with curiosity, for she had heard it said of Representative Chabot that he affected to attend the sittings of the Convention in a tattered shirt, with bare legs and wearing a scarlet cap. In fact, it was said of him that he owed most of his popularity to this display of cynicism: also, that he, like his brother-in-law Bazire, had before now paid a hired assassin to dig a knife between his ribs in order to raise the cry among his friends in the Convention: "See! the counter-revolutionists are murdering the patriots. Marat first, now the incorruptible Chabot. Whose turn will it be next?"

But Josette, though remembering all this, was in no mood to smile. Did not this damnable hypocrite hold Maurice's life in his ugly hands? Those same hands—large, bony, with greyish nails and spatulated fingers—were toying with the written message which Josette had sent in to him. They were perhaps the hands that had dealt the fatal blow to Bastien de Croissy. Josette glanced on them with horror and then quickly drew her eyes away.

The janitor had motioned her to a seat, then he retired, closing the door behind him. Josette was alone with the Citizen Representative.

He was sitting at a large desk which was littered with papers, and she sat opposite to him. He now raised his pale, shifty eyes to her, and she returned his searching glance fearlessly. He was obviously nervous; cleared his throat to give himself importance and shifted his position once or twice. The paper which he held between two fingers and pointed towards Josette rustled audibly.

"Your name?" he asked curtly after a time.

"Josephine Gravier," she replied.

"And occupation?"

"Seamstress in the Government workshops. I was also companion and housekeeper in the household of Maître Croissy—"

"Ah!"

". . . until the day of his death."

There was a pause. The man was as nervous as a cat. He made great efforts to appear at ease, and above all to control his voice, which after that first "Ah!" had sounded hoarse and choked.

The handsome Boule clock on the mantelpiece, obviously the spoils of a raid on a confiscated *château*, struck the hour with deliberate majesty. Chabot shifted his position again, crossed and uncrossed his legs, pushed his chair father away from the bureau, and went on fidgeting with Josette's written message, crushing it between his fingers.

"Advocate Croissy," he said at last with an effort, "committed suicide, I understand."

"It was said so, citizen."

"What do you mean by that?"

"Nothing beyond what I said."

They were like duellists, these two, measuring their foils in a preliminary passage of arms. Chabot's glance had in it now something malevolent, cruel. . . . the cruelty of a coward who is not sure yet of what it is he has to fear.

Suddenly he said, holding up the crumpled bit of paper:

"Why did you send me this?"

"To warn you, citizen," Josette replied quite quietly.

"Of what?"

"That certain letters of which you and others are cognisant have not been destroyed."

"Letters?" Chabot demanded roughly. "What letters?"

"Letters written by you, Citizen Representative, to Maître de Croissy, which prove you to be a shameless hypocrite and a traitor to your country."

She had shot this arrow at random, but at once she had the satisfaction of knowing that the shaft had gone home. Chabot's sallow cheeks had become the colour of lead, his thick lips quivered visibly. A slight scum appeared at the corner of his mouth.

"It's all a lie!" he protested, but his voice sounded forced and hollow. "An invention of that traitor Croissy."

"You know best, Citizen Representative," Josette retorted simply.

Chabot tried to put on an air of indifference.

"Croissy," he said as calmly as he could, "told you a deliberate lie if he said that certain letters of mine were anything but perfectly innocent. I personally should not care if anybody read them—"

He paused, then added: "If that is all you wished to tell me, my girl, the interview can end here."

"As you desire, citizen," Josette said, and made as if to rise.

"Stay a moment," Chabot commanded. "Merely from idle curiosity I would like to know where those famous letters are. Can you perchance tell me?"

"Oh, yes," she replied. "They are in England and out of your reach, Citizen Representative."

"What do you mean by 'in England'?"

"Just what I say. When the widow of Maître de Croissy went to England with her boy she took the packet of letters with her."

"She fled from Paris, I know," Chabot retorted, still trying to control his fury. "I know it. I had the report. That cursed English spy...!" He checked himself; this girl's slightly mocking glance was making a havoc of his nerves.

"The letters, such as they are, are probably destroyed by now," he said as coolly as he could.

"They are not destroyed."

"How do you know?"

Josette shrugged. Would she be here if the letters had been destroyed?

"Why did the woman Croissy run away like a traitor?"

"Her child was sick. It was imperative he should leave Paris for a healthier spot."

"I know. Croissy told me that tale. I didn't then believe a word of it. It was just blackmail, nothing more." Then as Josette was once more silent he reiterated roughly: "Why did the woman Croissy leave Paris in such haste? Why should she have taken the letters with her? You say she did, but I don't believe it."

"Perhaps she was afraid, citizen."

"Afraid of what? Only traitors need be afraid."

"Afraid of. . . . committing suicide like her husband."

This shaft, too, went straight home. Every drop of blood seemed to ebb from the man's face and left it ashen grey. His pale eyes wandered all round in the room as if in search of a hiding-place from that straight accusing glance. For the next minute or two he affected to busy himself with the papers on his desk, whilst the priceless Boule clock on the mantelshelf ticked away several fateful seconds.

Then he said abruptly, with an attempt at unconcern:

"Ah, bah! little woman. You think yourself very shrewd, what? No doubt you have some nice little project of blackmail in that pretty head of yours. But if you really did know all about the letters you speak of so glibly, you would also be aware that I am the man least concerned in them. There are others whose names apparently are unknown to you and who—"

"Their names are not unknown to me, Citizen Representative," Josette broke in with unruffled calm.

"Then why the hell haven't you been to them! Is it because you know less than you pretend?"

"If you, citizen, do not choose to bargain with me, I will certainly go to Citizen Bazire and Fabre d'Eglantine, but in that case—"

At mention of the two names Chabot had given a visible start: a nervous twitching of his lips showed how severely he had been hit. He still tried to bluster by reiterating gruffly:

"In that case?"

"I am treating separately with the writers of each individual letter," Josette said firmly. "Those who do not choose to bargain with me must accept the consequences."

"Which are?"

"Publication of the letters in the *Moniteur*, in *Père Duchesne* and other newspapers. They will make good reading, Citizen Representative."

"You little devil!"

He had jumped to his feet, and with clenched fists resting upon the bureau he leaned across, staring into her face. His pale brown eyes had glints in them now of cold, calculating cruelty. Had he dared he would have seized this weak woman by the throat and torn the life out of her, slowly, brutally, with hellish cunning until she begged for death.

"You devil!" he reiterated savagely. "You forget that I can make you suffer for this."

Josette gave her habitual shrug.

"You certainly can," she said calmly. "You can do the same to me as you did to Maître de Croissy. But not even a second murder will put you in possession of the letters."

Never for a moment had the girl lost her presence of mind. She knew well enough what she risked when she came to beard this hyena in his lair; but it was the only way to save Maurice. She had thought it all out and had deliberately chosen it. Throughout the interview she had remained perfectly calm and self-possessed; and now, when for the first time she had the feeling that she was winning the day, she still remained demure and apparently unmoved. But Chabot was pacing up and down the room like a caged beast, kicking savagely at anything that was in his way.

At one moment it seemed as if he was on the point of giving way to his fury, of being willing to risk everything, even his own neck, for the satisfaction of his revenge. During that fateful moment Josette's life did indeed hang in the balance, for already the man's hand was on the bell-pull. Another second and he was ready to send for his stalwart and to order him to summon the men of the National Guard who were always on duty in the streets outside the dwellings of the Representatives of the People: to summon the guard and order this woman to be thrown into the most noisome prison of the city, where mental and physical torture would punish her for her presumption.

With his hand on the bell-pull Chabot looked round and encountered the cool, unconcerned glance of a pair of eyes as deeply blue as the midnight sky in June, and other thoughts and desires, more foul than the first, distorted his ugly face. Had he read aught in those eyes but contempt and self-confidence the dark spirits that haunted this house of evil would have had their way with him. But it was the girl's evident complete sell-assurance that made him pause. . . . pause long enough to gauge the depth of the abyss into which he would fall if those compromising letters were by some chance given publicity.

He let go of the bell-pull and came back to his place by the bureau. He sat down and, leaning back in his chair, he allowed a minute or two to go by while he regained control over himself. Knitting his bony hands together he twisted them until all the finger-joints cracked. He took a handkerchief from his pocket and wiped the cold sweat from his brow.

Then at last he spoke:

"You said just now, *citizeness*," he rejoined with enforced calm, trying to emulate the girl's self-assurance and her show of contempt, "that when the widow Croissy ran away to England she took certain letters with her. Is that it?"

"Yes. She did."

"How do you know that?"

"She has told me so.... in a letter."

"A letter from England?"

"Yes."

"And that's a lie! How could you get a letter from England? We are at war with that accursed country, and—"

"Do not let us discuss the point, Citizen Representative. Let me assure you that the letters in question are in England: the Citizeness Croissy has not destroyed them—she has told me so. If you agree to my terms I will bring you the letters, otherwise they will be sent to the *Moniteur* and other newspapers for publication. And that," Josette added firmly, "is my last word."

"What are your terms?"

"First, a safe-conduct to enable me to travel to England without molestation—"

Chabot gave a harsh, ironical laugh.

"To travel to England? Fine idea, in very truth! Go to England and stay in England, what? And from thence make long noses at François Chabot, what? who was fool enough to let you hoodwink him!"

"Had you not best listen to me, Citizen Representative, before you jump to conclusions?"

"I listen. Indeed, I am vastly interested in your *naïve* project, my engaging young friend."

"My price for placing letters, which you would give your fortune to possess, in your hands, Citizen, is the liberty and life of one, Maurice Reversac, who was clerk to Maître de Croissy."

Chabot sneered. "Your lover, I suppose."

"What you choose to suppose is nothing to me. I have named my price for the letters."

Chabot, his elbow resting on the table, his chin cupped in his hand, was apparently wrapped in thought. He was contemplating that greatly daring woman who had delivered her ultimatum with no apparent consciousness of her danger. He could silence her, of course: send her to the guillotine, her and her lover, Reversac; but she seemed so sure that he would not do this that her assurance became disconcerting. The same reason which had stayed his and his friends' hands when they discussed the advisability of having Bastien de Croissy summarily arrested held good in this girl's case also. There was always the possibility of her getting a word in during her trial—a word which might prove the undoing of them all. How far was she telling the truth at this moment? How far was she lying in order to save her lover? These were the questions which François Chabot was putting to himself while he contemplated the beautiful woman before him.

And whilst he gazed on her she seemed slowly to vanish from his vision, both she and his luxurious surroundings, the costly furniture, the carpets, all the paraphernalia of his sybaritic life. Instead of this there appeared to his mental consciousness the Place de la Barrière du Trône, with the guillotine towering above a sea of faces. He saw himself mounting the fatal steps; he saw the executioner, the glint on the death-dealing knife, the horrible basket into which great and noble heads had often rolled at his, Chabot's, bidding. He heard the roll of drums ordered by Sauterre, the cries of execration of the mob, the strident laugh of those horrible hags who sat knitting and jabbering while the knife worked up and down, up and down. . . . A hoarse cry nearly escaped him. He passed his bony fingers under his choker for he felt stifled and sick. . .

The vision vanished. The girl was still sitting opposite to him, demure and silent—curse her!—waiting for him to speak. And looking on her he knew that he must have those letters or he would never know a moment's peace again. Once he had them, once he felt entirely safe, he would have his revenge. Let her look to herself, the miserable trollop! She will have brought her fate upon herself.

He said! "I'll give you the safe-conduct. You can start for England today."

"I will start tomorrow," she rejoined coolly. "I still must speak with Citizens Fabre and Bazire."

"I can make that right with them. You need not see them."

"I must have their signatures on the safe-conduct as well as yours, Citizen Chabot."

"You shall have them."

He was searching among the litter on his desk for the paper which he wanted. These men always had forms of safe-conduct made out with blank spaces for the name of a relation or friend who happened to be in trouble and hoped to leave the country before trouble materialised. Chabot found what he wanted. The paper was headed:

"COMMISSARIAT DE POLICE DE LA VIII^{ieme} SECTION DE PARIS."

and

"Laissez passer."

"Your name?" he asked once more.

"Josephine Madeleine Marie Gravier."

And Chabot, with a shaking hand, wrote these names in the blank space left for the purpose.

"Your residence?"

"Forty-Three Rue Picpus."

"Your age?"

"Twenty."

"The colour of your eyes?"

She looked at him and in the blank space he wrote the word "Blue"; and farther on he made note that the hair was burnished copper, her chin small, her teeth even.

When he had filled in all the blank spaces he stewed the writing with sand; then he said, "You can come and fetch this this evening."

"It will be signed?"

"By myself and by Citizens Fabre and Bazire."

"Then I will start tomorrow."

"You have money?"

"Yes, I thank you."

"When do you return?"

"It will take me a week probably to get to England and a week or more to come back. It will be close on three weeks, Citizen Representative, before your mind is set at rest."

He shrugged and sneered:

"And in the meanwhile, your lover—"

"In the meanwhile, citizen," Josette broke in firmly, "See to it that Maurice Reversac is safe and well. If on my return he is not there to greet me, if, in fact, you play me false in any way, it is the *Moniteur* who will have the letters, not you."

Chabot rose slowly from his chair. He stood for a moment quite still beside the desk, his spatulated fingers spread out upon the table-top. All his nervousness, his fury, his excitement seemed suddenly to drop away from him. His ugly face wore an air of cunning, almost of triumph, and there was a hideous leer around his thick lips. He appeared to be watching Josette intently while she rose, shook out her kirtle, smoothed down her *fichu* and straightened her cap. As she turned towards the door he said slowly:

"We shall see!" he added with mock courtesy, "*Au revoir*, little citizeness."

A few minutes later Josette was speeding up the street on her way home.

Chapter 19

Later in the day a meeting took place in the bare white-washed room of the *Club des Cordeliers* between three members of the National Convention—François Chabot, Claude Bazire and Fabre d'Eglantine—and an obscure member of the Committee of Public Safety named Armand Chauvelin. This man had at one time been highly influential in the councils of the revolutionary government; before the declaration of war he had been sent to England as secret envoy of the Republic; but conspicuous and repeated failures in various missions which had been entrusted to him had hopelessly ruined his prestige and hurled him down from his high position to one of almost ignoble dependence.

Many there were who marvelled how it had come to pass that Armand Chauvelin had kept his head on his shoulders: "The Republic," Danton had thundered more than once from the tribune, "has no use for failures." It is to be supposed, therefore, that the man possessed certain qualities which made him useful to those in power: perhaps he was in possession of secrets which would have made his death undesirable. Be that as it may, Chauvelin, dressed in seedy black, his pale face scored with lines of anxiety, his appearance that of a humble servant of these popular Representatives of the People, sat at one end of the deal table, listening with almost obsequious deference to the words of command from the other three.

He only put in a word now and again, for he had been summoned in order to take orders, not to give advice.

"The girl," Chabot said to him, "lives at No. 43 in the Rue Picpus. She will leave Paris tomorrow. You will shadow her from the moment that she leaves the house: never lose sight of her as you value your life. She is going to England; you will follow her. You have been in England before, Citizen Chauvelin," he added with a sarcastic grin, "so I understand, and are acquainted with the English tongue."

"That is so, Citizen Representative."

Chauvelin's eyes were downcast; not one of the three caught the feline gleam of hate that shot through their pale depths.

"Your safe-conduct is all in order. The wench will probably make for Tréport and take boat there for one of the English ports. It is up to you to board the same ship as she does. You must assume what disguise seems most suitable at the time. Our friend here, Fabre d'Eglantine, has been the means of finding you an English safe-conduct which was taken from one of that accursed nation who was trying to cross over our frontier from Belgium: he was an English spy. Our men caught and shot him; his papers remained in their hands: one of these was a safe-conduct signed by the English Minister of Foreign Affairs. Those stupid English don't usually trouble about passports or safe-conducts. They welcome the *émigrés* from France, and often among those traitors one or other of our spies have got through. Still, this document will probably serve you well, and you can easily make up to appear like the description of the original holder. Here are the two passports. Examine them carefully first, then I or one of my friends will give you further instructions."

Chabot handed two papers to Chauvelin across the table. Chauvelin took them, and for the next few minutes was absorbed in a minute examination of them. One bore the signature of Fabre d'Eglantine, who was representative for a section of Paris: it was counter-signed by François Chabot (Seine et loire) and by Claud Bazire (Côte d'Or). The second paper bore the seal of the English Foreign Office and was signed by Lord Grenville himself. It was made out in the name of Malcolm Russel Stone, and described the bearer of the safe-conduct as short and slight, with brown hair and a pale face—a description, in fact, which could apply to twenty men out of a hundred. It had the advantage of not being a forgery, but was a genuine passport issued to an unfortunate Secret Service man since dead. As Chabot had said, the English authorities cared little, if anything, about passports; nevertheless, the present one might prove useful.

Chauvelin folded the two papers and put them in the inside pocket of his coat.

"So far, so good," he said drily. "I await your further instructions, Citizen Representative."

Chabot was the spokesman of the party. He was, perhaps, sunk more deeply than the other two in the morass of treachery and venality which threatened to engulf them all. He it was who had summoned this conference and who had thought of Armand Chauvelin as the man most likely to be useful in this terrible emergency.

"He has a character to redeem," he had said to his friends when first the question was mooted of setting a sleuth-hound on the girl's tracks: "he speaks English, he knows his way about over there—"

"He failed signally," Bazire objected, "over that affair of the English spies."

"You mean the man they call the Scarlet Pimpernel?"

"Yes!"

"Chauvelin has sworn to lay him by the heels."

"But has never succeeded."

"No; but Robespierre tells me that he is the most tenacious tracker of traitors they have on the Committees—a real bloodhound, what!"

Thus, it was that Chauvelin had been called in to confer on the best means of circumventing a simple girl in the fateful undertaking she had in view. Four men to defeat one woman in her purpose! What chance would she have to accomplish it?

"It is on the return journey, my friend," Chabot was saying, "that your work will effectually begin. This wench, Josette Gravier, is going to England for the sole purpose of getting hold of a certain packet of letters—seven in all—which are now in the possession of a woman named Croissy, the widow of the lawyer Croissy who—er—committed suicide a month or so ago. You recollect?"

"I do recollect perfectly," Chauvelin remarked blandly.

Chabot cleared his throat, fidgeted in his usual nervous manner, but took good care not to encounter Chauvelin's quizzical glance.

"Those letters," he said after a moment or two, "were written by me and my two friends here in the strictest confidence to Croissy, who was acting as our lawyer at the time. None of us dreamed that he would turn traitor. Well, he did, and no doubt was subsequently stricken either with remorse or fright, for after threatening us all with the betrayal of our confidence he took his own miserable life."

Chabot paused, apparently highly satisfied with his peroration. Chauvelin, silent and with thin white hands folded in front of him, waited calmly for him to continue. But his pale steely eyes were no longer downcast: their glance, bitterly ironical, was fixed on the speaker, and there was no mistaking the question which that glance implied. "Why do you take the trouble to tell me those lies?" those eyes seemed to ask. No wonder that none of the three blackguards dared to look him straight in the face!

"I think," Chabot resumed after a time with added pompousness, "that I have told you enough to make you appreciate the importance of the task which we propose to entrust to you. My friends and I must regain possession of those confidential letters, but we look to you, Citizen Chauvelin, to put us in possession of them and not to the wench Gravier—you understand?"

"Perfectly."

"She is nothing but a trollop and a baggage who has shamelessly resorted to blackmail in order to save her gallant from justice. She has put a dagger at my throat—at the throat of my two friends here—and her dagger is more deadly than the one with which the traitor Charlotte Corday pierced the noble heart of Marat—"

He would have continued in this eloquent strain had not his brother-in-law, Bazire, put a restraining hand on his shoulder. Armand Chauvelin, with his arms tightly clasped over his chest, his thin legs crossed, his pale eyes looking up at the ceiling, presented a perfect picture of irony and contempt. The others dared not resent this attitude. They had need of this man for the furtherance of their schemes. Revenge was what they were looking for now. The wench had indeed put a dagger to their throats, and for this they were determined to make her suffer; and there was no man alive with such a marvellous capacity for tracking an enemy and bringing him to book as Armand Chauvelin, in spite of the fact that he had failed so signally in bringing the greatest enemy of the revolutionary government to the guillotine.

In this he certainly had failed. Not one of his colleagues, not one of the three who had need of his services now, knew how the recollection of that failure galled him. He was thankful for this mission which would take him to England once more. He had heart-breaking ill luck over his adventures with the Scarlet Pimpernel, but luck might take a turn at any time, and, anyway, he was the only man in his own country who had definitely identified the mysterious hero with that ballroom exquisite Sir Percy Blakeney. Given a modicum of luck it was still on the cards that he, Chauvelin, might yet be even with his arch-enemy whilst he was engaged in dogging the footsteps of Josette Gravier. That wench was just the type of "persecuted innocent" that would appeal to the chivalrous nature of the elusive Sir Percy.

Yes! on the whole Chauvelin felt satisfied with his immediate prospects, and as soon as Chabot had ceased perorating he put a few curt questions to him.

"When does the girl start?" he asked.

"Tomorrow," Chabot replied. "I have told her to call at my house this evening for her safe-conduct."

"It is made out in the name of. . . ?'

"Josephine Gravier."

"Josephine Gravier," Chauvelin iterated slowly; "and the safe-conduct is signed—?"

"By myself, by my friend Fabre and my brother-in-law Claude Bazire."

Chauvelin then rose and said: "That is all I need know for the moment." He paused a moment as if reflecting and then added: "Oh! by the way, I may need a man by me whom I can trust—a man who will give me a hand in an emergency, you understand; who will be discreet and above all obedient."

"I see no objection to that," Chabot said and turned to his colleagues: "do you?"

"No. None," they all agreed.

"Do you know the right sort of man?" one of them asked.

"Yes! Auguste Picard," was Chauvelin's reply: "a sturdy fellow, ready for any adventure. He is attached to the *gendarmerie* of the VIIIth section at the moment, but he can be spared—Picard would suit me well: he is never troubled with unnecessary scruples," he added with a curl of the lip.

"Auguste Picard. Why not?"

They all agreed as to the suitability of Auguste Picard as a satellite to their friend Chauvelin.

"So long as he is told nothing," one of them remarked.

"Why, of course," Chauvelin hastened to reassure them all. He then concluded with complacency: "You may rest assured, my friends, that in less than a month the letters will be in your hands."

Chabot and the others sighed in unison: "The devil speed you, friend Chauvelin." One of them said: "Not one of us will know a moment's peace until your return."

On which note of mutual confidence they parted. Chauvelin went his way; the other three stayed talking for a little while at the club; other members strolled in from time to time, Danton among them. The great man himself was none too easy over this affair of the letters which had been recounted to him by his satellite Fabre d'Eglantine. He was not dead sure whether his own name was mentioned or not in the correspondence between de Batz and Croissy. He had at the time been unpleasantly mixed up in those Austrian intrigues, and it was part of de Batz' game to compromise them and thus bring about the downfall of the revolutionary government and the restoration of the king.

Chabot, Fabre and Bazire were in it up to the neck, but the moment mud-slinging began, any of their friends might get spattered with the slime. Robespierre, the wily jackal, was only waiting for an opportunity to be at Danton's throat, to wrest from him that popularity which for the time being made him the master of the Convention. It would indeed be a strange freak of Destiny if the downfall of the great Danton—the lion of the Revolution—were brought about through the intervention of a woman, a chit of a girl more feeble even than Charlotte Corday, whose dagger had put an end to Marat's career.

"But we can leave all that with safety in Armand Chauvelin's hands," was the sum-total of the confabulation between the four men before they bade one another goodnight.

Chapter 20

The small diligence which had left Les Andelys in the early morning rattled into the courtyard of the Auberge du Cheval Blanc in Rouen soon after seven o'clock in the evening. It had encountered bad weather the whole of the way: torrential rain lashed by gusty north-westerly winds made going difficult for the horses. The roads were fetlock-deep in mud: on the other hand, the load had been light—two passengers in the front compartment and only four in the rear, and very little luggage on top.

In the rear of the coach the four passengers had sat in silence for the greater part of the journey, the grey sky and dreary outlook not being conducive to conversation. The desolation of the country, due to lack of agricultural labour, was apparent even along the fertile stretch of Normandy. The orchard trees were already bare of leaves and bent their boughs to the fury of the blast; their naked branches, weighted with the rain, were stretched out against the wind like the great gaunt arms of skinny old men suffering from rheumatism and doing their best to run away.

Of the two female travellers one looked like the middle-aged wife of some prosperous shopkeeper. She had rings on her fingers and a gold brooch was pinned to her shawl. Her hands were folded above the handle of a wicker basket out of which she extracted, from time to time, miscellaneous provisions with which she regaled herself on the journey. At one moment when the other woman who sat next to her, overcome with sleep, fell up against her shoulder, she drew herself up with obvious disgust and eyed the presumptuous creature up and down with the air of one unaccustomed to any kind of familiarity.

This other woman was Josette Gravier, *en route* for England, all alone, unprotected, ignorant of the country she was going to, of the districts she would have to traverse, of the sea which she had never seen and of which she had a vague dread; but her courage kept up by the determination to get to England, to wrest the letters from Louise de Croissy and, with them in her hand, to force those influential Terrorists into granting life and liberty to Maurice.

It was Josette Gravier who, overcome with sleep, had fallen against the shoulder of her fellow-traveller, but it was a very radically transformed Josette; not disguised, but transformed from the dainty, exquisite apparition she always was into an ugly, dowdy, uncouth-looking girl unlikely to attract the attention of those young gallants who are always ready for an adventure with any pretty woman they might meet on the way. She had dragged her hair out of curl, smeared it with grease till it hung in lankish strands down her cheeks and brows; over it she wore a black cap, frayed and green with age, and this she had tied under her chin with a tired bit of back ribbon. She had rubbed her little nose and held it out to the blast till the tip was blue: she hunched up her shoulders under a tattered shawl and forced her pretty mouth to wear an expression of boredom and discontent.

What she could not hide altogether was the glory of her eyes, but even so she contrived to dim their lustre by appearing to be half asleep the whole of the way. Like the other woman she kept her basket of provisions on her lap, and at different times she munched bits of stale bread and cheese and drank thin-looking wine out of a bottle, after which she passed the back of her hand over her mouth and nose and left marks of grease on her chin and cheeks.

Altogether she looked a most unattractive bit of goods, and this, apparently, was the opinion of the two male travellers who sat opposite, for after a quick survey of their fellow-passengers they each settled down in their respective corners and whiled away the dreary hours of the long day by sleep. They did not carry provisions with them but jumped out of the diligence for refreshments whenever the driver pulled up outside some village hostelry on the way.

At the Auberge du Cheval Blanc in Rouen everyone had to get down. The diligence went no farther, but another would start early the next morning and, in all probability, would reach Tréport in the late afternoon. Josette, like the other travellers, was obliged to go to the *commissariat* of the town for the examination of her papers before she could be allowed to hire a bed for the night. Her safe-conduct was in order, which seemed greatly to astonish the Chief *Commissary*, for he eyed with some curiosity this bedraggled, uncouth female who presented a permit signed by three of the most prominent members of the National Convention.

Laissez passer la citoyenne Josephine Gravier agée de vingt ans de-meurant a Paris Villieme section Rue Picpus No. 43, etc., etc. . . .

It was all in order; the *commissary* countersigned the safe-conduct, affixed the municipal seal to it and handed it back to Josette. She had been the last of the travellers to present her papers at the desk; she took them now from the *commissary* and turned to go out of the narrow stuffy room when a man's voice spoke gently close to her:

"Can I direct you to a respectable hostelry, *citizeness*?"

Josette glanced up and encountered a pair of light-coloured eyes that looked kindly and in no way provokingly at her: they were the eyes of one of her fellow-travellers who had entered the diligence at Les Andelys and had sat in the corner opposite to her, half asleep, taking no notice of anything or anybody. He was a small, thin man with pale cheeks and a sad, or perhaps discontented, expression round his thin lips: his hair was lank and plentifully streaked with grey. He was dressed in seedy black and looked quite insignificant and not at all the kind of man to scare a girl who was travelling alone.

Josette thanked him for his kindness:

"I have engaged a bed at the Cheval Blanc," she said, "which I am assured is a model of respectability: I shall be sharing a room with some of the maids at the hostelry, and the charge for this accommodation is not high. All the same," she added politely, "I thank you, sir, for your kind offer."

She was about to turn away when he spoke again:

"I am journeying to England, and if I can be of service there I pray you to command me."

It did not occur to Josette at the moment to wonder how this stranger came to know that she was journeying to England, but she could not help asking him who he was and why he should trouble about her.

"Before the war," he replied, "my business used often to take me to England and I was able to master its difficult language. Now, alas! my business is at an end, but I have friends over the water and, like yourself, I was lucky enough to obtain a permit to visit them."

Once more Josette thanked him: he seemed so very kind; but at the outset of her journey she had made up her mind very firmly not to enter into conversation with anyone, not to trust anyone, least of all one of her own nationality. She had no idea as yet of the difficulties which she might encounter when she landed in a strange country. Indeed, she had undertaken this journey without any thought of possible failure, but wariness and discretion were the rules of conduct which she had imposed on herself and to which she was determined to adhere rigidly. Having thanked her amiable friend, she bade him goodnight and hastened back to the hostelry.

She didn't see him again on the following morning when she took ticket for the diligence that was to take her to Tréport. An altogether different set of people were her fellow-travellers on this stage of her journey: they were a noisy crowd—three men and two women besides herself in the rear compartment of the coach; so they were rather crowded and jammed up against one another. Josette, being small and unobtrusive, was pushed into a corner by the other women, who were large and stout and took up a lot of room.

Talk was incessant, chiefly on the recent incidents at Nantes. Carrier, the abominable butcher, had been recalled, but his successors had carried on his infamous work. The war in the Vendée had drawn to its close: those who took part in it fell victims to their loyalty to the throne; their wives and children were murdered wholesale. Travellers who had come from those parts spoke of this with bated breath. Only a few had escaped butchery, and this through the agency of some English spies—so 'twas said—whose activities throughout Brittany had baffled the revolutionary government. One man especially, who went, it seems, by the strange name of a small scarlet flower, had been instrumental in effecting the escape of a number of women and children out of the plague-ridden prisons of Nantes, where such numbers of them died of disease and inanition even while the guillotine was being prepared for them.

Josette, huddled up in the corner of the compartment, listened to these tales with a beating heart. Ever since she had started on this fateful journey she had wondered in her mind whether somewhere or other, in a moment of distress or difficulty, she would suddenly find that unseen hand was there to succour or to help, whether she would hear a comforting voice to cheer her on her way, or catch unexpectedly a glance from eyes that, whilst revealing nothing to the uninitiated, would convey a world of meaning to her.

Now the tales that she heard dispelled any such hope. Women and children in greater distress than herself were claiming the aid and time of the gallant Scarlet Pimpernel. It was sad and terribly disappointing that she would not see him as she had so confidently hoped. Only in her dreams would she see him as she had done hitherto. The rumble of the coach-wheels, the heavy atmosphere made her drowsy: she shrank farther still into her corner and slept and dreamed; she dreamed of the gallant English hero and also of Maurice—Maurice who was so unselfish, so self-effacing, who was suffering somewhere in a dingy prison, pining for his little friend Josette, wondering, perhaps, what had become of her, and eating his heart out with anxiety on her account. And somehow in her dream Josette saw the English hero less clearly than she used to do; his imaginary face and form slowly faded and grew dim and were presently merged in the presentment of Maurice Reversac, who looked sad and ill—so sad and ill that Josette's heart ached for him in her sleep, and that her lips murmured his name "Maurice!" with exquisite longing and tenderness.

Chapter 21

Whenever Josette's thoughts in after years reverted to her memorable journey to England, she never felt that it had been real. It was all so like a dream: her start from Paris in the early morning; the diligence; the first halt at the barrier; the examination of the passports; and then the incessant rumble of wheels, the rain beating against the windows, the gusts of wind, the atmosphere reeking of stale provisions, of damp cloth and of leather; the murmur of voices; the halts outside village hostelries; the nights in the *auberge* at Meulan and Les Andelys, at Rouen and Tréport; and her fellow-travellers.

They were nothing but dream figures, and it was only when she closed her eyes very tight that Josette could vaguely recall their faces: the prosperous shopman's wife with her rings and her gold brooch and her wicker basket; the crowd in the diligence between Rouen and Tréport who chattered incessantly about the English spy and the horrors of Nantes; her neighbour, who squeezed her into a corner until she could hardly breathe; and then the small, thin man—he, surely, was nothing but a figure in a dream!

Dreams, dreams! they must all have been dreams! All those events, those happenings which memory had never properly recorded, they were surely only dreams; and all the way across the Channel she sat as in a dream: she saw other travellers being very seasick, and there was, indeed, a nasty gale blowing from the south-west, but it was a favourable wind for the packet-boat to Dover and she made excellent going, whilst to Josette the fresh sea air, the excitement of seeing the white cliffs of England looming out of the mist, the sense of contentment that she was nearing the end of her journey and that her efforts on behalf of Maurice would surely be crowned with success were all most welcome after the stuffiness and dreariness of those days passed in the diligence.

And how bright and lovely England seemed to her! It was indeed a dream world into which she had drifted. People looked happy and free! Yes, free! There was no look of furtiveness or terror on their faces; even children had shoes and stockings on their feet, and not one of them had that look of disease and hunger so prevalent—alas!—in revolutionary France. Peace and contentment reigned everywhere; ay! in spite of the war-clouds that hung over the land. And Josette's heart ached when she thought of her own beautiful country, her beloved France, which was all the more dear to all her children for the terrible time she was going through.

Poor little Josette! She felt very forlorn and very much alone when she stood on the quay at Dover with her modest little bundle and her wicker basket which contained all her worldly possessions. For the first time she realised the magnitude of the task which she had imposed on herself when all around her people talked and talked and she could not understand one word that was said. Never before had she been outside France, never before had she heard a language other than her native one. She felt as if she had been dropped down from somewhere into another world and knew not yet what would become of her, a stranger among its *denizens*. Frightened? Only a little, perhaps, was she frightened, but firm, nevertheless, in her resolve to succeed. But what had seemed like such a simple proposition in Paris looked distinctly complicated now.

She was forlorn and alone—and all round her people bustled and jostled; not that anyone was unkind—far from it—they but were all of them busy coming and going, collecting luggage, meeting friends, asking for information. She, Josette, was the only one who, perforce, was tongue-tied—a pathetic little figure in short kirtle, shawl and frayed-out black cap, with lanky hair and a red nose and a smear across one cheek, for much against her will tears would insist on coming to her eyes and they made the smear when they would roll down her face.

The crowd presently thinned out a bit: Josette could see these or those fellow-passengers hurrying hither or thither, either followed by a porter carrying luggage or shouldering their own valise. They all seemed to know where they were going; she alone was doubtful and ignorant. Indeed, she had never thought it would be as bad as this.

And suddenly a kind voice reached her ear:

"Can I be of service now, *Mademoiselle?* We all have to report at the constable's office, you know."

Just for the moment it seemed to Josette as if *le bon Dieu* had just taken pity on her and sent one of His angels to look after her. And yet it was only the thin little man in seedy black who had spoken, and there was nothing angelic about him. He had his papers in his hand and quite instinctively she took hers out from inside her bodice and gave them to him.

"Will you come with me, *Mademoiselle,*" he went on to say, "in case there is a little difficulty about your safe-conduct being entirely made out by the French Government, with which the English are at war! They welcome the *émigrés* as a matter of course; still, there might be a little trouble. But if you will come with me I feel sure I can see you through."

Josette gave him a look of trust and of gratitude out of her blue eyes. How could she help fancying that here was one of those English heroes of whom she had always dreamed and who were known in the remotest corners of France as angels of rescue to those unfortunates who were forced to flee from their own country and take refuge in hospitable England? Dreams! dreams! Could Josette Gravier be blamed for thinking that here were her dreams coming true? When she felt miserable, helpless and forlorn, a hand was suddenly stretched out to help her over her difficulties. Of course, she did not think that this pale-faced little man was the hero of her dreams—she had always thought of the Scarlet Pimpernel as magnificently tall and superbly handsome; but then she had also thought of him as mysterious and endowed with mystic powers that enabled him to assume any kind of personality at will.

There was enough talk about him among the girls in the government workshops: how he had driven through the barriers of Paris disguised as an old hag in charge of a refuse-cart in which the Marquis de Tournay and his family lay hidden: and there were other tales more wonderful still. Then why could he not diminish his stature and become a pale-faced little man who spoke both English and French and conducted her, Josette, to an office where he exhibited an English passport which evidently satisfied the official in charge not only as to his own identity, but also as to that of the girl with him?

Who but a hero of romance would have the power so to protect the weak as to smooth out every difficulty that beset Josette Gravier's path after her landing in England, from the finding her a respectably hostelry where she could spend the night to guiding her the next morning to the *Bureau des émigrés Français* in Dover, where he obtained for her all the information she wanted about her beloved Louise? Louise, indeed, lived and worked not very far from Dover, in a town called Maidstone, to which a public coach plied that very day. And into this coach did Josette Gravier step presently in the company of her new guardian angel, the thin-faced, pale-eyed little man with the soft voice, whose mysterious hints and utterances, now that she fell into more intimate conversation with him, clearly indicated that if he was not actually the Scarlet Pimpernel himself, he was, at any rate, very closely connected with him.

Chapter 22

Louise de Croissy was sitting in the bow-window of the small house in Milsom Street in the city of Maidstone when, looking up from her embroidery frame, she saw Josette Gravier coming down the street in the company of a little man in black who was evidently pointing out the way to her. Louise gave one cry of amazement, jumped up from her chair, and in less than half a minute was out in the street, with arms outstretched and a cry of "Josette! My darling one!" on her lips.

The next moment Josette was in her arms.

"Josette! My little Josette! I am not dreaming, am I? It really is you?"

But Josette, overcome with fatigue and emotion, could not yet speak. She let Louise lead her to the house. She appeared half-dazed; but when they came to the door she turned to look for the guiding angel who had brought her safely within sight of her beloved Louise. All she could see of him was his back in the seedy black coat a hundred yards away, hurrying down the street.

Louise was devoured with curiosity; question after question tumbled out of her mouth.

"Josette *chérie*, how did you come? And all alone? And who was that funny little man in black? What made you come? Why, why didn't you let me know?"

Josette had sunk into the armchair which Louise had dragged for her beside the fire—a lovely fire glowing with coal, the flames dancing as if with joy and putting life and warmth into the girl's stiffened limbs. And Louise, kneeling beside her, holding her little cold hands, went on excitedly:

"Of course, you mustn't talk now, *chérie*, and you must not heed my silly questions. But imagine my amazement! I thought I was dreaming. I had been thinking of you, too, all these days. . . . and to think of you here and now. . . . What will Charles-Léon say when he sees you?. . . . He is getting so strong and well and—"

Then she jumped to her feet, struck her forehead with her hand and exclaimed:

"But what a fool I am to keep on chattering when you are so weary and cold, my darling!. . . . Just wait a few minutes and close your eyes and I will get you some lovely hot tea. Everyone here in England drinks tea in the afternoon. . . . At first, I couldn't get used to it. . . . I hadn't drunk tea for years, and then not often—only when I had a headache. . . . but I soon got the way of it. . . . No, no! I won't chatter any more. . . . Just sit still, *chérie*, and I'll bring you something you'll like."

She trotted off, eager, excited and longing desperately to hear how Josette had come to travel alone all the way to England; through the instrumentality of that marvellous Scarlet Pimpernel, she decided within herself; and her active brain worked round and round, conjecturing, imagining all sorts of possibilities. "I wonder what has become of poor Maurice Reversac?" she mused at one moment.

She delighted on preparing the tea for Josette and prided herself in the way she made it—one spoonful of tea for each cup and one for the pot—and in the English way of making toast with butter on it. How Josette will love that! Darling, darling Josette! Life from now on would be just perfect; no more loneliness; no more anxiety for Charles-Léon. The angel of the house was present once more.

And in the little sitting-room, ensconced in the big winged chair, Josette Gravier sat with eyes closed, still living in her dream. Was it not marvellous how *le bon Dieu* had brought her safely to Louise; The events of her journey passed before her mental vision like a kaleidoscope of many shapes and colours. It seemed almost impossible to realise that all these things had truly happened to her, Josette Gravier, and that she was really here in England instead of in the dingy Rue

Picpus or stitching away at the government workshops. And thoughts of the workshop brought back a vision of Maurice, and terror gripped her heart because of what might be happening to him—terror, and then a great feeling of joy because she remembered what she was able to do for him. Maurice to her had become as a child, as Charles-Léon was to Louise, a being dependent on her for love and, in a sense, for protection.

It was a wonderful thing, in very truth, to be sitting in a large, comfortable easy-chair beside a lovely fire here in England, and to be drinking tea and eating *pain grillé* with delicious butter on it; and, above all, to have Louise sitting beside her and watching her with loving eyes whilst she ate and drank. Tea was lovely! Like Louise, she had not tasted it for years; it was a luxury unknown in France these terrible times, and even in the happy olden days in the farm by the Isère or in the convent school of the Visitation Josette had only been given tea when she had a headache.

After a little while she felt wonderfully comforted; she knew that Louise was consumed with curiosity and, in all conscience, she could not delay satisfying her.

"Can you not guess why I am here, Louise?" she asked abruptly.

"Of course, I can, *chérie!*" Louise replied. "You came to England for the same reason that I did—to get away from those abominable murderers."

But Josette shook her head.

"Should I have run away," she asked, "and left Maurice out there alone?"

"I don't understand, *chérie*. Where is Maurice?"

"In prison."

"In—?"

"He was arrested two days before I left Paris."

"But on what grounds?"

Josette gave a sigh and a shrug; she stared dreamily into the fire.

"Does one ever know?" she murmured, and then added: "I suppose that Maurice's connection with Bastien disturbed the complacency of some of those devils. They didn't know how much he knew—about those letters."

"The letters?"

"Yes—the letters. You have still got them, Louise?"

"Of course."

A deep sigh of relief came from little Josette's anxious heart. She turned her large, luminous eyes on her friend.

"That is why I came to England, *chérie*—to fetch those letters."

"Josette!" Louise exclaimed, "what do you mean?"

"Just that. Maurice has been arrested—you know what that means: a week or a fortnight in some dank prison, then the mockery of a trial, and, finally, the guillotine—"

"But—"

". . . so *le bon Dieu* inspired me and gave me courage. I thought of the letters. In order to try and get hold of them, men like Chabot and Fabre went to the length of murder. Fortunately, you had taken them away with you. I thought and thought until I remembered the names of those black-guards who had written them and who had murdered Bastien. Then I went to call on them."

"You—my little timid Josette?"

"Yes. I went and I was no longer timid. I went, first of all, to that horrible man Chabot. I told him that those compromising letters of his were still in existence and that I knew where they were. Then I proposed by bargain: complete immunity for Maurice with a safe-conduct to enable him to leave France as soon as I had retrieved the letters and placed them in the hands of their writers."

"You did that, Josette?"

"I did it for Maurice."

"But that was just the bargain which my poor Bastien proposed to those same men, and in consequence of it—"

". . . they murdered him in cold blood. I know that."

"Then how could you—?"

"I ran that risk, I know," Josette replied calmly; "but I also knew by then that possession of those letters had become a question of life and death to those assassins. I threatened them with the immediate publication of the letters in the *Moniteur* if anything happened to Maurice or to me. They didn't know where the letters were; all I told them was that they were in England and that you had kept them. Anyway, they gave me a safe-conduct to go to England and come back. And here I am, my Louise, and if you will give me the letters I will start on my journey back the day after tomorrow."

Louise made no immediate reply: she was staring at her little friend—the frail, modest girl who all alone and sustained only by her own courage had undertaken such a dangerous task for the sake of the man she loved. For, in truth, Louise was forced to the conclusion that Josette's heart, unbeknown to herself, had been touched at last by

Maurice Reversac's devotion. Only a woman in love could accomplish what Josette Gravier had done, could so calmly face difficulties and dangers and be ready to face them again without rest or respite. Neither did Josette speak; she was once more staring into the fire, and the dancing flames showed her visions of Maurice suffering in prison and longing for her.

"Josette darling," Louise said after a time, "you cannot possibly start on another long journey just yet."

"Why not?"

"You must have a few days' rest. You are so tired—"

Josette gave a slight shrug.

"Oh!—tired—"

"I cannot imagine how you ever found me—I mean, so quickly. Did you go to London?"

"No, I didn't have to."

"Then, how—?"

"A kind friend helped me."

"A friend? Who was it?"

"I don't know. He was a fellow-passenger first in the diligence and then on board ship."

"A stranger?"

"Why, yes! but you cannot imagine how kind he was. When I landed on the quay at Dover I felt terribly lonely and helpless; indeed, I don't know what was to become of me. Everything was horribly strange, and then I couldn't understand a word anyone said—"

"I know. I felt just like that at first, although, of course, I was in the hands of friends. I told you—in my letter—"

"I thought of you, Louise, and of the wonderful friends who were looking after you. What were they like, darling?"

"It is not easy to describe people, and I was terribly over-wrought at the time, but the two friends whom we met in the cottage on the cliffs and who took us across the sea in that beautiful ship were good-looking young English gentlemen. One was fair, the other had brown hair, and—"

"Was not one of them quite small and thin, with a very pale face and light-coloured eyes—?"

"No, dear, nothing like that."

"That was what my friend looked like. He spoke to me first at Rouen, and then again at Dover when I felt so lost I didn't know what to do. He took me to a nice hostelry where I could hire a bed

213

for the night. Then the next morning he went with me to the *Bureau des émigrés*, where they spoke French and where they looked up your name and told me where to find you. After that we took the coach for this town. My thin friend with the pale face arranged everything, and when we arrived in this city he walked through the streets with me to show me where you lived; and then—and then, while I ran to embrace you, darling, he hurried away. But I hope and pray that I may meet him again so that I can thank him properly for all the help he gave me."

"Do you think you will?"

"I think so. He told me that he would be in Dover for a couple of days and that a packet-boat would be leaving for Tréport on Thursday at two o'clock in the afternoon. That is the day after tomorrow. He said he would look out for me on the quay. So you see—"

"Josette darling," Louise exclaimed impulsively, "you must be wary of strangers!"

"But of course, Louise, I am wary—very wary. Whenever I spent the night in a hostelry, although I really had enough money to pay for a private room, I always chose to share one with other women or girls. I wouldn't sleep alone in a strange room for anything, although I did so long for privacy sometimes. But if you saw that insignificant little man, Louise, you would know that I had nothing to fear from him."

"I wonder who he is?"

"Sometimes I think—" Josette murmured.

"What, darling?"

"Oh, you will only laugh!"

"Not I. And I know what you were going to say."

"What?"

"That you think he has some connection with the Scarlet Pimpernel."

"Well, don't you?"

"I don't know, dear. You see the members of the League of the Scarlet Pimpernel with whom I came in contact were all English."

"My thin friend with the pale face might be a French member of the League. How otherwise can you explain his kindness to me?"

"I cannot explain it, *chérie*. Everything that happened to me was so wonderful that I am ready to accept all your theories of the super-natural powers of the mysterious Scarlet Pimpernel. But now, darling, we have chatted quite long enough. You are tired and you must have a rest. After that we'll have supper and you shall go to bed early, if you must leave me again so soon—"

"I must Louise, I must. And you understand, don't you?"

"I suppose I do; but it will break my heart to part from you again."

"I have to think of Maurice," Josette said softly.

"You love him, Josette?"

"I don't know," the girl replied with a sigh. "At one time I thought that my heart and soul belonged to the mysterious hero whom perhaps I would never see; but since Maurice has been in danger I have realised—"

"What, *chérie?*"

"That he is dear, very dear to me."

Chapter 23

It seemed so strange to be back in France once more, to hear again one's own tongue spoken and to understand everything that was said.

Josette, standing in the queue outside the *Commissariat de Police* at Rouen with the same little bundle and the same wicker basket in her hand, waiting to have her safe-conduct examined and stamped, was a very different person to the forlorn young creature who had felt so bewildered and so terribly lonely at Dover.

She had had two very happy days with Louise. Her arrival, her first sight of the beloved friend had been unalloyed joy; sitting by a cosy fire with Louise quite close to her and holding her hand brought back memories of the happiest days of her childhood. Then there was Charles-Léon looking so bright and bonny, with colour in his cheeks and all his pathetic listlessness gone. In a way, Josette had not altogether liked England; the grey clouds, the misty damp atmosphere were so unlike the brilliant blue skies of France and the sparkling clear air of her native Dauphiné that went to the head like wine; but, then, that atmosphere was pure and wholesome, Charles-Léon's bright eyes testified to that: he no longer suffered from the poisonous air of Pairs; and Louise, even in this short time, seemed to have recovered the elasticity of youth.

Yes! it had been a happy, a very happy time, brightened still further by thoughts of what she, Josette, was doing for Maurice. On the very first evening Louise had given her the sealed packet containing the precious letters: the precious, precious packet which would purchase Maurice's life and liberty. Josette turned it over and over in her hands and gazed down on the seals and on the wrapper as if her eyes could pierce them.

"What are you looking at so intently, darling?" Louise asked with a smile.

"I didn't recognise the seals," Josette replied.

"It must be the one that Bastien used at the office. I never looked closely at the impress before."

"You've never opened the packet?"

"Never. And it never left me since the moment I left our apartment."

"You had it inside your corsets?"

"In the big pocket inside my skirt; and at night I always slipped it under my pillow, or under whatever happened to be my pillow."

"That is what I will do, of course."

"Only once," Louise resumed after a moment or two, "I had a bad scare: one of the last days of our journey. We had reached the desolate region of the Artois and I was terribly, terribly tired. I remembered that the night before I had slipped the letters into my pocket as usual, nevertheless, when we halted the next day and the driver helped me out of the cart, I felt for the packet and imagine my horror when I found it was gone! A wild panic seized me: I don't know why, but I just turned ready to run away. I was suddenly convinced that I had been lured to this lonely spot for the sake of the letters and that Charles-Léon and I would now be murdered. However, I hadn't gone far when the kindest voice imaginable, accompanied by a delicious soft laugh, called me back and, my dear Josette, imagine my joy and surprise when I saw our driver coolly holding the packet out to me!"

"The driver?"

"Yes! I will leave you to guess who he was, just as I did."

They talked by the fire half the day and late into the night, dreaming dreams of happy times to come when that awful revolutionary government would be forced to give way to a spirit of good-will, charity and order—the true birth-right of the French nation. Indeed, it had all been a very happy time, and those two days at Maidstone went by like a dream. And now Josette was back, in France, on the last stage but one, of her journey to Paris. Within three, at most four days, Maurice would be free, and together they would come out to this fair land of England, for it would not be safe to remain in France any longer.

Here they would wait for the happy days that were sure to come: Maurice would find work to do, for he was clever and brave, and he would surely earn enough to support himself; then, just as they had always done in Pairs, they would wander together in the English woods, those lovely woods about Maidstone of which Josette had had a passing glimpse. In a few short months spring would come and the birds in England, just like those in France, would all be nesting, and under the trees the ground would be carpeted with snowdrops and anemones just as it was at Fontainebleau.

And if Maurice's heart was still unchanged, if the same words of love came to his lips which he had spoken before that awful tragedy had darkened both their lives, then she, Josette, would no longer laugh at him. She would listen silently and reverently to an avowal which she knew now would give her infinite happiness; and she would say "Yes!" to his request that she should become his wife, and together they would steal away in the very early morning to some little English church, and here before God's altar they would swear love and fealty to one another.

Dreams, dreams, which now of a surety would soon become a glowing reality; and all the way since she had left Maidstone in the coach and after she had cried her fill over parting from Louise, Josette had thoughts only of Maurice; and now and then her little hand went up to her bosom, where inside her corsets rested that precious packet; whereupon a look of real joy would gleam out of her eyes, and not even the devices wherewith she had contrived to make her pretty face seem almost ugly could altogether mar its beauty then.

Chapter 24

The little man with the pale sad face whom Josette looked on as a friend had been most kind and helpful at Dover. He had met Josette on the quay, helped her with her safe-conduct, saw her on the boat for Tréport, and promised that he would meet her again on the journey, probably at Rouen; he himself was bound for Calais, but he would be posting from there to Rouen, and if he was lucky he would get the diligence there for Paris.

Many a time during the next forty-eight hours had Josette longed for his company, not so much because she was lonely, but because the whole way from Dover she had been somewhat worried with the attentions of a stranger, and those attentions had filled her with vague mistrust. She had first caught sight of him on the packet-boat, striding up and down the deck with a swaggering, rolling gait. He was clad like a sailor and ogled all the women as he strode past them—Josette especially—and when he caught a woman's eye a hideous squint further disfigured his ugly face. Somehow, she had felt uncomfortable under his glance. Then at Tréport he had seemed to keep an eye on her, and when she boarded the diligence he took a seat in the same compartment and sat opposite to her. He certainly did not molest her in any way, but she felt all the time conscious of his presence.

He was very big and fat and entered into conversation with any of the other passengers who were willing to listen to him, telling tall sea yarns and expatiating on his own prowess in various adventures of which, according to his own showing, he was the hero. Oddly enough, he was a native of Nantes—so he informed one of his fellow-travellers—and had been in port there quite recently. Josette, at this, pricked up her ears, and, sure enough, the sailor had something to say about those English spies and their activity in helping *aristos* and other traitors to evade justice.

"Citizen Carrier," the man had gone on with a dry laugh which revealed some ugly gaps between his teeth, "grows livid with rage at the bare mention of English spies, and lashes about him with a horse-whip like an infuriated tiger with its tail. Only the other day—"

And there followed a long and involved story of how a whole family of *aristos*—an old man and his grandchildren—were spirited away out of the prison of Le Bouffay, how and when nobody ever knew; and Carrier was in such a rage that he had an epileptic fit on the spot. To all this Josette listened eagerly; but all the same she couldn't bear that ugly fat sailor and was vaguely afraid of him.

Josette felt quite happy and relieved when at Rouen she caught sight once more of her pale-faced little friend. She had been lucky enough to fall in on the way with two pleasant women—a mother and daughter—who were ready to share a room with her in the Traverne du Cheval Blanc, and thither the three women repaired after the necessary visit at the *commissariat*. It was here that Josette saw her friend again. He was standing in the little hall talking to a rough-looking fellow to whom he appeared to be giving instructions.

When he encountered Josette's glance, he gave her a nod and an encouraging smile.

Josette and the two women went into the public dining-room, where several of the smaller tables were already occupied. In the centre of the room there was one long table, and round it two people were sitting, waiting for supper to be served. They were for the most part a rough-looking crowd of men who were making a good deal of noise. The three women, however, were fortunate enough to find an unoccupied small table in a quiet corner where they could have their meal in comfort.

From where Josette sat she could see the door and watch the people coming in and going out. Two diligences had arrived in Rouen within the hour: the one from Tréport and the other from Paris, and a great number of weary and hungry travellers trooped into the public room, demanding supper. The big fat sailor was among these, and Josette was thankful that there was no seat available at her own table, for already she had seen the glance wherewith he had sought to catch her eye, and she had felt quite a cold wave of dread creep down her spine at sight of that ugly face with the leer and the hideous squint.

However, after that first searching glance round the room the fat sailor took no more notice of her; he lolled up to the centre table and sat down. He ate a hearty supper and continued to regale the rest of the company with his ridiculous tall yarns.

Half-way through supper Josette had the joy of seeing her small, pale-faced friend come into the room. He, too, gave a searching glance all round the room, and when he caught sight of Josette he gave her another of his pleasant smiles. Somehow at sight of him she felt comforted. Later on, she could not help noticing with what deference everyone at the Cheval Blanc had welcomed the insignificant-looking little man. The landlord, his wife and daughter all came bustling into the room and, in a trice, had prepared and laid a separate table for him in a corner by the hearth. Though the *table d'hôte* supper was practically over by then, they brought him steaming hot soup and after that what was obviously a specially prepared dish. Some of the travellers remarked on this and whispered among themselves, but quite unconsciously, no doubt, the deference shown by the landlord and his family communicated itself to them, and the rowdy hilarity of a while ago gave place to more sober and less noisy conversation.

Only the fat sailor tried for a time to foist his impossible tales on the company, but as no one appeared eager now to listen to him he subsided presently and remained silent and sulky, squinting at the new-coming and moodily picking his teeth. Josette could not help watching him—he was so very ugly and so very large, with his great loose paunch pressed against the table and the hideous black gaps in his mouth; and then those eyes which seemed to be looking both ways at once, one across the other and in no particular direction.

Presently he rose. Josette could not help watching him. She saw him pick up the pepper-pot and toy with it for a moment or two; then, with it in his hand, he lolled across to where Josette's little friend was quietly eating his supper. The latter didn't look up; continued to eat, even while that impudent sailor man stood looking down on him for a moment or two. On the part of a person of consideration this indifference would have seemed strange in the olden days, but now when mudlarks such as this ugly sailor were the virtual rulers of France it was never safe to resent their familiarity or even their impertinence.

The next moment, with slow deliberation, the sailor put the pepper-pot down in front of the stranger, and Josette saw her friend's pale eyes travel upwards from the pepper-pot to the ugly face leering down on him, and she could have sworn that he gave a start and that his thin hands were suddenly clenched convulsively round his knife and fork; also, that his pale cheeks took on a kind of grey, ashen hue. No one apparently noticed any of this except Josette, who was watching the two men. She could only see the broad back of the sailor, saw him give a shrug and heard something like a mocking laugh ring across the room.

A second or two later the sailor had lolled out of the door, and Josette might have thought she had imagined the whole scene but for the expression on her little friend's face. It still looked ghastly, and suddenly he put down his knife and fork and strode very quickly out of the room. What happened after that she didn't know, as her friend did not come back to finish his supper, and very soon the two women who were sharing a room with her gave the signal to go upstairs to bed.

The room which the three of them had secured for the night was at the top of the house under the roof. There were two beds in it: a large one in the far corner of the room which the mother and daughter claimed for themselves and a very small truckle bed for Josette which stood across the embrasure of the dormer window between it and the door. Josette, as was her wont, took the precaution of placing the precious packet of letters underneath her pillow; having said her prayers she slid between the coarse sheets and composed herself for sleep. Her room companions, who had the one and only candle by the side of their bed, soon put the light out, and presently their even breathing proclaimed that they had already travelled far in the land of Nod.

At first it seemed pitch-dark in the room, for outside the weather was rough and no light whatever came through the dormer window; but presently a tiny gleam became apparent underneath the door. It came from the lamp which was kept alight all night in the vestibule down below for the convenience of belated travellers. Josette welcomed the little gleam; her eyes soon became accustomed to what had become semi-gloom; she felt secure and comforted, and after a few minutes she, too, was fast asleep.

What woke her so suddenly she did not know, but wake she did, and for a while she lay quite still, with eyes wide open, her heart pounding away inside her and her hand seeking the precious packet underneath her pillow. At the far end of the room the two women were obviously asleep: one of them snoring lustily. And suddenly Josette perceived that the narrow streak of light under the door had considerably widened and had become triangular in shape; indeed, it was widening even now; she also perceived that there was now an upright shaft of light which also widened and widened as slowly, very slowly, the door swung open.

Josette in an instant sat straight up in bed and gave a cry which roused her roommates out of their sleep. From where they lay they couldn't see the door, but they called out: "What is it?"

"The door!" Josette gasped in a hoarse whisper, and then, "The light! the light!"

The women had a tinder-box on a chair near their bed: they fumbled for it whilst Josette's wide, terror-filled eyes remained fixed on the door. It was half-open now, but by whose hand? impossible to say, for there was no one to be seen. But it seemed to Josette's terrified senses as if she heard a furtive footstep making its way across the narrow landing and down the rickety stairs.

The older woman from her bed asked rather crossly:

"What is it frightened you, little *citizeness*?"

Her daughter was still trying to get a light from the tinder-box, which, as was very usual these days, refused to work.

Josette gave a gasp and murmured under her breath: "The door. . . someone opened it. . . . I heard—"

"Did you see anyone?"

"I don't know. . . . but the door is open and I heard—"

"The latch didn't go home," the woman said more testily. "That's what it was. I noticed last night it didn't look very safe. The draught blew the door open—"

She settled herself back on her pillow. Her daughter gave up trying to get a light and said as testily as her mother:

"Go and shut it, *citizeness*; put a chair to hold it if you are frightened and let's get to sleep again."

For a few moments after that Josette remained silent, sitting up in bed, staring at the door. Some evil-doer, she was sure, had tried it and perhaps, scared by her cry and by the women talking, had slunk away again. Certainly, there was no one behind the door now. For a time, it remained half-open just as it was and then it swayed gently in the draught and creaked on its rusty hinges. The two women had already turned over and were snoring peaceably once more.

What could Josette do but chide herself for her fears? But impossible, of course, to go to sleep again with one's nerves on edge and that door swinging and creaking all the time; so, Josette crept out of bed and tiptoed across the floor with the intention of closing the door. She moved about as softly as she could so as not to wake the others again. With her hand on the latch she ventured to peep out on the landing. The feeble glimmer emitted by the lamp down below cast a dim yellowish light up the well of the stairs.

The house appeared very still, save for the sounds of the stertorous breathings which came from one or other of the rooms on the various floors where tired travellers were sleeping. Outside a dog barked. Josette listened for a moment or two for that furtive footstep which she had heard before, but everything appeared perfectly peaceful and very still. She closed the door very gently and then she groped for a chair to prop against it, when suddenly there came a loud bang right behind her and a terrific current of air swept across the room; the door was once more torn open, quite wide this time, and continued to rattle and to creak. The chair fell out of Josette's hand and she remained standing in her shift, shivering with cold and fright, with her kirtle flapping about her bare legs and her hair blowing into her eyes. The women woke and grumbled, asked with obvious irritation why the *citizeness* didn't go to bed and let others sleep in peace.

Josette's heart was beating so fast that she could neither speak nor move; the weather outside was fairly rough and the draught took her breath away.

"Close the window!" the younger woman shouted to Josette. "The wind has blown it open."

At last Josette was able to get her bearings; she turned to the window and saw that in effect it was wide open and that wind and rain were beating in. She had to climb over her bed in order to get to the window and to secure it.

"I call it sheer robbery," the older woman muttered, half-asleep, "to put honest women in such a ramshackle hole."

But neither she nor her daughter offered to lend a hand to Josette, who, buffeted by the rough weather, had great difficulty in fastening the window. When she had done that she had to climb over her bed again in order to close the door; thus, several minutes went by before peace reigned once more in the attic room. Josette crept back to bed. Her first thought was for the precious packet: she slid her hand under the pillow to feel for it, but the packet was no longer there.

With an agonising sinking of the heart, in a state not so much of panic as of despair, she turned and ran just as she was in shift and kirtle without stockings or shoes out of the room and down the stairs, crying: "Thief! thief! thief!" She reached the bottom of the stairs without meeting anyone: she ran across the passage and the vestibule to the front door, tried to open it, but it was locked and bolted. She tore at the handle and at the bolts, still calling wildly: "Thief! thief!" in a voice broken by sobs.

Gradually the whole house was aroused. Doors were heard to open, testy voices wanted to know what all this noise was about. The night watchman came out of the public room, blinking his eyes. Mine host came along from his room down the passage, cursing and swearing at all this disturbance.

"Name of a name! Who is the miscreant who dares to disturb the peace of this highly respectable hostelry?"

Then he caught sight of Josette, who was still fumbling with the door and crying, "Thief! thief!" in a tear-choked voice. Her bare arms and her shoulders were wet, her clothes were wet, her wet hair fell all over her face.

"Name of a dog, wench!" the landlord thundered, and seized the disturber of the peace by the wrist, "what are you doing here? And pray why aren't you in bed where every respectable person should be at this hour?"

It was a blessing in disguise that Josette should be held so firmly by the wrist else she would certainly have measured her length on the floor. Her senses were reeling. Through the gloom she saw angry faces glowering at her. Quite a small crowd had collected in the vestibule: a crowd of angry men roused from their slumbers, clad in whatever garments they happened to have slept in; the women for the most part did not venture beyond the doorway of their rooms, and peeped out thence with eyes heavy with sleep to see what was happening. At sight of Josette most of them murmured:

"A trollop no doubt, caught in some turpitude."

The irate landlord gave Josette's arm a shake: "What were you doing here?" he demanded, "little str—"

He was going to say an ugly word, but just at the moment Josette raised her eyes to his, and Josette's eyes were bathed in tears and they had such an expression of childlike innocence in them that the worthy landlord could think of nothing but of the Madonna whose lovely image had been banished from the village church where he had been baptised and had made his first Communion, and which was now closed because the good *curé* of the village had refused to conform to the mockery of religion which an impious government was striving to force upon the people: and looking into Josette's eyes, the landlord's thoughts flew back to the Madonna, before whose picture he had worshipped as a child. How, then, could he speak an ugly word in this innocent angel's ear?

"You have got to tell me, you know," he said somewhat sheepishly, "why you are not in your room and asleep." He paused a moment while Josette made a great effort to collect her scattered senses; ashamed of her bare legs and shoulders she tried to get farther back into the gloom.

Someone in the crowd remarked: "Perhaps she is a sleep-walker and had a nightmare."

But at this suggestion Josette shook her head.

"Did something frighten you, little *citizeness?*" the landlord asked quite kindly.

Josette now found her voice again.

"Yes!" she said slowly, swallowing hard, for the last thing she wanted to do was to cry before all these people. "I woke very suddenly. I could see the door. It was being pushed open slowly from outside. I cried out. Then I heard footsteps shuffling down the stairs."

"Impossible!" the landlord said.

"I heard nothing," commented someone.

"Nor I," added another.

"I did hear a bang," remarked a third, "not many minutes ago."

"There was a bang," Josette went on slowly. "While I was closing the door, the window flew open behind me. I went to shut it. Then the door flew open, and I went to shut it too. When I crept back to bed I found—oh, *mon Dieu! mon Dieu!*"

"What is it? What happened?" they all asked.

"A packet of letters," she replied, "more precious to me than life itself—"

"Not stolen?"

"Yes—stolen."

"Where were they?"

"Underneath my pillow."

"And you say that when you went back to bed those letters—"

"Were not there."

"Impossible!" the landlord reiterated obstinately.

One of the men said, "The thief, whoever he was, must still be in the house then, since the front door is bolted on the inside."

"What about the back door?" another suggested.

Several of them, under the lead of the night watchman, went to investigate the back door. It was bolted and barred the same as the front door.

"I knew it was," the night watchman said somewhat illogically. "I pushed all the bolts in myself all over the house and saw to all the windows."

He felt that Josette's story reflected adversely upon his zeal.

"The thief must still be in the house," Josette murmured mechanically.

"Impossible!" the landlord reiterated for the third time.

The glances cast on Josette became anything but kind, and though the landlord and some of the men were under the influence of her innocent blue eyes, the women from their respective doorways had a good deal to say. One of them started the ball rolling by muttering:

"It's all a pack of lies."

After which the others went at it hammer and tongs. Women are like that. Let some vixen give a lead and there is no stopping the flow of evil tongues. Poor Josette felt this hostility growing around her. It added poignancy to her distress over the letters. Indeed, the little crowd had as usual behaved like sheep; after the first doubt had been cast on Josette's story hardly anyone believed her. The theory of her being a sleepwalker was incontinently rejected: she was just a little strumpet roaming through the house at night in search of adventure. In vain did she weep and protest; in vain did she beg that her room-mates be questioned as to the truth of her story: those two women refused to leave their bed, where they lay with their heads smothered under the blanket, wishing to God they had never set foot in this abominable hostelry.

Josette, overcome with misery and with shame, had shrunk back into a dark angle of the vestibule, trying with all her might to overcome her terror of all these angry faces, and, above all, to swallow her tears. In her heart she prayed as she had never prayed before that *le bon Dieu,* her patron saint and her guardian angel might guide her with safety out of this awful pass. The landlord stood by, undecided, scratching his head.

"It is a matter for the police, I say." It was a woman who made this suggestion. It was quickly taken up by others, for, indeed, this seemed the easiest solution to the present difficulty; after which everybody would be able to go back to bed and go through the rest of the night in peace.

"I agree," one of the men said. "Let the wench be taken to the nearest *Commissariat de Police.*"

And then a funny thing happened.

The suggestion that the disturber of the peace should be taken to the *Commissariat de Police* was received with approval, especially by the women. Some of the men were rather doubtful, and there ensued quite a considerable hubbub and a good deal of argument: the women holding to their opinion with loud, shrill voices, the men muttering and cursing.

The landlord stood by scratching his head, not knowing what to do: the casting vote as to Josette's fate would of course rest with him.

And suddenly a quiet vote broke in on the hubbub, saying authoritatively:

"Certainly not. Never shall it be said that a respectable *citizeness* of the Republic had been put to the indignity of being dragged before the police in the middle of the night."

It was the voice of one accustomed to command and to being obeyed—very quiet and low but peremptory. A small, thin man with pale face and hard penetrating eyes pressed his way through the small crowd. Unlike the rest of them he had slipped on his coat over his shirt, he had stockings on and shoes, and his hair was brushed back tidily. Under his coat and round his waist he wore a tricolour sash. The landlord gave a big sigh of relief: he was truly thankful that decision in this difficult case was taken out of his hands. The girl's story certainly sounded very lame. . . . but, then, she had such lovely blue eyes. . . . and her little mouth—well, well!

Anyway, he would not have the unpleasant task of taking her to the police on an ugly charge. The others were all deeply impressed by the little man's authority and by his tricolour sash—badge of service under the government. As for Josette, she just clasped her tiny hands together and gazed on that insignificant, pale-faced little man as would a devotee upon her favourite saint; her eyes were bathed in tears, her lips already murmured words of gratitude, but actually she was not yet able to speak.

"Where is your wife, landlord?" the little man went on to say in the same peremptory tone.

"At your service, citizen," the woman replied for herself. She had slipped her bare feet into her shoes and she had on her kirtle and a shawl round her shoulders. Unlike the female guests of the hostelry, she felt that this matter concerned her, and she had dressed herself ready in case of an emergency.

"You will give Citizeness Gravier a bed in your daughter's room, where she will, I hope, spend the rest of the night in peace." So spake the little man with the tricolour sash, and it was marvellous with what alacrity his orders were obeyed. That tricolour sash did indeed work wonders! And now he added curtly: "Remember that the *citizeness* is under the special protection of the Central Committee of Public Safety."

Josette could only stare at him with wide-open eyes that looked of a deep luminous blue in this half-light. The little man caught her glance and came over to her. He took her limp, moist hand in his and patted it gently:

"Try and get a little rest now, little woman," he said kindly. "You shall have your letters back, I promise you, even if," he added with a curious smile, "even if we have to set the whole machinery of the law going in order to recover them for you."

He said this so lightly and with so much confidence that Josette felt comforted and almost reassured; indeed, her unsophisticated heart was so full of gratitude that instinctively like a child she raised the thin, clawlike hand which patted her own to her lips. She was on the point of imprinting a kiss upon it when from somewhere in the house there resounded a tremendous crash as of falling furniture. It was immediately followed by loud and prolonged laughter. All the heads were turned towards the stairs as the noise seemed to have come from somewhere above.

"What in the world—?" and other expressions of amazement came to everyone's lips.

"I believe it's that drunken sailor," someone remarked.

"Let me get at him," the landlord said grimly, and pushed his way through the small crowd in the direction of the stairs.

"It can't be him," the night watchman asserted. "I let him out myself by the back door two hours ago and bolted the door after him."

But the little man with the tricolour scarf had snatched his hand out of Josette's grasp. For a moment it seemed as if he was about to join the landlord in his quest after the sailor, but apparently, he thought better of it; probably he felt that it would be beneath the dignity of a Government official to chase a mudlark up and down the stairs of a tavern; besides which he well knew in his heart of hearts that no sailor or mudlark would be found inside the house. The laughter had come from outside—there must be an open window somewhere—and its ringing tone was only too familiar to this same Government official with the pale sad face and the badge of office round his waist: it came from a personage that had always proved elusive, whenever the utmost resources of his enemy's intelligence were set to work to run him to earth.

The only thing to do now in this present crisis—for crisis it certainly would prove to be—was to think things over very carefully, to lay plans so secretly and so carefully that no power on earth could counter them. The girl, Josette Gravier, was a magnificent pawn in the game that was to follow the events of this night, just the sort of pawn that would appeal to the so-called chivalry of those damnable English spies: a decoy—what?

So the little man, whose pale face reflected something of the inward rage that tortured him at this moment, turned fiercely on the small crowd of quidnuncs who still stood about quizzing and whispering, and with a peremptory wave of the arm ordered everyone off to bed. They immediately scattered like sheep. The landlord's wife took hold of Josette's hand.

"Come along, little girl," she said; "there is a nice couch in Annette's room: you'll sleep well on that."

"And remember, both of you," the little man said in the end when Josette meekly allowed herself to be led away, "that you are responsible with your lives—your lives," he iterated emphatically, "for the safety of Citizeness Gravier."

The man and woman both shuddered: their ruddy faces became sallow with terror. They understood the threat well enough, even though the amazing turn which the events of this night had taken was past their comprehension.

Silent and obedient the little crowd had dispersed. They all slunk back to bed, there to exchange surmises, conjectures, gossip with their respective roommates. Josette lay down on the couch in Annette's room. She could not sleep, for her brain was working all the time and her heart still beating with the many emotions to which she had succumbed this night. There were moments when, lying here in the darkness, she doubted and feared. That was because of the tricolour sash and the authority which her friend seemed to wield. Before his appearance in this new guise of authority she had almost persuaded herself that he was intimately connected with the hero of her dreams, but there was no reconciling the badge of officialdom of the Terrorist Government with the personality of the Scarlet Pimpernel.

Nevertheless, it was this same little man who had saved her from the ill-will of all those horrid people who said such awful things about her and threatened her with the police. It was he who had given her a solemn promise that the precious letters would be restored to her; so, what was an ignorant, unsophisticated girl like Josette Gravier to make of all these mysteries? What she did do was to turn her thoughts to Maurice. Surely *le bon Dieu* would not be so cruel as to snatch from her the means by which she could demand his life and liberty. Surely not at this hour when she was so near her goal.

And in a private room on the floor above, Citizen Chauvelin was pacing up and down the floor, with hands clasped tightly behind his back, his pale face set, his thin lips murmuring over and over again:

"Now then, *à nous deux* once more, my gallant Scarlet Pimpernel."

After a time there came a knock at the door. In response to a peremptory "*Entrez!*" a rough-looking fellow in jersey and breeches undone at the knee came into the room. He had a sealed packet in his large, grimy hands, and this he handed to Chauvelin.

Neither of the men spoke for some time. The man had remained standing in the middle of the room waiting for the other to speak, while Chauvelin sat at the table, his thin delicate hands toying with the packet, his pale eyes hiding their expression of triumph behind their blue-veined lids.

The silence threatened to become oppressive. The newcomer was the first to break it. He pointed a grimy finger at the sealed packet in Chauvelin's hand.

"That is what you wanted," he asked, "was it not, Citizen?"

"Yes," the other replied curtly.

"It was difficult to get. If I had known—"

"Well!" Chauvelin broke in impatiently; "the wind and rain helped you, didn't they?"

"But if I had been caught—"

"You weren't. So why talk about it?"

"And I injured my knee climbing down again from that cursed window," Picard muttered with a surely glance at his employer.

"Your knee will mend," Chauvelin rejoined curtly; "and you have earned good money."

He gave a quiet chuckle at recollection of the night's events. He and Picard. The open door. The open window. The draught. Josette in her shift and kirtle struggling with the door while Picard stole in at the window, and he, Chauvelin, tip—toed noiselessly back down the stairs. Yes! the whole thing had worked wonderfully well, better even than he had hoped. It had been a perfect example of concerted action.

Picard was waiting for his money. Chauvelin gave him the promised two hundred *livres*—a large sum in these days. The man tried to grumble, but it was no use, and after a few moments he slouched, still grumbling, out of the room.

For close on half an hour after that did Chauvelin remain sitting at the table, toying with the stolen packet. There was a lighted candle on the table, its feeble light flickered in the draught. Chauvelin's pale, expressive eyes were fixed upon the seals. He did not break them, for it was part of the tortuous scheme which he had evolved that these seals should remain intact. He looked at them closely, wondering whose hand had fixed them there: Bastien de Croissy's probably, who had been murdered for his pains, or else the wife's before she entrusted the packet to Josette. The seals told him nothing, and he did not mean to break them: he laid the precious packet down on the table. Then he opened the table drawer. Out of it he took a small lump of soft wax. With the utmost care he took an impression of one of the seals: he examined his work when it was done and was satisfied that it was well done. He then returned the wax impression into the table drawer and locked it.

The stolen packet he slipped into the breast pocket of his coat, and he laid the coat under the mattress in the adjoining room. After which he went to bed.

Chapter 25

The imaginative brain that invented the torment meted out to Damocles could not in very truth have invented torture more unendurable. Poor old Damocles! All he wanted was to taste for a time the splendour and joys of kingship, and Dionysius, the tyrant King of Sicily, thought to gratify his whim and his own sense of humour by giving the ambitious courtier charge of the kingdom for a while.

So good old Damocles ascended the throne which he had coveted and licked his chops in anticipation of all the luxury that was going to be his, until suddenly he perceived that a sword was hanging over his head by nothing but a hair from a horse's tail. Now we must take it, though legend doesn't say so, that this sword followed the poor man about wherever he went, else all he need have done was to wonder through his kingdom and avoid sitting immediately under that blessed sword. As to how the business of the horse's hair was accomplished, say in an open field, is perhaps a little difficult to imagine.

Be that as it may, three worthy Representatives of the People in the autumn of 1793 did in very truth go about their avocations with, figuratively speaking, a sword of doom hanging over their heads.

Three weeks had gone by since Chabot's memorable interview with Josette Gravier, and there was no news of her, no news of Armand Chauvelin, no news, alas! of those compromising letters which were enough to send the whole batch of them to the guillotine.

The Club of the Cordeliers had of late lost a great deal of its prestige, and consequently was not frequented by the most influential members of the Government: it was, therefore, an admirable meeting-place for those who desired to talk things over in the peace and quiet of the club's deserted rooms. Many a time in the past weeks did those three reprobates, quaking in their shoes, hold conclave among themselves, trying to infuse assurance and even hope into one another. Sometimes the great Danton would join them, knowing well that if his three satellites fell, he, too, would be involved in the general *débâcle* that would ensue. Late into the night they would sit and talk, wondering what had become of the little she-devil who had dared to threaten them, hoping against hope that one of the many accidents attendant on a voyage across France had put an end to her.

Then one day there came a letter from Citizen Chauvelin. It was sent to François Chabot, the unfrocked monk turned traitor, renegade and Terrorist, as being the most deeply involved in the affair of the compromising letters. With trembling fingers Chabot broke the seals of this welcome message, for he had already recognised the thin Italian calligraphy of the writer: he was alone in his luxuriously furnished study. At first, he could hardly see what he was doing: the words of the letter danced before his eyes, the blood rushed up to his temples, and the paper rustled in his trembling hands. Then slowly he was able to decipher the writing. The first sentence that he read caused him to utter a gurgle of joy: "I have the girl here—"

That was good news indeed. Chabot closed his eyes so as to savour all the more thoroughly the intense joy produced to him by this
message. With the girl in his power Chauvelin could have no possible
difficulty in getting hold of the letters as well. Now Chabot came to
think of it, it was strange that his colleague chose this enigmatic way
of commencing his letter. The girl! Yes! the girl was well enough! But
what about the letters? He suddenly felt uncomfortable. . . . vaguely
frightened of he knew not what. He blinked his eyes once or twice
because they had become blurred, and beads of perspiration stood
out at the roots of his hair and trickled down his nose. Then at last he
settled down to read, and this is what Citizen Armand Chauvelin had
written to him from Rouen:

Citizen and Dear Colleague.
I have the girl here under my eye, and by this you will gather
that my mission has been successfully accomplished. I am now
in Rouen at the hostelry of the Cheval Blanc, under the same
roof as the little blackmailer. So far I have done nothing about
the letters. I can get hold of them any moment, but there are
other very grave matters that command my attention. Owing
to the inclement weather the diligence cannot ply for some
days, and this enforced delay suits my purpose admirably, for
I do not wish to leave Rouen just now. The wench cannot in
any case escape me and, if you will believe me, I have such high
quarry close to my hand that I cannot leave this city until I
have secured it. This is not a personal matter but one that affects
the very safety of the Republic: how, then, could I risk that by
deserting my post?
You must try and read between the lines, and then explain the
matter to all those who are involved in the affair of the Croissy
letters. As I have already told you, I can, of course, get hold of the
letters at any time, and I suggest that you give me leave in that
case to destroy them before any further mischief is wrought. If
you agree to this wise course, send me a courier immediately
to the hostelry of the Cheval Blanc here in Rouen. But I beg
of you not to delay. There are inimical powers at work here
of which you can have no conception, and if, as I believe, the
safety of the Republic is as dear to you as it is to me, you will
be ready to fall in with my views.

François Chabot read and re-read this letter, which did certainly in some of its phrases appear ambiguous. What, for instance, did Chauvelin mean by the closing sentence? To Chabot it seemed to contain a veiled threat, and there were other points, too. . . .

That evening the four men sat in a corner of the club-room in a very different mood to that of the past few weeks. There they were— François Chabot (Loire et Cher), Fabre d'Eglantine (Paris) and Claud Bazire (Côte d'Or), as unprincipled a lot of rascals as ever defamed the country of their birth. The great Danton had joined them at their earnest request—not so much a scoundrel he, as an infuriated wild animal, smarting under many wrongs, lashing out savagely against guilty and innocent alike, and with old ideals long since laid in the dust.

"I would not trust that old fox farther than I could see him," Danton had said as soon as the matter of Chauvelin's letter had been put before him.

"But he can get hold of the letters at any time—there's no doubt about that," one of the others remarked.

"He has probably got them inside his coat pocket by now," the great man retorted, "ready to sell them or use them for his own ends."

"Then what had one better do?"

"Let us send a courier over to Rouen," Fabre d'Eglantine suggested, "with orders to Citizen Chauvelin to come to Paris immediately."

"Suppose he refuses?" Danton said with a shrug.

"He wouldn't dare. . . ."

"And would you dare threaten him if he really has the letters and holds them over you?"

They were silent after that because they knew quite well—in fact had just realised it for the first time—that it was Armand Chauvelin now instead of Bastien de Croissy or Josette Gravier who held the sword of Damocles over their heads.

After a time, Chabot murmured, looking to the great Danton for guidance now that the emergency appeared more fateful than before: "What shall we do, then?"

"If you take my advice," Danton said, and strove to appear as if the whole matter did not greatly concern him, "if you take my advice, one of you will go straight to Rouen, see Citizen Chauvelin and get the packet of letters straight from the girl. After that the sooner the wretched things are destroyed the better."

That seemed sound advice, and after discussion it was decided to act upon it, François Chabot declaring his willingness, in spite of the weather, to journey to Rouen by special coach on the morrow.

Chapter 26

From Meulon, where he spent the night, Chabot sent a courier with a letter over to Rouen to prepare Chauvelin for his arrival, he wrote:

Devoured with impatience, I am coming in person to receive the precious letters from your hands and discuss with you the terms of your reward, which my friends and I are determined shall be as great as your service to our party.

An ironic smile twisted Chauvelin's thin lips when he read this short epistle. The events had not turned out any differently to what he had expected. Those cowardly fools over there were, in fact, playing into his hands.

He had been interrupted by the courier in an important work which had demanded a great deal of time and skill. Five days had gone by since poor little Josette had been robbed of her precious letters, and today Chauvelin was sitting at the table in the private room which he still occupied in the hostelry of the Cheval Blanc. Though it was day-light there was a lighted candle on the table, and when the courier arrived, Chauvelin's deft fingers had been busy making up a small parcel which looked like a packet of letters and which he had been engaged in sealing down with red wax and a brand-new seal.

When the courier was announced he blew out the candle and threw the packet into the table-drawer.

Now that he was alone again he took the packet out of the drawer, and then drew another out of the breast-pocket of his coat. The two packets now lay side by side on the table. Chauvelin applied himself sedulously to a final examination of them. To all intents and purposes, they were exactly alike. None but a specially trained eye could detect the slightest difference in them. In shape, in size, in the soiled and crumpled appearance of the outside covering, in the disposition of the five seals they were absolutely interchangeable. It was only to Chauvelin's lynx-like eyes that the difference in the seals was apparent. A very minute difference indeed in the sharpness and clearness of the impress.

He gave a deep sigh of satisfaction. All was well. The work of die-sinking had been admirably done from the wax impression of the original, by a skilled workman of Rouen. Chauvelin could indeed be satisfied: his deep-laid scheme was working admirably: he could await the arrival of Chabot with absolute calm and the certainty that his own delicate hands held all the threads of as neat an intrigue as he had ever devised for the ultimate undoing of his own most bitter enemy.

He slipped the two packets inside his coat pockets; the original one stolen from under the pillow of Josette Gravier he thrust against his breast, the other he put into a side pocket. After which he settled his sharp features into an expression of kindliness and went in search of Josette.

He knew just where to find her, sitting on the bench under the chestnut trees—that beautiful avenue which had once formed part of the old convent garden of the Ursulines, driven away by the relentless edicts of the revolutionary government. The mediaeval building, still splendid in its desolation, showed already signs of decay. The garden was untended, the paths overgrown with weeds, the grass rank and covered with a carpet of fallen leaves, the statuary broken, but nothing could mar the beauty of the age-old trees, of the chestnuts already half-denuded of leaves. And the *vista* over the river was beautiful, with the two islands and the sleepy backwater, and the sight of the ships gliding with such stately majesty down-stream towards the sea.

The place was not lonely, for the riverside was a favourite walk of the townsfolk, and on the quay, boatmen plied their trade of letting pleasure boats out on hire. The convent itself had been turned into a communal school for the children of Rouennais soldiers who were fighting for their country, and, after school hours or during recreation time, crowds of children trooped out of the building and ran playing up and down the avenue. Indeed, Josette did not come here for solitude: she liked to watch the children and the passers-by and, anyway, it was nicer than sitting in that stuffy public room of the hostelry where prying eyes scanned her none too kindly.

Her pale-faced little friend had insisted that she should continue to share a room with the landlord's daughter: this room had no egress save through the larger one occupied by the landlord himself and his wife, and Josette was quite aware that her friend had made these people responsible for her safety as well as for her comfort. This, of course, had greatly reassured her, and his promise that he would get the letters back for her had cheered her up—especially for the first twenty-four hours. She had such implicit faith not only in his friendship, but also, since that fateful night, in his power; but for that tricolour sash she would have felt happier still, but somehow, she didn't like to think of that kind, sad, gentle creature as a member of a government of assassins.

This was the fifth day that Josette had spent in Rouen, waiting and hoping almost against hope. Once or twice she had caught sight of her friend either in the garden or while he wandered along the riverside, with head bent, hands clasped behind his back, evidently wrapped in thought. When he passed by in front of Josette he always looked up and gave her an encouraging smile. And then, again, she saw him in the public room at meal-times, and always he gave her a smile and a nod.

Then yesterday, here in the old garden, he came and sat down beside her under the chestnut tree, and he was so gentle and so kind that she was tempted to confide in him. She told him about the contents of the stolen packet—about the letters, the possession of which had cost brave Bastien de Croissy his life, and about her own journey to England in order to get the letters from Louise. And as he listened with so much attention and sympathy she went so far as to tell him about Maurice, and how it had been the object of her journey—nay! the object of her life—to use the letters as Bastien had intended to use them: as a leverage to obtain what she desired more than anything in the world—the life and liberty of Maurice Reversac.

"I am not afraid of what I mean to do," she concluded. "I have already bearded Citizen Chabot once, and I know that I can get from him everything I want—" She paused and added with a sigh of longing, "if only I have those letters. . . !"

Her friend had been more than kind after that, and so confident and reassuring that she slept that night more soundly and peacefully than she had done since she arrived in Rouen.

"Have no doubt whatever, little one," he had said in the end. "You shall have your precious letters back very soon."

And then, today, even while she sat at her accustomed place under the chestnut tree, and with dreamy glance watched the people coming and going up and down the riverside all intent on affairs of their own, heedless of this poor little waif with the gnawing anxiety in her heart, she suddenly caught sight of the little man coming towards her with a light, springy step. Somehow, directly she saw his face, she knew that he was the bearer of good news. And so, it turned out to be. Even before he came close to her he thrust his hand into the side pocket of his coat and she guessed that he had the letters. She could not repress a cry of joy which caused the passers-by to cast astonished glances at the pretty wench, but she paid no heed to them. She was so excited that she jumped up and ran to her friend.

He had indeed drawn the sealed packet from the pocket of his coat, and now he actually put it into her hands. It was so wonderful—almost unbelievable. Josette pressed the packet against her cheek and her young palpitating bosom—the precious, precious packet! She was so happy, so marvellously, so completely happy! She didn't care who watched her; just like a child she spread out her arms and would have hugged that kind peerless friend to her breast only that he put up a warning hand, for, in truth, she was attracting too much attention from the quidnuncs on the quay. At once she asked his pardon for her vehemence.

"I am so happy," she murmured 'twixt laughter and tears, "so happy! I was forgetting—"

"I told you I would get the letters for you, didn't I?" he said, and with kindly indulgence patted her trembling little hands.

"And I shall pray God every day of my life," she responded, sinking her voice to a whisper, "to give you due reward."

"So long as you are happy, my child—"

"I could fall at your feet now," she murmured earnestly, "and thank you on my knees."

None but a hardened, stony heart as that which beat in the Terrorist's breast could have resisted the charm, the exquisite sentiment of this beautiful woman's gratitude. To his enduring shame, be it said that Chauvelin felt neither remorse nor pity as he looked on the lovely young face with the glowing eyes and tender mouth quivering with emotion. His tortuous schemes would presently land her on the hideous platform of the guillotine; that beautiful head with the soft chestnut curls would presently fall into the ghoulish basket which already had received so many lovely heads.

What cared he? All these people—men, women, young and old— were so many pawns in the game which he had devised; and he, Chauvelin, was still engaged in moving the pieces: he still had his hold on the pawns. Away with them if they proved to be in the way or merely useless. It was more often than not a scramble as to which party would push the other up the steps of the guillotine.

Chauvelin sat himself down quite coolly on the bench and, with a sneer round his lips which he took care the girl should not see, he watched her as she tucked the precious packet away underneath her *fichu*.

"I have further good news for you, *citizeness*," he said as soon as she had sat down beside him.

"More good news!" she exclaimed; then pulled herself together and turned big inquiring eyes on her friend: "I won't hear it," she said resolutely, "until I know your name."

He gave a light shrug and a laugh: "Suppose you call me Armand," he replied, "Citizen Armand."

"Is that your name?"

"Why, yes?"

Josette murmured the name once or twice to herself.

"It will be easier like this for me," she said with *naïve* seriousness, "when I pray to *le bon Dieu* for you. And now," she went on gaily, "Citizen Armand, I am ready for your news."

"It is just this: you won't need to go to Paris."

"What do you mean?"

"Just what I say. A courier has just come from Meulon with news that François Chabot, representative of the people, will be in Rouen this evening."

"This—evening?"

"So you see—"

"Yes. . . . I see," she murmured, awed at the prospect of this unexpected event.

"It all becomes so much safer," he hastened to reassure her. "I succeeded in getting that packet back for you this time, but I could not journey all the way to Paris with you, and you might have been robbed again."

"Oh, I see—I do see!" Josette sighed. "Isn't it wonderful?"

She felt rather bewildered. It was all so unexpected and not a little startling. Instinctively her hand sought the packet in the bosom of her gown. She drew it out. The outside wrapper was very soiled and crumpled—it had been through so many hands—but the seals were intact.

"I wouldn't break the seals if I were you, little girl," Chauvelin said. "It will be better for you, I think, also for your friend—what's his name?—Reversac, isn't that it?—if the Citizen Representative is allowed to think that you have not actually read those compromising letters. It will make him less ill-disposed towards you personally. Do you see what I mean?"

"I think I do, but even if I didn't," Josette added *naïvely*, "I should do as you tell me."

No compunction, no pity for this guileless child who trusted him! Chauvelin patted her on the shoulder:

"That's brave!" was all he said. He appeared ready to go, but Josette put a timid hand on his arm.

"Citizen Armand—"

"Yes? What is it now?"

"Shall I see you before—"

"Before the arrival of François Chabot?"

"Yes."

"I will certainly let you know, and see you if I can. . . . By the way," he added as if in after-thought, "would it not be wiser for you to leave the packet with me until this evening?. . . . No?" he went on with a smile as Josette quickly crossed her little hands over her bosom as if some powerful instinct had suddenly prompted her not to part again from her precious possession. "No. . . ? Well, just as you like, my child; but take care of them: those spies and thieves are still about, you know."

"Spies?"

"Of course. Surely you guessed that your letters were not stolen by ordinary thieves?"

"No, I did not. I just thought—"

"What?"

"That being a sealed packet a thief would think that it contained money."

"Enough to warrant such an elaborate plot," Chauvelin remarked drily, "and you so obviously not a wealthy traveller?"

"I hadn't thought of that. But, then, of course, Citizen Armand, you must know who stole the packet since—"

"Since I got it back for you? I do know, of course."

"Who was it?" Josette asked and gazed on Chauvelin with wide-open frightened eyes.

"If I were to tell you, you wouldn't understand."

"I think I would," she murmured. "Try me!"

"Well," he replied, sinking his voice to a whisper, "did you happen to notice on the first evening you arrived here a big man dressed as a sailor, who made himself conspicuous in the public room of the Cheval Blanc?"

"Yes, I did—a horrid man, I thought. But surely he—?"

"That man, who I admit wore a clever disguise, is the head of an English organisation whose aim is the destruction of France."

"You don't mean—?" she gasped.

Chauvelin nodded. "I see," he said, "that you have heard of those people. They call themselves the League of the Scarlet Pimpernel and, under the pretence of chivalry and benevolence, are nothing but a pestilential pack of English spies who take money from both sides—their own Governments or ours whichever suits their pocket."

"I'll not believe it!" Josette protested hotly.

"Did you not notice that night as soon as I entered the room that the fat sailor beat a hasty retreat?"

"I noticed," she admitted, "that he did leave the public room soon after you sat down to supper."

"I sent the police after him then, but he had a marvellous faculty for disappearing when he is afraid for his own skin."

"I'll not believe it!" Josette protested again, thinking of Louise's letter and of the hero of her dreams. "Had it not been for the Scarlet Pimpernel—"

"Your friend Louise de Croissy," Chauvelin broke in with a sneer, "would have never reached England—I know that. Did I not tell you just now that pretence of chivalry is one of that man's stock-in-trade? No doubt he wanted to get Citizeness Croissy away, thinking that she would leave the letters with you: when he realised that you hadn't them and that you were journeying to England obviously in order to get them, he followed you. I know he did, and I did my best to circumvent him. I befriended you as far as I could, for he dared not approach you while I was on the watch."

"Oh, I know," Josette sighed, "you have been more than kind."

She felt as if she were floundering in a morass of doubt and misery, tortured by suspicion, wounded in her most cherished ideals. Ignorant, unsophisticated as she was, how could she escape out of this sea of trouble? How could she know whom to trust or in whom to believe? This friend had been so kind, so kind! The precious letters had been stolen from her and he had got them back. Without him where would she be at this hour? Without him she would have nothing wherewith to obtain life and liberty for Maurice. Tears welled up to her eyes; never, perhaps, had she felt quite so unhappy, because never before had she been brought up in such close contact with all that was most hideous in life—treachery and deceit.

She turned her head away because she was half-ashamed of her tears. After all, what was the destruction of an illusion in these days when one saw all one's beliefs shattered, all one's ideals crumbled to dust? Josette had almost deified the Scarlet Pimpernel in her mind, and Louise's letter had confirmed her belief in his wonderful personality with the fascinating mystery that surrounded it and the almost legendary acts of bravery and chivalry which characterised it. If any other man had spoken about her hero in the way this pale-faced little friend of hers had done she would have dubbed him a liar and done battle for her ideal; but she owed so much to Citizen Armand, he had been such a wonderful friend, such a help in all her difficulties, and now, but for him, she would have been in the depths of despair.

He was wrong—Josette was certain that he was wrong—in his estimate of the Scarlet Pimpernel, but never for a moment did she doubt his sincerity. She owed him too much to think of doubting him. Whatever he said—and his words had been like cruel darts thrust into her heart—he had said because he was convinced of the truth, and he had spoken only because of his friendship for her. Even now he seemed to divine her thoughts and the reason of her tears.

"It is always sad," he said gently, "to see an illusion shattered; but think of it like this, my child: you have lost a—shall I say friend, though I do not like to misuse the word?—who in very truth had no existence save in your imagination; against that you have found one who, if I may venture to say so, has already proved his worth by restoring to you the magic key which will open the prison doors for the man you love. Am I not right in supposing that Maurice Reversac is that lucky man?"

Josette nodded and smiled up at the hypocrite through her tears.

"I hadn't meant to tell you so much," he said, rising ready to go, "only that I felt compelled to warn you. The man who stole your letters once will try to do so again, and I might not be able to recover them a second time."

It was getting late afternoon now, the shadows were deep under the trees, but on the river, twilight lingered still. The girl sat with her head bent, her fingers interlocked and hot tears fell upon her hands. The kind friend who had done so much for her was still standing there about to go, and she could not find it in her heart to look up into his face and to speak the words of gratitude which his marvellous solicitude for her should have brought so readily to her lips. Her thoughts were far away with Louise in her pretty room in England, telling her story of the astounding prowess of the Scarlet Pimpernel, his resourcefulness, his devotion, the glamour that surrounded his mysterious personality in his own country; how could all that be true if this kind and devoted friend over here did not deceive himself and her? And if he did not, then were all the tales she had heard tell of the

241

mystic hero nothing but legends or lies?

A confused hum of sounds was in her ears; the boatmen gossiping on the quay, the shuffling footsteps of passers-by the shrieks and laughter of children up and down the avenue and, suddenly through it all, a stentorian voice chanting the first strains of the *Marseillaise* completely out of tune. Josette felt rather than saw Citizen Armand give a distinct start: she looked up just in time to see him cross over rapidly to the quay. The ear-splitting song had come from that direction. The boatmen were all laughing and pointing to a boat just putting off the shore, in which a fat sailor in tattered coat and shiny black hat thrust at the back of his head was plying the oars. He it was who was singing so intolerably out of tune; his voice resounded right across the intervening space: even when he reached midstream and headed toward the islands, some of the stentorian notes echoed down the avenue. Josette couldn't help smiling. Was that the man who had stolen the letters from under her pillow—the dangerous spy whom it took all her friend's ingenuity to track? Could, in fact, that ugly uncouth creature, with the lank hair, the tattered clothes and the toothless mouth, be the mysterious and redoubtable Scarlet Pimpernel?

Josette could not help laughing to herself at the very thought. Citizen Armand must indeed be moonstruck to think of connecting that buffoon with the most gallant figure of all times. She glanced anxiously about her to find her friend Armand, for she wanted to speak with him again, to convince him how wrong he was, how utterly mistaken he had been. All at once her big sea of troubles ebbed away. She felt happy and light-hearted once more. Her illusions were not shattered: she could still worship her ideal and yet retain her affection for the sad-faced and kindly man who had befriended her. She was happy—oh, so happy!—and her lips were ready now to speak the words of gratitude.

But look where she might, there was no longer any sign of Citizen Armand.

Chapter 27

It was now eight o'clock in the evening. An hour ago, a postchaise had driven into the courtyard of the Cheval Blanc and from it descended Citizen François Chabot, Representative of the People for the department of Loire et Cher. He had been received by the landlord of the tavern with all the honours due to his exalted station and to his influence and had supped in the public room in the company of that pale-faced little man who had already created so much attention in the hostelry and who went by the name of Citizen Armand.

Josette sitting at another table in a dark angle of the room watched the two men with mixed feelings in her heart. She couldn't eat any supper, for inwardly she was terribly excited. The hour had come when all her efforts on behalf of Maurice would come to fruit. Her friend had sent her word that he would summon her when the Citizen Representative was ready to receive her, so she waited as patiently as she could. Watching Chabot, she recalled every moment of her first interview with him; she had been perfectly calm and self-possessed then, and she would be calm now when she found herself once more face to face with him. Though ignorant and unsophisticated, Josette was no fool. She knew well what risk she ran by consenting to meet Chabot here in Rouen with the letters actually upon her person. Events had turned out differently from what she had planned. She had meant to meet Chabot in Paris on neutral ground, conducts for herself and Maurice safely put away. Here it was different.

Danger? There always was danger in coming in conflict with these men who ruled France by terror and the ever-present threat of the guillotine, but there was also that other danger, the risk of the precious letters being stolen again during the final stage of the journey, and no chance of getting them back a second time. Even so, Josette would perhaps have refused to meet Chabot till she could do so in Paris had it not been for Citizen Armand; but it never entered her mind that this faithful and powerful friend would not be there to protect her and to see fair play.

As on that other occasion in the luxurious room of the Rue d'Anjou she was not the least afraid: it was only the waiting that was so trying to her nerves. While she made pretence to eat her supper she tried to catch her friend's eye, but he was deeply absorbed in conversation with Chabot. Once or twice the latter glanced in her direction, then turned back to Armand with a sneer and a shrug.

After supper the two men went out of the room together, and Josette waited quietly for the summons from her friend. At last it came. Looking up, she saw him standing in the doorway: he beckoned to her and she followed him out of the room. She was absolutely calm now, as calm as she had been during the first interview when the precious letters were not yet in her possession. Now she felt the paper crackling against her bosom—the golden key her friend had called the packet, which would open the prison gates for Maurice.

Armand conducted her to a small room at the back of the house, one which had been put at the disposal of the Citizen Representative by the landlord, who probably used it in a general way as a place where he could receive his friends with the privacy which the public room could not offer. It was sparsely furnished with a deal table covered by a faded cloth, on which past libations had left a number of sticky stains: on the table a bottle of ink, a mangy quill pen, a jar of sand and a couple of pewter sconces in which flickered and guttered the tallow candles. There were a few chairs ranged about the place and a wooden bench, all somewhat rickety, covered in grime and innocent of polish.

From a small iron stove in an angle of the room a wood fire shed a welcome glow. The only nice bit of furniture in the place was an old Normandy grandfather clock, standing against the wall and ticking away with solemn majesty. There was only one window, and that was shuttered and bolted. The walls had once been whitewashed: they were bare of ornament save for a cap of liberty roughly drawn in red just above the clock and below it the device of the Terrorist Government: "*Liberté, Égalité, Fraternité.*" Recently a zealous hand had chalked up below this the additional words: "*Ou la mort.*"

When Chauvelin ushered Josette into this room Chabot was sitting at the table. The girl came forward and without waiting to be asked she sat down opposite of Chabot and waited for him to speak. She looked him fearlessly in the face, and he returned her glance with an unmistakable sneer. Chauvelin, who had followed Josette into the room, now put the question:

"Shall I go, or would you like me to stay?"

Josette, looking up at him, did not know to whom he had addressed the question, but in case it was to her she hastened to say: "Do please stay, Citizen Armand."

Chauvelin then sat down on the bench against the wall behind Josette but facing his colleague. For a minute or two no one spoke, and the only sound that broke the fateful silence was the solemn ticking of the old clock. Then Chabot said abruptly:

"Well, little baggage, so you've been in England, I understand."

"Yes, citizen, I have," Josette replied coolly.

Chabot, his ugly head on one side, was eyeing her quizzically, his thick lips were curled in a sneer. He picked up the pen from the table and toyed with it: stroked his unshaven chin with the quill.

"Let me see," he went on slowly, "what exactly was the object of your journey?"

"To get certain letters, citizen," she rejoined, unmoved by his attitude of contempt, "which you were anxious to possess."

"H'm!" was Chabot's curt comment. Then he added drily, "Ah! I was anxious to possess those letters, was I?"

"You certainly were, Citizen."

"And it was in order to relieve my anxiety that you travelled all the way to England, what?"

"We'll put it that way if you like, Citizen Representative."

The girl's coolness seemed to exasperate Chabot as it had done in their first interview. Even now at this hour when she was entirely in his power, when his scheme of vengeance against this impudent baggage had matured to such perfection, he could not control that feeling of irritation against his victim, and he envied his colleague over there who sat looking perfectly placid and entirely at his ease. Suddenly he said:

"Where are those letters, *citizeness*?"

"I have them here," she answered with disconcerting coldness.

"Let's see them," he commanded.

But she was not to be moved into easy submission.

"You remember, citizen," she said, "under what conditions I agreed to hand you over the letters?'

"Conditions?" he retorted with a harsh laugh. "Conditions? Say, I have forgotten those conditions. Will you be so gracious as to let me hear them again?"

"I told you, Citizen Representative," Josette proceeded wearily, for she was getting tired of this word play, "I told you at the time; I want a safe-conduct in the name of Maurice Reversac and one in mine to enable us both to quit this country and travel whither we please."

"Is that all?"

"Enough for my purpose. Shall we conclude, Citizen Representative? You must be as tired as I am of all this quibble."

"You are right there, you impudent trollop!" Chabot snapped at her with a short laugh. "Give me those letters!"

Then as she made no answer, only glanced at him with contempt and shrugged, he iterated hoarsely:

"Did you hear me? Give me those letters!"

"Not till I have the safe-conducts written out and signed by your hand."

"So that's it, is it?" Chabot snarled, and leaned right across the table, peering into her face. He looked hideous in the dim, unsteady light of the candles, with his thick lips quivering, a slight scum gathering at the corners of his mouth and his thin face bilious and sallow with rage. Thus, he remained for the space of a minute, gloating over his triumph. The wench was in his power—nothing could save her now; the vengeance for which he had thirsted was his at last; but there was exquisite pleasure in the anticipation of it, in looking at that slender neck so soon to be severed by the knife of the guillotine, on that dainty head with its wealth of golden curls soon to fall into the gruesome basket while those luminous eyes were closed in death-agony.

"Ah!" he murmured hoarsely, "you thought you had François Chabot in your power, you little fool, you little idiot! You thought that you could frighten him, torture him with doubts and fears? You triple, triple fool!"

His voice rose to a shriek: he jumped to his feet and, thumping the table with the palm of his hand, he shouted: "Here! Guard! À *moi!*"

The door flew open: two men of the Republican Guard appeared under the lintel, and there were others standing in the passage. Josette saw it all. While Chabot was raving and spitting venom at her like an angry serpent she had kept hold on herself. She was not frightened because she knew that Armand, her friend, was close by and that Chabot, even though, or perhaps because he was a Representative of the People would not dare to commit a flagrant act of treachery before his colleague: would not dare to provoke her, Josette Gravier, into revealing the existence of letters compromising to himself here and now. But when the door flew open and she caught sight of the soldiers, she jumped to her feet and turned to the friend to whom she looked so confidently for protection. Chabot now was laughing loudly; with head thrown back he laughed as if his sides would split.

"You little fool!" he continued to snarl. "You egregious little idiot!" He paused, and then commanded: "Search her!" The two soldiers advanced. Josette stood quite still and did not utter a single cry. Her great eyes were fixed on her friend—the friend who was playing her false, who had already betrayed her. At first her glance had pleaded to him: "Save me!" Her dark blue eyes, dark as a midsummer's night, had seemed to say: "Are you not my friend?"

But gradually entreaty gave place to horror and then to a stony stare; for Citizen Armand, the friend and protector who had wormed himself into her secrets, gained her trust and stolen her gratitude, sat there silent and unmoved, stroking his chin with his talon-like fingers, an enigmatic smile round his thin lips. Slowly Josette averted her gaze: she turned from the treacherous friend to the gloating enemy. The soldiers now stood one on each side of her—she could actually feel their breath upon her neck; the hand of one of them fell upon her shoulder. With a smothered cry of revolt, she shook it off and deliberately took the packet of letters from inside her bodice and laid it on the table.

A hoarse sigh of satisfaction broke from Chabot's throat. His thick, coarse hand closed over the fateful packet; the soldiers stood by like wooden dummies, one on each side of Josette.

"Can I go now?" the girl asked.

Chabot threw her a mocking glance.

"Go?" he mimicked with a sneer. Then the sarcasm died on his lips, and his ugly face, which he thrust forward within an inch of hers, became distorted with a look of almost bestial rage. "Go? No, you evil-minded young jade—you are not going. Like a born idiot you have placed yourself in my power. For the past month you have been laughing at me and my friends in your sleeve, relishing like a debauched little glutton the torment which you were inflicting upon us. Well, it is our turn to laugh at you now, and laugh we will while you rot in gaol, you and your lover, aye! rot, until the day on which your heads fall under the guillotine will be welcomed by you as the happiest one of your lives."

Except that she recoiled with the feeling of physical disgust when the man's venom-laden breath fanned her cheeks, Josette had not departed for one moment from her attitude of absolute calm. The moment that earthly protection failed her and the friend whom she trusted proved to be a traitor, she knew that she and Maurice were lost. Nothing on earth could save either of them now from whatever fate these assassins chose to mete out to them. She prayed to *le bon Dieu* to give her courage to bear it all and, above all, she prayed for strength not to let this monster see what she suffered. The name of Maurice thrown at her with such cruelty had made her wince. It was indeed for Maurice's sake that she suffered most acutely. She had built such high hopes—such fond and foolish hopes apparently—on what she could do for him that the disappointment did for the moment seem greater than she could bear.

She no longer looked at the betrayer of her trust: in her innocent mind she thought that he must be overwhelmed with shame at his own cowardice. *Le bon Dieu* alone would know how to punish him.

At a sign from Chabot the soldiers each placed a hand once more upon the girl's shoulder. They waited for another sign to lead her away. Their officer was standing in the doorway: Chabot spoke to him.

"What accommodation have they got in this city," he asked with a leer at Josette and a refinement of cruelty worthy of the murderer of Bastien de Croissy, "for hardened criminals?"

"There is the town jail, citizen," the man replied.

"Safe, I suppose?"

"Very well guarded, anyway. It is built underneath the town hall."

"Who is in charge?'

"I am, citizen, with a score of men."

"And in the town hall?"

"There is a detachment of the National Guard under the command of Captain Favret."

"Quartered there?"

"Yes, Citizen."

Chabot gave another harsh laugh and a shrug.

"That should be enough to guard a wench," he said, "but one never knows—you men are such fools—"

While he spoke, Chabot had been idly fingering the packet, breaking the seals one by one. Now the outside wrapper fell apart and disclosed a small bundle of letters—letters. . . ? Letters? Chabot's hand shook as he took up each scrap of paper and unfolded it, and while he did so every drop of blood seemed to be drained from his ugly face and his bilious skin took on a grey ashen hue; for the packet contained only scraps of paper folded to look like letters with not a word on any of them. Chabot's eyes as he looked down on those empty scraps seemed to start out of his head: his face had been distorted before, now it seemed like a mask of death—grey, parchment-like, rigid. He raised his eyes and fixed them on Josette, while one by one the scraps of paper fluttered out of his hand.

But Josette herself was no longer the calm, self-possessed woman of a moment ago. When Chabot fingered the fateful packet and broke the seals one by one, when the outside wrapper fell apart and disclosed what should have been the famous letters, a cruel stab went through her heart at the thought of how different it would all have been if only the man she had trusted had not proved to be a Judas. Then suddenly she saw there here were no letters, only empty scraps of paper: her amazement was as great as that of her tormentor himself. She had received that packet from Louise: she had never parted from it since Louise placed it in her hands—never. But, of course. . . . the last five days. . . . the theft. . . . the miraculous recovery. . . . Oh, *mon Dieu! mon Dieu!* what did it all mean? Her brain was in a whirl. She could only stare and stare on those scraps of paper which fell out of Chabot's bony hands one by one.

No one spoke: the soldiers stood at attention, waiting for further orders. At the end of the room the old grandfather clock ticked away the minutes with slow and majestic monotony. At last a husky groan came from Chabot's quivering lips. He pointed a finger at Josette and then at the papers on the table.

"So," he murmured in a hoarse whisper, "you thought to fool me again?"

"No, no!" she protested involuntarily.

"You thought," he insisted in the same throaty voice, "to extract a safe-conduct from me and to fool me with these worthless scraps—"

He paused and then his voice rose to a shriek.

"Where are the letters?" he shouted stridently.

"I don't know," Josette protested. "I swear I do not know."

"Bring me those letters now," he iterated, "or by Satan—"

Once more he paused, for the words had died on his lips; indeed, how could he threaten his victim further when already he had promised her all the torments, mental and physical, that it was in his power to inflict. "Or by Satan—" What further threat could he utter? Jail? Death for her and her lover? What else was there?

"Bring me those letters!" he snarled, like a wild cat robbed of its prey, "or I'll have you branded, publicly whipped. I'll have you—I—I thank my stars that we've not given up in France all means of punishing hell-hounds like you."

"I cannot give you what I haven't got, Citizen," Josette declared calmly, "and I swear to you that I believed that the letters were in the packet which I have given you."

"You lie! You—"

Chabot turned to the officer-in-charge. "Take the strumpet away and remember—" He checked himself and for the next few moments swore and blasphemed; then suddenly changing his tone he said to Josette:

"Listen, little *citizeness*; I was only trying to frighten you," and the tiger's snarl became a tabby's purr. "I can see that you are a clever wench. You thought you would fool poor old Chabot, did you not? Thought you would have a bit of a game with him, what?"

He tiptoed round the table till he stood close to Josette; he thrust his grimy finger under her chin, forced her to raise her head: "Pretty dear!" he ejaculated, and pursed his thick lips as if to frame a kiss. But it must be supposed that something in the girl's expression of face caused him to spare her this final outrage: or did he really wish to cajole her? Certain it is that he contented himself with leering at her and ogling the sweet pale face which would have stirred compassion in any heart but that of a fiend.

"So now you've had your fun," he resumed with an artful chuckle, "and we are where we were before, eh? You are going to give me the letters which you went all the way to England to fetch, and I will give you a perfectly bee-ee-autiful safe-conduct for yourself and that handsome young lover of yours—lucky dog!—so that you can go and cuddle and kiss each other wherever you like. Now, I suppose you have hidden those naughty letters somewhere in your pretty little bed and we'll just go there together to fetch them, what?"

Josette made no reply and no movement. What could she do or say? She had only listened with half an ear to that abominable hypocrite's cajoleries. She had no more idea than he had what had become of the letters, or how it was that a packet in appearance exactly like the one which Louise had given her came to be substituted for the original one. She guessed—but only in a vague way—that Citizen Armand had something to do with the substitution, but she could not imagine what his object could possibly have been. While she stood mute and in an absolute whirl of conjecture and of doubt, Chabot waxed impatient.

"Now then, you little baggage," he said, and already he had dropping his insinuating tone, "don't stand there like a wooden image. Do not force me to send you marching along between two soldiers. Lead the way to your room. My friend and I will follow."

"I have already told you, Citizen," Josette maintained firmly, "I know nothing about any packet except the one which I have given you."

"It's a lie!"

"The truth, so help me God! And," she added solemnly, "I do still believe in God."

"Tshah!"

It was just an ejaculation of baffled rage and disappointment. For the next few seconds Chabot, with his hands behind his back, paced up and down the narrow room like a caged panther. He came to a halt presently in front of his colleague.

"What would you do, friend Chauvelin," he asked him, "if you were in my shoes?"

Chauvelin, during all this time, had remained absolutely quiescent, sitting on the bench immediately behind Josette. It was difficult indeed to conjecture if he had taken in all the phases of the scene which had been enacted in this room in the last quarter of an hour: Chabot's violence, Josette's withering contempt had alike left him unmoved. At one time it almost looked as if he slept: his head was down on his breast, his arms were crossed, his eyes closed. But now when directly interpellated by his colleague he seemed to rouse himself and glanced up at the angry face before him.

"Eh?" he queried vaguely. "What did you say, Citizen Representative?"

"Don't go to sleep, man!" the other retorted furiously. "Your neck and mine are in jeopardy while that baggage is allowed to defy me. What shall I do with her?"

"Keep her under guard and perquisition in her room: 'tis simple enough." And Chauvelin's lips curled in a sarcastic smile.

"Perquisition? Why, yes of course! The simplest thing, is it not?" And Chabot turned to the officer once more. "Sergeant," he commanded, "some of you go find the landlord of this hostelry. Order him to conduct you to the room occupied by the girl Gravier. You will search that room and never leave it until you have found a sealed packet exactly like the one which she laid on the table just now. You understand?"

"Yes, Citizen."

"Then go; and remember," he added significantly, "that packet must be found or there'll be trouble for your lack of zeal."

"There will be no trouble," the soldier retorted drily.

He turned on his heel and was about to march off with his men when Chauvelin said in a whisper to his friend:

"I would go with them if I were you. You'll want to see that the packet is given to you with the seals unbroken, what?"

"You are right, my friend," the other assented. He signalled to the sergeant, who stood at attention and waited for the distinguished Representative to go out of the room in front of him. In the doorway Chabot turned once more to Chauvelin:

"Look after the hussy while I'm gone," he said, and nodded in the direction of Josette. "I'm leaving some men outside to guard her."

"Have no fear," Chauvelin responded drily; "she'll not run away."

Chabot strode out of the room; the sergeant followed him, and some of the men fell into step and marched in their wake up the passage.

"You can wait outside, Citizen Soldiers!" Chauvelin said to the two men who were standing beside Josette. He had his tricolour scarf on, so there was no questioning his command: the soldiers fell back, turned and marched out of the room, closing the door behind them. And between those four white-washed walls Josette was now alone with Chauvelin.

Chapter 28

"Was I not right, little one, to carry out that small deception?"

If at the moment when Mother Eve was driven out from the Garden of Eden she had suddenly heard the serpent's voice whispering: "Was I not right to suggest your eating that bit of apple?" she would not have been more astonished than was Josette when that gentle, insinuating voice reached her ears.

She woke as from a dream—from a kind of coma into which she had been plunged by despair. She turned and encountered the kindly familiar glance of Citizen Armand, sitting cross-legged, unmoved on the bench, his head propped against the wall. In the feeble light of the guttering candles he appeared if anything paler than usual, and very tired. Josette gazed on him tongue-tied and puzzled, indeed more puzzled than she had ever felt before during these last few days so full of unexplainable events. As she did not attempt to speak he continued after a moment's pause:

"But for the substitution which I thought it best to effect, your precious letters would now be in the hands of that rogue, and nothing in the world could have saved you and your friend Reversac from death." And again, he continued: "The situation would be the same as now but we shouldn't have the letters."

He thrust his long thin hand into the inner pocket of his coat and half drew out a packet, wrapped and sealed just as was the other which had contained the pretended letters. Josette gave a gasp, and with her habitual, pathetic gesture pressed her hands against her heart. It had begun to beat furiously. She would have moved only that Armand put a finger quickly to his lips.

"Sh-sh!" he admonished and slipped the packet back inside his coat.

There was a murmur of voices outside; one of the soldiers cleared his throat, others shuffled their feet. There were sounds of whisperings, of movements and heavy footsteps the other side of the closed door— reminders that watch was being kept there by order of the Citizen Representative. Josette sank her voice to a whisper:

"And you did that. . . ? For me. . . ? Whilst I—"

"Whilst you called me a traitor and a Judas in your heart," he concluded with a wan smile. "Let's say no more about it."

"You may forgive me. . . . I cannot. . . ."

"Don't let's talk of that," he resumed with a show of impatience. "I only wished you to know that the reason why I didn't interfere between Chabot and yourself was because in the existing state of our friend's temper my interference would have been not only useless but harmful to you and your friend. All I could do was to manoeuvre him into ordering the perquisition in your room and get him to superintend it so as to have the chance of saying these few words to you in private."

"You are right, as you always have been, Citizen Armand," Josette rejoined fervently. "I cannot imagine how I ever came to doubt you."

As if in response to her unspoken request he rose and came across the room to her, gave her the kindest and most gentle of smiles and patted her shoulder.

"Poor little girl!" he murmured softly.

She took hold of his hand and managed to imprint a kiss upon it before he snatched it away.

"You have been such a wonderful friend to me," she sighed. "I shall never doubt you again."

"Even though I were to put your trust to a more severe test than before?" he asked.

"Try me," she rejoined simply.

"Suppose I were to order your arrest. . . . now?. . . . It would only be for a few days," he hastened to assure her.

"I would not doubt you," she declared firmly.

"Only until I can order young Reversac to be brought here."

"Maurice?"

"Yes! For your ultimate release I must have you both here together. You understand?"

"I think I do."

"While one of you is here and the other in Paris, complications can so easily set in, and those fiends might still contrive to play us a trick. But with both of you here, and the letters in my hands, I can negotiate with Chabot for your release and for the necessary safe-conducts. After which you can take the diligence together to Tréport and be in England within three days."

"Yes! yes! I do understand," Josette reiterated, tears of happiness and gratitude welling to her eyes. "And I don't mind prison one little bit, dear Citizen Armand," she added *naïvely*. "Indeed, I don't mind anything that you order me to do. I do trust you absolutely. Absolutely."

"I'll try and make it as easy for you as I can, and with luck I hope to have our friend Reversac here within the week."

Excited and happy, not the least bit frightened, and without the slightest suspicion, Josette saw Chauvelin go to the door, open it and call to the soldiers who were on guard in the passage. She heard him call: "Which of you is in command here?" She saw one of them step briskly forward; heard his smart reply: "I am, citizen!" and finally her friend's curt command:

"Corporal, you will take this woman, Josephine Gravier, to the *Commissariat de Police*. You will give her in charge of the Chief *Commissary* with orders that she be kept under strict surveillance until further orders." He then came across to the table, took up the quill pen that was lying there and a printed paper out of his pocket, scribbled a few words, signed his name and strewed the writing with sand. The tallow candles had now guttered so low, and emitted such a column of black smoke, that he could hardly see: he tried to re-read what he had written and was apparently satisfied, for he handed the paper to the soldier, saying curtly:

"This will explain to the Chief *Commissary* that the order for this arrest is issued by a member of the Third Sectional Committee of Public Safety—Armand Chauvelin—and that I hereby denounce Josephine Gravier as suspect of treason against the Republic."

The corporal—a middle-aged man in somewhat shabby uniform—took the paper and stood at attention, while Chauvelin, with a peremptory gesture, beckoned to Josette to fall in with the men. Loyal and trusting until the end, the girl even forbore to throw a glance on the treacherous friend who was playing her this cruel trick: she even went to the length of appearing overcome with terror, indeed she played to perfection the *rôle* of an unfortunate *aristo* confronted with treason and preparing for death.

"Now then, young woman," the corporal commanded curtly. Three men were waiting in the passage. With faltering steps and her face buried in her hands, Josette allowed herself to be led out of the room. The corporal was the last to go; the door fell to behind him with a bang. Chauvelin stood for a moment in the centre of the room, listening. He heard the brief word of command, the tramp of heavy feet along the passage in the direction of the front door, the shooting of bolts and rattle of chains. He rubbed his pale, talon-like hands together, and a curious smile played round his thin lips.

"You'll have your work cut out, my gallant Pimpernel," he murmured to himself, "to get the wench away. And even if you do, her lover is still in Paris, and what will you do about him? I think this time—" he added complacently.

Then he paused and once more lent an attentive ear to the sounds that came to him from the other side of the house; to the banging and stamping, the thuds and thunderings, the loud and strident shoutings and medley of angry voices, all gradually merging into a terrific uproar.

And as he listened the enigmatic smile on his lips turned to a contemptuous sneer.

Chapter 29

It was late in the evening by now and most of the clients of the hostelry had already retired for the night. Awakened by the terrible hubbub some of them had ventured outside their doors, only to find that the corridors and stairs were patrolled by soldiers, who promptly ordered them back into their rooms. On the downstairs floor the landlord and his wife, in the room adjoining the one on which their daughter had shared with Josette Gravier, had been rudely ordered to give up all keys and on peril of their lives not to interfere with the soldiers in the discharge of their duty. The Representative of the People, who had arrived at the hostelry that very evening, appeared to be in a towering rage: he it was who ordered a rigorous search of both the rooms, the landlord vaguely protesting against this outrage put upon his house.

He and his family were, however, soon reduced to silence, as were the guests on the floors above, and the stamping and the banging, the thuds and thunderings, the shouts and imprecations were confined to the two rooms in the house where a squad of soldiers, under the command of their sergeant and egged on by Chabot, carried on a perquisition with ruthless violence.

Within a quarter of an hour there was not a single article of furniture left whole in the place. The men had broken up the flooring, pulled open every drawer, smashed every lock; they had ripped up the mattresses and pillows and pulled the curtains down from their rods. Chabot, stalking about from one room to the other with great strides and arms *akimbo*, cursed the soldiers loudly for their lack of zeal.

"Did I not say," he bellowed like a raging bull, "that those letters must be found?"

The sergeant was at his wits' ends. The two rooms did, indeed, look in the feeble light of the hanging lamp above as if a Prussian cannon had exploded in their midst. The landlord with his wife and daughter cowered terror-stricken in a corner.

"Never," they protested with sobs, "never has such an indignity been put upon this house."

"You should not have taken in such baggage," Chabot retorted roughly.

"Citizen Chauvelin gave orders—"

"Never mind about Citizen Chauvelin. I am giving you orders, here and now."

He strode across the room and came to a halt in front of the three unfortunates. They struggled to their feet and clung to one another in terror before the fearsome Representative of the People. Indeed, Chabot at this moment, with face twisted into a mask of fury, with hair hanging in fantastic curls over his brow, with eyes bloodshot and curses spluttering out of his quivering lips, looked almost inhuman in his overwhelming rage.

"The hussy who slept here—?" he demanded.

"Yes, citizen?"

"She had a sealed packet—a small packet about the size of my hand—?"

"Yes, citizen."

"What did she do with it?"

"It was stolen from her, Citizen Representative, the first night she slept in this house," the landlord explained, his voice quaking with fear.

"So, she averred," the woman put in trembling.

"Did any of you see it?"

They all three shook their heads.

"The girl didn't sleep in this room that night, citizen," the woman explained. "She shared a room with two female travellers who left the next day on the diligence. Citizen Chauvelin then gave orders for her to sleep in my daughter's room and made us responsible for her safety."

Chabot glanced over his shoulder at the sergeant.

"Find out in the morning," he commanded, "at the *commissariat* all about the female travellers and whither they went, and report to me." He then turned back to the landlord. "And do you mean to tell me that none of you saw anything of that sealed packet supposed to have been stolen? Think again," he ordered roughly.

"I never set eyes on it, citizen," the man declared.

"Nor I, I swear it!" both the two women averred.

Chabot kept the wretched family in suspense for a few minutes after that, gloating over their misery and their fear of him, while his bloodshot eyes glared into their faces. Behind him the sergeant now stood at attention, waiting for further orders. There was nothing to be done, since every nook and cranny had been ransacked, and short of pulling down the walls no further search was possible. But Chabot's lust of destruction was not satisfied. He had the feeling at this moment that he wanted to set fire to the house and see it burned to the ground, together with that elusive packet of letters which meant more than life to him.

"Sergeant!" he cried, and was on the point of giving the monstrous order when a quiet, dry voice suddenly broke in:

"There are other ways than fire and brimstone, my friend, of recovering what you desire to possess."

Chabot swung round with an angry snarl and saw Armand Chauvelin standing in the doorway, a placid, slender figure in sober black with inscrutable face and smooth unruffled hair.

"The hussy?" Chabot yelled, his voice husky with choler.

"She is safer than she was when you left her half an hour ago, for I've had her arrested and sent to the *commissary* of the district under a denunciation from me. She is safe there for the present, but she certainly won't be for long if you spend your time raving and swearing and pulling the house down about our ears."

"What the devil do you mean—she won't be safe for long? Why not?"

"Because," Chauvelin replied with earnest significance, "there are influences at work about here which will be exerted to their utmost power to get the wench out of your clutches."

"I care nothing about the wench," Chabot muttered under his breath. "It's those accursed letters—"

"Exactly," Chauvelin broke in quietly, "the letters."

Chabot was silent for a moment or two, swallowing the blasphemies that forced themselves to his lips. He glared with mixed feelings of wrath and vague terror into those pale, deep-set eyes that regarded him with unconcealed contempt. Something in their glance seemed to hypnotise him and to weaken his will. After a time, his own glance fell; he cleared his throat, tugged at his waistcoat and passed his grimy, moist palm over his curly hair. And in order to gain further control over his nerves he buried his hands in his breeches pockets and started once more to pace up and down the room. The soldiers had lined up the passage outside: their sergeant had stepped back against the door-way and was doing his best not to smile at the Citizen Representative's discomfiture.

"You are right," Chabot said at last to Chauvelin with a semblance of calm. "We must talk the matter of letters over before we can decide what we do with the baggage."

Then he turned to the sergeant.

"Which are the men who took the wench to the *commissariat?*" he asked.

"I don't think they are back, citizen," the sergeant replied.

"Don't think!" Chabot snarled. "Go and find out."

The man moved away and Chabot called after him:

"Report to me in the public room—you'll find me there."

He gave a sign to Chauvelin. "Let's go!" he said curtly. "The sight of this room makes me see red."

He did not throw another glance on the unfortunate landlord and his family, the victims of his unreasoning rage. They stood in the midst of their devastated room looking utterly forlorn, not knowing yet if they had anything more to fear. The house appeared singularly still after the uproar of a while ago, only the measured tread of soldiers patrolling the corridors echoed weirdly through the gloom.

Chabot stalked on ahead of his colleague and made his way to the public room. There he threw himself into a convenient chair and sprawled across the nearest table, ordering the man in charge to bring him a bottle of wine. Then he called loudly to his colleague to come and join him.

But Chauvelin did not respond to the call. He turned into the small private room where the fateful interview had just taken place. He closed the door, locked and bolted it. He then went across to the window and examined its shutter. It was barred as before. There was no fear that he would be interrupted in the task which now lay before him. The candles had burned down almost to their sockets: Chauvelin picked up the snuffers and trimmed the wicks. Then he sat down at the table and drew the original sealed packet out of his breast pocket.

The time had come to break the seals. There was no longer any reason to keep the packet intact. The first act in the drama which he had devised for his own advancement and the destruction of his powerful enemy had been a brilliant success. The wench Josette Gravier and her lover were both in prison—one in Rouen, the other in Paris. Such a situation would of a certainty arouse the sympathy of the Scarlet Pimpernel and induce him to exert that marvellous ingenuity of his for the rescue of the two young people.

But this time Chauvelin was more accurately forewarned than he had ever been before. All he need do was keep a close eye on the wench; the English spy, however elusive he might be, must of necessity attempt to get in touch with the girl, and unless he had the power of rendering himself invisible, his capture was bound to follow. It may safely be said that no fear of failure assailed Chauvelin at this hour. He considered his enemy as good as captured already. It would be a triumph for his perseverance, his inventive genius and his patriotism! Once more he would become a power in the land, the master of these men—these venal cowardly fools—who would again fawn at his feet after this and suffer at his hands for all the humiliation they had heaped upon him these past two years.

The compromising letters would be an additional weapon wherewith to chastise these arrogant upstarts—not excluding the powerful Danton himself, perhaps not even Robespierre. Armand Chauvelin saw himself on the very pinnacle of popularity, the veritable ruler of France. To what height of supreme power could not he aspire, who had brought such an inveterate enemy of revolutionary France to death?

And all the while that these pleasant thoughts, these happy anticipations ran through Armand Chauvelin's mind, his delicate hands toyed with the packet of letters—the keystone that held together the edifice of his future. He fingered it lovingly as he had done many a time before. Here it was just as it had been when Picard placed it in his hands: he had never broken the seals, never seen its contents, never set eyes on the letters which caused men like Chabot, Bazire, and Fabre d'Eglantine and even the popular Danton to tremble for their lives. But now that the first act of the little comedy which he had devised had been successfully enacted in this very room, he felt that he could indulge his natural curiosity to probe into the secrets of these men. He felt eager and excited. These letters might reveal secrets that would be a still more powerful leverage than he had hoped for the fulfilment of his ambition.

His fingers shook slightly as they broke the seals. The wrapper fell apart just as that other had done in Chabot's hands, and the contents were revealed to Chauvelin's horror-filled gaze. For here were no letters either; like the wrapper and like the seals the contents were the same as those which had turned Citizen Chabot from a human being into a raging beast: scraps of paper made to appear like letters—nothing more!

Chauvelin stared at them and stared; his pale, deep-set eyes were aflame, his temples throbbed, his whole body shook as with ague. What did the whole thing mean? Where did this monstrous deception begin? What was the initial thread which bound this amazing conspiracy together? Did it have its origin in Bastien de Croissy's tortured brain—in that of his despairing widow? Or did that seemingly guileless girl after all. . . ? But no! this, of course, was nonsense. Chauvelin passed his trembling hand over his burning forehead. He felt as if he had been stunned by a heavy blow on the head. Idly he allowed the scraps of paper to glide in and out between his fingers.

There was not a word written on any of them. Mere empty scraps of paper!....All save one!....Mechanically Chauvelin picked that one up.... it was soiled and creased, more so than the others. He passed his hand over it to smooth it out. The candles were guttering and smoking again.. he could hardly see. . . . his eyes, too, were dim—not with tears, of course; just with a kind of film which threw a crimson blur over everything. He was compelled to blink once or twice before he could decipher the words on that one scrap of paper. He did succeed in the end, but only read the first few words:

We seek him here. . .

That maddening doggerel, the sight of which had so often been to him the precursor of some awful disaster! For the first time in his career Chauvelin felt a sense of discouragement. He had been so full of hope only a few minutes ago—so full of certainty. This awful disappointment came like a terrific, physical crash upon his aching head. With arms stretched out upon the table, that one scrap of paper crushed in his hand, he thought of the many failures which had gradually brought him down from his exalted rank to one of humiliation. Calais, Boulogne, Paris, Nantes, and many more—and now this! He had felt it coming when his enemy had so impudently faced him in the public room of this hostelry. The big fat sailor—that unmistakable laugh—the pepper-pot to remind him of his greatest discomfiture over at the Chat Gris in Calais: these and more all seemed to flit past Chauvelin's fevered brain in this moment of bitter disappointment. He had even ceased to think of Josette, communing only with the past. The minutes sped by; the old Normandy clock ticked away, majestic and indifferent.

A few minutes later Chabot's clamorous voice broke in on the lonely man's meditations. He roused himself from his apathy, threw a quick glance around. Then as the familiar voice drew nearer and nearer he gathered the scraps of paper hastily together and thrust them in his pocket out of sight. He went to the door and opened it just in time to meet his colleague, whose walk was not as steady as it had been when rage alone had governed his movements. Since then a bottle of red wine and one of heady Normandy cider had gone to his head; his lips sagged and his eyes were bleary. Lurching forward he nearly fell into Chauvelin's arms.

"I have been waiting for you for half an hour," the latter said with a show of reproach. "What in the world have you been doing?"

"I was in a high fever," Chabot muttered thickly. "A raging thirst I had—must have a drink—"

"Sit down there," Chauvelin commanded, for the man could hardly stand. "We must have more light."

"Yes. . . . more light. . . . I hate this gloom—"

Chabot fell into a chair; he stretched his arms over the table and buried his head in the crook of his elbow and was soon breathing audibly. Chauvelin looked down on him with bitter contempt. What a partner in this great undertaking which he already had in mind! However, there was nothing for it now. . . . this drunken lout was the only man who could lend him a hand in this juncture. He clapped his hands, and after a moment or two the maid in charge appeared. Chauvelin ordered her to bring more candles and a jug of cold water.

Chabot was snoring. With scant ceremony Chauvelin dashed the water over his head. The maid retired, grinning.

"What in hell—?" Chabot cried out, thus rudely awakened from his slumbers.

The cold water had partially sobered him. He blinked for a time into the fluttering candle-light, the water dripping down the tousled strands of his hair and the furrows of his cheeks.

"We've got to review the situation," Chauvelin began drily.

He sat down opposite Chabot, leaning his elbows on the table, his thin veined hands tightly clasped together.

"The situation?" Chabot iterated dully. "Yes, by Satan!. . . . that hussy. . . . what?"

"Never mind about the hussy now! You are still anxious, I imagine, that certain letters which gravely compromise you and your party do not fall into the hands, say, of the *Moniteur* or the *Pére Duchesne* for publication."

Chauvelin spoke slowly and deliberately so as to allow every word to sink into the consciousness of that sot. In this he succeeded, for at mention of those fateful letters the last cloud of drunkenness seemed to vanish from the man's sodden brain. Rage and fear had once more sole possession of him.

"You swore," he countered roughly, "that you would get those letters—"

"And so, I will," Chauvelin returned calmly, "but you must do your best to help."

"You have allowed yourself to be hoodwinked by a young baggage—you—"

"If you take up that tone with me, my friend," Chauvelin suddenly said in a sharp, peremptory tone, fixing his colleague with a stern eye, "I will throw up the sponge at once and let the man who now has the letters do his damndest with them."

The threat had the same effect on Chabot as the douche of cold water. He swallowed his choler and said almost humbly:

"What is it you want me to do?"

"I'll tell you. First, about the packet of letters—"

"Yes!. . . . the packet of letters—the real packet. . . . Who has it—where is it?. . . . I want to know—" And with each phrase he uttered Chabot beat on the table with the palm of his hand, while Chauvelin's quick brain was at work on the last phases of his tortuous scheme.

"I'll tell you," he replied quietly, "who stole the packet of letters from the girl Gravier. It was the English spy who is known under the name of 'The Scarlet Pimpernel.'"

"How do you know?"

"Never mind how I know: I do know. Let that be sufficient! But as true as that you and I are alive at this moment the Scarlet Pimpernel has those letters in his possession—"

"And he can send the lot of us to the guillotine?" Chabot interposed in a raucous whisper.

"He certainly will," Chauvelin retorted drily, "unless—"

"Unless what? Speak, man, unless you wish to see me fall dead at your feet!"

". . . unless we can capture him, of course."

"But they say he is as elusive as a ghost. Why, you yourself—"

"I know that. He is not as elusive as you think. I have tried—and failed—that is true. But never before have I had the help of an influential man like you."

Chabot bridled at the implied flattery.

"I'll help you," he said, "of course."

"Then listen, citizen. Although we have not got the letters, we hold what we might call the trump card in this game—"

"The trump card?"

"Yes, the girl Gravier. I told you I had ordered her arrest—"

"True, but—"

"She is at the present moment at the *commissariat*, under strict surveillance—"

Chabot jumped to his feet, glared into his colleague's pale face and brought his heavy fist crashing down upon the table.

"You lie!" he shrieked at the top of his voice. "She is not at the *commissariat*."

Chauvelin shrugged.

"Where, then?" he asked coolly.

"The devil knows—I don't!"

It was Chauvelin's turn to stare into his colleague's eyes. Was the man still drunk, or had he gone mad?

"You'd oblige me, citizen," he said coolly, "by not talking in riddles."

"Riddles?" the other mocked. "Tscha! I tell you that that bit of baggage whom you ordered to be taken to the *commissariat* never got there at all."

"Never got there?" Chauvelin queried with a frown. "You are joking, Citizen."

"Joking, am I? Let me tell you this: the sergeant and the soldiers whom I sent to inquire after the wench came back half an hour ago and this is what they reported: neither the soldiers nor the hussy were seen at the *commissariat*—"

"But where—?"

"Where the wench is no one knows. The *commissary* at once sent out a patrol. They found the four soldiers in the public garden behind the St. Ouen, their legs tied together by their belts, their caps doing duty as gags in their mouths; but not a sign of the girl."

"Well—and?"

"The soldiers were interrogated. They are all under arrest now, the cowardly traitors! They declared that while they crossed the garden on their way to the *commissariat* they were suddenly attacked from behind without any warning. They had seen no one and hadn't heard a sound: the place was pitch dark and entirely deserted. It seems that the lights have been abolished in this God-forsaken city ever since oil and tallow got so dear, and the townsfolk avoid going through the garden, as it is the haunt of every evil-doer in Rouen. The men swore that they did their best to defend themselves, but that they were outnumbered and outclassed. Anyway, the miscreants, whoever they were, brought them down, bound and gagged them and then made off in the darkness, taking the wench with them."

"But didn't the men see anything? Were they footpads who attacked them, or—or—?"

"The devil only knows! Two of the soldiers declared that they were attacked by men in the same uniform that they wore themselves, and one thought that he recognised a sailor whom he had seen about on the quay the last day or two—a huge, powerful fellow, whose fist would fell an ox."

"Ah?"

"Anyway, the hell-hounds made off in the direction of the river."

"Ah?" Chauvelin remarked again.

"Why do you say 'Ah?' like that?" Chabot queried roughly. "Do you know anything of this affair?"

"No, but it does confirm what I said just now."

"What's that?"

"That those infernal English spies are at work here."

"Why do you say that?"

"Everything points to it: the mode of attack, the disappearance of the girl, the big sailor. Footpads would not have attacked soldiers with empty pockets, nor would they have carried off a girl who has neither friends nor relations to pay ransom for her."

"That's true."

"When did the sergeant tell you all this?"

"Not so long ago—might be a quarter of an hour—"

"Why didn't you let me know at once?"

"It was none of your business. I am here to give orders, not you."

"And what orders did you give? You didn't seem to be in a fit condition to give any orders at all."

"Rage at being baffled again went to my head. If you had not taken it upon yourself to order that girl's arrest—"

"You were about to tell me," Chauvelin broke in harshly, "what orders you gave to the sergeant."

"I ordered them to bring the four delinquents here, as I wish to interrogate them."

"Well—and are they here?"

"Wait, citizen—all in good time! The sergeant had to go to the *commissariat*—then he would have to—"

"I know all that," the other interrupted impatiently. He went to the door and opened it, clapped his hands and waited until the night-watchman came shuffling along the corridor.

"As soon as the sergeant returns," he said to the man, "bring him in here."

Chabot opened his mouth in order to protest; he was jealous of his prerogatives as a Representative of the People, a position of far greater authority than a mere member of the Committee of Public Safety. But there was something in Chauvelin's quiet assumption of command that overawed him and he felt shrunken and insignificant under the other's contemptuous glance. His ugly mouth closed with a snap, and he saw the watchman depart with a glowering look in his eyes. He sat down again by the table and stared stupidly into vacancy; his clumsy fingers toyed with the objects on the table; his thin legs were stretched straight out before him. Now and then he glanced towards the open door and listened to the several sounds which still resounded through the house.

Although the guests had been peremptorily ordered to keep to their rooms they could not be prevented from moving about and whispering among themselves, since sleep had become impossible. The uproar of a while ago, when furniture was being smashed and floors and walls were battered, had awakened them all from their first sleep. Since then vague terror and the ceaseless tramping of soldiers who patrolled the house had kept everyone on the alert. The unfortunate landlord and his family had taken refuge in a vacant room, but for them, more so than for any of their clients, sleep was impossible.

Thus, a constant, if subdued, hubbub reigned throughout the house. Chabot seemed to find a measure of comfort in listening to it all. Like so many persons who profess atheism, he was very superstitious, and all the talk about the mysterious spy, who worked in the dark and was as elusive as a ghost, had exacerbated his nerves. Chauvelin, on the other hand, paced up and down the room; his thin hands were tightly clasped behind his back, his head was down on his chest. His busy mind was ceaselessly at work.

Obviously, he had lost the first round in this new game which he had engaged in against the Scarlet Pimpernel. And not only that: he had lost what he had so aptly termed the trump card in the game. Josette Gravier was just the type of female in distress who would appeal to the adventurous spirit of Sir Percy Blakeney: while she was a prisoner in Rouen the Scarlet Pimpernel would not vacate the field, and there would have been a good chance of laying him by the heels. There was none now that the girl was in safety, for Chauvelin knew from experience that there was no getting prisoners like her out of the clutches of the Scarlet Pimpernel, once that prince of adventures had them under his guard.

Indeed, the Terrorist would have felt completely baffled but for one fact—yet another trump card which he still held and which if judiciously played...

At this point his reflections were interrupted by the arrival of the sergeant, followed by the four delinquent soldiers. This time Chauvelin made no attempt to interfere. Let Chabot question the men if he wished. He, Chauvelin, knew everything they could possibly say. He listened with half an ear to the interrogatory, only catching a word or a phrase here and there: "We saw nothing. . . . we heard nothing. . . . They were on us like a lightning flash. . . . Yes, we had our bayonets. . . . impossible to use them. . . . It was dark as pitch. . . . They wore the uniform of the National Guard. . . . the same as ours, at least as far as one could see in the dark. . . . All except one, and he looked like a boatman. . . . a huge fellow with a powerful fist. . . . I had seen him on the quay before. . . . and here in the public room. . . . How could we use our bayonets?. . . . They were dressed the same as we were. . . . They hit about with their fists. . . . the big sailor felled me down. . . . and me too. . . . I saw stars. . . . So did I. . . . When I recovered my legs were tied together and my woollen cap was stuffed into my mouth—" and more in the same strain.

The city gates being closed after dark no one could possibly pass them before dawn on the morrow, but there was always the river and no end to the ingenuity and daring of the Scarlet Pimpernel. But there was that last trump card—the ace, Chauvelin fondly hoped.

When Chabot finally dismissed the soldiers the two men once more put their heads together.

"There is not much we can do about the girl Gravier," Chauvelin remarked drily. "Luckily, we hold the man Reversac. It is with him we can deal now."

"The girl's lover?" the other asked.

"Of course."

"I see what you mean."

"Lucky that you do," Chauvelin mocked. "You know where he is, I presume."

"In the *abbaye*. I had him taken there myself. A stroke of genius, methinks," he added complacently, "to have the fellow arrested."

"Well, you have had a pretty free hand these last few weeks while that cursed English spy turned his attention to our friend Carrier at Nantes."

"I suppose the death of all those priests and women appealed to him. . . . As for me—"

"So, did Josette Gravier as your victim appeal to him, and so will Maurice Reversac."

"Thank our friend Satan, we've got him safe enough!"

"Yes, he is our trump card," Chauvelin concluded, "and we must play him for all he is worth."

He renewed his pacing up and down the room, while Chabot, quite sober now but with not two ideas in his muddled brain, stared stupidly in front of him.

"Paris will not do," Chauvelin resumed after a little while, mumbling to himself rather than speaking to his colleague. That damned Pimpernel has too many spies and friends there and hidden lairs we know nothing about.

"Eh? What did you say?" Chabot queried tartly.

"I said that we must get Reversac away from Paris."

"Why? We've got him safe enough."

"You have not," Chauvelin asserted forcefully. He came to a halt the other side of the table, and fixing his pale eyes on Chabot asked him: "Have you ever asked Fouquier-Tinville how many prisoners have escaped from Paris alone through the agency of the Scarlet Pimpernel?"

"No, but—"

"Considerably over two hundred since the beginning of this year."

"I don't believe it!"

"It's true, I tell you; and the same number from Nantes. Carrier is at his wits' end."

"Carrier is a fool."

"Perhaps. But you understand now why I want to get Reversac away from Paris. By dint of bribery if nothing else, the Scarlet Pimpernel will drag him out of your clutches."

Chabot reflected for a moment, and Chauvelin, guessing the workings of his mind, added with earnest significance:

"If we lose Reversac we shall have nothing to offer in exchange for the letters."

"The letters—" Chabot murmured vaguely.

"Yes," Chauvelin remarked drily: "you haven't found them, have you?"

By way of a reply Chabot uttered a savage oath.

"Where the girl is, there are the letters," the other went on, "get that into your head, and the letters are in the possession of the English spies. Now remember one thing, my friend: while we hold the girl's lover we can still get the letters, by offering a safe-conduct in exchange for them. And incidentally—don't forget that—we have the chance of laying our hands on the Scarlet Pimpernel, for whose capture there is a reward of ten thousand *livres.*"

As Chabot had exhausted his vocabulary of curses he relieved his feelings this time by blaspheming.

"Ten thousand," he ejaculated.

"Not to mention the glory."

"Damn the glory! But I hate to let the baggage and her lover go."

"You need not."

"How do you mean—I need not? You've just mentioned safe-conducts—"

"So, I did. But I can endorse those with a secret sign. It is known to every Chief *Commissary* in France and nullifies every safe-conduct."

"Splendid!" Chabot exclaimed and beat the table with the palm of his hand. "Splendid!" he exclaimed and jumped to his feet. "Now I begin to understand."

The two men exchanged *rôles* for the moment. It was Chabot now who paced up and down the room, mumbling to himself, while Chauvelin sat down at the table and with idle hands toyed with the quill pen, the snuffers, or anything that was handy. Presently Chabot came to a standstill in front of him.

"You want to get Reversac away from Paris?" he asked.

"Yes."

"And bring him here?"

"Yes."

"The journey down will be dangerous if, as you say, the English spies are on the war-path."

"We must minimise the danger as far as we can."

"How?"

"A strong escort. And there will be the additional chance of capturing the Scarlet Pimpernel."

"You think he will be sure to try and get at Reversac?"

"Absolutely certain."

"And forewarned is forearmed, what?"

"Exactly."

"Splendid!" Chabot reiterated gleefully.

"And if we succeed in capturing one or more of those confounded spies, just think how marvellous our position will be with regard to the letters. We shall have something to bargain with, eh?"

"The Scarlet Pimpernel himself?"

"The whole damned crowd of them, as well as the girl and her lover!"

"You can have the lot," Chabot ejaculated, "so long as I have the accursed letters!"

"If you follow my instructions, point by point," Chauvelin concluded, "I can safely promise you those."

They sat together for another hour after that, elaborating Chauvelin's plan, lingering over every detail, leaving nothing to chance, gloating over the victory which they felt was assured.

It was midnight before they finally went to bed. And at break of day Chabot was already posting for Paris armed with instructions from Chauvelin to the secret agents of the Committee of Public Safety.

Chapter 30

Snow lay thick on the ground; it was heavy going up the hills and slippery coming down. In an ordinary way the diligence between Meulon and Rouen would have ceased to ply in weather as severe as this. Already at Meulon, when an early start was made, the clouds had looked threatening. "We'll have more snow, for sure," everyone had declared, the driver included, who muttered something about its being madness to attempt the journey with those leaden-coloured clouds hanging overhead.

But in spite of these protests and warnings a start was made in the early dawn. Such were the orders of Citizen Representative Chabot (Loire et Cher), who was travelling in the diligence, and his word, of course, was law. Outside the hostelry of the Mouton Blanc a small crowd had gathered despite the early hour, to watch the departure of the diligence. All along people, who stood about at a respectful distance because of the soldiers, declared that this was no ordinary diligence. Though it was one of the small ones with just the *coupé* and the *rotonde*, it was drawn by four horses with postilion and all the *banquette* behind the driver was unoccupied, although the awning was up, and this was odd, declared the gaffers, because the *banquette* places being the cheapest, three of four passengers usually crowded there, under the lee, too, of the luggage piled upon the top.

In the *coupé* sat the Citizen Representative himself, and he had that compartment entirely to himself. In the *rotonde* there was a young man sitting between two soldiers in uniform, and three other men were on the seats opposite. Moreover, and this was the most amazing circumstance of all, what looked at first sight like the usual pile of luggage on the top was no luggage at all, but three men lying huddled up under the tarpaulin, wrapped in greatcoats, for it was bitterly cold up there.

No! It decidedly was on ordinary diligence. And it was under strong escort, too: six mounted men under the command of an officer—a captain, what? So not only was the traveller in the *coupé* a great personage, but the prisoner must also be one of consequence, for no sooner was he installed with the soldiers in the *rotonde* than the blinds were at once drawn down, nor was anyone allowed to come nigh the vehicle after that. Naturally all this secrecy and the unusual proceedings created further amazement still, but those *quidnuncs* who came as near as they dared were quickly and peremptorily ordered back by the soldiers: and later in the day, at Vernon outside the Boule d'Or, two boys, who had after the manner of such youngsters succeeded in crawling underneath the coach, were caught when on the point of stepping on the foot-board.

The captain in command of the guards seized them both by the ears and ordered them to be soundly flogged then and there, which was done by a couple of soldiers with a will and the buckle end of their belts. The howls that ensued and the sudden report of a pistol-shot, discharged no one could ever tell whence, startled the horses into a panic. The leaders reared, the ostler unable to hold them fell, and fortunately rolled over unhurt in the snow. A more serious catastrophe was just averted through the presence of mind of a passer-by, a poor old vagabond shivering with cold, who did not look as if he had any vitality in him, let alone the pluck to seize the near leader by the bridle as he did and bring the frightened team to a standstill.

The driver and the postilion were having a drink of mulled cider at the moment that all this commotion was going on. They came rushing out of the hostelry just in time to witness the prowess of that miserable old man. The driver was gracious enough to murmur approbation, and even the captain of the guard had something pleasant to say.

It had been so very neatly done.

"I was a stud-groom once," the old man explained with a self-deprecating shrug, "in the house of *aristos*. 'Tis not much I don't know about horses."

The captain tendered him a few *sous*.

"This is for your pains, citizen," he said, and nodded in the direction of the hostelry close by: "you'd better go in there and get a hot drink."

"Thank you kindly, Citizen Captain," the man rejoined as his thin hands, blue with cold, closed over the money. He seemed loth to go away from the horses. They were fine, strong beasts, relays just taken up here and very fresh. The poor man had evidently spoken the truth: there was not much he did not know about horses. One could see that from the way he looked at them and handled them, adjusting a buckle here and there, fondling the beasts' manes, their ears and velvety noses, inspecting their fetlocks and their shoes.

"Good smith's work here," he said approvingly, tapping one shoe after another.

"That's all right, my man," the captain broke in impatiently. "We must be off now. You go and get your drink."

The vagabond demurred and looked down with a rueful glance on his ragged clothes.

"I can't go in there," he said with a woebegone shake of the head, "not in these rags. The landlord doesn't like it," he went on, "because of other customers—"

The captain gave a shrug. He didn't really care what happened to that wretched *caitiff*. Indeed, he was anxious to get away as he had been ordered by the Citizen Representative to make Gaillon before dark. Citizen Chabot was not a man to be lightly disobeyed, and as he had suffered much from cold and discomfort his temper throughout this journey had been of the vilest. So, losing no more time the captain now turned on his heel and went to give orders to his men. The young postilion, more charitably disposed, perhaps, towards the poor wretch, or in less of a hurry to make a start, said:

"I'll bring you out a drink, old gaffer," and he ran back into the hostelry, leaving the driver and the whilom stud-groom to exchange reminiscences of past *aristo* stablings. He returned after a couple of minutes with a mug of steaming cider in his hand.

"Here you are, citizen," he said.

The vagabond took the mug but seemed in no hurry to drink. He had a fit of coughing and swayed backwards and forwards on his long legs as if already he had a drop too much. The driver, in the meanwhile, took the opportunity of administering correction to the ostler for failing to hold the horses properly when they shied, and for rolling about in the snow when he should have held on tightly to the bridles.

"Call yourself a stableman," he said contemptuously while the postilion stood by, grinning: "why, look at this poor man here—"

But the "poor man here" seemed in a sorry plight just now. The coughing fit shook him so that the steaming cider squirted out of the mug.

"Let me hold the mug for you, old man," the postilion suggested.

"You drink it, citizen," the man said between gasps. "I can't. It makes me sick."

Nothing loth, the postilion had a drink, was indeed on the point of draining the mug when the driver with a "Here! I say!" took the mug from him and drank the remainder of the cider down.

Chabot put his head out of the window: "Now then, over there!" he called out with a loud curse. And "*En avant!*" came in peremptory command from the captain of the guard. The driver made ready to climb up on the box when the old vagabond touched him on the shoulder: "You wouldn't give me a lift," he suggested timidly, "would you, citizen?"

"Not I," the other retorted gruffly. "I daren't. . . . not without orders." And he nodded in the direction of the captain.

"He wouldn't know," the poor man whispered. "When you move off I'll climb on the step. I'll keep close behind you and hide in the *banquette* under cover of the luggage. They couldn't see from the back. . . . My home is in Gaillon and it's three leagues to walk in this damnable weather!"

He looked so sick and so miserable that the driver hesitated. He was possessed of bowels of compassion, even though he was a paid servant of the most cruel, most ruthless government in the world. But despite his feelings of pity for a fellow-creature he would probably have refused point-blank to take up an extra passenger without permission but for the fact that he was not feeling very well just then.

That last mugful of steaming cider, coupled with the action of the cold frosty air, had sent the blood up to his head. His temples began to throb furiously and he felt giddy; indeed, he had some difficulty in climbing up to his box and never noticed that the vagabond was so close on his heels. Fortunately, the captain at the rear of the coach noticed nothing: he and the soldiers were busy getting to horse. As for Chabot, he had once more curled himself up in the corner of the *coupé* and was already fast asleep.

Once installed on the box with the reins in his hands the driver felt better, but even so he was comforted by the knowledge that the ex-stud-groom had installed himself behind him. The man was so handy with horses—far more handy than that young postilion—and if that giddy feeling were to return. . .

It did, about half a league beyond Vernon. That awful sense of giddiness and unconquerable drowsiness! And it was not a moment ago that he had noticed the postilion's strange antics on his horse, his swaying till he nearly fell, and the rolling of his head.

"What the devil can it be?" he muttered to himself when that nasty sick feeling seemed completely to master him. What a comfort it was to feel a pair of strong hands take the reins out of his. Whose those hands were he was too sleepy to guess, and it was so pleasant, so restful, to close one's eyes and to sleep. Daylight was fast drawing in, and with twilight down came the snow: not large, heavy, smooth flakes by nasty thin sleet, which a head wind drove straight into one's face, and which fretted and teased the horses already over-excited by certain judicious touches of the whip. As for the postilion, it was as much as he could do to keep his seat. It was only the instinct of self-preservation that kept him on the horse's back at all.

It was a bad time, too, for the soldiers. They had to keep their heads down against the wind and the driven snow, and to put spur to their horses at the same time, for the diligence, which had lumbered along slowly enough up to now, had taken on sudden speed, and the team galloped up every hill it came to in magnificent style.

Chabot once more thrust his head out of the window and shouted: "*Holà!*" He had been asleep ever since that halt at Vernon, but this abrupt lurching of the coach had not only wakened him but also frightened him.

"Why the hell are you driving like a fury?" he cried. But the head wind drowned his shouts and his reiterated cries of "*Holà!*"

The horses did not relax speed. Someone was holding the reins who knew how and when to urge them on, and the sensitive creatures responded with a will to the expert touch. It was as much as the mounted men could do to keep up with the coach.

It was not until the Captain chanced to look that way and caught sight of the Citizen Representative's head out of the *coupé* window, and of his arms gesticulating wildly, that he called out "*Halte-là!*" whereupon the diligence came immediately to a standstill. Instinct caused driver and postilion to pull themselves together, for the Citizen Representative's voice, husky with rage and fear, was raised above the howling of the wind.

"Tell that fool," he yelled, "not to drive like a fury! He will have us in the ditch directly."

"It is getting dark," the driver made effort to retort, "and this infernal snow is fretting the horses. We must make Gaillon soon."

"At least you know your way, citizen?" the captain asked.

"Know my way?" the other mumbled. "Haven't I been on this road for over fifteen years?"

"*En avant*, then!" the captain ordered once more.

The horses tossed their heads in the keen, cold air, and forward lurched the clumsy diligence. The driver clicked his tongue and made a feeble attempt at cracking his whip. It was not so much giddy that he felt now but more intolerably sleepy than before.

"Give me back the reins, citizen," a soothing voice whispered in his ear. The driver thought it might be the devil who had spoken, for who else could it be in this infernal weather and this blinding snow? Who but a devil would want to drive this cursed diligence? But he really didn't care. . . . devil or no he was too infernally sleepy to resist, and the reins were taken out of his hands as before and firmly held above his head. He ventured on a peep round under the awning of the banquette, but all he could see was a pair of legs, set wide apart, with the strong knees that looked as if chiselled in stone, and the powerful hands holding the reins. He remembered the vagabond who climbed up to the *banquette* behind him and had apparently escaped the officer's notice.

"That old vagabond," he muttered to himself, and then added

grudgingly: "He does know how to handle horses."

Another three leagues at galloping speed. But twilight was now sinking into the arms of night. Whoever was holding the reins had the eyes of a cat, for the postilion was mouse. But surely Gaillon would not be far. From Vernon it was only a matter of three leagues altogether, and why was the river on the left and not on the right of the road? And why was it so narrow, more like the Eure than the Seine? Its slender winding ribbon gleamed through the bare branches of the willow trees, its icy surface defying the gloom.

"Where the hell. . . !" the driver mumbled to himself from time to time as his bleary eyes roamed over the landscape. Some little way ahead a few cottages and a church with a square tower loomed out of the snow, the tiny windows blinking like sleepy eyes through the sparse intervening trees. But this was certainly not Gaillon. The driver rubbed his eyes. He was suddenly very wide awake. He snatched at the reins, held them tight and the team came to a halt, the steam rising like a cloud from their quivering cruppers. The captain swore and called loudly: "*En avant!*" and then: "Is this Gaillon?" He rode up abreast of the driver. "Is this Gaillon?" he iterated, pointing to the distant village.

"No, it's not," the driver replied. "At least—"

"Then where the devil are we?"

And the driver scratched his head and vowed he was damned if he knew!

"Must have taken the wrong turning," he said ruefully.

"You said you been on this road for over fifteen years."

"But not," the driver growled, "in such confounded weather." He went on muttering about the usual way of diligences. . . . they did not ply in the winter, save in settled weather. . . . sometimes one was caught in a snowstorm, but not often. . . . and it was not fit for horses with all that snow on the ground. . . . it had been madness to start from Mantes this morning and expect to make Gaillon by night-fall. And more to this effect, while the officer with eyes trying to pierce the gloom was evidently debating within himself whether he should beard the irate Representative of the People and rouse him from sleep.

"Where did you miss your road?" he asked roughly. And: "Can't we go back?"

"The only turning I know," the driver muttered, "is close to Vernon. We should have to go back three leagues—"

This time the captain blasphemed. Curses were no longer adequate.

"What's the name of that village?" he queried when he had exhausted most of his vocabulary. "Do you know?"

The driver did not.

"Is there a hostelry where we can commandeer shelter for the night?"

"Sure to be," the other rejoined.

"*En avant*, then!"

The driver did a good deal more muttering and grumbling and hard swearing when he heard the captain say finally: "The Citizen Representative will have something unpleasant to say to you about this delay."

Something unpleasant! Something unpleasant! He, too, would have something unpleasant to say to that old vagabond who did know all about horses and nothing about the way to Gaillon. Where they were now, the devil knew! He himself had been on the main road for fifteen years. Paris, Mantes, Vernon, Rouen, he knew all about them; and his home was in Paris; how, then, could he be supposed to know anything of these country roads and God-forsaken villages? Le Roger it was, probably, in which case he, the driver, had vaguely heard of a dirty hole there where bed and supper might be found. As for sta-bling for all these horses. . . . If he dared he would denounce that old vagabond for getting them into this trouble, but he was afraid of the punishment which, of course, he deserved for having taken the man on board without permission.

But the time would come, and very soon too, when the shoulders of the old villain would smart under the whip, so thought the driver as he clutched that whip with special gusto, and then cracked it and clicked his tongue. And the team made another fresh start—in dark-ness this time and with the wind howling as the lumbering vehicle sped in the teeth of the gale. The snow swirled round the heads of men and beasts and stung their faces as with myriads of tiny whip-lashes. Another ten minutes of this intolerable going through the ev-er-increasing gloom, with heads bent against the storm and stiffened hands clutching at the sodden reins. Then at last the driver's eyes were gladdened by the sight of a scaffolded pole on which dangled the dis-mal creakings an iron lantern: its feeble light revealed the sign beneath: *Le Bout du Monde.*

The End of the World! An appropriate as well as a welcome sign. A desolate conglomeration of isolated cottages, two or three barns grouped at some distance round the tumble-down *auberge* seemed all there was of the village, with the ice-bound river winding around it and a background of snow-covered fields.

The driver pulled up and looked about him with misgivings and choler. It didn't seem as if a good supper and comfortable beds could be got in this God-forsaken hole. There was only one thing to look forward to with glee, and that was the castigation to be administered to that infernal vagabond. There was any amount of noise and confusion going on to drown the howls of the victim—what with the soldiers dismounting, the horses fretting and stamping, chains rattling, hinges creaking, doors banging, the Representative of the People yelling and cursing and calling for the landlord, a rushing and a running and a swearing as the landlord came racing out of the *auberge*.

The driver called over his shoulder: "Now then, down you get!"

But there came no sign or movement from the *banquette*. The driver peered through the darkness and under the awning, but of a certainty the miserable vagabond was not there. Down clambered the driver in double quick time; he paid no heed to the orders shouted at him, to the curses from the irate Representative of the People; he pushed his way through the crowd of soldiers, he jostled the prisoner and the passengers: he even fell up against the sacrosanct person of Citizen Representative Chabot. Like a lunatic he ran hither and thither, peering in every angle, every barn, behind every tree, but there was no sign of that old rogue who had sprung out of the snow at Vernon only to disappear in the darkness around the *Bout du Monde*.

The End of the World! In very truth, had not such an action been forbidden by decree of the National Convention, the driver, when he finally realised that the man had really and truly vanished, would of a certainty have crossed himself.

The devil couldn't do more, what?

Chapter 31

There was, of a truth, a great deal of confusion and any amount of cursing and swearing before men and beasts, not to mention the coach and saddlery, were housed under in this poverty-stricken village and wholly inadequate at the hostelry itself. There were close on a score of men all requiring bed and supper and eleven horses to stable and to feed. The resources of the *Bout du Monde* were nowhere near equal to such a strain.

The landlord, indeed, was profuse in apologies. Never, never before had his poor house been honoured by such distinguished company. Le Roger was right off the main Paris-Rouen road; seldom did a coach come through the village at all, let alone with so numerous an escort: as for a diligence with a team and postilion, such a thing hadn't been seen here within memory of the oldest inhabitant. Sometimes travellers on horse-back bound for Elboeuf chose this route rather than the longer one by Gaillon, but. . .

At this point Chabot, fuming with impatience, broke in on the landlord's topographical dissertation and curtly ordered him to prepare the best food the house could muster for himself and the captain of the guard, together with a large jug of mulled cider. As for the rest of the party, they would have to make shift with whatever there was.

The captain and the landlord then worked with a will. There was a large thatched barn at some distance from the *Bout du Monde* where all the horses were presently jostled in, and such hay and fodder as could be mustered in the village was all commandeered by the soldiers for the poor tired beasts. A couple of men were told off to watch over them. Under the roof of another small barn close by and open to the four winds the coach and saddlery was then stowed. So far, so good. As for the men, they swarmed all over the small hostelry, snatching at what food they could get, raiding the outhouse for wood wherewith to pile up a good fire in the public room, where presently, after their scanty meal of lean pork, hard bread and dry beans, they would finally curl themselves up on the floor in their military cloaks, hoping to get some sleep.

The wretched prisoner was among them. No one had troubled to give him any food or drink. As presumably he was being taken to Rouen in order to be guillotined there was not much object in feeding him. But orders were very strict as to keeping watch over him; and the soldiers of the guard were commanded to take it in turns, two by two, all through the night to keep an eye on him. At the slightest disturbance all the men were to be aroused, the prisoner's safety being a matter of life and death for them all. Having given these orders and uttered these threats, Representative Chabot, in company of the captain, followed the landlord up a flight of rickety stairs to the floor above, where they were served with supper in a private room under the sloping roof.

In this room, which was not much more than a loft, there was a truckle bed hastily made up for the Citizen Representative, and in the corner a mattress and pillow for the Citizen Captain. This was the best the landlord could muster for the distinguished personages who were honouring his poor house, and anyway, a good fire was roaring in the iron stove, and the place was away from the noise and confusion of the overcrowded public room.

Chabot's temper was at its worst. Having eaten and drunk his fill, he lay down on the truckle bed and tried to get some sleep; but ne'er a wink did he get. All night he tossed about, furious with everything and everybody. From time to time he tumbled out of bed to throw a log on the fire, for it was very cold: he made as much noise as he could then and tramped heavily once or twice up and down the room so as to wake the captain, who was snoring lustily. During moments of fitful slumber, he was haunted by a ghostlike procession of all those who had contributed to his present discomfort: he dreamed of the time, not far distant he hoped, when he would belabour them with tongue and whiplash to his heart's content.

There was the hussy Josette Gravier, who had dared to threaten and then to hoodwink him; there was her lover, Reversac, the wretched prisoner downstairs, who, luckily, could not possibly escape the guillotine; there was, too, that fool of a driver who had landed him, François Chabot, Representative of the People, in this God-forsaken hole, and the captain of the guard, whose persistent snoring chased away even the semblance of sleep. Even his colleague, Chauvelin, were he here, should not escape the trouncing.

The hours of the night went by leaden-footed. At the slightest noise Chabot would rouse himself from his hard pillow and sit up in bed, listening. The prisoner—that valuable hostage for the return of the letters—was well guarded, but the very importance of his safety further exacerbated Chabot's nerves. But nothing happened, and after a while the silence of the night fell on the *Bout du Monde*.

At last in the distance and through the silence a church clock struck six. It was still quite dark; only the fire in the iron stove shed a modicum of light with its glow into the room. The getting away of the coach with its mounted escort would certainly take some time and, anyway, as he, Chabot, could not sleep there was no reason why anyone else should. He jumped out of bed and roused the captain.

"Why, what's the time?" the latter queried, his eyes still heavy with sleep.

"Damn the time!" Chabot retorted roughly. "'Tis, anyway, late enough for you to stop snoring and begin to see to things."

Very ill-humoured, but not daring to murmur, the captain rose and pulled on his boots. One slept in one's clothes these days, especially on a journey like this; and there was, of course, no question of washing at the *Bout du Monde* save, perhaps, at the pump outside, and it was much too cold for that. The captain's toilet on this occasion meant slipping on his coat, fastening his belt and smoothing his hair; and it all had to be done in the dark. He peeped out of the window.

"The wind has dropped," he remarked, "but there's a lot more snow to come down."

"Anyway," Chabot rejoined, "we start whatever the weather."

He, too, had pulled on his boots, but was still in his shirt-sleeves, and his coarse curly hair stood out from his head in tufts like an ill-combed poodle dog. He took to marching up and down the room, striding about in the darkness and swearing hard when he barked his shins against a chair. As the captain went out of the room he called to him:

"Tell the landlord to bring candles and a large jug of hot cider with plenty of spice in it."

He resumed his walk up and down the room, varying his oaths with blasphemies, and spat on the floor in the intervals of picking his teeth. He went to the door once or twice and listened to the confused sounds which came from below. A score of men roused from sleep, the inevitable swearing and shouting and tramping up and down the passage. The dormer window in this room gave on the back of the house where it was comparatively quiet; but after a time, Chabot heard the men's voices down there, the jingle of their spurs and their heavy footsteps as they went off evidently to see to the horses.

The barn where the horses were stabled was at some little distance in the village, and Chabot congratulated himself that he had roused that lazy lout of an officer in good time. He was hungry and cold in spite of the fire in the room and swore copiously at the landlord when the latter brought him the jug of steaming cider and a couple of lighted candles. The remnants of last night's supper were still on the table; he pushed the dirty plates and dishes impatiently on one side, then poured himself out a mugful of hot drink while the landlord excused himself on the plea that he had such a lot to do with so big a crowd in his small house. Should his daughter come up and attend to the distinguished Representative's commands?

But Chabot was, above all, impatient to get away.

"We must make Rouen before dark," he said tartly, "and the days are so short. I want no attention. You go and speed up the men and give a hand with the horses so that we can make a start within the hour."

He drank the cider and felt a little better, but he could not sit still. After marching up and down the room again once or twice he went to the window and tried to peer out, but the small panes were thick with grime and framed in with snow and it was pitch-dark outside. His nerves were terribly on edge and he cursed Chauvelin for having expected him to undertake this uncomfortable journey alone. Then there was the responsibility about the prisoner and this perpetual talk of English spies. "Bah!" he muttered to himself as if to instil courage into himself: "a score of these louts I've got here can easily grapple with them."

Then why this agonising nervousness, this unconquerable feeling of impending danger? Suddenly he felt hot: the blood had rushed to his head, beads of perspiration gathered on his forehead. He went to the window and unlatched it, but the cold rush of air made him shiver. He feared that he was sickening for a fever. He tried to close the window again, but the latch was stiff with rust and his fingers soon became numb with the cold.

"Curse the blasted thing!" he swore between his teeth as he fumbled with the latch.

"Let me do it for you, citizen," a pleasant voice said close to his ear.

Chabot swung round on his heel, smothering a cry of terror. A man—tall, broad-shouldered, dressed in sober black that fitted his magnificent figure to perfection—was in the act of closing the window. With firm dexterous fingers he got the latch into position.

"There! that's better now, is it not, my dear *Monsieur?* I forget your name," he said with a light laugh. Then added: "So now we can talk."

He brushed one slender hand against the other and with a lace-edged handkerchief flicked the dust off from his coat.

"Dirty place, this End of the World, what?" he remarked.

Chabot, tongue-tied and terror stricken, had collapsed upon the truckle bed. He gazed on this tall figure which he could only vaguely distinguish in the gloom. Like the driver of the diligence a while ago, he would have crossed himself if he dared, for this, of a surety, must be Lucifer: tall, slender, in black clothes that melted and merged into the surrounding darkness, allowing the flickering candlelight to play upon a touch of white at throat and wrist and on the highly polished leather of the boot.

"Who are you?" he gasped after a time, for the stranger had not moved, and Chabot felt that all the while a pair of eyes, cold and mocking, were fixed upon him from out of the gloom. "Who are you?" he reiterated under his breath.

"The devil you think I am," the other responded lightly, "but won't you come and sit down?"

He motioned towards a chair by the table.

"I haven't much time, I'm afraid; and," he went on lightly, "you'll be more comfortable than on that hard bed."

Then as Chabot made no effort to move, but sat there, one hand resting on the bed, the glow of the firelight upon him, the stranger remarked:

"Why, look at your hand, my dear *Monsieur* What's-your-name; it looks as if you had dipped it in a sanguinary mess."

Mechanically Chabot looked down on his hand to which the stranger was now pointing. In that crimson glow it certainly looked as if. . . . Hastily he withdrew it and rubbed it against his coat. Then, as if impelled by some unknown force, he rose and made a movement towards the table, but stopped half-way and suddenly made a dash for the door. But the stranger forestalled him, had him by the wrist before he could seize the latch, and with a grip that was irresistible drew him back to the table and forced him down upon a chair. He sat down opposite to him on the other side of the table and reiterated quietly:

"Now we can talk."

Chabot up to this moment was absolutely convinced that this was the devil made manifest. His education, conducted within the narrow limits of a seminary, had in a way prepared him for such a possibility, and during the brief years which he spent as a Capuchin friar he had had every belief implanted into him of demons and evil spirits, and maternal hell and bottomless pit. Cold, terror, discomfort of every sort all helped to unnerve him. Fascinated, he watched that tall dark figure, pouring with white slender hand the mulled cider into a mug and handing it over to him.

"Drink this, man," came the mellow voice out of the darkness, "and pull yourself together. We have no time to lose."

Chabot took the mug but set it down on the table untasted.

"Well," the stranger said lightly, "as you like; but try and listen to me. I am not a manifestation of your familiar as you suppose, only a plain English gentleman. I happen to have in my possession certain letters which in a moment of carelessness you were rash enough to write to a certain Bastien de Croissy—"

At mention of "letters" Chabot uttered a hoarse cry: his fingers went up to his necktie, for he suddenly felt as if he would choke.

"You!" he murmured, "you—?"

"Yes! I, at your service; I know all about those letters, for that is what you were about to say, was it not?"

He held Chabot with his eyes, and Chabot was fascinated by that glance. The eyes held him and he tried to defy them, made a supreme effort to pull himself together. Slowly it dawned upon him that here was no devil made manifest, but rather an enemy who was trying to hit at him to hoodwink him about those letters as that young baggage had tried to do. Another of her lovers probably—yes! that was it: an English lover picked up in England recently: one of those spies, perhaps, of whom his friend Armand Chauvelin was often wont to talk, but certainly another lover, and if he, Chabot, was fool enough to bargain he would be made a fool of once more.

This thought had the effect of soothing his nerves: he suddenly felt quite calm. That choking sensation was gone; he took up the mug of cider and drank it down. His hand was perfectly steady; and he was in no hurry. The captain would be back directly and together they would laugh over the discomfiture of this fool when he found himself securely bound with cords in the company of the other prisoner, Maurice Reversac, the hussy's latest lover.

It was all very easy and very amusing. No! there was no hurry. In fact, this hour would have been very dull and very long but for this diversion. The candles were guttering and Chabot took the snuffers and used them very efficiently and deliberately. He pretended not to notice the stranger's nonchalant attitude, sitting there opposite to him, with his arms resting on the table and his very clean white hands interlocked.

"That wick would be all the better for another snick," he remarked; and Chabot tried to imitate his careless manner by saying: "You think so, citizen?" and carefully trimmed the offending wick.

He really was enjoying every moment of this unexpected interview. How stupid he had been to be so scared! The devil, indeed! Just an English jackanape who had put his head in the lion's jaw previous to laying it under the knife of the guillotine; moreover, a spy could be shot without trial within the hour, in fact, and the captain could see to it that this one didn't talk. He, the captain, would be back directly, and, anyway, there were at least a dozen men in the public room down below, so what was there to fear when all was well and quite amusing?

The stranger had made no movement. Chabot leaned over the table, resting his head in his hand.

"You know, Mr. the Englishman," he said with a well-assumed unconcern, "that you have vastly interested me."

"I am glad," rejoined the other.

"About those letters, I mean."

"Indeed?"

"Now I should be very curious to know just how you came to be in possession of them."

"I will gratify your curiosity with all the pleasure in life," the stranger replied. "I took them out of the pocket of Madame de Croissy while she was asleep."

"Nonsense!" Chabot retorted with an assumption of indifference, although the name de Croissy had grated unpleasantly on his ear. "What in the world had the Widow Croissy got to do with any supposed letters of mine?"

"You forget, my dear sir," the Englishman retorted blandly, "that the letters were written by yourself to that lady's husband; that in order to obtain possession of them you murdered that unfortunate man in a peculiarly cruel and cowardly manner; the lady thereupon was persuaded for obvious reasons to leave for England, taking the letters with her."

"Bah! I've heard that story before."

"Have you now?" the stranger remarked with an engaging smile. "Isn't that funny?"

"Not nearly so funny as your lie that you took those letters—whatever they were—out of the woman's pocket, and that she never noticed the loss."

"How very clever of you to say that, my dear Citizen What's-your-name: a masterpiece, I call it, of skilful cross-examination. You would have made a wonderful advocate at any bar." He gave a short laugh, and Chabot spat like a cat that's being teased. "As a matter of fact," the stranger resumed, quite unperturbed, "the lady certainly might have noticed her loss. You were right there. But, you see, I took the precaution of substituting a sealed packet exactly similar to the one I had stolen and placed it in the lady's pocket."

Then as Chabot made no reply, was obviously thinking over what his next move should be in this singular encounter, the Englishman continued:

"In fact, you will observe, Sir, that my process was identical to the one employed by our mutual friend Chambertin when he stole what he thought was the precious packet of letters from little Josette Gravier and substituted for it another contrived by himself to look exactly similar. I am very fond really of Monsieur Chambertin; for a clever man he is sometimes such a silly fool, what?"

"Chambertin?" Chabot queried, frowning.

"Beg pardon—I should say Chauvelin."

"Do you pretend that it was he?"

"Why, of course. Who else?"

"And that he had those damned letters?"

"No, no, my dear *Monsieur* What-d'you-call-yourself," the stranger retorted with a light laugh. "I have those blessed—not damned—letters here, as I had the honour of explaining to you just now."

And with his elegant, slender hand he tapped the left breast of his coat. Chabot watched him for a moment or two under beetling brows. The man's coolness, his impudence had irritated him, and while he had thought that he was playing a cat's game with a mouse, somehow the *rôles* of cat and mouse had come to be reversed. But it had lasted too long already. It was time to put an end to it, and the moment was entirely opportune, for just then Chabot's ears were pleasantly tickled by the sound of the captain's voice down below ordering the landlord to bring him some hot cider. He had evidently returned from the barn, leaving the men to feed and saddle the horses.

Chabot chuckled at thought of the stranger's discomfiture when presently the caption would come tramping up the stairs, and, in anticipation of coming triumph, he fixed his antagonist with what he felt was a searching as well as an ironic glance.

"Suppose," he began slowly, "that before going any further you show me those supposed letters."

"With all the pleasure in life," the Englishman responded blandly. And to Chabot's intense amazement he drew out of his breast-pocket a small sealed packet exactly similarly in appearance to the one which poor little Josette Gravier had so trustingly kept in the bosom of her gown. Chabot chortled at sight of it.

"Will you break the seals, *Monsieur* the Englishman?" he queried with withering sarcasm, "or shall I?"

But already the stranger's finely shaped hands were busy with the seals. Chabot, his ugly face still wearing a sarcastic expression, drew the candles closer. Soon the seals were broken, the wrapper fell apart and displayed, not scraps of paper this time, but just a few letters, written by diverse hands. Chabot felt as if his eyes would drop out of his head as he gazed. The flickering candles illumined the topmost letter with its unmistakable signature—his own—François Chabot. And there were others: he remembered every one of them, gazed on the tell-tale signatures—his—Bazire's—Fabre's.

"Name of a dog!" he cried and made a quick grab for the letters. But the stranger's hands, delicate and slender though they were, were extraordinarily firm and quick. In a moment he had the letters all together, the wrapper round them, a piece of twine, picked out of the devil knew whence, holding the packet once more securely together. Chabot could not take his eyes off him. He watched him as if hypnotised, mute, blind to all else save that calm, high-bred face with the firm lips and the humorous twinkle in the eyes. But when he saw the stranger on the point of putting the packet back inside his coat, he cried, hoarse with passion: "Give me those letters!"

"All in good time, my dear sir. First, as I have already had the honour to remark, we must have a good talk."

Chabot rose slowly to his feet. The captain's voice rising from the public room below, the tramp of the soldiers' feet, his whole surroundings recalled him to himself. Fool that he was to fear anything from this insolent nincompoop!

"I give you one last chance," he said very quietly, even though he could not disguise the tremor of his voice. "Either you give me those letters now—at once—in which case you can go from here a free man and to the devil if you choose; or—"

At this same moment the sound of several voices was wafted upwards. Some of the soldiers had apparently assembled somewhere underneath the window and were talking over some momentous happening. Chabot and the stranger could hear snatches of what they said:

"Luckily the horses were not—"

"The wind unfortunately—"

"The saddles are—"

"So is the coach—"

"What in the world are we going—"

"Better see what the Citizen Captain—"

And so on, until after a time they moved away to the front entrance of the house, which was right the other side. The stranger was smiling while he lent an attentive ear. But Chabot only thought of the fact that now the guard would soon be assembled inside the house. Twenty trained men to cope with this insolent spy. His pale-yellow eyes gleamed in the dim light like those of a cat. He was gloating over his coming triumph, licking his chops like a greedy cur in sight of food.

"Or," he concluded between clenched teeth, "I'll call the captain of the guard and have you shot as a spy within the hour."

By way of reply the stranger rose slowly from the table. To Chabot's excited fancy he appeared immensely tall: terrifying in his air of power and physical strength, and instinctively this scrubby worm, this cowardly assassin, this unfrocked friar cowered before the tall, commanding figure of the stranger in abject terror of his own miserable life. He edged round the table, while the Englishman deliberately walked to the window; then he made a dart for the door, expecting every second to feel that steel-like grip once more upon his arm. With his hand already on the latch he looked over his shoulder at his enemy, who was at the moment engaged in opening the window.

The gust of wind that ensued was so strong that Chabot could not pull the door open; moreover, his hands were shaking and his knees felt as if they were about to give way under him: only later did he become aware that the door was locked. He heard the stranger give a curious call, like that of sea-mews who are wont to circle about the Pont-Neuf in Paris when the winter is very severe. The call was responded to in the same way from below, whereupon the stranger flung the packet out of the window. Three words were wafted upwards, words with a foreign sound which Chabot could not understand. Subsequently he averred that one of those words sounded something like "Raitt!" and the other like "Fouk's!" but of course that was nonsense.

The stranger then went back to the table and sat down. Once more he reiterated the irritating phrase which so exasperated the Terrorist: "Now we can talk."

Chabot fumbled with the door-knob. He had just heard the men trooping back into the house.

"No use, my friend," the stranger remarked drily. "I locked that door when I came in. And here's the key," he added, and put the rusty old key down on the table.

"Come and sit down," he resumed after a second or two as Chabot had not moved, had in fact seemed glued to that locked door; "or shall I have to come and fetch you?"

"You devil! You hound! You abominable—" Chabot muttered inarticulately. "Get me back those letters or—"

"Come and sit down," the other reiterated coolly. "You have exactly five minutes in which to save your skin. My friend is still outside, just under the window; if within the next five minutes he hears no signal from me he will speed to Paris with those letters, and three days after that they will be published in every newspaper in the city and shouted from every house-top in France."

"It's not true," Chabot muttered huskily. "He cannot do it. He couldn't pass the gates of Paris."

"Would you care to take your chance of that?" the stranger retorted blandly. "If so, here's the key. . . . call your guard. . . . do what you damn well like. . . ."

He laughed, a pleasant infectious laugh, full of the joy of living through this perilous, exciting adventure, full of self-assurance, of arrogance, as you will, a laugh to gladden the hearts of the brave and to strike terror in those of the craven.

"One minute nearly gone," he renewed, and from his breeches pocket drew a jewelled watch attached to a fob, and this he held out for the other man to see.

Birds and rabbits, 'tis averred, are so attracted by the python which is about to gulp them down that they do not attempt to flee from him but become hypnotised, and of themselves draw nearer and nearer to the devouring jaws. In very truth there was nothing snake-like about the tall Englishman with the merry, lazy eyes and the firm mouth so often curled in a pleasant smile, but Chabot was just like a hypnotised rabbit. He crossed the room slowly, very slowly, and presently sat down opposite his tormentor.

"Nearly two minutes gone out of the five," the latter said, "and I verily believe I can hear your friend the captain's footfall in the hall below."

It was then that Chabot had an inspiration. In this moment of crushing humiliation and of real peril he remembered that his friend Chauvelin, saw him as in a vision sitting with him in the small private room of the Cheval Blanc at Rouen. What did he say when there was talk of the prisoner Reversac and his sweetheart Josette? Something about safe-conducts for them to be offered in exchange for the letters. Safe-conducts? And in his quiet, incisive voice Chauvelin had added, "I can endorse those with a secret sign. It is known to every Chief *Commissary* in France and nullifies every safe-conduct."

Yes, that was it: "Nullifies every safe-conduct." And Chauvelin knew the secret sign as did every Chief *Commissary* in France. So now to play one's cards carefully, and above all not to show fear; on no account to show that one was afraid.

And Chabot, sitting at the table, stroked his scrubby chin and said:

"I suppose what you want is a safe-conduct for some traitor or other, what?"

But the inspiration proved only to be a mirage and the sense of triumph very short-lived. The very next moment Chabot's fond hopes were rudely dashed to the ground, for the stranger replied, still smiling:

"No, my friend, I want no safe-conduct endorsed by you or your colleague with a secret sign to render them valueless."

And Chabot fell back in his chair; he was sweating at every pore. He marvelled if after all his first impression had not been the true one; since this man appeared to be a reader of thought was he not truly the devil incarnate?

"What is it you do want?" he uttered, choking and gasping.

"That you unlock that door—here's the key—and call to the gallant captain of the guard."

He held the key out to Chabot, who, fascinated, hypnotised, took it from him.

"Go and unlock that door, *Monsieur* What's-your-name, and call your friend the captain."

Slowly, as if moved by some unseen and compelling power, Chabot tottered towards the door. The stranger spoke to him over his shoulder: "When he comes you will tell him that you desire someone to go over to the village to the house of Citizen Pailleron with a message from you. Pailleron has a nice covered wagonette which he uses for the purpose of his trade as carrier between here and Elboeuf. Your messenger will explain to him that Citizen Representative François Chabot requires the wagonette immediately for his personal use. A sum in compensation will be given to him before a start is made."

Chabot made a final effort to turn on his tormentor: "This is madness!" he cried. "I'll not do it. If I call the captain it will be to have you shot—"

"Another minute gone," quoth the stranger blandly, "and I am sure the captain is coming up the stairs."

"You hellish fiend!"

"My friend down below will be wondering if he should speed for Paris or—"

The key grated in the lock. Chabot's trembling hands were fumbling with the latch.

"Come! that is wise," the Englishman said, "but for you own sake I entreat you to command your nerves. The captain is coming up. You will explain to him about the wagonette, also that you will be leaving here within the hour in the company of two friends, one of them being the young man, Maurice Reversac, at present detained through an unfortunate misunderstanding, and the other your humble servant."

Chabot was like a whipped cur with its tail between its legs. He slunk away from the door and came back across the room, and, like a whipped cur, he made a final effort to bite the hand that smote him.

"You must think me a fool—" he began, trying to swagger.

"I do," the other broke in blandly. "But that is not the point. The point is that I am looking to you to effect the ultimate rescue of two innocent young people out of your murderous clutches. Josette Gravier is in comparative safety for the moment, and Maurice Reversac is close at hand. I propose to convey them to Havre and see them safely on board an English ship *en route* for our shores, which you must admit are more hospitable than yours. For this expedition your help, my dear *Monsieur* What's-your-name, will be invaluable, so you are coming with us, my friend, in Citizen Pailleron's wagonette, and I myself will have the honour to drive you.

"And when we are challenged at the gates of any city, or commune, or at a bridge-head, you will show the guard your pretty face and reveal your identity as Representative of the People in the National Convention and stand upon your rights as such to free passage and no molestation for yourself, your driver and your son—we'll call Maurice Reversac your son for convenience' sake—and at Elboeuf, as well as at Dieppe, on the quay or at any barrier your pleasant countenance and your gentle, authoritative voice will command the obsequiousness they deserve. So I pray you," he concluded with perfect suavity, "call the captain of the guard and explain to him all that is necessary. We ought soon to be getting on the way."

He leaned back in his chair, gave a slight yawn, then rose, and from his magnificent height looked down on the cringing figure of the unfrocked friar. Chabot tried vainly to collect his thoughts, to make some plan, to think, to think, my God! to think of something, and above all to gather courage from the fact that this man, this abominable spy, this arrogant devil, was still in his power: now, at this moment, he could still hand him over to be shot at sight. . . . or else at Rouen; with Chauvelin waiting for him, he could. . . . he could. . .

But the other, as if divining his thoughts, broke in on them by saying: "You could do nothing at Rouen, my friend, for let me assure you that within twenty-four hours my friend who now has your letters in his possession will be on his way to Paris, there to deliver them at the offices of the *Moniteur* and of *Père Duchnese*, unless I myself desire him to hand them over to you."

"And if I yield to your cowardly threats," Chabot hissed between his teeth, "if I lend myself to this dastardly comedy, how shall I know that your associate, as vile a craven as yourself, will give me the letters in the end?"

"You can't know that, my friend," the other retorted simply, "for I cannot expect such as you to know the meaning of a word of honour spoken by an English gentleman."

"How shall I know if I do get the letters that none have been kept back?"

"That's just it: you can't know. But remember, my friend, that there is one thing you do know with absolute certainty, and that is, if my plan to save those two young people fails, if I do not myself request my friend to give up the letters to you, then as sure as we are both alive at this moment those letters will be published in every news-sheet throughout France; your name will become a byword for every-thing that is most treacherous and most vile, and not even the dirtiest mudrake in the country will care to take you by the hand."

The stranger had spoken with unwonted earnestness, all the more impressive for the flippant way in which he had carried on the con-versation before. Chabot, always a bully, was nothing if not a coward. Any danger to himself reduced him to a wriggling worm. That his peril was great he knew well enough, and he had realised at last that there was no threat that he could utter which would shake that cursed English spy from his purpose.

There was a moment of tense silence in the room, whilst the cap-tain's footsteps were heard slowly coming up the stairs. The stranger gave a gay little laugh and sat down once more opposite his writhing victim. He poured out two mugfuls of cider, and the moment that the door was thrown open he was saying with easy familiarity:

"Your good health, my dear François, and to our proposed journey together."

He held the white-livered recreant with his magnetic eyes and made as if to raise the mug to his lips; then he paused and went on lightly:

"By the way, did you happen to see the *Moniteur* the day before yesterday? It had a scathing attack, inspired of certainty by Couthon, against Danton and some of his methods."

Chabot clenched his teeth. At this moment he would have sold his soul to the devil for the power to slay this over-weening rapscallion.

The captain, seeing the Citizen Representative in conversation with a friend, halted respectfully at the door. He stood at attention, until Chabot looked round at him with tired, bleary eyes.

"What is it, Citizen Captain?" he inquired in a thick, tired voice, while the stranger, as if suddenly aware of the officer's presence, rose courteously from the table.

"I have to report, Citizen Representative," the captain replied, "that during the night certain miscreants found their way to the coach and saddlery, to which they did a good deal of mischief."

"Mischief? What mischief?" Chabot muttered inarticulately, while the stranger gave a polite murmur of sympathy.

"They've cut the saddle-girths, the reins and the stirrup-leathers, and the spokes of two of the coach wheels are broken right across. The damage will take more than a day to repair."

"I hope, Citizen Captain," the stranger said affably, "that you have laid hands on the rascals."

"Alas, no! the mischief was done at night. The barn lies some way back from this house; no one heard anything. The ruffians got clean away."

Chabot was speechless; not only had the quantity of spiced cider got into his head, but rage and despair had made him dumb.

"My dear François," the Englishman commented with good-humoured urbanity, "this is indeed unfortunate for all these fine soldiers who will have to spend a day or two in this God-forsaken hole. I know what that means," he went on, turning once more to the captain, "as I have been through such experience before, travelling on my business in these outlying parts."

"Ah! You know Le Roger then, Citizen?" the captain asked.

"I have been here once before. I am a commercial traveller, you know, and go about the country a good deal. I only arrived last night from St. Pierre half an hour after you did and was happy to hear that my old friend François Chabot was putting up for the night. Then luckily, I happened to bespeak Citizen Pailleron's covered wagonette to take me on today to Louviers, but it will be a pleasure as well as an honour for me to drive the Citizen Representative to Rouen if he desires."

"It will be heavy going."

"Perhaps, but my friend Pailleron has excellent horses which he will let me have."

292

"This is indeed lucky," the captain assented.

Still he seemed to hesitate. As Chabot remained tongue-tied, the stranger touched him lightly on the shoulder.

"It is lucky, is it not, my dear François?" he asked.

Chabot looked up at his tormentor. "Go to hell!" he murmured under his breath.

"The Citizen Captain is waiting for orders, my friend."

"You give them, then."

The stranger gave a light laugh. "I am afraid the cider was rather heady," he explained to the officer. "Will you be so good, captain, as to send round to Citizen Pailleron and let him know that the Representative of the People is ready to start. I believe the snow has left off for the moment; we can make Louviers before noon."

There was nothing in this to rouse the captain's suspicions. The Citizen Representative, though suffering perhaps from an excess of hot, spiced drink, nodded his head as if to confirm the order given by his friend. That this tall stranger was his friend there could be no doubt; the two of them were conversing amicably when he, the captain, first entered the room. And it certainly was the most natural conclusion for any man to come to, that so distinguished a personage as the Representative of the People in the National Convention would not wish to remain snowed up in this desolate village for two days at least but would gladly avail himself of the means of transit offered to him by a friend. And certainly, whatever doubt the officer might have had in his mind was finally dissipated when the stranger spoke again to Citizen Chabot.

"My dear François," he said, once more touching the other on the shoulder, "you have forgotten to speak to our friend the captain about the young man, Reversac."

"The prisoner?" the captain asked.

"Even him."

"He is quite safe at this moment in the public room, and we—"

"That's just the point," the stranger rejoined; and, unseen by the captain, he tightened his grip on Chabot's shoulder. "Do, my dear François, explain to the Citizen Captain—"

Chabot winced under the grip, which seemed like a veritable strangle-hold upon his will-power. He had not an ounce of strength left in him, either moral or physical, to resist. It was as much as he could do to mutter a few words and to gaze with bleared vision on his smiling enemy.

"Do explain, my dear François," the latter insisted.

Chabot brought the palm of his hand down with a crash upon the table.

"Damn explanations!" he snapped savagely. "The prisoner Reversac comes with me. That's enough."

And as the captain, momentarily taken off his balance by this unexpected command, still stood by the door, Chabot shouted at him: "Get out!"

It was the stranger who, with perfect courtesy, went to the door and held it open for the officer to pass out.

"That cider was much too heady," he said, dropping his voice to a whisper, "but the Citizen Representative will be all right when he gets into the cold air." After which he added, "He does not wish to lose sight of the prisoner, and I shall be there to look after them both."

"Well! It is not for me to make comment," the soldier remarked drily, "so long as the Citizen Representative is satisfied—"

"Oh! He is quite satisfied, I do assure you. You are satisfied, are you not, you dear old François?"

But even while he asked this final question he quickly closed the door on the departing soldier, for in very truth the blasphemies which Chabot uttered after that would have polluted even the ears of an old Republican campaigner.

Chapter 32

Less than half an hour later a covered wagonette to which a couple of sturdy Normandy horses were harnessed drew up outside the front door of the *Bout de Monde*. The word had soon enough gone round the village and among the men that the Representative of the People was leaving Le Roger in company of a friend, taking the prisoner with him.

He came out of the hostelry wrapped in his big coat. He looked neither to right nor left, nor did he acknowledge the respectful salutes of the landlord and his family assembled at the door to bid him goodbye. The prisoner, hatless, coatless and shivering with cold, was close behind him. But it was the Representative's friend who created most attention. He was very tall and wore the finest of clothes. It was generally whispered among the quidnuncs that he was a commercial traveller who had made much money by smuggling French brandy into England.

While François Chabot and the prisoner stowed themselves away as best they could under the hood of the wagonette, the stranger climbed up on the box and took the reins. He clicked his tongue, tickled the horses with his whip, and the light vehicle bumped along the snow-covered road and was soon lost to sight.

Grey dawn was breaking just then; the sky was clear and gave promise of a fine sunny day. The men who had formed the escort for the diligence and those who had travelled inside in order to guard the prisoner sat around the fire in the public room in the intervals between scanty meals and discussed the amazing adventures of the past twenty-four hours. They had begun, so it was universally admitted, with the mysterious report of a pistol outside the hostelry at Vernon and the strange appearance of the whilom stud-groom who looked such a miserable tramp. What happened on the road after that no one could aver with any certainty, for the driver, who knew himself to be heavily at fault, never said a word about having taken the tramp aboard on the *banquette* and allowing the reins to slip out of his hands into the more capable ones of the stud-groom.

Indeed, while the others talked the driver seemed entrenched in complete dumbness. He drank copiously, and as he was known to become violent in his cups he was left severely alone. The damage done in the night to the coach and saddlery had further aggravated his ill-humour. He put it all down to spite directed against him by some power of evil made manifest in the person of that cursed vagabond. It was supposed that the villagers had set themselves the task to bring the miscreants to book, but the hours sped by and nothing was discovered that would lead to such a happy result. The snow all round the barn where coach and saddlery had been stowed had been trampled down so heavily that it was impossible to determine in which direction the rapscallions had made good their escape.

Chapter 33

To François Chabot the journey between Le Roger and the coast was nothing less than a nightmare. He was more virtually the prisoner of that impudent English spy than any *aristo* had ever been in the hands of Terrorists. And while thoughts and plans and useless desires went hammering through his fevered brain, the wagonette lumbered along on the snow-covered road, and on the driver's seat in front of him sat the man who was the cause of his humiliation and his despair. Oh, for the courage to end it all and plunge a knife into that broad back! But what was the good of wishing, for there was that terrible threat hanging over him of the letters to be published where all who wished could read, and the certainty of disgrace with the inevitable guillotine? Chabot could really thank his stars that he did not happen to have a knife handy. He might surely, in a moment of madness, have killed his tormentor and also the young man who sat squeezed beside him in the interior of the wagonette.

They reached Louvier's at noon. At the entrance to the city they were challenged by the sentry at the gate. The Englishman jumped down from the box. At a mere sign from him Chabot showed his papers of identity:—

"François Chabot, Representative of the People in the National Convention for the department of Loire et Cher—"

He declared the young man sitting next to him to be his son, and the other a friend under his own especial protection. The sentry stood at attention: the officer gave the word:

"Pass on in the name of the Republic!"

A nightmare, what? or else an outpost of hell!

They avoided Rouen, made a circuit of the town and turned into a country lane. Presently the driver pulled up outside a small, somewhat dilapidated house, which lay *perdu* in the midst of a garden all overgrown with weeds and surrounded by a wall broken down in many places and with a low iron gate dividing it from the road. He jumped down from the box, fastened the reins to a ring in the wall; then, with his usual impudent glance, peeped underneath the hood of the wagonette. He thrust a parcel and a bottle into Chabot's lap and said curtly:

"Eat and drink, my friend. Monsieur Reversac and I have business inside the house."

The whilom prisoner stepped out of the wagonette and together the two men went inside the house. One or two people passed by while Chabot sat shivering in the draughty vehicle. He ate and drank, for he was hungry and thirsty, but he had entirely ceased to think by now. He no longer felt that he was a real live man, but only an automaton made to move and to speak through the touch of a white slender hand and the glance of a pair of lazy deep-set blue eyes.

Many minutes went by before he heard the rickety door of the old house creak upon its hinges. The two men came down the path towards the wagonette, but they were not alone. There was a girl with them, and Chabot uttered a hoarse cry as he recognised the baggage, Josette Gravier, who had made a fool of him and was now a witness of his humiliation.

This, perhaps, was the most galling experience of all. He, the arrogant bully who had planned the destruction of these innocents, was now the means of their deliverance and their happiness. He closed his eyes so as not to see the triumph which he felt must be gleaming in theirs.

How little he understood human nature! Josette and Maurice had no thought of their enemy, none of the terrible torments which they had endured; their thoughts were of one another, of their happiness in holding each other by the hand; above all, of their love. In the hours of sorrow and peril of death they had realised at last the magnitude of that love, the joy that would be theirs if it pleased God to unite them in the end.

And this happiness they had now attained and owed it to the brave man who had been the hero of Josette's dreams. When first she discovered his identity, when she knew that she owed her rescue to him, and when today he had suddenly walked into the old house where she had been patiently waiting for him under the care of a kindly farmer and his wife, she would gladly, if he had allowed it, have knelt at his feet and kissed his hands in boundless gratitude.

For these two, also, the journey seemed like a dream, but it was a dream of earthly Paradise; hand in hand they sat and hardly were conscious of the presence of that ugly, ungainly creature huddled up, silent and motionless, in a corner of the wagonette.

For them, too, he was just an automaton, moved at will by the mysterious Scarlet Pimpernel. He only bestirred himself when the wagonette was challenged at a bridge-head or the barriers of a commune; then, in answer to a demand from the sentry, he would poke his ugly head, toneless voice recite his name and quality. And Josette and Maurice invariably giggled when they heard themselves described as the son and daughter of that hideous man, and that tall, handsome stranger as his friend.

The sentry then would give the word:

"Pass on in the name of the Republic!" and the wagonette, driven by the mysterious stranger, would once more lumber along on its way.

The journey was broken at a small hostelry, about half a league beyond Elboeuf. The food was scanty and ill-cooked, the beds were hard, the place squalid, the rooms cold; but the idea of sleeping under the same roof with Maurice made Josette in her narrow truckle-bed feel as if she were in heaven.

When they neared the coast of the first tang of the sea coming to Josette's nostrils brought with it recollections of that former journey which she had undertaken all alone for Maurice's sake. And when, presently, they came into Havre, and after the usual formalities at the gates of the city were able to leave the wagonette, these recollections turned to vivid memories. Guided by the tall mysterious stranger, they walked along the quay, whilst the past unrolled itself before Josette's mental vision like an ever-changing kaleidoscope. She remembered Citizen Armand, heard again his suave, lying tongue, met his pale eyes with their treacherous, deceptive glance. And she snuggled up close to Maurice, and he put his arm round her to guide her down the bridge to the packet-boat, which was on the point of starting for England.

To follow them thither were a sorry task. Many French men and women there were these days—Louise de Croissy and little Charles-Léon among them—who, fleeing from the terrors of a Government of assassins, found refuge in hospitable England. Helped by friends, made welcome by thousands of kindly hearts, the eked out their precarious existence by working in fields or factories until such time as the return of law and order in their own beautiful country enabled them to go back to their devastated homes.

Heureux la peuple qui n'a pas d'histoire. Of Maurice and Josette Reversac there is nothing further to record, save the fulfilment of their love-dream and their happiness.

Chapter 34

"And now we'll go and get those blessed letters."

Sir Percy Blakeney, known to the world as the Scarlet Pimpernel, had stood on the quay watching the packet-boat sailing down the mouth of the river. His arm was linked in that of François Chabot, once a Capuchin friar, now Representative of the People in the National Convention. He held Chabot by the arm, and Chabot stood beside him and also watched the boat gliding out of the range of his vision.

The nightmare was not yet ended, for there was the journey back to Rouen in the wagonette with himself, François Chabot, chained to the chariot wheel of his ruthless conqueror.

A halt was made on the road outside the same old house where they had picked up Josette Gravier. This time Sir Percy bade Chabot follow him into the house. How it all happened Chabot never knew. He never could remember how it came about that presently he found himself fingering those fateful letters: they were all there—three written by himself, two written by his brother-in-law, Bazire, and two by Fabre d'Eglantine—seven letters: mere scraps of paper; but what a price to pay for their possession! An immense wave of despair swept over the recreant. Perhaps at this hour the whole burden of his crimes weighed down his miserable soul and it received its first consciousness of inevitable retribution. The wretch spread his arms out on the table and, laying down his head, he burst into abject tears.

When the paroxysm of weeping was over and he looked about him the tall mysterious stranger was gone.

It was twilight of one of the most dismal days of the year. Looking up at the window, Chabot saw the leaden snow-laden clouds sweeping across the sky. Heavy flakes fell slowly, slowly. All round him absolute silence reigned. The house apparently was quite deserted. He staggered rather than walked to the door. He tramped across the path to the low gate in the wall. Here he stood for a moment looking up and down the narrow road and the heavy snowflakes covered his shoulders and his tufty, ill-kempt hair. There was no sign of the wagonette beyond the ruts made by the wheels in the snow, and for a long time not a soul came by. Presently, however, a couple of men—farm-labourers they were by the look of them—came along and Chabot asked them:

"Where are we?"

The men stopped and, in the twilight, peered curiously at this hatless man, half-covered with snow.

"What do you mean by 'Where are we?'" one of them asked.

"Just what I am asking," Chabot replied in that same dead tone of voice. "Which is the nearest town or village? I am stranded here and there is no one in this house."

The men seemed surprised.

"No one there?"

"Not a soul."

"Farmer Marron and his wife still live here," one of the men said, "two days ago, and they had a wench with them for a little while."

"They must have gone to Elboeuf where the old grandmother lives," the other suggested. "I know they talked of it."

"Elboeuf?" Chabot queried. "How far is that?"

A league and a quarter, and it was getting dark and snow was falling fast. It was so cold, so cold! and Chabot was very tired.

"Well, goodnight, Citizen," the men called out to him. "We are going part of the way to Elboeuf. Would you like to join us?"

A league and a quarter, and Chabot was so tired.

"No, thank you, Citizens," he murmured feebly. "I'll tramp thither tomorrow."

He turned on his heel and went back into the lonely house. The arch-fiend who had brought him hither had seemingly left him some provisions and a bottle of sour wine. There was a fire in the room and upstairs in a room above there was a truckle bed and on it a couple of blankets.

Chabot curled himself up in these and fell into a fitful sleep.

The next day he tramped to Elboeuf and the day after that took coach for Rouen to meet his colleague Armand Chauvelin and give him the trouncing he deserved, for it was because of him, his intrigues and his wild talk of the Scarlet Pimpernel, that he, François Chabot, had been brought to humiliation and despair. The interview between the two men was brief and stormy. They parted deadly enemies.

A week later Chabot was back in his luxurious apartment in the Rue d'Anjou and a month later he perished on the guillotine. He had been denounced as suspect by Armand Chauvelin of the Committee of Public Safety for having on the *15 Frimaire an II de la République* connived at the escape of two traitors condemned to death: Josette Gravier and Maurice Reversac, and for having failed to bring to justice the celebrated spy known as the Scarlet Pimpernel

Sir Percy Explains

1

It was not, Heaven help us all! a very uncommon occurrence these days: a woman almost unsexed by misery, starvation, and the abnormal excitement engendered by daily spectacles of revenge and of cruelty. They were to be met with every day, round every street corner, these harridans, more terrible far than were the men.

This one was still comparatively young, thirty at most; would have been good-looking too, for the features were really delicate, the nose chiselled, the brow straight, the chin round and small. But the mouth! Heavens, what a mouth! Hard and cruel and thin-lipped; and those eyes! sunken and rimmed with purple; eyes that told tales of sorrow and, yes! of degradation. The crowd stood round her, sullen and apathetic; poor, miserable wretches like herself, staring at her antics with lack-lustre eyes and an ever-recurrent contemptuous shrug of the shoulders.

The woman was dancing, contorting her body in the small circle of light formed by a flickering lanthorn which was hung across the street from house to house, striking the muddy pavement with her shoeless feet, all to the sound of a beribboned tambourine which she struck now and again with her small, grimy hand. From time to time she paused, held out the tambourine at arm's length, and went the round of the spectators, asking for alms. But at her approach the crowd at once seemed to disintegrate, to melt into the humid evening air; it was but rarely that a greasy token fell into the outstretched tambourine. Then as the woman started again to dance the crowd gradually reassembled, and stood, hands in pockets, lips still sullen and contemptuous, but eyes watchful of the spectacle. There were such few spectacles these days, other than the monotonous processions of tumbrils with their load of aristocrats for the guillotine!

So, the crowd watched, and the woman danced. The lanthorn overhead threw a weird light on red caps and tricolour cockades, on the sullen faces of the men and the shoulders of the women, on the dancer's weird antics and her flying, tattered skirts. She was obviously tired, as a poor, performing cur might be, or a bear prodded along to uncongenial buffoonery. Every time that she paused and solicited alms with her tambourine the crowd dispersed, and some of them laughed because she insisted.

"*Voyons*," she said with a weird attempt at gaiety, "a couple of *sous* for the entertainment, citizen! You have stood here half an hour. You can't have it all for nothing, what?"

The man—young, square-shouldered, thick-lipped, with the look of a bully about his well-clad person—retorted with a coarse insult, which the woman resented. There were high words; the crowd for the most part ranged itself on the side of the bully. The woman backed against the wall nearest to her, held feeble, emaciated hands up to her ears in a vain endeavour to shut out the hideous jeers and ribald jokes which were the natural weapons of this untamed crowd.

Soon blows began to rain; not a few fell upon the unfortunate woman. She screamed, and the more she screamed the louder did the crowd jeer, the uglier became its temper. Then suddenly it was all over. How it happened the woman could not tell. She had closed her eyes, feeling sick and dizzy; but she had heard a loud call, words spoken in English (a language which she understood), a pleasant laugh, and a brief but violent scuffle. After that the hurrying retreat of many feet, the click of *sabots* on the uneven pavement and patter of shoeless feet, and then silence.

She had fallen on her knees and was cowering against the wall, had lost consciousness probably for a minute or two. Then she heard that pleasant laugh again and the soft drawl of the English tongue.

"I love to see those beggars scuttling off, like so many rats to their burrows, don't you, Ffoulkes?"

"They didn't put up much fight, the cowards!" came from another voice, also in English. "A dozen of them against this wretched woman. What had best be done with her?"

"I'll see to her," rejoined the first speaker. "You and Tony had best find the others. Tell them I shall be round directly."

It all seemed like a dream. The woman dared not open her eyes lest reality—hideous and brutal—once more confronted her. Then all at once she felt that her poor, weak body, encircled by strong arms, was lifted off the ground, and that she was being carried down the street, away from the light projected by the lanthorn overhead, into the sheltering darkness of a yawning *porte cochère*. But she was not then fully conscious.

2

When she reopened her eyes, she was in what appeared to be the lodge of a *concierge*. She was lying on a horsehair sofa. There was a sense of warmth and of security around her. No wonder that it still seemed like a dream. Before her stood a man, tall and straight, surely a being from another world—or so he appeared to the poor wretch who, since uncountable time, had set eyes on none but the most miserable dregs of struggling humanity, who had seen little else but rags, and faces either cruel or wretched. This man was clad in a huge caped coat, which made his powerful figure seem preternaturally large. His hair was fair and slightly curly above his low, square brow; the eyes beneath their heavy lids looked down on her with unmistakable kindness.

The poor woman struggled to her feet. With a quick and pathetically humble gesture she drew her ragged, muddy skirts over her ankles and her tattered kerchief across her breast.

"I had best go now, *Monsieur* . . . . citizen," she murmured, while a hot flush rose to the roots of her unkempt hair. "I must not stop here . . . . I—"

"You are not going, *Madame*," he broke in, speaking now in perfect French and with a great air of authority, as one who is accustomed to being implicitly obeyed, "until you have told me how, a lady of culture and of refinement, comes to be masquerading as a street-dancer. The game is a dangerous one, as you have experienced tonight."

"It is no game, *Monsieur* . . . . citizen," she stammered; "nor yet a masquerade. I have been a street-dancer all my life, and—"

By way of an answer he took her hand, always with that air of authority which she never thought to resent.

"This is not a street-dancer's hand; *Madame*," he said quietly. "Nor is your speech that of the people."

She drew her hand away quickly, and the flush on her haggard face deepened.

"If you will honour me with your confidence, *Madame*," he insisted.

The kindly words, the courtesy of the man, went to the poor creature's heart. She fell back upon the sofa and with her face buried in her arms she sobbed out her heart for a minute or two. The man waited quite patiently. He had seen many women weep these days, and had dried many a tear through deeds of valour and of self-sacrifice, which were for ever recorded in the hearts of those whom he had succoured.

When this poor woman had succeeded in recovering some semblance of self-control, she turned her wan, tear-stained face to him and said simply:

"My name is Madeleine Lannoy, *Monsieur*. My husband was killed during the *émeutes* at Versailles, whilst defending the persons of the queen and of the royal children against the fury of the mob. When I was a girl I had the misfortune to attract the attentions of a young doctor named Jean Paul Marat. You have heard of him, *Monsieur*?"

The other nodded.

"You know him, perhaps," she continued, "for what he is: the most cruel and revengeful of men. A few years ago, he threw up his lucrative appointment as Court physician to Monseigneur le Comte d'Artois, and gave up the profession of medicine for that of journalist and politician. Politician! Heaven help him! He belongs to the most bloodthirsty section of revolutionary brigands. His creed is pillage, murder, and revenge; and he chooses to declare that it is I who, by rejecting his love, drove him to these foul extremities. May God forgive him that abominable lie! The evil we do, *Monsieur*, is within us; it does not come from circumstance. I, in the meanwhile, was a happy wife. My husband, M. de Lannoy, who was an officer in the army, idolised me. We had one child, a boy—"

She paused, with another catch in her throat. Then she resumed, with calmness that, in view of the tale she told, sounded strangely weird:

"In June last year my child was stolen from me—stolen by Marat in hideous revenge for the supposed wrong which I had done him. The details of that execrable outrage are of no importance. I was decoyed from home one day through the agency of a forged message purporting to come from a very dear friend whom I knew to be in grave trouble at the time. Oh! the whole thing was thoroughly well thought out, I can assure you!" she continued, with a harsh laugh which ended in a heartrending sob. "The forged message, the suborned servant, the threats of terrible reprisals if anyone in the village gave me the slightest warning or clue.

"When the whole miserable business was accomplished, I was just like a trapped animal inside a cage, held captive by immovable bars of obstinate silence and cruel indifference. No one would help me. No one ostensibly knew anything; no one had seen anything, heard anything. The child was gone! My servants, the people in the village—some of whom I could have sworn were true and sympathetic—only

304

shrugged their shoulders. '*Que voulez-vous, Madame?* Children of *bourgeois* as well as of *aristos* were often taken up by the State to be brought up as true patriots and no longer pampered like so many lap-dogs.'

"Three days later I received a letter from that inhuman monster, Jean Paul Marat. He told me that he had taken my child away from me, not from any idea of revenge for my disdain in the past, but from a spirit of pure patriotism. My boy, he said, should not be brought up with the same ideas of *bourgeois* effeteness and love of luxury which had disgraced the nation for centuries. No! he should be reared amongst men who had realised the true value of fraternity and equality and the ideal of complete liberty for the individual to lead his own life, unfettered by senseless prejudices of education and refinement. Which means, *Monsieur*," the poor woman went on with passionate misery, "that my child is to be reared up in the company of all that is most vile and most degraded in the disease-haunted slums of indigent Paris; that, with the connivance of that execrable fiend Marat, my only son will, mayhap, come back to me one day a potential thief, a criminal probably, a drink-sodden reprobate at best. Such things are done every day in this glorious Revolution of ours—done in the sacred name of France and of Liberty. And the moral murder of my child is to be my punishment for daring to turn a deaf ear to the indign passion of a brute!"

Once more she paused, and when the melancholy echo of her broken voice had died away in the narrow room, not another murmur broke the stillness of this far-away corner of the great city.

The man did not move. He stood looking down upon the poor woman before him, a world of pity expressed in his deep-set eyes. Through the absolute silence around there came the sound as of a gentle flutter, the current of cold air, mayhap, sighing through the ill-fitting shutters, or the soft, weird soughing made by unseen things. The man's heart was full of pity, and it seemed as if the Angel of Compassion had come at his bidding and enfolded the sorrowing woman with his wings.

A moment or two later she was able to finish her pathetic narrative.

"Do you marvel, *Monsieur*," she said, "that I am still sane—still alive? But I only live to find my child. I try and keep my reason in order to fight the devilish cunning of a brute on his own ground. Up to now all my inquiries have been in vain. At first, I squandered money, tried judicial means, set an army of sleuth-hounds on the track. I tried bribery, corruption. I went to the wretch himself and abased myself in the dust before him. He only laughed at me and told me that his love for me had died long ago; he now was lavishing its treasures upon the faithful friend and companion—that awful woman, Simonne Evrard—who had stood by him in the darkest hours of his misfortunes.

"Then it was that I decided to adopt different tactics. Since my child was to be reared in the midst of murderers and thieves, I, too, would haunt their abodes. I became a street-singer, dancer, what you will. I wear rags now and solicit alms. I haunt the most disreputable *cabarets* in the lowest slums of Paris. I listen and I spy; I question every man, woman, and child who might afford some clue, give me some indication. There is hardly a house in these parts that I have not visited and whence I have not been kicked out as an importunate beggar or worse. Gradually I am narrowing the circle of my investigations. Presently I shall get a clue. I shall! I know I shall! God cannot allow this monstrous thing to go on!"

Again, there was silence. The poor woman had completely broken down. Shame, humiliation, passionate grief, had made of her a mere miserable wreckage of humanity.

The man waited awhile until she was composed, then he said simply:

"You have suffered terribly, *Madame*; but chiefly, I think, because you have been alone in your grief. You have brooded over it until it has threatened your reason. Now, if you will allow me to act as your friend, I will pledge you my word that I will find your son for you. Will you trust me sufficiently to give up your present methods and place yourself entirely in my hands? There are more than a dozen gallant gentlemen, who are my friends, and who will help me in my search. But for this I must have a free hand, and only help from you when I require it. I can find you lodgings where you will be quite safe under the protection of my wife, who is as like an angel as any man or woman I have ever met on this earth. When your son is once more in your arms, you will, I hope, accompany us to England, where so many of your friends have already found a refuge. If this meets with your approval, *Madame*, you may command me, for with your permission I mean to be your most devoted servant."

Dante, in his wild imaginations of hell and of purgatory and fleeting glimpses of paradise, never put before us the picture of a soul that was lost and found heaven, after a cycle of despair. Nor could Madeleine Lannoy ever explain her feelings at that moment, even to herself. To begin with, she could not quite grasp the reality of this ray of hope, which came to her at the darkest hour of her misery. She stared at the man before her as she would on an ethereal vision; she fell on her knees and buried her face in her hands.

What happened afterwards she hardly knew; she was in a state of semi-consciousness. When she once more woke to reality, she was in comfortable lodgings; she moved and talked and ate and lived like a human being. She was no longer a pariah, an outcast, a poor, half-demented creature, insentient save for an infinite capacity for suffering. She suffered still, but she no longer despaired. There had been such marvellous power and confidence in that man's voice when he said: "I pledge you my word." Madeleine Lannoy lived now in hope and a sweet sense of perfect mental and bodily security. Around her there was an influence, too, a presence which she did not often see, but always felt to be there: a woman, tall and graceful and sympathetic, who was always ready to cheer, to comfort, and to help. Her name was Marguerite. Madame Lannoy never knew her by any other. The man had spoken of her as being as like an angel as could be met on this earth, and poor Madeleine Lannoy fully agreed with him.

3

Even that bloodthirsty tiger, Jean Paul Marat, has had his apologists. His friends have called him a martyr, a selfless and incorruptible exponent of social and political ideals. We may take it that Simonne Evrard loved him, for a more impassioned obituary speech was, mayhap, never spoken than the one which she delivered before the National Assembly in honour of that sinister demagogue, whose writings and activities will for ever sully some of the really fine pages of that revolutionary era.

But with those apologists we have naught to do. History has talked its fill of the inhuman monster. With the more intimate biographists alone has this true chronicle any concern. It is one of these who tells us that on or about the eighteenth day of *Messidor*, in the year 1 of the Republic (a date which corresponds with the sixth of July, 1793, of our own calendar), Jean Paul Marat took an additional man into his service, at the instance of Jeannette Maréchal, his cook and maid-of-all-work. Marat was at this time a martyr to an unpleasant form of skin disease, brought on by the terrible privations which he had endured during the few years preceding his association with Simonne Evrard, the faithful friend and housekeeper, whose small fortune subsequently provided him with some degree of comfort.

The man whom Jeannette Maréchal, the cook, introduced into

the household of No. 30, Rue des Cordeliers, that worthy woman had literally picked one day out of the gutter where he was grabbing for scraps of food like some wretched starving cur. He appeared to be known to the police of the section, his identity book proclaiming him to be one Paul Molé, who had served his time in gaol for larceny. He professed himself willing to do any work required of him, for the merest pittance and some kind of roof over his head. Simonne Evrard allowed Jeannette to take him in, partly out of compassion and partly with a view to easing the woman's own burden, the only other domestic in the house—a man named Bas—being more interested in politics and the meetings of the Club des Jacobins than he was in his master's ailments. The man Molé, moreover, appeared to know something of medicine and of herbs and how to prepare the warm baths which alone eased the unfortunate Marat from pain. He was powerfully built, too, and though he muttered and grumbled a great deal, and indulged in prolonged fits of sulkiness, when he would not open his mouth to anyone, he was, on the whole, helpful and good-tempered.

There must also have been something about his whole wretched personality which made a strong appeal to the "Friend of the People," for it is quite evident that within a few days Paul Molé had won no small measure of his master's confidence.

Marat, sick, fretful, and worried, had taken an unreasoning dislike to his servant Bas. He was thankful to have a stranger about him, a man who was as miserable as he himself had been a very little while ago; who, like himself, had lived in cellars and in underground burrows, and lived on the scraps of food which even street-curs had disdained.

On the seventh day following Molé's entry into the household, and while the latter was preparing his employer's bath, Marat said abruptly to him:

"You'll go as far as the Chemin de Pantin today for me, citizen. You know your way?"

"I can find it, what?" muttered Molé, who appeared to be in one of his surly moods.

"You will have to go very circumspectly," Marat went on, in his cracked and feeble voice. "And see to it that no one spies upon your movements. I have many enemies, citizen . . . . one especially . . . . a woman . . . . She is always prying and spying on me . . . . So beware of any woman you see lurking about at your heels."

Molé gave a half-audible grunt in reply.

"You had best go after dark," the other rejoined after a while. "Come back to me after nine o'clock. It is not far to the Chemin de Pantin—just where it intersects the Route de Meaux. You can get there and back before midnight. The people will admit you. I will give you a ring—the only thing I possess . . . . . It has little or no value," he added with a harsh, grating laugh. "It will not be worth your while to steal it. You will have to see a brat and report to me on his condition—his appearance, what? . . . . Talk to him a bit . . . . See what he says and let me know. It is not difficult."

"No, citizen."

Molé helped the suffering wretch into his bath. Not a movement, not a quiver of the eyelid betrayed one single emotion which he may have felt—neither loathing nor sympathy, only placid indifference. He was just a half-starved menial, thankful to accomplish any task for the sake of satisfying a craving stomach. Marat stretched out his shrunken limbs in the herbal water with a sigh of well-being.

"And the ring, citizen?" Molé suggested presently.

The demagogue held up his left hand—it was emaciated and disfigured by disease. A cheap-looking metal ring, set with a false stone, glistened upon the fourth finger.

"Take it off," he said curtly.

The ring must have all along been too small for the bony hand of the once famous Court physician. Even now it appeared embedded in the flabby skin and refused to slide over the knuckle.

"The water will loosen it," remarked Molé quietly.

Marat dipped his hand back into the water, and the other stood beside him, silent and stolid, his broad shoulders bent, his face naught but a mask, void and expressionless beneath its coating of grime.

One or two seconds went by. The air was heavy with steam and a medley of evil-smelling fumes, which hung in the close atmosphere of the narrow room. The sick man appeared to be drowsy, his head rolled over to one side, his eyes closed. He had evidently forgotten all about the ring.

A woman's voice, shrill and peremptory, broke the silence which had become oppressive:

"Here, Citizen Molé, I want you! There's not a bit of wood chopped up for my fire, and how am I to make the coffee without firing, I should like to know?"

"The ring, citizen," Molé urged gruffly.

Marat had been roused by the woman's sharp voice. He cursed her for a noisy harridan; then he said fretfully:

"It will do presently—when you are ready to start. I said nine o'clock . . . . it is only four now. I am tired. Tell Citizeness Evrard to bring me some hot coffee in an hour's time . . . .You can go and fetch me the *Moniteur* now, and take back these proofs to Citizen Dufour. You will find him at the 'Cordeliers,' or else at the printing works . . . . Come back at nine o'clock . . . . I am tired now . . . . too tired to tell you where to find the house which is off the Chemin de Pantin. Presently will do . . . . "

Even while he spoke he appeared to drop into a fitful sleep. His two hands were hidden under the sheet which covered the bath. Molé watched him in silence for a moment or two, then he turned on his heel and shuffled off through the ante-room into the kitchen beyond, where presently he sat down, squatting in an angle by the stove, and started with his usual stolidness to chop wood for the *citizeness'* fire.

When this task was done, and he had received a chunk of sour bread for his reward from Jeannette Maréchal, the cook, he shuffled out of the place and into the street, to do his employer's errands.

4

Paul Molé had been to the offices of the *Moniteur* and to the printing works of *L'Ami du Peuple*. He had seen the Citizen Dufour at the Club and, presumably, had spent the rest of his time wandering idly about the streets of the quartier, for he did not return to the Rue des Cordeliers until nearly nine o'clock.

As soon as he came to the top of the street, he fell in with the crowd which had collected outside No. 30.With his habitual slouchy gait and the steady pressure of his powerful elbows, he pushed his way to the door, whilst gleaning whisperings and rumours on his way.

"The Citizen Marat has been assassinated."

"By a woman."

"A mere girl."

"A wench from Caen. Her name is Corday."

"The people nearly tore her to pieces a while ago."

"She is as much as guillotined already."

The latter remark went off with a loud guffaw and many a ribald joke.

Molé, despite his great height, succeeded in getting through unperceived. He was of no account, and he knew his way inside the house. It was full of people: journalists, gaffers, women and men—the usual crowd that come to gape. The Citizen Marat was a great personage. The Friend of the People. An Incorruptible, if ever there was one. Just look at the simplicity, almost the poverty, in which he lived! Only the *aristos* hated him, and the fat *bourgeois* who battened on the people. Citizen Marat had sent hundreds of them to the guillotine with a stroke of his pen or a denunciation from his fearless tongue.

Molé did not pause to listen to these comments. He pushed his way through the throng up the stairs, to his late employer's lodgings on the first floor.

The anteroom was crowded, so were the other rooms; but the greatest pressure was around the door immediately facing him, the one which gave on the bathroom. In the kitchen on his right, where a while ago he had been chopping wood under a flood of abuse from Jeannette Maréchal, he caught sight of this woman, cowering by the hearth, her filthy apron thrown over her head, and crying—yes! crying for the loathsome creature, who had expiated some of his abominable crimes at the hands of a poor, misguided girl, whom an infuriated mob was even now threatening to tear to pieces in its rage.

The parlour and even Simonne's room were also filled with people: men, most of whom Molé knew by sight; friends or enemies of the ranting demagogue who lay murdered in the very bath which his casual servant had prepared for him. Everyone was discussing the details of the murder, the punishment of the youthful assassin. Simonne Evrard was being loudly blamed for having admitted the girl into Citizen Marat's room. But the wench had looked so simple, so innocent, and she said she was the bearer of a message from Caen. She had called twice during the day, and in the evening the citizen himself said that he would see her. Simonne had been for sending her away. But the citizen was peremptory. And he was so helpless . . . . in his bath . . . . name of a name, the pitiable affair!

No one paid much attention to Molé. He listened for a while to Simonne's impassioned voice, giving her version of the affair; then he worked his way stolidly into the bathroom.

It was some time before he succeeded in reaching the side of that awful bath wherein lay the dead body of Jean Paul Marat. The small room was densely packed—not with friends, for there was not a man or woman living, except Simonne Evrard and her sisters, whom the bloodthirsty demagogue would have called "friend"; but his powerful personality had been a menace to many, and now they came in crowds to see that he was really dead, that a girl's feeble hand had actually done the deed which they themselves had only contemplated. They stood about whispering, their heads averted from the ghastly spectacle of this miserable creature, to whom even death had failed to lend his usual attribute of tranquil dignity.

The tiny room was inexpressibly hot and stuffy. Hardly a breath of outside air came in through the narrow window, which only gave on the bedroom beyond. An evil-smelling oil-lamp swung from the low ceiling and shed its feeble light on the upturned face of the murdered man.

Molé stood for a moment or two, silent and pensive, beside that hideous form. There was the bath, just as he had prepared it: the board spread over with a sheet and laid across the bath, above which only the head and shoulders emerged, livid and stained. One hand, the left, grasped the edge of the board with the last convulsive clutch of supreme agony.

On the fourth finger of that hand glistened the shoddy ring which Marat had said was not worth stealing. Yet, apparently, it roused the cupidity of the poor wretch who had served him faithfully for these last few days, and who now would once more be thrown, starving and friendless, upon the streets of Paris.

Molé threw a quick, furtive glance around him. The crowd which had come to gloat over the murdered Terrorist stood about whispering, with heads averted, engrossed in their own affairs. He slid his hand surreptitiously over that of the dead man. With dexterous manipulation he lifted the finger round which glistened the metal ring. Death appeared to have shrivelled the flesh still more upon the bones, to have contracted the knuckles and shrunk the tendons. The ring slid off quite easily. Molé had it in his hand, when suddenly a rough blow struck him on the shoulder.

"Trying to rob the dead?" a stern voice shouted in his ear. "Are you a disguised *aristo*, or what?"

At once the whispering ceased. A wave of excitement went round the room. Some people shouted, others pressed forward to gaze on the abandoned wretch who had been caught in the act of committing a gruesome deed.

"Robbing the dead!"

They were experts in evil, most of these men here. Their hands were indelibly stained with some of the foulest crimes ever recorded in history. But there was something ghoulish in this attempt to plunder that awful thing lying there, helpless, in the water. There was also a great relief to nerve-tension in shouting Horror and Anathema with self-righteous indignation; and additional excitement in the suggested "*aristo* in disguise."

Molé struggled vigorously. He was powerful and his fists were heavy. But he was soon surrounded, held fast by both arms, whilst half a dozen hands tore at his tattered clothes, searched him to his very skin, for the booty which he was thought to have taken from the dead.

"Leave me alone, curse you!" he shouted, louder than his aggressors. "My name is Paul Molé, I tell you. Ask the Citizeness Evrard. I waited on Citizen Marat. I prepared his bath. I was the only friend who did not turn away from him in his sickness and his poverty. Leave me alone, I say! Why," he added, with a hoarse laugh, "Jean Paul in his bath was as naked as on the day he was born!"

"'Tis true," said one of those who had been most active in rummaging through Molé's grimy rags. "There's nothing to be found on him."

But suspicion once aroused was not easily allayed. Molé's protestations became more and more vigorous and emphatic. His papers were all in order, he vowed. He had them on him: his own identity papers, clear for anyone to see. Someone had dragged them out of his pocket; they were dank and covered with splashes of mud—hardly legible. They were handed over to a man who stood in the immediate circle of light projected by the lamp. He seized them and examined them carefully. This man was short and slight, was dressed in well-made cloth clothes; his hair was held in at the nape of the next in a modish manner with a black taffeta bow. His hands were clean, slender, and claw-like, and he wore the tricolour scarf of office round his waist which proclaimed him to be a member of one of the numerous Committees which tyrannised over the people.

The papers appeared to be in order, and proclaimed the bearer to be Paul Molé, a native of Besancon, a carpenter by trade. The identity book had recently been signed by Jean Paul Marat, the man's latest employer, and been counter-signed by the *commissary* of the section.

The man in the tricolour scarf turned with some acerbity on the crowd who was still pressing round the prisoner.

"Which of you here," he queried roughly, "levelled an unjust accusation against an honest citizen?"

But, as usual in such cases, no one replied directly to the charge. It was not safe these days to come into conflict with men like Molé. The Committees were all on their side, against the *bourgeois* as well as against the *aristos*. This was the reign of the proletariat, and the sansculotte always emerged triumphant in a conflict against the well-to-do. Nor was it good to rouse the ire of Citizen Chauvelin, one of the most powerful, as he was the most pitiless members of the Committee of Public Safety. Quiet, sarcastic rather than aggressive, something of the *aristo*, too, in his clean linen and well-cut clothes, he had not even yielded to the defunct Marat in cruelty and relentless persecution of aristocrats.

Evidently his sympathies now were all with Molé, the out-at-elbows, miserable servant of an equally miserable master. His pale-coloured, deep-set eyes challenged the crowd, which gave way before him, slunk back into the corners, away from his coldly threatening glance. Thus, he found himself suddenly face to face with Molé, somewhat isolated from the rest, and close to the tin bath with its grim contents. Chauvelin had the papers in his hand.

"Take these, citizen," he said curtly to the other. "They are all in order."

He looked up at Molé as he said this, for the latter, though his shoulders were bent, was unusually tall, and Molé took the papers from him. Thus, for the space of a few seconds the two men looked into one another's face, eyes to eyes—and suddenly Chauvelin felt an icy sweat coursing down his spine. The eyes into which he gazed had a strange, ironical twinkle in them, a kind of good-humoured arrogance, whilst through the firm, clear-cut lips, half hidden by a dirty and ill-kempt beard, there came the sound—oh! a mere echo—of a quaint and inane laugh.

The whole thing—it seemed like a vision—was over in a second. Chauvelin, sick and faint with the sudden rush of blood to his head, closed his eyes for one brief instant. The next, the crowd had closed round him; anxious inquiries reached his re-awakened senses.

But he uttered one quick, hoarse cry:

"Hébert! À *moi!* Are you there?"

"Present, citizen!" came in immediate response. And a tall figure in the tattered uniform affected by the revolutionary guard stepped briskly out of the crowd. Chauvelin's claw-like hand was shaking visibly.

"The man Molé," he called in a voice husky with excitement. "Seize him at once! And, name of a dog! do not allow a living soul in or out of the house!"

Hébert turned on his heel. The next moment his harsh voice was heard above the din and the general hubbub around:

"Quite safe, citizen!" he called to his chief. "We have the rogue right enough!"

There was much shouting and much cursing, a great deal of bustle and confusion, as the men of the Sûreté closed the doors of the defunct demagogue's lodgings. Some two score men, a dozen or so women, were locked in, inside the few rooms which reeked of dirt and of disease. They jostled and pushed, screamed and protested. For two or three minutes the din was quite deafening. Simonne Evrard pushed her way up to the forefront of the crowd.

"What is this I hear?" she queried peremptorily. "Who is accusing Citizen Molé? And of what, I should like to know? I am responsible for everyone inside these apartments . . . . and if Citizen Marat were still alive—"

Chauvelin appeared unaware of all the confusion and of the woman's protestations. He pushed his way through the crowd to the corner of the anteroom where Molé stood, crouching and hunched up, his grimy hands idly fingering the papers which Chauvelin had returned to him a moment ago. Otherwise he did not move.

He stood, silent and sullen; and when Chauvelin, who had succeeded in mastering his emotion, gave the peremptory command: "Take this man to the depot at once. And do not allow him one instant out of your sight!" he made no attempt at escape.

He allowed Hébert and the men to seize him, to lead him away. He followed without a word, without a struggle. His massive figure was hunched up like that of an old man; his hands, which still clung to his identity papers, trembled slightly like those of a man who is very frightened and very helpless. The men of the Sûreté handled him very roughly, but he made no protest. The woman Evrard did all the protesting, vowing that the people would not long tolerate such tyranny. She even forced her way up to Hébert. With a gesture of fury, she tried to strike him in the face, and continued, with a loud voice, her insults and objurgations, until, with a movement of his bayonet, he pushed her roughly out of the way.

After that Paul Molé, surrounded by the guard, was led without ceremony out of the house. Chauvelin gazed after him as if he had been brought face to face with a ghoul.

5

Chauvelin hurried to the depot. After those few seconds wherein he had felt dazed, incredulous, almost under a spell, he had quickly regained the mastery of his nerves, and regained, too, that intense joy which anticipated triumph is wont to give.

In the out-at-elbows, half-starved servant of the murdered Terror-ist, Citizen Chauvelin, of the Committee of Public Safety, had recog-nised his arch enemy, that Meddlesome and adventurous Englishman who chose to hide his identity under the pseudonym of the Scarlet Pimpernel. He knew that he could reckon on Hébert; his orders not to allow the prisoner one moment out of sight would of a certainty be strictly obeyed.

Hébert, indeed, a few moments later, greeted his chief outside the doors of the depot with the welcome news that Paul Molé was safely under lock and key.

"You had no trouble with him?" Chauvelin queried, with ill-con-cealed eagerness.

"No, no! citizen, no trouble," was Hébert's quick reply. "He seems to be a well-known rogue in these parts," he continued with a com-placent guffaw; "and some of his friends tried to hustle us at the cor-ner of the Rue de Tourraine; no doubt with a view to getting the prisoner away. But we were too strong for them, and Paul Molé is now sulking in his cell and still protesting that his arrest is an outrage against the liberty of the people."

Chauvelin made no further remark. He was obviously too excited to speak. Pushing past Hébert and the men of the Sûreté who stood about the dark and narrow passages of the depot, he sought the *Com-missary* of the Section in the latter's office.

It was now close upon ten o'clock. The Citizen Commissary Cui-sinier had finished his work for the day and was preparing to go home and to bed. He was a family man, had been a respectable *bourgeois* in his day, and though he was a rank opportunist and had sacrificed not only his political convictions but also his conscience to the exigencies of the time, he still nourished in his innermost heart a secret contempt for the revolutionary brigands who ruled over France at this hour.

To any other man than Citizen Chauvelin, the Citizen Commis-sary would, no doubt, have given a curt refusal to a request to see a prisoner at this late hour of the evening. But Chauvelin was not a man to be denied, and whilst muttering various objections in his ill-kempt beard, Cuisinier, nevertheless, gave orders that the citizen was to be conducted at once to the cells.

Paul Molé had in truth turned sulky. The turnkey vowed that the prisoner had hardly stirred since first he had been locked up in the common cell. He sat in a corner at the end of the bench, with his face turned to the wall, and paid no heed either to his fellow-prisoners or to the facetious remarks of the warder.

Chauvelin went up to him, made some curt remark. Molé kept an obstinate shoulder turned towards him—a grimy shoulder, which showed naked through a wide rent in his blouse. This portion of the cell was well-nigh in total darkness; the feeble shaft of light which came through the open door hardly penetrated to this remote angle of the squalid burrow. The same sense of mystery and unreality overcame Chauvelin again as he looked on the miserable creature in whom, an hour ago, he had recognised the super-exquisite Sir Percy Blakeney. Now he could only see a vague outline in the gloom: the stooping shoulders, the long limbs, that naked piece of shoulder which caught a feeble reflex from the distant light. Nor did any amount of none too gentle prodding on the part of the warder induce him to change his position.

"Leave him alone," said Chauvelin curly at last. "I have seen all that I wished to see."

The cell was insufferably hot and stuffy. Chauvelin, finical and queasy, turned away with a shudder of disgust. There was nothing to be got now out of a prolonged interview with his captured foe. He had seen him: that was sufficient. He had seen the super-exquisite Sir Percy Blakeney locked up in a common cell with some of the most scrubby and abject rogues which the slums of indigent Paris could yield, having apparently failed in some undertaking which had demanded for its fulfilment not only tattered clothes and grimy hands, but menial service with a beggarly and disease-ridden employer, whose very propinquity must have been positive torture to the fastidious dandy.

Of a truth this was sufficient for the gratification of any revenge. Chauvelin felt that he could now go contentedly to rest after an evening's work excellently done.

He gave order that Molé should be put in a separate cell, denied all intercourse with anyone outside or in the depot, and that he should be guarded on sight day and night. After that he went his way.

6

The following morning Citizen Chauvelin, of the Committee of Public Safety, gave due notice to Citizen Fouquier-Tinville, the Public Prosecutor, that the dangerous English spy, known to the world as the Scarlet Pimpernel, was now safely under lock and key, and that he must be transferred to the Abbaye prison forthwith and to the guillotine as quickly as might be. No one was to take any risks this time; there must be no question either of discrediting his famous League or of obtaining other more valuable information out of him. Such methods had proved disastrous in the past.

There were no safe Englishmen these days, except the dead ones, and it would not take Citizen Fouquier-Tinville much thought or time to frame an indictment against the notorious Scarlet Pimpernel, which would do away with the necessity of a prolonged trial. The revolutionary government was at war with England now, and short work could be made of all poisonous spies.

By order, therefore, of the Committee of Public Safety, the prisoner, Paul Molé, was taken out of the cells of the depot and conveyed in a closed carriage to the Abbaye prison. Chauvelin had the pleasure of watching this gratifying spectacle from the windows of the *Commissariat*. When he saw the closed carriage drive away, with Hébert and two men inside and two others on the box, he turned to Citizen Commissary Cuisinier with a sigh of intense satisfaction.

"There goes the most dangerous enemy our glorious revolution has had," he said, with an accent of triumph which he did not attempt to disguise.

Cuisinier shrugged his shoulders.

"Possibly," he retorted curtly. "He did not seem to me to be very dangerous and his papers were quite in order."

To this assertion Chauvelin made no reply. Indeed, how could he explain to this stolid official the subtle workings of an intriguing brain? Had he himself not had many a proof of how little the forging of identity papers or of passports troubled the members of that accursed League? Had he not seen the Scarlet Pimpernel, that exquisite Sir Percy Blakeney, under disguises that were so grimy and so loathsome that they would have repelled the most abject, suborned spy?

Indeed, all that was wanted now was the assurance that Hébert—who himself had a deadly and personal grudge against the Scarlet Pimpernel—would not allow him for one moment out of his sight.

Fortunately, as to this, there was no fear. One hint to Hébert and the man was as keen, as determined, as Chauvelin himself.

"Set your mind at rest, citizen," he said with a rough oath. "I guessed how matters stood the moment you gave me the order. I knew you would not take all that trouble for a real Paul Molé. But have no fear! That accursed Englishman has not been one second out of my sight, from the moment I arrested him in the late Citizen Marat's lodgings, and by Satan! he shall not be either, until I have seen his impudent head fall under the guillotine."

He himself, he added, had seen to the arrangements for the disposal of the prisoner in the Abbaye: an inner cell, partially partitioned off in one of the guard-rooms, with no egress of its own, and only a tiny grated air-hole high up in the wall, which gave on an outside corridor, and through which not even a cat could manage to slip. Oh! the prisoner was well guarded! The Citizen Representative need, of a truth, have no fear! Three or four men—of the best and most trustworthy—had not left the guard-room since the morning. He himself (Hébert) had kept the accursed Englishman in sight all night, had personally conveyed him to the Abbaye, and had only left the guard-room a moment ago in order to speak with the Citizen Representative. He was going back now at once, and would not move until the order came for the prisoner to be conveyed to the Court of Justice and thence to summary execution.

For the nonce, Hébert concluded with a complacent chuckle, the Englishman was still crouching dejectedly in a corner of his new cell, with little of him visible save that naked shoulder through his torn shirt, which, in the process of transference from one prison to another, had become a shade more grimy than before.

Chauvelin nodded, well satisfied. He commended Hébert for his zeal, rejoiced with him over the inevitable triumph. It would be well to avenge that awful humiliation at Calais last September. Nevertheless, he felt anxious and nervy; he could not comprehend the apathy assumed by the factitious Molé. That the apathy was assumed Chauvelin was keen enough to guess. What it portended he could not conjecture. But that the Englishman would make a desperate attempt at escape was, of course, a foregone conclusion. It rested with Hébert and a guard that could neither be bribed nor fooled into treachery, to see that such an attempt remained abortive.

What, however, had puzzled Citizen Chauvelin all along was the motive which had induced Sir Percy Blakeney to play the role of menial to Jean Paul Marat. Behind it there lay, undoubtedly, one of those subtle intrigues for which that insolent Scarlet Pimpernel was famous; and with it was associated an attempt at theft upon the murdered body of the demagogue . . . . an attempt which had failed, seeing that the supposititious Paul Molé had been searched and nothing suspicious been found upon his person.

Nevertheless, thoughts of that attempted theft disturbed Chauvelin's equanimity. The old legend of the crumpled roseleaf was applicable in his case. Something of his intense satisfaction would pale if this final enterprise of the audacious adventurer were to be brought to a triumphant close in the end.

7

That same forenoon, on his return from the Abbaye and the depot, Chauvelin found that a visitor was waiting for him. A woman, who gave her name as Jeannette Maréchal, desired to speak with the Citizen Representative. Chauvelin knew the woman as his colleague Marat's maid-of-all-work, and he gave orders that she should be admitted at once.

Jeannette Maréchal, tearful and not a little frightened, assured the Citizen Representative that her errand was urgent. Her late employer had so few friends; she did not know to whom to turn until she bethought herself of Citizen Chauvelin. It took him some little time to disentangle the tangible facts out of the woman's voluble narrative. At first the words: "Child .... Chemin de Pantin .... Leridan," were only a medley of sounds which conveyed no meaning to his ear. But when occasion demanded, Citizen Chauvelin was capable of infinite patience. Gradually he understood what the woman was driving at.

"The child, citizen!" she reiterated excitedly. "What's to be done about him? I know that Citizen Marat would have wished—"

"Never mind now what Citizen Marat would have wished," Chauvelin broke in quietly. "Tell me first who this child is."

"I do not know, citizen," she replied.

"How do you mean, you do not know? Then I pray you, *citizeness*, what is all this pother about?"

"About the child, citizen," reiterated Jeannette obstinately.

"What child?"

"The child whom Citizen Marat adopted last year and kept at that awful house on the Chemin de Pantin."

"I did not know Citizen Marat had adopted a child," remarked Chauvelin thoughtfully.

"No one knew," she rejoined. "Not even Citizeness Evrard. I was the only one who knew. I had to go and see the child once every month. It was a wretched, miserable brat," the woman went on, her shrivelled old breast vaguely stirred, mayhap, by some atrophied feeling of motherhood. "More than half-starved .... and the look in its eyes, citizen! It was enough to make you cry! I could see by his poor little emaciated body and his nice little hands and feet that he ought

320

never to have been put in that awful house, where—"

She paused, and that quick look of furtive terror, which was so often to be met with in the eyes of the timid these days, crept into her wrinkled face.

"Well, *citizeness*," Chauvelin rejoined quietly, "why don't you proceed? That awful house, you were saying. Where and what is that awful house of which you speak?"

"The place kept by Citizen Leridan, just by Bassin de l'Ourcq," the woman murmured. "You know it, citizen."

Chauvelin nodded. He was beginning to understand.

"Well, now, tell me," he said, with that bland patience which had so oft served him in good stead in his unavowable profession. "Tell me. Last year Citizen Marat adopted—we'll say adopted—a child, whom he placed in the Leridans' house on the Pantin road. Is that correct?"

"That is just how it is, citizen. And I—"

"One moment," he broke in somewhat more sternly, as the woman's garrulity was getting on his nerves. "As you say, I know the Leridans' house. I have had cause to send children there myself. Children of *aristos* or of fat *bourgeois*, whom it was our duty to turn into good citizens. They are not pampered there, I imagine," he went on drily; "and if Citizen Marat sent his—er—adopted son there, it was not with a view to having him brought up as an *aristo*, what?"

"The child was not to be brought up at all," the woman said gruffly. "I have often heard Citizen Marat say that he hoped the brat would prove a thief when he grew up, and would take to alcoholism like a duck takes to water."

"And you know nothing of the child's parents?"

"Nothing, citizen. I had to go to Pantin once a month and have a look at him and report to Citizen Marat. But I always had the same tale to tell. The child was looking more and more like a young reprobate every time I saw him."

"Did Citizen Marat pay the Leridans for keeping the child?"

"Oh, no, citizen! The Leridans make a trade of the children by sending them out to beg. But this one was not to be allowed out yet. Citizen Marat's orders were very stern, and he was wont to terrify the Leridans with awful threats of the guillotine if they ever allowed the child out of their sight."

Chauvelin sat silent for a while. A ray of light had traversed the dark and tortuous ways of his subtle brain. While he mused the woman became impatient. She continued to talk on with the volubility peculiar to her kind. He paid no heed to her, until one phrase struck his ear.

"So now," Jeannette Maréchal was saying, "I don't know what to do. The ring has disappeared, and the Leridans are suspicious."

"The ring?" queried Chauvelin curtly. "What ring?"

"As I was telling you, citizen," she replied querulously, "when I went to see the child, the Citizen Marat always gave me this ring to show to the Leridans. Without I brought the ring they would not admit me inside their door. They were so terrified with all the citizen's threats of the guillotine."

"And now you say the ring has disappeared. Since when?"

"Well, citizen," replied Jeannette blandly, "since you took poor Paul Molé into custody."

"What do you mean?" Chauvelin riposted. "What had Paul Molé to do with the child and the ring?"

"Only this, citizen, that he was to have gone to Pantin last night instead of me. And thankful I was not to have to go. Citizen Marat gave the ring to Molé, I suppose. I know he intended to give it to him. He spoke to me about it just before that execrable woman came and murdered him. Anyway, the ring has gone and Molé too. So, I imagine that Molé has the ring and—"

"That's enough!" Chauvelin broke in roughly. "You can go!"

"But, citizen—"

"You can go, I said," he reiterated sharply. "The matter of the child and the Leridans and the ring no longer concerns you. You understand?"

"Y—y—yes, citizen," murmured Jeannette, vaguely terrified.

And of a truth the change in Citizen Chauvelin's demeanour was enough to scare any timid creature. Not that he raved or ranted or screamed. Those were not his ways. He still sat beside his desk as he had done before, and his slender hand, so like the talons of a vulture, was clenched upon the arm of his chair. But there was such a look of inward fury and of triumph in his pale, deep-set eyes, such lines of cruelty around his thin, closed lips, that Jeannette Maréchal, even with the picture before her mind of Jean Paul Marat in his maddest moods, fled, with the unreasoning terror of her kind, before the sternly controlled, fierce passion of this man.

Chauvelin never noticed that she went. He sat for a long time, silent and immovable. Now he understood. Thank all the Powers of Hate and Revenge, no thought of disappointment was destined to embitter the overflowing cup of his triumph. He had not only brought his arch-enemy to his knees, but had foiled one of his audacious ventures. How clear the whole thing was! The false Paul Molé, the newly acquired menial in the household of Marat, had wormed himself into the confidence of his employer in order to wrest from him the secret of the *aristo's* child. Bravo! bravo! my gallant Scarlet Pimpernel! Chauvelin now could see it all. Tragedies such as that which had placed an *aristo's* child in the power of a cunning demon like Marat were not rare these days, and Chauvelin had been fitted by nature and by temperament to understand and appreciate an execrable monster of the type of Jean Paul Marat.

And Paul Molé, the grimy, degraded servant of the indigent demagogue, the loathsome mask which hid the fastidious personality of Sir Percy Blakeney, had made a final and desperate effort to possess himself of the ring which would deliver the child into his power. Now, having failed in his machinations, he was safe under lock and key—guarded on sight. The next twenty-four hours would see him unmasked, awaiting his trial and condemnation under the scathing indictment prepared by Fouquier-Tinville, the unerring Public Prosecutor. The day after that, the tumbril and the guillotine for that execrable English spy, and the boundless sense of satisfaction that his last intrigue had aborted in such a signal and miserable manner.

Of a truth Chauvelin at this hour had every cause to be thankful, and it was with a light heart that he set out to interview the Leridans.

8

The Leridans, anxious, obsequious, terrified, were only too ready to obey the Citizen Representative in all things.

They explained with much complacency that, even though they were personally acquainted with Jeannette Maréchal, when the *citizeness* presented herself this very morning without the ring they had refused her permission to see the brat.

Chauvelin, who in his own mind had already reconstructed the whole tragedy of the stolen child, was satisfied that Marat could not have chosen more efficient tools for the execution of his satanic revenge than these two hideous products of revolutionary Paris.

Grasping, cowardly, and avaricious, the Leridans would lend themselves to any abomination for a sufficiency of money; but no money on earth would induce them to risk their own necks in the process. Marat had obviously held them by threats of the guillotine. They knew the power of the "Friend of the People," and feared him accordingly. Chauvelin's scarf of office, his curt, authoritative manner, had an equally awe-inspiring effect upon the two miserable creatures. They became absolutely abject, cringing, maudlin in their protestations of good-will and loyalty. No one, they vowed, should as much as see the child—ring or no ring—save the Citizen Representative himself. Chauvelin, however, had no wish to see the child. He was satisfied that its name was Lannoy—for the child had remembered it when first he had been brought to the Leridans. Since then he had apparently forgotten it, even though he often cried after his "*Maman!*"

Chauvelin listened to all these explanations with some impatience. The child was nothing to him, but the Scarlet Pimpernel had desired to rescue it from out of the clutches of the Leridans; had risked his all—and lost it—in order to effect that rescue! That in itself was a sufficient inducement for Chauvelin to interest himself in the execution of Marat's vengeance, whatever its original mainspring may have been.

At any rate, now he felt satisfied that the child was safe, and that the Leridans were impervious to threats or bribes which might land them on the guillotine.

All that they would own to was to being afraid.

"Afraid of what?" queried Chauvelin sharply.

That the brat may be kidnapped . . . . stolen. Oh! he could not be decoyed . . . . they were too watchful for that! But apparently there were mysterious agencies at work . . . .

"Mysterious agencies!" Chauvelin laughed aloud at the suggestion. The "mysterious agency" was even now rotting in an obscure cell at the Abbaye. What other powers could be at work on behalf of the brat?

Well, the Leridans had had a warning!

What warning?

"A letter," the man said gruffly. "But as neither my wife nor I can read—"

"Why did you not speak of this before?" broke in Chauvelin roughly. "Let me see the letter."

The woman produced a soiled and dank scrap of paper from beneath her apron. Of a truth she could not read its contents, for they were writ in English in the form of a doggerel rhyme which caused Chauvelin to utter a savage oath.

"When did this come?" he asked. "And how?"

"This morning, citizen," the woman mumbled in reply. "I found it outside the door, with a stone on it to prevent the wind from blowing it away. What does it mean, citizen?" she went on, her voice shaking with terror, for of a truth the Citizen Representative looked as if he had seen some weird and unearthly apparition.

He gave no reply for a moment or two, and the two *caitiffs* had no conception of the tremendous effort at self-control which was hidden behind the pale, rigid mask of the redoubtable man.

"It probably means nothing that you need fear," Chauvelin said quietly at last. "But I will see the *Commissary* of the Section myself, and tell him to send a dozen men of the Sûreté along to watch your house and be at your beck and call if need be. Then you will feel quite safe, I hope."

"Oh, yes! quite safe, citizen!" the woman replied with a sigh of genuine relief. Then only did Chauvelin turn on his heel and go his way.

9

But that crumpled and soiled scrap of paper given to him by the woman Leridan still lay in his clenched hand as he strode back rapidly citywards. It seemed to scorch his palm. Even before he had glanced at the contents he knew what they were. That atrocious English doggerel, the signature—a five-petalled flower traced in crimson! How well he knew them!

"*We seek him here, we seek him there!*"

The most humiliating moments in Chauvelin's career were associated with that silly rhyme, and now here it was, mocking him even when he knew that his bitter enemy lay fettered and helpless, caught in a trap, out of which there was no escape possible; even though he knew for a positive certainty that the mocking voice which had spoken those rhymes on that far-off day last September would soon be stilled for ever.

No doubt one of that army of abominable English spies had placed this warning outside the Leridans' door. No doubt they had done that with a view to throwing dust in the eyes of the Public Prosecutor and causing a confusion in his mind with regard to the identity of the prisoner at the Abbaye, all to the advantage of their chief.

The thought that such a confusion might exist, that Fouquier-Tinville might be deluded into doubting the real personality of Paul Molé, brought an icy sweat all down Chauvelin's spine. He hurried along the interminably long Chemin de Pantin, only paused at the Barrière du Combat in order to interview the *Commissary* of the Section on the matter of sending men to watch over the Leridans' house. Then, when he felt satisfied that this would be effectively and quickly done, an unconquerable feeling of restlessness prompted him to hurry round to the lodgings of the Public Prosecutor in the Rue Blanche—just to see him, to speak with him, to make quite sure.

Oh! he must be sure that no doubts, no pusillanimity on the part of any official would be allowed to stand in the way of the consummation of all his most cherished dreams. Papers or no papers, testimony or no testimony, the incarcerated Paul Molé was the Scarlet Pimpernel—of this Chauvelin was as certain as that he was alive. His every sense had testified to it when he stood in the narrow room of the Rue des Cordeliers, face to face—eyes gazing into eyes—with his sworn enemy.

Unluckily, however, he found the Public Prosecutor in a surly and obstinate mood, following on an interview which he had just had with Citizen Commissary Cuisinier on the matter of the prisoner Paul Molé.

"His papers are all in order, I tell you," he said impatiently, in answer to Chauvelin's insistence. "It is as much as my head is worth to demand a summary execution."

"But I tell you that, those papers of his are forged," urged Chauvelin forcefully.

"They are not," retorted the other. "The *commissary* swears to his own signature on the identity book. The *concierge* at the Abbaye swears that he knows Molé, so do all the men of the Sûreté who have seen him. The *commissary* has known him as an indigent, good-for-nothing lubbard who has begged his way in the streets of Paris ever since he was released from gaol some months ago, after he had served a term for larceny. Even your own man Hébert admits to feeling doubtful on the point. You have had the nightmare, citizen," concluded Fouquier-Tinville with a harsh laugh.

"But, name of a dog!" broke in Chauvelin savagely. "You are not proposing to let the man go?"

"What else can I do?" the other rejoined fretfully. "We shall get into terrible trouble if we interfere with a man like Paul Molé. You know yourself how it is these days. We should have the whole of the rabble of Paris clamouring for our blood. If, after we have guillotined him, he is proved to be a good patriot, it will be my turn next. No! I thank you!"

"I tell you, man," retorted Chauvelin desperately, "that the man is not Paul Molé—that he is the English spy whom we all know as the Scarlet Pimpernel."

"*Eh Bien!*" riposted Fouquier-Tinville. "Bring me more tangible proof that our prisoner is not Paul Molé and I'll deal with him quickly enough, never fear. But if by tomorrow morning you do not satisfy me on the point . . . . I must let him go his way."

A savage oath rose to Chauvelin's lips. He felt like a man who has been running, panting to reach a goal, who sees that goal within easy distance of him, and is then suddenly captured, caught in invisible meshes which hold him tightly, and against which he is powerless to struggle. For the moment he hated Fouquier-Tinville with a deadly hatred, would have tortured and threatened him until he wrung a consent, an admission, out of him.

Name of a name! when that damnable English spy was actually in his power, the man was a pusillanimous fool to allow the rich prize to slip from his grasp! Chauvelin felt as if he were choking; his slender fingers worked nervily around his cravat; beads of perspiration trickled unheeded down his pallid forehead.

Then suddenly he had an inspiration—nothing less! It almost seemed as if Satan, his friend, had whispered insinuating words into his ear. That scrap of paper! He had thrust it a while ago into the breast pocket of his coat. It was still there, and the Public Prosecutor wanted a tangible proof . . . . Then, why not . . . . ?

Slowly, his thoughts still in the process of gradual coordination, Chauvelin drew that soiled scrap of paper out of his pocket. Fouquier-Tinville, surly and ill-humoured, had his back half-turned towards him, was moodily picking at his teeth. Chauvelin had all the leisure which he required. He smoothed out the creases in the paper and spread it out carefully upon the desk close to the other man's elbow. Fouquier-Tinville looked down on it, over his shoulder.

"What is that?" he queried.

"As you see, citizen," was Chauvelin's bland reply. "A message, such as you yourself have oft received, methinks, from our mutual enemy, the Scarlet Pimpernel."

But already the Public Prosecutor had seized upon the paper, and of a truth Chauvelin had no longer cause to complain of his colleague's indifference. That doggerel rhyme, no less than the signature, had the power to rouse Fouquier-Tinville's ire, as it had that of disturbing Chauvelin's well-studied calm.

"What is it?" reiterated the Public Prosecutor, white now to the lips.

"I have told you, citizen," rejoined Chauvelin imperturbably. "A message from that English spy. It is also the proof which you have demanded of me—the tangible proof that the prisoner, Paul Molé, is none other than the Scarlet Pimpernel."

"But," ejaculated the other hoarsely, "where did you get this?"

"It was found in the cell which Paul Molé occupied in the depot of the Rue de Tourraine, where he was first incarcerated. I picked it up there after he was removed . . . . the ink was scarcely dry upon it."

The lie came quite glibly to Chauvelin's tongue. Was not every method good, every device allowable, which would lead to so glorious an end?

"Why did you not tell me of this before?" queried Fouquier-Tinville, with a sudden gleam of suspicion in his deep-set eyes.

"You had not asked me for a tangible proof before," replied Chauvelin blandly. "I myself was so firmly convinced of what I averred that I had well-nigh forgotten the existence of this damning scrap of paper."

Damning indeed! Fouquier-Tinville had seen such scraps of paper before. He had learnt the doggerel rhyme by heart, even though the English tongue was quite unfamiliar to him. He loathed the English— the entire nation—with all that deadly hatred which a divergence of political aims will arouse in times of acute crises. He hated the English government, Pitt and Burke and even Fox, the happy-go-lucky apologist of the young Revolution. But, above all, he hated that League of English spies—as he was pleased to call them—whose courage, resourcefulness, as well as reckless daring, had more than once baffled his own hideous schemes of murder, of pillage, and of rape.

Thank Beelzebub and his horde of evil spirits, Citizen Chauvelin had been clear-sighted enough to detect that elusive Pimpernel under the disguise of Paul Molé.

"You have deserved well of your country," said Fouquier-Tinville with lusty fervour, and gave Chauvelin a vigorous slap on the shoulder. "But for you I should have allowed that abominable spy to slip through our fingers."

"I have succeeded in convincing you, citizen?" Chauvelin retorted dryly.

"Absolutely!" rejoined the other. "You may now leave the matter to me. And 'twill be friend Molé who will be surprised tomorrow," he added with a harsh guffaw, "when he finds himself face to face with me, before a Court of Justice."

He was all eagerness, of course. Such a triumph for him! The indictment of the notorious Scarlet Pimpernel on a charge of espionage would be the crowning glory of his career! Let other men look to their laurels! Those who brought that dangerous enemy of revolution to the guillotine would for ever be proclaimed as the saviours of France.

"A short indictment," he said, when Chauvelin, after a lengthy discussion on various points, finally rose to take his leave, "but a scathing one! I tell you, Citizen Chauvelin, that tomorrow you will be the first to congratulate me on an unprecedented triumph."

He had been arguing in favour of a sensational trial and no less sensational execution. Chauvelin, with his memory harking back on many mysterious abductions at the very foot of the guillotine, would have liked to see his elusive enemy quietly put to death amongst a batch of traitors, who would help to mask his personality until after the guillotine had fallen, when the whole of Paris should ring with the triumph of this final punishment of the hated spy.

In the end, the two friends agreed upon a compromise, and parted well pleased with the turn of events which a kind Fate had ordered for their own special benefit.

10

Thus satisfied, Chauvelin returned to the Abbaye. Hébert was safe and trustworthy, but Hébert, too, had been assailed with the same doubts which had well-nigh wrecked Chauvelin's triumph, and with such doubts in his mind he might slacken his vigilance.

Name of a name! every man in charge of that damnable Scarlet Pimpernel should have three pairs of eyes wherewith to watch his movements. He should have the alert brain of a Robespierre, the physical strength of a Danton, the relentlessness of a Marat. He should be a giant in sheer brute force, a tiger in caution, an elephant in weight, and a mouse in stealthiness!

Name of a name! but 'twas only hate that could give such powers to any man!

Hébert, in the guard-room, owned to his doubts. His comrades, too, admitted that after twenty-four hours spent on the watch, their minds were in a whirl. The Citizen Commissary had been so sure—so was the chief *concierge* of the Abbaye even now; and the men of the Sûreté! .... they themselves had seen the real Molé more than once .. .. and this man in the cell .... Well, would the Citizen Representative have a final good look at him?

"You seem to forget Calais, Citizen Hébert," Chauvelin said sharply, "and the deadly humiliation you suffered then at the hands of this man who is now your prisoner. Surely your eyes should have been, at least, as keen as mine own."

Anxious, irritable, his nerves well-nigh on the rack, he nevertheless crossed the guard-room with a firm step and entered the cell where the prisoner was still lying upon the palliasse, as he had been all along, and still presenting that naked piece of shoulder through the hole in his shirt.

"He has been like this the best part of the day," Hébert said with a shrug of the shoulders. "We put his bread and water right under his nose. He ate and he drank, and I suppose he slept. But except for a good deal of swearing, he has not spoken to any of us."

He had followed his chief into the cell, and now stood beside the paillasse, holding a small dark lantern in his hand. At a sign from Chauvelin he flashed the light upon the prisoner's averted head.

Molé cursed for a while, and muttered something about "good patriots" and about "retribution." Then, worried by the light, he turned slowly round, and with fish-like, bleary eyes looked upon his visitor.

The words of stinging irony and triumphant sarcasm, all fully prepared, froze on Chauvelin's lips. He gazed upon the prisoner, and a weird sense of something unfathomable and mysterious came over him as he gazed. He himself could not have defined that feeling: the very next moment he was prepared to ridicule his own cowardice— yes, cowardice! because for a second or two he had felt positively afraid.

Afraid of what, forsooth? The man who crouched here in the cell was his arch-enemy, the Scarlet Pimpernel—the man whom he hated most bitterly in all the world, the man whose death he desired more than that of any other living creature. He had been apprehended by the very side of the murdered man whose confidence he had all but gained. He himself (Chauvelin) had at that fateful moment looked into the factitious Molé's eyes, had seen the mockery in them, the lazy insouciance which was the chief attribute of Sir Percy Blakeney. He had heard a faint echo of that inane laugh which grated upon his nerves. Hébert had then laid hands upon this very same man; agents of the Sûreté had barred every ingress and egress to the house, had conducted their prisoner straightway to the depot and thence to the Abbaye, had since that moment guarded him on sight, by day and by night. Hébert and the other men as well as the chief warder, all swore to that!

No, no! There could be no doubt! There was no doubt! The days of magic were over! A man could not assume a personality other than his own; he could not fly out of that personality like a bird out of its cage. There on the *palliasse* in the miserable cell were the same long limbs, the broad shoulders, the grimy face with the three days' growth of stubbly beard—the whole wretched personality of Paul Molé, in fact, which hid the exquisite one of Sir Percy Blakeney, Bart. And yet! . . .

A cold sweat ran down Chauvelin's spine as he gazed, mute and immovable, into those fish-like, bleary eyes, which were not—no! they were not those of the real Scarlet Pimpernel.

The whole situation became dreamlike, almost absurd. Chauvelin was not the man for such a mock-heroic, melodramatic situation. Common-sense, reason, his own cool powers of deliberation, would soon reassert themselves. But for the moment he was dazed. He had worked too hard, no doubt; had yielded too much to excitement, to triumph, and to hate. He turned to Hébert, who was standing stolidly by, gave him a few curt orders in a clear and well-pitched voice. Then he walked out of the cell, without bestowing another look on the prisoner.

Molé had once more turned over on his *palliasse* and, apparently, had gone to sleep. Hébert, with a strange and puzzled laugh, followed his chief out of the cell.

11

At first Chauvelin had the wish to go back and see the Public Prosecutor—to speak with him—to tell him—what? Yes, what? That he, Chauvelin, had all of a sudden been assailed with the same doubts which already had worried Hébert and the others?—that he had told a deliberate lie when he stated that the incriminating doggerel rhyme had been found in Molé's cell? No, no! Such an admission would not only be foolish, it would be dangerous now, whilst he himself was scarce prepared to trust to his own senses. After all, Fouquier-Tinville was in the right frame of mind for the moment. Paul Molé, whoever he was, was safely under lock and key.

The only danger lay in the direction of the house on the Chemin de Pantin. At the thought Chauvelin felt giddy and faint. But he would allow himself no rest. Indeed, he could not have rested until something approaching certainty had once more taken possession of his soul. He could not—would not—believe that he had been deceived. He was still prepared to stake his very life on the identity of the prisoner at the Abbaye. Tricks of light, the flash of the lantern, the perfection of the disguise, had caused a momentary illusion—nothing more.

Nevertheless, that awful feeling of restlessness which had possessed him during the last twenty-four hours once more drove him to activity. And although common sense and reason both pulled one way, an eerie sense of superstition whispered in his ear the ominous words, "If, after all!"

At any rate, he would see the Leridans, and once more make sure of them; and, late as was the hour, he set out for the lonely house on the Pantin Road.

Just inside the Barrière du Combat was the Poste de Section, where Commissary Burban was under orders to provide a dozen men of the Sûreté, who were to be on the watch round and about the house of the Leridans. Chauvelin called in on the *commissary*, who assured him that the men were at their post.

Thus satisfied, he crossed the Barrière and started at a brisk walk down the long stretch of the Chemin de Pantin. The night was dark. The rolling clouds overhead hid the face of the moon and presaged the storm. On the right, the irregular heights of the Buttes Chaumont loomed out dense and dark against the heavy sky, whilst to the left, on ahead, a faintly glimmering, greyish streak of reflected light revealed the proximity of the canal.

Close to the spot where the main Route de Meux intersects the Chemin de Pantin, Chauvelin slackened his pace. The house of the Leridans now lay immediately on his left; from it a small, feeble ray of light, finding its way no doubt through an ill-closed shutter, pierced the surrounding gloom. Chauvelin, without hesitation, turned up a narrow track which led up to the house across a field of stubble. The next moment a peremptory challenge brought him to a halt.

"Who goes there?"

"Public Safety," replied Chauvelin. "Who are you?"

"Of the Sûreté," was the counter reply. "There are a dozen of us about here."

"When did you arrive?"

"Some two hours ago. We marched out directly after you left the orders at the *Commissariat*."

"You are prepared to remain on the watch all night?"

"Those are our orders, citizen," replied the man.

"You had best close up round the house, then. And, name of a dog!" he added, with a threatening ring in his voice. "Let there be no slackening of vigilance this night. No one to go in or out of that house, no one to approach it under any circumstances whatever. Is that understood?"

"Those were our orders from the first, citizen," said the man simply.

"And all has been well up to now?"

"We have seen no one, citizen."

The little party closed in around their chief and together they marched up to the house. Chauvelin, on tenterhooks, walked quicker than the others. He was the first to reach the door. Unable to find the bell-pull in the dark, he knocked vigorously.

The house appeared silent and wrapped in sleep. No light showed from within save that one tiny speck through the cracks of an ill-fitting shutter, in a room immediately overhead.

In response to Chauvelin's repeated summons, there came *anon* the sound of someone moving in one of the upstairs rooms, and presently the light overhead disappeared, whilst a door above was heard to open and to close and shuffling footsteps to come slowly down the creaking stairs.

A moment or two later the bolts and bars of the front door were unfastened, a key grated in the rusty lock, a chain rattled in its socket, and then the door was opened slowly and cautiously.

The woman Leridan appeared in the doorway. She held a guttering tallow candle high above her head. Its flickering light illumined Chauvelin's slender figure.

"Ah! the Citizen Representative!" the woman ejaculated, as soon as she recognised him. "We did not expect you again today, and at this late hour, too. I'll tell my man—"

"Never mind your man," broke in Chauvelin impatiently, and pushed without ceremony past the woman inside the house. "The child? Is it safe?"

He could scarcely control his excitement. There was a buzzing, as of an angry sea, in his ears. The next second, until the woman spoke, seemed like a cycle of years.

"Quite safe, citizen," she said placidly. "Everything is quite safe. We were so thankful for those men of the Sûreté. We had been afraid before, as I told the Citizen Representative, and my man and I could not rest for anxiety. It was only after they came that we dared go to bed."

A deep sigh of intense relief came from the depths of Chauvelin's heart. He had not realised himself until this moment how desperately anxious he had been. The woman's reassuring words appeared to lift a crushing weight from his mind. He turned to the man behind him.

"You did not tell me," he said, "that some of you had been here already."

"We have not been here before," the sergeant in charge of the little platoon said in reply. "I do not know what the woman means."

"Some of your men came about three hours ago," the woman retorted; "less than an hour after the Citizen Representative was here. I remember that my man and I marvelled how quickly they did come, but they said that they had been on duty at the Barrière du Combat when the citizen arrived, and that he had dispatched them off at once. They said they had run all the way. But even so, we thought it was quick work—"

The words were smothered in her throat in a cry of pain, for, with an almost brutal gesture, Chauvelin had seized her by the shoulders.

"Where are those men?" he queried hoarsely. "Answer!"

"In there, and in there," the woman stammered, well-nigh faint with terror as she pointed to two doors, one on each side of the passage. "Three in each room. They are asleep now, I should say, as they seem so quiet. But they were an immense comfort to us, citizen . . . . we were so thankful to have them in the house . . . . "

But Chauvelin had snatched the candle from her hand. Holding it high above his head, he strode to the door on the right of the passage. It was ajar. He pushed it open with a vicious kick. The room beyond was in total darkness.

"Is anyone here?" he queried sharply.

Nothing but silence answered him. For a moment he remained there on the threshold, silent and immovable as a figure carved in stone. He had just a sufficiency of presence of mind and of will power not to drop the candle, to stand there motionless, with his back turned to the woman and to the men who had crowded in, in his wake. He would not let them see the despair, the rage and grave superstitious fear, which distorted every line of his pallid face.

He did not ask about the child. He would not trust himself to speak, for he had realised already how completely he had been baffled. Those abominable English spies had watched their opportunity, had worked on the credulity and the fears of the Leridans and, playing the game at which, they and their audacious chief were such unconquerable experts, they had made their way into the house under a clever ruse.

The men of the Sûreté, not quite understanding the situation, were questioning the Leridans. The man, too, corroborated his wife's story. Their anxiety had been worked upon at the moment that it was most acute. After the Citizen Representative left them, earlier in the evening, they had received another mysterious message which they had been unable to read, but which had greatly increased their alarm. Then, when the men of the Sûreté came . . . . Ah! they had no cause to doubt that they were men of the Sûreté! . . . . their clothes, their speech, their appearance . . . . figure to yourself, even their uniforms! They spoke so nicely, so reassuringly. The Leridans were so thankful to see them! Then they made themselves happy in the two rooms below, and for additional safety the Lannoy child was brought down from its attic and put to sleep in the one room with the men of the Sûreté.

After that the Leridans went to bed. Name of a dog! how were they to blame? Those men and the child had disappeared, but they (the Leridans) would go to the guillotine swearing that they were not to blame.

Whether Chauvelin heard all these jeremiads, he could not afterwards have told you. But he did not need to be told how it had all been done. It had all been so simple, so ingenious, so like the methods usually adopted by that astute Scarlet Pimpernel! He saw it all so clearly before him. Nobody was to blame really, save he himself—he, who alone knew and understood the adversary with whom he had to deal.

But these people here should not have the gratuitous spectacle of a man enduring the torments of disappointment and of baffled revenge. Whatever Chauvelin was suffering now would for ever remain the secret of his own soul. *Anon*, when the Leridans' rasping voices died away in one of the more distant portions of the house and the men of the Sûreté were busy accepting refreshment and gratuity from the two terrified wretches, he had put down the candle with a steady hand and then walked with a firm step out of the house.

Soon the slender figure was swallowed up in the gloom as he strode back rapidly towards the city.

12

Citizen Fouquier-Tinville had returned home from the Palais at a very late hour that same evening. His household in his simple lodgings in the Place Dauphine was already abed: his wife and the twins were asleep. He himself had sat down for a moment in the living-room, in dressing-gown and slippers, and with the late edition of the *Moniteur* in his hand, too tired to read.

It was half-past ten when there came a ring at the front door bell. Fouquier-Tinville, half expecting Citizen Chauvelin to pay him a final visit, shuffled to the door and opened it.

A visitor, tall, well-dressed, exceedingly polite and urbane, requested a few minutes' conversation with Citizen Fouquier-Tinville.

Before the Public Prosecutor had made up his mind whether to introduce such a late-comer into his rooms, the latter had pushed his way through the door into the ante-chamber, and with a movement as swift as it was unexpected, had thrown a scarf round Fouquier-Tinville's neck and wound it round his mouth, so that the unfortunate man's call for help was smothered in his throat.

So dexterously and so rapidly indeed had the miscreant acted, that his victim had hardly realised the assault before he found himself securely gagged and bound to a chair in his own ante-room, whilst that dare-devil stood before him, perfectly at his ease, his hands buried in the capacious pockets of his huge caped coat, and murmuring a few casual words of apology.

"I entreat you to forgive, citizen," he was saying in an even and pleasant voice, "this necessary violence on my part towards you. But my errand is urgent, and I could not allow your neighbours or your household to disturb the few minutes' conversation which I am obliged to have with you. My friend Paul Molé," he went on, after a slight pause, "is in grave danger of his life owing to a hallucination on the part of our mutual friend Citizen Chauvelin; and I feel confident that you yourself are too deeply enamoured of your own neck to risk it wilfully by sending an innocent and honest patriot to the guillotine."

Once more he paused and looked down upon his unwilling interlocutor, who, with muscles straining against the cords that held him, and with eyes nearly starting out of their sockets in an access of fear and of rage, was indeed presenting a pitiful spectacle.

"I dare say that by now, citizen," the brigand continued imperturbably, "you will have guessed who I am. You and I have oft crossed invisible swords before; but this, methinks, is the first time that we have met face to face. I pray you, tell my dear friend M. Chauvelin that you have seen me. Also, that there were two facts which he left entirely out of his calculations, perfect though these were. The one fact was that there were two Paul Molés—one real and one factitious. Tell him that, I pray you. It was the factitious Paul Molé who stole the ring and who stood for one moment gazing into clever Citizen Chauvelin's eyes.

But that same factitious Paul Molé had disappeared in the crowd even before your colleague had recovered his presence of mind. Tell him, I pray you, that the elusive Pimpernel whom he knows so well never assumes a fanciful disguise. He discovered the real Paul Molé first, studied him, learned his personality, until his own became a perfect replica of the miserable *caitiff*. It was the false Paul Molé who induced Jeannette Maréchal to introduce him originally into the household of Citizen Marat. It was he who gained the confidence of his employer; he, for a consideration, borrowed the identity papers of his real prototype. He again who for a few *francs* induced the real Paul Molé to follow him into the house of the murdered demagogue and to mingle there with the throng. He who thrust the identity papers back into the hands of their rightful owner whilst he himself was swallowed up by the crowd. But it was the real Paul Molé who was finally arrested and who is now lingering in the Abbaye prison, whence you, Citizen Fouquier-Tinville, must free him on the instant, on pain of suffering yourself for the nightmares of your friend."

"The second fact," he went on with the same good-humoured pleasantry, "which our friend Citizen Chauvelin had forgotten was that, though I happen to have aroused his unconquerable ire, I am but one man amongst a league of gallant English gentlemen. Their chief, I am proud to say; but without them, I should be powerless. Without one of them near me, by the side of the murdered Marat, I could not have rid myself of the ring in time, before other rough hands searched me to my skin. Without them, I could not have taken Madeleine Lannoy's child from out that terrible hell, to which a miscreant's lustful revenge had condemned the poor innocent. But while Citizen Chauvelin, racked with triumph as well as with anxiety, was rushing from the Leridans' house to yours, and thence to the Abbaye prison, to gloat over his captive enemy, the League of the Scarlet Pimpernel carefully laid and carried out its plans at leisure.

"Disguised as men of the Sûreté, we took advantage of the Leridans' terror to obtain access into the house. Frightened to death by our warnings, as well as by Citizen Chauvelin's threats, they not only admitted us into their house, but actually placed Madeleine Lannoy's child in our charge. Then they went contentedly to bed, and we, before the real men of the Sûreté arrived upon the scene, were already safely out of the way. My gallant English friends are some way out of Paris by now, escorting Madeleine Lannoy and her child into safety. They will return to Paris, citizen," continued the audacious adventurer, with a laugh full of joy and of unconquerable vitality, "and be my henchmen as before in many an adventure which will cause you and Citizen Chauvelin to gnash your teeth with rage. But I myself will remain in Paris," he concluded lightly. "Yes, in Paris; under your very nose, and entirely at your service!"

The next second, he was gone, and Fouquier-Tinville was left to marvel if the whole apparition had not been a hideous dream. Only there was no doubt that he was gagged and tied to a chair with cords: and here his wife found him, an hour later, when she woke from her first sleep, anxious because he had not yet come to bed.

A Question of Passports

Bibot was very sure of himself. There never was, never had been, there never would be again another such patriotic citizen of the Republic as was Citizen Bibot of the Town Guard.

And because his patriotism was so well known among the members of the Committee of Public Safety, and his uncompromising hatred of the aristocrats so highly appreciated, Citizen Bibot had been given the most important military post within the city of Paris.

He was in command of the Porte Montmartre, which goes to prove how highly he was esteemed, for, believe me, more treachery had been going on inside and out of the Porte Montmartre than in any other quarter of Paris. The last commandant there, Citizen Ferney, was guillotined for having allowed a whole batch of aristocrats—traitors to the Republic, all of them—to slip through the Porte Montmartre and to find safety outside the walls of Paris. Ferney pleaded in his defence that these traitors had been spirited away from under his very nose by the devil's agency, for surely that meddlesome Englishman who spent his time in rescuing aristocrats—traitors, all of them—from the clutches of Madame la Guillotine must be either the devil himself, or at any rate one of his most powerful agents.

"*Nom de Dieu!* just think of his name! The Scarlet Pimpernel they call him! No one knows him by any other name! and he is preternaturally tall and strong and superhumanly cunning! And the power which he has of being transmuted into various personalities—rendering himself quite unrecognisable to the eyes of the most sharp-seeing patriot of France, must of a surety be a gift of Satan!"

But the Committee of Public Safety refused to listen to Ferney's explanations. The Scarlet Pimpernel was only an ordinary mortal—an exceedingly cunning and meddlesome personage it is true, and endowed with a superfluity of wealth which enabled him to break the thin crust of patriotism that overlay the natural cupidity of many captains of the Town Guard—but still an ordinary man for all that! and no true lover of the Republic should allow either superstitious terror or greed to interfere with the discharge of his duties which at the Porte Montmartre consisted in detaining any and every person—aristocrat, foreigner, or otherwise traitor to the Republic—who could not give a satisfactory reason for desiring to leave Paris. Having detained such persons, the patriot's next duty was to hand them over to the Committee of Public Safety, who would then decide whether Madame la Guillotine would have the last word over them or not.

And the guillotine did nearly always have the last word to say, unless the Scarlet Pimpernel interfered.

The trouble was, that that same accursed Englishman interfered at times in a manner which was positively terrifying. His impudence, *certes*, passed all belief. Stories of his daring and of his impudence were abroad which literally made the lank and greasy hair of every patriot curl with wonder. 'Twas even whispered—not too loudly, forsooth—that certain members of the Committee of Public Safety had measured their skill and valour against that of the Englishman and emerged from the conflict beaten and humiliated, vowing vengeance which, of a truth, was still slow in coming.

Citizen Chauvelin, one of the most implacable and unyielding members of the Committee, was known to have suffered overwhelming shame at the hands of that daring gang, of whom the so-called Scarlet Pimpernel was the accredited chief. Some there were who said that Citizen Chauvelin had for ever forfeited his prestige, and even endangered his head by measuring his well-known astuteness against that mysterious League of spies.

But then Bibot was different!

He feared neither the devil, nor any Englishman. Had the latter the strength of giants and the protection of every power of evil, Bibot was ready for him. Nay! he was aching for a tussle, and haunted the purlieus of the Committees to obtain some post which would enable him to come to grips with the Scarlet Pimpernel and his League.

Bibot's zeal and perseverance were duly rewarded, and *anon* he was appointed to the command of the guard at the Porte Montmartre.

A post of vast importance as aforesaid; so much so, in fact, that no less a person than Citizen Jean Paul Marat himself came to speak with Bibot on that third day of *Nivose* in the year 1 of the Republic, with a view to impressing upon him the necessity of keeping his eyes open, and of suspecting every man, woman, and child indiscriminately until they had proved themselves to be true patriots.

"Let no one slip through your fingers, Citizen Bibot," Marat admonished with grim earnestness. "That accursed Englishman is cunning and resourceful, and his impudence surpasses that of the devil himself."

"He'd better try some of his impudence on me!" commented Bibot with a sneer, "he'll soon find out that he no longer has a Ferney to deal with. Take it from me, Citizen Marat, that if a batch of aristocrats escape out of Paris within the next few days, under the guidance of the d—d Englishman, they will have to find some other way than the Porte Montmartre."

"Well said, citizen!" commented Marat. "But be watchful tonight .... tonight especially. The Scarlet Pimpernel is rampant in Paris just now."

"How so?"

"The *ci-devant* Duc and Duchesse de Montreux and the whole of their brood—sisters, brothers, two or three children, a priest, and several servants—a round dozen in all, have been condemned to death. The guillotine for them tomorrow at daybreak! Would it could have been tonight," added Marat, whilst a demoniacal leer contorted his face which already exuded lust for blood from every pore. "Would it could have been tonight. But the guillotine has been busy; over four hundred executions today .... and the tumbrils are full—the seats bespoken in advance—and still they come .... But tomorrow morning at daybreak Madame la Guillotine will have a word to say to the whole of the Montreux crowd!"

"But they are in the *Conciergerie* prison surely, citizen! out of the reach of that accursed Englishman?"

"They are on their way, an I mistake not, to the prison at this moment. I came straight on here after the condemnation, to which I listened with true joy. Ah, Citizen Bibot! the blood of these hated aristocrats is good to behold when it drips from the blade of the guillotine. Have a care, Citizen Bibot, do not let the Montreux crowd escape!"

"Have no fear, Citizen Marat! But surely there is no danger! They have been tried and condemned! They are, as you say, even now on their way—well guarded, I presume—to the *Conciergerie* prison!—tomorrow at daybreak, the guillotine! What is there to fear?"

"Well! well!" said Marat, with a slight tone of hesitation, "it is best, Citizen Bibot, to be over-careful these times."

Even whilst Marat spoke his face, usually so cunning and so vengeful, had suddenly lost its look of devilish cruelty which was almost superhuman in the excess of its infamy, and a greyish hue—suggestive of terror—had spread over the sunken cheeks. He clutched Bibot's arm, and leaning over the table he whispered in his ear:

"The Public Prosecutor had scarce finished his speech today, judgment was being pronounced, the spectators were expectant and still, only the Montreux woman and some of the females and children were blubbering and moaning, when suddenly, it seemed from nowhere, a small piece of paper fluttered from out the assembly and alighted on the desk in front of the Public Prosecutor. He took the paper up and glanced at its contents. I saw that his cheeks had paled, and that his hand trembled as he handed the paper over to me."

"And what did that paper contain, Citizen Marat?" asked Bibot, also speaking in a whisper, for an access of superstitious terror was gripping him by the throat.

"Just the well-known accursed device, citizen, the small scarlet flower, drawn in red ink, and the few words:

'Tonight the innocent men and women now condemned by this infamous tribunal will be beyond your reach!'"

"And no sign of a messenger?"

"None."

"And when did——"

"Hush!" said Marat peremptorily, "no more of that now. To your post, citizen, and remember—all are suspect! let none escape!"

The two men had been sitting outside a small tavern, opposite the Porte Montmartre, with a bottle of wine between them, their elbows resting on the grimy top of a rough wooden table. They had talked in whispers, for even the walls of the tumble-down *cabaret* might have had ears.

Opposite them the city wall—broken here by the great gate of Montmartre—loomed threateningly in the fast-gathering dusk of this winter's afternoon. Men in ragged red shirts, their unkempt heads crowned with Phrygian caps adorned with a tricolour cockade, lounged against the wall, or sat in groups on the top of piles of refuse that littered the street, with a rough deal plank between them and a greasy pack of cards in their grimy fingers. Guns and bayonets were propped against the wall. The gate itself had three means of egress; each of these was guarded by two men with fixed bayonets at their shoulders, but otherwise dressed like the others, in rags—with bare legs that looked blue and numb in the cold—the *sans-culottes* of revolutionary Paris.

Bibot rose from his seat, nodding to Marat, and joined his men.

From afar, but gradually drawing nearer, came the sound of a ribald song, with chorus accompaniment sung by throats obviously surfeited with liquor.

For a moment—as the sound approached—Bibot turned back once more to the Friend of the People.

"Am I to understand, citizen," he said, "that my orders are not to let anyone pass through these gates tonight?"

"No, no, citizen," replied Marat, "we dare not do that. There are a number of good patriots in the city still. We cannot interfere with their liberty or—"

And the look of fear of the demagogue—himself afraid of the human whirlpool which he has let loose—stole into Marat's cruel, piercing eyes.

"No, no," he reiterated more emphatically, "we cannot disregard the passports issued by the Committee of Public Safety. But examine each passport carefully, Citizen Bibot! If you have any reasonable ground for suspicion, detain the holder, and if you have not——"

The sound of singing was quite near now. With another wink and a final leer, Marat drew back under the shadow of the *cabaret*, and Bibot swaggered up to the main entrance of the gate.

"*Qui va la?*" he thundered in stentorian tones as a group of some half-dozen people lurched towards him out of the gloom, still shouting hoarsely their ribald drinking song.

The foremost man in the group paused opposite Citizen Bibot, and with arms *akimbo*, and legs planted well apart tried to assume a rigidity of attitude which apparently was somewhat foreign to him at this moment.

"Good patriots, citizen," he said in a thick voice which he vainly tried to render steady.

"What do you want?" queried Bibot.

"To be allowed to go on our way unmolested."

"What is your way?"

"Through the Porte Montmartre to the village of Barency."

"What is your business there?"

This query delivered in Bibot's most pompous manner seemed vastly to amuse the rowdy crowd. He who was the spokesman turned to his friends and shouted hilariously:

"Hark at him, citizens! He asks me what is our business. Oh, Citizen Bibot, since when have you become blind? A dolt you've always been, else you had not asked the question."

343

But Bibot, undeterred by the man's drunken insolence, retorted gruffly:

"Your business, I want to know."

"Bibot! my little Bibot!" cooed the bibulous orator now in dulcet tones, "dost not know us, my good Bibot? Yet we all know thee, citizen—Captain Bibot of the Town Guard, eh, citizens! Three cheers for the Citizen Captain!"

When the noisy shouts and cheers from half a dozen hoarse throats had died down, Bibot, without more ado, turned to his own men at the gate.

"Drive these drunken louts away!" he commanded; "no one is allowed to loiter here."

Loud protest on the part of the hilarious crowd followed, then a slight scuffle with the bayonets of the Town Guard. Finally, the spokesman, somewhat sobered, once more appealed to Bibot.

"Citizen Bibot! you must be blind not to know me and my mates! And let me tell you that you are doing yourself a deal of harm by interfering with the citizens of the Republic in the proper discharge of their duties, and by disregarding their rights of egress through this gate, a right confirmed by passports signed by two members of the Committee of Public Safety."

He had spoken now fairly clearly and very pompously. Bibot, somewhat impressed and remembering Marat's admonitions, said very civilly:

"Tell me your business then, citizen, and show me your passports. If everything is in order you may go your way."

"But you know me, Citizen Bibot?" queried the other.

"Yes, I know you—unofficially, Citizen Durand."

"You know that I and the citizens here are the carriers for Citizen Legrand, the market gardener of Barency?"

"Yes, I know that," said Bibot guardedly, "unofficially."

"Then, unofficially, let me tell you, citizen, that unless we get to Barency this evening, Paris will have to do without cabbages and potatoes tomorrow. So now you know that you are acting at your own risk and peril, citizen, by detaining us."

"Your passports, all of you," commanded Bibot.

He had just caught sight of Marat still sitting outside the tavern opposite, and was glad enough, in this instance, to shelve his responsibility on the shoulders of the popular "Friend of the People." There was general searching in ragged pockets for grimy papers with official

344

seals thereon, and whilst Bibot ordered one of his men to take the six passports across the road to Citizen Marat for his inspection, he himself, by the last rays of the setting winter sun, made close examination of the six men who desired to pass through the Porte Montmartre.

As the spokesman had averred, he—Bibot—knew every one of these men. They were the carriers to Citizen Legrand, the Barency market gardener. Bibot knew every face. They passed with a load of fruit and vegetables in and out of Paris every day. There was really and absolutely no cause for suspicion, and when Citizen Marat returned the six passports, pronouncing them to be genuine, and recognising his own signature at the bottom of each, Bibot was at last satisfied, and the six bibulous carriers were allowed to pass through the gate, which they did, arm in arm, singing a wild *carmagnole*, and vociferously cheering as they emerged out into the open.

But Bibot passed an unsteady hand over his brow. It was cold, yet he was in a perspiration. That sort of thing tells on a man's nerves. He rejoined Marat, at the table outside the drinking booth, and ordered a fresh bottle of wine.

The sun had set now, and with the gathering dusk a damp mist descended on Montmartre. From the wall opposite, where the men sat playing cards, came occasional volleys of blasphemous oaths. Bibot was feeling much more like himself. He had half forgotten the incident of the six carriers, which had occurred nearly half an hour ago.

Two or three other people had, in the meanwhile, tried to pass through the gates, but Bibot had been suspicious and had detained them all.

Marat having commended him for his zeal took final leave of him. Just as the demagogue's slouchy, grimy figure was disappearing down a side street there was the loud clatter of hoofs from that same direction, and the next moment a detachment of the mounted Town Guard, headed by an officer in uniform, galloped down the ill-paved street.

Even before the troopers had drawn rein the officer had hailed Bibot.

"Citizen," he shouted, and his voice was breathless, for he had evidently ridden hard and fast, "this message to you from the Citizen Chief Commissary of the Section. Six men are wanted by the Committee of Public Safety. They are disguised as carriers in the employ of a market gardener, and have passports for Barency! . . . . The passports are stolen: the men are traitors—escaped aristocrats—and their spokesman is that d—d Englishman, the Scarlet Pimpernel."

Bibot tried to speak; he tugged at the collar of his ragged shirt; an awful curse escaped him.

"Ten thousand devils!" he roared.

"On no account allow these people to go through," continued the officer. "Keep their passports. Detain them! . . . . Understand?"

Bibot was still gasping for breath even whilst the officer, ordering a quick "Turn!" reeled his horse round, ready to gallop away as far as he had come.

"I am for the St. Denis Gate—Grosjean is on guard there!" he shouted. "Same orders all round the city. No one to leave the gates! . . . Understand?"

His troopers fell in. The next moment he would be gone, and those cursed aristocrats well in safety's way.

"Citizen Captain!"

The hoarse shout at last contrived to escape Bibot's parched throat. As if involuntarily, the officer drew rein once more.

"What is it? Quick!—I've no time. That confounded Englishman may be at the St. Denis Gate even now!"

"Citizen Captain," gasped Bibot, his breath coming and going like that of a man fighting for his life. "Here! . . . . at this gate! . . . . not half an hour ago . . . . six men . . . . carriers . . . . market gardeners . . . . I seemed to know their faces . . . . "

"Yes! yes! market gardener's carriers," exclaimed the officer glee-fully, "aristocrats all of them . . . . and that d—d Scarlet Pimpernel. You've got them? You've detained them? . . . . Where are they? . . . . Speak, man, in the name of hell! . . . ."

"Gone!" gasped Bibot. His legs would no longer bear him. He fell backwards on to a heap of street debris and refuse, from which lowly vantage ground he contrived to give away the whole miserable tale.

"Gone! half an hour ago. Their passports were in order! . . . . I seemed to know their faces! Citizen Marat was here . . . . He, too—"

In a moment the officer had once more swung his horse round, so that the animal reared, with wild forefeet pawing the air, with champing of bit, and white foam scattered around.

"A thousand million curses!" he exclaimed. "Citizen Bibot, your head will pay for this treachery. Which way did they go?"

A dozen hands were ready to point in the direction where the merry party of carriers had disappeared half an hour ago; a dozen tongues gave rapid, confused explanations.

"Into it, my men!" shouted the officer; "they were on foot! They can't have gone far. Remember the Republic has offered ten thousand *francs* for the capture of the Scarlet Pimpernel."

Already the heavy gates had been swung open, and the officer's voice once more rang out clear through a perfect thunder-clap of fast galloping hoofs:

"*Ventre à terre!* Remember!—ten thousand *francs* to him who first sights the Scarlet Pimpernel!"

The thunder-clap died away in the distance, the dust of four score hoofs was merged in the fog and in the darkness; the voice of the captain was raised again through the mist-laden air. One shout .... a shout of triumph .... then silence once again.

Bibot had fainted on the heap of debris.

His comrades brought him wine to drink. He gradually revived. Hope came back to his heart; his nerves soon steadied themselves as the heavy beverage filtrated through into his blood.

"Bah!" he ejaculated as he pulled himself together, "the troopers were well-mounted .... the officer was enthusiastic; those carriers could not have walked very far. And, in any case, I am free from blame. Citizen Marat himself was here and let them pass!"

A shudder of superstitious terror ran through him as he recollected the whole scene: for surely, he knew all the faces of the six men who had gone through the gate. The devil indeed must have given the mysterious Englishman power to transmute himself and his gang wholly into the bodies of other people.

More than an hour went by. Bibot was quite himself again, bullying, commanding, detaining everybody now.

At that time there appeared to be a slight altercation going on, on the farther side of the gate. Bibot thought it his duty to go and see what the noise was about. Someone wanting to get into Paris instead of out of it at this hour of the night was a strange occurrence.

Bibot heard his name spoken by a raucous voice. Accompanied by two of his men he crossed the wide gates in order to see what was happening. One of the men held a lanthorn, which he was swinging high above his head. Bibot saw standing there before him, arguing with the guard by the gate, the bibulous spokesman of the band of carriers.

He was explaining to the sentry that he had a message to deliver to the citizen commanding at the Porte Montmartre.

"It is a note," he said, "which an officer of the mounted guard gave me. He and twenty troopers were galloping down the great North

Road not far from Barency. When they overtook the six of us they drew rein, and the officer gave me this note for Citizen Bibot and fifty *francs* if I would deliver it tonight."

"Give me the note!" said Bibot calmly.

But his hand shook as he took the paper; his face was livid with fear and rage.

The paper had no writing on it, only the outline of a small scarlet flower done in red—the device of the cursed Englishman, the Scarlet Pimpernel.

"Which way did the officer and the twenty troopers go," he stammered, "after they gave you this note?"

"On the way to Calais," replied the other, "but they had magnificent horses, and didn't spare them either. They are a league and more away by now!"

All the blood in Bibot's body seemed to rush up to his head, a wild buzzing was in his ears . . . .

And that was how the Duc and Duchesse de Montreux, with their servants and family, escaped from Paris on that third day of *Nivose* in the year I of the Republic.

Two Good Patriots

*Being the deposition of Citizeness Fanny Roussell, who was brought
up, together with her husband, before the Tribunal of the Revolution on
a charge of treason—both being subsequently acquitted.*

My name is Fanny Roussell, and I am a respectable married woman, and as good a patriot as any of you sitting there.

Aye, and I'll say it with my dying breath, though you may send me to the guillotine . . . . as you probably will, for you are all thieves and murderers, every one of you, and you have already made up your minds that I and my man are guilty of having sheltered that accursed Englishman whom they call the Scarlet Pimpernel . . . . and of having helped him to escape.

But I'll tell you how it all happened, because, though you call me a traitor to the people of France, yet am I a true patriot and will prove it to you by telling you exactly how everything occurred, so that you may be on your guard against the cleverness of that man, who, I do believe, is a friend and confederate of the devil . . . . else how could he have escaped that time?

Well! it was three days ago, and as bitterly cold as anything that my man and I can remember. We had no travellers staying in the house, for we are a good three leagues out of Calais, and too far for the folk who have business in or about the harbour. Only at midday the coffee-room would get full sometimes with people on their way to or from the port.

But in the evenings the place was quite deserted, and so lonely that at times we fancied that we could hear the wolves howling in the forest of St. Pierre.

It was close on eight o'clock, and my man was putting up the shutters, when suddenly we heard the tramp of feet on the road outside, and then the quick word, "Halt!"

The next moment there was a peremptory knock at the door. My man opened it, and there stood four men in the uniform of the 9th Regiment of the Line . . . . the same that is quartered at Calais. The uniform, of course, I knew well, though I did not know the men by sight.

"In the name of the People and by the order of the Committee of Public Safety!" said one of the men, who stood in the forefront, and who, I noticed, had a corporal's stripe on his left sleeve.

He held out a paper, which was covered with seals and with writing, but as neither my man nor I can read, it was no use our looking at it.

Hercule—that is my husband's name, citizens—asked the corporal what the Committee of Public Safety wanted with us poor *hôteliers* of a wayside inn.

"Only food and shelter for tonight for me and my men," replied the corporal, quite civilly.

"You can rest here," said Hercule, and he pointed to the benches in the coffee-room, "and if there is any soup left in the stockpot, you are welcome to it."

Hercule, you see, is a good patriot, and he had been a soldier in his day .... No! no .... do not interrupt me, any of you .... you would only be saying that I ought to have known .... but listen to the end.

"The soup we'll gladly eat," said the corporal very pleasantly. "As for shelter .... well! I am afraid that this nice warm coffee-room will not exactly serve our purpose. We want a place where we can lie hidden, and at the same time keep a watch on the road. I noticed an outhouse as we came. By your leave we will sleep in there."

"As you please," said my man curtly.

He frowned as he said this, and it suddenly seemed as if some vague suspicion had crept into Hercule's mind.

The corporal, however, appeared unaware of this, for he went on quite cheerfully:

"Ah! that is excellent! *Entre nous*, citizen, my men and I have a desperate customer to deal with. I'll not mention his name, for I see you have guessed it already. A small red flower, what? .... Well, we know that he must be making straight for the port of Calais, for he has been traced through St. Omer and Ardres. But he cannot possibly enter Calais city tonight, for we are on the watch for him. He must seek shelter somewhere for himself and any other aristocrat he may have with him, and, bar this house, there is no other place between Ardres and Calais where he can get it. The night is bitterly cold, with a snow blizzard raging round. I and my men have been detailed to watch this road, other patrols are guarding those that lead toward Boulogne and to Gravelines; but I have an idea, citizen, that our fox is making for Calais, and that to me will fall the honour of handing that tiresome scarlet flower to the Public Prosecutor *en route* for Madame la Guillotine."

Now I could not really tell you, citizens, what suspicions had by this time entered Hercule's head or mine; certainly, what suspicions we did have were still very vague.

I prepared the soup for the men and they ate it heartily, after which my husband led the way to the outhouse where we sometimes stabled a traveller's horse when the need arose.

It is nice and dry, and always filled with warm, fresh straw. The entrance into it immediately faces the road; the corporal declared that nothing would suit him and his men better.

They retired to rest apparently, but we noticed that two men remained on the watch just inside the entrance, whilst the two others curled up in the straw.

Hercule put out the lights in the coffee-room, and then he and I went upstairs—not to bed, mind you—but to have a quiet talk together over the events of the past half-hour.

The result of our talk was that ten minutes later my man quietly stole downstairs and out of the house. He did not, however, go out by the front door, but through a back way which, leading through a cabbage-patch and then across a field, cuts into the main road some two hundred metres higher up.

Hercule and I had decided that he would walk the three leagues into Calais, despite the cold, which was intense, and the blizzard, which was nearly blinding, and that he would call at the post of *gendarmerie* at the city gates, and there see the officer in command and tell him the exact state of the case. It would then be for that officer to decide what was to be done; our responsibility as loyal citizens would be completely covered.

Hercule, you must know, had just emerged from our cabbage-patch on to the field when he was suddenly challenged:

"*Qui va là?*"

He gave his name. His certificate of citizenship was in his pocket; he had nothing to fear. Through the darkness and the veil of snow he had discerned a small group of men wearing the uniform of the 9th Regiment of the Line.

"Four men," said the foremost of these, speaking quickly and commandingly, "wearing the same uniform that I and my men are wearing

. . . . have you seen them?"

"Yes," said Hercule hurriedly.

"Where are they?"

"In the outhouse close by."

The other suppressed a cry of triumph.

"At them, my men!" he said in a whisper, "and you, citizen, thank your stars that we have not come too late."

"These men. . . ." whispered Hercule. "I had my suspicions."

"Aristocrats, citizen," rejoined the commander of the little party, "and one of them is that cursed Englishman—the Scarlet Pimpernel."

Already the soldiers, closely followed by Hercule, had made their way through our cabbage-patch back to the house.

The next moment they had made a bold dash for the barn. There was a great deal of shouting, a great deal of swearing and some firing, whilst Hercule and I, not a little frightened, remained in the coffee-room, anxiously awaiting events.

Presently the group of soldiers returned, not the ones who had first come, but the others. I noticed their leader, who seemed to be exceptionally tall.

He looked very cheerful, and laughed loudly as he entered the coffee-room. From the moment that I looked at his face I knew, somehow, that Hercule and I had been fooled, and that now, indeed, we stood eye to eye with that mysterious personage who is called the Scarlet Pimpernel.

I screamed, and Hercule made a dash for the door; but what could two humble and peaceful citizens do against this band of desperate men, who held their lives in their own hands? They were four and we were two, and I do believe that their leader has supernatural strength and power.

He treated us quite kindly, even though he ordered his followers to bind us down to our bed upstairs, and to tie a cloth round our mouths so that our cries could not be distinctly heard.

Neither my man nor I closed an eye all night, of course, but we heard the miscreants moving about in the coffee-room below. But they did no mischief, nor did they steal any of the food or wines.

At daybreak we heard them going out by the front door, and their footsteps disappearing toward Calais. We found their discarded uniforms lying in the coffee-room. They must have entered Calais by daylight, when the gates were opened—just like other peaceable citizens. No doubt they had forged passports, just as they had stolen uniforms.

Our maid-of-all-work released us from our terrible position in the course of the morning, and we released the soldiers of the 9th Regiment of the Line, whom we found bound and gagged, some of them wounded, in the outhouse.

That same afternoon we were arrested, and here we are, ready to die if we must, but I swear that I have told you the truth, and I ask you, in the name of justice, if we have done anything wrong, and if we did not act like loyal and true citizens, even though we were pitted against an emissary of the devil?

The Old Scarecrow

1

Nobody in the *quartier* could quite recollect when it was that the new Public Letter-Writer first set up in business at the angle formed by the Quai des Augustins and the Rue Dauphine, immediately facing the Pont Neuf; but there he certainly was on the 28th day of February, 1793, when Agnès, with eyes swollen with tears, a market basket on her arm, and a look of dreary despair on her young face, turned that self-same angle on her way to the Pont Neuf, and nearly fell over the rickety construction which sheltered him and his stock-in-trade.

"Oh, *mon Dieu!* Citizen Lépine, I had no idea you were here," she exclaimed as soon as she had recovered her balance.

"Nor I, *citizeness*, that I should have the pleasure of seeing you this morning," he retorted.

"But you were always at the other corner of the Pont Neuf," she argued.

"So, I was," he replied, "so I was. But I thought I would like a change. The Faubourg St. Michel appealed to me; most of my clients came to me from this side of the river—all those on the other side seem to know how to read and write."

"I was just going over to see you," she remarked.

"You, *citizeness*," he exclaimed in unfeigned surprise, "what should procure a poor public writer the honour of—"

"Hush, in God's name!" broke in the young girl quickly as she cast a rapid, furtive glance up and down the *quai* and the narrow streets which converged at this angle.

She was dressed in the humblest and poorest of clothes, her skimpy shawl round her shoulders could scarce protect her against the cold of this cruel winter's morning; her hair was entirely hidden beneath a frilled and starched cap, and her feet were encased in coarse worsted stockings and *sabots*, but her hands were delicate and fine, and her face had that nobility of feature and look of patient resignation in the midst of overwhelming sorrow which proclaimed a lofty refinement both of soul and of mind.

The old Letter-Writer was surveying the pathetic young figure before him through his huge horn-rimmed spectacles, and she smiled on him through her fast-gathering tears. He used to have his pitch at the angle of the Pont Neuf, and whenever Agnès had walked past it, she had nodded to him and bidden him "Good morrow!" He had at times done little commissions for her and gone on errands when she needed a messenger; today, in the midst of her despair, she had suddenly thought of him and that rumour credited him with certain knowledge which she would give her all to possess.

She had sallied forth this morning with the express purpose of speaking with him; but now suddenly she felt afraid, and stood looking at him for a moment or two, hesitating, wondering if she dared tell him—one never knew these days into what terrible pitfall an ill-considered word might lead one.

A scarecrow he was, that old Public Letter-Writer, more like a great, gaunt bird than a human being, with those spectacles of his, and his long, very sparse and very lanky fringe of a beard which fell from his cheeks and chin and down his chest for all the world like a crumpled grey bib. He was wrapped from head to foot in a caped coat which had once been green in colour, but was now of many hues not usually seen in rainbows. He wore his coat all buttoned down the front, like a dressing-gown, and below the hem there peeped out a pair of very large feet encased in boots which had never been a pair. He sat upon a rickety, straw-bottomed chair under an improvised awning which was made up of four poles and a bit of sacking. He had a table in front of him—a table partially and very insecurely propped up by a bundle of old papers and books, since no two of its four legs were completely whole—and on the table there was a neckless bottle half-filled with ink, a few sheets of paper and a couple of quill pens.

The young girl's hesitation had indeed not lasted more than a few seconds.

Furtively, like a young creature terrified of lurking enemies, she once more glanced to right and left of her and down the two streets and the river bank, for Paris was full of spies these days—human bloodhounds ready for a few *sous* to sell their fellow-creatures' lives. It was middle morning now, and a few passers-by were hurrying along wrapped to the nose in mufflers, for the weather was bitterly cold.

Agnès waited until there was no one in sight, then she leaned forward over the table and whispered under her breath:

"They say, citizen, that you alone in Paris know the whereabouts of the English milor'—of him who is called the Scarlet Pimpernel . . . ."

"Hush-sh-sh!" said the old man quickly, for just at that moment two men had gone by, in ragged coats and torn breeches, who had leered at Agnès and her neat cap and skirt as they passed. Now they had turned the angle of the street and the old man, too, sank his voice to a whisper.

"I know nothing of any Englishman," he muttered.

"Yes, you do," she rejoined insistently. "When poor Antoine Carré was somewhere in hiding and threatened with arrest, and his mother dared not write to him lest her letter be intercepted, she spoke to you about the English milor', and the English milor' found Antoine Carré and took him and his mother safely out of France. Mme. Carré is my godmother . . . . I saw her the very night when she went to meet the English milor' at his commands. I know all that happened then . . . . I know that you were the intermediary."

"And if I was," he muttered sullenly as he fiddled with his pen and paper, "maybe I've had cause to regret it. For a week after that Carré episode I dared not show my face in the streets of Paris; for nigh on a fortnight I dared not ply my trade . . . . I have only just ventured again to set up in business. I am not going to risk my old neck again in a hurry . . . ."

"It is a matter of life and death," urged Agnès, as once more the tears rushed to her pleading eyes and the look of misery settled again upon her face.

"Your life, *citizeness*?" queried the old man, "or that of Citizen-Deputy Fabrice?"

"Hush!" she broke in again, as a look of real terror now overspread her face. Then she added under her breath: "You know?"

"I know that Mademoiselle Agnès de Lucines is *fiancée* to the Citizen-Deputy Arnould Fabrice," rejoined the old man quietly, "and that it is Mademoiselle Agnès de Lucines who is speaking with me now."

"You have known that all along?"

"Ever since *mademoiselle* first tripped past me at the angle of the Pont Neuf dressed in wincey kirtle and wearing *sabots* on her feet . . . ."

"But how?" she murmured, puzzled, not a little frightened, for his knowledge might prove dangerous to her. She was of gentle birth, and as such an object of suspicion to the Government of the Republic and of the Terror; her mother was a hopeless cripple, unable to move: this together with her love for Arnould Fabrice had kept Agnès de Lucines in France these days, even though she was in hourly peril of arrest.

"Tell me what has happened," the old man said, unheeding her last anxious query. "Perhaps I can help ..."

"Oh! you cannot—the English milor' can and will if only we could know where he is. I thought of him the moment I received that awful man's letter—and then I thought of you ...."

"Tell me about the letter—quickly," he interrupted her with some impatience. "I'll be writing something—but talk away, I shall hear every word. But for God's sake be as brief as you can."

He drew some paper nearer to him and dipped his pen in the ink. He appeared to be writing under her dictation. Thin, flaky snow had begun to fall and settled in a smooth white carpet upon the frozen ground, and the footsteps of the passers-by sounded muffled as they hurried along. Only the lapping of the water of the sluggish river close by broke the absolute stillness of the air.

Agnès de Lucines' pale face looked ethereal in this framework of white which covered her shoulders and the shawl crossed over her bosom: only her eyes, dark, appealing, filled with a glow of immeasurable despair, appeared tensely human and alive.

"I had a letter this morning," she whispered, speaking very rapidly, "from Citizen Hériot—that awful man—you know him?"

"Yes, yes!"

"He used to be valet in the service of Deputy Fabrice. Now he, too, is a member of the National Assembly .... he is arrogant and cruel and vile. He hates Arnould Fabrice and he professes himself passionately in love with me."

"Yes, yes!" murmured the old man, "but the letter?"

"It came this morning. In it he says that he has in his possession a number of old letters, documents and manuscripts which are quite enough to send Deputy Fabrice to the guillotine. He threatens to place all those papers before the Committee of Public Safety unless . ... unless I ...."

She paused, and a deep blush, partly of shame, partly of wrath, suffused her pale cheeks.

"Unless you accept his grimy hand in marriage," concluded the man dryly.

Her eyes gave him answer. With pathetic insistence she tried now to glean a ray of hope from the old scarecrow's inscrutable face. But he was bending over his writing: his fingers were blue with cold, his great shoulders were stooping to his task.

"Citizen," she pleaded.

"Hush!" he muttered, "no more now. The very snowflakes are made up of whispers that may reach those bloodhounds yet. The English milor' shall know of this. He will send you a message if he thinks fit."

"Citizen—"

"Not another word, in God's name! Pay me five *sous* for this letter and pray Heaven that you have not been watched."

She shivered and drew her shawl closer round her shoulders, then she counted out five *sous* with elaborate care and laid them out upon the table. The old man took up the coins. He blew into his fingers, which looked paralysed with the cold. The snow lay over everything now; the rough awning had not protected him or his wares.

Agnès turned to go. The last she saw of him, as she went up the rue Dauphine, was one broad shoulder still bending over the table, and clad in the shabby, caped coat all covered with snow like an old Santa Claus.

2

It was half-an-hour before noon, and Citizen-Deputy Hériot was preparing to go out to the small tavern round the corner where he habitually took his *déjeuner*. Citizen Rondeau, who for the consideration of ten *sous* a day looked after Hériot's paltry creature-comforts, was busy tidying up the squalid apartment which the latter occupied on the top floor of a lodging-house in the Rue Cocatrice. This apartment consisted of three rooms leading out of one another; firstly there was a dark and narrow *antichambre* wherein slept the aforesaid citizen-servant; then came a sitting-room sparsely furnished with a few chairs, a centre table and an iron stove, and finally there was the bedroom wherein the most conspicuous object was a large oak chest clamped with wide iron hinges and a massive writing-desk; the bed and a very primitive washstand were in an alcove at the farther end of the room and partially hidden by a tapestry curtain.

At exactly half-past seven that morning there came a peremptory knock at the door of the *anti-chambre*, and as Rondeau was busy in the bedroom, Hériot went himself to see who his unexpected visitor might be. On the landing outside stood an extraordinary-looking individual—more like a tall and animated scarecrow than a man—who in a tremulous voice asked if he might speak with the Citizen Hériot.

"That is my name," said the deputy gruffly, "what do you want?"

He would have liked to slam the door in the old scarecrow's face, but the latter, with the boldness which sometimes besets the timid,

had already stepped into the *antichambre* and was now quietly sauntering through to the next room into the one beyond. Hériot, being
a representative of the people and a social democrat of the most advanced type, was supposed to be accessible to everyone who desired
speech with him. Though muttering sundry curses, he thought it best
not to go against his usual practice, and after a moment's hesitation he
followed his unwelcome visitor.

The latter was in the sitting-room by this time; he had drawn a
chair close to the table and sat down with the air of one who has
a perfect right to be where he is; as soon as Hériot entered he said
placidly:

"I would desire to speak alone with the Citizen-Deputy."

And Hériot, after another slight hesitation, ordered Rondeau to
close the bedroom door.

"Keep your ears open in case I call," he added significantly.

"You are cautious, citizen," merely remarked the visitor with a
smile.

To this Hériot vouchsafed no reply. He, too, drew a chair forward
and sat opposite his visitor, then he asked abruptly: "Your name and
quality?"

"My name is Lépine at your service," said the old man, "and by
profession I write letters at the rate of five *sous* or so, according to
length, for those who are not able to do it for themselves."

"Your business with me?" queried Hériot curtly.

"To offer you two thousand *francs* for the letters which you stole
from deputy Fabrice when you were his valet," replied Lépine with
perfect calm.

In a moment Hériot was on his feet, jumping up as if he had been
stung; his pale, short-sighted eyes narrowed till they were mere slits,
and through them he darted a quick, suspicious glance at the extraordinary out-at-elbows figure before him. Then he threw back his
head and laughed till the tears streamed down his cheeks and his sides
began to ache.

"This is a farce, I presume, citizen," he said when he had recovered
something of his composure.

"No farce, citizen," replied Lépine calmly. "The money is at your
disposal whenever you care to bring the letters to my pitch at the angle of the Rue Dauphine and the Quai des Augustins, where I carry
on my business."

"Whose money is it? Agnès de Lucines' or did that fool Fabrice send you?"

"No one sent me, citizen. The money is mine—a few savings I possess—I honour Citizen Fabrice—I would wish to do him service by purchasing certain letters from you."

Then as Hériot, moody and sullen, remained silent and began pacing up and down the long, bare floor of the room, Lépine added persuasively, "Well! what do you say? Two thousand *francs* for a packet of letters—not a bad bargain these hard times."

"Get out of this room," was Hériot's fierce and sudden reply.

"You refuse?"

"Get out of this room!"

"As you please," said Lépine as he, too, rose from his chair. "But before I go, Citizen Hériot," he added, speaking very quietly, "let me tell you one thing. Mademoiselle Agnès de Lucines would far sooner cut off her right hand than let yours touch it even for one instant. Neither she nor Deputy Fabrice would ever purchase their lives at such a price."

"And who are you—you mangy old scarecrow?" retorted Hériot, who was getting beside himself with rage, "that you should assert these things? What are those people to you, or you to them, that you should interfere in their affairs?"

"Your question is beside the point, citizen," said Lépine blandly; "I am here to propose a bargain. Had you not better agree to it?"

"Never!" reiterated Hériot emphatically.

"Two thousand *francs*," reiterated the old man imperturbably.

"Not if you offered me two hundred thousand," retorted the other fiercely. "Go and tell that, to those who sent you. Tell them that I—Hériot—would look upon a fortune as mere dross against the delight of seeing that man Fabrice, whom I hate beyond everything in earth or hell, mount up the steps to the guillotine. Tell them that I know that Agnès de Lucines loathes me, that I know that she loves him. I know that I cannot win her save by threatening him. But you are wrong, Citizen Lépine," he continued, speaking more and more calmly as his passions of hatred and of love seemed more and more to hold him in their grip; "you are wrong if you think that she will not strike a bargain with me in order to save the life of Fabrice, whom she loves. Agnès de Lucines will be my wife within the month, or Arnould Fabrice's head will fall under the guillotine, and you, my interfering friend, may go to the devil, if you please."

"That would be but a tame proceeding, citizen, after my visit to you," said the old man, with unruffled *sang-froid*. "But let me, in my turn, assure you of this, Citizen Hériot," he added, "that Mlle. de Lucines will never be your wife, that Arnould Fabrice will not end his valuable life under the guillotine—and that you will never be allowed to use against him the cowardly and stolen weapon which you possess."

Hériot laughed—a low, cynical laugh and shrugged his thin shoulders:

"And who will prevent me, I pray you?" he asked sarcastically.

The old man made no immediate reply, but he came just a step or two closer to the Citizen-Deputy and, suddenly drawing himself up to his full height, he looked for one brief moment down upon the mean and sordid figure of the ex-valet. To Hériot it seemed as if the whole man had become transfigured; the shabby old scarecrow looked all of a sudden like a brilliant and powerful personality; from his eyes there flashed down a look of supreme contempt and of supreme pride, and Hériot—unable to understand this metamorphosis which was more apparent to his inner consciousness than to his outward sight, felt his knees shake under him and all the blood rush back to his heart in an agony of superstitious terror.

From somewhere there came to his ear the sound of two words: "I will!" in reply to his own defiant query. Surely those words uttered by a man conscious of power and of strength could never have been spoken by the dilapidated old scarecrow who earned a precarious living by writing letters for ignorant folk.

But before he could recover some semblance of presence of mind Citizen Lépine had gone, and only a loud and merry laugh seemed to echo through the squalid room.

Hériot shook off the remnant of his own senseless terror; he tore open the door of the bedroom and shouted to Rondeau, who truly was thinking that the Citizen-Deputy had gone mad:

"After him!—after him! Quick! curse you!" he cried.

"After whom?" gasped the man.

"The man who was here just now—an *aristo*."

"I saw no one—but the Public Letter-Writer, old Lépine—I know him well—-"

"Curse you for a fool!" shouted Hériot savagely, "the man who was here was that cursed Englishman—the one whom they call the Scarlet Pimpernel. Run after him—stop him, I say!"

"Too late, citizen," said the other placidly; "whoever was here before is certainly half-way down the street by now."

"No use, Ffoulkes," said Sir Percy Blakeney to his friend half-an-hour later, "the man's passions of hatred and desire are greater than his greed."

The two men were sitting together in one of Sir Percy Blakeney's many lodgings—the one in the Rue des Petits Pères—and Sir Percy had just put Sir Andrew Ffoulkes *au fait* with the whole sad story of Arnould Fabrice's danger and Agnès de Lucines' despair.

"You could do nothing with the brute, then?" queried Sir Andrew.

"Nothing," replied Blakeney. "He refused all bribes, and violence would not have helped me, for what I wanted was not to knock him down, but to get hold of the letters."

"Well, after all, he might have sold you the letters and then denounced Fabrice just the same."

"No, without actual proofs he could not do that. Arnould Fabrice is not a man against whom a mere denunciation would suffice. He has the grudging respect of every faction in the National Assembly. Nothing but irrefutable proof would prevail against him—and bring him to the guillotine."

"Why not get Fabrice and Mlle. de Lucines safely over to England?"

"Fabrice would not come. He is not of the stuff that *émigrés* are made of. He is not an aristocrat; he is a republican by conviction, and a demmed honest one at that. He would scorn to run away, and Agnès de Lucines would not go without him."

"Then what can we do?"

"Filch those letters from that brute Hériot," said Blakeney calmly.

"House-breaking, you mean!" commented Sir Andrew Ffoulkes dryly.

"Petty theft, shall we say?" retorted Sir Percy. "I can bribe the lout who has charge of Hériot's rooms to introduce us into his master's *sanctum* this evening when the National Assembly is sitting and the Citizen-Deputy safely out of the way."

And the two men—one of whom was the most intimate friend of the Prince of Wales and the acknowledged darling of London society—thereupon fell to discussing plans for surreptitiously entering a man's room and committing larceny, which in normal times would entail, if discovered, a long term of imprisonment, but which, in these days, in Paris, and perpetrated against a member of the National Assembly, would certainly be punished by death.

Citizen Rondeau, whose business it was to look after the creature comforts of Deputy Hériot, was standing in the *antichambre* facing the two visitors whom he had just introduced into his master's apartments, and idly turning a couple of gold coins over and over between his grimy fingers.

"And mind, you are to see nothing and hear nothing of what goes on in the next room," said the taller of the two strangers; "and when we go there'll be another couple of *louis* for you. Is that understood?"

"Yes! it's understood," grunted Rondeau sullenly; "but I am running great risks. The Citizen-Deputy sometimes returns at ten o'clock, but sometimes at nine . . . . I never know."

"It is now seven," rejoined the other; "we'll be gone long before nine."

"Well," said Rondeau surlily, "I go out now for my supper. I'll return in half an hour, but at half-past eight you must clear out."

Then he added with a sneer:

"Citizens Legros and Desgas usually come back with deputy Hériot of nights, and Citizens Jeanniot and Bompard come in from next door for a game of cards. You wouldn't stand much chance if you were caught here."

"Not with you to back up so formidable a *quintette* of stalwarts," assented the tall visitor gaily. "But we won't trouble about that just now. We have a couple of hours before us in which to do all that we want. So *au revoir*, friend Rondeau . . . . two more *louis* for your complaisance, remember, when we have accomplished our purpose."

Rondeau muttered something more, but the two strangers paid no further heed to him; they had already walked to the next room, leaving Rondeau in the *anti-chambre*.

Sir Percy Blakeney did not pause in the sitting-room where an oil lamp suspended from the ceiling threw a feeble circle of light above the centre table. He went straight through to the bedroom. Here, too, a small lamp was burning which only lit up a small portion of the room—the writing-desk and the oak chest—leaving the corners and the alcove, with its partially drawn curtains, in complete shadow.

Blakeney pointed to the oak chest and to the desk.

"You tackle the chest, Ffoulkes, and I will go for the desk," he said quietly, as soon as he had taken a rapid survey of the room. "You have your tools?"

Ffoulkes nodded, and *anon* in this squalid room, ill-lit, ill-ventilated, barely furnished, was presented one of the most curious spectacles of these strange and troublous times: two English gentlemen, the acknowledged dandies of London drawing-rooms, busy picking locks and filing hinges like any common house-thieves.

Neither of them spoke, and a strange hush fell over the room—a hush only broken by the click of metal against metal, and the deep breathing of the two men bending to their task. Sir Andrew Ffoulkes was working with a file on the padlocks of the oak chest, and Sir Percy Blakeney, with a bunch of skeleton keys, was opening the drawers of the writing-desk. These, when finally opened, revealed nothing of any importance; but when *anon* Sir Andrew was able to lift the lid of the oak chest, he disclosed an innumerable quantity of papers and documents tied up in neat bundles, docketed and piled up in rows and tiers to the very top of the chest.

"Quick to work, Ffoulkes," said Blakeney, as in response to his friend's call he drew a chair forward and, seating himself beside the chest, started on the task of looking through the hundreds of bundles which lay before him. "It will take us all our time to look through these."

Together now the two men set to work—methodically and quietly—piling up on the floor beside them the bundles of papers which they had already examined, and delving into the oak chest for others. No sound was heard save the crackling of crisp paper and an occasional ejaculation from either of them when they came upon some proof or other of Hériot's propensity for blackmail.

"Agnès de Lucines is not the only one whom this brute is terrorising," murmured Blakeney once between his teeth; "I marvel that the man ever feels safe, alone in these lodgings, with no one but that weak-kneed Rondeau to protect him. He must have scores of enemies in this city who would gladly put a dagger in his heart or a bullet through his back."

They had been at work for close on half an hour when an exclamation of triumph, quickly smothered, escaped Sir Percy's lips.

"By Gad, Ffoulkes!" he said, "I believe I have got what we want!"

With quick, capable hands he turned over a bundle which he had just extracted from the chest. Rapidly he glanced through them. "I have them, Ffoulkes," he reiterated more emphatically as he put the bundle into his pocket; "now everything back in its place and—"

Suddenly he paused, his slender hand up to his lips, his head turned toward the door, an expression of tense expectancy in every line of his face.

"Quick, Ffoulkes," he whispered, "everything back into the chest, and the lid down."

"What ears you have," murmured Ffoulkes as he obeyed rapidly and without question. "I heard nothing."

Blakeney went to the door and bent his head to listen.

"Three men coming up the stairs," he said; "they are on the landing now."

"Have we time to rush them?"

"No chance! They are at the door. Two more men have joined them, and I can distinguish Rondeau's voice, too."

"The *quintette*," murmured Sir Andrew. "We are caught like two rats in a trap."

Even as he spoke the opening of the outside door could be distinctly heard, then the confused murmur of many voices. Already Blakeney and Ffoulkes had with perfect presence of mind put the finishing touches to the tidying of the room—put the chairs straight, shut down the lid of the oak chest, closed all the drawers of the desk.

"Nothing but good luck can save us now," whispered Blakeney as he lowered the wick of the lamp. "Quick now," he added, "behind that tapestry in the alcove and trust to our stars."

Securely hidden for the moment behind the curtains in the dark recess of the alcove the two men waited. The door leading into the sitting-room was ajar, and they could hear Hériot and his friends making merry irruption into the place. From out the confusion of general conversation they soon gathered that the debates in the Chamber had been so dull and uninteresting that, at a given signal, the little party had decided to adjourn to Hériot's rooms for their habitual game of cards. They could also hear Hériot calling to Rondeau to bring bottles and glasses, and vaguely they marvelled what Rondeau's attitude might be like at this moment. Was he brazening out the situation, or was he sick with terror?

Suddenly Hériot's voice came out more distinctly.

"Make yourselves at home, friends," he was saying; "here are cards, dominoes, and wine. I must leave you to yourselves for ten minutes whilst I write an important letter."

"All right, but don't be long," came in merry response.

"Not longer than I can help," rejoined Hériot. "I want my revenge against Bompard, remember. He did fleece me last night."

"Hurry on, then," said one of the men. "I'll play Desgas that return game of dominoes until then."

"Ten minutes and I'll be back," concluded Hériot.

He pushed open the bedroom door. The light within was very dim. The two men hidden behind the tapestry could hear him moving about the room muttering curses to himself. Presently the light of the lamp was shifted from one end of the room to the other. Through the opening between the two curtains Blakeney could just see Hériot's back as he placed the lamp at a convenient angle upon his desk, divested himself of his overcoat and muffler, then sat down and drew pen and paper closer to him. He was leaning forward, his elbow resting upon the table, his fingers fidgeting with his long, lank hair. He had closed the door when he entered, and from the other room now the voices of his friends sounded confused and muffled. Now and then an exclamation: *"Double!" "Je . . . . tiens!" "Cinq-deux!"* an oath, a laugh, the click of glasses and bottles came out more clearly; but the rest of the time these sounds were more like a droning accompaniment to the scraping of Hériot's pen upon the paper when he finally began to write his letter.

Two minutes went by and then two more. The scratching of Hériot's pen became more rapid as he appeared to be more completely immersed in his work. Behind the curtain the two men had been waiting: Blakeney ready to act, Ffoulkes equally ready to interpret the slightest signal from his chief. The next minute Blakeney had stolen out of the alcove, and his two hands—so slender and elegant looking, and yet with a grip of steel—had fastened themselves upon Hériot's mouth, smothering within the space of a second the cry that had been half-uttered. Ffoulkes was ready to complete the work of rendering the man helpless: one handkerchief made an efficient gag, another tied the ankles securely. Hériot's own coat-sleeves supplied the handcuffs, and the blankets off the bed tied around his legs rendered him powerless to move. Then the two men lifted this inert mass on to the bed and Ffoulkes whispered anxiously: "Now, what next?"

Hériot's overcoat, hat, and muffler lay upon a chair. Sir Percy, placing a warning finger upon his lips, quickly divested himself of his own coat, slipped that of Hériot on, twisted the muffler round his neck, hunched up his shoulders, and murmuring: "Now for a bit of luck!" once more lowered the light of the lamp and then went to the door.

"Rondeau!" he called. "Hey, Rondeau!" And Sir Percy himself was surprised at the marvellous way in which he had caught the very inflection of Hériot's voice.

"Hey, Rondeau!" came from one of the players at the table, "the

Citizen-Deputy is calling you!"

They were all sitting round the table: two men intent upon their game of dominoes, the other two watching with equal intentness. Rondeau came shuffling out of the *antichambre*. His face, by the dim light of the oil lamp, looked jaundiced with fear.

"Rondeau, you fool, where are you?" called Blakeney once again.

The next moment Rondeau had entered the room. No need for a signal or an order this time. Ffoulkes knew by instinct what his chief's bold scheme would mean to them both if it succeeded. He retired into the darkest corner of the room as Rondeau shuffled across to the writing-desk. It was all done in a moment. In less time than it had taken to bind and gag Hériot, his henchman was laid out on the floor, his coat had been taken off him, and he was tied into a mummy-like bundle with Sir Andrew Ffoulkes' elegant coat fastened securely round his arms and chest. It had all been done in silence. The men in the next room were noisy and intent on their game; the slight scuffle, the quickly smothered cries had remained unheeded.

"Now, what next?" queried Sir Andrew Ffoulkes once more.

"The impudence of the d—l, my good Ffoulkes," replied Blakeney in a whisper, "and may our stars not play us false. Now let me make you look as like Rondeau as possible—there! Slip on his coat—now your hair over your forehead—your coat-collar up—your knees bent—that's better!" he added as he surveyed the transformation which a few deft strokes had made in Sir Andrew Ffoulkes' appearance. "Now all you have to do is to shuffle across the room—here's your prototype's handkerchief—of dubious cleanliness, it is true, but it will serve—blow your nose as you cross the room, it will hide your face. They'll not heed you—keep in the shadows and God guard you—I'll follow in a moment or two . . . . but don't wait for me."

He opened the door, and before Sir Andrew could protest his chief had pushed him out into the room where the four men were still intent on their game. Through the open door Sir Percy now watched his friend who, keeping well within the shadows, shuffled quietly across the room. The next moment Sir Andrew was through and in the *anti-chambre*. Blakeney's acutely sensitive ears caught the sound of the opening of the outer door. He waited for a while, then he drew out of his pocket the bundle of letters which he had risked so much to obtain. There they were neatly docketed and marked: "The affairs of Arnould Fabrice."

Well! if he got away tonight Agnès de Lucines would be happy and free from the importunities of that brute Hériot; after that he must persuade her and Fabrice to go to England and to freedom.

For the moment his own safety was terribly in jeopardy; one false move—one look from those players round the table ....Bah! even then—!

With an inward laugh he pushed open the door once more and stepped into the room. For the moment no one noticed him; the game was at its most palpitating stage; four shaggy heads met beneath the lamp and four pairs of eyes were gazing with rapt attention upon the intricate maze of the dominoes.

Blakeney walked quietly across the room; he was just midway and on a level with the centre table when a voice was suddenly raised from that tense group beneath the lamp: "Is it thou, friend Hériot?"

Then one of the men looked up and stared, and another did likewise and exclaimed: "It is not Hériot!"

In a moment all was confusion, but confusion was the very essence of those hair-breadth escapes and desperate adventures which were as the breath of his nostrils to the Scarlet Pimpernel. Before those four men had had time to jump to their feet, or to realise that something was wrong with their friend Hériot, he had run across the room, his hand was on the knob of the door—the door that led to the *antichambre* and to freedom.

Bompard, Desgas, Jeanniot, Legros were at his heels, but he tore open the door, bounded across the threshold, and slammed it to with such a vigorous bang that those on the other side were brought to a momentary halt. That moment meant life and liberty to Blakeney; already he had crossed the *antichambre*. Quite coolly and quietly now he took out the key from the inner side of the main door and slipped it to the outside. The next second—even as the four men rushed helter-skelter into the *antichambre* he was out on the landing and had turned the key in the door.

His prisoners were safely locked in—in Hériot's apartments—and Sir Percy Blakeney, calmly and without haste, was descending the stairs of the house in the Rue Cocatrice.

The next morning Agnès de Lucines received, through an anonymous messenger, the packet of letters which would so gravely have compromised Arnould Fabrice. Though the weather was more inclement than ever, she ran out into the streets, determined to seek out the old Public Letter-Writer and thank him for his mediation with the English milor, who surely had done this noble action.

But the old scarecrow had disappeared.

A Fine Bit of Work

1

"Sh! . . . . sh! . . . . It's the Englishman. I'd know his footstep any-where—"

"God bless him!" murmured *petite maman* fervently.

Père Lenègre went to the door; he stepped cautiously and with that stealthy foot-tread which speaks in eloquent silence of daily, hourly danger, of anguish and anxiety for lives that are dear.

The door was low and narrow—up on the fifth floor of one of the huge tenement houses in the Rue Jolivet in the Montmartre quarter of Paris. A narrow stone passage led to it—pitch-dark at all times, but dirty, and evil-smelling when the *concierge*—a free citizen of the new democracy—took a week's holiday from his work in order to spend whole afternoons either at the wine-shop round the corner, or on the Place du Carrousel to watch the guillotine getting rid of some twenty aristocrats an hour for the glorification of the will of the people.

But inside the small apartment everything was scrupulously neat and clean. *Petite maman* was such an excellent manager, and Rosette was busy all the day tidying and cleaning the poor little home, which Père Lenègre contrived to keep up for wife and daughter by working fourteen hours a day in the government saddlery.

When Père Lenègre opened the narrow door, the entire frame-work of it was filled by the broad, magnificent figure of a man in heavy caped coat and high leather boots, with dainty frills of lace at throat and wrist, and elegant *chapeau-bras* held in the hand.

Père Lenègre at sight of him, put a quick finger to his own quiver-ing lips.

"Anything wrong, *vieux papa*?" asked the newcomer lightly.

The other closed the door cautiously before he made reply. But *petite maman* could not restrain her anxiety.

"My little Pierre, milor?" she asked as she clasped her wrinkled hands together, and turned on the stranger her tear-dimmed restless eyes.

"Pierre is safe and well, little mother," he replied cheerily. "We got him out of Paris early this morning in a coal cart, carefully hidden among the sacks. When he emerged he was black but safe. I drove the cart myself as far as Courbevoie, and there handed over your Pierre and those whom we got out of Paris with him to those of my friends who were going straight to England. There's nothing more to be afraid of, *petite maman*," he added as he took the old woman's wrinkled hands in both his own; "your son is now under the care of men who would die rather than see him captured. So, make your mind at ease, Pierre will be in England, safe and well, within a week."

Petite maman couldn't say anything just then because tears were choking her, but in her turn, she clasped those two strong and slender hands—the hands of the brave Englishman who had just risked his life in order to save Pierre from the guillotine—and she kissed them as fervently as she kissed the feet of the Madonna when she knelt before her shrine in prayer.

Pierre had been a footman in the household of unhappy Marie Antoinette. His crime had been that he remained loyal to her in words as well as in thought. A hot-headed but nobly outspoken harangue on behalf of the unfortunate queen, delivered in a public place, had at once marked him out to the spies of the Terrorists as suspect of intrigue against the safety of the Republic. He was denounced to the Committee of Public Safety, and his arrest and condemnation to the guillotine would have inevitably followed had not the gallant band of Englishmen, known as the League of the Scarlet Pimpernel, succeeded in effecting his escape.

What wonder that *petite maman* could not speak for tears when she clasped the hands of the noble leader of that splendid little band of heroes? What wonder that Père Lenègre, when he heard that his son was safe murmured a fervent: "God bless you, milor, and your friends!" and that Rosette surreptitiously raised the fine caped coat to her lips, for Pierre was her twin-brother, and she loved him very dearly.

But already Sir Percy Blakeney had, with one of his characteristic cheery words, dissipated the atmosphere of tearful emotion which oppressed these kindly folk.

"Now, Papa Lenègre," he said lightly, "tell me why you wore such a solemn air when you let me in just now."

"Because, milor," replied the old man quietly, "that d——d *concierge*, Jean Baptiste, is a black-hearted traitor."

Sir Percy laughed, his merry, infectious laugh.

"You mean that while he has been pocketing bribes from me, he has denounced me to the Committee."

Père Lenègre nodded: "I only heard it this morning," he said, "from one or two threatening words the treacherous brute let fall. He knows that you lodge in the Place des Trois Maries, and that you come here frequently. I would have given my life to warn you then and there," continued the old man with touching earnestness, "but I didn't know where to find you. All I knew was that you were looking after Pierre."

Even while the man spoke there darted from beneath the Englishman's heavy lids a quick look like a flash of sudden and brilliant light out of the lazy depths of his merry blue eyes; it was one of those glances of pure delight and exultation which light up the eyes of the true soldier when there is serious fighting to be done.

"*La*, man," he said gaily, "there was no cause to worry. Pierre is safe, remember that! As for me," he added with that wonderful *insouciance* which caused him to risk his life a hundred times a day with a shrug of his broad shoulders and a smile upon his lips; "as for me, I'll look after myself, never fear."

He paused awhile, then added gravely: "So long as you are safe, my good Lenègre, and *petite maman*, and Rosette."

Whereupon the old man was silent, *petite maman* murmured a short prayer, and Rosette began to cry. The hero of a thousand gallant rescues had received his answer.

"You, too, are on the black list, Père Lenègre?" he asked quietly.

The old man nodded.

"How do you know?" queried the Englishman.

"Through Jean Baptiste, milor."

"Still that demmed *concierge*," muttered Sir Percy.

"He frightened *petite maman* with it all this morning, saying that he knew my name was down on the Sectional Committee's list as a 'suspect.' That's when he let fall a word or two about you, milor. He said it is known that Pierre has escaped from justice, and that you helped him to it.

"I am sure that we shall get a domiciliary visit presently," continued Père Lenègre, after a slight pause. "The *gendarmes* have not yet been, but I fancy that already this morning early I saw one or two of the Committee's spies hanging about the house, and when I went to the workshop I was followed all the time."

The Englishman looked grave: "And tell me," he said, "have you got anything in this place that may prove compromising to any of you?"

"No, milor. But, as Jean Baptiste said, the Sectional Committee know about Pierre. It is because of my son that I am suspect."

The old man spoke quite quietly, very simply, like a philosopher who has long ago learned to put behind him the fear of death. Nor did *petite maman* cry or lament. Her thoughts were for the brave milor who had saved her boy; but her fears for her old man left her dry-eyed and dumb with grief.

There was silence in the little room for one moment while the angel of sorrow and anguish hovered round these faithful and brave souls, then the Englishman's cheery voice, so full of spirit and merriment, rang out once more—he had risen to his full, towering height, and now placed a kindly hand on the old man's shoulder:

"It seems to me, my good Lenègre," he said, "that you and I haven't many moments to spare if we mean to cheat those devils by saving your neck. Now, *petite maman*," he added, turning to the old woman, "are you going to be brave?"

"I will do anything, milor," she replied quietly, "to help my old man."

"Well, then," said Sir Percy Blakeney in that optimistic, light-hearted yet supremely authoritative tone of which he held the secret, "you and Rosette remain here and wait for the *gendarmes*. When they come, say nothing; behave with absolute meekness, and let them search your place from end to end. If they ask you about your husband say that you believe him to be at his workshop. Is that clear?"

"Quite clear, milor," replied *petite maman*.

"And you, Père Lenègre," continued the Englishman, speaking now with slow and careful deliberation, "listen very attentively to the instructions I am going to give you, for on your implicit obedience to them depends not only your own life but that of these two dear women. Go at once, now, to the Rue Ste. Anne, round the corner, the second house on your right, which is numbered thirty-seven. The *porte cochère* stands open, go boldly through, past the *concierge's* box, and up the stairs to apartment number twelve, second floor. Here is the key of the apartment," he added, producing one from his coat pocket and handing it over to the old man. "The rooms are nominally occupied by a certain Maitre Turandot, maker of violins, and not even the *concierge* of the place knows that the hunchbacked and snuffy violinmaker and the meddlesome Scarlet Pimpernel, whom the Committee of Public Safety would so love to lay by the heels, are one and the same person. The apartment, then, is mine; one of the many which I occupy in Paris at different times," he went on. "Let yourself in quietly with this key, walk straight across the first room to a wardrobe, which you will see in front of you. Open it. It is hung full of shabby clothes; put these aside, and you will notice that the panels at the back do not fit very closely, as if the wardrobe was old or had been badly put together. Insert your fingers in the tiny aperture between the two middle panels. These slide back easily: there is a recess immediately behind them. Get in there; pull the doors of the wardrobe together first, then slide the back panels into their place. You will be perfectly safe there, as the house is not under suspicion at present, and even if the revolutionary guard, under some meddlesome sergeant or other, chooses to pay it a surprise visit, your hiding-place will be perfectly secure. Now is all that quite understood?"

"Absolutely, milor," replied Lenègre, even as he made ready to obey Sir Percy's orders, "but what about you? You cannot get out of this house, milor," he urged; "it is watched, I tell you."

"*La!*" broke in Blakeney, in his light-hearted way, "and do you think I didn't know that? I had to come and tell you about Pierre, and now I must give those worthy *gendarmes* the slip somehow. I have my rooms downstairs on the ground floor, as you know, and I must make certain arrangements so that we can all get out of Paris comfortably this evening. The demmed place is no longer safe either for you, my good Lenègre, or for *petite maman* and Rosette. But wherever I may be, meanwhile, don't worry about me. As soon as the *gendarmes* have been and gone, I'll go over to the Rue Ste. Anne and let you know what arrangements I've been able to make. So, do as I tell you now, and in Heaven's name let me look after myself."

Whereupon, with scant ceremony, he hustled the old man out of the room.

Père Lenègre had contrived to kiss *petite maman* and Rosette before he went. It was touching to see the perfect confidence with which these simple-hearted folk obeyed the commands of milor. Had he not saved Pierre in his wonderful, brave, resourceful way? Of a truth he would know how to save Père Lenègre also. But, nevertheless, anguish gripped the women's hearts; anguish doubly keen since the saviour of Pierre was also in danger now.

When Père Lenègre's shuffling footsteps had died away along the flagged corridor, the stranger once more turned to the two women.

"And now, *petite maman*," he said cheerily, as he kissed the old woman on both her furrowed cheeks, "keep up a good heart, and say your prayers with Rosette. Your old man and I will both have need of them."

He did not wait to say goodbye, and *anon* it was his firm footstep that echoed down the corridor. He went off singing a song, at the top of his voice, for the whole house to hear, and for that traitor, Jean Baptiste, to come rushing out of his room marvelling at the impudence of the man, and cursing the Committee of Public Safety who were so slow in sending the soldiers of the Republic to lay this impertinent Englishman by the heels.

2

A quarter of an hour later half dozen men of the Republican Guard, with corporal and sergeant in command, were in the small apartment on the fifth floor of the tenement house in the Rue Jolivet. They had demanded an entry in the name of the Republic, had roughly hustled *petite maman* and Rosette, questioned them to Lenègre's whereabouts, and not satisfied with the reply which they received, had turned the tidy little home topsy-turvy, ransacked every cupboard, dislocated every bed, table or sofa which might presumably have afforded a hiding place for a man.

Satisfied now that the "suspect" whom they were searching for was not on the premises, the sergeant stationed four of his men with the corporal outside the door, and two within, and himself sitting down in the centre of the room ordered the two women to stand before him and to answer his questions clearly on pain of being dragged away forthwith to the St. Lazare house of detention.

Petite maman smoothed out her apron, crossed her arms before her, and looked the sergeant quite straight in the face. Rosette's eyes were full of tears, but she showed no signs of fear either, although her shoulder—where one of the *gendarmes* had seized it so roughly—was terribly painful.

"Your husband, *citizeness*," asked the sergeant peremptorily, "where is he?"

"I am not sure, citizen," replied *petite maman*. "At this hour he is generally at the government works in the Quai des Messageries."

"He is not there now," asserted the sergeant. "We have knowledge that he did not go back to his work since dinner-time."

Petite maman was silent.

"Answer," ordered the sergeant.

"I cannot tell you more, Citizen Sergeant," she said firmly. "I do not know."

"You do yourself no good, woman, by this obstinacy," he continued roughly. "My belief is that your husband is inside this house, hidden away somewhere. If necessary I can get orders to have every apartment searched until he is found: but in that case it will go much harder with you and with your daughter, and much harder too with your husband than if he gave us no trouble and followed us quietly."

But with sublime confidence in the man who had saved Pierre and who had given her explicit orders as to what she should do, *petite maman*, backed by Rosette, reiterated quietly:

"I cannot tell you more, Citizen Sergeant, I do not know."

"And what about the Englishman?" queried the sergeant more roughly, "the man they call the Scarlet Pimpernel, what do you know of him?"

"Nothing, citizen," replied *petite maman*, "what should we poor folk know of an English milor?"

"You know at any rate this much, *citizeness*, that the English milor helped your son Pierre to escape from justice."

"If that is so," said *petite maman* quietly, "it cannot be wrong for a mother to pray to God to bless her son's preserver."

"It behoves every good citizen," retorted the sergeant firmly, "to denounce all traitors to the Republic."

"But since I know nothing about the Englishman, Citizen Sergeant—?"

And *petite maman* shrugged her thin shoulders as if the matter had ceased to interest her.

"Think again, *citizeness*," admonished the sergeant, "it is your husband's neck as well as your daughter's and your own that you are risking by so much obstinacy."

He waited a moment or two as if willing to give the old woman time to speak: then, when he saw that she kept her thin, quivering lips resolutely glued together he called his corporal to him.

"Go to the Citizen Commissary of the Section," he commanded, "and ask for a general order to search every apartment in No. 24 Rue Jolivet. Leave two of our men posted on the first and third landings of this house and leave two outside this door. Be as quick as you can. You can be back here with the order in half an hour, or perhaps the committee will send me an extra squad; tell the Ctizen Commissary that this is a big house, with many corridors. You can go."

The corporal saluted and went.

Petite maman and Rosette the while were still standing quietly in the middle of the room, their arms folded underneath their aprons, their wide-open, anxious eyes fixed into space. Rosette's tears were falling slowly, one by one down her cheeks, but *petite maman* was dry-eyed. She was thinking, and thinking as she had never had occasion to think before.

She was thinking of the brave and gallant Englishman who had saved Pierre's life only yesterday. The sergeant, who sat there before her, had asked for orders from the Citizen Commissary to search this big house from attic to cellar. That is what made *petite maman* think and think.

The brave Englishman was in this house at the present moment: the house would be searched from attic to cellar and he would be found, taken, and brought to the guillotine.

The man who yesterday had risked his life to save her boy was in imminent and deadly danger, and she—*petite maman*—could do nothing to save him.

Every moment now she thought to hear milor's firm tread resounding on stairs or corridor, every moment she thought to hear snatches of an English song, sung by a fresh and powerful voice, never after today to be heard in gaiety again.

The old clock upon the shelf ticked away these seconds and minutes while *petite maman* thought and thought, while men set traps to catch a fellow-being in a deathly snare, and human carnivorous beasts lay lurking for their prey.

3

Another quarter of an hour went by. *Petite maman* and Rosette had hardly moved. The shadows of evening were creeping into the narrow room, blurring the outlines of the pieces of furniture and wrapping all the corners in gloom.

The sergeant had ordered Rosette to bring in a lamp. This she had done, placing it upon the table so that the feeble light glinted upon the belt and buckles of the sergeant and upon the tricolour cockade which was pinned to his hat. *Petite maman* had thought and thought until she could think no more.

Anon there was much commotion on the stairs; heavy footsteps were heard ascending from below, then crossing the corridors on the various landings. The silence which reigned otherwise in the house, and which had fallen as usual on the squalid little street, void of traffic at this hour, caused those footsteps to echo with ominous power.

Petite maman felt her heart beating so vigorously that she could hardly breathe. She pressed her wrinkled hands tightly against her bosom.

There were the quick words of command, alas! so familiar in France just now, the cruel, peremptory words that invariably preceded an arrest, preliminaries to the dragging of some wretched—often wholly harmless—creature before a tribunal that knew neither pardon nor mercy.

The sergeant, who had become drowsy in the close atmosphere of the tiny room, roused himself at the sound and jumped to his feet. The door was thrown open by the men stationed outside even before the authoritative words, "Open! in the name of the Republic!" had echoed along the narrow corridor.

The sergeant stood at attention and quickly lifted his hand to his forehead in salute. A fresh squad of some half-dozen men of the Republican Guard stood in the doorway; they were under the command of an officer of high rank, a rough, uncouth, almost bestial-looking creature, with lank hair worn the fashionable length under his greasy *chapeau-bras,* and unkempt beard round an ill-washed and bloated face. But he wore the tricolour sash and badge which proclaimed him one of the military members of the Sectional Committee of Public Safety, and the sergeant, who had been so overbearing with the women just now, had assumed a very humble and even obsequious manner.

"You sent for a general order to the Sectional Committee," said the newcomer, turning abruptly to the sergeant after he had cast a quick, searching glance round the room, hardly condescending to look on *petite maman* and Rosette, whose very souls were now gazing out of their anguish-filled eyes.

"I did, Citizen Commandant," replied the sergeant.

"I am not a *commandant,*" said the other curtly. "My name is Rouget, member of the Convention and of the Committee of Public Safety. The sectional Committee to whom you sent for a general order of search thought that you had blundered somehow, so they sent me to put things right."

"I am not aware that I committed any blunder, citizen," stammered the sergeant dolefully. "I could not take the responsibility of making a domiciliary search all through the house. So, I begged for fuller orders."

"And wasted the Committee's time and mine by such nonsense," retorted Rouget harshly. "Every citizen of the Republic worthy of the name should know how to act on his own initiative when the safety of the nation demands it."

"I did not know—I did not dare—" murmured the sergeant, obviously cowed by this reproof, which had been delivered in the rough, overbearing tones peculiar to these men who, one and all, had risen from the gutter to places of importance and responsibility in the new-ly-modelled State.

"Silence!" commanded the other peremptorily. "Don't waste any more of my time with your lame excuses. You have failed in zeal and initiative. That's enough. What else have you done? Have you got the man Lenègre?"

"No, citizen. He is not in hiding here, and his wife and daughter will not give us any information about him."

"That is their look-out," retorted Rouget with a harsh laugh. "If they give up Lenègre of their own free will the law will deal leniently with them, and even perhaps with him. But if we have to search the house for him, then it means the guillotine for the lot of them."

He had spoken these callous words without even looking on the two unfortunate women; nor did he ask them any further questions just then, but continued speaking to the sergeant:

"And what about the Englishman? The sectional Committee sent down some spies this morning to be on the look-out for him on or about this house. Have you got him?"

"Not yet, citizen. But—"

"*Ah ça*, Citizen Sergeant," broke in the other brusquely, "meseems that your zeal has been even more at fault than I had supposed. Have you done anything at all, then, in the matter of Lenègre or the Eng-lishman?"

"I have told you, citizen," retorted the sergeant sullenly, "that I believe Lenègre to be still in this house. At any rate, he had not gone out of it an hour ago—that's all I know. And I wanted to search the whole of this house, as I am sure we should have found him in one of the other apartments. These people are all friends together, and will always help each other to evade justice. But the Englishman was no concern of mine. The spies of the Committee were ordered to watch for him, and when they reported to me I was to proceed with the arrest. I was not set to do any of the spying work. I am a soldier, and obey my orders when I get them."

"Very well, then, you'd better obey them now, Citizen Sergeant," was Rouget's dry comment on the other man's surly explanation, "for you seem to have properly blundered from first to last, and will be hard put to it to redeem your character. The Republic, remember, has no use for fools."

The sergeant, after this covert threat, thought it best, apparently, to keep his tongue, whilst Rouget continued, in the same aggressive, peremptory tone:

"Get on with your domiciliary visits at once. Take your own men with you, and leave me the others. Begin on this floor, and leave your sentry at the front door outside. Now let me see your zeal atoning for your past slackness. Right turn! Quick march!"

Then it was that *petite maman* spoke out. She had thought and thought, and now she knew what she ought to do; she knew that that cruel, inhuman wretch would presently begin his tramp up and down corridors and stairs, demanding admittance at every door, entering every apartment. She knew that the man who had saved her Pierre's life was in hiding somewhere in the house—that he would be found and dragged to the guillotine, for she knew that the whole governing body of this abominable Revolution was determined not to allow that hated Englishman to escape again.

She was old and feeble, small and thin—that's why everyone called her *petite maman*—but once she knew what she ought to do, then her spirit overpowered the weakness of her wizened body.

Now she knew, and even while that arrogant member of an execrated murdering Committee was giving final instructions to the sergeant, *petite maman* said, in a calm, piping voice:

"No need, Citizen Sergeant, to go and disturb all my friends and neighbours. I'll tell you where my husband is."

In a moment Rouget had swung round on his heel, a hideous gleam of satisfaction spread over his grimy face, and he said, with an ugly sneer:

"So! you have thought better of it, have you? Well, out with it! You'd better be quick about it if you want to do yourselves any good."

"I have my daughter to think of," said *petite maman* in a feeble, querulous way, "and I won't have all my neighbours in this house made unhappy because of me. They have all been kind neighbours. Will you promise not to molest them and to clear the house of soldiers if I tell you where Lenègre is?"

"The Republic makes no promises," replied Rouget gruffly. "Her citizens must do their duty without hope of a reward. If they fail in it, they are punished. But privately I will tell you, woman, that if you save us the troublesome and probably unprofitable task of searching this rabbit-warren through and through, it shall go very leniently with you and with your daughter, and perhaps—I won't promise, remember—perhaps with your husband also."

"Very good, citizen," said *petite maman* calmly. "I am ready."

"Ready for what?" he demanded.

"To take you to where my husband is in hiding."

"Oho! He is not in the house, then?"

"No."

"Where is he, then?"

"In the Rue Ste. Anne. I will take you there."

Rouget cast a quick, suspicious glance on the old woman, and exchanged one of understanding with the sergeant.

"Very well," he said after a slight pause. "But your daughter must come along too. Sergeant," he added, "I'll take three of your men with me; I have half a dozen, but it's better to be on the safe side. Post your fellows round the outer door, and on my way to the rue Ste. Anne I will leave word at the *gendarmerie* that a small reinforcement be sent on to you at once. These can be here in five minutes; until then you are quite safe."

Then he added under his breath, so that the women should not hear: "The Englishman may still be in the house. In which case, hearing us depart, he may think us all gone and try to give us the slip. You'll know what to do?" he queried significantly.

"Of course, citizen," replied the sergeant.

"Now, then, *citizeness*—hurry up."

Once more there was tramping of heavy feet on stone stairs and corridors. A squad of soldiers of the Republican Guard, with two women in their midst, and followed by a member of the Committee of Public Safety, a sergeant, corporal and two or three more men, excited much anxious curiosity as they descended the steep flights of steps from the fifth floor.

Pale, frightened faces peeped shyly through the doorways at sound of the noisy tramp from above, but quickly disappeared again at sight of the grimy scarlet facings and tricolour cockades.

The sergeant and three soldiers remained stationed at the foot of the stairs inside the house. Then Citizen Rouget roughly gave the order to proceed. It seemed strange that it should require close on a dozen men to guard two women and to apprehend one old man, but as the member of the Committee of Public Safety whispered to the sergeant before he finally went out of the house: "The whole thing may be a trap, and one can't be too careful. The Englishman is said to be very powerful; I'll get the *gendarmerie* to send you another half-dozen men, and mind you guard the house until my return."

4

Five minutes later the soldiers, directed by *petite maman*, had reached No. 37 Rue Ste. Anne. The big outside door stood wide open, and the whole party turned immediately into the house.

The *concierge*, terrified and obsequious, rushed—trembling—out of his box.

"What was the pleasure of the citizen soldiers?" he asked.

"Tell him, *citizeness*," commanded Rouget curtly.

"We are going to apartment No. 12 on the second floor," said *petite maman* to the *concierge*.

"Have you a key of the apartment?" queried Rouget.

"No, citizen," stammered the *concierge*, "but—"

"Well, what is it?" queried the other peremptorily.

"Papa Turandot is a poor, harmless maker of volins," said the *concierge*. "I know him well, though he is not often at home. He lives with a daughter somewhere Passy way, and only uses this place as a workshop. I am sure he is no traitor."

"We'll soon see about that," remarked Rouget dryly.

Petite maman held her shawl tightly crossed over her bosom: her hands felt clammy and cold as ice. She was looking straight out before her, quite dry-eyed and calm, and never once glanced on Rosette, who was not allowed to come anywhere near her mother.

As there was no duplicate key to apartment No. 12, Citizen Rouget ordered his men to break in the door. It did not take very long: the house was old and ramshackle and the doors rickety. The next moment the party stood in the room which a while ago the Englishman had so accurately described to Père Lenègre in *petite maman*'s hearing.

There was the wardrobe. *Petite maman*, closely surrounded by the soldiers, went boldly up to it; she opened it just as milor had directed, and pushed aside the row of shabby clothes that hung there. Then she pointed to the panels that did not fit quite tightly together at the back. *Petite maman* passed her tongue over her dry lips before she spoke.

"There's a recess behind those panels," she said at last. "They slide back quite easily. My old man is there."

"And God bless you for a brave, loyal soul," came in merry, ringing accent from the other end of the room. "And God save the Scarlet

Pimpernel!"

These last words, spoken in English, completed the blank amazement which literally paralysed the only three genuine Republican soldiers there—those, namely, whom Rouget had borrowed from the sergeant. As for the others, they knew what to do. In less than a minute they had overpowered and gagged the three bewildered soldiers.

Rosette had screamed, terror-stricken, from sheer astonishment, but *petite maman* stood quite still, her pale, tear-dimmed eyes fixed upon the man whose gay "God bless you!" had so suddenly turned her despair into hope.

How was it that in the hideous, unkempt and grimy Rouget she had not at once recognised the handsome and gallant milor who had saved her Pierre's life? Well, of a truth he had been unrecognisable, but now that he tore the ugly wig and beard from his face, stretched out his fine figure to its full height, and presently turned his lazy, merry eyes on her, she could have screamed for very joy.

The next moment he had her by the shoulders and had imprinted two sounding kisses upon her cheeks.

"Now, *petite maman*," he said gaily, "let us liberate the old man."

Père Lenègre, from his hiding-place, had heard all that had been going on in the room for the last few moments. True, he had known exactly what to expect, for no sooner had he taken possession of the recess behind the wardrobe than milor also entered the apartment and then and there told him of his plans not only for *père's* own safety, but for that of *petite maman* and Rosette who would be in grave danger if the old man followed in the wake of Pierre.

Milor told him in his usual light-hearted way that he had given the Committee's spies the slip.

"I do that very easily, you know," he explained. "I just slip into my rooms in the Rue Jolivet, change myself into a snuffy and hunchback violin-maker, and walk out of the house under the noses of the spies. In the nearest wine-shop my English friends, in various disguises, are all ready to my hand: half a dozen of them are never far from where I am in case they may be wanted."

These half-dozen brave Englishmen soon arrived one by one: one looked like a coal-heaver, another like a seedy musician, a third like a coach-driver. But they all walked boldly into the house and were soon all congregated in apartment No. 12. Here fresh disguises were assumed, and soon a squad of Republican Guards looked as like the real thing as possible.

Père Lenègre admitted himself that though he actually saw milor transforming himself into Citizen Rouget, he could hardly believe his eyes, so complete was the change.

"I am deeply grieved to have frightened and upset you so, *petite maman*," now concluded milor kindly, "but I saw no other way of getting you and Rosette out of the house and leaving that stupid sergeant and some of his men behind. I did not want to arouse in him even the faintest breath of suspicion, and of course if he had asked me for the written orders which he was actually waiting for, or if his corporal had returned sooner than I anticipated, there might have been trouble. But even then," he added with his usual careless *insouciance*, "I should have thought of some way of baffling those brutes."

"And now," he concluded more authoritatively, "it is a case of getting out of Paris before the gates close. Père Lenègre, take your wife and daughter with you and walk boldly out of this house. The sergeant and his men have not vacated their post in the Rue Jolivet, and no one else can molest you. Go straight to the Porte de Neuilly, and on the other side wait quietly in the little *café* at the corner of the Avenue until I come. Your old passes for the barriers still hold good; you were only placed on the 'suspect' list this morning, and there has not been a hue and cry yet about you. In any case some of us will be close by to help you if needs be."

"But you, milor," stammered Père Lenègre, "and your friends—?"

"*La*, man," retorted Blakeney lightly, "have I not told you before never to worry about me and my friends? We have more ways than one of giving the slip to this demmed government of yours. All you've got to think of is your wife and your daughter. I am afraid that *petite maman* cannot take more with her than she has on, but we'll do all we can for her comfort until we have you all in perfect safety—in England—with Pierre."

Neither Père Lenègre, nor *petite maman*, nor Rosette could speak just then, for tears were choking them, but *anon* when milor stood nearer, *petite maman* knelt down, and, imprisoning his slender hand in her brown, wrinkled ones, she kissed it reverently.

He laughed and chided her for this.

"'Tis I should kneel to you in gratitude, *petite maman*," he said earnestly, "you were ready to sacrifice your old man for me."

"You have saved Pierre, milor," said the mother simply.

A minute later Père Lenègre and the two women were ready to go. Already milor and his gallant English friends were busy once more transforming themselves into grimy workmen or seedy middle-class professionals.

As soon as the door of apartment No. 12 finally closed behind the three good folk, my lord Tony asked of his chief:

"What about these three wretched soldiers, Blakeney?"

"Oh! they'll be all right for twenty-four hours. They can't starve till then, and by that time the *concierge* will have realised that there's something wrong with the door of No. 12 and will come in to investigate the matter. Are they securely bound, though?"

"And gagged! Rather!" ejaculated one of the others. "Odds life, Blakeney!" he added enthusiastically, "that was a fine bit of work!"

How Jean Pierre Met the Scarlet Pimpernel
As told by Himself

1

Ah, *monsieur!* the pity of it, the pity! Surely there are sins which *le bon Dieu* Himself will condone. And if not—well, I had to risk His displeasure anyhow. Could I see them both starve, *monsieur?* I ask you! and M. le Vicomte had become so thin, so thin, his tiny, delicate bones were almost through his skin. And Mme. la Marquise! an angel, *monsieur!* Why, in the happy olden days, before all these traitors and assassins ruled in France, M. and Mme. la Marquise lived only for the child, and then to see him dying—yes, dying, there was no shutting one's eyes to that awful fact—M. le Vicomte de Mortain was dying of starvation and of disease.

There we were all herded together in a couple of attics—one of which little more than a cupboard—at the top of a dilapidated half-ruined house in the Rue des Pipots—Mme. la Marquise, M. le Vicomte and I—just think of that, *monsieur!* M. le Marquis had his *château*, as no doubt you know, on the outskirts of Lyons. A loyal high-born gentleman; was it likely, I ask you, that he would submit passively to the rule of those execrable revolutionaries who had murdered their king, outraged their queen and royal family, and, God help them! had already perpetrated every crime and every abomination for which of a truth there could be no pardon either on earth or in Heaven? He joined that plucky but, alas! small and ill-equipped army of royalists who, unable to save their king, were at least determined to avenge him.

Well, you know well enough what happened. The counter-revolution failed; the revolutionary army brought Lyons down to her knees after a siege of two months. She was then marked down as a rebel city, and after the abominable decree of October 9th had deprived her of her very name, and Couthon had exacted bloody reprisals from the entire population for its loyalty to the king, the infamous Laporte was sent down in order finally to stamp out the lingering remnants of the rebellion. By that time, *monsieur,* half the city had been burned down, and one-tenth and more of the inhabitants—men, women, and children—had been massacred in cold blood, whilst most of the others had fled in terror from the appalling scene of ruin and desolation. Laporte completed the execrable work so ably begun by Couthon. He was a very celebrated and skilful doctor at the Faculty of Medicine, now turned into a human hyena in the name of Liberty and Fraternity.

M. le Marquis contrived to escape with the scattered remnant of the Royalist army into Switzerland. But Mme la Marquise throughout all these strenuous times had stuck to her post at the *château* like the valiant creature that she was. When Couthon entered Lyons at the head of the revolutionary army, the whole of her household fled, and I was left alone to look after her and M. le Vicomte.

Then one day when I had gone into Lyons for provisions, I suddenly chanced to hear outside an eating-house that which nearly froze the marrow in my old bones. A captain belonging to the Revolutionary Guard was transmitting to his sergeant certain orders, which he had apparently just received.

The orders were to make a perquisition at ten o'clock this same evening in the Château of Mortaine as the *marquis* was supposed to be in hiding there, and in any event to arrest every man, woman, and child who was found within its walls.

"Citizen Laporte," the captain concluded, "knows for a certainty that the *ci-devant marquise* and her brat are still there, even if the *marquis* has fled like the traitor that he is. Those cursed English spies who call themselves the League of the Scarlet Pimpernel have been very active in Lyons of late, and Citizen Laporte is afraid that they might cheat the guillotine of the carcase of those *aristos*, as they have already succeeded in doing in the case of a large number of traitors."

I did not, of course, wait to hear any more of that abominable talk. I sped home as fast as my old legs would carry me. That self-same evening, as soon as it was dark, Mme. la Marquise, carrying M. le Vicomte in her arms and I carrying a pack with a few necessaries on my back, left the ancestral home of the Mortaines never to return to it again: for within an hour of our flight a detachment of the revolutionary army made a descent upon the *château*; they ransacked it from attic to cellar, and finding nothing there to satisfy their lust of hate, they burned the stately mansion down to the ground.

We were obliged to take refuge in Lyons, at any rate for a time. Great as was the danger inside the city, it was infinitely greater on the high roads, unless we could arrange for some vehicle to take us a considerable part of the way to the frontier, and above all for some sort of passports—forged or otherwise—to enable us to pass the various toll-gates on the road, where vigilance was very strict. So, we wandered through the ruined and deserted streets of the city in search of shelter, but found every charred and derelict house full of miserable tramps and destitutes like ourselves. Half dead with fatigue, Mme. la Marquise was at last obliged to take refuge in one of these houses which was situated in the Rue des Pipots. Every room was full to overflowing with a miserable wreckage of humanity thrown hither by the tide of anarchy and of bloodshed. But at the top of the house we found an attic. It was empty save for a couple of chairs, a table and a broken-down bedstead on which were a ragged mattress and pillow.

Here, *monsieur*, we spent over three weeks, at the end of which time M. le Vicomte fell ill, and then there followed days, *monsieur*, through which I would not like my worst enemy to pass.

Mme. la Marquise had only been able to carry away in her flight what ready money she happened to have in the house at the time. Securities, property, money belonging to aristocrats had been ruthlessly confiscated by the revolutionary government in Lyons. Our scanty resources rapidly became exhausted, and what was left had to be kept for milk and delicacies for M. le Vicomte. I tramped through the streets in search of a doctor, but most of them had been arrested on some paltry charge or other of rebellion, whilst others had fled from the city. There was only that infamous Laporte—a vastly clever doctor, I knew—but as soon take a lamb to a hungry lion as the Vicomte de Mortaine to that bloodthirsty cut-throat.

Then one day our last *franc* went and we had nothing left. Mme. la Marquise had not touched food for two days. I had stood at the corner of the street, begging all the day until I was driven off by the *gendarmes*. I had only obtained three *sous* from the passers-by. I bought some milk and took it home for M. le Vicomte. The following morning when I entered the larger attic I found that Mme. la Marquise had fainted from inanition.

I spent the whole of the day begging in the streets and dodging the guard, and even so I only collected four *sous*. I could have got more perhaps, only that at about midday the smell of food from an eating-house turned me sick and faint, and when I regained consciousness I found myself huddled up under a doorway and evening gathering in fast around me. If Mme. la Marquise could go two days without food I ought to go four. I struggled to my feet; fortunately, I had retained possession of my four *sous*, else of a truth I would not have had the courage to go back to the miserable attic which was the only home I knew.

I was wending my way along as fast as I could—for I knew that Mme. la Marquise would be getting terribly anxious—when, just as I turned into the Rue Blanche, I spied two gentlemen—obviously strangers, for they were dressed with a luxury and care with which we had long ceased to be familiar in Lyons—walking rapidly towards me. A moment or two later they came to a halt, not far from where I was standing, and I heard the taller one of the two say to the other in English—a language with which I am vaguely conversant: "All right again this time, what, Tony?"

Both laughed merrily like a couple of schoolboys playing truant, and then they disappeared under the doorway of a dilapidated house, whilst I was left wondering how two such elegant gentlemen dared be abroad in Lyons these days, seeing that every man, woman and child who was dressed in anything but threadbare clothes was sure to be insulted in the streets for an aristocrat, and as often as not summarily arrested as a traitor.

However, I had other things to think about, and had already dismissed the little incident from my mind, when at the bottom of the Rue Blanche I came upon a knot of gaffers, men and women, who were talking and gesticulating very excitedly outside the door of a cook-shop. At first, I did not take much notice of what was said: my eyes were glued to the front of the shop, on which were displayed sundry delicacies of the kind which makes a wretched, starved beggar's mouth water as he goes by; a roast capon especially attracted my attention, together with a bottle of red wine; these looked just the sort of luscious food which Mme. la Marquise would relish.

Well, sir, the law of God says: "Thou shalt not covet!" and no doubt that I committed a grievous sin when my hungry eyes fastened upon that roast capon and that bottle of Burgundy. We also know the stories of Judas Iscariot and of Jacob's children who sold their own brother Joseph into slavery—such a crime, *monsieur*, I took upon my conscience then; for just as the vision of Mme. la Marquise eating that roast capon and drinking that Burgundy rose before my eyes, my ears caught some fragments of the excited conversation which was going on all around me.

"He went this way!" someone said.

"No; that!" protested another.

"There's no sign of him now, anyway."

The owner of the shop was standing on his own doorstep, his legs wide apart, one arm on his wide hip, the other still brandishing the knife wherewith he had been carving for his customers.

"He can't have gone far," he said, as he smacked his thick lips.

"The impudent rascal, flaunting such fine clothes—like the *aristo* that he is."

"Bah! these cursed English! They are *aristos* all of them! And this one with his followers is no better than a spy!"

"Paid by that damned English Government to murder all our patriots and to rob the guillotine of her just dues."

"They say he had a hand in the escape of the *ci-devant* Duc de Sermeuse and all his brats from the very tumbril which was taking them to execution."

A cry of loathing and execration followed this statement. There was vigorous shaking of clenched fists and then a groan of baffled rage.

"We almost had him this time. If it had not been for these confounded, ill-lighted streets—"

"I would give something," concluded the shopkeeper, "if we could lay him by the heels."

"What would you give, Citizen Dompierre?" queried a woman in the crowd, with a ribald laugh, "one of your roast capons?"

"Aye, little mother," he replied jovially, "and a bottle of my best Burgundy to boot, to drink confusion to that meddlesome Englishman and his crowd and a speedy promenade up the steps of the guillotine."

Monsieur, I assure you that at that moment my heart absolutely stood still. The tempter stood at my elbow and whispered, and I deliberately smothered the call of my conscience. I did what Joseph's brethren did, what brought Judas Iscariot to hopeless remorse. There was no doubt that the hue and cry was after the two elegantly dressed gentlemen whom I had seen enter the dilapidated house in the Rue Blanche. For a second or two I closed my eyes and deliberately conjured up the vision of Mme. la Marquise fainting for lack of food, and of M. le Vicomte dying for want of sustenance; then I worked my way to the door of the shop and accosted the burly proprietor with as much boldness as I could muster.

"The two Englishmen passed by me at the top of the Rue Blanche," I said to him. "They went into a house . . . . I can show you which it is—"

In a moment I was surrounded by a screeching, gesticulating

crowd. I told my story as best I could; there was no turning back now from the path of cowardice and of crime. I saw that brute Dompierre pick up the largest roast capon from the front of his shop, together with a bottle of that wine which I had coveted; then he thrust both these treasures into my trembling hands and said:

"*En avant!*"

And we all started to run up the street, shouting: "Death to the English spies!" I was the hero of the expedition. Dompierre and another man carried me, for I was too weak to go as fast as they wished. I was hugging the capon and the bottle of wine to my heart; I had need to do that, so as to still the insistent call of my conscience, for I felt a coward—a mean, treacherous, abominable coward!

When we reached the house and I pointed it out to Dompierre, the crowd behind us gave a cry of triumph. In the topmost storey a window was thrown open, two heads appeared silhouetted against the light within, and the cry of triumph below was answered by a merry, prolonged laugh from above.

I was too dazed to realise very clearly what happened after that. Dompierre, I know, kicked open the door of the house, and the crowd rushed in, in his wake. I managed to keep my feet and to work my way gradually out of the crowd. I must have gone on mechanically, almost unconsciously, for the next thing that I remember with any distinctness was that I found myself once more speeding down the Rue Blanche, with all the yelling and shouting some little way behind me.

With blind instinct, too, I had clung to the capon and the wine, the price of my infamy. I was terribly weak and felt sick and faint, but I struggled on for a while, until my knees refused me service and I came down on my two hands, whilst the capon rolled away into the gutter, and the bottle of Burgundy fell with a crash against the pavement, scattering its precious contents in every direction.

There I lay, wretched, despairing, hardly able to move, when suddenly I heard rapid and firm footsteps immediately behind me, and the next moment two firm hands had me under the arms, and I heard a voice saying:

"Steady, old friend. Can you get up? There! Is that better?"

The same firm hands raised me to my feet. At first, I was too dazed to see anything, but after a moment or two I was able to look around me, and, by the light of a street lanthorn immediately overhead, I recognised the tall, elegantly dressed Englishman and his friend, whom I had just betrayed to the fury of Dompierre and a savage mob.

I thought that I was dreaming, and I suppose that my eyes betrayed the horror which I felt, for the stranger looked at me scrutinisingly for a moment or two, then he gave the quaintest laugh I had ever heard in all my life, and said something to his friend in English, which this time I failed to understand.

Then he turned to me:

"By my faith," he said in perfect French—so that I began to doubt if he was an English spy after all—"I verily believe that you are the clever rogue, eh? who obtained a roast capon and a bottle of wine from that fool Dompierre. He and his boon companions are venting their wrath on you, old *compeer*; they are calling you liar and traitor and cheat, in the intervals of wrecking what is left of the house, out of which my friend and I have long since escaped by climbing up the neighbouring gutter-pipes and scrambling over the adjoining roofs."

Monsieur, will you believe me when I say that he was actually saying all this in order to comfort me? I could have sworn to that because of the wonderful kindliness which shone out of his eyes, even through the good-humoured mockery wherewith he obviously regarded me. Do you know what I did then, *monsieur*? I just fell on my knees and loudly thanked God that he was safe; at which both he and his friend once again began to laugh, for all the world like two schoolboys who had escaped a whipping, rather than two men who were still threatened with death.

"Then it *was* you!" said the taller stranger, who was still laughing so heartily that he had to wipe his eyes with his exquisite lace handkerchief.

"May God forgive me," I replied.

The next moment his arm was again round me. I clung to him as to a rock, for of a truth I had never felt a grasp so steady and withal so gentle and kindly, as was his around my shoulders. I tried to murmur words of thanks, but again that wretched feeling of sickness and faintness overcame me, and for a second or two it seemed to me as if I were slipping into another world. The stranger's voice came to my ear, as it were through cotton-wool.

"The man is starving," he said. "Shall we take him over to your lodgings, Tony? They are safer than mine. He may be able to walk in a minute or two, if not I can carry him."

My senses at this partly returned to me, and I was able to protest feebly:

"No, no! I must go back—I must—kind sirs," I murmured. "Mme.

La Marquise will be getting so anxious."

No sooner were these foolish words out of my mouth than I could have bitten my tongue out for having uttered them; and yet, somehow, it seemed as if it was the stranger's magnetic personality, his magic voice and kindly act towards me, who had so basely sold him to his enemies, which had drawn them out of me. He gave a low, prolonged whistle.

"Mme. la Marquise?" he queried, dropping his voice to a whisper.

Now to have uttered Mme. la Marquise de Mortaine's name here in Lyons, where every aristocrat was termed a traitor and sent without trial to the guillotine, was in itself an act of criminal folly, and yet— you may believe me, *monsieur*, or not—there was something within me just at that moment that literally compelled me to open my heart out to this stranger, whom I had so basely betrayed, and who requited my abominable crime with such gentleness and mercy. Before I fully realised what I was doing, *monsieur*, I had blurted out the whole history of Mme. la Marquise's flight and of M. le Vicomte's sickness to him. He drew me under the cover of an open doorway, and he and his friend listened to me without speaking a word until I had told them my pitiable tale to the end.

When I had finished he said quietly:

"Take me to see Mme. la Marquise, old friend. Who knows? perhaps I may be able to help."

Then he turned to his friend.

"Will you wait for me at my lodgings, Tony," he said, "and let Ffoulkes and Hastings know that I may wish to speak with them on my return?"

He spoke like one who had been accustomed all his life to give command, and I marvelled how his friend immediately obeyed him. Then when the latter had disappeared down the dark street, the stranger once more turned to me.

"Lean on my arm, good old friend," he said, "and we must try and walk as quickly as we can. The sooner we allay the anxieties of Mme. la Marquise the better."

I was still hugging the roast capon with one arm, with the other I clung to him as together we walked in the direction of the Rue des Pipots. On the way we halted at a respectable eating-house, where my protector gave me some money wherewith to buy a bottle of good wine and sundry provisions and delicacies which we carried home with us.

Never shall I forget the look of horror which came in Mme. la Marquise's eyes when she saw me entering our miserable attic in the company of a stranger. The last of the little bit of tallow candle flickered in its socket. *Madame* threw her emaciated arms over her child, just like some poor hunted animal defending its young. I could almost hear the cry of terror which died down in her throat ere it reached her lips. But then, *monsieur*, to see the light of hope gradually illuminating her pale, wan face as the stranger took her hand and spoke to her—oh! so gently and so kindly—was a sight which filled my poor, half-broken heart with joy.

"The little invalid must be seen by a doctor at once," he said, "after that only can we think of your ultimate safety."

Mme. la Marquise, who herself was terribly weak and ill, burst out crying. "Would I not have taken him to a doctor ere now?" she murmured through her tears. "But there is no doctor in Lyons. Those who have not been arrested as traitors have fled from this stricken city. And my little Jose is dying for want of medical care."

"Your pardon, *madame*," he rejoined gently, "one of the ablest doctors in France is at present in Lyons—"

"That infamous Laporte," she broke in, horrified. "He would snatch my sick child from my arms and throw him to the guillotine."

"He would save your boy from disease," said the stranger earnestly, "his own professional pride or professional honour, whatever he might choose to call it, would compel him to do that. But the moment the doctor's work was done, that of the executioner would commence."

"You see, milor," moaned *Madame* in pitiable agony, "that there is no hope for us."

"Indeed, there is," he replied. "We must get M. le Vicomte well first—after that we shall see."

"But you are not proposing to bring that infamous Laporte to my child's bedside!" she cried in horror.

"Would you have your child die here before your eyes," retorted the stranger, "as he undoubtedly will this night?"

This sounded horribly cruel, and the tone in which it was said was commanding. There was no denying its truth. M. le Vicomte was dying. I could see that. For a moment or two *madame* remained quite still, with her great eyes, circled with pain and sorrow, fixed upon the stranger. He returned her gaze steadily and kindly, and gradually that frozen look of horror in her pale face gave place to one of deep puzzlement, and through her bloodless lips there came the words, faintly murmured: "Who are you?"

He gave no direct reply, but from his little finger he detached a ring and held it out for her to see. I saw it too, for I was standing close by Mme. la Marquise, and the flickering light of the tallow candle fell full upon the ring. It was of gold, and upon it there was an exquisitely modelled, five-petalled little flower in vivid red enamel.

Madame la Marquise looked at the ring, then once again up into his face. He nodded assent, and my heart seemed even then to stop its beating as I gazed upon his face. Had we not—all of us—heard of the gallant Scarlet Pimpernel? And did I not know—far better than Mme. la Marquise herself—the full extent of his gallantry and his self-sacrifice? The hue and cry was after him. Human bloodhounds were even now on his track, and he spoke calmly of walking out again in the streets of Lyons and of affronting that infamous Laporte, who would find glory in sending him to death. I think he guessed what was passing in my mind, for he put a finger up to his lip and pointed significantly to M. le Vicomte.

But it was beautiful to see how completely Mme. la Marquise now trusted him. At his bidding she even ate a little of the food and drank some wine—and I was forced to do likewise. And even when *anon* he declared his intention of fetching Laporte immediately, she did not flinch. She kissed M. le Vicomte with passionate fervour, and then gave the stranger her solemn promise that the moment he returned she would take refuge in the next room and never move out of it until after Laporte had departed.

When he went I followed him to the top of the stairs. I was speechless with gratitude and also with fears for him. But he took my hand and said, with that same quaint, somewhat inane laugh which was so characteristic of him:

"Be of good cheer, old fellow! Those confounded murderers will not get me this time."

3

Less than half an hour later, *monsieur*, Citizen Laporte, one of the most skilful doctors in France and one of the most bloodthirsty tyrants this execrable Revolution has known, was sitting at the bedside of M. le Vicomte de Mortaine, using all the skill, all the knowledge he possessed in order to combat the dread disease of which the child was dying, ere he came to save him—as he cynically remarked in my hearing—for the guillotine.

I heard afterwards how it all came about.

Laporte, it seems, was in the habit of seeing patients in his own house every evening after he had settled all his business for the day. What a strange contradiction in the human heart, eh, *monsieur?* The tiger turned lamb for the space of one hour in every twenty-four—the butcher turned healer. How well the English milor had gauged the strange personality of that redoubtable man! Professional pride—interest in intricate cases—call it what you will—was the only redeeming feature in Laporte's abominable character. Everything else in him, every thought, every action was ignoble, cruel and vengeful.

Milor that night mingled with the crowd who waited on the human hyena to be cured of their hurts. It was a motley crowd that filled the dreaded pro-consul's ante-chamber—men, women and children—all of them too much preoccupied with their own troubles to bestow more than a cursory glance on the stranger who, wrapped in a dark mantle, quietly awaited his turn. One or two muttered curses were flung at the *aristo*, one or two spat in his direction to express hatred and contempt, then the door which gave on the inner chamber would be flung open—a number called—one patient would walk out, another walk in—and in the ever-recurring incident the stranger for the nonce was forgotten.

His turn came—his number being called—it was the last on the list, and the ante-chamber was now quite empty save for him. He walked into the presence of the pro-consul. Claude Lemoine, who was on guard in the room at the time, told me that just for the space of two seconds the two men looked at one another. Then the stranger threw back his head and said quietly:

"There's a child dying of pleurisy, or worse, in an attic in the Rue des Pipots. There's not a doctor left in Lyons to attend on him, and the child will die for want of medical skill. Will you come to him, Citizen Doctor?"

It seems that for a moment or two Laporte hesitated.

"You look to me uncommonly like an *aristo*, and therefore a traitor," he said, "and I've half a mind—"

"To call your guard and order my immediate arrest," broke in milor with a whimsical smile, "but in that case a citizen of France will die for want of a doctor's care. Let me take you to the child's bedside, Citizen Doctor, you can always have me arrested afterwards."

But Laporte still hesitated.

"How do I know that you are not one of those English spies?" he began.

"Take it that I am," rejoined milor imperturbably, "and come and see the patient."

Never had a situation been carried off with so bold a hand. Claude Lemoine declared that Laporte's mouth literally opened for the call which would have summoned the sergeant of the guard into the room and ordered the summary arrest of this impudent stranger. During the veriest fraction of a second life and death hung in the balance for the gallant English milor. In the heart of Laporte every evil passion fought the one noble fibre within him. But the instinct of the skilful healer won the battle, and the next moment he had hastily collected what medicaments and appliances he might require, and the two men were soon speeding along the streets in the direction of the Rue des Pipots.

★★★★★★

During the whole of that night, milor and Laporte sat together by the bedside of M. le Vicomte. Laporte only went out once in order to fetch what further medicaments he required. Mme. la Marquise took the opportunity of running out of her hiding-place in order to catch a glimpse of her child. I saw her take milor's hand and press it against her heart in silent gratitude. On her knees she begged him to go away and leave her and the boy to their fate. Was it likely that he would go? But she was so insistent that at last he said:

"*Madame*, let me assure you that even if I were prepared to play the coward's part which you would assign to me, it is not in my power to do so at this moment. Citizen Laporte came to this house under the escort of six picked men of his guard. He has left these men stationed on the landing outside this door."

Madame la Marquise gave a cry of terror, and once more that pathetic look of horror came into her face. Milor took her hand and then pointed to the sick child.

"*Madame*," he said, "M. le Vicomte is already slightly better. Thanks to medical skill and a child's vigorous hold on life, he will live. The rest is in the hands of God."

Already the heavy footsteps of Laporte were heard upon the creaking stairs. Mme. la Marquise was forced to return to her hiding-place.

Soon after dawn he went. M. le Vicomte was then visibly easier. Laporte had all along paid no heed to me, but I noticed that once or twice during his long vigil by the sick-bed his dark eyes beneath their overhanging brows shot a quick suspicious look at the door behind which cowered Mme. la Marquise. I had absolutely no doubt in my mind then that he knew quite well who his patient was.

He gave certain directions to milor—there were certain fresh medicaments to be got during the day. While he spoke, there was a sinister glint in his eyes—half cynical, wholly menacing—as he looked up into the calm, impassive face of milor.

"It is essential for the welfare of the patient that these medicaments be got for him during the day," he said dryly, "and the guard have orders to allow you to pass in and out. But you need have no fear," he added significantly, "I will leave an escort outside the house to accompany you on your way."

He gave a mocking, cruel laugh, the meaning of which was unmistakable. His well-drilled human bloodhounds would be on the track of the English spy, whenever the latter dared to venture out into the streets.

Mme. la Marquise and I were prisoners for the day. We spent it in watching alternately beside M. le Vicomte. But milor came and went as freely as if he had not been carrying his precious life in his hands every time that he ventured outside the house.

In the evening Laporte returned to see his patient, and again the following morning, and the next evening. M. le Vicomte was making rapid progress towards recovery.

The third day in the morning Laporte pronounced his patient to be out of danger, but said that he would nevertheless come again to see him at the usual hour in the evening. Directly he had gone, milor went out in order to bring in certain delicacies of which the invalid was now allowed to partake. I persuaded *Madame* to lie down and have a couple of hours' good sleep in the inner attic, while I stayed to watch over the child.

To my horror, hardly had I taken up my stand at the foot of the bed when Laporte returned; he muttered something as he entered about having left some important appliance behind, but I was quite convinced that he had been on the watch until milor was out of sight, and then slipped back in order to find me and *Madame* here alone.

He gave a glance at the child and another at the door of the inner attic, then he said in a loud voice:

"Yes, another twenty-four hours and my duties as doctor will cease and those of patriot will re-commence. But Mme. la Marquise de Mortaine need no longer be in any anxiety about her son's health, nor will Mme. la Guillotine be cheated of a pack of rebels."

He laughed, and was on the point of turning on his heel when the door which gave on the smaller attic was opened and Mme. la Marquise appeared upon the threshold.

Monsieur, I had never seen her look more beautiful than she did now in her overwhelming grief. Her face was as pale as death, her eyes, large and dilated, were fixed upon the human monster who had found it in his heart to speak such cruel words. Clad in a miserable, threadbare gown, her rich brown hair brought to the top of her head like a crown, she looked more regal than any queen.

But proud as she was, *monsieur*, she yet knelt at the feet of that wretch. Yes, knelt, and embraced his knees and pleaded in such pitiable accents as would have melted the heart of a stone. She pleaded, *monsieur*—ah, not for herself. She pleaded for her child and for me, her faithful servant, and she pleaded for the gallant gentleman who had risked his life for the sake of the child, who was nothing to him.

"Take me!" she said. "I come of a race that have always known how to die! But what harm has that innocent child done in this world? What harm has poor old Jean-Pierre done, and, oh . . . . is the world so full of brave and noble men that the bravest of them all be so unjustly sent to death?"

Ah, *monsieur*, any man, save one of those abject products of that hideous Revolution, would have listened to such heartrending accents. But this man only laughed and turned on his heel without a word.

★★★★★★

Shall I ever forget the day that went by? Mme. la Marquise was well-nigh prostrate with terror, and it was heartrending to watch the noble efforts which she made to amuse M. le Vicomte. The only gleams of sunshine which came to us out of our darkness were the brief appearances of milor. Outside we could hear the measured tramp of the guard that had been set there to keep us close prisoners. They were relieved every six hours, and, in fact, we were as much under arrest as if we were already incarcerated in one of the prisons of Lyons.

At about four o'clock in the afternoon milor came back to us after a brief absence. He stayed for a little while playing with M. le Vicomte. Just before leaving he took *Madame's* hand in his and said very earnestly, and sinking his voice to the merest whisper:

"Tonight! Fear nothing! Be ready for anything! Remember that the League of the Scarlet Pimpernel have never failed to succour, and that I hereby pledge you mine honour that you and those you care for will be out of Lyons this night."

He was gone, leaving us to marvel at his strange words. Mme. la Marquise after that was just like a person in a dream. She hardly spoke to me, and the only sound that passed her lips was a quaint little lullaby which she sang to M. le Vicomte ere he dropped off to sleep.

The hours went by leaden-footed. At every sound on the stairs, *Madame* started like a frightened bird. That infamous Laporte usually paid his visits at about eight o'clock in the evening, and after it became quite dark, *Madame* sat at the tiny window, and I felt that she was counting the minutes which still lay between her and the dreaded presence of that awful man.

At a quarter before eight o'clock we heard the usual heavy footfall on the stairs. *Madame* started up as if she had been struck. She ran to the bed—almost like one demented, and wrapping the one poor blanket round M. le Vicomte, she seized him in her arms. Outside we could hear Laporte's raucous voice speaking to the guard. His usual query: "Is all well?" was answered by the brief: "All well, citizen." Then he asked if the English spy were within, and the sentinel replied: "No, citizen, he went out at about five o'clock and has not come back since."

"Not come back since five o'clock?" said Laporte with a loud curse. "*Pardi!* I trust that that fool Caudy has not allowed him to escape."

"I saw Caudy about an hour ago, citizen," said the man.

"Did he say anything about the Englishman then?"

It seemed to us, who were listening to this conversation with bated breath, that the man hesitated a moment ere he replied; then he spoke with obvious nervousness.

"As a matter of fact, citizen," he said, "Caudy thought then that the Englishman was inside the house, whilst I was equally sure that I had seen him go downstairs an hour before."

"A thousand devils!" cried Laporte with a savage oath, "if I find that you, Citizen Sergeant, or Caudy have blundered there will be trouble for you."

To the accompaniment of a great deal more swearing he suddenly kicked open the door of our attic with his boot, and then came to a standstill on the threshold with his hands in the pockets of his breeches and his legs planted wide apart, face to face with Mme. la Marquise, who confronted him now, herself like a veritable tigress who is defending her young.

He gave a loud, mocking laugh.

"Ah, the *aristos!*" he cried, "waiting for that cursed Englishman, what? to drag you and your brat out of the claws of the human tiger . . . . Not so, my fine *ci-devant marquise.* The brat is no longer sick—he is well enough, anyhow, to breathe the air of the prisons of Lyons for a few days pending a final rest in the arms of Mme. la Guillotine. Citizen Sergeant," he called over his shoulder, "escort these *aristos* to my carriage downstairs. When the Englishman returns, tell him he will find his friends under the tender care of Doctor Laporte. *En avant,* little mother," he added, as he gripped Mme. la Marquise tightly by the arm, "and you, old scarecrow," he concluded, speaking to me over his shoulder, "follow the Citizen Sergeant, or——"

Mme. la Marquise made no resistance. As I told you, she had been, since dusk, like a person in a dream; so, what could I do but follow her noble example? Indeed, I was too dazed to do otherwise.

We all went stumbling down the dark, rickety staircase, Laporte leading the way with Mme. la Marquise, who had M. le Vicomte tightly clasped in her arms. I followed with the sergeant, whose hand was on my shoulder; I believe that two soldiers walked behind, but of that I cannot be sure.

At the bottom of the stairs through the open door of the house I caught sight of the vague outline of a large *barouche*, the lanthorns of which threw a feeble light upon the cruppers of two horses and of a couple of men sitting on the box.

Mme. la Marquise stepped quietly into the carriage. Laporte followed her, and I was bundled in in his wake by the rough hands of the soldiery. Just before the order was given to start, Laporte put his head out of the window and shouted to the sergeant:

"When you see Caudy tell him to report himself to me at once. I will be back here in half an hour; keep strict guard as before until then, Citizen Sergeant."

The next moment the coachman cracked his whip, Laporte called loudly, "*En avant!*" and the heavy *barouche* went rattling along the ill-paved streets.

Inside the carriage all was silence. I could hear Mme. la Marquise softly whispering to M. le Vicomte, and I marvelled how wondrously calm—nay, cheerful, she could be. Then suddenly I heard a sound which of a truth did make my heart stop its beating. It was a quaint and prolonged laugh which I once thought I would never hear again on this earth. It came from the corner of the *barouche* next to where Mme. la Marquise was so tenderly and gaily crooning to her child.

And a kindly voice said merrily:

"In half an hour we shall be outside Lyons. Tomorrow we'll be across the Swiss frontier. We've cheated that old tiger after all. What say you, Mme. la Marquise?"

It was milor's voice, and he was as merry as a schoolboy.

"I told you, old Jean-Pierre," he added, as he placed that firm hand which I loved so well upon my knee, "I told you that those confounded murderers would not get me this time."

And to think that I did not know him, as he stood less than a quarter of an hour ago upon the threshold of our attic in the hideous guise of that abominable Laporte. He had spent two days in collecting old clothes that resembled those of that infamous wretch, and in taking possession of one of the derelict rooms in the house in the Rue des Pipots. Then while we were expecting every moment that Laporte would order our arrest, milor assumed the personality of the monster, hoodwinked the sergeant on the dark staircase, and by that wonderfully audacious coup saved Mme. la Marquise, M. le Vicomte and my humble self from the guillotine.

Money, of which he had plenty, secured us immunity on the way, and we were in safety over the Swiss frontier, leaving Laporte to eat out his tigerish heart with baffled rage.

Out of the Jaws of Death

*(Being a fragment from the diary of Valentine Lemercier, in the posses-
sion of her great-granddaughter.)*

We were such a happy family before this terrible Revolution broke
out; we lived rather simply, but very comfortably, in our dear old home
just on the borders of the forest of Compiègne. Jean and Andre were
the twins; just fifteen years old they were when King Louis was deposed from the throne of France which God had given him, and sent
to prison like a common criminal, with our beautiful Queen Marie
Antoinette and the royal children, and Madame Elizabeth, who was so
beloved by the poor!

Ah! that seems very, very long ago now. No doubt you know better than I do all that happened in our beautiful land of France and in
lovely Paris about that time: goods and property confiscated, innocent
men, women, and children condemned to death for acts of treason
which they had never committed.

It was in August last year that they came to "*Mon Repos*" and arrested papa, and *maman*, and us four young ones and dragged us to
Paris, where we were imprisoned in a narrow and horribly dank vault
in the Abbaye, where all day and night through the humid stone walls
we heard cries and sobs and moans from poor people, who no doubt
were suffering the same sorrows and the same indignities as we were.

I had just passed my nineteenth birthday, and Marguerite was only
thirteen. *Maman* was a perfect angel during that terrible time; she kept
up our courage and our faith in God in a way that no one else could
have done. Every night and morning we knelt round her knee and
papa sat close beside her, and we prayed to God for deliverance from
our own afflictions, and for the poor people who were crying and
moaning all the day.

But of what went on outside our prison walls we had not an idea,
though sometimes poor papa would brave the warder's brutalities and
ask him questions of what was happening in Paris every day.

"They are hanging all the *aristos* to the street-lamps of the city," the man would reply with a cruel laugh, "and it will be your turn next."

We had been in prison for about a fortnight, when one day—oh! shall I ever forget it?—we heard in the distance a noise like the rumbling of thunder; nearer and nearer it came, and soon the sound became less confused, cries and shrieks could be heard above that rumbling din; but so weird and menacing did those cries seem that instinctively—though none of us knew what they meant—we all felt a nameless terror grip our hearts.

Oh! I am not going to attempt the awful task of describing to you all the horrors of that never-to-be-forgotten day. People, who today cannot speak without a shudder of the September massacres, have not the remotest conception of what really happened on that awful second day of that month.

We are all at peace and happy now, but whenever my thoughts fly back to that morning, whenever the ears of memory recall those hideous yells of fury and of hate, coupled with the equally horrible cries for pity, which pierced through the walls behind which the six of us were crouching, trembling, and praying, whenever I think of it all my heart still beats violently with that same nameless dread which held it in its deathly grip then.

Hundreds of men, women, and children were massacred in the prisons of that day—it was a St. Bartholomew even more hideous than the last.

Maman was trying in vain to keep our thoughts fixed upon God—papa sat on the stone bench, his elbows resting on his knees, his head buried in his hands; but *maman* was kneeling on the floor, with her dear arms encircling us all and her trembling lips moving in continuous prayer.

We felt that we were facing death—and what a death, O my God!

Suddenly the small grated window—high up in the dank wall—became obscured. I was the first to look up, but the cry of terror which rose from my heart was choked ere it reached my throat.

Jean and Andre looked up, too, and they shrieked, and so did Marguerite, and papa jumped up and ran to us and stood suddenly between us and the window like a tiger defending its young.

But we were all of us quite silent now. The children did not even cry; they stared, wide-eyed, paralysed with fear.

Only *maman* continued to pray, and we could hear papa's rapid and stertorous breathing as he watched what was going on at that window above.

Heavy blows were falling against the masonry round the grating, and we could hear the nerve-racking sound of a file working on the iron bars; and farther away, below the window, those awful yells of human beings transformed by hate and fury into savage beasts.

How long this horrible suspense lasted I cannot now tell you; the next thing I remember clearly is a number of men in horrible ragged clothing pouring into our vault-like prison from the window above; the next moment they rushed at us simultaneously—or so it seemed to me, for I was just then recommending my soul to God, so certain was I that in that same second I would cease to live.

It was all like a dream, for instead of the horrible shriek of satisfied hate which we were all expecting to hear, a whispering voice, commanding and low, struck our ears and dragged us, as it were, from out the abyss of despair into the sudden light of hope.

"If you will trust us," the voice whispered, "and not be afraid, you will be safely out of Paris within an hour."

Papa was the first to realise what was happening; he had never lost his presence of mind even during the darkest moment of this terrible time, and he said quite calmly and steadily now:

"What must we do?"

"Persuade the little ones not to be afraid, not to cry, to be as still and silent as may be," continued the voice, which I felt must be that of one of God's own angels, so exquisitely kind did it sound to my ear.

"They will be quiet and still without persuasion," said papa; "eh, children?"

And Jean, Andre, and Marguerite murmured: "Yes!" whilst *maman* and I drew them closer to us and said everything we could think of to make them still more brave.

And the whispering, commanding voice went on after a while:

"Now will you allow yourselves to be muffled and bound, and, after that, will you swear that whatever happens, whatever you may see or hear, you will neither move nor speak? Not only your own lives, but those of many brave men will depend upon your fulfilment of this oath."

Papa made no reply save to raise his hand and eyes up to where God surely was watching over us all. *Maman* said in her gentle, even voice:

"For myself and my children, I swear to do all that you tell us."

A great feeling of confidence had entered into her heart, just as it had done into mine. We looked at one another and knew that we were both thinking of the same thing: we were thinking of the brave Englishman and his gallant little band of heroes, about whom we had heard many wonderful tales—how they had rescued a number of innocent people who were unjustly threatened with the guillotine; and we all knew that the tall figure, disguised in horrible rags, who spoke to us with such a gentle yet commanding voice, was the man whom rumour credited with supernatural powers, and who was known by the mysterious name of "The Scarlet Pimpernel."

Hardly had we sworn to do his bidding than his friends most unceremoniously threw great pieces of sacking over our heads, and then proceeded to tie ropes round our bodies. At least, I know that that is what one of them was doing to me, and from one or two whispered words of command which reached my ear I concluded that papa and *maman* and the children were being dealt with in the same summary way.

I felt hot and stifled under that rough bit of sacking, but I would not have moved or even sighed for worlds. Strangely enough, as soon as my eyes and ears were shut off from the sounds and sights immediately round me, I once more became conscious of the horrible and awful din which was going on, not only on the other side of our prison walls, but inside the whole of the Abbaye building and in the street beyond.

Once more I heard those terrible howls of rage and of satisfied hatred, uttered by the assassins who were being paid by the government of our beautiful country to butcher helpless prisoners in their hundreds.

Suddenly I felt myself hoisted up off my feet and slung up on to a pair of shoulders that must have been very powerful indeed, for I am no light weight, and once more I heard the voice, the very sound of which was delight, quite close to my ear this time, giving a brief and comprehensive command:

"All ready!—remember your part—*en avant!*"

Then it added in English. "Here, Tony, you start kicking against the door whilst we begin to shout!"

I loved those few words of English, and hoped that *maman* had heard them too, for it would confirm her—as it did me—in the happy knowledge that God and a brave man had taken our rescue in hand.

But from that moment we might have all been in the very antechamber of hell. I could hear the violent kicks against the heavy door of our prison, and our brave rescuers seemed suddenly to be transformed into a cageful of wild beasts. Their shouts and yells were as horrible as any that came to us from the outside, and I must say that the gentle, firm voice which I had learnt to love was as execrable as any I could hear.

Apparently, the door would not yield, as the blows against it became more and more violent, and presently from somewhere above my head—the window presumably—there came a rough call, and a raucous laugh:

"Why? what in the name of —— is happening here?"

And the voice near me answered back equally roughly: "A quarry of six—but we are caught in this confounded trap—get the door open for us, citizen—we want to get rid of this booty and go in search for more."

A horrible laugh was the reply from above, and the next instant I heard a terrific crash; the door had at last been burst open, either from within or without, I could not tell which, and suddenly all the din, the cries, the groans, the hideous laughter and bibulous songs which had sounded muffled up to now burst upon us with all their hideousness.

That was, I think, the most awful moment of that truly fearful hour. I could not have moved then, even had I wished or been able to do so; but I knew that between us all and a horrible, yelling, murdering mob there was now nothing—except the hand of God and the heroism of a band of English gentlemen.

Together they gave a cry—as loud, as terrifying as any that were uttered by the butchering crowd in the building, and with a wild rush they seemed to plunge with us right into the thick of the awful *mêlée*.

At least, that is what it all felt like to me, and afterwards I heard from our gallant rescuer himself that that is exactly what he and his friends did. There were eight of them altogether, and we four young ones had each been hoisted on a pair of devoted shoulders, whilst *maman* and papa were each carried by two men.

I was lying across the finest pair of shoulders in the world, and close to me was beating the bravest heart on God's earth.

Thus burdened, these eight noble English gentlemen charged right through an army of butchering, howling brutes, they themselves howling with the fiercest of them.

All around me I heard weird and terrific cries: "What ho! citizens—what have you there?"

"Six *aristos!*" shouted my hero boldly as he rushed on, forging his way through the crowd.

"What are you doing with them?" yelled a raucous voice.

"Food for the starving fish in the river," was the ready response. "Stand aside, citizen," he added, with a round curse; "I have my orders from Citizen Danton himself about these six *aristos*. You hinder me at your peril."

He was challenged over and over again in the same way, and so were his friends who were carrying papa and *maman* and the children; but they were always ready with a reply, ready with an invective or a curse; with eyes that could not see, one could imagine them as hideous, as vengeful, as cruel as the rest of the crowd.

I think that soon I must have fainted from sheer excitement and terror, for I remember nothing more till I felt myself deposited on a hard floor, propped against the wall, and the stifling piece of sacking taken off my head and face.

I looked around me, dazed and bewildered; gradually the horrors of the past hour came back to me, and I had to close my eyes again, for I felt sick and giddy with the sheer memory of it all.

But presently I felt stronger and looked around me again. Jean and Andre were squatting in a corner close by, gazing wide-eyed at the group of men in filthy, ragged clothing, who sat round a deal table in the centre of a small, ill-furnished room.

Maman was lying on a horsehair sofa at the other end of the room, with Marguerite beside her, and papa sat in a low chair by her side, holding her hand.

The voice I loved was speaking in its quaint, somewhat drawly cadence:

"You are quite safe now, my dear Monsieur Lemercier," it said; "after *Madame* and the young people have had a rest, some of my friends will find you suitable disguises, and they will escort you out of Paris, as they have some really genuine passports in their possessions, which we obtain from time to time through the agency of a personage highly placed in this murdering government, and with the help of English banknotes. Those passports are not always unchallenged, I must confess," added my hero with a quaint laugh; "but tonight everyone is busy murdering in one part of Paris, so the other parts are comparatively safe."

Then he turned to one of his friends and spoke to him in English:

"You had better see this through, Tony," he said, "with Hastings and Mackenzie. Three of you will be enough; I shall have need of the others."

No one seemed to question his orders. He had spoken, and the others made ready to obey. Just then papa spoke up:

"How are we going to thank you, sir?" he asked, speaking broken English, but with his habitual dignity of manner.

"By leaving your welfare in our hands, *Monsieur*," replied our gallant rescuer quietly.

Papa tried to speak again, but the Englishman put up his hand to stop any further talk.

"There is no time now, *Monsieur*," he said with gentle courtesy. "I must leave you, as I have much work yet to do."

"Where are you going, Blakeney?" asked one of the others.

"Back to the Abbaye prison," he said; "there are other women and children to be rescued there!"

The Traitor

1

Not one of them had really trusted him for some time now. Heaven and his conscience alone knew what had changed my Lord Kulmsted from a loyal friend and keen sportsman into a surly and dissatisfied adherent—adherent only in name.

Some say that lack of money had embittered him. He was a confirmed gambler, and had been losing over-heavily of late; and the League of the Scarlet Pimpernel demanded sacrifices of money at times from its members, as well as of life if the need arose. Others averred that jealousy against the chief had outweighed Kulmsted's honesty. Certain it is that his oath of fealty to the League had long ago been broken in the spirit. Treachery hovered in the air.

But the Scarlet Pimpernel himself, with that indomitable optimism of his, and almost maddening *insouciance*, either did not believe in Kulmsted's disloyalty or chose not to heed it.

He even asked him to join the present expedition—one of the most dangerous undertaken by the League for some time, and which had for its object the rescue of some women of the late unfortunate Marie Antoinette's household: maids and faithful servants, ruthlessly condemned to die for their tender adherence to a martyred queen. And yet eighteen pairs of faithful lips had murmured words of warning.

It was towards the end of November, 1793. The rain was beating down in a monotonous *drip, drip, drip* on to the roof of a derelict house in the Rue Berthier. The wan light of a cold winter's morning peeped in through the curtainless window and touched with its weird grey brush the pallid face of a young girl—a mere child—who sat in a dejected attitude on a rickety chair, with elbows leaning on the rough deal table before her, and thin, grimy fingers wandering with pathetic futility to her tearful eyes.

In the farther angle of the room a tall figure in dark clothes was made one, by the still lingering gloom, with the dense shadows beyond.

"We have starved," said the girl, with rebellious tears. "Father and I and the boys are miserable enough, God knows; but we have always been honest."

From out the shadows in that dark corner of the room there came the sound of an oath quickly suppressed.

"Honest!" exclaimed the man, with a harsh, mocking laugh, which made the girl wince as if with physical pain. "Is it honest to harbour the enemies of your country? Is it honest——"

But quickly he checked himself, biting his lips with vexation, feeling that his present tactics were not like to gain the day.

He came out of the gloom and approached the girl with every outward sign of eagerness. He knelt on the dusty floor beside her, his arms stole round her meagre shoulders, and his harsh voice was subdued to tones of gentleness.

"I was only thinking of your happiness, Yvonne," he said tenderly; "of poor blind papa and the two boys to whom you have been such a devoted little mother. My only desire is that you should earn the gratitude of your country by denouncing her most bitter enemy—an act of patriotism which will place you and those for whom you care for ever beyond the reach of sorrow or of want."

The voice, the appeal, the look of love, was more than the poor, simple girl could resist. Milor was so handsome, so kind, so good.

It had all been so strange: these English aristocrats coming here, she knew not whence, and who seemed fugitives even though they had plenty of money to spend. Two days ago, they had sought shelter like malefactors escaped from justice—in this same tumbledown, derelict house where she, Yvonne, with her blind father and two little brothers, crept in of nights, or when the weather was too rough for them all to stand and beg in the streets of Paris.

There were five of them altogether, and one seemed to be the chief. He was very tall, and had deep blue eyes, and a merry voice that went echoing along the worm-eaten old rafters. But milor—the one whose arms were encircling her even now—was the handsomest among them all. He had sought Yvonne out on the very first night when she had crawled shivering to that corner of the room where she usually slept.

The English aristocrats had frightened her at first, and she was for flying from the derelict house with her family and seeking shelter elsewhere; but he who appeared to be the chief had quickly reassured her. He seemed so kind and good, and talked so gently to blind papa, and made such merry jests with Francois and Clovis that she herself could scarce refrain from laughing through her tears.

But later on, in the night, milor—her milor, as she soon got to call him—came and talked so beautifully that she, poor girl, felt as if no music could ever sound quite so sweetly in her ear.

That was two days ago, and since then milor had often talked to her in the lonely, abandoned house, and Yvonne had felt as if she dwelt in Heaven. She still took blind papa and the boys out to beg in the streets, but in the morning, she prepared some hot coffee for the English aristocrats, and in the evening, she cooked them some broth. Oh! they gave her money lavishly; but she quite understood that they were in hiding, though what they had to fear, being English, she could not understand.

And now milor—her milor—was telling her that these Englishmen, her friends, were spies and traitors, and that it was her duty to tell Citizen Robespierre and the Committee of Public Safety all about them and their mysterious doings. And poor Yvonne was greatly puzzled and deeply distressed, because, of course, whatever milor said, that was the truth; and yet her conscience cried out within her poor little bosom, and the thought of betraying those kind Englishmen was horrible to her.

"Yvonne," whispered milor in that endearing voice of his, which was like the loveliest music in her ear, "my little Yvonne, you do trust me, do you not?"

"With all my heart, milor," she murmured fervently.

"Then, would you believe it of me that I would betray a real friend?"

"I believe, milor, that whatever you do is right and good."

A sigh of infinite relief escaped his lips.

"Come, that's better!" he said, patting her cheek kindly with his hand. "Now, listen to me, little one. He who is the chief among us here is the most unscrupulous and daring rascal whom the world has ever known. He it is who is called the 'Scarlet Pimpernel!'"

"The Scarlet Pimpernel!" murmured Yvonne, her eyes dilated with superstitious awe, for she too had heard of the mysterious Englishman and of his followers, who rescued aristocrats and traitors from the death to which the tribunal of the people had justly condemned them, and on whom the mighty hand of the Committee of Public Safety had never yet been able to fall.

"This Scarlet Pimpernel," said milor earnestly after a while, "is also mine own most relentless enemy. With lies and promises he induced me to join him in his work of spying and of treachery, forcing me to do this work against which my whole soul rebels. You can save me from this hated bondage, little one. You can make me free to live again, make me free to love and place my love at your feet."

His voice had become exquisitely tender, and his lips, as he whispered the heavenly words, were quite close to her ear. He, a great gentleman, loved the miserable little waif whose kindred consisted of a blind father and two half-starved little brothers, and whose only home was this miserable hovel, whence milor's graciousness and bounty would soon take her.

Do you think that Yvonne's sense of right and wrong, of honesty and treachery, should have been keener than that primeval instinct of a simple-hearted woman to throw herself trustingly into the arms of the man who has succeeded in winning her love?

Yvonne, subdued, enchanted, murmured still through her tears:

"What would milor have me do?"

Lord Kulmsted rose from his knees satisfied.

"Listen to me, Yvonne," he said. "You are acquainted with the Englishman's plans, are you not?"

"Of course," she replied simply. "He has had to trust me."

"Then you know that at sundown this afternoon I and the three others are to leave for Courbevoie on foot, where we are to obtain what horses we can whilst awaiting the chief."

"I did not know whither you and the other three gentlemen were going, milor," she replied; "but I did know that some of you were to make a start at four o'clock, whilst I was to wait here for your leader and prepare some supper against his coming."

"At what time did he tell you that he would come?"

"He did not say; but he did tell me that when he returns he will have friends with him—a lady and two little children. They will be hungry and cold. I believe that they are in great danger now, and that the brave English gentleman means to take them away from this awful Paris to a place of safety."

"The brave English gentleman, my dear," retorted milor, with a sneer, "is bent on some horrible work of spying. The lady and the two children are, no doubt, innocent tools in his hands, just as I am, and when he no longer needs them he will deliver them over to the Committee of Public Safety, who will, of a surety, condemn them to death. That will also be my fate, Yvonne, unless you help me now."

"Oh, no, no!" she exclaimed fervently. "Tell me what to do, milor, and I will do it."

"At sundown," he said, sinking his voice so low that even she could scarcely hear, "when I and the three others have started on our way, go straight to the house I spoke to you about in the Rue Dauphine—you know where it is?"

"Oh, yes, milor."

"You will know the house by its tumbledown portico and the tattered red flag that surmounts it. Once there, push the door open and walk in boldly. Then ask to speak with Citizen Robespierre."

"Robespierre?" exclaimed the child in terror.

"You must not be afraid, Yvonne," he said earnestly; "you must think of me and of what you are doing for me. My word on it— Robespierre will listen to you most kindly."

"What shall I tell him?" she murmured.

"That a mysterious party of Englishmen are in hiding in this house—that their chief is known among them as the Scarlet Pimpernel. The rest leave to Robespierre's discretion. You see how simple it is?"

It was indeed very simple! Nor did the child recoil any longer from the ugly task which milor, with suave speech and tender voice, was so ardently seeking to impose on her.

A few more words of love, which cost him nothing, a few kisses which cost him still less, since the wench loved him, and since she was young and pretty, and Yvonne was as wax in the hands of the traitor.

2

Silence reigned in the low-raftered room on the ground floor of the house in the Rue Dauphine.

Citizen Robespierre, chairman of the Cordeliers Club, the most bloodthirsty, most Evolutionary club of France, had just re-entered the room.

He walked up to the centre table, and through the close atmosphere, thick with tobacco smoke, he looked round on his assembled friends.

"We have got him," he said at last curtly.

"Got him! Whom?" came in hoarse cries from every corner of the room.

"That Englishman," replied the demagogue, "the Scarlet Pimpernel!"

A prolonged shout rose in response—a shout not unlike that of a caged herd of hungry wild beasts to whom a succulent morsel of flesh has unexpectedly been thrown.

"Where is he?" "Where did you get him?" "Alive or dead?" And many more questions such as these were hurled at the speaker from every side.

Robespierre, calm, impassive, immaculately neat in his tightly fitting coat, his smart breeches, and his lace cravat, waited awhile until the din had somewhat subsided. Then he said calmly:

"The Scarlet Pimpernel is in hiding in one of the derelict houses in the Rue Berthier."

Snarls of derision as vigorous as the former shouts of triumph drowned the rest of his speech.

"Bah! How often has that cursed Scarlet Pimpernel been said to be alone in a lonely house? Citizen Chauvelin has had him at his mercy several times in lonely houses."

And the speaker, a short, thick-set man with sparse black hair plastered over a greasy forehead, his shirt open at the neck, revealing a powerful chest and rough, hairy skin, spat in ostentatious contempt upon the floor.

"Therefore, will we not boast of his capture yet, Citizen Roger," resumed Robespierre imperturbably. "I tell you where the Englishman is. Do you look to it that he does not escape."

The heat in the room had become intolerable. From the grimy ceiling an oil-lamp, flickering low, threw lurid, ruddy lights on tricolour cockades, on hands that seemed red with the blood of innocent victims of lust and hate, and on faces glowing with desire and with anticipated savage triumph.

"Who is the informer?" asked Roger at last.

"A girl," replied Robespierre curtly. "Yvonne Lebeau, by name; she and her family live by begging. There are a blind father and two boys; they herd together at night in the derelict house in the Rue Berthier. Five Englishmen have been in hiding there these past few days. One of them is their leader. The girl believes him to be the Scarlet Pimpernel."

"Why has she not spoken of this before?" muttered one of the crowd, with some scepticism.

"Frightened, I suppose. Or the Englishman paid her to hold her tongue."

"Where is the girl now?"

"I am sending her straight home, a little ahead of us. Her presence should reassure the Englishman whilst we make ready to surround the house. In the meanwhile, I have sent special messengers to every gate of Paris with strict orders to the guard not to allow anyone out of the city until further orders from the Committee of Public Safety. And now," he added, throwing back his head with a gesture of proud challenge, "citizens, which of you will go man-hunting tonight?"

This time the strident roar of savage exultation was loud and deep enough to shake the flickering lamp upon its chain.

A brief discussion of plans followed, and Roger—he with the broad, hairy chest and that gleam of hatred for ever lurking in his deep-set, shifty eyes—was chosen the leader of the party.

Thirty determined and well-armed patriots set out against one man, who mayhap had supernatural powers. There would, no doubt, be some aristocrats, too, in hiding in the derelict house—the girl Lebeau, it seems, had spoken of a woman and two children. Bah! These would not count. It would be thirty to one, so let the Scarlet Pimpernel look to himself.

From the towers of Notre Dame, the big bell struck the hour of six, as thirty men in ragged shirts and torn breeches, shivering beneath a cold November drizzle, began slowly to wend their way towards the Rue Berthier.

They walked on in silence, not heeding the cold or the rain, but with eyes fixed in the direction of their goal, and nostrils quivering in the evening air with the distant scent of blood.

3

At the top of the Rue Berthier the party halted. On ahead—some two hundred metres farther—Yvonne Lebeau's little figure, with her ragged skirt pulled over her head and her bare feet pattering in the mud, was seen crossing one of those intermittent patches of light formed by occasional flickering street lamps, and then was swallowed up once more by the inky blackness beyond.

The Rue Berthier is a long, narrow, ill-paved and ill-lighted street, composed of low and irregular houses, which abut on the line of fortifications at the back, and are therefore absolutely inaccessible save from the front.

Midway down the street a derelict house rears ghostly debris of roofs and chimney-stacks upward to the sky. A tiny square of yellow light, blinking like a giant eye through a curtainless window, pierced the wall of the house. Roger pointed to that light.

"That," he said, "is the quarry where our fox has run to earth."

No one said anything; but the dank night air seemed suddenly alive with all the passions of hate let loose by thirty beating hearts.

The Scarlet Pimpernel, who had tricked them, mocked them, fooled them so often, was there, not two hundred metres away; and they were thirty to one, and all determined and desperate.

The darkness was intense.

Silently now the party approached the house, then again, they halted, within sixty metres of it.

"Hist!"

The whisper could scarce be heard, so low was it, like the sighing of the wind through a misty veil.

"Who is it?" came in quick challenge from Roger.

"I—Yvonne Lebeau!"

"Is he there?" was the eager whispered query.

"Not yet. But he may come at any moment. If he saw a crowd round the house, mayhap he would not come."

"He cannot see a crowd. The night is as dark as pitch."

"He can see in the darkest night," and the girl's voice sank to an awed whisper, "and he can hear through a stone wall."

Instinctively, Roger shuddered. The superstitious fear which the mysterious personality of the Scarlet Pimpernel evoked in the heart of every Terrorist had suddenly seized this man in its grip.

Try as he would, he did not feel as valiant as he had done when first he emerged at the head of his party from under the portico of the Cordeliers Club, and it was with none too steady a voice that he ordered the girl roughly back to the house. Then he turned once more to his men.

The plan of action had been decided on in the Club, under the presidency of Robespierre; it only remained to carry the plans through with success.

From the side of the fortifications there was, of course, nothing to fear. In accordance with military regulations, the walls of the houses there rose sheer from the ground without doors or windows, whilst the broken-down parapets and dilapidated roofs towered forty feet above the ground.

The derelict itself was one of a row of houses, some inhabited, others quite abandoned. It was the front of that row of houses, therefore, that had to be kept in view. Marshalled by Roger, the men flattened their meagre bodies against the walls of the houses opposite, and after that there was nothing to do but wait.

To wait in the darkness of the night, with a thin, icy rain soaking through ragged shirts and tattered breeches, with bare feet frozen by the mud of the road—to wait in silence while turbulent hearts beat well-nigh to bursting—to wait for food whilst hunger gnaws the bowels—to wait for drink whilst the parched tongue cleaves to the roof of the mouth—to wait for revenge whilst the hours roll slowly by and the cries of the darkened city are stilled one by one!

Once—when a distant bell tolled the hour of ten—a loud prolonged laugh, almost impudent in its suggestion of merry *insouciance*, echoed through the weird silence of the night.

Roger felt that the man nearest to him shivered at that sound, and he heard a volley or two of muttered oaths.

"The fox seems somewhere near," he whispered. "Come within. We'll wait for him inside his hole."

He led the way across the street, some of the men following him.

The door of the derelict house had been left on the latch. Roger pushed it open.

Silence and gloom here reigned supreme; utter darkness, too, save for a narrow streak of light which edged the framework of a door on the right. Not a sound stirred the quietude of this miserable hovel, only the creaking of boards beneath the men's feet as they entered.

Roger crossed the passage and opened the door on the right. His friends pressed closely round to him and peeped over his shoulder into the room beyond.

A guttering piece of tallow candle, fixed to an old tin pot, stood in the middle of the floor, and its feeble, flickering light only served to accentuate the darkness that lay beyond its range. One or two rickety chairs and a rough deal table showed vaguely in the gloom, and in the far corner of the room there lay a bundle of what looked like heaped-up rags, but from which there now emerged the sound of heavy breathing and also a little cry of fear.

"Yvonne," came in feeble, querulous accents from that same bundle of wretchedness, "are these the English milors come back at last?"

"No, no, father," was the quick whispered reply.

Roger swore a loud oath, and two puny voices began to whimper piteously.

"It strikes me the wench has been fooling us," muttered one of the men savagely.

The girl had struggled to her feet. She crouched in the darkness, and two little boys, half-naked and shivering, were clinging to her skirts.

The rest of the human bundle seemed to consist of an oldish man, with long, gaunt legs and arms blue with the cold. He turned vague, wide-open eyes in the direction whence had come the harsh voices.

"Are they friends, Yvonne?" he asked anxiously.

The girl did her best to reassure him.

"Yes, yes, father," she whispered close to his ear, her voice scarce above her breath; "they are good citizens who hoped to find the English milor here. They are disappointed that he has not yet come."

"Ah! but he will come, of a surety," said the old man in that querulous voice of his. "He left his beautiful clothes here this morning, and surely he will come to fetch them." And his long, thin hand pointed towards a distant corner of the room.

Roger and his friends, looking to where he was pointing, saw a parcel of clothes, neatly folded, lying on one of the chairs. Like so many wild cats snarling at sight of prey, they threw themselves upon those clothes, tearing them out from one another's hands, turning them over and over as if to force the cloth and satin to yield up the secret that lay within their folds.

In the skirmish a scrap of paper fluttered to the ground. Roger seized it with avidity, and, crouching on the floor, smoothed the paper out against his knee.

It contained a few hastily scrawled words, and by the feeble light of the fast-dying candle Roger spelt them out laboriously:

"If the finder of these clothes will take them to the cross-roads opposite the foot-bridge which leads straight to Courbevoie, and will do so before the clock of Courbevoie Church has struck the hour of midnight, he will be rewarded with the sum of five hundred *francs*."

"There is something more, Citizen Roger," said a raucous voice close to his ear.

"Look! Look, citizen—in the bottom corner of the paper!"

"The signature."

"A scrawl done in red," said Roger, trying to decipher it.

"It looks like a small flower."

"That accursed Scarlet Pimpernel!"

And even as he spoke the guttering tallow candle, swaying in its socket, suddenly went out with a loud splutter and a sizzle that echoed through the desolate room like the mocking laugh of ghouls.

4

Once more the tramp through the dark and deserted streets, with the drizzle—turned now to sleet—beating on thinly clad shoulders.

Fifteen men only on this tramp. The others remained behind to watch the house. Fifteen men, led by Roger, and with a blind old man, a young girl carrying a bundle of clothes, and two half-naked children dragged as camp-followers in the rear.

Their destination now was the sign-post which stands at the cross-roads, past the footbridge that leads to Courbevoie.

The guard at the Maillot Gate would have stopped the party, but Roger, member of the Committee of Public Safety, armed with his papers and his tricolour scarf, overruled Robespierre's former orders, and the party marched out of the gate.

They pressed on in silence, instinctively walking shoulder to shoulder, vaguely longing for the touch of another human hand, the sound of a voice that would not ring weirdly in the mysterious night.

There was something terrifying in this absolute silence, in such intense darkness, in this constant wandering towards a goal that seemed for ever distant, and in all this weary, weary fruitless waiting; and these men, who lived their life through, drunken with blood, deafened by the cries of their victims, satiated with the moans of the helpless and the innocent, hardly dared to look around them, lest they should see ghoulish forms flitting through the gloom.

Soon they reached the cross-roads, and in the dense blackness of the night the gaunt arms of the sign-post pointed ghostlike towards the north.

The men hung back, wrapped in the darkness as in a pall, while Roger advanced alone.

"*Hola!* Is anyone there?" he called softly.

Then, as no reply came, he added more loudly:

"*Hola!* A friend—with some clothes found in the Rue Berthier. Is anyone here? *Hola!* A friend!"

But only from the gently murmuring river far away the melancholy call of a waterfowl seemed to echo mockingly:

"A friend!"

Just then the clock of Courbevoie Church struck the midnight hour.

"It is too late," whispered the men.

They did not swear, nor did they curse their leader. Somehow it seemed as if they had expected all along that the Englishman would evade their vengeance yet again, that he would lure them out into the cold and into the darkness, and then that he would mock them, fool them, and finally disappear into the night.

It seemed futile to wait any longer. They were so sure that they had failed again.

"Who goes there?"

The sound of naked feet and of wooden *sabots* pattering on the distant footbridge had caused Roger to utter the quick challenge.

"*Hola! Hola!* Are you there?" was the loud, breathless response.

The next moment the darkness became alive with men moving quickly forward, and raucous shouts of "Where are they?" "Have you got them?" "Don't let them go!" filled the air.

"Got whom?" "Who are they?" "What is it?" were the wild counter-cries.

"The man! The girl! The children! Where are they?"

"What? Which? The Lebeau family? They are here with us."

"Where?"

Where, indeed? To a call to them from Roger there came no answer, nor did a hasty search result in finding them—the old man, the two boys, and the girl carrying the bundle of clothes had vanished into the night.

"In the name of ——, what does this mean?" cried hoarse voices in the crowd.

The newcomers, breathless, terrified, shaking with superstitious fear, tried to explain.

"The Lebeau family—the old man, the girl, the two boys—we discovered after your departure, locked up in the cellar of the house—prisoners."

"But, then—the others?" they gasped.

"The girl and the children whom you saw must have been some aristocrats in disguise. The old man who spoke to you was that cursed Englishman—the Scarlet Pimpernel!"

And as if in mocking confirmation of these words there suddenly rang, echoing from afar, a long and merry laugh.

"The Scarlet Pimpernel!" cried Roger. "In rags and barefooted! At him, citizens; he cannot have got far!"

"Hush! Listen!" whispered one of the men, suddenly gripping him by the arm.

And from the distance—though Heaven only knew from what direction—came the sound of horses' hoofs pawing the soft ground; the next moment they were heard galloping away at breakneck speed.

The men turned to run in every direction, blindly, aimlessly, in the dark, like bloodhounds that have lost the trail.

One man, as he ran, stumbled against a dark mass prone upon the ground. With a curse on his lips, he recovered his balance.

"Hold! What is this?" he cried.

Some of his comrades gathered round him. No one could see anything, but the dark mass appeared to have human shape, and it was bound round and round with cords. And now feeble moans escaped from obviously human lips.

"What is it? Who is it?" asked the men.

"An Englishman," came in weak accents from the ground.

"Your name?"

"I am called Kulmsted."

"Bah! An aristocrat!"

"No! An enemy of the Scarlet Pimpernel, like yourselves. I would have delivered him into your hands. But you let him escape you. As for me, he would have been wiser if he had killed me."

They picked him up and undid the cords from round his body, and later on took him with them back into Paris.

But there, in the darkness of the night, in the mud of the road, and beneath the icy rain, knees were shaking that had long ago forgotten how to bend, and hasty prayers were muttered by lips that were far more accustomed to blaspheme.

The Cabaret de la Liberté

1

"Eight!"

"Twelve!"

"Four!"

A loud curse accompanied this last throw, and shouts of ribald laughter greeted it.

"No luck, Guidal!"

"Always at the tail end of the cart, eh, citizen?"

"Do not despair yet, good old Guidal! Bad beginnings oft make splendid ends!"

Then once again the dice rattled in the boxes; those who stood around pressed closer round the gamesters; hot, avid faces, covered with sweat and grime, peered eagerly down upon the table.

"Eight and eleven—nineteen!"

"Twelve and zero! By Satan! Curse him! Just my luck!"

"Four and nine—thirteen! Unlucky number!"

"Now then—once more! I'll back Merri! Ten *assignats* of the most worthless kind! Who'll take me that Merri gets the wench in the end?"

This from one of the lookers-on, a tall, cadaverous-looking creature, with sunken eyes and broad, hunched-up shoulders, which were perpetually shaken by a dry, rasping cough that proclaimed the ravages of some mortal disease, left him trembling as with ague and brought beads of perspiration to the roots of his lank hair. A recrudescence of excitement went the round of the spectators. The gamblers sitting round a narrow deal table, on which past libations had left marks of sticky rings, had scarce room to move their elbows.

"Nineteen and four—twenty-three!"

"You are out of it, Desmonts!"

"Not yet!"

"Twelve and twelve!"

"There! What did I tell you?"

"Wait! wait! Now, Merri! Now! Remember I have backed you for ten *assignats*, which I propose to steal from the nearest Jew this very night."

"Thirteen and twelve! Twenty-five, by all the demons and the ghouls!" came with a triumphant shout from the last thrower.

"Merri has it! *Vive* Merri!" was the unanimous and clamorous response.

Merri was evidently the most popular amongst the three gamblers. Now he sprawled upon the bench, leaning his back against the table, and surveyed the assembled company with the air of an Achilles having vanquished his Hector.

"Good luck to you and to your *aristo!*" began his backer lustily—would, no doubt, have continued his song of praise had not a violent fit of coughing smothered the words in his throat. The hand which he had raised in order to slap his friend genially on the back now went with a convulsive clutch to his own chest.

But his obvious distress did not apparently disturb the equanimity of Merri, or arouse even passing interest in the lookers-on.

"May she have as much money as rumour avers," said one of the men sententiously.

Merri gave a careless wave of his grubby hand.

"More, citizen; more!" he said loftily.

Only the two losers appeared inclined to scepticism.

"Bah!" one of them said—it was Desmonts. "The whole matter of the woman's money may be a tissue of lies!"

"And England is a far cry!" added Guidal.

But Merri was not likely to be depressed by these dismal croakings.

"'Tis simple enough," he said philosophically, "to disparage the goods if you are not able to buy."

Then a lusty voice broke in from the far corner of the room:

"And now, Citizen Merri, 'tis time you remembered that the evening is hot and your friends thirsty!"

The man who spoke was a short, broad-shouldered creature, with crimson face surrounded by a shock of white hair, like a ripe tomato wrapped in cotton wool.

"And let me tell you," he added complacently, "that I have a cask of rum down below, which came straight from that accursed country, England, and is said to be the nectar whereon feeds that confounded Scarlet Pimpernel. It gives him the strength, so 'tis said, to intrigue successfully against the representatives of the people."

"Then by all means, citizen," concluded Merri's backer, still hoarse and spent after his fit of coughing, "let us have some of your nectar. My friend, Citizen Merri, will need strength and wits too, I'll warrant, for, after he has married the *aristo*, he will have to journey to England to pluck the rich dowry which is said to lie hidden there."

"Cast no doubt upon that dowry, Citizen Rateau, curse you!" broke in Merri, with a spiteful glance directed against his former rivals, "or Guidal and Desmonts will cease to look glum, and half my joy in the *aristo* will have gone."

After which, the conversation drifted to general subjects, became hilarious and ribald, while the celebrated rum from England filled the close atmosphere of the narrow room with its heady fumes.

2

Open to the street in front, the locality known under the pretentious title of "*Cabaret de la Liberté*" was a favoured one among the flotsam and jetsam of the population of this corner of old Paris; men and sometimes women, with nothing particular to do, no special means of livelihood save the battening on the countless miseries and sorrows which this Revolution, which was to have been so glorious, was bringing in its train; idlers and loafers, who would crawl desultorily down the few worn and grimy steps which led into the *cabaret* from the level of the street. There was always good brandy or *eau de vie* to be had there, and no questions asked, no scares from the revolutionary guards or the secret agents of the Committee of Public Safety, who knew better than to interfere with the citizen host and his dubious *clientèle*. There was also good Rhine wine or rum to be had, smuggled across from England or Germany, and no interference from the spies of some of those countless Committees, more autocratic than any *ci-devant* despot.

It was, in fact, an ideal place wherein to conduct those shady transactions which are unavoidable corollaries of an unfettered democracy. Projects of burglary, pillage, rapine, even murder, were hatched within this underground burrow, where, as soon as evening drew in, a solitary, smoky oil-lamp alone cast a dim light upon faces that liked to court the darkness, and whence no sound that was not meant for prying ears found its way to the street above. The walls were thick with grime and smoke, the floor mildewed and cracked; dirt vied with squalor to make the place a fitting abode for thieves and cut-throats, for some of those sinister night-birds, more vile even than those who shrieked with satisfied lust at sight of the tumbril, with its daily load of unfortunates for the guillotine.

On this occasion the project that was being hatched was one of the most abject. A young girl, known by some to be possessed of a fortune, was the stake for which these workers of iniquity gambled across one of mine host's greasy tables. The latest decree of the Convention, encouraging, nay, commanding, the union of aristocrats with so-called patriots, had fired the imagination of this nest of jail-birds with thoughts of glorious possibilities. Some of them had collected the necessary information; and the report had been encouraging.

That self-indulgent *aristo*, the *ci-devant* banker Amédé Vincent, who had expiated his villainies upon the guillotine, was known to have been successful in abstracting the bulk of his ill-gotten wealth and concealing it somewhere—it was not exactly known where, but thought to be in England—out of the reach, at any rate, of deserving patriots.

Some three or four years ago, before the glorious principles of Liberty, Equality, and Fraternity had made short shrift of all such pestilential aristocrats, the *ci-devant* banker, then a widower with an only daughter, Esther, had journeyed to England. He soon returned to Paris, however, and went on living there with his little girl in comparative retirement, until his many crimes found him out at last and he was made to suffer the punishment which he so justly deserved. Those crimes consisted for the most part in humiliating the aforesaid deserving patriots with his benevolence, shaming them with many kindnesses, and the simplicity of his home-life, and, above all, in flouting the decrees of the Revolutionary Government, which made every connection with *ci-devant* churches and priests a penal offence against the security of the State.

Amédé Vincent was sent to the guillotine, and the representatives of the people confiscated his house and all his property on which they could lay their hands; but they never found the millions which he was supposed to have concealed. Certainly, his daughter Esther—a young girl, not yet nineteen—had not found them either, for after her father's death she went to live in one of the poorer quarters of Paris, alone with an old and faithful servant named Lucienne. And while the Committee of Public Safety was deliberating whether it would be worthwhile to send Esther to the guillotine, to follow in her father's footsteps, a certain number of astute jail-birds plotted to obtain possession of her wealth.

The wealth existed, over in England; of that they were ready to take their oath, and the project which they had formed was as ingenious as it was diabolic: to feign a denunciation, to enact a pretended arrest, to place before the unfortunate girl the alternative of death or marriage with one of the gang, were the chief incidents of this iniquitous project, and it was in the *Cabaret de la Liberté* that lots were thrown as to which among the herd of miscreants should be the favoured one to play the chief role in the sinister drama.

The lot fell to Merri; but the whole gang was to have a share in the putative fortune—even Rateau, the wretched creature with the hacking cough, who looked as if he had one foot in the grave, and shivered as if he were stricken with ague, put in a word now and again to remind his good friend Merri that he, too, was looking forward to his share of the spoils. Merri, however, was inclined to repudiate him altogether.

"Why should I share with you?" he said roughly, when, a few hours later, he and Rateau parted in the street outside the *Cabaret de la Liberté*. "Who are you, I would like to know, to try and poke your ugly nose into my affairs? How do I know where you come from, and whether you are not some crapulent spy of one of those pestilential committees?"

From which eloquent flow of language, we may infer that the friendship between these two worthies was not of very old duration. Rateau would, no doubt, have protested loudly, but the fresh outer air had evidently caught his wheezy lungs, and for a minute or two he could do nothing but cough and splutter and groan, and cling to his unresponsive comrade for support. Then at last, when he had succeeded in recovering his breath, he said dolefully and with a ludicrous attempt at dignified reproach:

"Do not force me to remind you, Citizen Merri, that if it had not been for my suggestion that we should all draw lots, and then play hazard as to who shall be the chosen one to woo the *ci-devant* millionairess, there would soon have been a free fight inside the *cabaret*, a number of broken heads, and no decision whatever arrived at; whilst you, who were never much of a fighter, would probably be lying now helpless, with a broken nose, and deprived of some of your teeth, and with no chance of entering the lists for the heiress. Instead of which, here you are, the victor by a stroke of good fortune, which you should at least have the good grace to ascribe to me."

Whether the poor wretch's argument had any weight with Citizen Merri, or whether that worthy patriot merely thought that procrastination would, for the nonce, prove the best policy, it were impossible to say. Certain it is that in response to his companion's tirade he contented himself with a dubious grunt, and without another word turned on his heel and went slouching down the street.

3

For the persistent and optimistic romanticist, there were still one or two idylls to be discovered flourishing under the shadow of the grim and relentless Revolution. One such was that which had Esther Vincent and Jack Kennard for hero and heroine. Esther, the orphaned daughter of one of the richest bankers of pre-Revolution days, now a daily governess and household drudge at ten *francs* a week in the house of a retired butcher in the Rue Richelieu, and Jack Kennard, formerly the representative of a big English firm of woollen manufacturers, who had thrown up his employment and prospects in England in order to watch over the girl whom he loved.

He, himself an alien enemy, an Englishman, in deadly danger of his life every hour that he remained in France; and she, unwilling at the time to leave the horrors of revolutionary Paris while her father was lingering at the *Conciergerie* awaiting condemnation, as such forbidden to leave the city. So, Kennard stayed on, unable to tear himself away from her, and obtained an unlucrative post as accountant in a small wine shop over by Montmartre. His life, like hers, was hanging by a thread; any day, any hour now, some malevolent denunciation might, in the sight of the Committee of Public Safety, turn the eighteen years old "suspect" into a living peril to the State, or the alien enemy into a dangerous spy.

Some of the happiest hours these two spent in one another's company were embittered by that ever-present dread of the peremptory knock at the door, the portentous: "Open, in the name of the Law!" the perquisition, the arrest, to which the only issue, these days, was the guillotine.

But the girl was only just eighteen, and he not many years older, and at that age, in spite of misery, sorrow, and dread, life always has its compensations. Youth cries out to happiness so insistently that happiness is forced to hear, and for a few moments, at the least, drives care and even the bitterest anxiety away.

For Esther Vincent and her English lover there were moments when they believed themselves to be almost happy. It was in the evenings mostly, when she came home from her work and he was free to spend an hour or two with her. Then old Lucienne, who had been

427

Esther's nurse in the happy, olden days, and was an unpaid maid-of-all-work and a loved and trusted friend now, would bring in the lamp and pull the well-darned curtains over the windows. She would spread a clean cloth upon the table and bring in a meagre supper of coffee and black bread, perhaps a little butter or a tiny square of cheese. And the two young people would talk of the future, of the time when they would settle down in Kennard's old home, over in England, where his mother and sister even now were eating out their hearts with anxiety for him.

"Tell me all about the South Downs," Esther was very fond of saying; "and your village, and your house, and the rambler roses and the clematis arbour."

She never tired of hearing, or he of telling. The old Manor House, bought with his father's savings; the garden which was his mother's hobby; the cricket pitch on the village green. Oh, the cricket! She thought that so funny—the men in high, sugar-loaf hats, grown-up men, spending hours and hours, day after day, in banging at a ball with a wooden bat!

"Oh, Jack! The English are a funny, nice, dear, kind lot of people. I remember—"

She remembered so well that happy summer which she had spent with her father in England four years ago. It was after the Bastille had been stormed and taken, and the banker had journeyed to England with his daughter in something of a hurry. Then her father had talked of returning to France and leaving her behind with friends in England. But Esther would not be left. Oh, no! Even now she glowed with pride at the thought of her firmness in the matter. If she had remained in England she would never have seen her dear father again. Here remembrances grew bitter and sad, until Jack's hand reached soothingly, consolingly out to her, and she brushed away her tears, so as not to sadden him still more.

Then she would ask more questions about his home and his garden, about his mother and the dogs and the flowers; and once more they would forget that hatred and envy and death were already stalking their door.

4

"Open, in the name of the Law!"

It had come at last. A bolt from out the serene blue of their happiness. A rough, dirty, angry, cursing crowd, who burst through the heavy door even before they had time to open it. Lucienne collapsed into a chair, weeping and lamenting, with her apron thrown over her head. But Esther and Kennard stood quite still and calm, holding one another by the hand, just to give one another courage.

Some half dozen men stalked into the little room. Men? They looked like ravenous beasts, and were unspeakably dirty, wore soiled tricolour scarves above their tattered breeches in token of their official status. Two of them fell on the remnants of the meagre supper and devoured everything that remained on the table—bread, cheese, a piece of home-made sausage. The others ransacked the two attic-rooms which had been home for Esther and Lucienne: the little living-room under the sloping roof, with the small hearth on which very scanty meals were wont to be cooked, and the bare, narrow room beyond, with the iron bedstead, and the *palliasse* on the floor for Lucienne.

The men poked about everywhere, struck great, spiked sticks through the poor bits of bedding, and ripped up the palliasse. They tore open the drawers of the rickety chest and of the broken-down wardrobe, and did not spare the unfortunate young girl a single humiliation or a single indignity.

Kennard, burning with wrath, tried to protest.

"Hold that cub!" commanded the leader of the party, almost as soon as the young Englishman's hot, indignant words had resounded above the din of overturned furniture. "And if he opens his mouth again throw him into the street!" And Kennard, terrified lest he should be parted from Esther, thought it wiser to hold his peace.

They looked at one another, like two young trapped beasts—not despairing, but trying to infuse courage one into the other by a look of confidence and of love. Esther, in fact, kept her eyes fixed on her good-looking English lover, firmly keeping down the shudder of loathing which went right through her when she saw those awful men coming nigh her. There was one especially whom she abominated worse than the others, a bandy-legged ruffian, who regarded her with a leer that caused her an almost physical nausea. He did not take part in the perquisition, but sat down in the centre of the room and sprawled over the table with the air of one who was in authority.

The others addressed him as "Citizen Merri," and alternately ridiculed and deferred to him. And there was another, equally hateful, a horrible, cadaverous creature, with huge bare feet thrust into *sabots*, and lank hair, thick with grime. He did most of the talking, even though his loquacity occasionally broke down in a racking cough, which literally seemed to tear at his chest, and left him panting, hoarse, and with beads of moisture upon his low, pallid forehead.

Of course, the men found nothing that could even remotely be termed compromising. Esther had been very prudent in deference to Kennard's advice; she also had very few possessions. Nevertheless, when the wretches had turned every article of furniture inside out, one of them asked curtly:

"What do we do next, Citizen Merri?"

"Do?" broke in the cadaverous creature, even before Merri had time to reply. "Do? Why, take the wench to—to—"

He got no further, became helpless with coughing. Esther, quite instinctively, pushed the carafe of water towards him.

"Nothing of the sort!" riposted Merri sententiously. "The wench stays here!"

Both Esther and Jack had much ado to suppress an involuntary cry of relief, which at this unexpected pronouncement had risen to their lips.

The man with the cough tried to protest.

"But—" he began hoarsely.

"I said, the wench stays here!" broke in Merri peremptorily. "*Ah ça!*" he added, with a savage imprecation. "Do you command here, Citizen Rateau, or do I?"

The other at once became humble, even cringing.

"You, of course, citizen," he rejoined in his hollow voice. "I would only remark—"

"Remark nothing," retorted the other curtly. "See to it that the cub is out of the house. And after that put a sentry outside the wench's door. No one to go in and out of here under any pretext whatever. Understand?"

Kennard this time uttered a cry of protest. The helplessness of his position exasperated him almost to madness. Two men were holding him tightly by his sinewy arms. With an Englishman's instinct for a fight, he would not only have tried, but also succeeded in knocking these two down, and taken the other four on after that, with quite a reasonable chance of success. That tuberculous creature, now! And that bandy-legged ruffian! Jack Kennard had been an amateur middle-weight champion in his day, and these brutes had no more science than an enraged bull! But even as he fought against that instinct he realised the futility of the struggle. The danger of it, too—not for himself, but for her. After all, they were not going to take her away to one of those awful places from which the only egress was the way to the guillotine; and if there was that amount of freedom there was bound to be some hope. At twenty there is always hope!

So when, in obedience to Merri's orders, the two ruffians began to drag him towards the door, he said firmly:

"Leave me alone. I'll go without this unnecessary struggling."

Then, before the wretches realised his intention, he had jerked himself free from them and run to Esther.

"Have no fear," he said to her in English, and in a rapid whisper. "I'll watch over you. The house opposite. I know the people. I'll manage it somehow. Be on the look-out."

They would not let him say more, and she only had the chance of responding firmly: "I am not afraid, and I'll be on the look-out." The next moment Merri's *compeers* seized him from behind—four of them this time.

Then, of course, prudence went to the winds. He hit out to the right and left. Knocked two of those recreants down, and already was prepared to seize Esther in his arms, make a wild dash for the door, and run with her, whither only God knew, when Rateau, that awful consumptive reprobate, crept slyly up behind him and dealt him a swift and heavy blow on the skull with his weighted stick. Kennard staggered, and the bandits closed upon him. Those on the floor had time to regain their feet. To make assurance doubly sure, one of them emulated Rateau's tactics, and hit the Englishman once more on the head from behind. After that, Kennard became inert; he had partly lost consciousness. His head ached furiously. Esther, numb with horror, saw him bundled out of the room. Rateau, coughing and spluttering, finally closed the door upon the unfortunate and the four brigands who had hold of him.

Only Merri and that awful Rateau had remained in the room. The latter, gasping for breath now, poured himself out a mugful of water and drank it down at one draught. Then he swore, because he wanted rum, or brandy, or even wine. Esther watched him and Merri, fascinated. Poor old Lucienne was quietly weeping behind her apron.

"Now then, my wench," Merri began abruptly, "suppose you sit down here and listen to what I have to say."

He pulled a chair close to him and, with one of those hideous leers which had already caused her to shudder, he beckoned her to sit. Esther obeyed as if in a dream. Her eyes were dilated like those of one in a waking trance. She moved mechanically, like a bird attracted by a serpent, terrified, yet unresisting. She felt utterly helpless between these two villainous brutes, and anxiety for her English lover seemed further to numb her senses. When she was sitting she turned her gaze, with an involuntary appeal for pity, upon the bandy-legged ruffian beside her. He laughed.

"No! I am not going to hurt you," he said with smooth condescension, which was far more loathsome to Esther's ears than his comrades' savage oaths had been. "You are pretty and you have pleased me. 'Tis no small matter, forsooth!" he added, with loud-voiced bombast, "to have earned the good-will of Citizen Merri. You, my wench, are in luck's way. You realise what has occurred just now. You are amenable to the law which has decreed you to be suspect. I hold an order for your arrest. I can have you seized at once by my men, dragged to the *Conciergerie*, and from thence nothing can save you—neither your good looks nor the protection of Citizen Merri. It means the guillotine. You understand that, don't you?"

She sat quite still; only her hands were clutched convulsively together. But she contrived to say quite firmly:

"I do, and I am not afraid."

Merri waved a huge and very dirty hand with a careless gesture.

"I know," he said with a harsh laugh. "They all say that, don't they, Citizen Rateau?"

"Until the time comes," assented that worthy dryly.

"Until the time comes," reiterated the other. "Now, my wench," he added, once more turning to Esther, "I don't want that time to come. I don't want your pretty head to go rolling down into the basket, and to receive the slap on the face which the Citizen Executioner has of late taken to bestowing on those aristocratic cheeks which Mme. la Guillotine has finally blanched for ever. Like this, you see."

And the inhuman wretch took up one of the round cushions from the nearest chair, held it up at arm's length, as if it were a head which he held by the hair, and then slapped it twice with the palm of his left hand. The gesture was so horrible and withal so grotesque, that Esther closed her eyes with a shudder, and her pale cheeks took on a leaden hue. Merri laughed aloud and threw the cushion down again.

"Unpleasant, what? my pretty wench! Well, you know what to expect .... unless," he added significantly, "you are reasonable and will listen to what I am about to tell you."

Esther was no fool, nor was she unsophisticated. These were not times when it was possible for any girl, however carefully nurtured and tenderly brought up, to remain ignorant of the realities and the brutalities of life. Even before Merri had put his abominable proposition before her, she knew what he was driving at. Marriage—marriage to him! that ignoble wretch, more vile than any dumb creature! In exchange for her life!

It was her turn now to laugh. The very thought of it was farcical in its very odiousness. Merri, who had embarked on his proposal with grandiloquent phraseology, suddenly paused, almost awed by that strange, hysterical laughter.

"By Satan and all his ghouls!" he cried, and jumped to his feet, his cheeks paling beneath the grime.

Then rage seized him at his own cowardice. His egregious vanity, wounded by that laughter, egged him on. He tried to seize Esther by the waist. But she, quick as some panther on the defence, had jumped up, too, and pounced upon a knife—the very one she had been using for that happy little supper with her lover a brief half hour ago. Unguarded, unthinking, acting just with a blind instinct, she raised it and cried hoarsely:

"If you dare touch me, I'll kill you!"

It was ludicrous, of course. A mouse threatening a tiger. The very next moment Rateau had seized her hand and quietly taken away the knife. Merri shook himself like a frowsy dog.

"Whew!" he ejaculated. "What a vixen! But," he added lightly, "I like her all the better for that—eh, Rateau? Give me a wench with a temperament, I say!"

But Esther, too, had recovered herself. She realised her helplessness, and gathered courage from the consciousness of it! Now she faced the infamous villain more calmly.

"I will never marry you," she said loudly and firmly. "Never! I am not afraid to die. I am not afraid of the guillotine. There is no shame attached to death. So now you may do as you please—denounce me, and send me to follow in the footsteps of my dear father, if you wish. But whilst I am alive you will never come nigh me. If you ever do but lay a finger upon me, it will be because I am dead and beyond the reach of your polluting touch. And now I have said all that I will ever say to you in this life. If you have a spark of humanity left in you, you will, at least, let me prepare for death in peace."

She went round to where poor old Lucienne still sat, like an insentient log, panic-stricken. She knelt down on the floor and rested her arm on the old woman's knees. The light of the lamp fell full upon her, her pale face, and mass of chestnut-brown hair. There was nothing about her at this moment to inflame a man's desire. She looked pathetic in her helplessness, and nearly lifeless through the intensity of her pallor, whilst the look in her eyes was almost maniacal.

Merri cursed and swore, tried to hearten himself by turning on his friend. But Rateau had collapsed—whether with excitement or the ravages of disease, it were impossible to say. He sat upon a low chair, his long legs, his violet-circled eyes staring out with a look of hebetude and overwhelming fatigue. Merri looked around him and shuddered. The atmosphere of the place had become strangely weird and uncanny; even the tablecloth, dragged half across the table, looked somehow like a shroud.

"What shall we do, Rateau?" he asked tremulously at last.

"Get out of this infernal place," replied the other huskily. "I feel as if I were in my grave-clothes already."

"Hold your tongue, you miserable coward! You'll make the *aristo* think that we are afraid."

"Well?" queried Rateau blandly. "Aren't you?"

"No!" replied Merri fiercely. "I'll go now because .... because ... . well! because I have had enough today. And the wench sickens me. I wish to serve the Republic by marrying her, but just now I feel as if I should never really want her. So, I'll go! But, understand!" he added, and turned once more to Esther, even though he could not bring himself to go nigh her again. "Understand that tomorrow I'll come again for my answer. In the meanwhile, you may think matters over, and, maybe, you'll arrive at a more reasonable frame of mind. You will not leave these rooms until I set you free. My men will remain as sentinels at your door."

He beckoned to Rateau, and the two men went out of the room without another word.

5

The whole of that night Esther remained shut up in her apartment in the Petite Rue Taranne. All night she heard the measured tramp, the movements, the laughter and loud talking of men outside her door. Once or twice she tried to listen to what they said. But the doors and walls in these houses of old Paris were too stout to allow voices to filter through, save in the guise of a confused murmur. She would have felt horribly lonely and frightened but for the fact that in one window on the third floor in the house opposite the light of a lamp appeared like a glimmer of hope. Jack Kennard was there, on the watch. He had the window open and sat beside it until a very late hour; and after that he kept the light in, as a beacon, to bid her be of good cheer.

In the middle of the night he made an attempt to see her, hoping to catch the sentinels asleep or absent. But, having climbed the five stories of the house wherein she dwelt, he arrived on the landing outside her door and found there half a dozen ruffians squatting on the stone floor and engaged in playing hazard with a pack of greasy cards. That wretched consumptive, Rateau, was with them, and made a facetious remark as Kennard, pale and haggard, almost ghostlike, with a white bandage round his head, appeared upon the landing.

"Go back to bed, citizen," the odious creature said, with a raucous laugh. "We are taking care of your sweetheart for you."

Never in all his life had Jack Kennard felt so abjectly wretched as he did then, so miserably helpless. There was nothing that he could do, save to return to the lodging, which a kind friend had lent him for the occasion, and from whence he could, at any rate, see the windows behind which his beloved was watching and suffering.

When he went a few moments ago, he had left the *porte cochère* ajar. Now he pushed it open and stepped into the dark passage beyond. A tiny streak of light filtrated through a small curtained window in the *concierge's* lodge; it served to guide Kennard to the foot of the narrow stone staircase which led to the floors above. Just at the foot of the stairs, on the mat, a white paper glimmered in the dim shaft of light. He paused, puzzled, quite certain that the paper was not there five minutes ago when he went out. Oh! it may have fluttered in from the courtyard beyond, or from anywhere, driven by the draught. But, even so, with that mechanical action peculiar to most people under like circumstances, he stooped and picked up the paper, turned it over between his fingers, and saw that a few words were scribbled on it in pencil. The light was too dim to read by, so Kennard, still quite mechanically, kept the paper in his hand and went up to his room. There, by the light of the lamp, he read the few words scribbled in pencil:

"Wait in the street outside."

Nothing more. The message was obviously not intended for him, and yet . . . . A strange excitement possessed him. If it should be! If . . . He had heard—everyone had—of the mysterious agencies that were at work, under cover of darkness, to aid the unfortunate, the innocent, the helpless. He had heard of that legendary English gentleman who had before now defied the closest vigilance of the Committees, and snatched their intended victims out of their murderous clutches, at times under their very eyes.

435

If this should be…! He scarce dared put his hope into words. He could not bring himself really to believe. But he went. He ran downstairs and out into the street, took his stand under a projecting doorway nearly opposite the house which held the woman he loved, and leaning against the wall, he waited.

After many hours—it was then past three o'clock in the morning, and the sky of an inky blackness—he felt so numb that despite his will a kind of trance-like drowsiness overcame him. He could no longer stand on his feet; his knees were shaking; his head felt so heavy that he could not keep it up. It rolled round from shoulder to shoulder, as if his will no longer controlled it. And it ached furiously. Everything around him was very still. Even "Paris-by-Night," that grim and lurid giant, was for the moment at rest. A warm summer rain was falling; its gentle, pattering murmur into the gutter helped to lull Kennard's senses into somnolence. He was on the point of dropping off to sleep when something suddenly roused him. A noise of men shouting and laughing—familiar sounds enough in these squalid Paris streets.

But Kennard was wide awake now; numbness had given place to intense quivering of all his muscles, and super-keenness of his every sense. He peered into the darkness and strained his ears to hear. The sound certainly appeared to come from the house opposite, and there, too, it seemed as if something or things were moving. Men! More than one or two, surely! Kennard thought that he could distinguish at least three distinct voices; and there was that weird, racking cough which proclaimed the presence of Rateau.

Now the men were quite close to where he—Kennard—still stood cowering. A minute or two later they had passed down the street. Their hoarse voices soon died away in the distance. Kennard crept cautiously out of his hiding-place. Message or mere coincidence, he now blessed that mysterious scrap of paper. Had he remained in his room, he might really have dropped off to sleep and not heard these men going away. There were three of them at least—Kennard thought four. But, anyway, the number of watch-dogs outside the door of his beloved had considerably diminished. He felt that he had the strength to grapple with them, even if there were still three of them left. He, an athlete, English, and master of the art of self-defence; and they, a mere pack of drink-sodden brutes! Yes! He was quite sure he could do it. Quite sure that he could force his way into Esther's rooms and carry her off in his arms—whither? God alone knew. And God alone would provide.

Just for a moment he wondered if, while he was in that state of somnolence, other bandits had come to take the place of those that were going. But this thought he quickly dismissed. In any case, he felt a giant's strength in himself, and could not rest now till he had tried once more to see her. He crept very cautiously along; was satisfied that the street was deserted.

Already he had reached the house opposite, had pushed open the *porte cochère*, which was on the latch—when, without the slightest warning, he was suddenly attacked from behind, his arms seized and held behind his back with a vice-like grip, whilst a vigorous kick against the calves of his legs caused him to lose his footing and suddenly brought him down, sprawling and helpless, in the gutter, while in his ear there rang the hideous sound of the consumptive ruffian's racking cough.

"What shall we do with the cub now?" a raucous voice came out of the darkness.

"Let him lie there," was the quick response. "It'll teach him to interfere with the work of honest patriots."

Kennard, lying somewhat bruised and stunned, heard this decree with thankfulness. The bandits obviously thought him more hurt than he was, and if only they would leave him lying here, he would soon pick himself up and renew his attempt to go to Esther. He did not move, feigning unconsciousness, even though he felt rather than saw that hideous Rateau stooping over him, heard his stertorous breathing, the wheezing in his throat.

"Run and fetch a bit of cord, Citizen Desmonts," the wretch said presently. "A trussed cub is safer than a loose one."

This dashed Kennard's hopes to a great extent. He felt that he must act quickly, before those brigands returned and rendered him completely helpless. He made a movement to rise—a movement so swift and sudden as only a trained athlete can make. But, quick as he was, that odious, wheezing creature was quicker still, and now, when Kennard had turned on his back, Rateau promptly sat on his chest, a dead weight, with long legs stretched out before him, coughing and spluttering, yet wholly at his ease.

Oh! the humiliating position for an amateur middle-weight champion to find himself in, with that drink-sodden—Kennard was sure that he was drink-sodden—consumptive sprawling on the top of him!

"Don't trouble, Citizen Desmonts," the wretch cried out after his retreating companions. "I have what I want by me."

Very leisurely he pulled a coil of rope out of the capacious pocket of his tattered coat. Kennard could not see what he was doing, but felt it with supersensitive instinct all the time. He lay quite still beneath the weight of that miscreant, feigning unconsciousness, yet hardly able to breathe. That tuberculous *caitiff* was such a towering weight. But he tried to keep his faculties on the alert, ready for that surprise spring which would turn the tables, at the slightest false move on the part of Rateau.

But, as luck would have it, Rateau did not make a single false move. It was amazing with what dexterity he kept Kennard down, even while he contrived to pinion him with cords. An old sailor, probably, he seemed so dexterous with knots.

My God! the humiliation of it all. And Esther a helpless prisoner, inside that house not five paces away! Kennard's heavy, wearied eyes could perceive the light in her window, five stories above where he lay, in the gutter, a helpless log. Even now he gave a last desperate shriek:

"Esther!"

But in a second the abominable brigand's hand came down heavily upon his mouth, whilst a raucous voice spluttered rather than said, right through an awful fit of coughing:

"Another sound, and I'll gag as well as bind you, you young fool!"

After which, Kennard remained quite still.

6

Esther, up in her little attic, knew nothing of what her English lover was even then suffering for her sake. She herself had passed, during the night, through every stage of horror and of fear. Soon after midnight that execrable brigand Rateau had poked his ugly, cadaverous face in at the door and peremptorily called for Lucienne. The woman, more dead than alive now with terror, had answered with mechanical obedience.

"I and my friends are thirsty," the man had commanded. "Go and fetch us a litre of *eau-de-vie.*"

Poor Lucienne stammered a pitiable: "Where shall I go?"

"To the house at the sign of '*Le fort Samson*,' in the Rue de Seine," replied Rateau curtly. "They'll serve you well if you mention my name."

Of course, Lucienne protested. She was a decent woman, who had never been inside a *cabaret* in her life.

"Then it's time you began," was Rateau's dry comment, which was greeted with much laughter from his abominable companions.

Lucienne was forced to go. It would, of course, have been futile and madness to resist. This had occurred three hours since. The Rue de Seine was not far, but the poor woman had not returned. Esther was left with this additional horror weighing upon her soul. What had happened to her unfortunate servant? Visions of outrage and murder floated before the poor girl's tortured brain. At best, Lucienne was being kept out of the way in order to make her—Esther—feel more lonely and desperate! She remained at the window after that, watching that light in the house opposite and fingering her prayer-book, the only solace which she had. Her attic was so high up and the street so narrow, that she could not see what went on in the street below. At one time she heard a great to-do outside her door. It seemed as if some of the bloodhounds who were set to watch her had gone, or that others came. She really hardly cared which it was. Then she heard a great commotion coming from the street immediately beneath her: men shouting and laughing, and that awful creature's rasping cough.

At one moment she felt sure that Kennard had called to her by name. She heard his voice distinctly, raised as if in a despairing cry.

After that, all was still.

So still that she could hear her heart beating furiously, and then a tear falling from her eyes upon her open book. So still that the gentle patter of the rain sounded like a soothing lullaby. She was very young, and was very tired. Out, above the line of sloping roofs and chimney pots, the darkness of the sky was yielding to the first touch of dawn. The rain ceased. Everything became deathly still. Esther's head fell, wearied, upon her folded arms.

Then, suddenly, she was wide awake. Something had roused her. A noise. At first, she could not tell what it was, but now she knew. It was the opening and shutting of the door behind her, and then a quick, stealthy footstep across the room. The horror of it all was unspeakable. Esther remained as she had been, on her knees, mechanically fingering her prayer-book, unable to move, unable to utter a sound, as if paralysed. She knew that one of those abominable creatures had entered her room, was coming near her even now. She did not know who it was, only guessed it was Rateau, for she heard a raucous, stertorous wheeze. Yet she could not have then turned to look if her life had depended upon her doing so.

The whole thing had occurred in less than half a dozen heartbeats. The next moment the wretch was close to her. Mercifully she felt that her senses were leaving her. Even so, she felt that a handkerchief was being bound over her mouth to prevent her screaming. Wholly unnecessary this, for she could not have uttered a sound. Then she was lifted off the ground and carried across the room, then over the threshold. A vague, subconscious effort of will helped her to keep her head averted from that wheezing wretch who was carrying her. Thus, she could see the landing, and two of those abominable watch-dogs who had been set to guard her.

The ghostly grey light of dawn came peeping in through the narrow dormer window in the sloping roof, and faintly illumined their sprawling forms, stretched out at full length, with their heads buried in their folded arms and their naked legs looking pallid and weird in the dim light. Their stertorous breathing woke the echoes of the bare, stone walls. Esther shuddered and closed her eyes. She was now like an insentient log, without power, or thought, or will—almost without feeling.

Then, all at once, the coolness of the morning air caught her full in the face. She opened her eyes and tried to move, but those powerful arms held her more closely than before. Now she could have shrieked with horror. With returning consciousness the sense of her desperate position came on her with its full and ghastly significance, its awe-inspiring details. The grey dawn, the abandoned wretch who held her, and the stillness of this early morning hour, when not one pitying soul would be astir to lend her a helping hand or give her the solace of mute sympathy. So great, indeed, was this stillness that the click of the man's *sabots* upon the uneven pavement reverberated, ghoul-like and weird.

And it was through that awesome stillness that a sound suddenly struck her ear, which, in the instant, made her feel that she was not re-ally alive, or, if alive, was sleeping and dreaming strange and impossible dreams. It was the sound of a voice, clear and firm, and with a wonder-ful ring of merriment in its tones, calling out just above a whisper, and in English, if you please:

"Look out, Ffoulkes! That young cub is as strong as a horse. He will give us all away if you are not careful."

A dream? Of course it was a dream, for the voice had sounded very close to her ear; so close, in fact, that . . . . well! Esther was quite sure that her face still rested against the hideous, tattered, and grimy coat which that repulsive Rateau had been wearing all along. And there was the click of his *sabots* upon the pavement all the time. So, then, the voice and the merry, suppressed laughter which accompanied it, must

440

all have been a part of her dream. How long this lasted she could not have told you. An hour and more, she thought, while the grey dawn yielded to the roseate hue of morning. Somehow, she no longer suffered either terror or foreboding. A subtle atmosphere of strength and of security seemed to encompass her. At one time she felt as if she were driven along in a car that jolted horribly, and when she moved her face and hands they came in contact with things that were fresh and green and smelt of the country. She was in darkness then, and more than three parts unconscious, but the handkerchief had been removed from her mouth. It seemed to her as if she could hear the voice of her Jack, but far away and indistinct; also, the tramp of horses' hoofs and the creaking of cart-wheels, and at times that awful, rasping cough, which reminded her of the presence of a loathsome wretch, who should not have had a part in her soothing dream.

Thus, many hours must have gone by.

Then, all at once, she was inside a house—a room, and she felt that she was being lowered very gently to the ground. She was on her feet, but she could not see where she was. There was furniture; a carpet; a ceiling; the man Rateau with the *sabots* and the dirty coat, and the merry English voice, and a pair of deep-set blue eyes, thoughtful and lazy and infinitely kind.

But before she could properly focus what she saw, everything began to whirl and to spin around her, to dance a wild and idiotic *saraband*, which caused her to laugh, and to laugh, until her throat felt choked and her eyes hot; after which she remembered nothing more.

7

The first thing of which Esther Vincent was conscious, when she returned to her senses, was of her English lover kneeling beside her. She was lying on some kind of couch, and she could see his face in profile, for he had turned and was speaking to someone at the far end of the room.

"And was it you who knocked me down?" he was saying, "and sat on my chest, and trussed me like a fowl?"

"*La!* my dear sir," a lazy, pleasant voice riposted, "what else could I do? There was no time for explanations. You were half-crazed, and would not have understood. And you were ready to bring all the nightwatchmen about our ears."

"I am sorry!" Kennard said simply. "But how could I guess?"

"You couldn't," rejoined the other. "That is why I had to deal so summarily with you and with Mademoiselle Esther, not to speak of good old Lucienne, who had never, in her life, been inside a *cabaret*. You must all forgive me ere you start upon your journey. You are not out of the wood yet, remember. Though Paris is a long way behind, France itself is no longer a healthy place for any of you."

"But how did we ever get out of Paris? I was smothered under a pile of cabbages, with Lucienne on one side of me and Esther, unconscious, on the other. I could see nothing. I know we halted at the barrier. I thought we would be recognised, turned back! My God! how I trembled!"

"Bah!" broke in the other, with a careless laugh. "It is not so difficult as it seems. We have done it before—eh, Ffoulkes? A market-gardener's cart, a villainous wretch like myself to drive it, another hideous object like Sir Andrew Ffoulkes, Bart., to lead the scraggy nag, a couple of forged or stolen passports, plenty of English gold, and the deed is done!"

Esther's eyes were fixed upon the speaker. She marvelled now how she could have been so blind. The cadaverous face was nothing but a splendid use of grease paint! The rags! the dirt! the whole assumption of a hideous character was masterly! But there were the eyes, deep-set, and thoughtful and kind. How did she fail to guess?

"You are known as the Scarlet Pimpernel," she said suddenly. "Suzanne de Tournai was my friend. She told me. You saved her and her family, and now . . . . oh, my God!" she exclaimed, "how shall we ever repay you?"

"By placing yourselves unreservedly in my friend Ffoulkes' hands," he replied gently. "He will lead you to safety and, if you wish it, to England."

"If we wish it!" Kennard sighed fervently.

"You are not coming with us, Blakeney?" queried Sir Andrew Ffoulkes, and it seemed to Esther's sensitive ears as if a tone of real anxiety and also of entreaty rang in the young man's voice.

"No, not this time," replied Sir Percy lightly. "I like my character of Rateau, and I don't want to give it up just yet. I have done nothing to arouse suspicion in the minds of my savoury *compeers* up at the *Cabaret de la Liberté*. I can easily keep this up for some time to come, and frankly I admire myself as Citizen Rateau. I don't know when I have enjoyed a character so much!"

"You mean to return to the *Cabaret de la Liberté!*" exclaimed Sir Andrew.

"Why not?"

"You will be recognised!"

"Not before I have been of service to a good many unfortunates, I hope."

"But that awful cough of yours! Percy, you'll do yourself an injury with it one day."

"Not I! I like that cough. I practised it for a long time before I did it to perfection. Such a splendid wheeze! I must teach Tony to do it someday. Would you like to hear it now?"

He laughed, that perfect, delightful, lazy laugh of his, which carried every hearer with it along the path of light-hearted merriment. Then he broke into the awful cough of the consumptive Rateau. And Esther Vincent instinctively closed her eyes and shuddered.

"Needs Must—"

1

The children were all huddled up together in one corner of the room. Etienne and Valentine, the two eldest, had their arms round the little one. As for Lucile, she would have told you herself that she felt just like a bird between two snakes—terrified and fascinated—oh! especially by that little man with the pale face and the light grey eyes and the slender white hands unstained by toil, one of which rested lightly upon the desk, and was only clenched now and then at a word or a look from the other man or from Lucile herself.

But Commissary Lebel just tried to browbeat her. It was not difficult, for in truth she felt frightened enough already, with all this talk of "traitors" and that awful threat of the guillotine.

Lucile Clamette, however, would have remained splendidly loyal in spite of all these threats, if it had not been for the children. She was little mother to them; for father was a cripple, with speech and mind already impaired by creeping paralysis, and *maman* had died when little Josephine was born. And now those fiends threatened not only her, but Etienne who was not fourteen, and Valentine who was not much more than ten, with death, unless she—Lucile—broke the solemn word which she had given to M. le Marquis. At first, she had tried to deny all knowledge of M. le Marquis' whereabouts.

"I can assure M. le Commissaire that I do not know," she had persisted quietly, even though her heart was beating so rapidly in her bosom that she felt as if she must choke.

"Call me Citizen Commissary," Lebel had riposted curtly. "I should take it as a proof that your aristocratic sentiments are not so deeprooted as they appear to be."

"Yes, citizen!" murmured Lucile, under her breath.

Then the other one, he with the pale eyes and the slender white hands, leaned forward over the desk, and the poor girl felt as if a mighty and unseen force was holding her tight, so tight that she could neither move, nor breathe, nor turn her gaze away from those pale, compelling eyes. In the remote corner little Josephine was whimpering, and Etienne's big, dark eyes were fixed bravely upon his eldest sister.

"There, there! little *citizeness*," the awful man said, in a voice that sounded low and almost caressing, "there is nothing to be frightened of. No one is going to hurt you or your little family. We only want you to be reasonable. You have promised to your former employer that you would never tell anyone of his whereabouts. Well! we don't ask you to tell us anything.

"All that we want you to do is to write a letter to M. le Marquis—one that I myself will dictate to you. You have written to M. le Marquis before now, on business matters, have you not?"

"Yes, *monsieur*—yes, citizen," stammered Lucile through her tears. "Father was bailiff to M. le Marquis until he became a cripple and now I—"

"Do not write any letter, Lucile," Etienne suddenly broke in with forceful vehemence. "It is a trap set by these miscreants to entrap M. le Marquis."

There was a second's silence in the room after this sudden outburst on the part of the lad. Then the man with the pale face said quietly:

"Citizen Lebel, order the removal of that boy. Let him be kept in custody till he has learned to hold his tongue."

But before Lebel could speak to the two soldiers who were standing on guard at the door, Lucile had uttered a loud cry of agonised protest.

"No! no! *monsieur!*—that is citizen!" she implored. "Do not take Etienne away. He will be silent . . . . I promise you that he will be silent . . . . only do not take him away! Etienne, my little one!" she added, turning her tear-filled eyes to her brother, "I entreat thee to hold thy tongue!"

The others, too, clung to Etienne, and the lad, awed and subdued, relapsed into silence.

"Now then," resumed Lebel roughly, after a while, "let us get on with this business. I am sick to death of it. It has lasted far too long already."

He fixed his blood-shot eyes upon Lucile and continued gruffly:

"Now listen to me, my wench, for this is going to be my last word. Citizen Chauvelin here has already been very lenient with you by allowing this letter business. If I had my way I'd make you speak here and now. As it is, you either sit down and write the letter at Citizen Chauvelin's dictation at once, or I send you with that impudent brother of yours and your imbecile father to jail, on a charge of trea-son against the State, for aiding and abetting the enemies of the Re-public; and you know what the consequences of such a charge usually are. The other two brats will go to a House of Correction, there to be detained during the pleasure of the Committee of Public Safety. That is my last word," he reiterated fiercely. "Now, which is it to be?"

He paused, the girl's wan cheeks turned the colour of lead. She moistened her lips once or twice with her tongue; beads of perspira-tion appeared at the roots of her hair. She gazed helplessly at her tor-mentors, not daring to look on those three huddled-up little figures there in the corner. A few seconds sped away in silence. The man with the pale eyes rose, and pushed his chair away. He went to the window, stood there with his back to the room, those slender white hands of his clasped behind him. Neither the *commissary* nor the girl appeared to interest him further. He was just gazing out of the window.

The other was still sprawling beside the desk, his large, coarse hand—how different his hands were!—was beating a devil's tattoo upon the arm of his chair.

After a few minutes, Lucile made a violent effort to compose her-self, wiped the moisture from her pallid forehead and dried the tears which still hung upon her lashes. Then she rose from her chair and walked resolutely up to the desk.

"I will write the letter," she said simply.

Lebel gave a snort of satisfaction; but the other did not move from his position near the window. The boy, Etienne, had uttered a cry of passionate protest.

"Do not give M. le Marquis away, Lucile!" he said hotly. "I am not afraid to die."

But Lucile had made up her mind. How could she do otherwise, with these awful threats hanging over them all? She and Etienne and poor father gone, and the two young ones in one of those aw-ful Houses of Correction, where children were taught to hate the Church, to shun the Sacraments, and to blaspheme God!

"What am I to write?" she asked dully, resolutely closing her ears against her brother's protest.

Lebel pushed pen, ink and paper towards her and she sat down, ready to begin.

"Write!" now came in a curt command from the man at the window. And Lucile wrote at his dictation:

"Monsieur le Marquis,—We are in grave trouble. My brother

Etienne and I have been arrested on a charge of treason. This means the guillotine for us and for poor father, who can no longer speak; and the two little ones are to be sent to one of those dreadful Houses of Correction, where children are taught to deny God and to blaspheme. You alone can save us, M. le Marquis; and I beg you on my knees to do it. The Citizen Commissary here says that you have in your possession certain papers which are of great value to the State, and that if I can persuade you to give these up, Etienne, father and I and the little ones will be left unmolested. M. le Marquis, you once said that you could never adequately repay my poor father for all his devotion in your service. You can do it now, M. le Marquis, by saving us all. I will be at the *château* a week from today. I entreat you, M. le Marquis, to come to me then and to bring the papers with you; or if you can devise some other means of sending the papers to me, I will obey your behests.—I am, M. le Marquis' faithful and devoted servant,

Lucile Clamette."

The pen dropped from the unfortunate girl's fingers. She buried her face in her hands and sobbed convulsively. The children were silent, awed and subdued—tired out, too. Only Etienne's dark eyes were fixed upon his sister with a look of mute reproach.

Lebel had made no attempt to interrupt the flow of his colleague's dictation. Only once or twice did a hastily smothered "What the—!" of astonishment escape his lips. Now, when the letter was finished and duly signed, he drew it to him and strewed the sand over it. Chauvelin, more impassive than ever, was once more gazing out of the window.

"How are the *ci-devant aristos* to get this letter?" the *commissary* asked.

"It must be put in the hollow tree which stands by the side of the stable gate at Montorgueil," whispered Lucile.

"And the *aristos* will find it there?"

"Yes. M. le Vicomte goes there once or twice a week to see if there is anything there from one of us."

"They are in hiding somewhere close by, then?"

But to this the girl gave no reply. Indeed, she felt as if any word now might choke her.

"Well, no matter where they are!" the inhuman wretch resumed, with brutal cynicism. "We've got them now—both of them. *Marquis! Vicomte!*" he added, and spat on the ground to express his contempt of such titles. "Citizens Montorgueil, father and son—that's all they are! And as such they'll walk up in state to make their bow to Mme.

447

la Guillotine!"

"May we go now?" stammered Lucile through her tears.

Lebel nodded in assent, and the girl rose and turned to walk towards the door. She called to the children, and the little ones clustered round her skirts like chicks around the mother-hen. Only Etienne remained aloof, wrathful against his sister for what he deemed her treachery. "Women have no sense of honour!" he muttered to himself, with all the pride of conscious manhood. But Lucile felt more than ever like a bird who is vainly trying to evade the clutches of a fowler. She gathered the two little ones around her. Then, with a cry like a wounded doe she ran quickly out of the room.

2

As soon as the sound of the children's footsteps had died away down the corridor, Lebel turned with a grunt to his still silent companion.

"And now, Citizen Chauvelin," he said roughly, "perhaps you will be good enough to explain what is the meaning of all this tomfoolery."

"Tomfoolery, citizen?" queried the other blandly. "What tomfoolery, pray?"

"Why, about those papers!" growled Lebel savagely. "Curse you for an interfering busybody! It was I who got information that those pestilential *aristos*, the Montorgueils, far from having fled the country are in hiding somewhere in my district. I could have made the girl give up their hiding-place pretty soon, without any help from you. What right had you to interfere, I should like to know?"

"You know quite well what right I had, Citizen Lebel," replied Chauvelin with perfect composure. "The right conferred upon me by the Committee of Public Safety, of whom I am still an unworthy member. They sent me down here to lend you a hand in an investigation which is of grave importance to them."

"I know that!" retorted Lebel sulkily. "But why have invented the story of the papers?"

"It is no invention, citizen," rejoined Chauvelin with slow emphasis. "The papers do exist. They are actually in the possession of the Montorgueils, father and son. To capture the two *aristos* would be not only a blunder, but criminal folly, unless we can lay hands on the papers at the same time."

"But what in Satan's name are those papers?" ejaculated Lebel with a fierce oath.

"Think, Citizen Lebel! Think!" was Chauvelin's cool rejoinder.

"Methinks you might arrive at a pretty shrewd guess." Then, as the other's bluster and bounce suddenly collapsed upon his colleague's calm, accusing gaze, the latter continued with impressive deliberation:

"The papers which the two *aristos* have in their possession, citizen, are receipts for money, for bribes paid to various members of the Committee of Public Safety by Royalist agents for the overthrow of our glorious Republic. You know all about them, do you not?"

While Chauvelin spoke, a look of furtive terror had crept into Lebel's eyes; his cheeks became the colour of lead. But even so, he tried to keep up an air of incredulity and of amazement.

"I?" he exclaimed. "What do you mean, Citizen Chauvelin? What should I know about it?"

"Some of those receipts are signed with your name, Citizen Lebel," retorted Chauvelin forcefully. "Bah!" he added, and a tone of savage contempt crept into his even, calm voice now. "Hériot, Foucquier, Ducros and the whole gang of you are in it up to the neck: trafficking with our enemies, trading with England, taking bribes from every quarter for working against the safety of the Republic. Ah! if I had my way, I would let the hatred of those *aristos* take its course. I would let the Montorgueils and the whole pack of Royalist agents publish those infamous proofs of your treachery and of your baseness to the entire world, and send the whole lot of you to the guillotine!"

He had spoken with so much concentrated fury, and the hatred and contempt expressed in his pale eyes were so fierce that an involuntary ice-cold shiver ran down the length of Lebel's spine. But, even so, he would not give in; he tried to sneer and to keep up something of his former surly defiance.

"Bah!" he exclaimed, and with a lowering glance gave hatred for hatred, and contempt for contempt. "What can you do? An I am not mistaken, there is no more discredited man in France today than the unsuccessful tracker of the Scarlet Pimpernel."

The taunt went home. It was Chauvelin's turn now to lose countenance, to pale to the lips. The glow of virtuous indignation died out of his eyes, his look became furtive and shamed.

"You are right, Citizen Lebel," he said calmly after a while. "Recriminations between us are out of place. I am a discredited man, as you say. Perhaps it would have been better if the Committee had sent me long ago to expiate my failures on the guillotine. I should at least not have suffered, as I am suffering now, daily, hourly humiliation at thought of the triumph of an enemy, whom I hate with a passion which consumes my very soul. But do not let us speak of me," he went on quietly. "There are graver affairs at stake just now than mine own."

Lebel said nothing more for the moment. Perhaps he was satisfied at the success of his taunt, even though the terror within his craven soul still caused the cold shiver to course up and down his spine. Chauvelin had once more turned to the window; his gaze was fixed upon the distance far away. The window gave on the North. That way, in a straight line, lay Calais, Boulogne, England—where he had been made to suffer such bitter humiliation at the hands of his elusive enemy. And immediately before him was Paris, where the very walls seemed to echo that mocking laugh of the daring Englishman which would haunt him even to his grave.

Lebel, unnerved by his colleague's silence, broke in gruffly at last:

"Well then, citizen," he said, with a feeble attempt at another sneer, "if you are not thinking of sending us all to the guillotine just yet, perhaps you will be good enough to explain just how the matter stands?"

"Fairly simply, alas!" replied Chauvelin dryly. "The two Montorgueils, father and son, under assumed names, were the Royalist agents who succeeded in suborning men such as you, citizen—the whole gang of you. We have tracked them down, to this district, have confiscated their lands and ransacked the old *château* for valuables and so on. Two days later, the first of a series of pestilential anonymous letters reached the Committee of Public Safety, threatening the publication of a whole series of compromising documents if the *Marquis* and the Vicomte de Montorgueil were in any way molested, and if all the Montorgueil property is not immediately restored."

"I suppose it is quite certain that those receipts and documents do exist?" suggested Lebel.

"Perfectly certain. One of the receipts, signed by Hériot, was sent as a specimen."

"My God!" ejaculated Lebel, and wiped the cold sweat from his brow.

"Yes, you'll all want help from somewhere," retorted Chauvelin coolly. "From above or from below, what? if the people get to know what miscreants you are. I do believe," he added, with a vicious snap of his thin lips, "that they would cheat the guillotine of you and, in the end, drag you out of the tumbrils and tear you to pieces limb from limb!"

Once more that look of furtive terror crept into the *commissary's* bloodshot eyes.

"Thank the Lord," he muttered, "that we were able to get hold of the wench Clamette!"

"At my suggestion," retorted Chauvelin curtly. "I always believe in threatening the weak if you want to coerce the strong. The Montorgueils cannot resist the wench's appeal. Even if they do at first, we can apply the screw by clapping one of the young ones in gaol. Within a week we shall have those papers, Citizen Lebel; and if, in the meanwhile, no one commits a further blunder, we can close the trap on the Montorgueils without further trouble."

Lebel said nothing more, and after a while Chauvelin went back to the desk, picked up the letter which poor Lucile had written and watered with her tears, folded it deliberately and slipped it into the inner pocket of his coat.

"What are you going to do?" queried Lebel anxiously.

"Drop this letter into the hollow tree by the side of the stable gate at Montorgueil," replied Chauvelin simply.

"What?" exclaimed the other. "Yourself?"

"Why, of course! Think you I would entrust such an errand to another living soul?"

3

A couple of hours later, when the two children had had their dinner and had settled down to play in the garden, and father been cosily tucked up for his afternoon sleep, Lucile called her brother Etienne to her. The boy had not spoken to her since that terrible time spent in the presence of those two awful men. He had eaten no dinner, only sat glowering, staring straight out before him, from time to time throwing a look of burning reproach upon his sister. Now, when she called to him, he tried to run away, was halfway up the stairs before she could seize hold of him.

"Etienne, *mon petit!*" she implored, as her arms closed around his shrinking figure.

"Let me go, Lucile!" the boy pleaded obstinately.

"*Mon petit*, listen to me!" she pleaded. "All is not lost, if you will stand by me."

"All is lost, Lucile!" Etienne cried, striving to keep back a flood of passionate tears. "Honour is lost. Your treachery has disgraced us all. If M. le Marquis and M. le Vicomte are brought to the guillotine, their blood will be upon our heads."

"Upon mine alone, my little Etienne," she said sadly. "But God alone can judge me. It was a terrible alternative: M. le Marquis, or you and Valentine and little Josephine and poor father, who is so helpless! But don't let us talk of it. All is not lost, I am sure. The last time that I spoke with M. le Marquis—it was in February, do you remember?— he was full of hope, and oh! so kind. Well, he told me then that if ever I or any of us here were in such grave trouble that we did not know where to turn, one of us was to put on our very oldest clothes, look as like a bare-footed beggar as we could, and then go to Paris to a place called the *Cabaret de la Liberté* in the Rue Christine. There we were to ask for the Citizen Rateau, and we were to tell him all our troubles, whatever they might be. Well! we are in such trouble now, *mon petit*, that we don't know where to turn. Put on thy very oldest clothes, little one, and run bare-footed into Paris, find the Citizen Rateau and tell him just what has happened: the letter which they have forced me to write, the threats which they held over me if I did not write it—everything. Dost hear?"

Already the boy's eyes were glowing. The thought that he individually could do something to retrieve the awful shame of his sister's treachery spurred him to activity. It needed no persuasion on Lucile's part to induce him to go. She made him put on some old clothes and stuffed a piece of bread and cheese into his breeches pocket.

It was close upon a couple of leagues to Paris, but that run was one of the happiest which Etienne had ever made. And he did it bare-footed, too, feeling neither fatigue nor soreness, despite the hardness of the road after a two weeks' drought, which had turned mud into hard cakes and ruts into fissures which tore the lad's feet till they bled.

He did not reach the *Cabaret de la Liberté* till nightfall, and when he got there he hardly dared to enter. The filth, the squalor, the hoarse voices which rose from that cellar-like place below the level of the street, repelled the country-bred lad. Were it not for the desperate urgency of his errand he never would have dared to enter. As it was, the fumes of alcohol and steaming, dirty clothes nearly choked him, and he could scarce stammer the name of "Citizen Rateau" when a gruff voice presently demanded his purpose.

He realised now how tired he was and how hungry. He had not thought to pause in order to consume the small provision of bread and cheese wherewith thoughtful Lucile had provided him. Now he was ready to faint when a loud guffaw, which echoed from one end of the horrible place to the other, greeted his timid request.

"Citizen Rateau!" the same gruff voice called out hilariously. "Why, there he is! Here, citizen! there's a blooming *aristo* to see you."

Etienne turned his weary eyes to the corner which was being indicated to him. There he saw a huge creature sprawling across a bench, with long, powerful limbs stretched out before him. Citizen Rateau was clothed, rather than dressed, in a soiled shirt, ragged breeches and tattered stockings, with shoes down at heel and faded crimson cap. His face looked congested and sunken about the eyes; he appeared to be asleep, for stertorous breathing came at intervals from between his parted lips, whilst every now and then a racking cough seemed to tear at his broad chest.

Etienne gave him one look, shuddering with horror, despite himself, at the aspect of this bloated wretch from whom salvation was to come. The whole place seemed to him hideous and loathsome in the extreme. What it all meant he could not understand; all that he knew was that this seemed like another hideous trap into which he and Lucile had fallen, and that he must fly from it—fly at all costs, before he betrayed M. le Marquis still further to these drink-sodden brutes. Another moment, and he feared that he might faint. The din of a bibulous song rang in his ears, the reek of alcohol turned him giddy and sick. He had only just enough strength to turn and totter back into the open. There his senses reeled, the lights in the houses opposite began to dance wildly before his eyes, after which he remembered nothing more.

4

There is nothing now in the whole countryside quite so desolate and forlorn as the Château of Montorgueil, with its once magnificent park, now overgrown with weeds, its encircling walls broken down, its terraces devastated, and its stately gates rusty and torn.

Just by the side of what was known in happier times as the stable gate there stands a hollow tree. It is not inside the park, but just outside, and shelters the narrow lane, which skirts the park walls, against the blaze of the afternoon sun.

Its beneficent shade is a favourite spot for an afternoon siesta, for there is a bit of green sward under the tree, and all along the side of the road. But as the shades of evening gather in, the lane is usually deserted, shunned by the neighbouring peasantry on account of its eerie loneliness, so different to the former bustle which used to reign around the park gates when M. le Marquis and his family were still in residence. Nor does the lane lead anywhere, for it is a mere loop which gives on the main road at either end.

Henri de Montorgueil chose a peculiarly dark night in mid-September for one of his periodical visits to the hollow-tree. It was close on nine o'clock when he passed stealthily down the lane, keeping close to the park wall. A soft rain was falling, the first since the prolonged drought, and though it made the road heavy and slippery in places, it helped to deaden the sound of the young man's furtive footsteps. The air, except for the patter of the rain, was absolutely still. Henri de Montorgueil paused from time to time, with neck craned forward, every sense on the alert, listening, like any poor, hunted beast, for the slightest sound which might betray the approach of danger.

As many a time before, he reached the hollow tree in safety, felt for and found in the usual place the letter which the unfortunate girl Lucile had written to him. Then, with it in his hand, he turned to the stable gate. It had long since ceased to be kept locked and barred. Pillaged and ransacked by order of the Committee of Public Safety, there was nothing left inside the park walls worth keeping under lock and key.

Henri slipped stealthily through the gates and made his way along the drive. Every stone, every nook and cranny of his former home was familiar to him, and *anon* he turned into a shed where in former times wheelbarrows and garden tools were wont to be kept. Now it was full of debris, lumber of every sort. A more safe or secluded spot could not be imagined. Henri crouched in the furthermost corner of the shed. Then from his belt he detached a small dark lanthorn, opened its shutter, and with the aid of the tiny, dim light read the contents of the letter. For a long while after that he remained quite still, as still as a man who has received a stunning blow on the head and has partly lost consciousness. The blow was indeed a staggering one. Lucile Clamette, with the invincible power of her own helplessness, was demanding the surrender of a weapon which had been a safeguard for the Montorgueils all this while. The papers which compromised a number of influential members of the Committee of Public Safety had been the most perfect arms of defence against persecution and spoliation.

And now these were to be given up: Oh! there could be no question of that. Even before consulting with his father, Henri knew that the papers would have to be given up. They were clever, those revolutionaries. The thought of holding innocent children as hostages could only have originated in minds attuned to the villainies of devils. But it was unthinkable that the children should suffer.

After a while the young man roused himself from the torpor into which the suddenness of this awful blow had plunged him. By the light of the lanthorn he began to write upon a sheet of paper which he had torn from his pocket-book.

"My Dear Lucile," he wrote, "As you say, our debt to your father and to you all never could be adequately repaid. You and the children shall never suffer whilst we have the power to save you. You will find the papers in the receptacle you know of inside the chimney of what used to be my mother's *boudoir*. You will find the receptacle unlocked. One day before the term you name I myself will place the papers there for you. With them, my father and I do give up our lives to save you and the little ones from the persecution of those fiends. May the good God guard you all."

He signed the letter with his initials, H. de M. Then he crept back to the gate and dropped the message into the hollow of the tree.

A quarter of an hour later Henri de Montorgueil was wending his way back to the hiding place which had sheltered him and his father for so long. Silence and darkness then held undisputed sway once more around the hollow tree. Even the rain had ceased its gentle pattering. *Anon* from far away came the sound of a church bell striking the hour of ten. Then nothing more.

A few more minutes of absolute silence, then something dark and furtive began to move out of the long grass which bordered the roadside—something that in movement was almost like a snake. It dragged itself along close to the ground, making no sound as it moved. Soon it reached the hollow tree, rose to the height of a man and flattened itself against the tree-trunk. Then it put out a hand, felt for the hollow receptacle and groped for the missive which Henri de Montorgueil had dropped in there a while ago.

The next moment a tiny ray of light gleamed through the darkness like a star. A small, almost fragile, figure of a man, dressed in the mud-stained clothes of a country yokel, had turned up the shutter of a small lanthorn. By its flickering light he deciphered the letter which Henri de Montorgueil had written to Lucile Clamette.

"One day before the term you name I myself will place the papers there for you."

A sigh of satisfaction, quickly suppressed, came through his thin, colourless lips, and the light of the lanthorn caught the flash of triumph in his pale, inscrutable eyes.

Then the light was extinguished. Impenetrable darkness swallowed up that slender, mysterious figure again.

Six days had gone by since Chauvelin had delivered his cruel "either—or" to poor little Lucile Clamette; three since he had found Henri de Montorgueil's reply to the girl's appeal in the hollow of the tree. Since then he had made a careful investigation of the *château*, and soon was able to settle it in his own mind as to which room had been Madame la Marquise's *boudoir* in the past. It was a small apartment, having direct access on the first landing of the staircase, and the one window gave on the rose garden at the back of the house. Inside the monumental hearth, at an arm's length up the wide chimney, a receptacle had been contrived in the brickwork, with a small iron door which opened and closed with a secret spring. Chauvelin, whom his nefarious calling had rendered proficient in such matters, had soon mastered the workings of that spring. He could now open and close the iron door at will.

Up to a late hour on the sixth night of this weary waiting, the receptacle inside the chimney was still empty. That night Chauvelin had determined to spend at the *château*. He could not have rested elsewhere.

Even his colleague Lebel could not know what the possession of those papers would mean to the discredited agent of the Committee of Public Safety. With them in his hands, he could demand rehabilitation, and could purchase immunity from those sneers which had been so galling to his arrogant soul—sneers which had become more and more marked, more and more unendurable, and more and more menacing, as he piled up failure on failure with every encounter with the Scarlet Pimpernel.

Immunity and rehabilitation! This would mean that he could once more measure his wits and his power with that audacious enemy who had brought about his downfall.

"In the name of Satan, bring us those papers!" Robespierre himself had cried with unwonted passion, ere he sent him out on this important mission. "We none of us could stand the scandal of such disclosures. It would mean absolute ruin for us all."

And Chauvelin that night, as soon as the shades of evening had drawn in, took up his stand in the *château*, in the small inner room which was contiguous to the *boudoir*.

Here he sat, beside the open window, for hour upon hour, his every sense on the alert, listening for the first footfall upon the gravel path below. Though the hours went by leaden-footed, he was neither excited nor anxious. The Clamette family was such a precious hostage that the Montorgueils were bound to comply with Lucile's demand for the papers by every dictate of honour and of humanity.

"While we have those people in our power," Chauvelin had reiterated to himself more than once during the course of his long vigil, "even that meddlesome Scarlet Pimpernel can do nothing to save those cursed Montorgueils."

The night was dark and still. Not a breath of air stirred the branches of the trees or the shrubberies in the park; any footsteps, however wary, must echo through that perfect and absolute silence. Chauvelin's keen, pale eyes tried to pierce the gloom in the direction whence in all probability the *aristo* would come. Vaguely he wondered if it would be Henri de Montorgueil or the old *marquis* himself who would bring the papers.

"Bah! whichever one it is," he muttered, "we can easily get the other, once those abominable papers are in our hands. And even if both the *aristos* escape," he added mentally, "'tis no matter, once we have the papers."

Anon, far away a distant church bell struck the midnight hour. The stillness of the air had become oppressive. A kind of torpor born of intense fatigue lulled the Terrorist's senses to somnolence. His head fell forward on his breast . . . .

6

Then suddenly a shiver of excitement went right through him. He was fully awake now, with glowing eyes wide open and the icy calm of perfect confidence ruling every nerve. The sound of stealthy footsteps had reached his ear.

He could see nothing, either outside or in; but his fingers felt for the pistol which he carried in his belt. The *aristo* was evidently alone; only one solitary footstep was approaching the *château*.

Chauvelin had left the door ajar which gave on the *boudoir*. The staircase was on the other side of that fateful room, and the door leading to that was closed. A few minutes of tense expectancy went by. Then through the silence there came the sound of furtive foot-steps on the stairs, the creaking of a loose board and finally the stealthy opening of the door.

In all his adventurous career Chauvelin had never felt so calm. His heart beat quite evenly, his senses were undisturbed by the slightest tingling of his nerves. The stealthy sounds in the next room brought the movements of the *aristo* perfectly clear before his mental vision.

The latter was carrying a small dark lanthorn. As soon as he entered he flashed its light about the room. Then he deposited the lanthorn on the floor, close beside the hearth, and started to feel up the chimney for the hidden receptacle.

Chauvelin watched him now like a cat watches a mouse, savouring these few moments of anticipated triumph. He pushed open the door noiselessly which gave on the *boudoir*. By the feeble light of the lanthorn on the ground he could only see the vague outline of the *aristo's* back, bending forward to his task; but a thrill went through him as he saw a bundle of papers lying on the ground close by.

Everything was ready; the trap was set. Here was a complete victory at last. It was obviously the young Vicomte de Montorgueil who had come to do the deed. His head was up the chimney even now. The old *marquis's* back would have looked narrower and more fragile. Chauvelin held his breath; then he gave a sharp little cough, and took the pistol from his belt.

The sound caused the *aristo* to turn, and the next moment a loud and merry laugh roused the dormant echoes of the old *château*, whilst a pleasant, drawly voice said in English:

"I am demmed if this is not my dear old friend M. Chambertin! Zounds, sir! who'd have thought of meeting you here?"

Had a cannon suddenly exploded at Chauvelin's feet he would, I think, have felt less unnerved. For the space of two heart-beats he stood there, rooted to the spot, his eyes glued on his arch-enemy, that execrated Scarlet Pimpernel, whose mocking glance, even through the intervening gloom, seemed to have deprived him of consciousness. But that phase of helplessness only lasted for a moment; the next, all the marvellous possibilities of this encounter flashed through the Terrorist's keen mind.

Everything was ready; the trap was set! The unfortunate Clamettes were still the bait which now would bring a far more noble quarry into the mesh than even he—Chauvelin—had dared to hope.

He raised his pistol, ready to fire. But already Sir Percy Blakeney was on him, and with a swift movement, which the other was too weak to resist, he wrenched the weapon from his enemy's grasp.

"Why, how hasty you are, my dear M. Chambertin," he said lightly. "Surely you are not in such a hurry to put a demmed bullet into me!"

The position now was one which would have made even a braver man than Chauvelin quake. He stood alone and unarmed in face of an enemy from whom he could expect no mercy. But, even so, his first

458

thought was not of escape. He had not only apprised his own danger, but also the immense power which he held whilst the Clamettes remained as hostages in the hands of his colleague Lebel.

"You have me at a disadvantage, Sir Percy," he said, speaking every whit as coolly as his foe. "But only momentarily. You can kill me, of course; but if I do not return from this expedition not only safe and sound, but with a certain packet of papers in my hands, my colleague Lebel has instructions to proceed at once against the girl Clamette and the whole family."

"I know that well enough," rejoined Sir Percy with a quaint laugh. "I know what venomous reptiles you and those of your kidney are. You certainly do owe your life at the present moment to the unfortunate girl whom you are persecuting with such infamous callousness."

Chauvelin drew a sigh of relief. The situation was shaping itself more to his satisfaction already. Through the gloom he could vaguely discern the Englishman's massive form standing a few paces away, one hand buried in his breeches pockets, the other still holding the pistol. On the ground close by the hearth was the small lanthorn, and in its dim light the packet of papers gleamed white and tempting in the darkness. Chauvelin's keen eyes had fastened on it, saw the form of receipt for money with Hériot's signature, which he recognised, on the top.

He himself had never felt so calm. The only thing he could regret was that he was alone. Half a dozen men now, and this impudent foe could indeed be brought to his knees. And this time there would be no risks taken, no chances for escape. Somehow it seemed to Chauvelin as if something of the Scarlet Pimpernel's audacity and foresight had gone from him. As he stood there, looking broad and physically powerful, there was something wavering and undecided in his attitude, as if the edge had been taken off his former recklessness and enthusiasm. He had brought the compromising papers here, had no doubt helped the Montorgueils to escape; but while Lucile Clamette and her family were under the eye of Lebel no amount of impudence could force a successful bargaining.

It was Chauvelin now who appeared the more keen and the more alert; the Englishman seemed undecided what to do next, remained silent, toying with the pistol. He even smothered a yawn. Chauvelin saw his opportunity. With the quick movement of a cat pouncing upon a mouse he stooped and seized that packet of papers, would then and there have made a dash for the door with them, only that, as he

459

seized the packet, the string which held it together gave way and the papers were scattered all over the floor.

Receipts for money? Compromising letters? No! Blank sheets of paper, all of them—all except the one which had lain tantalisingly on the top: the one receipt signed by Citizen Hériot. Sir Percy laughed lightly:

"Did you really think, my good friend," he said, "that I would be such a demmed fool as to place my best weapon so readily to your hand?"

"Your best weapon, Sir Percy!" retorted Chauvelin, with a sneer. "What use is it to you while we hold Lucile Clamette?"

"While I hold Lucile Clamette, you mean, my dear Monsieur Chambertin," riposted Blakeney with elaborate blandness.

"You hold Lucile Clamette? Bah! I defy you to drag a whole family like that out of our clutches. The man a cripple, the children helpless! And you think they can escape our vigilance when all our men are warned! How do you think they are going to get across the river, Sir Percy, when every bridge is closely watched? How will they get across Paris, when at every gate our men are on the look-out for them?"

"They can't do it, my dear Monsieur Chambertin," rejoined Sir Percy blandly, "else I were not here."

Then, as Chauvelin, fuming, irritated despite himself, as he always was when he encountered that impudent Englishman, shrugged his shoulders in token of contempt, Blakeney's powerful grasp suddenly clutched his arm.

"Let us understand one another, my good M. Chambertin," he said coolly. "Those unfortunate Clamettes, as you say, are too helpless and too numerous to smuggle across Paris with any chance of success. Therefore, I look to you to take them under your protection. They are all stowed away comfortably at this moment in a conveyance which I have provided for them. That conveyance is waiting at the bridge-head now. We could not cross without your help; we could not get across Paris without your august presence and your tricolour scarf of office. So, you are coming with us, my dear M. Chambertin," he continued, and, with force which was quite irresistible, he began to drag his enemy after him towards the door. "You are going to sit in that conveyance with the Clamettes, and I myself will have the honour to drive you. And at every bridgehead you will show your pleasing countenance and your scarf of office to the guard and demand free passage for yourself and your family, as a representative member of the

Committee of Public Safety. And then we'll enter Paris by the Porte d'Ivry and leave it by the Batignolles; and everywhere your charming presence will lull the guards' suspicions to rest. I pray you, come! There is no time to consider! At noon tomorrow, without a moment's grace, my friend Sir Andrew Ffoulkes, who has the papers in his possession, will dispose of them as he thinks best unless I myself do claim them from him."

While he spoke, he continued to drag his enemy along with him, with an assurance and an impudence which were past belief. Chauvelin was trying to collect his thoughts; a whirl of conflicting plans were running riot in his mind. The Scarlet Pimpernel in his power! At any point on the road he could deliver him up to the nearest guard . . . . then still hold the Clamettes and demand the papers . . . .

"Too late, my dear Monsieur Chambertin!" Sir Percy's mocking voice broke in, as if divining his thoughts. "You do not know where to find my friend Ffoulkes, and at noon tomorrow, if I do not arrive to claim those papers, there will not be a single ragamuffin in Paris who will not be crying your shame and that of your precious colleagues upon the housetops."

Chauvelin's whole nervous system was writhing with the feeling of impotence. Mechanically, unresisting now, he followed his enemy down the main staircase of the *château* and out through the wide open gates. He could not bring himself to believe that he had been so completely foiled, that this impudent adventurer had him once more in the hollow of his hand.

"In the name of Satan, bring us back those papers!" Robespierre had commanded. And now he—Chauvelin—was left in a maze of doubt; and the vital alternative was hammering in his brain: "The Scarlet Pimpernel—or those papers—" Which, in Satan's name, was the more important? Passion whispered "The Scarlet Pimpernel!" but common sense and the future of his party, the whole future of the Revolution mayhap, demanded those compromising papers. And all the while he followed that relentless enemy through the avenues of the park and down the lonely lane. Overhead the trees of the forest of Sucy, nodding in a gentle breeze, seemed to mock his perplexity.

He had not arrived at a definite decision when the river came in sight, and when *anon* a carriage lanthorn threw a shaft of dim light through the mist-laden air. Now he felt as if he were in a dream. He was thrust unresisting into a closed chaise, wherein he felt the presence of several other people—children, an old man who was muttering ceaselessly. As in a dream he answered questions at the bridge to a guard whom he knew well.

"You know me—Armand Chauvelin, of the Committee of Public Safety!"

As in a dream, he heard the curt words of command:

"Pass on, in the name of the Republic!"

And all the while the thought hammered in his brain: "Something must be done! This is impossible! This cannot be! It is not I—Chauvelin—who am sitting here, helpless, unresisting. It is not that impudent Scarlet Pimpernel who is sitting there before me on the box, driving me to utter humiliation!"

And yet it was all true. All real. The Clamette children were sitting in front of him, clinging to Lucile, terrified of him even now. The old man was beside him—imbecile and not understanding. The boy Etienne was up on the box next to that audacious adventurer, whose broad back appeared to Chauvelin like a rock on which all his hopes and dreams must for ever be shattered.

The chaise rattled triumphantly through the Batignolles. It was then broad daylight. A brilliant early autumn day after the rains. The sun, the keen air, all mocked Chauvelin's helplessness, his humiliation. Long before noon they passed St. Denis. Here the *barouche* turned off the main road, halted at a small wayside house—nothing more than a cottage. After which everything seemed more dreamlike than ever. All that Chauvelin remembered of it afterwards was that he was once more alone in a room with his enemy, who had demanded his signature to a number of safe-conducts, ere he finally handed over the packet of papers to him.

"How do I know that they are all here?" he heard himself vaguely muttering, while his trembling fingers handled that precious packet.

"That's just it!" his tormentor retorted airily. "You don't know. I don't know myself," he added, with a light laugh. "And, personally, I don't see how either of us can possibly ascertain. In the meanwhile, I must bid you *au revoir*, my dear M. Chambertin. I am sorry that I cannot provide you with a conveyance, and you will have to walk a league or more ere you meet one, I fear me. We, in the meanwhile, will be well on our way to Dieppe, where my yacht, the *Day Dream*, lies at anchor, and I do not think that it will be worth your while to try and overtake us. I thank you for the safe-conducts. They will make our journey exceedingly pleasant. Shall I give your regards to M. le Marquis de Montorgueil or to M. le Vicomte? They are on board the *Day*

Dream, you know. Oh! and I was forgetting! Lady Blakeney desired to be remembered to you."

The next moment he was gone. Chauvelin, standing at the window of the wayside house, saw Sir Percy Blakeney once more mount the box of the chaise. This time he had Sir Andrew Ffoulkes beside him. The Clamette family were huddled together—happy and free—inside the vehicle. After which there was the usual clatter of horses' hoofs, the creaking of wheels, the rattle of chains. Chauvelin saw and heard nothing of that. All that he saw at the last was Sir Percy's slender hand, waving him a last *adieu*.

After which he was left alone with his thoughts. The packet of papers was in his hand. He fingered it, felt its crispness, clutched it with a fierce gesture, which was followed by a long-drawn-out sigh of intense bitterness.

No one would ever know what it had cost him to obtain these papers. No one would ever know how much he had sacrificed of pride, revenge and hate in order to save a few shreds of his own party's honour.

A Battle of Wits

What had happened was this:

Tournefort, one of the ablest of the many sleuth-hounds employed by the Committee of Public Safety, was out during that awful storm on the night of the twenty-fifth. The rain came down as if it had been poured out of buckets, and Tournefort took shelter under the portico of a tall, dilapidated-looking house somewhere at the back of St. Lazare. The night was, of course, pitch dark, and the howling of the wind and beating of the rain effectually drowned every other sound.

Tournefort, chilled to the marrow, had at first cowered in the angle of the door, as far away from the draught as he could. But presently he spied the glimmer of a tiny light some little way up on his left, and taking this to come from the *concierge's* lodge, he went cautiously along the passage intending to ask for better shelter against the fury of the elements than the rickety front door afforded.

Tournefort, you must remember, was always on the best terms with every *concierge* in Paris. They were, as it were, his subordinates; without their help he never could have carried on his unavowable profession quite so successfully. And they, in their turn, found it to their advantage to earn the good-will of that army of spies, which the Revolutionary Government kept in its service, for the tracking down of all those unfortunates who had not given complete adhesion to their tyrannical and murderous policy.

Therefore, in this instance, Tournefort felt no hesitation in claiming the hospitality of the *concierge* of the squalid house wherein he found himself. He went boldly up to the lodge. His hand was already on the latch, when certain sounds which proceeded from the interior of the lodge caused him to pause and to bend his ear in order to listen. It was Tournefort's *métier* to listen. What had arrested his attention was the sound of a man's voice, saying in a tone of deep respect:

"*Bien*, Madame la Comtesse, we'll do our best."

No wonder that the servant of the Committee of Public Safety remained at attention, no longer thought of the storm or felt the cold blast chilling him to the marrow. Here was a wholly unexpected piece of good luck. "Madame la Comtesse!" *Peste!* There were not many such left in Paris these days. Unfortunately, the tempest of the wind and the rain made such a din that it was difficult to catch every sound which came from the interior of the lodge. All that Tournefort caught definitely were a few fragments of conversation.

"My good M. Bertin ..." came at one time from a woman's voice. "Truly I do not know why you should do all this for me."

And then again: "All I possess in the world now are my diamonds. They alone stand between my children and utter destitution."

The man's voice seemed all the time to be saying something that sounded cheerful and encouraging. But his voice came only as a vague murmur to the listener's ears. Presently, however, there came a word which set his pulses tingling. *Madame* said something about "Gentilly," and directly afterwards: "You will have to be very careful, my dear M. Bertin. The *château*, I feel sure, is being watched."

Tournefort could scarce repress a cry of joy. "Gentilly? Madame la Comtesse? The *château?*" Why, of course, he held all the necessary threads already. The *ci-devant* Comte de Sucy—a pestilential *aristo* if ever there was one!—had been sent to the guillotine less than a fort-night ago. His *château*, situated just outside Gentilly, stood empty, it having been given out that the widow Sucy and her two children had escaped to England. Well! she had not gone apparently, for here she was, in the lodge of the *concierge* of a mean house in one of the desolate quarters of Paris, begging some traitor to find her diamonds for her, which she had obviously left concealed inside the *château*. What a haul for Tournefort! What commendation from his superiors! The chances of a speedy promotion were indeed glorious now! He blessed the storm and the rain which had driven him for shelter to this house, where a poisonous plot was being hatched to rob the people of valuable property, and to aid a few more of those abominable *aristos* in cheating the guillotine of their traitorous heads.

He listened for a while longer, in order to get all the information that he could on the subject of the diamonds, because he knew by experience that those perfidious *aristos*, once they were under arrest, would sooner bite out their tongues than reveal anything that might be of service to the Government of the people. But he learned little else. Nothing was revealed of where Madame la Comtesse was in hiding, or how the diamonds were to be disposed of once they were found. Tournefort would have given much to have at least one of his colleagues with him. As it was, he would be forced to act single-handed and on his own initiative. In his own mind he had already decided that he would wait until Madame la Comtesse came out of the *concierge's* lodge, and that he would follow her and apprehend her somewhere out in the open streets, rather than here where her friend Bertin might prove to be a stalwart as well as a desperate man, ready with a pistol, whilst he—Tournefort—was unarmed. Bertin, who had, it seemed, been entrusted with the task of finding the diamonds, could then be shadowed and arrested in the very act of filching property which by decree of the State belonged to the people.

So, he waited patiently for a while. No doubt the *aristo* would remain here under shelter until the storm had abated. Soon the sound of voices died down, and an extraordinary silence descended on this miserable, abandoned corner of old Paris. The silence became all the more marked after a while, because the rain ceased its monotonous pattering and the soughing of the wind was stilled. It was, in fact, this amazing stillness which set Citizen Tournefort thinking. Evidently the *aristo* did not intend to come out of the lodge tonight. Well! Tournefort had not meant to make himself unpleasant inside the house, or to have a quarrel just yet with the traitor Bertin, whoever he was; but his hand was forced and he had no option.

The door of the lodge was locked. He tugged vigorously at the bell again and again, for at first, he got no answer. A few minutes later he heard the sound of shuffling footsteps upon creaking boards. The door was opened, and a man in night attire, with bare, thin legs and tattered carpet slippers on his feet, confronted an exceedingly astonished servant of the Committee of Public Safety. Indeed, Tournefort thought that he must have been dreaming, or that he was dreaming now. For the man who opened the door to him was well known to every agent of the Committee. He was an ex-soldier who had been crippled years ago by the loss of one arm, and had held the post of *concierge* in a house in the Ruelle du Paradis ever since. His name was Grosjean. He was very old, and nearly doubled up with rheumatism, had scarcely any hair on his head or flesh on his bones. At this moment he appeared to be suffering from a cold in the head, for his eyes were streaming and his narrow, hooked nose was adorned by a drop of moisture at its tip. In fact, poor old Grosjean looked more like a dilapidated scarecrow than a dangerous conspirator. Tournefort literally gasped at sight of him, and Grosjean uttered a kind of croak, intended, no doubt, for complete surprise.

"Citizen Tournefort!" he exclaimed. "Name of a dog! What are you doing here at this hour and in this abominable weather? Come in! Come in!" he added, and, turning on his heel, he shuffled back into the inner room, and then returned carrying a lighted lamp, which he set upon the table. "Amelie left a sup of hot coffee on the hob in the kitchen before she went to bed. You must have a drop of that."

He was about to shuffle off again when Tournefort broke in roughly:

"None of that nonsense, Grosjean! Where are the *aristos*?"

"The *aristos*, citizen?" queried Grosjean, and nothing could have looked more utterly, more ludicrously bewildered than did the old *concierge* at this moment. "What *aristos*?"

"Bertin and Madame la Comtesse," retorted Tournefort gruffly. "I heard them talking."

"You have been dreaming, Citizen Tournefort," the old man said, with a husky little laugh. "Sit down, and let me get you some coffee—"

"Don't try and hoodwink me, Grosjean!" Tournefort cried now in a sudden access of rage. "I tell you that I saw the light. I heard the *aristos* talking. There was a man named Bertin, and a woman he called 'Madame la Comtesse,' and I say that some devilish royalist plot is being hatched here, and that you, Grosjean, will suffer for it if you try and shield those *aristos*."

"But, Citizen Tournefort," replied the *concierge* meekly, "I assure you that I have seen no *aristos*. The door of my bedroom was open, and the lamp was by my bedside. Amelie, too, has only been in bed a few minutes. You ask her! There has been no one, I tell you—no one! I should have seen and heard them—the door was open," he reiterated pathetically.

"We'll soon see about that!" was Tournefort's curt comment.

But it was his turn indeed to be utterly bewildered. He searched—none too gently—the squalid little lodge through and through, turned the paltry sticks of furniture over, hauled little Amelie, Grosjean's granddaughter, out of bed, searched under the mattresses, and even poked his head up the chimney.

Grosjean watched him wholly unperturbed. These were strange times, and friend Tournefort had obviously gone a little off his head. The worthy old *concierge* calmly went on getting the coffee ready. Only when presently Tournefort, worn out with anger and futile exertion, threw himself, with many an oath, into the one armchair, Grosjean

467

remarked coolly:

"I tell you what I think it is, citizen. If you were standing just by the door of the lodge you had the back staircase of the house immediately behind you. The partition wall is very thin, and there is a disused door just there also. No doubt the voices came from there. You see, if there had been any *aristos* here," he added *naively*, "they could not have flown up the chimney, could they?"

That argument was certainly unanswerable. But Tournefort was out of temper. He roughly ordered Grosjean to bring the lamp and show him the back staircase and the disused door. The *concierge* obeyed without a murmur. He was not in the least disturbed or frightened by all this blustering. He was only afraid that getting out of bed had made his cold worse. But he knew Tournefort of old. A good fellow, but inclined to be noisy and arrogant since he was in the employ of the Government. Grosjean took the precaution of putting on his trousers and wrapping an old shawl round his shoulders. Then he had a final sip of hot coffee; after which he picked up the lamp and guided Tournefort out of the lodge.

The wind had quite gone down by now. The lamp scarcely flickered as Grosjean held it above his head.

"Just here, Citizen Tournefort," he said, and turned sharply to his left. But the next sound which he uttered was a loud croak of astonishment.

"That door has been out of use ever since I've been here," he muttered.

"And it certainly was closed when I stood up against it," rejoined Tournefort, with a savage oath, "or, of course, I should have noticed it."

Close to the lodge, at right angles to it, a door stood partially open. Tournefort went through it, closely followed by Grosjean. He found himself in a passage which ended in a *cul de sac* on his right; on the left was the foot of the stairs. The whole place was pitch dark save for the feeble light of the lamp. The *cul de sac* itself reeked of dirt and fustiness, as if it had not been cleaned or ventilated for years.

"When did you last notice that this door was closed?" queried Tournefort, furious with the sense of discomfiture, which he would have liked to vent on the unfortunate *concierge*.

"I have not noticed it for some days, citizen," replied Grosjean meekly. "I have had a severe cold, and have not been outside my lodge since Monday last. But we'll ask Amelie!" he added more hopefully.

Amelie, however, could throw no light upon the subject. She certainly kept the back stairs cleaned and swept, but it was not part of her duties to extend her sweeping operations as far as the *cul de sac*. She had quite enough to do as it was, with grandfather now practically helpless. This morning, when she went out to do her shopping, she had not noticed whether the disused door did or did not look the same as usual.

Grosjean was very sorry for his friend Tournefort, who appeared vastly upset, but still more sorry for himself, for he knew what endless trouble this would entail upon him.

Nor was the trouble slow in coming, not only on Grosjean, but on every lodger inside the house; for before half an hour had gone by Tournefort had gone and come back, this time with the local *commissary* of police and a couple of agents, who had every man, woman and child in that house out of bed and examined at great length, their identity books searchingly overhauled, their rooms turned topsy-turvy and their furniture knocked about.

It was past midnight before all these perquisitions were completed. No one dared to complain at these indignities put upon peaceable citizens on the mere denunciation of an obscure police agent. These were times when every regulation, every command, had to be accepted without a murmur. At one o'clock in the morning, Grosjean himself was thankful to get back to bed, having satisfied the *commissary* that he was not a dangerous conspirator.

But of anyone even remotely approaching the description of the *ci-devant* Comtesse de Sucy, or of any man called Bertin, there was not the faintest trace.

2

But no feeling of discomfort ever lasted very long with Citizen Tournefort. He was a person of vast resource and great buoyancy of temperament.

True, he had not apprehended two exceedingly noxious *aristos*, as he had hoped to do; but he held the threads of an abominable conspiracy in his hands, and the question of catching both Bertin and Madame la Comtesse red-handed was only a question of time. But little time had been lost. There was always someone to be found at the offices of the Committee of Public Safety, which were open all night. It was possible that Citizen Chauvelin would be still there, for he often took on the night shift, or else Citizen Gourdon.

It was Gourdon who greeted his subordinate, somewhat ill-humouredly, for he was indulging in a little sleep, with his toes turned to the fire, as the night was so damp and cold. But when he heard Tournefort's story, he was all eagerness and zeal.

"It is, of course, too late to do anything now," he said finally, after he had mastered every detail of the man's adventures in the Ruelle du Paradis; "but get together half a dozen men upon whom you can rely, and by six o'clock in the morning, or even five, we'll be on our way to Gentilly. Citizen Chauvelin was only saying today that he strongly suspected the *ci-devant* Comtesse de Sucy of having left the bulk of her valuable jewellery at the *château*, and that she would make some effort to get possession of it. It would be rather fine, Citizen Tournefort," he added with a chuckle, "if you and I could steal a march on Citizen Chauvelin over this affair, what? He has been extraordinarily arrogant of late and marvellously in favour, not only with the Committee, but with Citizen Robespierre himself."

"They say," commented Tournefort, "that he succeeded in getting hold of some papers which were of great value to the members of the Committee."

"He never succeeded in getting hold of that meddlesome Englishman whom they call the Scarlet Pimpernel," was Gourdon's final dry comment.

Thus, was the matter decided on. And the following morning at daybreak, Gourdon, who was only a subordinate officer on the Committee of Public Safety, took it upon himself to institute a perquisition in the Château of Gentilly, which is situated close to the commune of that name. He was accompanied by his friend Tournefort and a gang of half a dozen ruffians recruited from the most disreputable *cabarets* of Paris.

The intention had been to steal a march on Citizen Chauvelin, who had been over arrogant of late; but the result did not come up to expectations. By midday the *château* had been ransacked from attic to cellar; every kind of valuable property had been destroyed, priceless works of art irretrievably damaged. But priceless works of art had no market in Paris these days; and the property of real value—the Sucy diamonds namely—which had excited the cupidity or the patriotic wrath of Citizens Gourdon and Tournefort could nowhere be found.

To make the situation more deplorable still, the Committee of Public Safety had in some unexplainable way got wind of the affair, and the two worthies had the mortification of seeing Citizen Chauvelin presently appear upon the scene.

It was then two o'clock in the afternoon. Gourdon, after he had snatched a hasty dinner at a neighbouring *cabaret*, had returned to the task of pulling the Château of Gentilly about his own ears if need be, with a view to finding the concealed treasure.

For the nonce he was standing in the centre of the finely proportioned hall. The rich ormolu and crystal chandelier lay in a tangled, broken heap of scraps at his feet, and all around there was a confused medley of pictures, statuettes, silver ornaments, tapestry and brocade hangings, all piled up in disorder, smashed, tattered, kicked at now and again by Gourdon, to the accompaniment of a savage oath.

The house itself was full of noises; heavy footsteps tramping up and down the stairs, furniture turned over, curtains torn from their poles, doors and windows battered in. And through it all the ceaseless hammering of pick and axe, attacking these stately walls which had withstood the wars and sieges of centuries.

Every now and then Tournefort, his face perspiring and crimson with exertion, would present himself at the door of the hall. Gourdon would query gruffly: "Well?"

And the answer was invariably the same: "Nothing!"

Then Gourdon would swear again and send curt orders to continue the search, relentlessly, ceaselessly.

"Leave no stone upon stone," he commanded. "Those diamonds must be found. We know they are here, and, name of a dog! I mean to have them."

When Chauvelin arrived at the *château* he made no attempt at first to interfere with Gourdon's commands. Only on one occasion he remarked curtly:

"I suppose, Citizen Gourdon, that you can trust your search party?"

"Absolutely," retorted Gourdon. "A finer patriot than Tournefort does not exist."

"Probably," rejoined the other dryly. "But what about the men?"

"Oh! they are only a set of barefooted, ignorant louts. They do as they are told, and Tournefort has his eye on them. I dare say they'll contrive to steal a few things, but they would never dare lay hands on valuable jewellery. To begin with, they could never dispose of it. Imagine a *va-nu-pieds* peddling a diamond tiara!"

"There are always receivers prepared to take risks."

"Very few," Gourdon assured him, "since we decreed that trafficking with *aristo* property was a crime punishable by death."

Chauvelin said nothing for the moment. He appeared wrapped in his own thoughts, listened for a while to the confused hubbub about the house, then he resumed abruptly:

"Who are these men whom you are employing, Citizen Gourdon?"

"A well-known gang," replied the other. "I can give you their names."

"If you please."

Gourdon searched his pockets for a paper which he found presently and handed to his colleague. The latter perused it thoughtfully.

"Where did Tournefort find these men?" he asked.

"For the most part at the *Cabaret de la Liberté*—a place of very evil repute down in the Rue Christine."

"I know it," rejoined the other. He was still studying the list of names which Gourdon had given him. "And," he added, "I know most of these men. As thorough a set of ruffians as we need for some of our work. Merri, Guidal, Rateau, Desmonds. *Tiens!*" he exclaimed. "Rateau! Is Rateau here now?"

"Why, of course! He was recruited, like the rest of them, for the day. He won't leave till he has been paid, you may be sure of that. Why do you ask?"

"I will tell you presently. But I would wish to speak with Citizen Rateau first."

Just at this moment Tournefort paid his periodical visit to the hall. The usual words, "Still nothing," were on his lips, when Gourdon curtly ordered him to go and fetch the Citizen Rateau.

A minute or two later Tournefort returned with the news that Rateau could nowhere be found. Chauvelin received the news without any comment; he only ordered Tournefort, somewhat roughly, back to his work. Then, as soon as the latter had gone, Gourdon turned upon his colleague.

"Will you explain—" he began with a show of bluster.

"With pleasure," replied Chauvelin blandly. "On my way hither, less than an hour ago, I met your man Rateau, a league or so from here."

"You met Rateau!" exclaimed Gourdon impatiently. "Impossible! He was here then, I feel sure. You must have been mistaken."

"I think not. I have only seen the man once, when I, too, went to recruit a band of ruffians at the *Cabaret de la Liberté*, in connection with some work I wanted doing. I did not employ him then, for he appeared to me both drink-sodden and nothing but a miserable, consumptive creature, with a churchyard cough you can hear half a league

472

away. But I would know him anywhere. Besides which, he stopped and wished me good morning. Now I come to think of it," added Chauvelin thoughtfully, "he was carrying what looked like a heavy bundle under his arm."

"A heavy bundle!" cried Gourdon, with a forceful oath. "And you did not stop him!"

"I had no reason for suspecting him. I did not know until I arrived here what the whole affair was about, or whom you were employing. All that the Committee knew for certain was that you and Tournefort and a number of men had arrived at Gentilly before daybreak, and I was then instructed to follow you hither to see what mischief you were up to. You acted in complete secrecy, remember, Citizen Gourdon, and without first ascertaining the wishes of the Committee of Public Safety, whose servant you are. If the Sucy diamonds are not found, you alone will be held responsible for their loss to the Government of the People."

Chauvelin's voice had now assumed a threatening tone, and Gourdon felt all his audacity and self-assurance fall away from him, leaving him a prey to nameless terror.

"We must round up Rateau," he murmured hastily. "He cannot have gone far."

"No, he cannot," rejoined Chauvelin dryly. "Though I was not specially thinking of Rateau or of diamonds when I started to come hither. I did send a general order forbidding any person on foot or horseback to enter or leave Paris by any of the southern gates. That order will serve us well now. Are you riding?"

"Yes. I left my horse at the tavern just outside Gentilly. I can get to horse within ten minutes."

"To horse, then, as quickly as you can. Pay off your men and dismiss them—all but Tournefort, who had best accompany us. Do not lose a single moment. I'll be ahead of you and may come up with Rateau before you overtake me. And if I were you, Citizen Gourdon," he concluded, with ominous emphasis, "I would burn one or two candles to your *compeer* the devil. You'll have need of his help if Rateau gives us the slip."

3

The first part of the road from Gentilly to Paris runs through the valley of the Bière, and is densely wooded on either side. It winds in and out for the most part, ribbon-like, through thick coppice of chestnut and birch. Thus, it was impossible for Chauvelin to spy his quarry from afar; nor did he expect to do so this side of the Hôpital de la Santé. Once past that point, he would find the road quite open and running almost straight, in the midst of arid and only partially cultivated land.

He rode at a sharp trot, with his caped coat wrapped tightly round his shoulders, for it was raining fast. At intervals, when he met an occasional wayfarer, he would ask questions about a tall man who had a consumptive cough, and who was carrying a cumbersome burden under his arm.

Almost everyone whom he thus asked remembered seeing a personage who vaguely answered to the description: tall and with a decided stoop—yes, and carrying a cumbersome-looking bundle under his arm. Chauvelin was undoubtedly on the track of the thief.

Just beyond Meuves he was overtaken by Gourdon and Tournefort. Here, too, the man Rateau's track became more and more certain. At one place he had stopped and had a glass of wine and a rest, at another he had asked how close he was to the gates of Paris.

The road was now quite open and level; the irregular buildings of the hospital appeared vague in the rain-sodden distance. Twenty minutes later Tournefort, who was riding ahead of his companions, spied a tall, stooping figure at the spot where the Chemin de Gentilly forks, and where stands a group of isolated houses and bits of garden, which belong to la Santé. Here, before the days when the glorious Revolution swept aside all such outward signs of superstition, there had stood a Calvary. It was now used as a signpost. The man stood before it, scanning the half-obliterated indications.

At the moment that Tournefort first caught sight of him he appeared uncertain of his way. Then for a while he watched Tournefort, who was coming at a sharp trot towards him. Finally, he seemed to make up his mind very suddenly and, giving a last, quick look round, he walked rapidly along the upper road. Tournefort drew rein, waited for his colleagues to come up with him. Then he told them what he had seen.

"It is Rateau, sure enough," he said. "I saw his face quite distinctly and heard his abominable cough. He is trying to get into Paris. That road leads nowhere but to the barrier. There, of course, he will be stopped, and—"

The other two had also brought their horses to a halt. The situation had become tense, and a plan for future action had at once to be decided on. Already Chauvelin, masterful and sure of himself, had assumed command of the little party. Now he broke in abruptly on Tournefort's vapid reflections.

"We don't want him stopped at the barrier," he said in his usual curt, authoritative manner. "You, Citizen Tournefort," he continued, "will ride as fast as you can to the gate, making a detour by the lower road. You will immediately demand to speak with the sergeant who is in command, and you will give him a detailed description of the man Rateau. Then you will tell him in my name that, should such a man present himself at the gate, he must be allowed to enter the city unmolested."

Gourdon gave a quick cry of protest.

"Let the man go unmolested? Citizen Chauvelin, think what you are doing!"

"I always think of what I am doing," retorted Chauvelin curtly, "and have no need of outside guidance in the process." Then he turned once more to Tournefort. "You yourself, citizen," he continued, in sharp, decisive tones which admitted of no argument, "will dismount as soon as you are inside the city. You will keep the gate under observation. The moment you see the man Rateau, you will shadow him, and on no account lose sight of him. Understand?"

"You may trust me, Citizen Chauvelin," Tournefort replied, elated at the prospect of work which was so entirely congenial to him. "But will you tell me—"

"I will tell you this much, Citizen Tournefort," broke in Chauvelin with some acerbity, "that though we have traced the diamonds and the thief so far, we have, through your folly last night, lost complete track of the *ci-devant* Comtesse de Sucy and of the man Bertin. We want Rateau to show us where they are."

"I understand," murmured the other meekly.

"That's a mercy!" riposted Chauvelin dryly. "Then quickly man. Lose no time! Try to get a few minutes' advance on Rateau; then slip in to the guard-room to change into less conspicuous clothes. Citizen Gourdon and I will continue on the upper road and keep the man in sight in case he should think of altering his course. In any event, we'll meet you just inside the barrier. But if, in the meanwhile, you have to get on Rateau's track before we have arrived on the scene, leave the usual indications as to the direction which you have taken."

Having given his orders and satisfied himself that they were fully understood, he gave a curt command, "*En avant*," and once more the three of them rode at a sharp trot down the road towards the city.

Citizen Rateau, if he thought about the matter at all, must indeed have been vastly surprised at the unwonted amiability or indifference of Sergeant Ribot, who was in command at the gate of Gentilly. Ribot only threw a very perfunctory glance at the greasy permit which Rateau presented to him, and when he put the usual query, "What's in that parcel?" and Rateau gave the reply: "Two heads of cabbage and a bunch of carrots," Ribot merely poked one of his fingers into the bundle, felt that a cabbage leaf did effectually lie on the top, and thereupon gave the formal order: "Pass on, citizen, in the name of the Republic!" without any hesitation.

Tournefort, who had watched the brief little incident from behind the window of a neighbouring *cabaret*, could not help but chuckle to himself. Never had he seen game walk more readily into a trap. Rateau, after he had passed the barrier, appeared undecided which way he would go. He looked with obvious longing towards the *cabaret*, behind which the keenest agent on the staff of the Committee of Public Safety was even now ensconced. But seemingly a halt within those hospitable doors did not form part of his programme, and a moment or two later he turned sharply on his heel and strode rapidly down the Rue de l'Oursine.

Tournefort allowed him a fair start, and then made ready to follow.

Just as he was stepping out of the *cabaret* he spied Chauvelin and Gourdon coming through the gates. They, too, had apparently made a brief halt inside the guard-room, where—as at most of the gates—a store of various disguises was always kept ready for the use of the numerous sleuth-hounds employed by the Committee of Public Safety. Here the two men had exchanged their official *garments* for suits of sombre cloth, which gave them the appearance of a couple of humble *bourgeois* going quietly about their business. Tournefort had donned an old blouse, tattered stockings, and shoes down at heel. With his hands buried in his breeches' pockets, he, too, turned into the long narrow Rue de l'Oursine, which, after a sharp curve, abuts on the Rue Mouffetard.

Rateau was walking rapidly, taking big strides with his long legs. Tournefort, now sauntering in the gutter in the middle of the road, now darting in and out of open doorways, kept his quarry well in sight. Chauvelin and Gourdon lagged some little way behind. It was still raining, but not heavily—a thin drizzle, which penetrated almost to the marrow. Not many passers-by haunted this forlorn quarter of old Paris. To right and left tall houses almost obscured the last, quick-ly-fading light of the grey September day.

At the bottom of the Rue Mouffetard, Rateau came once more to a halt. A network of narrow streets radiated from this centre. He looked all round him and also behind. It was difficult to know wheth-er he had a sudden suspicion that he was being followed; certain it is that, after a very brief moment of hesitation, he plunged suddenly into the narrow Rue Contrescarpe and disappeared from view.

Tournefort was after him in a trice. When he reached the corner of the street he saw Rateau, at the further end of it, take a sudden sharp turn to the right. But not before he had very obviously spied his pur-suer, for at that moment his entire demeanour changed. An air of fur-tive anxiety was expressed in his whole attitude. Even at that distance Tournefort could see him clutching his bulky parcel close to his chest.

After that the pursuit became closer and hotter. Rateau was in and out of that tight network of streets which cluster around the Place de Fourci, intent, apparently, on throwing his pursuers off the scent, for after a while he was running round and round in a circle. Now up the Rue des Poules, then to the right and to the right again; back in the Place de Fourci. Then straight across it once more to the Rue Con-trescarpe, where he presently disappeared so completely from view that Tournefort thought that the earth must have swallowed him up.

Tournefort was a man capable of great physical exertion. His call-ing often made heavy demands upon his powers of endurance; but never before had he grappled with so strenuous a task. Puffing and panting, now running at top speed, *anon* brought to a halt by the doubling-up tactics of his quarry, his great difficulty was the fact that Citizen Chauvelin did not wish the man Rateau to be apprehended; did not wish him to know that he was being pursued. And Tournefort had need of all his wits to keep well under the shadow of any project-ing wall or under cover of open doorways which were conveniently in the way, and all the while not to lose sight of that consumptive gi-ant, who seemed to be playing some intricate game which well-nigh exhausted the strength of Citizen Tournefort.

What he could not make out was what had happened to Chau-velin and to Gourdon. They had been less than three hundred metres behind him when first this wild chase in and out of the Rue Con-trescarpe had begun. Now, when their presence was most needed, they seemed to have lost track both of him—Tournefort—and of the very elusive quarry. To make matters more complicated, the shades of evening were drawing in very fast, and these narrow streets of the Faubourg were very sparsely lighted.

Just at this moment Tournefort had once more caught sight of Rateau, striding leisurely this time up the street. The worthy agent quickly took refuge under a doorway and was mopping his streaming forehead, glad of this brief respite in the mad chase, when that awful churchyard cough suddenly sounded so close to him that he gave a great jump and well-nigh betrayed his presence then and there. He had only just time to withdraw further still into the angle of the doorway, when Rateau passed by.

Tournefort peeped out of his hiding-place, and for the space of a dozen heart beats or so, remained there quite still, watching that broad back and those long limbs slowly moving through the gathering gloom. The next instant he perceived Chauvelin standing at the end of the street.

Rateau saw him too—came face to face with him, in fact, and must have known who he was for, without an instant's hesitation and just like a hunted creature at bay, he turned sharply on his heel and then ran back down the street as hard as he could tear. He passed close to within half a metre of Tournefort, and as he flew past he hit out with his left fist so vigorously that the worthy agent of the Committee of Public Safety, caught on the nose by the blow, staggered and measured his length upon the flagged floor below.

The next moment Chauvelin had come by. Tournefort, struggling to his feet, called to him, panting:

"Did you see him? Which way did he go?"

"Up the Rue Bordet. After him, citizen!" replied Chauvelin grimly, between his teeth.

Together the two men continued the chase, guided through the intricate mazes of the streets by their fleeing quarry. They had Rateau well in sight, and the latter could no longer continue his former tactics with success now that two experienced sleuth-hounds were on his track.

At a given moment he was caught between the two of them. Tournefort was advancing cautiously up the Rue Bordet; Chauvelin, equally stealthily, was coming down the same street, and Rateau, once more walking quite leisurely, was at equal distance between the two.

5

There are no side turnings out of the Rue Bordet, the total length of which is less than fifty metres; so Tournefort, feeling more at his

478

ease, ensconced himself at one end of the street, behind a doorway, whilst Chauvelin did the same at the other. Rateau, standing in the gutter, appeared once more in a state of hesitation. Immediately in front of him the door of a small *cabaret* stood invitingly open; its signboard, "*Le Bon Copain*," promised rest and refreshment. He peered up and down the road, satisfied himself presumably that, for the moment, his pursuers were out of sight, hugged his parcel to his chest, and then suddenly made a dart for the *cabaret* and disappeared within its doors.

Nothing could have been better. The quarry, for the moment, was safe, and if the sleuth-hounds could not get refreshment, they could at least get a rest. Tournefort and Chauvelin crept out of their hiding-places. They met in the middle of the road, at the spot where Rateau had stood a while ago. It was then growing dark and the street was innocent of lanterns, but the lights inside the *cabaret* gave a full view of the interior. The lower half of the wide shop-window was curtained off, but above the curtain the heads of the customers of "*Le Bon Copain*," and the general comings and goings, could very clearly be seen.

Tournefort, never at a loss, had already climbed upon a low projection in the wall of one of the houses opposite. From this point of vantage he could more easily observe what went on inside the *cabaret*, and in short, jerky sentences he gave a description of what he saw to his chief.

"Rateau is sitting down . . . . he has his back to the window . . . . he has put his bundle down close beside him on the bench . . . . he can't speak for a minute, for he is coughing and spluttering like an old walrus . . . . A wench is bringing him a bottle of wine and a hunk of bread and cheese . . . . He has started talking . . . . is talking volubly . . . . the people are laughing . . . . some are applauding . . . . And here comes Jean Victor, the landlord . . . . you know him, citizen . . . . a big, hulking fellow, and as good a patriot as I ever wish to see . . . . He, too, is laughing and talking to Rateau, who is doubled up with another fit of coughing—"

Chauvelin uttered an exclamation of impatience:

"Enough of this, Citizen Tournefort. Keep your eye on the man and hold your tongue. I am spent with fatigue."

"No wonder," murmured Tournefort. Then he added insinuatingly: "Why not let me go in there and apprehend Rateau now? We should have the diamonds and—"

"And lose the *ci-devant* Comtesse de Sucy and the man Bertin," retorted Chauvelin with sudden fierceness. "Bertin, who can be none other than that cursed Englishman, the—"

He checked himself, seeing Tournefort was gazing down on him, with awe and bewilderment expressed in his lean, hatchet face.

"You are losing sight of Rateau, citizen," Chauvelin continued calmly. "What is he doing now?"

But Tournefort felt that this calmness was only on the surface; something strange had stirred the depths of his chief's keen, masterful mind. He would have liked to ask a question or two, but knew from experience that it was neither wise nor profitable to try and probe Citizen Chauvelin's thoughts. So after a moment or two he turned back obediently to his task.

"I can't see Rateau for the moment," he said, "but there is much talking and merriment in there. Ah! there he is, I think. Yes, I see him! . . . . He is behind the counter, talking to Jean Victor . . . . and he has just thrown some money down upon the counter . . . . gold too! name of a dog . . . . "

Then suddenly, without any warning, Tournefort jumped down from his post of observation. Chauvelin uttered a brief:

"What the —— are you doing, citizen?"

"Rateau is going," replied Tournefort excitedly. "He drank a mug of wine at a draught and has picked up his bundle, ready to go."

Once more cowering in the dark angle of a doorway, the two men waited, their nerves on edge, for the reappearance of their quarry.

"I wish Citizen Gourdon were here," whispered Tournefort. "In the darkness it is better to be three than two."

"I sent him back to the station in the Rue Mouffetard," was Chauvelin's curt retort; "there to give notice that I might require a few armed men presently. But he should be somewhere about here by now, looking for us. Anyway, I have my whistle, and if—"

He said no more, for at that moment the door of the *cabaret* was opened from within and Rateau stepped out into the street, to the accompaniment of loud laughter and clapping of hands which came from the customers of the "*Bon Copain.*"

This time he appeared neither in a hurry nor yet anxious. He did not pause in order to glance to right or left, but started to walk quite leisurely up the street. The two sleuth-hounds quietly followed him. Through the darkness they could only vaguely see his silhouette, with the great bundle under his arm. Whatever may have been Rateau's fears of being shadowed a while ago, he certainly seemed free of them now. He sauntered along, whistling a tune, down the Montagne Ste.

Geneviève to the Place Maubert, and thence straight towards the river.

Having reached the bank, he turned off to his left, sauntered past the Ecole de Médecine and went across the Petit Pont, then through the New Market, along the Quai des Orfèvres. Here he made a halt, and for a while looked over the embankment at the river and then round about him, as if in search of something. But presently he appeared to make up his mind, and continued his leisurely walk as far as the Pont Neuf, where he turned sharply off to his right, still whistling, Tournefort and Chauvelin hard upon his heels.

"That whistling is getting on my nerves," muttered Tournefort irritably; "and I haven't heard the ruffian's churchyard cough since he walked out of the '*Bon Copain*.'"

Strangely enough, it was this remark of Tournefort's which gave Chauvelin the first inkling of something strange and, to him, positively awesome. Tournefort, who walked close beside him, heard him suddenly mutter a fierce exclamation.

"Name of a dog!"

"What is it, citizen?" queried Tournefort, awed by this sudden outburst on the part of a man whose icy calmness had become proverbial throughout the Committee.

"Sound the alarm, citizen!" cried Chauvelin in response. "Or, by Satan, he'll escape us again!"

"But—" stammered Tournefort in utter bewilderment, while, with fingers that trembled somewhat, he fumbled for his whistle.

"We shall want all the help we can," retorted Chauvelin roughly. "For, unless I am much mistaken, there's more noble quarry here than even I could dare to hope!"

Rateau in the meanwhile had quietly lolled up to the parapet on the right-hand side of the bridge, and Tournefort, who was watching him with intense keenness, still marvelled why Citizen Chauvelin had suddenly become so strangely excited. Rateau was merely lolling against the parapet, like a man who has not a care in the world. He had placed his bundle on the stone ledge beside him. Here he waited a moment or two, until one of the small craft upon the river loomed out of the darkness immediately below the bridge. Then he picked up the bundle and threw it straight into the boat. At that same moment Tournefort had the whistle to his lips. A shrill, sharp sound rang out through the gloom.

"The boat, Citizen Tournefort, the boat!" cried Chauvelin. "There are plenty of us here to deal with the man."

Immediately, from the quays, the streets, the bridges, dark figures emerged out of the darkness and hurried to the spot. Some reached the bridgehead even as Rateau made a dart forward, and two men were upon him before he succeeded in running very far. Others had scrambled down the embankment and were shouting to some unseen boatman to "halt, in the name of the people!"

But Rateau gave in without a struggle. He appeared more dazed than frightened, and quietly allowed the agents of the Committee to lead him back to the bridge, where Chauvelin had paused, waiting for him.

6

A minute or two later Tournefort was once more beside his chief. He was carrying the precious bundle, which, he explained, the boatman had given up without question.

"The man knew nothing about it," the agent said. "No one, he says, could have been more surprised than he was when this bundle was suddenly flung at him over the parapet of the bridge."

Just then the small group, composed of two or three agents of the Committee, holding their prisoner by the arms, came into view. One man was walking ahead and was the first to approach Chauvelin. He had a small screw of paper in his hand, which he gave to his chief.

"Found inside the lining of the prisoner's hat, citizen," he reported curtly, and opened the shutter of a small, dark lantern which he wore at his belt.

Chauvelin took the paper from his subordinate. A weird, unexplainable foreknowledge of what was to come caused his hand to shake and beads of perspiration to moisten his forehead. He looked up and saw the prisoner standing before him. Crushing the paper in his hand he snatched the lantern from the agent's belt and flashed it in the face of the quarry who, at the last, had been so easily captured.

Immediately a hoarse cry of disappointment and of rage escaped his throat.

"Who is this man?" he cried.

One of the agents gave reply:

"It is old Victor, the landlord of the 'Bon Copain.' He is just a fool, who has been playing a practical joke."

Tournefort, too, at sight of the prisoner had uttered a cry of dismay and of astonishment.

"Victor!" he exclaimed. "Name of a dog, citizen, what are you doing here?"

But Chauvelin had gripped the man by the arm so fiercely that the latter swore with the pain.

"What is the meaning of this?" he queried roughly.

"Only a bet, citizen," retorted Victor reproachfully. "No reason to fall on an honest patriot for a bet, just as if he were a mad dog."

"A joke? A bet?" murmured Chauvelin hoarsely, for his throat now felt hot and parched. "What do you mean? Who are you, man? Speak, or I'll—"

"My name is Jean Victor," replied the other. "I am the landlord of the '*Bon Copain.*' An hour ago, a man came into my *cabaret*. He was a queer, consumptive creature, with a churchyard cough that made you shiver. Some of my customers knew him by sight, told me that the man's name was Rateau, and that he was an *habitué* of the '*Liberté*,' in the Rue Christine. Well; he soon fell into conversation, first with me, then with some of my customers—talked all sorts of silly nonsense, made absurd bets with everybody. Some of these he won, and others he lost; but I must say that when he lost he always paid up most liberally. Then we all got excited, and soon bets flew all over the place.

"I don't rightly know how it happened at the last, but all at once he bet me that I would not dare to walk out then and there in the dark, as far as the Pont Neuf, wearing his blouse and hat and carrying a bundle the same as his under my arm. I not dare? . . . . I, Jean Victor, who was a fine fighter in my day! I bet him a gold piece that I would and he said that he would make it five if I came back without my bundle, having thrown it over the parapet into any passing boat.

"Well, citizen!" continued Jean Victor with a laugh, "I ask you, what would you have done? Five gold pieces means a fortune these hard times, and I tell you the man was quite honest and always paid liberally when he lost. He slipped behind the counter and took off his blouse and hat, which I put on. Then we made up a bundle with some cabbage heads and a few carrots, and out I came. I didn't think there could be anything wrong in the whole affair—just the tomfoolery of a man who has got the betting mania and in whose pocket money is just burning a hole. And I have won my bet," concluded Jean Victor, still unabashed, "and I want to go back and get my money. If you don't believe me, come with me to my *cabaret*. You will find the Citizen Rateau there, for sure; and I know that I shall find my five gold pieces."

Chauvelin had listened to the man as he would to some weird dream-story, wherein ghouls and devils had played a part. Tournefort, who was watching him, was awed by the look of fierce rage and grim hopelessness which shone from his chief's pale eyes. The other agents laughed. They were highly amused at the tale, but they would not let the prisoner go.

"If Jean Victor's story is true, citizen," their sergeant said, speaking to Chauvelin, "there will be witnesses to it over at '*Le Bon Copain*.' Shall we take the prisoner straightway there and await further orders?"

Chauvelin gave a curt acquiescence, nodding his head like some insentient wooden automaton. The screw of paper was still in his hand; it seemed to sear his palm. Tournefort even now broke into a grim laugh. He had just undone the bundle which Jean Victor had thrown over the parapet of the bridge. It contained two heads of cabbage and a bunch of carrots. Then he ordered the agents to march on with their prisoner, and they, laughing and joking with Jean Victor, gave a quick turn, and soon their heavy footsteps were echoing down the flagstones of the bridge.

★★★★★★

Chauvelin waited, motionless and silent, the dark lantern still held in his shaking hand, until he was quite sure that he was alone. Then only did he unfold the screw of paper.

It contained a few lines scribbled in pencil—just that foolish rhyme which to his fevered nerves was like a strong irritant, a poison which gave him an unendurable sensation of humiliation and impotence:

> *We seek him here, we seek him there!*
> *Chauvelin seeks him everywhere!*
> *Is he in heaven? Is he in hell?*
> *That demmed, elusive Pimpernel!*

He crushed the paper in his hand and, with a loud groan, of misery, fled over the bridge like one possessed.

7

Madame la Comtesse de Sucy never went to England. She was one of those French women who would sooner endure misery in their own beloved country than comfort anywhere else. She outlived the horrors of the Revolution and speaks in her memoirs of the man Bertin. She never knew who he was nor whence he came. All that she knew was that he came to her like some mysterious agent of God, bringing help, counsel, a semblance of happiness, at the moment when she was at the end of all her resources and saw grim starvation staring her and her children in the face. He appointed all sorts of strange places in out-of-the-way Paris where she was wont to meet him, and one night she confided to him the history of her diamonds, and hardly dared to trust his promise that he would get them for her.

Less than twenty-four hours later he brought them to her, at the poor lodgings in the Rue Blanche which she occupied with her children under an assumed name. That same night she begged him to dispose of them. This also he did, bringing her the money the next day.

She never saw him again after that.

But Citizen Tournefort never quite got over his disappointment of that night. Had he dared, he would have blamed Citizen Chauvelin for the discomfiture. It would have been better to have apprehended the man Rateau while there was a chance of doing so with success.

As it was, the impudent ruffian slipped clean away, and was never heard of again either at the "*Bon Copain*" or at the "*Liberté*." The customers at the *cabaret* certainly corroborated the story of Jean Victor. The man Rateau, they said, had been honest to the last. When time went on and Jean Victor did not return, he said that he could no longer wait, had work to do for the government over the other side of the water and was afraid he would get punished if he dallied. But, before leaving, he laid the five gold pieces on the table. Everyone wondered that so humble a workman had so much money in his pocket, and was withal so lavish with it. But these were not the times when one inquired too closely into the presence of money in the pocket of a good patriot.

And Citizen Rateau was a good patriot, for sure.

And a good fellow to boot!

They all drank his health in Jean Victor's sour wine; then each went his way.

Printed in the USA
CPSIA information can be obtained
at www.ICGtesting.com
LVHW041328211023
761731LV00004B/9/J